ERIC LUSTBADER

BLACK HEART

HarperCollins*Publishers*

HarperCollins*Publishers*
77–85 Fulham Palace Road,
Hammersmith, London W6 8JB

This paperback edition 1993
3 5 7 9 8 6 4 2

Previously published in paperback by Grafton 1984
Reprinted thirteen times

First published in Great Britain by
Granada Publishing 1983

Set in Bembo

Printed and bound in Great Britain by
Mackays of Chatham plc, Chatham, Kent

i

Author's Note

Researching the recent history of Cambodia is somewhat akin to reading *Rashomon*. No account, written or oral, can be automatically accepted as fact. Incidents and, especially, the motives of the principals involved shift like sand. There is no one who seems able to provide an unbiased and objective look at that time because the political ramifications of the situation were and continue to be nothing less than explosive, engendering in people rage, fear and what amounts to ideological hysteria.

In sifting through the 'evidence' of the sad and horrifying Cambodian holocaust it is therefore necessary to try to intuit the truth, for no other method appears to exist.

Whether or not what you read here is the truth is impossible for anyone to say. As for the depiction of the true nature of the Cambodian spirit, I am at least satisfied with that.

Eric Lustbader
New York City
June 1982

Acknowledgements

Black Heart is a work of fiction. However, the research that went into its creation was quite real. I would like to take this opportunity to thank the following people who were so graciously helpful to me. None of the real life people, needless to say, bear the slightest resemblance to the characters in this novel who, without exception, were drawn from my imagination.

Maureen Aung-Thwin, the Asia Society
Richard J. Mangan, Chief of Police, Solebury Twp.
Stephen Meredith, patrolman, Solebury Twp. Police
Phra Maha Ghosananda
Merrill Ashley
Helene Alexopoulos } The New York City Ballet
Leslie Bailey
Melina Hung, Hong Kong Tourist Association
Gordon Corrigan, stablemaster, and all at the Royal
     Hong Kong Jockey Club
and, especially,
Sichan Siv, who lived through his nation's holocaust
Milton Osborne, whose book *Before Kampuchea: Preludes
     to Tragedy* provided both historical background and
     ideas.

My thanks to V. for providing invaluable editorial assistance, and to my father for, as always, proof-reading the manuscript.

Translations: Sichan and Emily
Technical assistance: Dr Bertram Newman, Dr Brian
     Collier

There is a rose that I want to live for
Although God knows I may not have met her
        —*'The Call Up' by Joe Strummer*

Hana-no kage
  aka-no tanin wa
    nakari-keri

Thanks to cherry blossom
  in its shadow utter strangers—
    there are none!
        —Issa (1762–1826)

FOR VICTORIA
my love,
who makes it all seem so easy

Present
New York City

From within the eye of the Buddha all things could be seen. The night sky erupted in a crown of light. A garland of illumination to guide him. The shrouds of night parted and revealed to him the path he must take to remain undiscovered.

The rhythmic sounds of their animal coupling filled the space he had entered like the aromatic scents of a freshly prepared meal. He heard the woman groan and call the man's name.

'Oh, John. Oh!'

Her voice was husky, just this side of out of control. A voice filled with sex and promise. But despite that, he listened with a purely dispassionate ear; that fever was not for him now or ever. It fell on his ears like a litany out of an alien religion. A Christian mass, perhaps. Latin.

He crawled on his belly, silent as a serpent. His mind was cool and detached. Memories, habits, disciplines, all had their carefully nurtured place within. This is what made him what he was. This and, had he understood it, history. But he had no concept of that.

He lay on his back behind the sofa and prepared himself. The snufflings and gruntings pierced the air, built patterns of lust all around him like a web.

From his hip pocket he produced a soft plastic vial filled with a colourless liquid. As a conjurer might, his right hand blurred, the fingers turning in against the hard flesh of the palm, and he produced a steel needle of peculiar design Mizo had taught him to manufacture. It had a slightly curved T-bar base which fitted neatly between the first two fingers of his hand.

With a deliberate twist of his hand, he plunged the needle into the soft plastic vial, worked it around the viscous liquid. When he judged the needle to be completely covered, he withdrew it and stared sightlessly at the ceiling.

For a time, he listened to their gruntings and groanings, like tuning a radio into a distant station. He imagined them as they were, locked within their tightly spinning world of rising passion.

'Moira. Oh, Moira, I love you *so!*'

At length, he rose up, emerging over the back of the sofa. The man was on top, raised like a bull over the woman's writhing supine form. Sweat drenched them; the man's face was red with his effort. It would be soon now when he would lose his seed inside her.

Sooner than he thought.

The surgeon's eye and the practised hand came together and he lifted the needle up to a level with his ear. He felt the strength flowing through him like a shower of silver.

The man jounced up, down, up, riding the woman's damp powerful thighs. Her eyes were squeezed shut in ecstasy. She groaned deep and long.

Up again and the needle shot out, white in the lamplight, embedding itself as if of its own volition at the base of the man's neck.

The reaction was instantaneous even though the needle was with-drawn in a flash. Muscles bulged and the man began to gasp. At that moment, the woman's eyes opened; they were misty with desire and focusing was difficult. She grasped him more firmly as her orgasm began to grow, suffusing her lower body, spreading like a fire.

She cried out but not in ecstasy. Something was dreadfully wrong. She began to scream as her lover's sweat-soaked torso flopped down on her with the weight of a hammer. She saw his eyes, filming, staring sightlessly at her. He was still deep inside her, hard as a rock.

She went on screaming.

BOOK ONE

The Cockatrice

1

July, Present
New York City/Kenilworth/
Bucks County/Washington

'Just what the hell d'you think you're doing to me, Johnny-boy?'

Tracy Richter, prone on the meticulously polished wooden floor, did not pause. While the figure of Detective Sergeant Douglas Ralph Thwaite loomed over him, blotting out the streaming sunlight from the smallpaned skylight windows that illuminated the *dojo* in cloudlike patches, he continued with his knuckle pushups.

'I'm talking to you, Johnny-boy. You'd better be listening.'

Tracy was already up to sixty-five and he wasn't about to stop for Detective Sergeant Thwaite; not for anyone. There was a lot of anger and frustration to get out this morning, little more than forty-eight hours after John Holmgren's death.

'Johnny-boy, I haven't got all day. You'll be answering all my questions.'

Seventy-seven, seventy-eight. The rest of the *sensei*'s class was inquisitive but too well trained to stop their exercises. This was, after all, the most advanced class in karate and aikido given at the *dojo*.

Eighty-one, eighty-two. The *sensei* had taken one economical move towards the stranger but Thwaite had flashed his badge. That said it all. The *sensei* knew Tracy well. But even had he not, he would have understood the nature of the detective's presence. Everyone here had known John Holmgren. Up until approximately 10 p.m. the night before last, he had been the Governor of New York State.

'My mother, God keep her, used to tell me I had no patience whatsoever.' The figure of Detective Sergeant Thwaite leaned over slightly, the edges of his light raincoat brushing the ridged muscles along Tracy's back. 'But my friends know better.'

He was in the high nineties and working up quite a sweat. His pulse rate had accelerated, the effort he was expending sending jolts of adrenalin into the system until his body matched the state of his mind, seething with frustration. Everything he had worked for for almost ten years down the drain in the blink of an eye. It still seemed impossible. Unthinkable.

'Your time's run out.'

Tracy reached a hundred and got to his feet. A spasm of rage ripped through him.

'What d'you want?' His tone was curt. 'I'd've thought you'd gotten it all at the Governor's brownstone. You kept us there long enough.'

'The only thing I got outta you, Johnny-boy, was a lot of doubletalk. As the late Governor's media consultant, I kind of expected that. But the Monserrat woman was already partially sedated –'

'She'd become hysterical. She was with him when it happened.'

A flicker of a smile tinged the detective's large face. 'Yeah,' he said with a certain amount of calculated cynicism, 'Holmgren's heart attack.'

Tracy knew he was being baited but somehow he did not care anymore. This went far beyond the normal grief at the loss of a friend; his entire life had been rendered meaningless by John's death. 'That's right, his heart attack.'

Now Thwaite's eyes were alight; he knew he'd made contact. 'Oh, please, Richter. Come off it. The old boy was fucking the shit outta the Monserrat woman.' Again his words were calculated, this time with the vulgarism. 'He died in the saddle.'

'He died of a massive myocardial infarction –' Tracy said with a considerable amount of venom –'as the preliminary Medical Examiner's report stated – and if you plan to say anything to the contrary in public I'd think twice if I were you. I'll see to it you're cut down to my shoetops.'

'Now, see, Johnny-boy, that's just the thing I came here to see you about.' Thwaite's lined face had darkened in real anger now. He was a raw-boned, wide-shouldered man with a great deal of physical strength. But his inner forces, Tracy could tell, were in a state of turmoil. Tracy knew he could take the man without serious effort. That did not mean that Thwaite could not be dangerous; Tracy knew he'd have to guard against such thinking.

Thwaite's great mastiff's head with its wide-apart eyes and lined cheeks swung around and fixed Tracy. 'You've already done it to me, Johnny-boy. I just came from a meeting with my captain and d'you know what he told me?'

'You're going to tell me anyway, Thwaite. I think I can wait until you get around to it.'

Something seemed to snap within the cop and he took a abrupt step towards Tracy. His face was flushed. 'You high-and-mighty bastards're all alike, know that? You all think you're above the law. You know goddamned well what my meeting with Flaherty was about 'cause you were the bright spark set it in motion.

'As of now, I'm officially off the Holmgren case.'

'*What* Holmgren case?' Tracy said as calmly as he could. 'The Governor was working late with his personal assistant, much as he did almost three hundred and sixty days a year. We were just beginning our run for the presidential nomination. I think he –'

'I don't give a fuck what you think, Johnny-boy,' the detective said nastily. 'If that's all there was to it, then why all this fast footwork. I managed to get a semi-coherent statement from the Monserrat woman that night. Then I find she's been spirited away. By whom I ask? By Tracy Richter, I'm told. I want to go after her but a signed statement from the Holmgren family doctor assures my captain that the Monserrat woman is in no emotional condition to be "badgered by interrogations", I remember that phrase well.

'Now I'm told to forget it all just like it never happened.' His thick forefinger came up, pointing. 'You know what I think, Johnny-boy?' He smiled thinly. 'Oh, not think. *Know.* *You* composed that letter and had the doctor sign it. *You* controlled the death scene – 'cause by my reckoning there's about forty minutes unaccounted for in the Monserrat woman's story. Forty minutes when I just know she called you to clean up the mess.

'And now the pressure put on from upstairs to put the clamp on the case. My captain doesn't want to know anything except that I'm reassigned. Now that's either Albany or the Attorney-General's office.'

'The request,' Tracy said, vowing this would be the last civil answer he'd give this man today, 'came from Mary Holmgren, John's widow.'

'Well, here we got a third source you're hooked into, Richter,' Thwaite said, still needling. 'But one thing I know for sure. It's not anyone but you orchestrating this thing and, like I said before, you can twist the commissioner around . . . Captain Flaherty, too, 'cause he's got no balls whatsoever underneath his dress blues. But me, now that's another story entirely.'

'Listen, Thwaite,' Tracy said with an edge to his voice, 'I'm tired of your threats. They don't mean anything. My best friend has just died. By natural causes. That's it. I think you've been on the streets too long. You're seeing bogeymen where there's nothing but shadows.'

Thwaite laughed nastily. 'Yeah. That's just what you are, Johnny-boy. A bogeyman. You're like all politicians. Nothing better than the stinking dead cat put out with the rest of the garbage.'

Thwaite jabbed his finger at Tracy's chest. 'Wherever you've put the Monserrat woman, it doesn't matter. I'll find her. And when I do I'll get it all out of her. I'll crack her, Johnny-boy.'

'You've been ordered off, Thwaite. Stay away.'

The detective's eyes opened wide. 'Crack her, Richter.'

'Don't make me laugh, Thwaite. You're between a medical hands off and an official cease and desist order. If you even go near Moira Monserrat you'll be yanked off the force *and* hit with a civil suit for harassment. Just forget it. It's dead and buried.'

Thwaite came closer still. 'I wish it was, Johnny-boy. I wish the Governor *had* been buried, 'cause then sure as I'm standin' here I'd find a way to bring him up again.'

His forefinger pointed again and this time it shot out, poking Tracy in the ribs as if he were a side of beef. 'But you saw to that as well, didn't you, you bastard. You had Holmgren cremated immediately after the preliminary autopsy.'

'That was Mary's wish.'

'Oh, yeah, tell me about it, big shot. But I know the little voice put *that* bug in her ear. *You* flushed him down the toilet on us, Johnny-boy, just so there'd be no way anyone could attempt a full investigation.' The forefinger jabbed out again.

Tracy had had enough. He felt the rage in him again, the seething lava flow of frustration and he was close again to doing something irrational. He had actually set himself, moving fractionally in the attack stance. Only his intensive training saved Thwaite. Still Tracy's muscles jumped in galvanic response.

Thwaite sensed what was happening. 'Come on, Johnny-boy,' he said, lifting his fists. 'If it's a fight you want, that's what you'll get. You've caused me too much grief over the last coupla days.' His shoulder muscles bunched. 'On the Holmgren investigation or off, you've got big trouble.'

'I'm not the guy to fuck with, Thwaite.'

'You think I'm afraid of you and your candy-ass class?'

Tracy ignored him. 'I'll let you in on a secret. There's nothing I'd like more right now than to take you down hard. All I'd need is a tenth of a second. I think it'd make me feel a whole helluva lot better. But it would solve nothing.

'I spent almost ten years working with John Holmgren. First by putting the presidential seed into his mind, then by personally mapping out his campaign for the nomination. We had a fight on our hands, especially from Atherton Gottschalk but I'm convinced we had it nailed down tight. And now this.

'If you think I'm going to allow some vindictive cop to smear our names all over the *New York Post* you're sorely mistaken. Whatever John was doing with Moira Monserrat that night is none of your business or anyone else's but theirs. And God help you, Thwaite, if you do anything to jeopardize John's good name.'

The *sensei* was looking at him and he knew it was time. He went away from Thwaite without saying another word. He took up his position in the centre of the *dojo*, opposite the *sensei*. They bowed formally to each other then there was stillness.

Thwaite turned, was about to leave when the *sensei* exploded into motion. He pointed four times and four students left their positions.

'Form a circle around Richter-san,' the *sensei* said. His voice was soft and dry as sand. It was more commanding than a shout.

As the students took up their new places a sound lifted in the room as if it were a wind. It made the hair on the back of the detective's neck stand up, his scrotum tighten. It was something animal, of that he was certain, not unlike a great predator's warning growl. It seemed to penetrate right to the centre of his brain, rooting him to the spot.

The sound had grown considerably until now it seemed to fill the room with vibration as well as sound. Sweat broke out along Thwaite's hairline. Gradually he became aware that the source of this unsettling effect was Tracy Richter's half-opened mouth.

'This,' the *sensei* said, pointing towards Tracy's expanded chest, 'is *yo-ibuki* or hard-style breathing, used in combat. It is, as you all know, the opposite of *in-ibuki*, the meditation breathing. Yet both use the entire natural breathing apparatus, not merely the top of the lungs as is the norm in modern-day society. Here the whole body is tensed, including the throat and oesophagus, thus constricting the air passage, forcing the air out of the abdomen.'

The *sensei* took a balletic step backward, clearing the field. 'Now,' he said, 'you will knock him off his feet.'

Obediently the students moved in and, using arms and shoulders, came against Tracy. Thwaite noticed especially his toes which were curved and tensed, as immovable as stone. He reckoned that the four students, combined, weighed somewhere between 650 and 700 pounds.

'Use all your strength now!' the *sensei* cried.

For an instant Tracy seemed to give the smallest fraction and then one after another the students were flung from him as if by their own reverse momentum. Thwaite was reminded of the Whip at Coney Island.

'Yes!' the *sensei*'s voice conveyed carefully controlled excitement. 'Give and snap back! This is your lesson for today. You must study this most carefully. Now: one hour's meditation.'

Thwaite found that his body had tensed itself during the demonstration. He had thought of all manner of retorts to Tracy's

18

last comment but abruptly he felt the need to leave this place. His sense of alienness and isolation was threatening to suffocate him.

Senator Roland Burke delighted in theatricality. That was why, he supposed, he loved chiaroscuro. His house in Kenilworth, the most exclusive suburb of Chicago, was decorated entirely in blacks and whites, the lamps and overhead lights so placed that when turned on they created pools, shafts, oblique blocks of shadow and light.

These lights were never off until Senator Burke was in bed, ready for sleep. Then, with a flick of a master switch, the entire house was plunged into darkness at once.

This still warm evening in July the senator was particularly pleased to turn the key in the latch and open his front door. There the perfectly ordered pools of light and dark confronted him comfortingly.

The Senator turned and, sighing, closed the door. He walked slowly down the hallway, emerging from darkness into the light, disappearing into shadows again. It was good to be home.

It was quiet in Kenilworth, always. The wind through the well-tended trees, a nightbird or two and, in summer, the crickets and cicadas. That was all.

He lifted a hand, massaged his eyes beneath closed lids. The pandemonium of the morning's press conference still rang in his ears. In the living room, he crossed to the bar, began to fix himself a bourbon and water.

Christ, he thought, dropping a handful of ice cubes into an Old Fashioned glass, what a stink the press makes when a senator changes his mind! You'd think war had been declared. That particular thought made him smile. Well, it had in a way. His war on America's ailing economy, the disastrous fall-off in social services for the poor and the aged, environmental grants.

He sipped at his drink. Now it seemed odd to him that he could ever have consented to retire prematurely. Money could do that to you, he mused, and the thought of a lifetime of security working in the private sector.

He snorted. Private sector, indeed! Put out to pasture to graze contentedly was more like it.

He had spent three restless weeks with that public decision. He had not been able to concentrate on his work or sleep at night. His oath of office kept rolling around in his mind. What about his oath to his constitutents? They deserved better than this.

So yesterday he had had his office call a press conference, and now he was back in the re-election race. What an uproar the announcement had created!

He sighed again. At last he was beginning to relax, the brutally hectic pace of this day finally leaching away from him. Warmth from the bourbon stole through him, softening his tensed muscles and mind.

He kicked off his shoes, went across the room, feeling with delight the thickness of the wall-to-wall carpet's pile on the soles of his feet. It reminded him of when he was a boy. He had never liked to wear shoes then, either.

The curtains were drawn across the window and he stood there, lifting an arm, pulling the drapes aside a little. Out there was the lake, lapping softly against the shore. Sometimes, at night, he could just make out the faint pale gleam of moonlight on the water, like an ethereal stairway to heaven.

'*Vous n'avez pas été sage.*'

Burke jumped so hard, half his bourbon sloshed onto the carpet. He whirled around, peered across the room. Patterns of intense shadow and light. He saw no one. There was no movement whatsoever.

'Who is that?' he said, his voice a trifle unsteady. '*Qu'est ce que vous êtes venu faire ici?*' The French was forced out of him.

'*Vous n'avez pas été sage.*'

This time he was watching the room. Still he saw nothing. The muscles in his lower belly contracted uncomfortably. He decided to brazen it out.

'*Montrez-vous!*' he said with more force. '*Montrez-vous ou j'appelle la police!*' Silence. He took a step in the direction of the phone on the bartop.

'*NE BOUGEZ PAS!*'

Senator Burke froze. He had been in the armed forces. He knew a command when he heard it. Jesus, he thought.

'*Pourquoi l'avez vous fait?*' the voice asked. '*Qu'est ce qui vous fait agir comme ça? On était prêt à vous tout donner mais vous n'étiez pas fidèle à notre accord.*' The voice held overtones that brought the sweat out on Burke.

Again he peered into the layers of concealing shadows. It was terribly unsettling to confront a voice without any real substance.

'My conscience,' he said after a moment. 'I couldn't live with what I had done. I . . . I have people to protect. People I have sworn to help.' My God, he thought wildly. How lame this all sounds, even to my own ears. 'I . . . found I couldn't go through with it.'

'Confidence was put in you, Senator.' The voice was almost a purr, silky and quiet as a buzz. It made Burke shiver involuntarily. 'Plans set in motion because of you.'

'Well, you'll just have to change those plans. I'm running for re-election in the fall.'

'These plans,' the voice said, 'cannot be changed. All this was explained to you in the beginning. You agreed to everything.'

The soft reasonable tone was infuriating. 'Goddamnit, I don't care what I said then!' the senator cried. 'Get the hell out of here! If you think I owe you anything, you're sorely mistaken. I am a member of the United States Senate.' He began to smile. His own voice, strong and sure, was infusing him with confidence. 'You can do nothing to me.' He nodded as he walked towards the bar. 'Who could you tell without exposing yourself? No one.' In there was a nickel-plated .22 pistol he had a licence for. If he could reach it, he reasoned, he could gain the upper hand. 'There is nothing you can do.' He was almost there. 'Face the truth and leave.' His palm slid across the rough surface of the bartop. 'I promise you it will be as if you've never been here.'

Senator Burke froze, his eyes open wide. The air in front of him seemed to ripple, then sizzle as if a thousand animals were screaming in pain. He gasped and fell back, staggering under the invisible assault. He was convinced a hand of immense power had struck him in the chest.

'*Vous niez la vie.*'

'What –?' he managed to get out before the room exploded into blurred motion.

A patch of deep shadow obliquely across the room from him had seemed to come alive. It ballooned outward with the frightening rapidity of a dream. He tried to move, to get away but that awful, eerie sound had returned, pinning him to the front of the bar as he saw death approach.

He tried to scream then but it was as if his vocal chords had been ripped from his throat. He watched the shadow approach and he was drenched in terror. He fouled his trousers.

Eyes like glittering diamonds, lethal and inhuman from out of the dark – this creature seemed to bring the shadow with it as it crossed through the beams of light. It came faster than anything he thought possible.

The hideous sound was building, eating away at his brain. He threw up his arms and the glass with its contents went flying against the sofa, the liquor spilling like silent tears. He pressed his hands against his ears to blot out the noise but it did no good.

Then darkness blossomed from just in front of him, a violent sunset, his last chiaroscuro, as the heel of his attacker's hand smashed with incalculable force into his nose at just the right angle, ramming bone and cartilage like a missile into his brain.

The senator leapt off his feet, lifted by forces he could not have understood even had he still been alive.

What Tracy remembered most clearly about the night John Holmgren died was the tone of Moira's voice. She had called him from the brown-stone, pulled him out of sleep.

'Oh, God, he's dead. I really think he's dead.'

The *sound* of her had chilled him because she had released the shuddering terror that had suffused her. He got dressed and went to her.

John's corpse was laid out on the sofa. One leg dangled to the floor, the toes and ball of the foot flexed as if he were about to lower his weight onto it.

He was naked, of course, his skin peculiarly white save for an area around his heart, his neck and face. Those were suffused with colour.

He knelt beside his friend's body, put a hand out to touch the cool flesh. The face looked just the same as the dead men Tracy had seen in Southeast Asia. Caucasian, Vietnamese, Chinese or Cambodian, it did not seem to matter. Violent death gave their faces one terrible fixed expression.

He sighed inwardly. He had never really doubted Moira's assessment; she was a brilliant woman, one not given to hysterics or exaggeration. But the physical confirmation was like a vault door swinging shut in his mind. So it was, after all. What dreams they had shared! Gone, now, the way of all dreams.

He turned to look at Moira but she was turned partially away as if she could not bear to look at John anymore. It looked to him on the face of it as if John had had a heart attack; the bodily signs were all there. But he needed to hear from Moira just what had happened.

Tracy came around and sat in a chair opposite her, took her longfingered hands – so cold! – in his. 'Moira,' he said softly, gently, 'you must téll me what happened.' She stared at nothing. He could only see her long lashes, the bruised purple of her upper eyelids. He knew he had to get through to her in the next minute or two. A call to 911 had to be made and, he knew, the sooner the better. The ME, establishing a rough time of death, would provide a starting point for the detectives and surely they would ask why it took an hour between the time of the Governor's demise and the call to the police.

So he tried another avenue. 'Moira, if you don't help me now, I won't be able to protect him.

Her head came up and he saw those bright green eyes, the sharp nose, wide mouth, high cheekbones. 'What do you mean?' Her voice was still quavery and he could feel the tremors shuddering through her like quakes.

'You know just what I mean.' He kept his voice low but filled it with a defined urgency. 'I have to know, Moira. Now. I have to call 911. Every minute is working against us. You must tell me.'

'Yes.' The single word was like an abject surrender. 'He – That is, we –' she broke off, her voice choking and Tracy could feel the pressure of her fingers gripping his with all her strength.

23

'We were ... we were making love ... for the second time –'
Her eyes locked with his, a challenge but Tracy said nothing, his face revealed nothing and, apparently satisfied, she went on. 'We often ... did that. John often seemed, well, starved for sex if not love. Trace, do you understand me?'

'Yes, Moira, I do. Go on.'

Her face was clouded with pain. 'He reared up in the middle of it. My eyes were closed. I was not exactly all there. At first I thought ... he had come.' Lines had apppeared between her eyes, atop the bridge of her nose. The nostrils were slightly flared. 'But then *something* – I don't know what – made me open my eyes.'

'What kind of something, Moira? Did you see anyone else in the room?'

'It was what you feel when you wake up from a nightmare. You feel a presence but when you turn around and look, nothing's there.' Tracy felt her long nails digging into his flesh. 'I was looking right into his face and, Trace, I thought I was still dreaming. He was as white as a sheet of paper. His lips were dark, drawn back from his teeth. He was gnashing them together. He looked like ... Oh, God, he looked like some kind of animal!' Now the sobbing began and Tracy moved forward. He stroked her back, whispering words of solace that he did not believe.

'It didn't matter to me what he looked like,' Moira whispered in his ear. 'I held him like a baby, kissing his cheeks, his eyelids, his half-open lips. I called his name over and over again. But he was gone, Trace. Gone.' She held onto him tightly. 'I'll never hear his voice again. Never feel his gentle touch.'

And despite himself, Tracy shuddered at her words. He wanted very much to comfort her; he understood her loss well. But what could he really do? He hated himself for what he was about to burden her with, but he had no choice. It had to be her. So he told her in his calmest, most convincing voice with his arm around her imparting warmth and comfort.

'But you'll be here.' She looked into his eyes. 'Won't you?'

He shook his head. 'No. I can't. You can see that, Moira. I don't want any hint that you might have made a call before you spoke to 911. I don't want anyone to think you've been coached or there's been any kind of coverup. It's going to be difficult enough going for the first two weeks as it is. After that, everything'll die down.'

'Trace, I can't stay here. Not through all that.'

'No. Of course not. I've got a place in Bucks County. Just outside of New Hope. I'll give you my spare set of keys and you drive out there tomorrow morning. Stay there. You have money?'

She nodded.

'Okay. Now when I leave, give me five minutes, then make the call to 911. You know what to say and how to say it.' Moira nodded again and for the first time since he got her call, Tracy thought it was going to be all right. 'Good. Now help me get some clothes on the Governor.'

Machine hum. The brief hiss of tape running, emanating from the threefoot Yamaha studio monitor speakers, breaking into an almost palpable silence. Words running together in a blurred ribbon of alien sound, abruptly bursting forth like a clear bubble climbing out of brackish water: '. . . don't know. I just felt . . . something.' 'But what, exactly?' the second voice said. 'That's just it,' the first replied shakily. 'It isn't something I can . . . put into words.' The quaver in the voice threatened to disintegrate the words. 'Perhaps tomorrow I can think . . .'

The reproduction was astonishingly accurate. One could even feel the inner tension fuelling the exchange.

Moira's voice returned, clotted with emotion: 'It . . . well. It was what you feel when you wake up from a nightmare.' A deep, shuddering breath. 'You *feel* a presence but when you turn around and look, nothing's there. I —' The voice was cut off as easily and completely as one wipes words off a blackboard.

There was little light in the room and no sound at all save the barely audible hiss from the speakers. Shadows lay like a three-dimensional landscape.

'*Je ne crois rien à ce qu'elle dit. Son amant s'est fait tué; elle en est complètement hystérique.*' The young man said. When he was speaking French, he had no accent at all; it seemed a much more natural language for him than English. He was dark-skinned, his face impossible to discern in the gloom.

For just an instant it appeared as if he were talking to himself, a thinker's pensive appraisal. Then another voice was raised.

'*Non, au contraire, je crois qu'elle est au courant . . . de quelque chose.*'

There was no movement in the room so that this voice gave the impression of emanating from the very heart, the mind of the house. Then a shadowy figure stirred in the wing-backed leather chair near the young man and the arch of one cheekbone came into a shaft of what dim light there was. From the height at which it appeared, it was possible to conclude that the figure was tall, certainly slender, for there was no excess fat on that crescent of flesh. A bit of reflected light illuminated the long hands lying peacefully along the polished mahogany arms of the chair. An odd combination: polished nails and calloused skin.

'*Qu'est ce qu'elle pourrait en savoir?*' The young man moved with absolute silence across the room; as a professional might move. '*Pensez-y d'une façon logique.*'

'Your Cambodian mythos,' the figure in the wing chair said, 'has gotten lost within the *logical* teachings of the radical French. Yes, logic says that she saw nothing. Yet I believe her when she says she felt something.'

'It is impossible.' The young man knelt in front of the chair. 'I was invisible.'

'Invisible, yes. But not undetectable. She felt you, all right, though what, precisely, will surface we cannot determine.' He steepled his fingers. His voice was deep, resonant and, to the young man, infinitely reassuring.

Those steepled fingers began to flex in the regimented rhythms of isometric exercise. 'The human mind is the best computer on earth, always was and always will be. That's why man does the programming and not the other way around. But' – one of his fingers lifted away from its work, pointed at the other man's head – 'the mind's still a mystery to us – *any* of us.'

The exercise over, the long competent fingers laced in repose. 'She might not know anything *today*. But she suspects. Somewhere inside her, the animal – the million-year-old mechanism

26

for survival we all still carry around – has marked you. And tomorrow or perhaps the day after that, what then? Can you answer me that?'

The young man stared into the other's eyes for as long as he dared. Then he bowed his head. The scent of incense was very strong in the room at that moment as if a gust of wind from the other side of the world, some ancient age, had crept in through the window sash, to permeate the atmosphere.

'The pupil still respects the teacher,' the young man murmured. 'Obey him, show him esteem by word and deed, harken attentively to his teaching.'

The figure unfurled himself from the wing-back chair, a riding sail pushing against an unseen wind, ignorant of defeat. He hauled the other up so that they stood within an inch of one another. He seemed to tower over the young man, as if he were larger in every way.

'Goddamnit!' he bellowed. 'Don't you dare give me any of that Buddhist bullshit! If you've got a point to argue, say so. I won't have you hiding behind nonsense some old windbag taught you when you were a pup in Phnom Penh!'

The young man kept his head bowed beneath this verbal assault, as a child who submits to his parent's well-reasoned wrath.

'*Pardonnez-moi;*' he whispered, a reed bending to the force of a strong wind.

The tone, perhaps, rather than the words took all the tension out of the tall man's frame. 'Oh, now.' His arm came up, wrapped itself around the other's shoulders. 'Now, Khieu,' he said softly, the anger washed from his voice, 'just tell me what you think, that's all.'

Together they strolled towards the casement curtains covering the high fifteen-foot windows. They moved to the beat of an unheard metronome as if they had performed this act – a kind of ritual – many times before.

At last the young man spoke. 'We have both listened to this tape,' he said, 'many times over. But I still maintain that it is inconclusive.' In the faint glimmerings of streetlight, it was just possible to make out his black eyes, the unusual width of his cheekbones, the thickness of his softly pouting lips as if, like the brightest of stars piercing a misty night, these were all that really existed or were of any importance. Still, there was an overall effect of beauty and sensuality that was instantly arresting. 'I was there and I can tell you unequivocally that she did not see me. She could not. When I made the strike, she was ... otherwise occupied.' His hands came up, stroked the tautness of the ivory-coloured curtains. 'As you know, sex tends to limit the senses into a tight-fisted path.'

The tall man absorbed the other's words yet still he was haunted by what the woman had said. *I just felt ... something.* He knew who that 'something' was. Did she?

He tightened his grip on the young man. 'You have been away from me too long, Khieu.' His voice held an odd tone. It was lighter, drifting as if on reflected water. 'First at the Ecole des Hautes Etudes Commerciales in Paris, then Geneva, Weisbaden and, finally, Hong Kong for your ... less orthodox studies. A long time since "Operation Sultan", eh?' He looked fondly at the younger man. 'Now you are ready ... We both are. And events are moving with us ... All is in its proper place.'

He raised his gaze above their heads. Along the ceiling the street lights cast their pale illumination as a procession of diffuse circles like old-time illustrations of lit candles.

'I read in this morning's paper of Senator Burke's unfortunate demise. The place was also burgled, they say. Good. His punishment will not go unnoticed among his ... former colleagues. None of them will now dare contemplate the road he travelled. So –' He rubbed his hands together '– we are absolutely shut-ended. Our security is once again at one hundred per cent. But now it occurs to me that this woman may just be a walking timebomb.'

'Even if she remembers,' Khieu said reasonably, 'she cannot hurt us.'

'Perhaps not,' the figure agreed. 'But this man Tracy Richter is another story entirely. We must both be very careful.' He was looking out the window again. Mist had come against the panes, moistening the streets like the tongue of God. Khieu could see that the other man's eyes were focused on nothing. 'You see, right now he is sleeping and I want it kept that way. If there ever comes a time when he wakes I shall have to deal with him. But understand me, I do not want that unless it becomes unavoidable.

'That is why the Monserrat woman must not be allowed to rabbit on to him about her suspicions, however vague they may be at this moment.' His arm dropped away from Khieu's shoulders. 'Now is the time of ultimate risk for us. Now, when we are the strongest is when we are also the most vulnerable.

'I will not be intimidated by chance. I – *we* went into this *à ses risques et périls*. I have learned over the years not to add to that. *Il faudrait supprimer ce risque.*'

At that moment a force was rising in the room, an energy that had not been present a moment ago. It was as if the tall man had breathed some ancient and arcane incantation, summoning up a darkness that was more than night.

The young man with the black eyes, a predator's eyes, was on the move. Khieu had said his piece, his heart was calm; the ultimate decision had been made in another precinct.

The tall figure's eyes fluttered closed as if he had in some way divorced himself from the increasing disturbance within the room. He took a breath, five seconds later allowing it to be expelled through his opened lips. His ivory teeth gleamed. *Prana.*

'Like one tiny pebble thrown into a still lake gifted with perfect reflection. Ripples on and on, outward, distorting, marring that perfection.' His voice, though low, sought for and gained ascendancy in the room. 'Who may foresee the consequences then?'

Within the silence the disturbance renewed itself, rising in power and intensity. The air seemed to vibrate with dark energy. Khieu was almost at the door.

'The reward of power is not for the timid.' The tall man breathed slowly, deeply. 'The only certain way to avoid the ripples is to remove the pebble, the potential source.'

He swung fully towards the windows as the door closed behind his back. He felt the calm returning slowly.

*

Some men disappeared into bars, others into the desolate countryside. But when Thwaite could no longer deal with the pressure-cooker milieu he deliberately steeped himself in, it was to Melody's he went. To him it was like vanishing off the face of the earth.

She owned a attic apartment on Eleventh Street just off Fourth Avenue. Up there on the sixth floor, the space seemed enormous. She had had it painted in black enamel. Deep in the night, with the ceiling and all of the furniture shades of grey and blue, he found it cavelike and curiously comforting.

She buzzed him up from the lobby and he took the creaking industrial elevator with its open grill-work front, up to her floor. He massaged the bridge of his nose with two fingers. His meeting with Richter had not gone the way he had imagined it would. Somehow he had lost the initiative. He had been freaked by that sound and the sight of Richter throwing men from him as if shrugging off rain. Thwaite shivered slightly as if shaking off a bad dream.

Melody was waiting for him. She stood in front of her closed front door, a red silk kimono pulled hastily around her. She was a slim-hipped, small-breasted woman. Her straight black hair hung all the way down to the crease of her buttocks.

Her face was an almost perfect oval, with a small chin and a sharp nose with flaring delicate nostrils. She was not a classic beauty by any means, Thwaite thought, but she compensated for that in so many ways.

'What are you doing here, Doug?' In her voice were hidden echoes of other languages, eleven to be precise, including Russian, Japanese and at least three separate dialects of Chinese; that was how she spent her spare time. It gave her a sense of pride to be able to speak all the world's major languages.

'What d'you think?' he said tightly. 'I want in.'

He began to move forward but Melody but a palm firmly against his chest, shook her head.

'It's a bad time. I –'

'No such thing.' Off the case and nowhere to go; he didn't care. He leaned on her.

Melody fought him. 'Doug, would you please try to understand –'

'We have an arrangement.' He didn't want to understand.

'I know but that doesn't mean you can come in any time you –'

'I don't give a shit if the Prince of Wales is in there,' he said finally pushing past her into the apartment. 'Get him the hell out.'

Melody kicked the door shut, stared at him for a long minute. 'Christ,' she said under her breath. Then, louder, 'The least you can do is disappear.'

Thwaite went through the long living room, heading to the left and the kitchen. He rummaged through the refrigerator before realizing he wasn't hungry. He sat down heavily on a chair, put his forearms on the glass-topped dining table. He realized he wasn't much of anything these days. Take now, for instance. Why the hell was he here in a whore's apartment when he should be at the office . . . or home.

He heard quiet voices, the front door close. He put his head in his hands and thought about nothing, which was easier. He grunted when he heard Melody come into the kitchen. He did not look at her, heard instead her throwing pots and pans around just as if she were a miffed housewife.

'You've got some hell of a nerve, you know that?' she said with her back to him. 'I don't know how I ever got myself into this position.'

'You fuck men for a living, remember?' Thwaite said nastily and was instantly sorry.

Melody spun around, her cheeks flaming with shame. 'Yeah. And I'm the one *you're* with, Doug. It's convenient for you to forget that. Why don't you just go home to your wife and kid?'

He dug his thumbs into his eyes until he saw white spots jumping. 'Sorry,' he said softly. 'I didn't expect you to be with someone, that's all.'

'Oh, what *did* you expect?'

He looked up. 'I didn't think about it. All right?'

'No,' she said, coming towards him. 'It's not all right. We have the same kind of arrangement you have with other people

31

around town, I imagine, except with me you don't take money. Okay, I accept that. I have no choice. But when it comes down to you scaring off my bread and butter, I have to draw the line.'

'Don't tell me where to draw the line!' he screamed, leaping up so quickly that she jumped back. 'I make the rules around here. I'm your lord and master and if you doubt that for a minute then think about me taking you downtown and booking you!'

'And spite yourself?' Her voice was rising as well. 'Don't make me laugh. You know a good thing when you feel it. Free fun. It's got to be more than you get at home!'

'You stay out of that!' he screamed. 'I won't warn you again.'

'I'm tired of your warnings, Thwaite. I'm tired of you. Just leave me alone, why don't you? I'll give you a percentage of the take instead. Just fuck someone else.'

'Goddamn you!' He rushed at her from around the table.

'What's the matter?' she goaded. 'I'm offering you part of the gross. Isn't that enough to assuage your larcenous heart? That's all you bastards seem to do down at the precinct anyway, work out schedules of pay-offs.'

She did not, perhaps, understand how deeply she had pricked him until the last instant. She saw the murderous look in his eyes and backed up against the counter, reaching behind her with one hand for the bread knife in its long wooden sheath.

But he was already upon her, batting the weapon away from her with a stinging slap. He hit her across the face and she put up both arms. He pried them aside, bending her backward at the waist.

'Bastard!' she cried. 'Bastard!' Until she saw that he was weeping as he fought with her. 'Doug,' she said softly.

'Why don't you do something else with your time, for the love of God!' he sobbed, his big head coming down against her breasts, her raised hands touching tentatively his dark hair then, feeling his convulsions, hugging him to her warm body. She kissed his forehead, whispering, 'It's all right,' as much to herself as to him.

Her real name was not Melody, of course. She had been born Eva Rabinowitz in a tenement not more than a mile away from where she now lived. But only Thwaite knew that. He had come across her during a particularly thorny homicide investigation and, for a time, it appeared she was his prime suspect, hence the background check he ran on her.

'You went to Barnard, graduate school at Columbia,' he had said to her once. 'Why do you do what you do?'

'I graduated with my Ph.D. and nothing else,' she had said. 'I felt like the emperor with his new clothes. I had nowhere to go and nothing to do. You know I was brought up with no money. Now I make as much as I could possibly need.' She shrugged. 'Sometimes a lot more. I can afford to give myself whatever I want.' Her grey eyes had regarded him steadily. 'And what about you?' She seemed to have a way of being able to cut through all the layers of bullshit, until the bones were laid bare. Early on Thwaite had seen what a brilliant mind she had not only for languages; he envied her that very much. 'What do you get out of being a cop?'

Thwaite sat back on the couch. 'I've been in the department for almost twenty years. Homicide. I've been there almost ten.' He shook his head. 'Christ, but it's full of dirty deals. I heard about all of 'em, you know, while I was still in the academy.' He smiled, a touch wistfully, sadly even. 'I promised myself I wasn't gonna get involved in all that shit.' He looked away from her. 'But that was school, you know. I was young then. No idea what the world was really like. But I found out real soon.'

His eyes lifted, swung back to her. 'My first collar as a uniform was a bad one. Bastard pushing smack near two schools, one of them a Junior High. I was hot. I saw the kids he was feedin', had to get the ambulance for one little girl.

'So I wanted this one bad. I got him, did everything right. Read him the Miranda in English and Spanish just in case. He was holdin', all of that.

'But the bastard had enough muscle to hire a lawyer who knew his way around the courts. He plea-bargained and the judge was lenient . . . socially conscious and all that. Sonuvabitch was out on the streets in six weeks. *Six weeks.* Can you believe it?'

He shrugged. 'But that was only the beginning. The graft, the dirty dealing was all around. There was no place you could walk without stepping in shit.

'I began to think of myself as a rat in the sewer. I'd come home and shower for a half an hour in water hot enough to scald.'

'But you kept at it,' Melody said without reproach.

'It was what I was trained for. Outside the department, I'd be a functional idiot.' He put his hands together. 'Then I got married, my wife wanted a house. We had a kid. And so on. The bills were piling up ... just like they were for everyone. But then one morning I came into the precinct and took a look around me. There were some guys who seemed all right even though I knew they were in the same situation as I was. Then there were others who seemed to be breaking their backs, old before their time.

'I didn't want that for myself. Basically I think of myself as an honest guy.' He shrugged. 'Who knows, maybe that's just a form of selfpreservation. I put the arm on low-lifes here and there. It's okay with them, it's okay with me. I'm making the best of it, see. At least I'm getting something back for the gruelling hours I spend in that cesspool.

'And Homicide is the worst of them all because everyday you feel the madness drugs like horse and methedone put into these people causing them to murder in an emotionless and offhand way.' His voice was a whisper now. 'And every day I feel reduced some more.'

Moira Monserrat was crying. She had arrived at Tracy's house in the midst of a driving rainstorm and done nothing more than walk unsteadily upstairs and, seeking out the big double bed, had thrown herself headlong onto its giving surface.

She had slept fitfully only to awake in the middle of the night with a sharp cry, her fists clutched to her breast. Breathing like a bellows; heart pounding painfully. What had she heard? What had awakened her? A presence. A tendril of a dream, reaching out to scrape along her shoulder.

Oh, John, she thought. Where are you now to protect me from myself?

His deep rich voice filled her mind again, bringing with it warmth and life. 'I know you down to your core,' he said. 'I just hope . . . I often think about what it's like for you . . . after I go home to Mary. I still love her, you know.'

She smiled. 'In a way I don't mind. You're a loyal person, John. It's one of the qualities in you I love the most. I could no more imagine you abandoning your family than I could you hurting me.'

He kissed her tenderly. 'But with you I feel alive. I know I have enough strength to fulfil the dream Tracy's constructing for me.' He gave a low laugh, then, squeezing her fondly. 'You know, sometimes I think he ought to be the candidate. Yes, I have the experience. But he's the one with the brilliant mind. He's a unique kind of architect, all right. He knows people in a manner that's sometimes scary. He's rarely bluffed and never wrong in his evaluations.'

'Then why is he working for you? You make it sound as if he could clean up on his own.'

'That's a good question, Moira, and I'm not sure whether even I know the answer.' He rolled over so that he could look directly into her eyes. 'He was in Southeast Asia. But not as an ordinary grunt. He was some kind of ultrasensitive spook. Special Forces, I'd guess. I've never gotten any details out of him and I wouldn't try.

'But I do know one thing. He had a lot of power once. A great deal of power.'

'What do you think happened?'

'Oh, I don't think anyone but Tracy really knows. It's my guess, however, that he walked away from it. Maybe he saw too much death. Underneath it all, Tracy's a sensitive man. But he's troubled as well. His position with me was carefully thought out, I now realize. He's close enough to the power – he manipulates it still – without being in its centre. For the time being, it's what he wants or needs. When he sorts things out, though, it may not be enough.'

Moira was alarmed. 'He wouldn't turn against you.'

'Tracy?' John laughed. 'Good God, no. Tracy's even more loyal than I am, if that's possible. No, we've become something more than friends even. We're family. I want you to remember that.'

And so Moira had. At the moment of John Holmgren's death, when panic and terror had gripped her, it was the only thing she remembered.

Now standing in the kitchen of Tracy's house, she knew that John had been right in his assessment of him.

Oh my God, John, she said silently. What will I do without you?

Fighting back the tears, she opened the wood-framed windows over the sink, dispelling the musty air. She liked this place. It was neat and homey, filled with old, well-worn furniture that exuded a personal history like a scent.

The cedar-cabineted kitchen led directly into the dining room. A dark wood table with spindle legs with partly covered by a handmade mat of some nubbly cotton material. A pair of Cambodian candlesticks stood on it. In the highboy hutch in one corner, she saw several boxes of long ivory candles, glasses and dishes along with a crowd of Cambodian artifacts.

Moira knew Cambodia to be one of Tracy's passions. She wondered what had happened to him out there. If John had been right, perhaps it was something awful, a secret buried away in his past.

She went slowly into the large bright living room beyond, allowing the essence of the place to seep in. The blackened fireplace was filled with a nineteen-inch TV.

The space before the fireplace as well as the mantel was made of local tile in green and blue squares. On the wide mantel itself sat a rather large Buddha. It was lacquered in gold, though its obvious age had caused the dark wood from which it had been carved to peek through here and there in ill-defined streaks.

Moira stared into that enigmatic face. To her it had an otherworldly cast to it; she did not associate it with the face of a human being. Still a quality it possessed caught her. The morning light slanting in burnished one side of the face, throwing the other half into shadow. She picked out more details the longer she looked until she had the impression she was no longer staring at a man-made object.

With an effort, she turned her attention elsewhere. She went across the room to the caramel corduroy sofa, its pillows cloudy with use. She knelt atop it, pulled one of the pillows to her, hugging it against her chest. She stared out the windows directly behind the sofa. Across the rutted dirt road was what appeared to be a rather large apple orchard, the trees lined in perfect rows like a marching band. Beyond was the tassle-topped brush of a wide cornfield.

She threw open the window, closed her eyes as the soft breeze brushed her cheeks and hair. She inhaled deeply of the rich summer scents.

Curled up on the sofa, her cheek against the edge of the fluffy pillow, she cried for real now, feeling the awful ache of loneliness, of displacement, of a creeping kind of unreality she seemed powerless to stop, knowing that there was life out there, all around her, and she was not a part of it.

'This is the last time I will see you.'

Tracy gave a start. 'What d'you mean?'

Mai looked at him levelly, her black eyes glossy. 'Something has happened to you.'

Outside the chatter of Chinatown waxed and waned, unabated.

'I don't know why you insist on still living here. You have more than enough money to –'

'I don't think,' she said quietly, 'that this is any of your concern now.'

Tracy knew that he had hurt her just by walking in the door. What did she know about him that he himself had failed to see? He walked across the dimly lit room and took her into his arms. She was small and delicate with a flat face and enormous eyes. She had seemed more animal than human to him the first time they had met at the *dōjo*, her whiplike grace and speed, the almost gentle touch she had in throwing her opponents to the resilient wooden floor.

'Come on, Mai,' he said, cajoling. He smiled. 'Let's go out. We can get some dim sum. I want to have a good time.'

She turned her head up to him. 'Already it has the feel of the last night.' She smiled thinly, that odd almost twisted expression she knew hid the beauty of her face. 'Remember, I know what it's like. I was there.' She meant Southeast Asia during the war. 'You have that feel about you now.'

'You're crazy.'

'You had it when you walked through the door,' she persisted.

'Come on,' he said again. 'Dim sum's your favourite.'

'I'm not hungry,' she said. 'Besides eating across a table in some flyblown restaurant is not how I want to remember you. I already have too many of those memories. We'll stay in tonight.' She slid out of his embrace like a wraith and began to unbutton her dress.

Following her with his eyes, Tracy said, 'No, Mai. Not now.'

She turned around at that and smiled. Her arms opened wide. 'You see?' Her voice was triumphant. 'But you want to "have fun".' She could mimic him very well when she had a mind to. 'You want to go out and eat; you want to drink.' She went to the sideboard. 'You can drink just as well up here, you know.'

Tracy turned away from her, stared out the window. The smell of fresh squid and frying sesame oil, fragrant dumplings steaming, the sharp tang of chilli paste. There was an argument in Cantonese going on in the street just below and he followed it for a time, reluctant to return his attention to the room.

'Don't you think,' she said quite close to him, 'that I don't know why you started seeing me? I began to suspect after the first nightmare. By the time the second came and went, I was certain.'

Tracy turned from the window; the conversations were both going to get nasty. 'It was very uncomplicated,' he said. 'I liked you.'

'You liked something you saw in me you mean.'

'Bullshit. I –'

'Do I look so much like her then,' she said with enough force to check him. He had never seen her like this. She had always been sweetness and light. Her small teeth were bared and he felt her presence in a very kinetic way, just as if they were both within the precincts of the *dojo*. It was not that he thought she might physically assault him, merely that the rawness of emotion was forcing that inner core of energy outward into the room. Quite naturally, he was the target.

She turned her face quickly from one side to another as if she were facing a mirror. 'Tell me, Tracy. I want to know. How much of her do you see in me? Could I be her sister? Her niece, cousin, what?' He was tensed now because the intrinsic force was rising and he hoped she could control it or he would have to do it himself. He did not want to do that; she might get hurt. 'How much of Tisah do you see in me?'

'Too much.' Perhaps the truth would defuse her. He did not move, knowing she would just come after him with her power increasing.

'I can't help what I feel,' he said carefully. 'But you must know that wasn't the only reason I wanted you.'

'But it *was* a reason.'

'Yes,' he said without hesitation.

'Well.' The force was ebbing and he breathed a silent sigh of relief. It had been very close.

'She must've meant a great deal to you.' Mai returned to the sideboard as if nothing out of the ordinary had happened. There was no trace of hurt or anger in her voice. 'To dream about her now.'

'Once, yes.'

She turned, a partly-filled glass in her hand. 'But no more.' He said nothing. Their eyes locked. 'That is why you sought me out, why you were attracted to me.'

'It was easy,' he said softly. 'You're beautiful, smart and very efficient where your body is concerned. It was natural.'

Just like my attraction to John Holmgren, he thought. He had been deeply wounded when he had met the man. John had been his lifeline, his road to recovery. He could think and plan in the relative safety of the Governor's long shadow – except John had been a councilman then – resting up from his extended ordeal until the time was right to spread his own wings again.

Christ, but it seemed like another lifetime. What was it Jinsoku had told him on graduation day from the Mines? *They'll use you until you drop, if you let them. They've no compassion in them. They burn people out like batteries. I don't want that to happen to you. Not to you.*

But, he saw now, it *had* happened to him . . . without his even knowing it until it was far too late. They had conditioned him well, made him used to moving too hard and too fast. How glad he was to have got out. To have met John.

'Your thoughts are very far away,' Mai whispered, coming up against his back. He could feel the insistent press of her breasts, the nipples sharp. There was time enough for that now, he thought. Mai was right. His life had changed again. John Holmgren's death had made it so. It had been to his power base that Tracy had come, tapping in easily, expanding on it, turning a councilman into the governor and then . . . President. Or so it had seemed. Now it was nothing but ashes. He found that he had no desire to give everything up just like that.

'Your thoughts are in the past,' Mai said throatily. Her sinewy arms were around him, searching. 'There's nothing to be done about that, isn't that clear to you yet?'

'You're wrong,' he said, staring out the window in front of them. A chorus of children's cries broke through the clatter from below, full of exuberant joy. 'The past holds the key to everything.'

Mai put her head down, her cheek against him, in acknowledgement of the truth. 'Then let tonight be the last night for you to forget it all.'

January 1963
Phnom Penh, Cambodia

'To which religion do you belong?'

'I am a Buddhist, *Lok Kru*.'

'What is the formula for guidance?'

'I follow the Buddha as my guide, I follow the Doctrine as my guide, I follow the order as my guide.'

There was an ancient wooden box on a sill just above Preah Moha Panditto's left shoulder. Khieu Sokha tried not to look at it but he found it increasingly difficult. For one thing, it was exceedingly beautiful. It was lacquered a deep glossy maroon over which a graceful blossom of rich saffron and cool emerald had been painted.

'Who is the Buddha?'

For another, it was set on the sill in just the spot where the morning sun's rays slanting in illuminated it in a diffuse and unearthly glow.

'He who, of His own strength attained perfection, enlightenment, and deliverance in His life. The holy and wise proclaimer of the truth.' It drew his attention like a powerful magnet until he began to feel drowsy with its insistent pull.

'Is the Buddha a god who manifested himself to humanity?'

'No.' Movement near the box; a shadow falling across the stone of the sill.

'Or was He a god's messenger who came down upon earth in order to bring salvation to men?'

'No.' Khieu Sokha's dark eyes flicked towards the moving shadow, saw that it was a large beetle crawling across the stone towards the box. Its carapace was a shiny black, as round as a barrel. It crawled laboriously up the side of the box, across the field of yellow and green.

'Was he then a human being?'

Khieu Sokha's eyelids flickered ever so lightly as his concentration waned. 'Yes,' he intoned. 'He was born a human being;

41

but such a one as appears only once in many thousands of years. To the child-like perception of the people they may appear as "gods" or "god's messengers".' But as a consequence, the inflection in his voice had become stilted and wooden.

'What is the meaning of the word?'

The beetle had stopped at the brass latch. Khieu Sokha blinked his eyes in astonished disbelief. In the glow of the sunlight it actually appeared as if the insect were trying to open the latch to gain access to the inside of the box. Impossible!

'The awakened or the Enlightened One,' he said almost mechanically. 'It designates a being who, by His own power, has acquired the highest wisdom and moral perfection attainable by a living being.'

Preah Moha Panditto stirred at last. That was not the name he had been born with; that was one of the many things he had willingly discarded upon taking up the priesthood. It was Sanskrit terminology: *Preah* meant variously *king*, *Buddha*, *god*; *Moha* was the word for *great*; and *Panditto* was an inclusive designation for a Buddhist monk. However, Khieu Sokha addressed him as *Lok Kru*: the Khmer word for *teacher*.

Preah Moha Panditto was an old man but only in terms of mortal chronology. When he bothered to remember the date of his birth and count up the intervening years, which was less and less often as time obscured what meaning it had once had, he was surprised to realize that he had lived upon the earth more than eighty years.

He looked no more than fifty: his eyes were bright with life and energy, his skin still taut across his muscles and skull. But when one was fully integrated into the universe as Preah Moha Panditto was, one heard not the insistent buzz of the mortal clock but the slow tick of the cosmic metronome. Time no longer weighed heavily on him, pulling at his soul like gravity. This he had contemplated many times, believing it to be the true meaning of levitation.

'Sokha,' he said so softly that the boy's attention was returned to him immediately, 'when were you born?'

'On the full moon day of the month of May.' He used the formal designation.

'That also was the date of the Buddha's birth.' His liquid eyes, which seemed to Khieu Sokha to be the most remarkable eyes he had ever seen, containing every shade of colour he saw in the earth and sky, regarded him with intense expression. 'Of course the Buddha was born a long time ago, in the year 523 before the beginning of the Western Christian era.' Those fabulous eyes closed. 'Perhaps that accounts for the vast differences between you.'

'I do not understand.'

Preah Moha Panditto's eyes snapped open. 'I am certain you do not,' he said softly, sadly.

Khieu Sokha knew a rebuke when he heard one. 'You are angry with me, *Lok Kru*.'

'I am angry with no one,' the old monk said. His opened palm lifted from the harbour of his lap. 'But please be kind enough to tell me what it is that occupies your attention so completely that you recite your lessons by rote instead of from your heart.'

'Is it true, *Lok Kru*, that there are no secrets from you?'

Preah Moha Panditto was silent.

'Then you should already know.'

'Even if that be so, I would hear it from your own lips.'

Khieu Sokha leaned forward eagerly, his eyes alight. 'Does that mean you *do* know?'

The monk smiled. 'Perhaps.' He waited.

At last the boy pointed and said, 'That beetle on the lacquered box.'

Preah Moha Panditto did not turn around to look. 'What is it you think it wants?'

Khieu Sokha shrugged. 'I don't know. Who can say what is in the mind of an insect?'

'If it were you?' he whispered.

The boy thought a moment, concentrating. 'I'd want to get inside.'

'Yes,' the old monk said. 'If you want to open the box, that is what you must do.'

The boy stood up, went towards his teacher. At his side, he reached up onto the sill and, as the shadow of his hand crossed the crest of the lacquered box, the great black beetle fled along

43

the edge of the window, disappearing into the light of the morning sun.

Khieu Sokha stood on tiptoe, craning his neck as he opened the latch of the brass lock. The lid came away easily. 'I can see nothing.'

'Then bring down the box.'

This the boy did quite carefully with both hands wrapped around the warm wood. He turned the thing so that sunlight filled its interior. He gasped, then reluctantly lifted his eyes to Preah Moha Panditto's face.

'Dead beetles,' he whispered. 'I see a mound of empty husks.' He had to look again, the rainbows of light prisming off the glossy black of the lifeless carapaces, drawing him.

'Beautiful, are they not?'

'Yes. The light . . .'

'And when the light is gone?'

Khieu Sokha manoeuvred the box, tilting it away from the window. 'Nothing,' he said. 'A blackness deeper even than the night.'

A stillness had crept into the room. It made the boy look up, startled. He turned his head this way and that as if to find the source of that extraordinary stillness but he saw nothing out of the ordinary. He returned his attention to the contents of the box.

'But why would the beetle try to get in here?' he asked. 'I found only death.'

'You are the world,' Preah Moha Panditto said slowly. 'You eat the world. When you know this, you know everything.'

Khieu Sokha looked at his teacher and he was astonished for he saw emanating from him a certain light, an aura of power he felt rather than saw. It awed him and he found himself trembling. He placed the box back on the sill for fear of dropping it.

He was close to tears, frightened though he could not understand why. He wondered if any mortal man should have that power. But the *Lok Kru* was no mortal man; he was Preah Moha Panditto. Then he wondered what it would be like to have such a power himself. What would he have to do? What would he have to give up? For he knew that all life was a balance. One could not gain such power without shedding other things. Important things. What were they? he wondered.

'I see by your face,' the old monk said kindly, 'that I have your attention now.' And his hands came up, drawing Khieu to him in a loving embrace.

His older brother, Samnang, was waiting for him outside. They were within the grounds of Prince Sihanouk's Royal Palace. Khieu Sokha stopped where he was, turned to look behind him at the many-tiered golden pagoda on the roof of Botum Veddey, the temple he had just come from. Sunlight streaked down from the heavens, striking Botum Veddey, dazzling him with its intensity. To his left were carefully pruned trees, whispering a melodious song in the breeze; to his right was the enormous pillared structure of the Royal Palace itself. Khieu Sokha thought he had never really understood the true nature of its beauty before.

'Ho, *Own*, Little One,' Khieu Samnang said, smiling. 'You look as if you've lost your bearings.'

The decorative wall that separated this part of the compound from the entrance gardens appeared so white to him that he was obliged to squint. He felt an urge to put his arm up to shield his eyes from the aura but he resisted; he did not want to miss this moment but to drink it all in.

Finally his gaze fell upon his brother and he smiled up at him.

'What has Preah Moha Panditto been teaching you this day?' Samnang said. 'You no longer look like yourself.'

'No?' Sokha said. 'Who is it I look like?'

His older brother laughed and they began to walk. 'Here,' he said, handing Sokha a package. 'I brought you lunch.'

'Thank you, Sam.' He accepted the package, held it close to his chest. It made him happy to receive it.

Beyond the high tiered gate he could see the persimmon-coloured robes of the Buddhist priests as they walked the ground. Many of them held white parasols over their head to keep out the strong sunlight.

The two brothers walked the gardens, the red brick paths zigzagging through the new-mown lawns, the circular flower beds, the sculptured emerald hedges. Stone *naga* were everywhere, their seven-headed presences following the boys wherever they went.

At length they found a stone bench and sat. From there they could just make out the forest of stone *chedi* monolith monuments commemorating the dead; caskets for the ashes of the ancients.

Samnang produced his bowl of rice filled with cooked fish and shrimp paste. He began to eat. Sohka held his bowl in his lap, his two palms cupped around its cool and comforting underside. He was not hungry. His belly was filled with something other than food.

Almost without thinking, he said: 'I am the world. I eat the world. I know this; I know everything.'

His brother heard him and laughed, not unkindly. 'I encountered that same feeling once, myself,' he said, shovelling the rice into his mouth. 'I thought I understood everything then.'

'But it's true,' Sokha said. 'I know it is.' He noticed the laughter of his brother. 'Are you making fun of it?'

Samnang shook his head. 'No. I'm not making fun of it, Sok. I merely question it.'

Sokha turned towards his brother. 'Question it? How can you question something that is our life?' His lunch lay forgotten beside him on the stone bench. 'You speak about Buddhism as if it is a thing that we choose. Buddhism is what makes us . . . us. What would we be without it, tell me that? Ever since I could string words into a sentence I have studied the catechism.' He touched his chest with the end of a forefinger. 'I am it and it is me.'

Samnang smiled, ruffled his brother's hair. 'How much fervour you have, *Own*.' He laughed. 'But you are only eight years old. Every Khmer begins as you have begun. There is much yet for you to learn.'

'Yes. I know that,' Sokha said excitedly. 'And Preah Moha Panditto is my guide. You should've seen it, Sam! The power he has! He reached out to me. And when he touched me I felt

46

it running down all through my body like a heat. I *felt* it like it was alive!'

His brother was nodding. 'Yes. I know. *Stiap Stanisuk*. The Touch of Peace. It *is* alive, *Own*. Once, I too was thrilled with it, much the same way you are. But I am older; I see a little better.' He shrugged his shoulders. 'What good is the *Stiap Stanisuk* to us? How can it help us in the real world?'

'Help us? I don't understand,' Sokha said. 'Why do we need help?'

'Because,' Samnang said softly, 'there is change coming. René says that revolution is the only way towards change. He says that Cambodia is being slowly ground into dust through the corruption of Sihanouk and his family.'

René Evan was a rather young pale-faced Frenchman, one of the editors of *Réalités Cambodgiennes*. He had come to Phnom Penh from his native country via Saigon. What he had been doing there was anybody's guess but that mystery that had about it the air of outlaw activity, Sokha was to realize much later, was one of the main factors that attracted his older brother to the foreigner. In any event they had become close during the past year and though he had tried often to deny it, Khieu Sokha had begun to discern in his brother a difference of opinion.

'René says that the Vietnamese are our real enemies,' Samnang was saying, 'and he's right. Despite what Sihanouk may say, they are our hereditary enemy.' He put aside his empty bowl. 'All you need do is remember your history lessons.

'Chey Chetha, our ill-remembered king who foolishly married a Vietnamese princess. You remember, Sokha, it was a time before there was even the name Vietnam. They were called Annamese but they were devious all the same. The princess pleaded with her new husband to allow her people to live in the southern part of Cambodia and he, like the weak-willed fool that he was, complied. The Annamese moved in and that was the beginning of our long history of invasion. They would not leave, immediately claiming the territory theirs. You know as well as I do that part of Vietnam is really Cambodia. So you see, it's a historical fact that you cannot trust the Vietnamese.

'It burns me up inside when I see that Vietnamese family

living near to us in Chamcar Mon. What right have they to be there? It is Sihanouk's doing, I tell you. He lives in Chamcar Mon four days a week with Monique and her clique of followers. Why else would they be there?'

'I don't see anything wrong with them,' Sokha said with a child's simple logic. 'They've never hurt us; they've never been mean to me or you or any of us.'

Samnang looked at his brother's troubled face and felt inside himself the white hot spark of rage. He struggled to smile, to quell the fire inside him; he had just come from seeing René. Always René lit that fire within him with his words.

Smiling still, he put his arms around his brother's shoulders, squeezed him in an embrace. The love between them was very strong. 'There is no one else to talk to,' he said softly, 'so sometimes I talk to you. You're all I have; the only one who understands.'

'I understand, *Bawng*,' Khieu Sokha said, wanting desperately to be of help to his brother. It filled him with happiness that they should be here together talking. 'You know I do.'

'Yes,' Khieu Samnang said, closing his eyes. 'Now forget what I've said. It's nothing.' But soon, he thought. Soon it will be something.

2

Kim was down in the Library, taking notes on the 'Ragman' file when the summons from the Director came. The librarian relayed the message that he was wanted upstairs.

Kim nodded, looked once more at his notes to make certain he was at last on the right track. Then he closed the file, got up from the leather and wood chair, took his notes to the shredder, fed them in. Nothing written was allowed out of the Library without a double signing.

He returned the file to the Librarian, logging in the time and scribbling his signature just below it. He nodded again to the nondescript man and went out along the narrow corridor.

Everywhere there were deep pile carpets. It was very quiet in here on all levels; one of the Director's prerequisites. Even on the first two floors of the building housing the Dieter Ives Music Foundation and Library, open to the public, setting perhaps two dozen grants per year to young American composers – the façade behind which the real foundation did its work – the use of earphones when playing back musical selections was mandatory. Only on alternating Sundays, when recitals were held in the auditorium in the back of the building, was there any sound at all above a soft murmur.

For Kim this studied silence nurtured the memories of his long-dead family that were all that kept him alive now. These vivid memories had allowed him to be patient; time had a different meaning for him than it did for most people.

Ascending in the elevator, he thought of what his patience had brought him. Now was the time, he told himself, to set it all in motion. He had the last piece of the puzzle at last, felt the elemental urge of the hawk as its powerful wings flutter just before it takes to the air after spotting its prey. It had taken him a long time to run down this one. Many lifetimes, it seemed.

Emerging onto the top floor, he looked out the fortress-shaped window onto K Street, watching the pedestrian flow. To the east was Farragut Square and the YWCA, near enough to the White House to get more than tourists walking by.

Kim turned from the window without a backward glance. He went through the two doors, the first opening towards him, the second, opening away from him.

He stood on Astroturf but there was no impulse to smile. The Director engendered no such levity. He was a bear of a man, impressive even to Kim, who had been trained to ignore physiognomy. The Director had a prognathous jaw dominating everything but his hard glittery eyes. Kim did not like the Director's eyes; they reminded him too much of Tracy Richter's.

'Have a good time in Florida?' the Director said like thunder.

'Florida's intolerable in the summer,' Kim came into the room.

The Director came out from behind his battleship of a desk, folded his arms across his massive chest. He was as close as a mere human being could get to looking like one of the heads on Mt Rushmore.

'Kim,' he said, 'you and I go back a long way. I hired you against the recommendations of a number of people for whom I normally have a great deal of respect.'

The Director pushed off from the desk like a cruiser heading for deep water. 'Now I trust I don't have to reiterate what a unique position you hold in the foundation. In some ways you have more freedom than I do. So much so that if the President ever got wind of it, he'd have my nuts in a sling.'

'We both know why you allow it.'

'Hell, yes, don't we though.' The Director allowed a smile to break through the ice. 'Jesus, you do one *helluva* job for us where we need it the most.' His arms broke apart like roiling thunderheads. 'While all those other bastards're chasing their tails in Southeast Asia, we have you building up files thicker than my wrist on all the most militant Communist leaders.' He brought up one hand, cocked it like a pistol. 'And then one by one' – he closed one eye, aiming – 'boum, boum, boum, they disappear into the night like red flowers.'

He pushed his shirtsleeves up as if the most difficult work were yet ahead of him. 'But then again that's not all of it.'

Kim knew now what the Director was leading to but he would be goddamned if he'd give him any help. He stayed silent.

'Kim,' the Director said, in his most serious voice, 'you spend your life terminating people. You do it better than almost anyone else alive today. Fine. That's what you're paid to do.' The Director squinted and the sun went out. 'I think it's reasonable to assume that when you're back home on vacation you could think of something *else* to do.'

'Do you know –'

'Yes,' the Director interrupted, 'I know who Lon Nam was.'

'He was a slaughterer of babies!' Kim cried. 'A butcher in the forests of Cambodia. He deserved less than the execution I gave him.'

'What he deserved or did not deserve,' the Director said evenly, 'is not at issue. It was a sanctionless execution and *that* I will not tolerate. Even from you. Your value to me only goes so far. Just be damned glad you're not in the CIA. Timpson would take you down so hard you'd be crawling for the next six weeks.'

'You shouldn't've found out,' Kim said. 'There was no way –'

'But I *did* find out, didn't I?' The Director smiled without warmth. 'Don't let your position here inflate your ego, Kim, or one day you'll be looking into the sun with blind eyes.'

He turned away abruptly, a sign that the interview was at an end. 'That's *your* lesson for today.'

Three days a week Khieu worked for Pan Pacifica, a non-profit organization dedicated to bringing Americans and Asians closer together through cultural and artistic understanding.

Pan Pacifica occupied three floors of a modern office building on Madison Avenue in the mid-sixties. It thrived through corporate and individual sponsorships, in no small part due to the recent prodigious growth in trade with the Japanese, Chinese and Thais.

But much of the work it provided was less immediately visible to the public. That included succour and refuge, resettlement and reeducation for the stream of Vietnamese and Cambodian refugees coming into the country. Already it had, in great part, been responsible for setting up the first few Cambodian Buddhist temples in the United States: in Washington, DC, Los Angeles and, most recently, in New York City.

It was in this less public area that Khieu worked. He spent much of those three days a week confronting a seemingly endless parade of Cambodians with blasted, frightened eyes. The awful mirror their faces presented him was, he felt, a fitting reminder of all he had left behind; all his father had saved him from. And each evening when he left the office he felt an overwhelming gratitude for the safety he had been abruptly – and sometimes he felt miraculously – provided.

Khieu's exotic good looks were a source of comment at Pan Pacifica as it was everywhere he went. A large percentage of the organization's personnel was Caucasian and female. The executive director tended towards the younger applicants in her hiring principally because she felt they were more idealistic and more enthusiastic.

For his part Khieu took the inevitable brushes with flirtation with a mixture of cool grace and curiosity; he wondered what it was the women saw in him. This reaction only succeeded in fuelling the flames.

There came a time when a great deal more than flirtation was delivered to him. At about the same time Kim and the Director were deep in conversation almost three hundred miles away, Khieu looked up from his desk to see Diane Samson standing over him.

She was young and, being in the publicity department, quite beautiful. That was an attribute the executive director insisted on. The public face of Pan Pacifica was of paramount importance to her.

'Yes?' he said. He did not put down the pen he had been using to draw up plans for a second New York Cambodian enclave in Brooklyn.

'I'd like to talk to you about the refugee problem,' Diane said.

Behind the large-lensed glasses, her blue eyes shone. 'I think it's time we did some print promotion of that side of us. *The New Yorker*, *Business Week* and *Forbes* seem the most logical places to start but I need to talk to you about copy.' She leaned towards him, put her knuckles on the edge of his desk and said very directly, 'Can you give me some time?'

Khieu nodded. 'All right.'

'Let's see. You won't be here tomorrow.' She cocked her head. 'Could we do it now, d'you think?'

Khieu rarely made lunch plans; there was always too much work and he was conscious of the fact that he did not spend five days a week heré. He had not finished the enclave proposal but, all things considered, he thought it could wait. He stood up from behind his desk, stretched. 'Any place special in mind?' He watched her eyes straying to the play of his taut muscles beneath his shirt.

'How about my place?' Diane whispered, leaning in.

She was not kidding. She lived less than five blocks away on East Seventieth Street, in a small but well-kept brownstone. From the bedroom you could look out at the leafy backyard filled with an old lightbarked American elm.

He allowed her to lead him through the apartment to the bedroom, then stood looking at the sunlight dappling the ground below through the multitudes of boughs while she slowly unknotted his tie, unbuttoned his shirt.

He felt its brief tickle as it slid down his bare arms, turned his head to watch her as her coral lips opened and her tiny tongue came snaking out to surround his nipple.

It erected under her tender ministrations and she moaned, running her fingertips lightly over the muscles of his arms, shoulders and chest. But he felt nothing.

He felt nothing, too, when she slid his pants down, gasping at his hard length. He stepped out of the puddle of his trousers and picked her effortlessly up in his arms, carrying her to the bed.

He removed her blouse and was astonished to feel the force of her emotions when he bent his head towards her, sucked a nipple into his mouth as she had done for him. Obviously, she felt something; some powerful pull he was as yet unaware of.

He scooped her breasts together, licked up and down the cleavage until her restless body told him to return to her nipples. She moaned when he took them inside his mouth one by one, babying them.

'I feel it,' she whispered. 'I feel it all the way down to my thighs.' Her eyelids were fluttering.

Khieu wondered what it was she was feeling and put her fingertips up against his own nipples so that he might feel it himself. She played with them, twirling them and rubbing them but still he felt nothing.

Yet I am hard, he told himself, staring for a moment down at his rampant penis; I am always hard in these encounters. Yet what do I really feel?

He felt the momentary warmth at the moment of his penetration. He felt how moist she was. But he also saw in her eyes how much she wanted his penis and he did not understand that passion.

He charged into her and, knowing where it felt best for women, rose high inside her.

She groaned and clutched him, her legs coming up around him, her heels at the small of his back pushing and relaxing, pushing and relaxing.

Khieu felt her muscles tensing, bunching up and beginning to tremble. Then he backed off and she cried out for him to continue. Her hips pushed up against him until her damp buttocks were off the bed, clenched hard but he used his superior strength to keep himself from hilting her. He rubbed the tip of himself inside her while his head swooped down and he licked her breasts again.

'Oh, I can't ...' Her voice was aqueous with desire. She strained upward again. 'I can't ...' Eyes squeezed shut, arms drawn taut across the rippling muscles of his back. 'Stand it!'

And with a great effort, she levered herself all the way up, rubbing her pelvis hard against him.

Then Khieu pushed her flat down against the mattress,

54

moving very fast, high up within her to give her the maximum sensation.

He heard her gasp in his ear, gurgle like a small child who has difficulty swallowing. Her inner muscles clamped themselves around his penis as he slid back and forth inside her.

Abruptly, he was cast down into viscous shadow; his hand pained him in quick, bright bursts like the hideous blossoms of mortar fire. Firestorms of images coming and he fought them back.

She was gasping like an engine out of control and once he was certain she called out his name. Her rigidity fixed him, her enormous tension transfering itself to him at the last moment.

He knew that moment, understood it as the time when his penis would spurt its semen. He did, in retrospect, feel some pleasure then. A tiny ball of intense heat in the spot covered by his pubic hair. He expelled an indrawn breath at its reflexive force while Diane sobbed into his sweat-soaked chest.

But there was nothing else to it. He wondered again as he walked slowly back to the office just what strange emotion had suffused Diane Samson, overpowering her with its force. At the very end when he had released himself into her, he had felt just a breath of it like a heated desert wind that hinted of the furnace of its origin but did no more.

And that was the most curious part; the part most mysterious to him. He did not often choose to think about that dark area. It reminded him too much of vague unnamed feelings he would arise with some mornings. They seemed to come most often the day after he had his nightmares which continued to possess him every ten or eleven days like clockwork.

He would always awake from those in the dead of night, sweatdrenched, breathing as if he had just run twenty miles over hard terrain, his mind filled with the heat of the falling napalm like a strap across his back, the stench of cindered human flesh clogging his nostrils.

Then he would cross to the ancient wooden statue of the Amida Buddha in his room, light a prayer candle and sink down onto his knees, in front of the enlightened face. He would pray diligently and long, as he had been taught by Preah Moha Panditto. And at length his mind would be clear again.

And invariably the next night he would sleep all the way through only to awaken in the pale light of dawn with the disquiet he somehow associated with his lovemaking suffusing him, bringing a sharp constriction to his groin.

His right hand would ache and he'd look around wildly, feeling the heated breath of that unknown furnace closing on him, brushing past him just a heartbeat away.

On Madison and Fiftieth, a black man with hair like greased snakes danced on the spot to Rastafarian Judge Dread. Earphoned into his Sony Walkman tapeplayer, he offered leaflets for a massage parlour around the corner, to every male who came his way.

But just a block away, the polished limos were lining up like a black caravan from the East, about to unload in front of St Patrick's Cathedral on Fifth.

The recently sandblasted face rose upward majestically, its twin spires seeming pale and remote in the brilliant late morning light. A pride of policemen had sent the sidewalk vendors and the shining-faced Three Card Monte practitioners scurrying for more felicitous precincts.

Tracy, standing on the steps of St Patrick's, saw the limo he had sent to pick up Mary Holmgren slide to a halt and went down to get her.

She was a thin woman with chestnut hair, a hard chin and pale nononsense eyes. She was dressed in black, more formally than anyone else, with a small hat and attaching veil.

'Hello, Mary,' he said softly. 'How are you?'

Mary Holmgren stood up, faced him. She was completely oblivious to the ranks of reporters, television and still cameras emplanted outside a roped-off barrier. Her face looked fresh and healthy.

She eyed him, put her black-gloved hands on the shoulders of the teenage girl who emerged behind her. 'You know my daughter, Anne.'

'Of course.'

'Margaret,' Mary Holmgren said in a voice like granite, 'please take Anne inside. I shall join you momentarily.' A tall, white-fleshed creature nodded her small head, took Anne's head, leading her up the steps as cameras ground away for history and flashbulbs exploded like miniature suns.

'She'll emerge the heroine from all this,' Mary Holmgren said, watching the straight line of her daughter's back.

'Is there anything I can do, Mary?'

Mary Holmgren linked her arm through his. She accepted the con-dolences of the city's comptroller and borough president, nodded at a representative she knew only slightly. She pulled on Tracy's arm.

'Is she here?'

Tracy knew instantly that she meant Moira. 'No, she isn't.'

She patted the back of his hand. 'Good. I could always count on you to do the right thing, Tracy.'

'Mary —'

'No!' Her voice was sharp, though low; this conversation was only for the two of them. 'We'll have none of that. Today or any other day. I am no longer concerned with what John did. Why should I be? He no longer is.'

She took them up the steps slowly. 'I'm glad you met me,' she said more gently. 'You were John's best friend. I think he would have been lost without you and for that I am eternally grateful to you.' She turned to him, nodded across at the mayor while she said to him, 'She would have taken him away from me, in the end, I know that.' He saw tears at the corners of her eyes now like tiny diamonds shivering in the sunlight. 'But, oh, he had so much more to do. So much more!'

He gripped her arm more tightly, lifting her upward as they ascended each step as if it were another plateau on the way towards heaven. He wanted to put his arm around her but he knew her well enough to understand that she would view that as an unforgivable sin. It had always been John who cried on her shoulder, needing solace, not the other way around. Perhaps, Tracy thought now, whatever solace Mary had ever needed she found every Sunday in church.

At the top of the steps they paused and Mary Holmgren, very

uncharacteristically, pulled him close. He could feel the shivering of her flesh. 'Tracy,' she whispered, 'I'll tell you something no one knows, though John may have suspected. I wanted more than anything else to be the First Lady of this country. There was so much I could do, too. So much!' Her eyes opened and he saw the emptiness there.

They went through the open doors, into the dim cool echoing interior, dominated by the dusky multi-coloured light filtered through the stained glass.

'In remembering John Holmgren, each in our own way,' the Archbishop said, unconsciously echoing Mary Holmgren's sentiments, 'we should look not to the past but to the future that he has provided us. The list of John Holmgren's good works for this state and for this city are too numerous to recount here.' Then he proceeded to recount them.

Tracy, sitting directly behind Mary and Anne Holmgren, was thinking of Moira almost as much as he was about John. In his heart he felt slightly guilty for not smuggling her into St Patrick's. But it was not a potential confrontation with Mary Holmgren that had prevented him from bringing her in; that would have been easy enough to avoid.

It was Thwaite Tracy was concerned about. He had no wish to subject Moira to that bastard's idea of an interrogation. As long as she was out of the city she was safe from him.

Tracy was an excellent judge of people and he suspected that an official Hands Off would be insufficient to deter the detective. Whether it was because he was smart enough or stupid enough to continue, Tracy had not yet determined.

The Archbishop's eulogy droned on endlessly, prompting Tracy to consider the fact that if John himself were here he'd throw up his hands in disgust.

There were a brace of hymns and then, mercifully, it was over. It's just as well Moira was spared this farce. The whole thing, he recognized now, had been for Mary – as well as for the media.

'Mr Richter.'

Tracy turned. Hushed voices spiralled off the cathedral's high ceiling. The casket had been taken solemnly out and down the steps, Mary and Anne walking just behind.

'Yes?' He saw a man of average height with gold-rimmed glasses and a hard savvy face. He was wearing a dark grey suit and black loafers.

'I'm Stephen Jacks.' He did not extend his hand. 'Atherton Gottschalk's aide.'

'Gottschalk's in town?'

'Of course. He came to pay his respects to John Holmgren.'

Tracy looked around at the crush of people. 'I haven't seen him.'

'You wouldn't,' Jacks said. 'Unfortunately, he was called away for a strategy session.' Jacks grimaced. 'The road a presidential candidate must tread is difficult indeed.'

'Aren't you getting a little ahead of yourself?' Tracy said. 'Your boss doesn't even have his party's nomination yet.'

Jacks smiled. 'It's only a matter of time. I have no doubt he'll come out of the convention in August as the Republican candidate.'

'So Gottschalk sent you to convey his condolences.'

'In a manner of speaking only.' Jacks's teeth shone. 'We both know that he and the Governor were not exactly ready to climb into bed together, as it were, though they were both Republicans. He felt – quite rightly, I might add – that John Holmgren was becoming too powerful a force for the party's own good.'

'You mean for the direction Gottschalk is seeking for the party,' Tracy said. 'I don't think you'd be so confident of victory in August if John were still alive.'

'Be that as it may, Mr Richter, Mr Gottschalk is still here and Holmgren is not.'

'Get out of here, Jacks,' Tracy said, abruptly furious.

'Just as soon as I deliver my message.' He took a step closer to Tracy. 'Mr Gottschalk's car will pick you up outside your office in precisely' – he looked at his gold chronometer – 'twenty-five minutes. He wishes to see you.'

'I'm not interested.'

'You're being foolish, Mr Richter. One does not turn down such an invitation.'

'You've just seen it done.'

Cords of anger stood out along the side of Jacks's neck. 'Now listen to me, you sonuvabitch. I'm not one of those who feel you should be treated with kid gloves.' He lowered his voice even further but there was more force to it now. 'You're a fucking menace to the future of our party. We know how much influence you wielded over Holmgren. I'm not going to lie to you; we don't want that to happen again.'

'Happily that's not up to you.'

'We'll see,' Jacks said. 'You're playing a very dangerous game; I don't think you understand that yet.' He thrust his face forward. 'Just do as you're told. You'd – Oof!' Jacks's eyes opened wide behind the lenses of his glasses, magnified into fish's pop eyes.

Tracy, using his body as an intervening barrier to block out the movement from the milling people, had jammed the ends of his stiff fingers up into the soft flesh directly beneath Jacks's rib cage. 'Go on,' he whispered between clenched teeth. 'I'm really interested in what you have to say. Continue, old man.'

'Ak! Ak! Ak!' was all the aide could manage. The blood had drained from his face, leaving him ashen and sweating, and his breathing was none too healthy.

'What's that?' Tracy leaned in closer. 'I can't quite hear you.'

'I . . . can't –' The words ended in an explosion of breath as Tracy levered up again with his fingertips, his open hand hard as concrete.

'Of course you can't, you disgusting parasite.' Tracy took Jacks's head up by grabbing his jacket collar. To anyone watching it would seem as if one man were helping another regain his balance after an unfortunate slip. 'Because I say you can't.'

'Ak!' Jacks said, his tongue protruding between his lips.

'Now you're making sense, old boy. You've got the brain of a shark, primitive and one-dimensional. I know what you need to get your attention.' His fingertips came up again, a shadow of the previous blows but Jacks flinched back, his eyes fearful.

'You see what I mean?' Tracy said. He patted the aide's shoulder with his free hand. 'Now that we understand one another, you tell your boss I'll spare him exactly fifteen minutes.' He looked at his watch. 'I'll be outside my office at precisely 3.30.'

Tracy jerked at Jacks and he nodded. 'Good. Now we can both get on with our busy lives.' He let Jacks go. The man immediately doubled over, gasping for air. His eyes squeezed shut with pain. No one noticed in all the confusion.

'Have a good day,' Tracy said, walking briskly away.

'I'm glad you've got your mind prepared for bad news. It won't be such a jolt ... I mean, it's a cinch you're really sick, and it would be wrong dope to kid yourself.'

'I'm not. I know how rotten I feel, and the fever and chills I get at night are no joke. I think Doctor Hardy's last guess was right. It must be the damn malaria come back on me.'

'No, no, no,' the director shouted, stepping out from the shadows down below the proscenium of the stage. She was florid-faced and her clear dark eyes flashed with anger.

'Mr Macomber,' she said in a metallic voice that made everyone listening cringe, 'if at some stage in your lifetime you are going to call yourself an *actor*, you will have to do better than that.'

She advanced on Eliott Macomber like a field marshall on the enemy. 'I have told you time and again. *Emotional recall*.' She broke the phrase down into its component syllables, mouthing them slowly, with exaggerated care as if he were slightly retarded. 'Right now, a wooden board could put more emotion into that performance.'

'Could we ... try it again?' Eliott said hoarsely. He was sweating profusely and not from just the lights. 'I'm sure I can do better.'

The director looked at her watch, gave him a sad expression. 'I'm afraid none of us have that much time to spare, Mr Macomber.' There was a snickering from the darkness of the theatre where the rest of the students sat and Eliott felt an unpleasant heat suffuse his face and neck.

The director clapped her hands, turned away from the stage. 'All right, listen up. We'll meet one hour earlier next Friday because of our late start today.' She turned back. 'And Mr Macomber, please try to do some work in the interim.'

He watched her eyes, could not help himself. They were his mother's eyes. He blinked, on the verge of tears. Cool eyes he had seen in photographs his father had shown him when he was old enough to appreciate such things, photographs Eliott had had copied. What kind of world was it, he thought, where a son was denied his own mother? Sometimes, when he was very frightened, it calmed him to imagine reversals where his parents were concerned: that his father had died in her place.

He stepped down off the stage.

Why had he been given *Long Day's Journey into Night* to do? Christ, he knew he wasn't up to it. He felt out of his depth, frightened and somehow humiliated by the role.

He saw Nancy, one of the students in his class. She was by herself. Now, Eliott thought, is the time to ask her. He went over to her. 'Hi, Nance,' he said in his calmest voice. 'You doing anything tonight?'

She looked at him. She had long dark hair, the green eyes and the perfect white skin of a colleen. She smiled sweetly. 'No, Eliott.'

'How about us going out to a movie?'

She seemed to contemplate this for a moment. 'Well, let's see,' she said. 'My alternative is to paint my nails.' She glanced down at them, then quickly back to him. The smile was still plastered on her face. 'I think I'd rather do my nails.'

There was loud laughter from somewhere in the darkened theatre and Eliott knew he had been set up.

'Damnit!' Eliott said as Nancy disappeared into the shadows. He trembled with impotent rage. If only he could have thought of something clever and cutting to say to her. But his mind was frozen. He hit the side of his head with his fist, furious at himself.

'So filled with anger.'

He whirled around, blinked into the spotlights onstage.

There was movement from the shadows. '*C'est moi*,' Khieu said calmly.

'What the hell are you doing here?'

'I came to see you at work, Eliott.' Khieu was smiling. 'I

wanted to see for myself just what's so important that it kept you from completing your assignments.'

'Don't you worry yourself about that,' Eliott said hotly. 'I get done what I have to.'

Khieu looked around placidly. 'You gave up your work at Metronics for *this*?' He shook his head.

'I hated it there,' Eliott said, 'and you know why. I act because I love it.'

'But you're no good at it.' Khieu's tone was matter-of-fact.

'You're a bastard, you know that.'

'I only tell you the truth.' Khieu could not understand the storm he had raised. 'I would never lie to you, Eliott.'

'Huh,' Eliott grunted, 'and you have no vested interest in seeing me out of here. Expect me to believe that as well.'

Khieu shook his head. 'Not at all. You know better. But the fact remains that you showed real ability during the six months you worked at Metronics. You'd be able to see that, too, if your, er, personal feelings weren't getting in the way. The fact is,' he said quietly, 'you could have everything. Money. Power. Everything. But you feel you're being forced into it.'

He took a step towards the other. 'Take your assignments, for example. You know pieces of a larger whole. Sometimes, Eliott, I worry about that. The kind of life you live fills me with concern. There is no honour in it. Yet you are entrusted with information that is, shall we say, highly explosive in nature.'

Khieu looked hard into Eliott's dark eyes. 'Let me ask you a question. Would you tell anyone what you know about the *ankga*?'

'No,' Eliott said quickly, 'of course not.' He seemed indignant. 'Why should I?'

'Money's one reason that comes immediately to mind.'

'Listen, you sonuvabitch, I'd never do a thing like that. You don't understand the situation at all. I *couldn't* . . . it's just not in me.'

Khieu smile again. 'I'm happy to hear that, Eliott. Suspicion is an evil thing. It eats the soul.' His eyes searched Eliott's face. 'Better to get it all out in the open; to lay it to rest, don't you think?'

A figure came out of the shadows and Eliott's head turned. His heart skipped a beat. Nancy? She was smiling, looking at him. She had changed her mind, then; had come back to apologize.

'El,' she said in her sweetest voice. 'Who's your friend here?' And she turned her head towards Khieu.

Eliott tensed. His face constricted. Rage thundered through him. I should have known, a voice inside his head screamed. It's always the same story, isn't it?

'A friend of mine,' he said in a strangled voice. 'Khieu.'

Nancy studied Khieu closely. 'Are you Chinese?' She was intrigued.

'Cambodian.'

Nancy's eyes were alight. 'Were you there during the war? Did you lose your family?' She linked her arm through his, pressed the side of one breast against him. 'I'm just dying to hear all about you.'

Eliott watched them disappear into the darkness, his heart pounding hard.

'Goddamn him,' he whispered under his breath. 'Goddamn him to hell.'

Tracy emerged from the glass and marble entrance to 1230 Avenue of the Americas at precisely 3.30. He had tried, unsuccessfully, to reach Moira earlier in the day and resolved to try her again after his meeting with Atherton Gottschalk.

The gleaming black Lincoln limo was waiting for him at the kerb. As he left the building, a grey-uniformed chauffeur had got out of the off-side of the car and come around to hold open the back door for him.

Tracy stepped in, nodding at the driver, expecting to find Gottschalk reclining in one corner. However, the back of the limo was empty. As soon as he sat down, the driver started the car and they nosed noiselessly out into traffic.

They headed north, straight up Sixth Avenue towards the southernmost end of Central Park. At Central Park South, the driver took them north into the park itself, leaving the St Moritz and the rest of Hotel Row behind.

The trees were in full bloom and there were plenty of joggers even in the heat at this time of the day. Near Seventy-ninth Street, the limo slid over to the kerb, came to a stop.

Tracy got out, looked around. He saw Atherton Gottschalk standing in the shade of an umbrella attached to one of those rolling carts dispensing junk food. He was wearing a charcoal grey chalk-stripe suit. His grey wingtip shoes were highly polished. He was bare-headed, his rather longish silver hair ruffling slightly in the wind. He was eating a hot dog with apparent great relish.

On a grassy knoll beyond the horse path, the children played with a ball striped red, white and blue, laughing and giggling, not yet aware of a world filled with worry and fear. A sleek golden retriever sprang at their heels barking as if she, too, were joining in their wordless communication.

'Mr Richter,' Atherton Gottschalk said, 'it's good of you to come,' just as if he had specified the time. They began to walk across the black moist earth of a horse path, Gottschalk taking great pains not to mar the perfect gloss of his shoes.

'You know, July is a glorious month to be in New York,' he said. 'It's not yet the dog days of summer, everything is lush, and it's not nearly as stifling as it is in Washington. It truly is a shame I can't get up here more often.' He shrugged his shoulders. 'But you know what a candidate's life is like.'

Tracy studied Gottschalk as they went off the horse path, stood on the verge of a grassy knoll looking idly at the children playing.

His face was almost diamond-shaped, with a sharply prominent cleft chin, a wide mouth, dark bushy eyebrows, the skin deeply tanned and lined. He wore his hair brushed straight back off his face. He could not be more than fifty yet he possessed that depth of character and bearing rare in a man his age. He had the look, in short, of a model statesman, full of charisma and the kind of avuncular confidence that used to be Walter Cronkite's stock-in-trade.

In the sixteen years he had been in the Senate, he had had a meteoric rise and during the last two was the man to whom the President turned in seeking a positive response on the Hill to his important bills. He was a lobbying centre and, until recently, had been chairman of the Senate's select intelligence committee.

Gottschalk turned them from their contemplation of the children, said, 'You gave my man Jacks quite a reception, I understand.'

'I gave him what he asked for,' Tracy said. 'Nothing more.'

'Indeed.' Gottschalk put his hands behind his back, pushed his lips out as if giving great thought to Tracy's words. 'Well, Stephen can often be rather abusive.' The Senator gave a little laugh. 'It's one of his most useful qualities.'

Tracy said nothing.

'Well, he doesn't admire you the way I do.'

'I beg your pardon?'

'Sure I do. Is that so difficult to understand?' He turned more directly towards Tracy, his pure blue eyes shining. 'I may have hated John Holmgren's guts because his kind of pacifism and overriding attention to humanitarian concerns would have eventually torn apart our party. And had he managed to become President, I shudder to think of the disaster he would have brought us to in the international arena.

'But, hell, I knew just how much of a threat he was to me. I never made the mistake of underestimating him ... or *you*. I know what kind of talent you have for orchestrating campaigns and ongoing media attention. Hell, there isn't anyone better. That's why I came all this way. To ask you to join my campaign for the presidency.'

Tracy stared at him. He could scarcely believe what he was hearing. Atherton Gottschalk stood for everything Tracy had once walked away from.

'I'm afraid you've made the trip for nothing.'

'Now, hold on. Don't make any hasty decisions. I know what you and Holmgren were up to, trying to unseat me at the coming convention. I also know your plans extended beyond the convention. Holmgren would not have turned down his party's nomination, of that I'm quite certain.

'Why don't you think about it? The plans're already formulated. I'll just appropriate them, changing them a little, of course. What d'you say?' He smiled a campaign smile. 'It's the

66

chance of a lifetime, Tracy because I *am* going to be our party's nominee come August. And you'll be close to me. I place a very high value on a man such as yourself. You're a superlative combination of brains and guts. I like that. It touches something inside me.'

'You're talking about an impossibility,' Tracy said. 'You and I could never see eye to eye on the issues.'

'Hell, man, who cares about issues? We're not two politicians in the same race who've gotta lock horns. That's not the game here. You're my *media advisor*. Not the same thing at all.'

Tracy's gaze was unwavering. 'I think it is. I've got to believe in what I'm doing.'

'Then you're in the wrong ballgame, I'll tell you that straight out.'

Tracy shrugged.

Gottschalk stared at him. 'Since you're still in this I guess you'll be going to work for that squirt Bill Conley since he's going to run for the spot his former boss so untimely vacated.'

'I haven't made up my mind yet.'

'Oh, hell, sure. You're going to piss in the same john with Conley. I just *know* you are.'

'I just might.'

Gottschalk went very still. 'It's a whole new race now and I'm going be the one putting the first licks in, make no mistake.' A sudden streak of sunlight breaking out from behind a cloud made him squint. 'What I mean to say is, when a steamroller comes down the street, the smart man swings up onto it. Either that or he steps aside.

'The way I see it. Your only real choice is to come on in with me.' He patted Tracy on the shoulder. 'You think about it. You've got a helluva career ahead of you.'

And with that he was gone, crossing the horse path in long confident strides. In a moment, the gleaming black limo had slid away from the kerb, disappearing amid the greenery and the traffic.

In the east, clouds were piling up, their undersides bruised with incipient rain. The air had turned heavy with humidity and young mothers pushing prams now began to head out of the park towards the sheltering awnings on the east side of Fifth Avenue.

A figure in an olive trenchcoat came down off the grassy knoll and, as if on cue, walked towards Tracy. His hands were in his pockets and the gathering wind lifted the open tails of his coat so that they flapped at his Sears doubleknit suit trousers.

Even after all these years, Tracy thought, he still hasn't learned how to dress properly.

'A new career in a new town?' Kim said to him. 'And the body just cremated.'

'I thought I'd seen the last of you.' But even as he said it, Tracy knew that this meeting was perhaps inevitable. He knew what it was now that Mai had seen on him when he had come in. And it was true, they'd never see each other again. Kim had come and that meant the foundation. They weren't through with him yet.

'So did I.' Kim shrugged. 'Why don't we take a walk. Just a couple of friends out for a stroll.'

'We were never friends.'

Kim ducked his head. 'For old times' sake then.' He was careful not to touch Tracy. 'There was a time when I thought we didn't need you anymore. You see, I had always thought of you as a brilliant but highly erratic kid whose neuroses finally outweighed his usefulness.'

'But now you see it all in a different light.' Tracy could not keep the sardonic note out of his voice.

But Kim only nodded seriously. 'Yes, well, we're both older now. From this vantage point, we *do* see things differently.'

Like the muck at the bottom of a lake disturbed by a careless swimmer's kick, Tracy found unpleasant memories surfacing within tremulous bubbles. 'With maturity comes an ability to assess the past with objective eyes.'

Kim's sweating face beneath harsh lights, working his particular awful magic on a North Vietnamese. Magic was what they had decided to call it in Ban Me Thuot rather than acknowledge its real name.

Delicate, precise, vicious, Kim's expertise could extract information from even the most recalcitrant minds.

'I now understand the enormity of your contribution to the foundation,' Kim said turning up the collar of his coat as the rain came softly. 'Though I admit it shook me a bit when the Director asked me to come. I mean, why me, right? Know what he said? "I don't want someone in there who'll sweettalk him into it".'

'Whatever it is,' Tracy said quickly, 'I don't want any part of it.' He stopped, turned towards the other. They were beneath an old oak whose scarred trunk was covered in spray-paint graffiti. 'I know you very well, Kim. Your magic ... the massacres in the jungle. I used to think, Jesus, why'd they even bother to send me along with him? When it came to the Khmer you were a killing machine.'

'I was like anyone else at Ban Me Thuot.'

Tracy shook his head. 'Not at all. You went at it with a gusto that was appalling. Your interest was more than skin deep. It was cultural. You hate the Khmer just as you hate the Communists. It was the Communists who killed your family, wasn't it?'

Kim said nothing. He watched Tracy and listened to the soft patter of the rain slanting down all around them. His feet were already wet inside his shoes and socks. There was a quick sound and he turned his head to look in its direction. Tracy saw the white scar that slashed down from behind one ear along the side of his neck. When he turned back, he was smiling. 'That's all ancient history by now. What difference does it make?'

'Now you take me for a fool. It makes all the difference in the world to you. It's what makes you tick.'

'You misunderstand me, Tracy. But what is the point in explaining it. We stand here in the dampness trading insults like a couple of school boys.' All around them the world had turned grey; foliage rustled beneath the onslaught of the rain.

'You're quite correct. My family means everything to me. You who know me so well. *Too* well. I told that to the Director but he said that, too, was a plus.'

'Neither of us could ever talk him out of anything,' Tracy said by way of cutting the tension. After all, he didn't have to take the thing. He was no longer within the foundation; no longer under orders. He was his own man.

Kim caught the change in mood immediately and he relaxed somewhat. His tone softened. 'Frankly, I thought he was out of his mind to send anyone. I told him straight out I didn't think you wanted any part of us anymore.'

'You're right.'

'Then I heard what this was all about and I changed my mind.'

Tracy looked at him while a young boy bicycled through the rain, a yellow slicker pulled up over his head. There was a splash as the boy went through a puddle then he was lost within the pelting haze.

This is the moment, Tracy thought, when I should say good-bye and just walk away. Part of him wanted to, he knew that. But there was another part of him, the part that Mai had seen and reacted to. And that part was the stronger one.

'What's happening?'

Kim nodded. 'The call-up's come.' He paused for a moment as if marshalling his thoughts. 'The Buddhists have a saying. Health is the greatest blessing, contentment the best possession, a true friend the nearest of kin.' His head swung around. 'D'you believe that?'

'What is this?' Tracy said, abruptly fed up. He felt a sudden chill go through him at the idea of what he was contemplating, of what Kim had come here for. 'I was dying in the foundation. That's why I left. You didn't understand that at the time. Maybe you thought I was a coward. I don't care what you thought then or think now. It took John Holmgren to breathe the breath of life back into me.'

'Well, it's John Holmgren I've come to see you about, Tracy.' Kim said calmly. 'We think there was something unnatural about his death.'

There were more than a half dozen important matters awaiting his immediate attention when he returned to the office but Tracy was interested in none of them. After the explosive information Kim had delivered to him nothing else seemed important. They had agreed to meet later that night at John's brownstone but Tracy could not put it out of his mind.

What if it were true? The decision to cremate the body immediately had been his idea and Mary had jumped at it. She had no desire to see old rumours resurrected; she did not want John's last moments in life talked about in salacious terms, the ending of his life the punch line of smutty jokes.

Tracy punched out the number of his house in Bucks County. After three rings Moira answered. Her voice sounded soft and thin but it grew stronger after she heard his voice.

'I'm still shaky,' she said in his ear, 'but how I love this house, Tracy. I can't thank you enough for letting me stay here. I know what this place means to you.'

'Don't even think about it,' Tracy said honestly.

'What about that cop ... the detective. I don't think I'm up to seeing him yet.'

'Thwaite's out of the picture altogether. A call to the attorney-general axed him. No one's going to bother you.'

'I'm still so confused ... about what really happened.' He could hear her voice breaking apart and abruptly she was sobbing, saying brokenly, 'Oh, Tracy ... I miss him ... so much.'

'Moira,' Tracy said softly, 'in the best of all possible worlds John would still be alive and next January he would be sworn in as President. But that's not how it's going to happen now. We ... both of us have to face up to that. I know it's difficult but we have a special kinship to John. We'll miss him in special ways ... for a long time to come.'

'Yes,' came the whisper in his ear. 'I don't ...' Her voice was still thick with emotion. 'I don't know what I'd've done without you, Tracy. I want you to know that.'

'I do.'

'You know, at night when I'm inside the house, I curl up on the couch and watch the face of your Buddha. It's so beautiful, Tracy. I stare into those golden eyes and somehow I feel calmer, if only for a little while.'

They spoke for a few moments more and then said good-bye. As he hung up the receiver, Tracy swivelled in his chair, reached

71

out for a small stone carving on a stand on one of his book-shelves. It was a five-sided piece, slightly cracked along one edge. It was old, dating back to perhaps the seventeenth century. The back and sides were still rough-surfaced but the front had a rounded look, smoothed and darkened along the high ridged carving by the pressure and oils of constant rubbing.

On that face was the stylized bas-relief image of a Cambodian Buddha. He had carried this Buddha in his pocket throughout most of his stay in Southeast Asia.

He had not thought about the day he had acquired the piece in a long time. But now it seemed quite fitting for the memory to come up. He was not a believer in any religion; worship was simply foriegn to him but when Kim had recited that particular Buddhist saying, he knew just what he was doing. Tracy's sense of honour and loyalty was as deeply-rooted as the Vietnamese's hatred. There was obviously an element of Buddhism that touched him deeply.

Early on in his stay in Southeast Asia, he and three others had been dropped into the middle of the Cambodian jungle. A well-disciplined cadre of Khmer Rouge was disrupting a large sector of the US intelligence-gathering apparatus, leaving a trail of over a dozen dead agents. His mission had been to eradicate the band as swiftly as possible.

They had spent the first three days of what had been antici-pated as a highly dangerous but relatively short mission fouled in the dense and unforgiving jungles. It was just after the rainy season and the footing was treacherous. Worse, they found no signs of the Khmer Rouge band where they were supposed to have had their base camp.

Tracy had elected to push on. Although young, he was nevertheless already the leader of this small unit. None of the three was over nineteen. Tracy was just twenty-three.

By dusk of the fourth day, the boys in the unit were ready to call it quits; Tracy pushed them on. They came to the verge of dense foliage without warning.

Beyond rose ancient structures built of enormous blocks of stone. Cautiously Tracy motioned them forward.

Dusk turned the stone structures blue in the shadows as they crept along, their rifles at the ready. Tracy went up a wide flight of stairs into a gallery he judged to be at least three hundred feet long. On either side of him carvings of amazing intricacy flowered like blossoms. Mythological scenes of gods and men mingled with panoramas of ancient life. The last culture of Cambodia surrounded him, mute and impenetrable but moving for all that.

For a time devoid of seconds or minutes, he wandered the halls of history, marvelling at what had once been. But outside the gallery, the livid scars of war were everywhere in evidence. The black acid stains of napalm obscured a frieze here, a string of machine gun bullet holes had chipped away stone bodies of a line of Buddhas there.

Tracy wondered whether he had inadvertently stumbled upon fabled Angkor Wat, built by the Khmer King Suryavarman II somewhere between 1113 and 1152 AD. A temple for the god Vishnu, if he remembered correctly. But he could not place Angkor Wat on his internal map of Cambodia.

He heard a crack to his left and turned. Peters, one of the urban nomads from Detroit, had lifted the butt of his rifle, smashing off the face of one of the sculptures on the side of the building.

Tracy ran towards him, grabbed his shirt-front with his left hand, spinning him towards him, slammed the leading edge of his right knuckles into the boy's face.

Peters went down as if he had run into a sack of cement. His rifle clattered out of his hands. He looked up at Tracy and, rubbing his reddened cheek, said, 'I don't know what the hell you're getting so hot about.' He picked himself up. 'It's not like it was made by Michelangelo or something. It's a fucking slant carving, not worth a damn.' He gestured. 'I mean it's not even Christian, for Christ's sake.'

'This's history,' Tracy said. Anger clotted his voice. 'It's not yours to disfigure or destroy.'

He turned away, looked at the damage. The head of the sculpture was shattered on the stone walkway at his feet. He looked up at the newly disfigured wall, saw it was the image of Shiva Peters had wrecked. What was it the Khmer believed? The world will be all right or not depending on the rhythm of Shiva's eternal dance.

He took them cautiously through the ruined city, feeling dwarfed and somehow insubstantial among the relics time had cast up. On the far side of the city they came upon a small building that was not deserted. It was a temple.

Tracy signalled his men to keep themselves hidden. He left his weapons with them and advanced on the structure. By comparison to the looming edifices around it, the temple was a simple structure of stone. The furry edges of the snaking foliage which its one doorway faced were already creeping back over parts of it.

He heard the high palms ruffled by the wind, the echoes of the monkey's chattering which had followed them for so many days. He wished he could stay here and explore the ruins with the delight of a child.

He saw Khmer villagers emerging from the forest greenery. They laid food before the doorway of the temple for it was a basic tenet of Buddhism that the priest could not till the soil to grow his own food lest he inadvertently take the life of an innocent insect or worm.

Tracy needed information badly. He entered the temple. Inside it was dark, the atmosphere thick and smoky with incense. A gold image of the Amida Buddha dominated the room, set on a rough stone plinth.

Soldiers had come to the village where this particular Buddha had originally resided, the priest told him. They had thrown it over, scratching its face with the points of their bayonets to determine if it was solid gold.

'When they found that it had merely been gold-washed and was but stone underneath, they burned the altar on which it had sat for two centuries.' He spoke in French.

The man was small, garbed in an orange robe that covered his entire body. His scalp was shaved and as shiny as if he had oiled it. Black stubble showed there.

His face was extraordinary. It seemed to Tracy as if his features had been forged by another force besides genetics. He appeared to be part of the earth, the sky, the jungle around him. He seemed . . . in tune with everything.

But it was not until he reached out and touched Tracy that the full extent of his uniqueness became apparent. It was a touch of infinite gentleness: the caress a loving mother imparts to her child. Yet it was filled with the most awesome power Tracy had ever encountered. He was convinced that had the priest wanted to he could have bowled Tracy over with a poke of his forefinger. He seemed invincible, unstoppable, eternal.

Yet there was nothing godlike about him. He was humble, calm, as watchful as a doe at a stream. No fear flowed through him; and no hostility either. It was as if all these powerful emotions had been leached from him. As if his detachment from them had been a source of his energy. You give up a thing to gain another.

'I know why you have come here,' the priest said softly. He had switched to Khmer.

Tracy bowed his head. 'I am sorry now that I came,' he said in the same language.

'Do not feel sorry,' the priest said and something in his touch made Tracy look up. His eyes were pools that seemed to reflect the world. 'I will tell you what you wish to know.'

Unaccountably, Tracy felt the hot pressure of tears welling up behind his eyes. He wondered at it for a moment and then he understood. The calm he felt here was ageless but it was only a small oasis in the midst of a sea of spilt blood and napalm. Death and destruction and the Khmer Rouge's new order sought to stamp it out. And he understood for the first time the nature of Buddhism; that it was more than a religion. It was a way of life.

Tracy's eyes refocused. His thumb ran back and forth over the raised figure of the Buddha given to him by that priest. That unexpected visit had stayed with him, its vividness and power undiminished by the intervening years. He wondered where that priest was now. He hoped he was safe.

His intercom buzzed. 'Yes, Irene.'

'Miss Marshall's here to see you.'

Christ, Tracy thought. What else could happen today? Maybe the sky would fall in. Or perhaps it already had. He had not seen Lauren Marshall for, what?, nine, ten months. Not since the night she had walked out on him. Now she was back.

'All right, Irene,' he said. 'Send her in.'

In the split second before she entered, He imagined her as she had been, slim and lithe, the sleek dancer's body more supple than he thought any human being could be. He saw her long neck, her oval face, her long straight hair the colour of the dying sun pulled straight back from her face in a long ponytail. But mostly, he thought about how she moved from her thighs and hips. She could set his heart on fire just by walking across the room.

He was unprepared for her now. The first thing he noticed was that she had put on weight. Not much, but on the athlete's frame it did not have to be to show. Her thighs were thicker, her hips a trifle wider and Tracy wondered at that. In ballet, there was no room for even an extra pound.

Her wide-apart inquisitive eyes, contemplated him from across the room. Her hair was pulled back tightly across her scalp, the ponytail at least the same. She work a dark blue Danskin top and a simple wraparound skirt below it. The kind of thing she wore to rehearsals. On her small feet were low, heelless dancer's shoes. An emerald satin jacket with the sleeves pushed up on her forearms made her look as vulnerable as a little girl, quite a bit younger than her twenty-seven years.

She opened her mouth, said, 'Tracy', so low that had he not been looking directly at her he would not have known she had spoken. He said nothing, stared at her as if mesmerized.

She took two hesitant steps towards him and his pulse rose. 'I'm . . . surprised you'd see me.' Her voice had gained in volume somewhat. She was trying to smile. 'I didn't know whether . . . what to expect.' She was grasping the strap of her sling shoulder bag with both hands as if holding onto a lifeline. 'I'm glad. I . . .' Her voice faltered and she looked quickly around the room. 'This place hasn't changed, I see.'

'Except John's no longer in it.'

Her head jerked and she took another step forward. 'I heard about his death, naturally. I'm so sorry, Tracy. I . . . know what he meant to you.'

'Yes. I know that. Thank you.' His voice sounded so formal, so distant to his own ears. He knew he was holding himself in check.

'I don't know what else to say,' She circled the desk as if afraid if she got too close he might take a swipe at her. 'In the face of . . . this, words are so . . . foolish sounding, so inadequate.' She gave him a small brave smile but it was the first honest gesture she had made. 'I've never been very good with . . . deep emotion between people. I've had no practice, you see. No experience. I've only known one thing: ballet. I'm just no good at anything else.'

It finally dawned on Tracy that she was no longer talking about John Holmgren's death but about their love affair. 'I thought you'd be dancing,' he said by way of self-preservation.

A peculiar look came over Lauren's face. 'I haven't danced for nine months.' And now her voice was filled with an unutterable sadness. 'I hurt my hip just after I . . . we broke up.' She looked away for a moment. 'A leap during *Ballo della Regina*. I don't even know what happened.' She shrugged. 'I wasn't concentrating fully.'

'That doesn't sound like you, Lauren.'

'And that's just the trouble,' she cried. 'It *isn't* me. But I don't know who I am any more.' Her shoulders were trembling. 'I don't know what's important to me any more. I practise eight hours a day. I should be back into it but . . . I'm not.'

Her green eyes were large and luminous and for no good reason he could think of Tracy stood up, came around from behind the fortress of his desk. They stood close enough to touch but did not.

'I dance,' Lauren whispered, 'and the technique is there, it's flawless. But something's missing. And it's you.' She took a deep shuddering sigh. 'It took me all this time to realize.' She was crying now. 'I go to practise and at the *barre* I think of you.

77

Putting on my leg warmers, I think of you. Onstage, in front of the audience, I think of you.'

Her fists clenched whitely at her sides. 'Damnit,' she cried, 'now you know why I ran away. I couldn't face what was happening to me ... I still don't know ...' Her eyes searched his. 'But I had to come back,' she breathed. 'I have to find out. I know I can't exist this way any longer ...'

'Remember what you said to me that night?' Tracy said, watching her eyes close, the jewelled tears spilling out from beneath the long lashes. '"Ballet's all I know", isn't that it, Lauren? "It's all I've been taught. It has to be my first and only love".'

Lauren was sobbing now. 'But it's not enough, Tracy. I can't dance anymore. Not the way I want to, not the way I always have. I was fine while you were there. Then I ... shut you out of my life.

'It was wrong, I know that now. But my God, I was scared! I sat up nights for weeks afterwards, afraid to go to sleep.' Her eyes were pleading. 'I can't do that anymore, Tracy. You were right and I was wrong. I admit it.'

He wanted so much to take her in his arms, enfold her and protect her. But he could not. Something hard and unyielding inside of him could not forget what she had done to him, the hurt she had suffered him to endure.

'I don't know, Lauren,' he said. 'So much has happened.'

'Please,' she whispered, 'I'm not asking the impossible. Just let's *try* it together. Spend a little time getting to know each other again.'

'I'm not sure it's possible,' Tracy said and saw the hurt look in her eyes.

'I guess I was a fool to come,' she said. 'But you can't blame me for thinking you were strong enough to accept how I feel now. We all make mistakes, Tracy. Even you.'

He said nothing, hating himself. Her eyes were dull as she turned away. 'You seeing anybody?'

The question was so unexpected he answered it truthfully. 'No.'

'Then maybe I'll see you sometime.' She tried that small

brave smile again but this time she missed. 'Good-bye, Tracy.'
She walked to the door, closed it softly behind her.

And Tracy said her name aloud to the empty room.

June 1966
Phnom Penh, Cambodia

Because the Khieus were a family of intellectuals it was not at all surprising that Khieu Khemara, Sokha's father, worked for Chau Seng. He was the head of Prince Sihanouk's private secretariat.

When Chau Seng returned from France in the fifties, Khemara helped him prepare a report on the complex problems of secondary education within Cambodia. Sihanouk seized upon this report, recognizing the brilliance of it and brought Chau Seng into his inner circle. Khieu Khemara came with him.

In fact, Sokha's father was one of the few men in Phnom Penh who could tolerate Chau Seng. He was a great progressive, a great thinker but he also possessed a remarkably abrasive personality. He was virtually anti-imperialist as was his prince but he exhibited none of the temperance Sihanouk, because of his position, was obliged to take from time to time.

It was a Thursday. Khieu Sokha had come to the Royal Palace to pick up his sister, Malis. Because of the Khieus' standing in the royal circle, Malis practised every Thursday in the Chau Chhaya, the moon shadow pavilion within the splendid palace. She was part of the Royal Cambodian Ballet.

Sokha had deliberately arrived early so that he could see some of the dance. He watched the lines of girls with their white short-sleeved shirts and their red *samput chang kheu*, skirts rolled in front and pulled up between their legs.

He saw Bopha Devi first. She was Sihanouk's daughter and as such the star of the ballet. There was no denying her dancing skills but still Sokha's eyes roamed the hall for a sign of Malis.

She was in the midst of the dance, one leg raised off the ground, her bare foot pointed. Her elbows were slightly bent, the fingers and palms of her hands perfectly straight and at a forty-five degree angle to her wrist. A teacher was instructing her on the hand motions which were the method of all communication in Khmer dancing.

Sokha watched, entranced. How exquisite she looked, how perfectly balanced. She moved as if she were a cloud, without weight or substance. Did her feet really press against the cool intricate tiles of the floor or did she float as it seemed to him? He could not say; he did not wish to know. He continued to watch until the lesson was completed, then he waited patiently for her.

She kissed him lightly on each cheek in the French manner and accompanied him to the car. While they were being driven past the multitudes of *cyclopousse* – Phnom Penh's omnipresent pedicabs – crosstown to Chamcar Mon, Sokhar thought about the French. In this year of the mid-sixties, Phnom Penh was still very much like a tiny French protectorate. Though there were perhaps only two thousand five hundred Frenchmen in the country as against six million nationals, their presence was felt quite heavily, especially within the precincts of Phnom Penh.

The French embassy's senior staff consisted mainly of men who had personally served with the Prince in various areas of what the French colonials had once termed 'our Indochina'. The Foreign Ministry, the Quai d'Orsay and, especially, the master of the Elysée Palace, Charles de Gaulle, half a world away, served as the link within the high embassy walls. They had a great stake in seeing Cambodia remain as it once had been: a direct colonial possession.

Some felt, Samnang and René among them, that de Gaulle served as a spiritual as well as a political mentor for Sihanouk. This they could not understand nor long tolerate.

However, at this point in time, the Gallic influence on this rather provincial city was enormous and all-pervading. Khmers in the highest political echelons took *café filtre* and *croissants* in the cool and unhurried splendour of the Hôtel le Royal's dining room each morning just as if they were in the centre of Parisian culture instead of in its brackish backwater bay ten thousand miles away.

Sokha's own father breakfasted there almost twice a week

and, often, the entire family would be guests of Chau Seng at his rubber plantation in the provinces. An intellectual he might be – a progressive as well; but neither stopped him from acquiring wealth.

Sokha blinked, looking out the car's window. They were just entering Chamcar Mon. This was an area of the city where only the élite lived. Those close to the prince were granted residence here: great villas in the Western style with orange, green and yellow tiled roofs like colours on an artist's palette, surrounded by whitewashed stone walls within which were inset copies of the bas-relief work at Bayon, the main temple at Angkor Thom.

Within the Khieus' villa was a garden with a banyan tree in its centre. To the left was a swimming pool that had been carved into the shape of a lotus blossom, its sloping bottom engraved with the radiating leaves.

Set within the inside of the walls were plaques in the twelfth-century style of Bayon depicting, variously, fish and game, scenes from ancient daily life. Often Sokha would come out early in the morning and stare at these replicas in an attempt to fathom the past of Cambodia.

The lives and times of those bygone kings such as Suryavarman II were not taught as a matter of course at the Lycée Descartes where he and his brothers and sisters went to school with the rest of the children who lived in Chamcar Mon. Sokha felt no connection with this part of his country's past. One day he promised himself he would go to Angkor Wat and Bayon and see for himself the real blocks and sculptures steeped in age and lore. He felt that perhaps his disconnection came from the fact that these artifacts in his garden were merely copies. If he could see the real thing; if he could just touch the stones with his fingertips he knew he would understand it all; he knew that he would find his place just as Preah Moha Panditto had found his place in the world.

As he alighted from the car, turned to help Malis from the back seat, he found himself anticipating dinner. But when he discovered that Samnang's guest was René Evan his excitement faded. It was not that he did not like the Frenchman but the man's almost constant discord with Khemara upset Sokha. He saw his father as having absolute authority, outside the villa as well as inside. Anyone who threatened that made him feel uncomfortable.

René was a slight man with the milk-white skin and reddish lips of a woman. His hair was dark-coloured and silken. His eyes were dark brown and considerably exophthalmic behind the round lenses of his steel-rimmed spectacles. Yet he more than made up for this unprepossessing exterior by the extraordinary manner of his rhetoric.

'There are rumblings in some quarters,' René said as they sat down to eat, 'that Kou Roun is feeling some pressure from other elements within the court.' René was constantly exposed to the veritable flood of gossip that invariably made its way around the inner circles of the city. Gossip and gambling were major trades of the times and it was said by many foreigners living within the precincts of Phnom Penh that the only people who loved gambling more than the Khmer were the Chinese, who were positively mad for it.

René was speaking now about the Minister of Internal Security. A heavyset man with a deep booming voice who seemed to have neither humour nor grace. He was also Chau Seng's chief enemy and it seemed to amuse René to needle his host in such a manner.

'Take this Kep Casino incident. You all know how the prince frowns upon gambling during the Chaul Chhnam festival.' Chaul Chhnam, lasting from 13 to 15 April, was the Khmer new year celebration.

'But just several months ago, Sihanouk opened two casinos – one of them in Kep, near the Gulf of Thailand.' His face was animated only when he spoke. At rest, the wan colour of his skin combined with the bulging eyes to make him appear quite dead. 'Well, you know, Monsieur Khemara, how this entire country runs on graft and illegal payoffs. So the casino continued to run at an immense profit to all concerned. But last week that came to an abrupt end.'

René leaned his slight frame forward. 'A gang of thugs entered the place and destroyed it all. Not just smashed some mirrors and glasses, mind you, as might be the case if it had been a warning. No, they destroyed it all.'

'We all heard about it at the same time,' Sokha's father said stolidly, attempting not to lose his temper with this graceless foreigner. They all spoke French not only in deference to their guest but because it was also their custom. 'We all read the newspapers. What of it?'

'Ah' – René lifted a thin forefinger into the air, jabbing – 'but what you do *not* know is that the casino's owner himself ordered the destruction of his business.'

'Excuse me, but I don't see how that could be possible,' Hema, Sokha's mother said seriously. 'What possible reason could he have for doing such a thing?'

'An excellent question, Madame Khemara,' René said. 'One that has been occupying us for the better part of this past week. Finally, through a leak in the office of the Minister of Internal Security I have discovered the answer. Next week, Kou Roun will deliver a public report on the matter. He will announce that the Chinese concessionaire at Kep was paying to a "high personality" in Phnom Penh as much as $40,000 a month to keep his casino running.' The Frenchman made a face, an odd sort of moue that made Sokha squirm in his chair. 'That is normal enough in these times but when this "high personality" demanded a higher payment, the Chinese refused; a bribe is a bribe but this was squeezing him out of business. A threat was then apparently made: the police would be summoned to the casino and not just once ... however many times it took for the Chinese to capitulate. Instead, he marked his own business for destruction.'

Khieu Khemara waved a hand. 'This is all foolishness, beneath our attention. I don't want to hear any more of it, Monsieur Evan.'

'But there's more,' René persisted. 'The most important part for those of you here.' He paused for a moment to see if Khieu Khemara would reiterate his objection; he did not. Silently, the family watched the Frenchman.

'It has happened that Chau Seng himself,' René continued looking directly at Sokha's father, 'has seen fit to bring to the prince his own report that consists mainly of the words of the Chinese concessionaire. He has done this, it is further said, on the behest of a "high feminine bourgeois personality of the capital".'

'Monique!' Khemara exclaimed. He was speaking of one of Prince Sihanouk's two wives; the low-born one, despised by many for surrounding herself with what was said to be a clique of money-hungry sycophants. Sokha did not know what, if any, was the truth of this. He found himself wondering now if his father did.

'You said it, I didn't.' René was smiling slyly. 'However, I do know that Kou Roun is furious with Chau Seng over this. I do not have to tell you, Monsieur Khemara, that the two are hardly the best of friends. But now ...' He let those two last words linger on. They had a taste in the mouth like wine turned to vinegar.

Hema, frightened, busied herself with sending the two youngest of her children, Boryia and Ratha, from the room.

'I don't think it is anything to concern yourselves with,' Khieu Kemara said lightly. 'These kinds of scandals are always raising their heads like ugly *naga*. It will all blow over. You will see. And then in August, when de Gaulle comes here for his visit, we shall see an upturn in our prosperity.'

'Tell me, Monsieur Khemara, is it true that the Prince is putting such great store on de Gaulle's visit here?'

'And why not?' Sokha's father said with a touch of pride. 'The very fact that one of the world's great and most respected leaders is coming to Cambodge will give us the kind of world-class status we have been seeking for many years. He has promised us substantial aid and his foreign minister, Couve de Muirville, will meet with representatives from Hanoi. The French influence can still serve to keep us secure.'

René made a disgusted face. 'He's a throwback, your Prince Sihanouk. A product of an older generation. He does not understand that the times are changing; that *new* methods must be sought to achieve true independence for Cambodge.

'First, he allows the *Yuons* to infiltrate the country.' He was

Using the colloquial term for the Vietminh and the Vietcong. 'Then he –'

'Excuse me, Monsieur,' Khemara said, 'but the Prince's policy of allowing North Vietnam sanctuary in Cambodge can only ensure our own sovereignty. Their gratitude –'

'Do you really think that Ho Chi Minh, Le Duan or Pham Van Dong will even remember this *great favour* Cambodge is granting them?' The Frenchman was incredulous. 'How many times must Sihanouk witness for himself their lies and deceits before he will cease to trust them.' His voice lowered, the sibilants increasing with the force of his emotions. 'They are *Vietnamese*. For the love of God, Monsieur, they *hate* the Khmer. You think if you knuckle under to them you will –'

'Not knuckle under,' Khemara said softly. 'They are our neighbours.' His words came slower as if he were speaking to a slightly retarded child. 'They always will be. We *must* be able to make our peace with them. The two–thousand–year war we have fought with them *must* cease for all of us to survive. *This* is what Prince Sihanouk believes most fervently.

'Look here, Monsieur Evan, even the French – even de Gaulle – has made his peace with Germany. They are neighbours; the war is over. Even a hero of the war must seek another road.

'Peace, Monsieur Evan, is a much more difficult course than war.'

'You speak to me of the French President as if he were the saviour of Cambodge. I am no Gaullist; I have no desire to return to France. It is no longer my home. Thirteen years after this country achieved its independence from France, it still seeks to return to a protectorate status. Don't you think that a bit odd?'

'We seek aid from our allies,' Khemara said steadfastly. 'That is all.'

'And I tell you that these times will not bear such a burden. Cambodians are starving, workless in the countryside while "high personalities" within the splendid villas of Chamcar Mon demand higher bribes from the enjoyment of the masses.

'This is an intolerable situation. Already the *montagnards* –'

86

'The *montagnards*,' Khemara interrupted, annoyed, 'are, in Kou Roun's own words, "being Khmerized".' The *montagnards* were groups of ethnic minorities within Cambodia, undifferentiated hill people given that name by the French.

'Oh, yes!' René laughed harshly. 'And listen to how proud you are of those words while they are being herded into camps, vilely maltreated.' René's eyes slid to slits. 'You've heard of the *maquis*?'

'I want no such talk in my house!' Khemara exlaimed. He was at last alarmed. The Frenchman's needling had done its work after all.

'Why not?' René persevered. 'Your children should know, surely, what lies in store for them.'

'Monsieur Evan, I must ask that you –'

'You mark my words, Monsieur Khemara. Your régime's maltreatment of the *montagnards* will be part of your own undoing. Revolution will come and all the sooner because those people will join with the *maquis*. Perhaps not this year but the next.'

'Silence!' Khemara thundered.

Those around the table were thunderstruck. For himself, Sokha could never remember his father raising his voice in that manner.

Samnang was first to clear his throat. Sokha had noticed that he had not said a word all through dinner.

'I think we had better go now, René.' He touched his friend lightly on his forearm.

René Evan stood up. He was shaking, white-faced. He stared at the man across the table from him. 'Knowledge is a dangerous thing, eh, Monsieur?'

'Please leave my house,' Khemara said softly. He did not look at the Frenchman.

René gave a small ironic nod of the head, almost a formal bow. 'Thank you for your gracious hospitality.'

Samnang touched his arm again and he turned away from the table. When the eldest son had followed him out of the room, Hema said, 'Dinner is over, children. I'm sure you all have schoolwork to attend to.' She had deliberately switched to

Khmer as if to wipe out the memory of the recent dialogue in French. But Sokha, for one, did not forget.

As he left the room, he saw his mother with her arm around his father.

'*Own*,' his father said, smiling softly. Then Sokha had left the room.

He did indeed have work to do, not only from the Lycée Descartes but that given to him by Preah Moha Panditto. Some time later, he did not know how long, Samnang put his head inside the doorway to his room.

'Still up, *Own*?'

'Yes. I'm just finishing.' He looked up. 'Is it late?'

Sam nodded, came into the room. He sat on the edge of Sokha's bed. 'That was some scene tonight.'

'You ought to know better by now, Sam.'

'I'm doing it for Pa's own good.'

'What?'

Sam nodded. 'René's right in everything he says. I think our world is going to change radically during the next year.'

'I don't believe you,' Sokha said but he felt a warning tightening in his stomach. Was Sam right? Then what would happen to them all?

'Well, it's true, *Own*. The *marquis* forces in the northwest are already beginning to build. There's revolution coming, all right. It's in the air.'

Sokha felt frightened. 'Even if it *is* true, Pa will protect us. He won't let anything happen to us.'

Sam looked at his younger brother and said nothing. The silence became intolerable for Sokha so he said, 'Where were you all this time? With René?'

'No. He had his own car. He gave me a lift ... to where I was going.'

There was an odd look in Sam's eyes. Sokha cocked his head. 'A girl's house,' he said with that odd intuitive thrust Sam had come to expect from him.

He laughed softly now, an easy sound. 'Yes. A new girl but a special one, *Own*. I think I'm in love. I want to marry her.'

Now Sokha laughed himself. 'Well, I wouldn't ask for Pa's permission tonight.'

Sam smiled, nodded. 'In a few months, when this has all blown over. You know how traditional he is in some ways. He'll want to know everything about the girl and her family.'

'Do I know her?'

Sam thought a moment. 'I think you met her once. At Le Royal; a reception for the French ambassador. Do you remember?'

Sokha did. 'Tall and slender. Very pretty.'

'Yes. That's Rattana.'

'A diamond,' Sokha said, translating the Khmer name into French. 'Beautiful,' he mused. 'Almost as beautiful as our Malis.'

Sam laughed. 'It's good you have a crush on her. You're too young to be getting into trouble with a real girl.'

'Like you and Diep.' It was out before he could think about it. Diep was the eldest daughter of the Vietnamese family two villas down the street. Sokha had seen the look on his brother's face on those occasions when she would pass by.

Sam's face darkened. 'Whatever it is you think you know, *Own*, I would forget it if I were you. I could feel nothing for Nguyan Van Diep. She is Vietnamese, after all.

'Remember the story of the poor Khmer peasant who found a baby croc lost and alone, without its mother. Out of the goodness of his heart, he took the creature home with him and fed it well every day, even though he could not really spare the food.

'Naturally, the croc grew ever larger. The peasant would feed it rabbit and monkey, picking fruit and vegetables for himself long after the creature, sated, was fast asleep.

'But one day, the croc grew bored with his fare and at dinner-time it pushed aside the fresh-killed monkey the peasant had set before it and gobbled him down in one enormous gulp.'

He stood up. 'Crocs and Vietnamese – they're both the same.'

He went out and down the dark hallway. The villa was quite still, just the chirrupping of the crickets and the wheezing drone of the flying insects, the humidity hanging in the air like sopping laundry.

Sokha closed his books and began to undress for bed. Naked from the waist up, he padded silently down the hall towards the bathroom. On the way he passed Malis' room. Tonight the door was slightly ajar and he stopped opposite it.

He felt his heart thudding in his chest. He had no clear conscious thought. He listened, heard only his own unquiet breathing. Then a thought came to him that seemed to whoosh all the air out of his lungs. He took a step towards the door before he could stop himself. As if in a dream, he saw his hand reach out and press against the partially opened door.

Visions of Malis dancing dazzled his mind as the door opened further so that he could see in an arc that moved inexorably towards the right and her bed.

His head strained forward on his neck. His mouth was dry with anticipation. He pushed gently at the door so that it gave even more.

Now he could see fully a third of the room. The bed. And on it, Malis. She slept with her feet towards him. She had thrown off the covers, had drawn back the curtains to allow whatever air there was this night to circulate.

Sokha strained to see in the semi-darkness and as his eyes adjusted to the lack of light, he bit down on his lower lip to stifle the gasp that rushed up into his throat. Malis was naked on the bed. He saw the swell of her budding breasts, the curve of her belly and below that, lying in deep shadow, what?

As he watched, he saw her toss and turn. Had her eyes opened? Was she awake? He felt a chill go through him. He wanted to turn and run but he was rooted to the spot. He could not avert his eyes. What if she *were* awake and saw him? He tried to bring saliva to his parched mouth. He could not even think of such a possibility.

She was moving on the bed now, her legs whispering apart, her hands snaking to the dark mound that swelled just below her belly. And then, abruptly, startlingly, she had flopped over on her stomach. Both hands were between her legs and it seemed to Sokha that her hips were moving up and down in a kind of slow rhythm he found hypnotic.

Her rounded buttocks were clear in the werelight, tensing and relaxing. The crease between them was very, dark; it drew his gaze like a magnet. He felt a curious heat suffusing him and he saw that his outstretched arm was trembling like a bough in a storm. His legs felt weak and his penis felt funny, as if it had grown heavier and enlarged as he watched. He put his free hand down there, felt that great lump forming, pushing out the fabric of his trousers. There was a kind of pressure there that hurt and felt good at the same time.

Malis was slightly arched now, alternating pushing her groin up against her working fingers and down against the giving support of the mattress. Sokha was not certain but he thought he could hear her breathing heavily or moaning slightly every so often.

Her buttocks worked in fascinating rhythm, swaying and clenching dramatically. Now her thighs were split wide and she began to draw her knees up under her so that he could now clearly see her fingers plunged into the core of her. Sokha had no idea what she was doing, he only understood that whatever it was moved him in a new and terribly exciting way.

He could hear her moaning now, a breathy kind of soft sighing that shivered him all through his body. His erection was bending him over slightly and he fought without thinking to open the front of his trousers in an effort to relieve the tension building there. Freed, he held on to his engorged penis, enjoying its silky feel and heated wetness.

Malis had opened herself so wide that he could make out the matted wet hairs around her pubis. The fingers of one hand had spread apart the hidden secret folds of silken flesh, stroking madly there. The other hand now reached upward spreading apart the tensing mounds of her buttocks. Into the infinitely dark crack they slipped so that Sokha could not believe his eyes.

A great wetness seemed to engulf him and his legs failed him. He slipped silently to the floor, his eyes on his own jerking member but his ear still linked to the soft guttural sounds that emanated from the partially opened doorway.

His palms were filled with a hot viscous fluid; his insides felt as if they had survived a sandstorm. The heated night beat on around him to its own rhythm, synchronized to the steady thump–thump of his rapid heartbeat.

Outside the hallway window a night bird trilled sweetly.

When Thwaite left the office early that afternoon everyone on his floor breathed a deep sigh of relief. Something had really got under his skin today and he had been downright nasty. Speculation was high that his Holmgren impasse was driving him crazy.

Actually, the rumours were not far from the truth. The plain fact was Thwaite could not get the entire deal off his mind. To his way of thinking, the Governor's death had been cockeyed from the word go.

It was Thwaite's considered opinion that the Monserrat woman had called Richter first, not 911, as she had stated. That would account for the forty minute discrepancy. There was nothing to go on but his nose – the instinct of years – but he could feel the set-up. He wanted to nail Richter for that. He wanted it badly.

That was what made him writhe all day, snapping at anyone who was unfortunate to get in his way. It was also what made him grab his jacket and leave the precinct early. He was going to take another crack at Richter.

He parked illegally on Sixth Avenue, pulling down his POLICE BUSINESS card pinned to one sun visor and went quickly into the building housing Tracy's office.

Tracy was on his way out when the elevator door opened and Thwaite emerged onto the floor.

Tracy checked when he saw the detective. 'Thwaite,' he said, 'you've caught me at a bad time. I'm already late for an appointment. What d'you want?'

'For starters I'll take a coupla hours with the Monserrat woman to go over her story again.'

'Haven't you given up yet?'

'Why should I? My job's to get at the truth.'

'You know what your job is and I think your captain should be informed you're not doing it. This city's filled with criminals,

Thwaite. Do something about them instead of standing here and butting heads with me.'

'Look, what's the big deal? If, like you said, everything went down as the Monserrat woman said, what could hurt if I talk to her again.'

'I just spoke to her,' Tracy said. 'She breaks down after every other sentence. Frankly, I don't think you'd get anything coherent from her. Does that satisfy you?'

Thwaite stared hard at him. 'Why should it? I only have your word to go on. I want to see her for myself. There's nothing else tangible left of this case.'

'What is it with you, Thwaite? The Governor dies of a heart attack and you get your bowels in an uproar.'

Thwaite took a step forward. 'In case you forgot, Johnny-boy, the Governor of New York State is news no matter what he did, including dying.' He took a deep breath. 'So what about it?'

'Moira Monserrat is off limits. Period.'

'Okay. Have it your way. But there're a coupla reporters on the *Post* who'd just love to take down my suspicions and put it into print.'

'That's suicide, Thwaite, and you know it. The force would bounce you halfway to Cleveland for that.'

'Only if they had proof it was me. And who's gonna tell them. Me? Reporters don't reveal their sources. It's me against you.'

'I've got more than enough clout,' Tracy said. He was thinking of Mary Holmgren now. He knew he had to protect John's good name and Mary's peace of mind at all costs. It was his duty. 'You'll get bounced, believe me.'

'I do,' Thwaite said steadily. 'But you know something? I don't give a shit anymore. I want the truth on this one and by Christ I'm gonna get it.'

'No matter who gets hurt.'

'You betcha, Johnny-boy.'

Tracy's intuition told him that Thwaite was bluffing. All he knew of the man told him that this was a career cop. What could he do out on the streets if the force dumped him? Become an industrial security guard for $125 a week and lose his pension? He'd often gambled on his intuition but now he had other people to think of. If there was even one chance in a thousand that Thwaite might carry out his threat, there was only one choice open to him.

'All right,' he said. 'If you give me a couple of days I'll see what I can do. I wasn't kidding about her emotional state.'

'I don't wanna wait, Richter.'

Tracy felt the tension returning to his body and, unconsciously he went into an aggressive stance. 'Well, you'll just have to, Thwaite, won't you? That's all you'll get from me. Take it or leave it.' That was no gamble at all.

Thwaite grunted. 'Don't take too long,' he said and, turning went down the corridor, disappearing into an open elevator.

Out on Sixth Avenue, the traffic was piling up, making an unholy stink in the heat. The air was blue with exhaust. Thwaite took the light, went quickly west. He held his breath as a bus cruised slowly by behind him.

He headed towards the honky tonk of Broadway with its glitter of huge movie marquees and giant advertising billboards. Between Eighth and Ninth Avenues the old turn-of-the-century tenements still proliferated with their worn stone stoops cracking under layers of cheap enamel. Rock and Latin music blared from wide open windows, battling with each other, and groups of young muscled men in sleeveless shirts joked and growled in the gutter Spanish of the neighbourhood while daydreaming of fast cars and even faster women.

Three-quarters of the way down the block, Thwaite crossed the street to the south side. He passed an open doorway strewn with garbage, went up the gritty steps of the next building.

He went quickly down the long narrow hall. He smelled the sour stench of old cabbage, the sharp hint of Tabasco. One unshielded 40-watt bulb hung, burning, high above his head, washing the confines in its sickly glow. He knocked on the last door on the right. Through the thin wood panels he could hear a brief welter of voices, abruptly cut short. He glanced at his watch. He was a half-hour early but he didn't care. His confrontation with Tracy Richter had left him frustrated and angry.

Lovely Leonard was not a bad person to take his wrath out on, Thwaite figured; in fact, his profession made him a better choice than most.

The door creaked open on its chain and Thwaite jammed his shoe into the gap.

'Open up, Lenny.'

'Yo' early, man.'

Thwaite reached beneath his jacket, produced the hardwood baton he had had made for himself. He brought it up in front of him. 'You see this, my man?' He waved the thing back and forth like a metronome. 'This says time don't mean a thing.'

'Hey, hey.' Lovely Leonard's voice dropped to a stage whisper. 'Yo' caught me wif ma pants down.' And when Thwaite made to comment, he went on. 'Got me a *bitch* in here, man. Bangin' her brains out, y'know? Gimme a break, will y _'

Thwaite's raised arm was already descending in a thick white and brown blur. The meat part of the baton crashed into the thin cheap chain, jerking it, mooring and all, from the inside wall. He lowered his shoulder and launched himself through the widening gap, smashing his way into the apartment.

'Fuck!' Lovely Leonard said, losing his balance. He stumbled backward into the threadbare rug. True to his word, he was naked from the waist up. His trousers had been hastily put on, the zipper still open, the waist button still undone. He clutched the top part now with one hand to keep the material from falling away from his private parts. His thin, hairless chest gleamed in the light.

'Get up from the floor, Lenny,' Thwaite said. 'You look like a fool down there.' He waited until the black had regained his feet and had done up his trousers, then he reached out and gripping the chocolate flesh at the base of the neck, he brought the man closer towards him.

'Now listen to me.' Thwaite's voice was soft, silky, nevertheless filled with menace. 'You open your door to me when I come. No matter what time it is, right? Remember that, Lovely Leonard' – he brandished the baton – 'or I'm likely to rearrange those beautiful facial features so that someone'll have to give you a new nickname.' He let the pimp go; he rippled his fingertips. 'Give it over.'

Lovely Leonard grunted, went to the far corner of the room, stopping to reach underneath the mattress of the day bed.

'Very original,' Thwaite commented as the other returned. He stood before Thwaite, counting out hundred dollar bills. When he got to five, he stopped, folded them over, put the wad into Thwaite's fist.

'Easy as pie,' Thwaite said, pocketing the cash. He saw the unhappy look on Lovely Leonard's face. 'Jesus,' he said lightly, 'you oughta be jumping for joy, Lenny. For this little monthly shot in the arm neither you nor any of your girls gets hassled by Vice. Your profits go up and I take a piece of it. Why worry? We all get a little richer.' The wad of bills seemed hot high up on his thigh. He put his hand in his trousers pocket, covering the cash with his palm. Somehow it didn't make him feel as good as it once did. 'Cheer up.'

At that moment, he heard the flushing of the toilet from behind the closed door to the bathroom: once, twice, three times.

He looked at Lovely Leonard. 'Your girl got the trots, Lenny?' The other's face was slick with sweat; his eyes were wide and rolling.

'The bitch's cleanin' herself.'

But Thwaite wasn't having any. In three swift strides he was at the door. 'Open up!' he called and immediately threw himself shoulder first at the door. It burst open and he saw a young white woman on her knees over the open toilet. She had one hand on the lever, the water was still spinning around.

She had been staring intently into the bowl but as he burst in on her, her head whipped around. He saw her pinched face filled with fear. Her small sharp teeth were bared.

He took a step towards the bowl and she growled low down in her throat. She leaped at him, fingers like claws, nails aimed at his eyes. He brought the baton up, tapped her as gently as he could on the side of her head at the apex of her arc. She let out a little moan, fell away from him against the tiled wall.

Thwaite ignored her for the moment, bent down and rescued

the small spinning objects from going down the toilet. He shook water off them: two glassine envelopes. He opened one carefully tasted a bit of the white powder inside.

'Shit!' he coughed.

He made a grab for the girl who was just beginning to stir. He took a look at the insides of her arms, then the insides of her legs. That's where he found them. An army of track marks.

'Goddamn shit!'

He pulled the girl to her feet, began to guide her out of the bathroom.

'What yo' doin', Thwaite?' Lovely Leonard called plaintively. 'She my best bitch by far. I pay you. No hassles.'

'That's vice,' Thwaite said nastily. The sight of the wretch he had his arm around made him ill. She couldn't've been more than seventeen. 'You do what you do, Lenny and that's fine by me. But you start foolin' with this shit' – he dangled the open bag in front of the pimp's face – 'and you got to pay. I told you in the beginning that you were buying yourself a limited insurance policy.' He held the half-conscious girl up in front of him. 'She's just a goddamned kid, Lenny. For Chrissakes, I got a daughter at home just about the same age. What the fuck's the matter with you, ain't you got any sense?'

'But *she* came to *me*,' the black man said. 'Hey, hey, they all do, y'know? They got no one, got nowhere t'go. They wanna make some bread. This's the way.' He danced around nervously. 'Hey, man, don't take her in now. I mean, shit, the bitch's worth a thousand a week to me, clean.'

Thwaite was almost at the door. 'You're goddamned lucky I'm not taking you in, too, Lenny.' Thwaite opened the front door with his free hand. 'But the truth is you're small potatoes. You and the others like you don't amount to shit in the cesspool I work in.' He lifted the girl up onto one meaty shoulder. 'You must've been born under a lucky sign, my man. This's your one and only warning.'

He took the girl out of there. She seemed as light as a feather. Downtown, at the precinct, he had her booked, gave over the evidence, then waited with her until the matron from Juvenile showed up.

Staring into that narrow, battlescarred face, he could see the beauty hidden underneath but not truly defeated yet. He was inured to her savagery; what did that mean, after all? The street had done that to her, the mean cruel street. But like a patina, he knew that wildness could be stripped away, leaving what had always been there.

She was just a girl, a thin frightened creature with no home, no family, no ties. She would not give him her name and Lovely Leonard said that 'Nina' was all he knew her by. Still Thwaite had run her description through Missing Persons just in case. He had come up with a blank but that meant nothing.

Somewhere, perhaps in Ohio or Michigan, Nina did have a family. But that hardly mattered. They were as good as dead to her and what was she left with? A needle filled with dream-sleep and death. She might have been treated better in a zoo.

He stood up when the matron arrived. He briefed her and all the while his gaze was on Nina. The girl stared at the floor at her feet. Her dirty blonde hair was tousled, clumped strands wisping her wide forehead. She appeared quite docile now.

And that was the last he saw of her. He said goodbye but either she did not hear him or did not care. She made no reply.

He became aware of how weary he felt. The combination of that pathetic girl and Tracy Richter's enormous energy had drained him. Locking horns with that man was like fighting a battalion.

He took the Chevy towards the Brooklyn-Battery Tunnel, thinking back to the confrontation. He was surprised to find that he had not been bluffing with Richter. He had actually put his job on the line! Amazing! Why did this case mean so much to him? Why not just forget all about the ugly mess and get on with his life. Shake down a few small time pimps and bookies. That was much more his speed, wasn't it? He was just a grimy slab, the department had turned into hamburger like it did everybody else. He had no business sticking his nose into this.

And that, he told himself, was just why he was doing it. He was enclosed in a tiny world of filth and once, just once, he wanted to stretch his neck out and get above it all. Just once he'd like to be able to clean up a patch of the shit instead of dumping more on the floor.

Every day, he pulled in junkies with weapons who cut up people. He went through the motions of giving a case to the DA's office only to see it disintegrate into a plea bargain or a slap on the wrists from an 'enlightened' judge who had absolutely no idea what was happening to the quality of life on the streets.

If it was up to him, he'd take every goddamned judge on the circuit and shove them out there for a month or two. He had no doubt they'd return to the bench with a different attitude.

Out through the tunnel. Thwaite took the Brooklyn-Queens Expressway south towards Park Slope. The lights of Manhattan twinkled into the gathering dusk, smeared by haze.

So now he'd made the Holmgren thing into a cause. The truth. He wanted only the truth, and by that, be cleansed by it.

At the western edge of Park Slope, the highways described a wide arc to the southwest. Unconsciously, he began to hum an odd, inverted rendition of 'The Man I Love'.

Up ahead, he could see the glow and glint of the Narrows, the water soft and gentle-looking; the night concealing the luridly iridescent oil stains scarring its surface. He was in Bay Ridge now; home.

He exited just south of Owls Head Park, taking Shore Road back down Sixty-ninth Street. His house, a white clapboard and shingle affair looking very much like the others, stood midway down the block. There was a maple tree out front that was making a valiant attempt to stay alive.

He sat in the car, staring at nothing. It was not yet time to go into the house. He could see the lights on here and there, the steel blue of TV sets flickering, giving out the news of the day. It was all bad.

Thwaite shut off the engine of the Chevy, got out and locked the door. The heat hit him hard; it was a stifling night even out here, across the river from the city.

He went north along Bliss Terrace, heading towards Owls Head Park. At the edge of the park he paused, wondering whether or not to go in. It was Wednesday, time for his weekly payoff, something he had come to think of as a normal clock-

-k part of his life. Tonight, however, he felt different. Per-

..ps it was the Holmgren thing and the promise it held out to
him; perhaps he was changing.

He almost turned away then but his roving eye caught the
movement within the park and he thought, Ah, what the hell,
I can always use the extra cash. He went slowly down the path
with the certain knowledge that this would be the last time. He
felt like he was shedding an old and filthy skin, leaving it on the
ground behind him.

Ships' horns hooted in ghostly concert as he left the stone path
and went over the low black iron railing. Past a large oak, he
saw Antonio's familiar silhouette with its wide-brimmed hat
and puffy-sleeved shirt. Spic dandy, Thwaite thought, disgusted
with himself. Yet he could not stop and turn around.

Now he could see the two girls: Spanish, big-breasted, wide-
hipped with the kind of animal sensuality he found typical of
their kind.

'Hey Thwaite,' the pimp said by way of greeting. 'You a little
late. Got business elsewhere now?'

'Always, 'Tonio,' Thwaite said. 'I got more important things
to do.'

Antonio gave him a sour grin. 'Yo Thwaite. You better be
careful what you say, man. I keep you in business.' He handed
over a clutch of bills.

Thwaite, counting them, said, 'You couldn't keep an old lady
welfare afloat with payments like this.'

The pimp spread his hands, shrugged. 'Yo Thwaite. What
can I say, man? Business sucks.'

Thwaite looked up. 'You're not thinking of holding out on
me, are you, 'Tonio? You got more brains than that.'

'Hold it right there.'

Thwaite swung his head around. One of the girls, her high
heels planted wide, had a small .32 calibre pistol levelled at his
stomach.

Antonio was grinning, his yellow teeth clacking together in
delight. 'Yo Thwaite. Now we see who's boss.' He came forward, prancing a little in his pointed-toed boots. 'I figure, this

here's my turf. You been runnin' me around, givin' me grief for too long a time, y'know? I had it with you, bro'.' He reached out a hand. 'Now be a good boy and hand over *all* your cash.'

'You're out of your mind,' Thwaite said. 'You won't have an operation left, you do this.'

'Shows just how fucked up you are, man. The PD, they don't like to hear about this kinda shit, you know? What d'you think, I'm ignorant or something? I watch the news on TV. They don't want no bad press: cops on the take, makes 'em sweat right through their blues, am I right? I squeal about this deal an' you dead an' buried, bro'.' His fingers made quick curling motions. 'Now hand it over. Move!'

Thwaite reached out towards the pimp's open hand and spread apart his fingers. The crumpled bills fluttered to the ground.

Antonio was lightning swift. His right leg came up in a blur, the pointed-toed boot burying itself in Thwaite's groin. '*Puerco!*' he cried.

The breath whooshed out of Thwaite's lungs as he grabbed himself. Bright lights danced in his head. Blinding pain filled him up so that he gasped uncontrollably.

'You think I'll get down on my knees for that?' Antonio watched the other bowed before him. He grinned. 'Yo not me, bro'. Now you know who's boss around here.' He leaned over slightly, his cupped palm coming down. 'Give me my fucking bread, man.' His voice was full of menace.

'Here!' Thwaite said, uncoiling. His polished hardwood baton shot upward and out, slamming the pimp in the ribs. He felt the percussion through his wrist and arm, heard the *snap-crunch* and felt the give at the same time.

Antonio moaned and collapsed where he was standing, a look of disbelief frozen on his face. On his way down, Thwaite used his kneecap against the pimp's cheekbone. Antonio spun, his arms pinwheeling.

Thwaite was aware of movement to his right and he crouched down, using Antonio's body as a shield. The pimp moaned as Thwaite manhandled him.

There was no sign of the two girls and Thwaite whispered

in the other's ear. 'You better pray they took themselves out of here, Johnny-boy.'

'*Madre de Dios!*' Antonio shivered in pain.

Thwaite took the surrounding terrain in by quadrants. A siren wailed somewhere behind him, diminishing. Then it was still. There was almost no wind but the crickets were up. Mournful hooting of the ships through the Narrows.

Lines of trees and shrubbery confronted him, looking oddly two-dimensional in the sputtering mercury lamps' harsh light. He was sitting in the middle of a vast shooting gallery and he was the duck. He dropped his baton and drew his service revolver. He put it in front of Antonio's face.

'Listen, shit-for-brains, I'm giving you the chance to end it here before someone really gets hurt.'

'I ain't gonna do no time, man.' Antonio spit blood. It looked black in the artifical light. He coughed, his body convulsing. 'Shit, you hurt me bad, bro'.'

Thwaite scanned the immediate vicinity. 'You shouldn't've been so greedy, 'Tonio. You had to be taught a lesson.'

'Last one to try to teach me a lesson, bro', was my old man.' He spit more blood. 'I carved him up good, man.'

Thwaite said nothing. He thought he had caught a glimpse of reflection moving among the maples. 'All right,' he called. 'I've got my gun drawn. Come out with you hands up and no one will get –' He ducked down, one hand grabbing the back of the pimp's shirt. A clod of dirt exploded to one side.

Antonio was giggling quietly now. 'Youn for it now, bro'. Sonia, she don't like *puercos*. She gon' put you away, man.'

But Thwaite had seen the bright orange blossom as the pistol had been fired. A second shot ploughed into the ground, nearer this time.

''Tonio, she'll listen to you,' he said quietly. 'Tell her to come out nice and easy and we'll forget the whole thing.'

The pimp twisted around. His nose and mouth were smeared with blood and he was holding the side where Thwaite's baton had cracked his ribs. His eyes were bright with life. 'Oh, no, man.' His lips twitched into a semblance of a smile. 'Now way. You scared, Thwaite. I can see that.'

Thwaite let go of Antonio and, keeping his eyes focussed on where Sonia was, began to move crabwise to his left. She was on that side of the tree and now she began to shift her position to get a clear shot at him. That was when he lifted the gun and, using both hands, the arms extended like rods, squeezed off two shots in succession. *Boom! Boom!* Like thunder in his ears.

'*Sonia! Anda! Anda!*' It was Antonio's strident voice. 'You stupid whore. Run!'

Thwaite stood up. 'It's too late for that now, 'Tonio.' He began to walk towards the trees, on the lookout for the other girl.

'*Puerco!*' the pimp screamed, struggling to his feet. 'Your mother was a whore, you sonuvabitch!'

Thwaite stood over the body. He had put the girl's gun in his jacket pocket. There was no sign of the other one. She lay with her legs spread wide as if he were a customer. His heart beat hard; how he wished he had turned around at the edge of the park and gone home.

He heard the noises as Antonio approached.

'*Madre de dios!*' He collapsed beside her, touched her face. '*Muerte!*' His head whipped up. 'You killed her, *puerco!*'

Thwaite was suddenly filled with rage. He gripped the pimp's greasy hair in his fingers and pulled hard. 'Listen to me, you little piece of snot, I warned you!' There were tears in his eyes. 'You were too stupid to know what you were fooling around with!'

With a violent gesture, he flung the man from him and, ignoring the hate he saw burning in those brown eyes, said, 'You take that other girl and get the hell out of my sight. Because if I ever see you again, 'Tonio, I'll blow your head off and no one will have to ask why I did it!'

He was breathing hard, his chest constricted and he made himself turn and walk away on stiff legs. Out on the streets, he called 911 from a pay phone and gave them all the information. Then he went home, turning in along his front walk, going past the tattered grass that needed attention, to finally lie down and sleep beside his wife.

*

'Kill me.'

Tracy stood stock still watching the man in front of him. Bright white bars of light slanted in through the long windows, touching each of them slightly.

'I should not have to tell you again.'

It was very still in the room. Tracy could hear the sound of his own breathing but not that of the man facing him. He dug his toes into the nap of the mat beneath his bare feet.

'You do not believe you can do it.'

'No.'

The *sensei*'s eyes glittered darkly. 'What makes you hesitate then.'

Tracy said nothing.

Higure, the *sensei*, parted his lips. 'The nature of what we do here hardly requires conscious thought ... that gets in the way of what the body must perform ... *without* thought.' Higure regarded Tracy. 'I am not telling you anything new.'

Tracy's body had begun quivering as particular muscles began to react to the stress of the situation.

'Surely,' the *sensei* said, 'you would obey a command from Jinsoku.' His eyes were guarded, careful in their surveillance. In a moment, he had seen what he was looking for and he made his formal bow, requiring Tracy to do the same thus ending their two hours together on the mats.

'Tea, I think, is called for.'

Tracy followed him into a back room, towelled himself off.

It was not until they were both seated on the tatami mats, drinking the frothy light green tea, so bitter it set the teeth on edge that anything else was said.

Higure carefully put down his tiny handleless cup. 'We must get to the bottom. You know that.' Tracy nodded briefly and the old man seemed satisfied.

'Can you tell me,' he said slowly, 'why you went to war in the first place.'

'I didn't go to war,' Tracy said quickly.

'No, of course not. Pardon me.'

The silence built itself around them; the world had faded into the distance of long-ago.

'I went to escape,' Tracy said after a time.

But already Higure was shaking his head back and forth. 'No. Listen to your heartbeat ... listen to your pulse. You went because you wanted to go. You –'

'No!' It was almost a kid shout and the walls seemed to tremble.

'You *wanted* to kill.'

Tracy was wide-eyed. 'How can you say that?'

'How can you deny it? It is your nature.'

Tracy got up, turned away. There was a small window that looked out onto a tiny back garden. Out there a chipmunk clung to the scaly bark of a maple tree as if for dear life. In a moment it had vanished, safe at home.

'Perhaps you believe it to be evil.'

'Of course it's evil.'

'Why?' Higure said.

Tracy's voice was strangled. 'The war.'

'It was your duty –'

'Don't you understand?' he said whirling to face his *sensei*. 'I *enjoyed* it.'

At last Higure rose; he did so without the least effort. 'And after all this time you're still haunted.'

Tracy watched him warily. He knew this was one man from whom the truth could not be hidden. He had begun to sweat profusely. 'It comes and goes,' he said at last.

'Well,' Higure said quietly, '*something* comes.'

'Yes.' It was a broken whisper. 'It's begun all over again. The call-up.'

Higure was close now; his face was shadowed, out of the line of light. 'They want you again.'

'That's it.'

'And what will you do?'

Tracy closed his eyes for a moment. His heart was hammering. 'I want to do it ... a friend is involved.'

'You feel a duty.'

'Yes.'

'And so you should.' His eyes narrowed slightly.

'There was murder,' Tracy said. His fists were clenched his

arms rigid. 'I can feel it though I don't know how or by whom.'

'Trust that,' Higure said. 'We both are aware of your strengths.'

'There will be more murder.' Silence, for a long time, unspooling. 'I think I'm talking about myself.'

'I know you are.' And Higure reached out, took Tracy gently by the arm. 'Your journey is not done yet. Do what you must and be accepting of it. You must learn to trust yourself again as you once did in the jungles of Cambodia.' He broke the contact. 'Trust yourself as I trust you.'

He set himself, bowed formally. 'Now,' he said, 'come and kill me.'

Lauren sat slumped over on a slat-seated wooden bench. Sunlight filtered in over her left shoulder from the high, small-paned translucent windows. Her hands trembled.

She wore a leotard, woollen legwarmers over white tights and a pair of Capezio point shoes. Her auburn hair was twisted into a long braid, curled in a tight circle on the top of her head.

Fascinated, she watched her hands tremble. From several yards away Martin Vlasky shot her a penetrating glance even as he said to one of a pair of new dancers practising the *entrée* from a *pas de deux* he had created more than fifty years ago. 'No, no, dear. You are grimacing.' He stepped forward, righting the exaggerated tilt of her head. 'Don't act – *dance*. That is what you do: dance. Your technique is your art.' He meant this for the cavalier as well. 'Don't be afraid of your technique. Through it, you must find the timing for the entire *pas de deux*. That is essential, yes?'

The girl – she could not be more than nineteen – inclined her head in silent agreement but she looked shaken nonetheless. Martin sighed inwardly. It always happened this way with the newcomers. You had to press all their preconceptions out of them in order to forge the vessel of pure expression. He turned his head away slightly as he signalled the pair to begin the *entrée* another time. His thoughts were with Lauren. What was it, he wondered, that caused her so much pain that it interfered with her work? For as long as Martin had known her – five years now in the impossibly compressed time signature of ballet life – she had lived for only one thing: the dance. That was as it should be.

But now, ever since her fall, the injury to her hip, her attitude had changed subtly. Martin had known many dancers whose entire personalities had been changed by serious falls. Confidence could be shaken; laziness could set in. Inactivity was often disastrous for the performing personality. Yet he had not expected this from Lauren Marshall.

He felt concern deep in his heart as a father will for a saddened daughter. It was not only of Lauren's unique gift he was thinking. He knew he held a special fondness for her though his company had seven prima ballerinas and he was publicly known for discouraging the star treatment other ballet ensembles used. He had created more than one ballet primarily for Lauren and he did not want to lose her.

Lauren, unaware of the master's scrutiny, was fighting to hold back the tears she felt welling up behind her mascaraed eyes. She clamped her teeth shut and whispered silently to herself. *You will not cry. You will not cry.*

It had taken more will power than she had believed she possessed to walk into Tracy's office and see him again. To say what she had said to him. She had no idea what kind of a front she had put up, only recognized the inner trembling, the sickening rollovers of her stomach that had still not quite ceased.

She got up and put in four shaky hours of practice that she found she had no memory of when she returned home to her small, highceilinged apartment on Seventy-sixth Street just west of Broadway.

She flopped down on her bed belly first without taking off her clothes. For a long time she thought of nothing, allowing the warm childlike feeling of the mattress pressed all along her front to suffuse her. For those moments she felt safe and secure.

But there was really no security for her here now. If she could not work she was through. What else could she do in life but dance? The answer to that was simple and terrifying: Nothing.

She turned her face into the pillow, balling a corner of it up against her cheek. Oh, God, what was she going to do?

'For Christ's sake, Adele, you can't allow this.'

Lauren could still hear her father's voice drifting into her from the living room. It was late at night and her parents had assumed she had long ago drifted off to sleep. She was six.

'Ballet. I mean – what the hell! It's not logical; it's not practical. It makes no goddamned sense!'

'It's what she wants,' Lauren's mother said calmly. 'It's what she'll have.'

'But how d'you know she's any good?'

'I know it as surely as I know I love you.'

'But, Hell, Adele, you know what that training's like. She'll have to give up being a kid. She'll have to give up everything.'

'If you want to be great,' Adele Marshall said, 'you have to sacrifice for it. It's a fact of life. And she has more discipline than Bobby will ever have.'

'Bobby's only four-and-a-half.'

'And sometimes he acts like he's two,' Adele said. 'That won't change, you'll see. He's immature; Lauren's got every right to tease him. He's got to toughen up.'

Lauren's father had not replied to that. She heard a taut crinkle of the newspaper and then the crisp clip-clop of her mother's high heels along the wood parquet of the hall. She dived back under the covers, closed her eyes and pretended to be asleep.

She heard the small creak of the partially open door swinging wider on its hinges, the faint rustle of her mother's skirts as she came across the thick pile carpeting.

She felt the bed give slightly as her mother sat on the edge, stroked her side with the flat of her hand, crooning, 'You, you, you', as if it were some sort of magical incantation.

Lauren blinked and she was back in her own small apartment. It was a studio in a dingy building. She could have afforded a large sunny one-bedroom apartment if she had accepted the money her mother wanted to give her on making the company five years ago. But she did not want that. And, although she pocketed the ten-dollar bills her father sneaked her when they came to visit, she never took a penny from her mother. She did not know why nor did she want to know. But maybe, she thought now, it had something to do with that magical incantation; maybe she had taken enough already.

Kim dealt almost exclusively in emotionalism. That was how he conducted a session of articulated interrogation; it was how he went out on a mission; it was the only way he could bring them back the dead meat they required of him. He was high and low like a manic depressive. It seemed odd in a man who should have been quite even-tempered. Perhaps it had something to do with the scar.

Looking at the Vietnamese now, on their way to the Governor's brownstone, Tracey thought of that. Once, just before. Kim had been betrayed. Starting across the Cambodian border on a vital mission of assassination, he had been ambushed by the Khmer Rouge. They knew about him; knew how much blood he himself had shed.

They had no cause to keep him alive – but they did. Perhaps he had become such an object of hate to them that they could not bear to part with him so soon; perhaps they meant to make an object lesson of him. Whatever the case, they did not execute him as was their wont.

They bound him, staked him to the earth in the middle of their seminomadic encampment and cut him. It was nothing systematic, nothing professional; merely a slash here or there at erratic intervals when they thought about it or were not otherwise occupied. They stabbed him in the thigh or the arm, rending his black cotton clothes.

For Kim that was far more humiliating than being subjected to articulated interrogation. At least then he would have been up against a professional with whom he could match wits, feel a bit of pride. The Khmer Rouge stripped him of pride and therefore of his manhood. Kim was a warrior and they treated him as if he were an animal not even worth spitting on.

When Tracy discovered his whereabouts, he infiltrated the Chet Khmau encampment, cut Kim's bonds and, throwing him over his shoulder, carried him out into the twisting concealing shadows of the jungle.

There had been no wound on the side of Kim's neck then. By crying out constantly, Kim had forced Tracy to stop, put him down. He asked for Tracy's knife 'to cut off some of these hanging rags I have for clothes'. Taking it, he had gone a few feet away into the jungle. Tracy turned, concentrated on enemy infiltration while he waited.

Kim, the knife held blade inward with one hand, cocked his head to the right as far as he could. The taste of bile was in his mouth like beaten brass, his saliva dried up. He was a warrior and they had beaten him; those animal Cambodians. His mind stank of hate.

No one could know what indignities he had suffered; that loss of face would literally kill Kim. The wounds he had suffered were only minor now that he had been saved. As the days had progressed and without any kind of medical attention they would have turned septic, swelling, darkening as infection set in. A slow lingering death by a thousand insignificant cuts. That was what the Khmer Rouge had planned for him. Kim could never forgive them for that. It was too early yet to formulate the structure of his revenge; time would bring that to blossom like an exquisite flower turning its widening face into the sun.

For now he must give evidence to Tracy and all those at Ban Me Thuot that he had been put through a gruelling, damaging mill; they must have no doubts that he had been treated like a warrior, had resisted like a warrior and, ultimately had triumphed as a warrior.

He turned his eyes once on Tracy who was looking off into the distance, the back of his head towards Kim; he would not see, he could not know. In that instant, much of the hatred Kim felt for his Cambodian captors fell on Tracy's shoulders. He had been, after all, the one who was bringing Kim back, who had witnessed first-hand Kim's humiliation. He was the one who had made Kim do now what he had to do and for that Kim could not, *would* not forgive him.

He jerked his eyes away, staring into the middle distance at nothing more substantial than the shifting shadows of the night.

Kim closed his eyes while opening his warrior's mind. He thought of the days and nights of his capture, the slow wheel of humiliation on which he had been crucified. Hate welled inside him like pent-up water sluicing through a collapsing dam.

Without conscious thought, through the will of his warrior's mind, his right hand blurred inward and the point of the knife blade buried itself in his own flesh. Kim bit his lip at the hot slice of pain, willed himself to move his hand, though it had gone numb. Everything was numb, numb but moving inexorably, down and down, from just behind the left ear to the base of his neck: a wound that would inevitably scar, a brand he would always wear and, outwardly at least, feel pride in. A scar that all at Ban Me Thuot would comment on, describing with just a hint of awe what Kim the Vietnamese had suffered for his white brothers. How he had come through his trial by fire like the great warrior he was.

Kim shuddered heavily as he drew away the knife blade. Blood trickled down, hot and salty, from where he had bit into his lower lip.

His eyes lit on Tracy again, afraid for the first time in his life. If Tracy had seen, if he should suspect. How could Kim ever live with that shame? The answer was simple; he could not. He would end his own life here, accomplishing what the Khmer Rouge could not, rather than suffer the non-privacy of his own shameful act.

Kim did not want to die; he was not insane. Yet to him life could only be lived one rigid way, bound in the iron of honour; otherwise, it was not life at all, at least not the life of a warrior, merely existence such as the animals endure.

Carefully, Kim bent down, feeling an intense stab of vertigo as he did. Blood hot and wet streamed down the side of his neck. He ran the smeared blade again and again over the high foliage, ridding it of all the blood stains.

'Kim!' He started at Tracy's urgent whisper; blood swam in his head like a school of darting fish. 'We've got to get going. I hear the Khmer Rouge coming!'

'Yes,' Kim said through dry lips. He stood up and the world whirled around him, shadow and light breaking up into asymetric patterns. With an audible gasp, he reached out wildly with one hand, gripped the hairy bole of a tree, felt as if he were swinging from it like an ape.

'Kim!' Tracy whispered. 'There's no more time! They'll be here any moment!'

Gritting his teeth, Kim moved away from his anchor. He tripped over an arching exposed root, almost smashed his front teeth. Picked himself up, went, stumbling, to Tracy. He felt the other's grip, strong and oddly reassuring and allowed himself to be half-carried through the jungle he knew so well. Home and the admiring glances of the others. Home a hero.

What Kim could not know as that Tracy felt the other's blood on his fingers as he gripped Kim, guiding him through the arboreal night. Kim's powerful self-discipline had already anaesthetized the new wound; otherwise he never would have been able to function. He did not, therefore, feel Tracy's fingers exploring his flesh, was not aware of the discovery Tracy made, the correct conclusion he was forming in his mind about what had just transpired. Thus Kim's dread secret was shared by another; a man he hated and who had come to hate him.

Now as they went up the steps to the Governor's brownstone, showed their passes, signed by Captain Michael C. Flaherty, to the patrolmen on duty. Tracy looked again at that whitely livid scar and wondered at the other man. How had he managed to bring Tracy here, to bring him back once again into the foundation's fold? Kim had struck at the vulnerable point, as always using emotionalism. Holmgren was Tracy's key. Kim knew it and so did Tracy but he was powerless to stop himself.

To hell with Kim, Tracy thought angrily as they went inside the house. I'm doing this for me, not for him. But he could not shake the feeling that he was stepping off into a black abyss the nature of which not even Higure could fathom.

When Atherton Gottschalk emerged from the Capitol Hilton after addressing a meeting of labour's top lobbyists who daily swarmed across the Hill making every senator's life miserable, he knew precisely what he needed.

He dismissed his car and driver and, under the scrutiny of

labour's eyes and ears in Washington, took a cab far enough north to be out of their sight. He got out abruptly, telling the cabby he had changed his mind.

He crossed the street and took a bus south, emerging forty minutes later in the heart of Alexandria's Old Town across the Potomac. He walked the rest of the way, falling into the rapid yet comfortable pace from his college athletics days.

It was unremittingly hot and muggy in Washington but he did not mind. My God, but he felt good tonight! His address had gone moderately well in front of a body of people if not exactly hostile then definitely cool towards his nomination. He thought they had listened. Perhaps some of them would even think about what he had told them.

But the main feeling he was experiencing today was, he realized, an enormous sense of relief. John Holmgren's death was like a great weight lifted from his shoulders. Holmgren had been part of the Eastern establishment in politics and, therefore, virtually unassailable. How Gottschalk had feared the man! He had known full well the kind of fight he had been in for at the Republican National Convention and he was not looking forward to it. He would have preferred to face major surgery.

But now that was all behind him. John Holmgren was dead and buried. So long and farewell. It couldn't have happened to a bigger son of a bitch. No lights in the darkness. He turned into the driveway of the four-bedroom house, tucked away amid high trees and shrubbery. A sixteen-foot-high bamboo fence screened out most of the lower storey and all of the well-kept grounds. Two stone pillars flanked an arching black iron gate. On the left-hand pillar was a small discreet brass plaque that read: CHRISTIAN.

He used a key he kept on a separate ring in the pocket of his Casio calculator case. He did not look around as he opened the small door in the gate; the nearest neighbour was over three thousand yards away.

He went up the octagonal tiled walkway, past the lines of acacia and magnolia. The double porch was supported by columns that reminded him of the Deep South. He liked that.

It was what had decided him to buy the place for Kathleen. Oh, not in any direct, traceable way. He could not be implicated. Which was just as it was meant to be. Gottschalk loved his wife. But he loved what Kathleen gave him as well.

He went down the long Italian-tiled hallway and into the master bedroom. As soon as he had alighted from the bus, he had pressed a button on the tiny beeper he carried with him. It had sent its brief electronic signal to its twin, lying at the bottom of Kathleen's handbag. Wherever she was, whatever she was doing, she would know. And she would come.

He stripped off his clothes, went across the room to a recessed closet, pulled down from wooden hangers a black nylon jogging suit.

He turned, gave a last look at his street clothes stretched out on the bed as neatly as he had been taught when he was a child. Then he crossed to a closed door.

He entered a rather large windowless, mirrored room. It was ringed with a complete set of Nautilus equipment. The floor was padded with tough black industrial rubber. A grillwork of speakers were hung at the far corners of the room like a spider-web where the walls met the ceiling.

Gottschalk walked with quick confident strides through the steel and chrome maze. It smelled faintly of sweat and energy. He reached an open section of the room and began his stretching routine down on the rubber floor, groaning with the effort. He sweated freely and was glad of it.

Then he got up and began his Nautilus routine, working on his lower body first, then twenty minutes later, transferring to the upper body equipment. This took another twenty minutes or so, ending up on the double chest machine.

This was set up in the centre of the room, width-wise but somewhat towards the back. It was directly in front of a section of mirror that did not look at all like the rest.

Gottschalk stared at its dark enigmatic face as he climbed aboard the machine and strapped himself in. He had already set the weights at twenty pounds, far below his usual sixty. He sat for a time, feeling the flow of energy hot through his body. He felt the pump. His muscles were tight, seeming to glow with a kind of radiance that pulsated with the triphammer beat of his heart.

Gradually he focused on the mirror before him whose face appeared to be the surface of a still lake, filled with moving shadows, life beneath its glassy skin. His body gleamed with sweat, slippery as oil. He could scent himself.

He heard the front door open and close. There was no need to wonder who it was.

There was a part of him he revealed to no one save her. His public must not know, nor his political allies and his enemies . . . not even his wife.

Only Kathleen could fulfil a need he had, a perverse need that filled him with shame and exaltation at the same time. He supposed it was akin to wanting to be beaten by a woman. He wouldn't know about that. All he knew was what was coming now and his body was on fire.

He began his repetitions, his muscles quivering just below the surface of his skin. Staring straight ahead as if he had X-ray and could look clear down to the bottom of the lake. And then in a lightning-like instant, he *could* see through it as lights came on in the adjacent room.

Kathleen! He could discern the chiselled bones of her face, the sharp angularity of her body. She did not have an ounce of spare fat on her. Impossibly long slim legs, a swan's neck, the heart-shaped face with its dominant blue eyes and above it the cap of shining black hair, cut as short as a man's, an animal's coat. She was lean and mean. He gave a short bark of laughter. Yes, that defined Kathleen, all right.

She was wearing a dark blue poplin dress, the colour setting off her glowing skin. Its semi-Mandarin collar displaying her long neck to its best advantage. A solitaire diamond glittered in the shadowed hollow there. On her feet were high-heeled open-toed shoes of crocodile skin in the same shade as her dress. She wore no rings but one wide gold band clasped tightly around her left wrist.

Dimly he could make out the shapes of the furniture behind her. He was reminded of his mother's bedroom in their old house in rural Virginia. Horse country.

The sweat was coming stronger now as he worked the machine. He licked his lips as, beyond the ghost-like barrier of the two-way mirror, Kathleen stood before him in three-quarters view, her back towards him. She did not once look in his direction; he was not there.

Her hands came up and, hidden from his sight, began to work at the buttons of her dress. He watched, unblinking as, slowly, they went down and down her body until her lips opened slightly and Gottschalk could swear he heard her sigh. Now her head was in profile. One shoulder lifted, grazing her chin, the other falling as if in afterthought and, as if by total accident, the poplin dress slid off the low shoulder.

Kathleen now seemed draped, and Gottschalk had the impression that he was peering through some arcane time-warp viewing Aphrodite at her toilet. He could see clearly the slope of her bare shoulder, the angled shadow that underscored the bone. Then without seeming to have moved at all, Kathleen caused the dress to fall from her other shoulder.

She stood naked from the waist up, the muscles of her back rippling. Her hands came down and she turned around. Gottschalk's breath escaped in a quick high hiss. Kathleen's fingers had spread the dress so that she was completely nude in a thick swath down the centre of her. Only the cincture at her waist erotically hid her navel as if that were her most intimate and secret treasure.

Kathleen's pubic hair was fully as black as the hair on her head. It grew up from between her thighs in thick languorous curls, reaching high onto her underbelly in wisps like black fire, framing but somehow not hiding the tattoo there.

For what seemed to him a long time, she did nothing, merely stood, posed, hands on hips, one knee bent, her head tilted. As a young boy, returning home full of sweat and horse smell from a full day's riding, he had often caught a glimpse of his mother in just such a pose, talking no doubt with his father as they dressed for a social evening out in Washington's most exclusive circles.

Then, imperceptibly, her powerful thighs began to separate, more and more, until her knees were bent so that it seemed as

117

if she were about to squat. Abruptly, her pelvis shot out and up just as if she were delivering the treasure between her thighs to his trembling lips.

All the dark, thundercloudy Virginian days he had spent with a sharp pain in his groin, not knowing why, unable to sleep for the evil visions webbing him of stockinged legs and pantied crotches, exploded in his brain like fireworks, releasing him; his throbbing adolescent steelband headaches ceased to prowl his memory. It was not Kathleen he was watching now but a beautiful Virginian woman: his mother.

He was reborn again in her primal dance. Nothing else existed but her cupped breasts, her long erect nipples, pulled this way and that by her own fingertips. Her sweat-streaked belly, her parted lips, shiny with saliva, her tiny pink tongue, flicking. Her blue eyes glazed with lust and the sensual jerking thrust of her mons. Nothing existed but this image, burning in his skull, and his own painfully hard penis.

He pumped all the harder at the machine, feeling his chest on fire, the tendons along the insides of his thighs beginning to ache, a spot between his shoulderblades daggered with agony.

But this, too, was good. He had to pay for the pleasure that was coming, for the supreme thrill that would soon suffuse him. The more he hurt, the more he paid ... and the greater the pleasure in the end.

From the speakers hung all about the room, he heard her cries and whispers of passion, building and building as her hips dipped and circled, as she offered up her stiff-nippled breasts, as she stroked her long thighs with her nails.

Oh, but he could stand it no more. Except he must, he must! For he knew what lay beyond and he would not spurt his seed before it came. But Kathleen's dance had become so frantic, her cries and groans so insistent that he felt his iron will dissolving in the delicious firestorm of his need.

With a cry, he tore his hands from the moist rubber grips of the machine, clawed down his nylon sweat pants. Beneath, his huge erection painfully twisted within the confines of his sport jock.

At that moment, as if she could sense what was transpiring

behind the thin barrier between them, Kathleen whirled around and in one blur of movement, bent over from the waist, pulled apart the cheeks of her behind and jammed them against the glass.

Gottschalk had only time enough to free his penis from its prison before the touch of his own trembling fingers combined with the sight his eyes were drinking in to set him off.

He jerked powerfully, grunting again and again, aiming his semen at the exposed pucker of flesh between Kathleen's buttocks. He groaned long and loud and, with that, slid off the machine onto his knees in front of her swaying image, his chin lolling against his heaving, sweatribboned chest.

'You know I always meant to read this.' Kim held up a slim hardbacked volume of *The Sailor Who Fell from Grace with the Sea* he had just slipped from one of John Holmgren's bookshelves. 'Yukio Mishima, it is said by many, was a true literary genius.' He looked up at Tracy. 'What do you think?'

'Kim,' Tracy said as his eyes searched about the Governor's study, 'I have neither the time nor the patience for your rhetorical questions.'

'Oh, no,' Kim said as if shocked by Tracy's words. 'Not rhetorical at all. No, I have never read this particular book.' He opened the covers, turned to a page at random. 'I have no idea what it's about. Do you?'

Tracy was staring at the sofa on which his friend had died – or been murdered. The chalk combined with strips of white surgical tape to define the last known position of the deceased; the position in which he had, presumably, died. Beyond, he saw the hardwood coffee table with its silver salver containing a chased silver coffee pot, a pair of bone china cups, saucers and demi-tasse spoons. The familiar square glass bottle of pear brandy, half-filled, the miniature fruit sitting shrivelled and lifeless in the brownish sediment on the bottom stood nearby. It made Tracy think of his friend's body, another bit of human detritus now.

The ruffle of pages. 'Really,' Kim said in an even tone, 'this Mishima person is utterly opaque.'

'It's about a man like you, Kim,' Tracy said. 'A traditionalist gone wrong. A man who breaks his vows and is devoured by the minions of his own fate.'

Kim looked up sharply, slammed the book shut with a whack. 'What the hell d'you mean by that?' he said, switching to French.

Tracy had spoken without thinking; out of anger. Kim's idiot prattlings had got to him. Not a very good sign. He was going into something dark and indefinable. It was a place in which he would be continually questing, his senses tuned and sensitive for the slightest thing out of place. In a red sector you had better make damned sure you were operating at optimal levels, otherwise you were likely never to have to make sure about anything else again.

'Nothing,' Tracy said calmly in the same language. 'Just telling you what you wanted to know.'

Kim put the book back where he had found it. 'You think I break my vows.' He had returned to English.

'I only know what I know.'

Kim came away from the bookcase. 'How I hate you.' His voice was low and deadly.

The tone made Tracy look up at last. He faced Kim squarely. 'It's not me you hate, Kim. You hate yourself. For what, I have no idea.'

Tracy went back to his work. Against the wall to his right was a bronze and glass sideboard on which was a three-tiered rack with perhaps a dozen pipes of varying shapes standing at attention.

Red tulips and mauve lilacs in a fluted crystal vase stood at one end of the sideboard. There had always been fresh flowers there, changed daily by Anna, the maid. Now the flowers were drooped and wilted, their colours softened and paled by time; the stench of decay was hard about them.

Tracy began to move then, Kim forgotten, in his own private world, as he carefully went through all the other rooms of the brownstone, one by one, through the four bedrooms, the two bathrooms, the kitchen, maid's rooms, living room, cellar, wound up back where he had started with no more knowledge.

He closed his eyes. Instinct cried out to him that if the truth about John Holmgren's death were to be found, it would be in here, the room in which he had died.

Kim looked on, sleepy-eyed. 'Now if we only had the corpse to work on, we wouldn't have to go through this mumbo-jumbo.'

Tracy's eyes snapped open and he glared at Kim. 'It really pisses you off to have to use me, doesn't it? I mean deep down inside. This is *my* speciality, not yours. *That's* what you hate.' Kim said nothing. 'Well, we're here and the body's been cremated. Why don't we try to make the best of what we have.'

'Of course.'

'Then shut up and let me do my work.'

Tracy did not cut into anything – at least, not noticeably. But he probed at the seams of all the cushions of the couch and the chairs to see if they had been opened or tampered with.

After the pillows, he went to work on the bottoms of the furniture, checking seams there, too, as well as keeping a sharp lookout for any stray bit of stuffing or sawdust in the carpet: sure signs of recent intrusion.

Next, he tackled the desk and its contents, the bookshelves, the sideboard, outward from the spot where the Governor had died in an everwidening circle. But an hour-and-a-quarter later he found himself back on the chair next to the sofa and the coffee table. Kim had poured himself a small glass of the clear brandy and was sipping it slowly as if he had nothing more on his mind than a relaxing dinner and a good night's sleep.

'Not ready to give up yet, are you?' There was a bantering note to his voice.

'Who said anything about giving up?'

Kim spread his arms. 'You've been everywhere, seen everything. What more can you do?'

Tracy was angry; he had been doing all the work while Kim sat back, talked about Yukio Mishima and drank brandy. 'Why don't you stop being such a goddamned hard case.'

'Me?' Kim raised his eyebrows.

'You're still in such a rush to prove your Orientalism.' His rush of emotion caused him to lean forward. 'Inscrutable Kim. Talking in oblique asides, spouting aphorisms you're convinced no Caucasian will fully understand. It gives you a kind of continuity, doesn't it? Yes. A feeling of specialness when you're in the West.'

'You don't have a clue how it is with me,' Kim said tightly. 'I don't care how much you know about the Khmer.' His lips curled up in a sneer. 'How much you love them. What can a Westerner feel? You're an outsider. You know nothing of the agony we carry around inside of us like a second aching heart.'

'That's right,' Tracy said hotly. 'Just keep on pretending you're the only one who's been scarred.' Something on the periphery of his vision. 'Poor Kim. The only Vietnamese whose family was killed in the war.' Insistence of image, a shifted pattern, resolving itself inside his head. 'Christ but you make me –'

Tracy froze as his head had turned slightly to the right. The brain had had time to focus, identify, classify and the warning bells had begun to clang stridently.

'What is it?' Kim had already forgotten their verbal fencing.

Tracy moved slowly towards the bottle of brandy. He supposed Kim's lifting it had done it. The small pear on the bottom had shifted, turning slightly on its side, exposing part of its bottom. What Tracy saw there interested him very much.

'Go upstairs to the bathroom,' he ordered, 'and get me a large towel. Then go to the kitchen and get me a paring knife.'

'What've you got there?'

'Just do it!' Tracy's eyes never left the pear's underside. He studied it while Kim was gone but through the imperfect lens of the bottle, the liquid and the sediment, it was impossible to decipher just what he was looking at.

With mounting excitement he picked up the bottle, un-screwing the top with his free hand and, flipping up the top of the chased silver coffee pot, poured the brandy inside in one long stream.

Kim had returned by then and Tracy took the soft towel from

him, wrapping the liquidless bottle again and again in its cocoon.

He set the cylindrical mass down and, lifting his right leg up, took a deep breath, a hissing exhale, and brought it down squarely on the centre with a swift sharp motion. The resulting muffled sound seemed no louder than the snap of a dry twig.

He bent down, slowly unwrapped the parcel layer by layer, fighting the urge to rip the shroud completely off in one jerk. He took the paring knife from Kim and with its gleaming tip deftly lifted away the shards of glass from the pear.

Kim looked on as Tracy reached for the small *demi-tasse* spoon alongside of the bone china cups, using it lift the mummified fruit onto the silver salver.

He stared at it for a moment. There was a dark line in its underside. It was definitely not a rip or a tear but an incision, the kind of perfectly straight slash nature was incapable of inflicting.

Carefully, he brought the tip of the blade to bear on the incision. He was very close to the pear now, inhaling its aromatic scent. The perfume of the brandy was heady in the room, drifting. Patiently he probed into the scar, trying to widen it without bruising the soft skin.

For long minutes he worked over the operation, sweating, biting his lower lip in concentration. Almost immediately, he had felt a solid obstruction, had determined that it was quite small, estimating it at less than an inch in length. But he had no clear idea of its shape and this was what he was spending so long in determining. He had no desire to lever out only part of what was in there, severing it by accident.

At last he had worked his way around the circumference of the thing and now he began to urge it outward into the light. He lost it once, his makeshift scalpel slicing through the soft wet flesh at a tangent, and he cursed mighty. Then he had it again and, at length, was rewarded.

Light shone on a curve of shining metal and then Pop! it dropped to the surface of the silver salver like an infant from the womb.

'Christ Almighty!' Tracy said while Kim bent over him.

Tracy sat back on his haunches and contemplated the gleaming thing. A cluster of muscles high up in his back was aching from the position he had been in; he ignored that. Nothing was as important as what he saw before him.

Neither of them spoke. But Kim reached into the breast pocket of his jacket, produced an immaculate white linen handkerchief. Tracy took it from him and, using the spoon, transferred the thing into its new bed. He wrapped it up, put it away in his pocket.

He looked at Kim. 'Did you know something like this might be here?' Even now, when they were safe, there was still a tendency to speak softly.

Kim shook his head. 'I told you everything we knew. It wasn't much but you've got to admit now that it was right on the button.'

They stared at each other for a time. Then Kim said, 'You know who that has to go to for analysis.'

Tracy knew. Though he did not want him involved in this, not now, especially, he saw no other choice. 'He's ill,' he said in an almost dreamlike voice. The ramifications of what he had just found were still echoing in his mind.

'I didn't know,' Kim said. 'How bad?'

'The worst.'

Kim got up. 'The Director will be upset.'

Tracy nodded absently. All of his attention was focused on the flat disc lying swathed in his pocket like a button from a general's dress jacket. But this was no button, he knew. It was an electronic listening device.

Khieu knew the moment Tracy found the bug. He was almost out the door when he heard the alarm sound. It occurred at the precise instant Tracy's knife tip had touched the tiny flat disc secreted within the pre-served pear.

He turned around and went up the wide staircase to the second floor of the house on Gramercy Park South, down the hall and into his bedroom. Beside the golden-skinned Buddha with the worn black face, his neat line of astrological texts and charts, was a small brown box he had built himself. It had at its heart a pair of microchips. On its face was a ruby red LED digital display. It was not a clock, though the readout showed: 21.06. Below the facia, was a cassette recorder.

Khieu pressed a hidden stud on the box's side. A cassette slid out into his cupped palm. Silently, he took it out of his room, down the hall to the study where the other man stood tall and firm.

'I thought you had left.' He glanced at his gold watch.

'The bug's been discovered,' Khieu said without preamble. He was already on the move, inserting the plastic cassette into a player on one of the bookshelves. He turned towards the other, got a nod of assent and depressed the 'play' bar.

'. . . I hate you,' they heard from the speakers.

'It's not me you hate, Kim,' a second voice said. 'You hate yourself. For what, I have no idea.'

The voice was wiped away by the tall man's curt gesture. He turned towards the high windows, his fingertips plucking at the taut cream curtains. 'Kim, eh? That means the foundation's become involved.' He turned back into the room, his cool grey eyes regarding Khieu. 'But we know that to be impossible, don't we?'

'So why is Kim here?'

The tall man grunted ruminatively. 'That may not be our real problem. Now the sleeper's been awakened. That was Tracy Richter with him. I know the two worked together for some time in Ban Me Thuot and Cambodia before Richter so mysteriously dropped out of sight.'

'Do you want me to stay here now?' Khieu asked.

The tall man shook his head. 'No. Of course not. What you have to do tonight cannot be delayed. You of all people understand that. The planets have dictated your actions. Go on with what you have to do. Now that we have this recording, we are in the perfect position again.' He smiled at the other. 'While you're gone I'll devise the proper course of action to take regarding the two of them.'

'I think we both know what Tracy will do with the bug now.' Mizo had told Khieu of the man in New York, had even shown him some of his handiwork.

'Oh, yes,' the tall man said. 'There's no doubt of it. The only question remaining is if Richter should be allowed to get that far.'

September 1966–April 1967
Phnom Penh, Cambodia

Like the backwash from a garbage-ridden scow, the aftermath of President de Gaulle's much-heralded visit to Cambodia threw most of the knowledgeable population of Phnom Penh into a deep depression. All of the euphoria that had gripped them during the grand days of his presence had slipped away like a thief in the night.

The anticipated aid the general had promised took the form of finance for a second *lycée*, a proposed phosphate factory and new uniforms for the terribly outfitted Khmer Army. And that was all.

The French foreign minister's meeting with the selected representatives of Hanoi ended without noticeable result. And as for de Gaulle's presence itself, it did nothing in the way of swaying sentiment in either the North Vietnamese or the Americans.

In short, it became clear that Prince Sihanouk's days were numbered. He had made his last stand, as pitiful as it was, and had nothing to show for it save perhaps a new school which would eventually turn out more well-educated but unemployable young men who would soon become disaffected with the régime that had supported them, albeit somewhat shakily.

As the tenor of life changed within the city so, too, did it change within the walls of the Khieu villa. The internecine battle of political wits between the Chau Sang and Kou Roun had been joined in earnest and it did not take a soothsayer to divine who the eventual winner would be.

During those heated days, filled with anxiety and discord, Sokha had cause to recall that brief moment on the night René Evan had come to dinner in June when, on leaving the dining room, he had glimpsed his father putting his arm around his mother's shoulders and, with an almost wistful smile, say, '*Own*'. In remembrance, that moment seemed all the more poignant painted as it was against the backdrop of rapidly escalating events.

Increasingly, Sokha felt adrift. There was a kind of semi-hysterical hush waiting in the air. Almost everyone knew something was coming but what it was they could not say. Sam said it was revolution but Sokha was not so certain. Often, he would ask Preah Moha Panditto his opinion at the conclusion of his lessons. The old monk would look at him and say, 'I do not think on such matters; politics are no concern of ours.' In the years ahead Sokah would cause to remember those words and weep bitter tears for his *Lok Kru*.

Terror was an uninvited guest, hanging like a fearful *kmoch* in his mind. What will happen to us? That phrase echoed in his mind like a chill wind so that his nights were filled with restless tossings and he would awaken ten or twelve times in the course of several hours.

During this time, his only solace was Malis or, more accurately, his one-way sexual communion with her. Almost every night and, especially when his anxiety became unbearable, he would creep silently down the dark hall and push open the door to her room. Then he would fill himself with her scent and the sight of her sexuality released like a bright kite, sizzling the air.

Then one evening Sam came home with a tall slender girl in tow. It was Rattana, full of smiles and happiness. Sam was uncharacteristically silent during dinner, leaving it to Khemara and Hema to make polite conversation with his girlfriend.

But Sokha saw in his older brother's eyes the tension of something building. At last Sam spoke up. He told the family how he and Rattana felt about each other; he asked his parents' permission to marry her.

Afterwards, when he had taken her home, Sam appeared in Sokha's doorway.

'I don't like it, *Own*,' he said softly. 'They didn't give their consent right away.'

'Oh, you know how they are. Especially Pa. You said yourself he was very traditional.'

That did not change the troubled look on Sam's face.

'They're going to consult a soothsayer . . . I have a bad feeling about it.'

'Don't worry,' Sokha soothed. 'It's just pre-marriage nerves. Everything will turn out all right.'

But, as it happened, Sam's apprehension was well-founded. The soothsayer Khemara and Hema consulted could not, he said, approve of the marriage and Sam flew into a rage when his parents told him.

'Do you mean to tell me that because I was born in the year of the rat and she was born in the year of the snake, we cannot get married?'

'The astrologer was quite specific about that, I'm afraid,' Khemara said. 'Because of that, the two of you are not compatible. I cannot give my permission for the marriage.'

'But we love each other.'

'Please understand, Sam, it is for your own good.'

'Pa, do you understand what I just said?'

Khemara put his arm around his son, tried to smile. 'I heard, Sam. But according to the astrologer that cannot last. The snake must devour the rat. It is the way of things. You must accept this.'

'No!' Sam pulled away from his father's embrace.

'Samnang!'

And it was as simple as that. Khemara raised his voice and Sam shut his mouth, bowed his head.

'You'll see, Sam,' Khemara said, 'this will pass. You'll find another girl for whom you are better suited.'

That night, through his field of view through the hallway window, Sokha saw Sam slip out of the house and move like the flitting shadow of some great nocturnal bird in the direction of Nguyan Van Diep's villa. Sokha went away from Malis' doorway for a moment in order to follow his brother's path but Sam had been swallowed up by the foliage and it was impossible for Sokha to say whether indeed his destination was the Vietnamese villa or whether he was sneaking out to see Rattana or René.

Sokha was already in bed, feeling the afterglow of sexual release, drifting off into a fitful half-sleep, when Sam returned.

At first, Sokha thought he was dreaming but then Sam had bent over him, delivered a kiss to each cheek.

'Where have you been?' His voice was furred with sleep.

'You won't tell that you saw me?'

Sokha shook his head back and forth. 'Bawng . . .' It was an endearment he did not often use with Sam. 'I'm frightened. I don't know what's going to happen.'

Sam knelt down beside him, put a strong arm across his chest. 'Hey, Own, didn't you say Pa would take care of us?'

They stared at each other for a long moment and perhaps for the first time Sam understood that Sokha knew what was going to occur soon. He put his head close to Sokha's, whispered, 'No time to feel frightened now, Own. You're going to have to take care of the family.'

Sokha rolled over, his eyes opened wide. 'What do you mean?'

'I mean I'm leaving. I can't stay here any longer. I can't bear to see what is happening. The elections are soon. The National Assembly will elect Lon Nol Prime Minister. Sihanouk will still be Chief of State, of course, just as he has been for the past six years. General Lon Nol will take more power and I think that is the beginning of the end for us. Already the General is slaughtering hundreds in the countryside. It will only get worse when he comes to power.'

'But what can you do?'

'I can join the maquis. René has made some contacts for me in a unit to the northwest, in Battambang. That's where I'll go.'

'But why?'

'Because, Sok, it is the only way to gain freedom for Cambodia. The Sihanouk régime is riddled with graft. The stink of corruption is all around us. Lon Nol is a vicious bastard; he'll try to wipe us out if he can. We can't allow that. That's why I must go.'

Sokha shivered. 'You're more than blood to me, Sam,' he said softly. 'You're my best friend. What will I do without you?'

Sam got up; he squeezed his brother's hand. 'Live, Sok. Live.'

He went across the room. Sokha saw him limned against the blackness of the hallway beyond. 'Bawng . . .'

'Yes, little one.'

'I'm sorry . . . about Rattana. That you can't marry her.'

Sam said nothing but after a time he raised his hand to his eyes, wiped them. 'Perhaps it's just as well.' His voice had a quality to stir the leaves on a tree. 'The revolution calls.'

With that he was gone and it was a long, long time before Sokha drifted off to sleep.

Sam had said nothing of his departure to Khemara or Hema or to any other member of the family. They were, quite naturally, distraught and Khemara first sought for him at Rattana's family villa.

He reported that she had said she had not seen or heard from Sam since the night of the dinner party. He said he believed her. He was reluctant to call in the police. In today's atmosphere who knew what conclusion they might jump to?

Sokha held his secret tight to him, anguishing at the torment this not knowing put his parents through. Yet he could not bring himself to tell them. Sam had not wanted them to know else he would have at least left them a note. And Sokha correctly concluded that they were better off not knowing what he had done.

The next night, he could not sleep and, feeling in need of solace, got out of bed, padding silently down the dark hall in his place of intimate communion in front of Malis' partly opened door.

He had already freed his penis which, in anticipation of the sight of his naked sister, was rapidly growing in size and girth. He reached a palm out and slowly pushed the door open.

It was a stifling night, hot, the air laden with humidity. All the windows were wide open, the curtains pushed back to allow the maximum flow of air inside the house.

The bedcovers were pushed to the end of the bed in an uneven roll. Malis' naked flesh seemed to glow with an inner radiance.

Sokha was already gripping his erection, starting to stroke. This was his time; he began to calm down, feeling a kind of inner peace steal over him.

Then out of the corner of his eye he thought he saw a shadow move. He turned his head to the right, towards the window.

Yes, it was true! Just outside the pushed-apart jalousie, he could just discern some movement. It was blacker than the surrounding night. Someone was out there.

He was about to make a noise to frighten the other away when he saw his sister raise her head off the bed, look towards the window. She sat up, her breasts hanging deliciously and then, incredibly, her crooked finger beckoned the shadow into her room!

Sokha was stunned. The shape of a man entered and they embraced. The man picked Malis up in his arms and gently placed her in the centre of the bed. Then, climbing up himself, he knelt over her, straddling her form. Malis' long arms reached up, snakelike, and, wrapped across his muscled back, pulled him down to her.

Sokha's penis hung limp and flaccid in his damp palm. Oh, Amida! he thought. He felt sick to his stomach. The spell had been broken and now he saw himself as someone observing. He saw what he had been doing night after night. How could he have done that? How could he?

He rushed from his place to sanctuary, a sanctuary no more but a place of vile, foul memories. In his own room, he leaped upon his bed and, jamming the fingers of his right hand between bedpost and wall, pushed hard at the bed with all his strength, using the force of his whole body, sandwiching his fingers, gritting his teeth against the rising tide of pain. It grew and grew like a terrible spectre, ribboning his entire frame but still he continued while blood from the torn flesh dribbled slowly to the floor, while the images assailed his mind, until he thought he could bear it no more.

He passed out.

He was awakened by the loud shout of voices raised in alarm. He turned his head slowly. His hand throbbed unmercifully. He blinked, becoming aware that his room was bathed in a flickering crimson glow.

He groaned and, holding his injured hand in his lap, looked out the window. The sky seemed to be on fire. Cinders fluttered through the air and it was so hot the beads of sweat were rolling down his back and beneath his arms.

'Sok!' His mother came into the room. 'Are you all right?'

'Yes, *Maman*,' he said automatically. He hid his right hand from her sight.

Hema put her arm around his shoulders. 'Come away from there,' she said. 'I want all the children out of this wing of the house. The firemen said there's little danger of the blaze spreading but I don't want to take any chances. You'll sleep with your father and me tonight.'

'But what happened, *Maman*? Whose villa is on fire?'

Hema said nothing, pushing him before her. In the living room he saw Malis with her arms around Ratha and sleepy Soryia, peering out the windows which his father had apparently closed against the heat and smoke and filtering debris.

Sokha stayed well away from her, circling around, trying to find his father. He found him at the front door.

'Don't go near there,' he heard his mother call anxiously. 'Khemara . . . !'

His father turned briefly towards him. Half his face seemed as if it was burning along with the night. Flames danced in one eye. 'Do as your mother says, Sok.' His voice was soft.

'What's burning, Pa?' Sokha asked him.

Khemara's face was filled with an infinite sadness and something more: terror. 'It's the villa of the Vietnamese, Nguyan Van Chinh.'

At the end of that week, barely a month before the elections, they came and took Khemara away. Officers of the Internal Security arrived at the villa without warning just as the family was getting ready for bed.

Sokha had never seen such a look in anyone's eyes as he saw in his mother's that night.

'It is nothing to worry about, *Own*,' Khemara said as he got dressed under the scrutiny of the officers. 'I am a loyal supporter of the Prince. Look at all my years of devoted service. It is an error, that is all.'

Tears filled Hema's eyes; she could say nothing. Khemara

came and kissed each of his children good-bye. When he came to Sokha he kissed his cheek, whispering in his ear, 'Take care of the family until I return.'

Deep in the night, Sokha was reminded of what Sam had said to him:

You're going to have to take care of the family. Had he known what was going to happen to Pa? he wondered. And if so, how could he bring himself to abandon them?

At last he drifted off to sleep but his unquiet mind was filled with a vivid dream. He was seated at the dinner table, Hema beside him. He put his arm around her shoulders and said softly, smiling, '*Own*'.

In the hard months that followed, Sokha found himself wondering with more and more frequency what he was doing in Phnom Penh. As Sam had predicted, General Lon Nol had been elected Prime Minister and the steel clamp of his growing influence was felt all over.

By December it was clear from all reports that the government's hold on the population in the countryside was eroding. At the beginning of the new year, Lon Nol took it upon himself to nationalize the rice crop. Soldiers were dispatched to take from the peasants as much of the recently harvested rice crop as they could for a vastly undervalued sum of money.

This '*ramassage du paddy*' as the new régime dubbed it found increasing resistance and, in retaliation, was pursued with increasing fervour and brutality. Daily, reports filtered into the city of new slaughters in the surrounding countryside.

With this, Sokha grew increasingly restless. It was clear to him after the first week that his father was never coming. But his mother would believe none of that. She spent most of her time at the Royal Palace trying to learn some news of her husband. There had been nothing forthcoming from the Sihanouk régime and then when Lon Nol came into power, his cabinet had no time for her.

Once, the soldiers beat her so severely that she could not walk and, fearful for her life, Sokha had set out to find her. He brought her back to the villa and a doctor was summoned. Still she went back as soon as she was able to sit on the government's doorstep until she got an answer.

But she found nothing but contempt and at last, white-faced and defeated, she returned to the villa and never set foot outside the compound again.

Sokha tried to comfort her but she was beyond that. He saw René once, near the Central Market.

'I am sorry about your father,' the Frenchman said. 'I tried to warn him. I did my best.'

Sokha knew that René was telling the truth but he could not find it in his heart to thank him or even acknowledge his remark.

Spring was coming and with it the heat of war. Preah Moha Panditto was gone from Botum Veddey. Like the forest of funeral chedi behind it, the temple was already considered a relic of Cambodia's unfortunate past.

Phnom Penh was falling apart. It seemed to Sokha that the life he and his family had once known was a figment of his imagination, merely a dream he had once conjured up. For the present was a nightmare.

He tried to tell his mother why he was leaving, what he felt he had to do. He had to stand up and fight for his father, for her, for Preah Moha Panditto. The old codes were being swept away on an unquenchable tide. There was no time now for peace and understanding and the teachings of his past. The Buddha would have to wait for another time to hold sway. But he would never forget, he told her that too.

Hema heard nothing of what he said. She stared out the window at the ancient banyan tree, unblinking, her old head trembling slightly on the thin stalk of its neck. Her eyes had gone milky, like the orbs of a blind person.

Sokha kissed her on each cheek, whispering still to her, seeking her permission and, without a word to Malis, who was picking Soryia and Ratha up from school, he slipped out of the door, out of Chamcar Mon, out of Phnom Penh, disappearing into the jungle to the northwest on the same route his brother had taken before him, on a collision course with the revolution.

Far downtown sirens wailed, carrying in the humid air. Accumulated heat radiated from the sidewalks, buildings' sides so that, even nearing midnight, it was as hot as afternoon.

Tracy was tired as he turned west on Thirtieth Street. His apartment was on the second floor of a small, neat brownstone tucked away within shouting distance of the Chief Medical Examiner's turquoise-façaded building on the east side of First.

Outside his building was adorned with a mullioned black wroughtiron trellis that rose the entire four stories. Its ornamental blossoms gave the place an odd New Orleans air. The fine latticework shadows dropped around his shoulders like a skein, rippling over his back, given life by his passage. He put his key in the lock, opened the front door.

He collected his mail, went up the flight of steps. The weariness in his body had not penetrated his head. His mind was buzzing with reflected thoughts, set off by the electronic listening device he had found in John's study.

He came up on the second floor landing. It was at the opposite end of the hallway from his apartment but he had a clear view of his front door. There was a crack of light seeping out onto the hall carpet from beneath his front door. He had not left the lights on when he had gone to work this morning.

Walking on the sides of his feet, went quickly and silently down the hallway. He stood on one side of the door, put the key into the lock, turned it over. Moving his hand quickly down, he snapped open the door.

He pressed his back hard against the hallway while the door swung on its hinges. He held his breath. Nothing happened.

Light spilled out, unwavering. No shadow played across it. He listened hard but heard nothing.

He went into the apartment sideways, moving out of the doorway as soon as he was inside. The apartment was as he had left it except that there was a half-filled glass on the dining room table. White wine. Standing next to it, staring wide-eyed at him was Lauren.

'Jesus Christ,' he breathed. He kicked the door shut behind him. 'Don't tell me. You bribed the super.'

She tried a smile. 'I told him who I was. I think he got a kick out of that.'

'I'm sure he did.'

'Meaning?' Her head seemed to be stiff and quivery.

'Balaban's a dirty old man; he thinks all ballet dancers are virgins. It seems to help his fantasy life.'

Lauren laughed despite her nervousness. 'I'm glad he doesn't know the truth, then. He might not've let me in.'

Tracy had an urge to say, You've got a hell of a nerve, but he just turned away.

Staring taut as a bow, Lauren reacted instantly. 'You're not angry, are you?' She took a step towards him when he did not turn back to her. 'I've missed you.' It was a whisper, searching him out across the chasm time had eroded like a powerful river, separating them. 'More than words can say.'

Why did you leave me? he longed to say. *Why did you hurt me so?* Though she had already told him, it was not enough. 'Why should I trust you now?' he said.

Lauren shuddered as if a cold wind had passed between them. This was what she had feared, what had caused her hand to tremble. Still, she persevered. 'There's no reason at all,' she said truthfully. 'Except to say that things are different now. I've . . . I don't know, I've found you inside of myself.'

Tears spilled down across her cheeks and her eyes glittered in the lamplight. 'But what can that mean to you? I suppose . . . words. Words can lie, say half-truths, who knows?'

She went silently towards him, willing herself not to shrink away. The thought that he would do to her what she had already done to him, lay heavily on her chest; the fright was ancient, therefore more powerful. She fought against it. 'But what,' she said softly, 'do you feel when I do this?'

And she touched him, sliding first her fingertips, then the soft palm of her hand across his upper arm and over his chest. She knew what she was doing; knew that she had never touched another man in such a manner, with such love and such tenderness.

Tracy turned when he felt the nature of her touch. He was somehow reminded of the Khmer priest's outpouring of affection. A stranger in a strange and hostile land, he had been shocked then by its comfort as well as its power. Now, with Lauren, he felt a kinship across the years in her touch.

'We've really been through the wars together, haven't we?' She nodded silently, glad that he was talking. 'We've lied to each other, cheated, turned our anger into hate.' He had not touched her yet. 'And hate into hurt.'

His silence frightened her and, instinctively, she moved closer so that her right hip pressed against his. She wore a pair of thin dark green silk trousers, a man's shirt. A ribbon with a tiny spray of purple heather held her long auburn hair back from her face in a shining ponytail. She wore just a touch of lipstick and blush. Her eyes needed no makeup except onstage. Diamond studs pierced the lobes of her ears.

'But I'm here.' Her voice was slightly tremulous as if she were again on the verge of tears. 'I've come back.' The lamplight threw shadows away from her face as if they were not for her. Her cheeks shone. 'And it feels like home.'

She knew she had said what she had come here to say. She had not practised it or even thought about it beforehand; she had been too terrified to think that clearly. Life would have been intolerable had she not come. Dance and, in between, stare at the floor while she listened to the boom of her empty heart as if she had been thrown up on some cruel foreign shore.

She shivered, felt the connection between them now as tenuous as one lone candle flame flickering in the night wind. Who knew when a sudden gust would swirl in and lick it out? She suspected the moment was close. So close she held her breath leaving only the thunderous marker of her heartbeat to count the seconds. Time seemed to attenuate. As if in a dream, she lost control of where she was and how long she had been there. Minutes, hours, days, there was no difference for her. Her longing for him, the certain knowledge that she did not want to leave him, the utter fragility of the moment in which they now existed terrified her.

In a panic, she wondered wildly what she would do if he sent her away. She would survive, of course, but, she asked herself, to what purpose.

She watched his eyes for clues, saw a stirring there. Her anxiety caused her to move and the strand – so thin and vulnerable – was broken and his arms came out, held her at arm's length.

'What is it?' she said a little breathlessly. Her lungs seemed unwilling to perform their function.

'Just . . . give me some time,' he said. 'It's too much, too soon. I don't know whether I'm ready for this.' He shook his head. 'There's been too much between us to just let it go all at once like this; too much feeling built up over too long a time.'

'Do you want me to go?' It was out before she had a chance to snatch it back. She almost cried out then in her agony and anger at herself.

He said nothing and she moved across the room to the stereo, selecting an album at random. She flicked on switches, placed the tone arm down, turned up the volume.

She came back to him and without artifice took his hand in hers. There was nothing seductive in the gesture, she was careful about that. The music began and she lifted his arm up, pulled gently.

Early Bruce Springsteen, 'Spirits in the Night,' billowed through the room like fog off the Hudson, bringing back the ghosts of their recent past, the innocence of what once had been, reminders of melodic thread, Bruce's gravelly, heartfelt voice, and the beat, the beat . . . she had chosen well.

She smiled at him, willing her fright down, and, putting her head to one side, mouthed *Come on* silently to him.

The music was infectious and they danced, as they had in the beginning before all the hurts. Lauren dancing all the day, dancing at night, too, to a different beat entirely. Rock'n'roll could fuel her just as well, the energy taking over at darkness' coming from the iron discipline of the day.

The music moved them both, powering them across the floor of whatever jammed and glittering latenight clubs they had frequented then; she could not remember the name of one. Perhaps they had all changed their names, or, more likely, it was she who had changed.

That jazz-influenced sax break he had loved so much flowed from the end of one of Bruce's verses and she thought, That's right, darling, let the music take you, let it bring you back to where we once started, on the other side of the pain and the sleepless nights.

Tracy held her in his arms and felt the trembling race through his muscles, tumbling and gusting like a summer storm. A heated kiss beneath the haloed glow of a city streetlight somewhere in Soho or beyond, the night so late he could feel dawn on its way. His eyes drank her in, the high-cheekboned face, the wide-apart eyes, uptilted like a Eurasian's, her long swan's neck, the ripeness of her lips and he knew that she had managed to crack through the cement job he had performed on his heart. An ache was gone from inside him and with it a deadness he only now with its absence had become aware of.

He swung her around, entering into himself again, and drew her to him. She lifted one leg, the other, and spun. In the air, he caught her, one arm around her narrow waist, the other beneath her knees.

'Lauren,' he whispered, and she heard it as music, lifting her face upward, burnished in the lamplight, her lips opening slightly. She did not take her eyes off him till he was too close to focus on, and by that time she felt his mouth against the side of her neck.

Tracy's tongue felt the pulse thrumming inside her through the soft skin. He felt her fingers stroking the back of his neck, twining themselves in his hair. He felt her against him like a hot engine, felt the quiver like a jolt down her spine.

Her scent was strong and sweet, bringing back in a flash all their shared intimacies like a drawerful of precious photographs. He remembered what she loved best, and his lips slid downward into the V formed by the opened buttons of her man's shirt, licking the saltness of her skin while her head went back and her eyes fluttered closed.

On the sofa, she tried to undo his trousers, but he pushed her back, and when she opened her mouth to question him he kissed her with so much passion it took her breath away and, dizzied, she allowed him to open the rest of the buttons on her shirt.

His hot tongue made a delicious trail down to her breasts. He circled them with his lips until she arched up against him. Her nipples were hard, burning for his touch. She gasped and guided his head.

He lifted her buttocks off the cushion, stripped down her pants. He raised Lauren's thighs, hearing her fluttering sigh like a murmur of her heart. His hands reached up across her belly to rub her nipples while his head swooped down toward her high mount.

He licked her, gently at first, then with increasing force as his ardour escalated, while Lauren shuddered and moaned beneath him. He felt the tensing of her muscles, and left her dampness to suck her nipples back into his mouth.

He repeated this over and over until she was jerking uncontrollably, her fingers twining with his with all her strength, pulling him closer, closer.

She called out his name, unashamedly drew her legs up even further. He heard every breath she took. He frictioned his tongue faster against her silken flesh.

'Ohhh ... Oh, I'm coming,' gusted out with a fountain's force, her hips up off the sofa, bucking against him. 'Oh, oh, oh, darling!' Her thighs clamped together around his ears and cheeks, rocking him back and forth with her in the aftermath. Her sighs.

And tears as she drew him up, whispering, 'Darling, darling, my darling,' as she kissed his eyes, cheeks, and lips. Her fingers tracing the outline of him hard and hot beneath the barrier of his trousers. She stroked up and down, cupping his balls from underneath, using the V of her thumb and forefinger to press against just the head until he gasped. She snaked her body around, her eyes wide and shining, her skin sheened with released oils, never losing touch with him, magically opening his trousers, slipping them down his legs as she caressed his muscles like a masseuse.

She mouthed the flesh along his hard belly, pulled back on her haunches to lick his nipples as he had hers. She wrapped her palm around the thick base of him, and her hand rose and fell in concert with his breathing.

She moved back down so that she was spread out against him, one heating the other. Her lips were very close to his quivering length. She let go of him long enough to reach down between her own thighs, wet her fingers in her own lubrication. She coated his penis, returned to her languorous stroking.

Her mouth opened and she breathed against him, forcing her breath out hot and hard. She had not directly touched the upper half of his penis as yet, and now her head moved so that he thought it was about to happen, arching up to help make the connection.

But Lauren had another goal in mind, her open lips engulfing his balls, humming slightly so that he felt the vibrations and his eyes squeezed shut.

Tracy felt his heart hammering so hard against his chest he thought the skin and flesh above it beat with its force. Cords along the insides of his thighs seemed stretched, elongated in a kind of pleasurable pain that built but somehow seemed incomplete.

Then Lauren moved her head back up and took him inside her mouth, groaning deep in her throat at the taste and texture. The reactions the prolongation of his ecstasy brought out in him stirred her so strongly that she suspected she might come again when he did. She had thought that impossible without any direct physical manipulation, but now it seemed to be happening.

As she felt him expanding inside her mouth, his balls tightening just beneath, she felt the familiar throbbing between her thighs, about to radiate through her whole body. She clamped her legs together, twisting slightly so that her mount pressed against the rough fabric of the sofa pillow.

'Oh!' she almost cried, swallowing the exclamation as Tracy exploded in her mouth. She licked and sucked, using her tongue as well as the insides of her cheeks, loving the feel of him there, the pleasure she was giving him after all the pain.

She wanted him. Again. She had never felt so sexually wild in her life. She had never felt so alive.

He might have been an animal but he was not, though he was totally at home in the wood. He stood within its silver-dappled confluence: ancient oak and maple joined together some distance from the river, petering slowly out into tangled undergrowth at the end of the far slope where the cornfield began.

As he moved through the forest's dark serpentine depths no bird lifted away from his line of passage or was disturbed from its slumber, no nocturnal creature – rabbit or vole, chipmunk or stoat – bounded from his path. He was accepted and therefore ignored.

Through the dense night the flat expanse of the cornfield could be seen, still and skyed. He scented the lingering dampness of the rain as he wound his way through the wood. He found a comfortable spot and sat down, crosslegged. Directly above his head, a horned owl ceased preening its wing feathers, swivelled its great icon head, its enormous golden eyes watching him with passive curiosity.

The pale watery moonlight passed over him as if he were merely another undulation in the ridge. He was hidden as completely as if he were cloaked in the darkness of the night.

He felt the peace envelop him as if it were a component of the wood itself. He thought of *Lok Kru*: Preah Moha Panditto as he slid to the forest's floor. He felt the dampness of the soil through his thin trousers, the soft mattress of windblown leaves, sprinklings of bark and nut husks. They were home to him, he felt as one with them. He began to chant, to cleanse his mind and, more importantly, his spirit. He called to the *vinheanakhan*, the spirits of his ancestors, to gather around him, to add their enormous strength to his. He felt them as he began to expand outward into the void, lifting his head to kiss the sky. His lips opened

Namo tassa Bhagavato, Arahato. Sammā-Sambuddhassa!
Namo tassa Bhagavato, Arahato. Sammā-Sambuddhassa!
Namo tassa Bhagavato, Arahato. Sammā-Sambuddhassa!

and encompassed the world.

Beyond the cornfield, the warm yellow lights of a house could be seen, two tiny squares of illumination, a second night sky.

From the inside of his black cotton blouse he extracted two sheets of onionskin paper. On each was drawn a circle divided up into twelve equal sections. Glyphs were drawn within some of these, more glyphs ran down the right side of each sheet.

Carefully he spread out each sheet so that they lay side by side. These were horoscopes, prepared by him several days before. On the left was his own. It showed the heartbeat of his life, the ridges and rills, the valleys and clefts. Like all such charts it did not predict the future but, rather, personal tendencies. This was most important to remember. It had been the first lesson he had been taught as a child learning the difficult art. It was so difficult primarily because it depended so much upon interpretation. It took years of training and, beyond even that, a sensitive's touch, to accurately read the portents.

His eyes shifted to the second chart. The tall man had obtained for him the birth place and date of Moira Monserrat. Those bits of information were all he needed. From both charts he had been able to fathom the right day and time their paths should cross.

Quickly he gathered up the onionskins, set fire to them, rubbing the black ash between his fingertips. His head turned. He had become aware of another presence. A small brown hare sat crouched on its hind legs within the labyrinth of the cornfield. Its long ears twitched as it looked nervously this way and that. Its sides were panting as if it had had a long run.

The night beat on quite still – almost no wind coming down into the cornfield through a swale in the hillock.

His nostrils flared briefly as the red fox came trotting through the stalks of corn. His head turned as if he, too, were searching for something; in that moment he seemed like a blind man, an ascetic in simple robes of dirt-scrubbed cloth.

The fox's quick knowing face lifted somewhat, one eye sparking in moonlight as it scented. Then it was off at a dangerous sprint. At that moment, the hare ceased washing its face with jerky erratic swipes of his forepaws. Its flanks quivered, its forepaws coming down hard on the tilled earth.

It jerked suddenly, its body lifted into the air by the force of the fox's vicious attack. A sharp crack like a bolt of heat lighting resounded, doubling, trebling across the ordered expanse.

He sat immobile, listening. There was nothing left in the cornfield but the chirrupping of the insects and a dark path of moisture that was soon absorbed by the earth.

The first erratic gusts of a freshening northerly wind touched his cheeks, ruffled his black hair in a mother's caress. He lifted his head as the fox had moments before. Already gauzy tendrils were extending skyward to diffuse the moonlight. Soon the moon. He could feel the sharp drop in pressure and he knew there would be rain soon.

He looked beyond the cornfield to the night sky with the two moons. The house lights were blinking on and off as a branch from a Japanese maple on its lawn swayed back and forth in the wind. It seemed to beckon him onward. The universe knew what was about to happen.

Rain stuttered against the leaded windowpanes, driven like tears along the glass. The wind coughed like a hound on the hunt, the sky was filthy with storm.

Moira lay on the high bed, the covers thrown off. Despite the change in weather she felt hot and uncomfortable. Unable to sleep, she had reluctantly swallowed a sleeping pill, lay down to await its effects. But it had not relaxed her and sleep was still far away.

Moira got up off the bed. Her legs were trembling with fatigue and an excess of emotion and she could feel the triphammer of her heart banging inside her ribcage. In a daze she walked unsteadily over to the window, drew back the curtains, peered out.

Darkness. Shadows on shadows, shifting in the wind eddies. Nightsounds and the rush of rain came to her. Nothing more.

She turned away and went downstairs; the thought of sleep now made her itch and the rumpled bed, so large and empty, brought back images of John.

Her lips opened and she spoke his name in prayer. 'Why?' she whispered. 'Why did you leave me?' She hated him then, more than she had hated anyone in her life. And the force of that staggered her, a physical blow that brought her to her knees. She sat heavily on the stairs, the cold wood against her buttocks and the backs of her thighs. She put her head in her hands, running her fingers through her thick hair. 'Oh, Christ,' she breathed.

Of course she did not hate him; not really. She loved him with the fierce abandoned pride one feels for one's first true love of adulthood; felt now that most terrible of pains when that love is gone.

She wrapped her arms around herself, rocked gently back and forth. She had given herself to him, opened up her heart and he had responded with the cruellest deed of all: he had forsaken her with all her desires opened rawly to the world.

'Oh, God, oh, God!' she cried softly. 'What will become of me now?'

'All right. That's enough,' Atherton Gottschalk said. He twisted around in his chair. 'Come on over here.'

'Just a minute,' his wife said. She was deftly manipulating the controls on an Atari unit. On the twenty-four-inch TV screen facing the foot of the bed, the last four evil ships of the Space Invaders were blown to electronic dust.

'Roberta,' Gottschalk said. It was late, well past midnight. But his evenings always seemed as long as his days. Work piled up while he made his clandestine visits to Kathleen and it just had to be dealt with. 'Enough already.'

They both knew he did not mean it. Gottschalk loved the upsurge in these computer games. That the generation currently growing up should be addicted to such games of obvious military bent encouraged him.

Yet he missed being with his wife. If only he did not have to sleep. Then he could have his cake and eat it, too. His most severe inner voice admonished. Now is that a way for the next President of the United States to think? You are not lusting in your heart, boy, but in other, more productive areas. He laughed. If it was good enough for that reprobate Jack Kennedy, hell, what was wrong with him doing it? Kennedy's trouble, Gottschalk knew, was that he didn't keep his mind on business. Otherwise the foul-ups at the Bay of Pigs and in Vietnam never would have happened. Had they been planned correctly who knows where we'd be now, Gottschalk thought. A sight more secure in the world than we are now, that's for sure.

He watched his wife as she scrambled across the bed towards him. She was in every way a physical contrast to Kathleen. Her body was fleshy where Kathleen's was trim, her hair was long and brown, her eyes black.

'It's about time you were finished,' she said in her low, throaty voice. 'It's a quarter to two. Time all decent folk were safely in bed.' She made a lunge for him, laughing. 'But not asleep!'

Her palm struck him just over his heart as her lips closed over his and, despite himself, he shuddered.

Once, in the middle of an awesome time of monsoons off the coast of Southeast Asia, the then future senator had thought he was having a heart attack. His father had died of massive coronary occlusion, his grandfather of a debilitating stroke. Gottschalk had heard that such things were hereditary. However, since he lacked the courage to discuss the topic with his doctor, it forever remained a nebulous, and therefore much more terrifying fear, inside him.

Roberta's salacious grab had made him feel again the acute vulnerability he suspected lurked within his heart. It was an ungovernable fear which he could admit to no one, not even his wife.

Gottschalk took her in his arms, rolled her back onto the bed. They grappled like teenagers, laughing while beside them, unattended, the lasers shooting at random were at length overcome by Space Invaders landing.

Roberta touched him between his thighs and he growled low in his throat, relaxing. The phone rang.

147

Gottschalk, cursing mightily, disentangled himself and, rolling to one side, picked up the receiver.

'What is it?' he barked testily into the instrument.

'It's late, I know. But I thought it would be the best time.'

He recognized Eliott's voice. 'Oh, it's you.' His tone softened immediately. 'What d'you have?'

'The *Vampire*'s aloft.'

'Terrific.' Everything was right on schedule.

'I'll have a packet for you in a week or two at the outside. We just want to build up enough data. But, unofficially, I can tell you the plane's fully operational.'

'In every aspect?'

'Yes.'

Gottschalk was thinking of LITLIS. Incredible. He was already thinking of a bullet vote.

'Good news, I take it?' Roberta said when he put down the phone.

'The best,' he said, smiling. And reached for her. The Space Invaders were massing again, lowering on the screen.

Moira, on the edge of sleep, might have fallen into a black hole. She contemplated the end of all things. Sitting still on the stairs, the study of dust consumed her. She hovered at the precipice of time, horrified.

Without John, she wondered what there was about life that should hold her. And should she find someone else, what would be the point? Death lurked around every corner, delighted to snatch away not only life but joy and hope as well.

Moira felt there was none of those within her now.

Abruptly, not even this benign house in the country seemed friendly any more. She was as alienated from it as she was from everything else. The night closed in claustrophobically. She desperately wanted to get up and turn on all the lights, to banish the darkness from this, her domain, but she lacked even the strength for that simple act.

Rain lashed the windowpanes, struck the roof like an angry beast and the wind howled eerily through the cracks in the house, just as if the world were singing the dirge she felt welling up inside her.

With a great effort, she dragged herself downstairs. No lights were on and when she reached the ground floor landing she heard a curious banging. At first, she thought that one of the shutters had come loose in the storm but she found they were all intact. She stood very still then, naked and shivering, her skin raised in gooseflesh. She listened.

The phone began to ring and she started. She felt sweat break out on her upper lip, in her armpits. She felt very exposed. She went into the kitchen, reached for the receiver.

It was then that she saw the kitchen door was unlocked and open. It was swinging back and forth, banging against the wall with the gusts of wind.

She took one step towards it to close it. She felt the wetness of the floor against her bare soles, rain running in on her, spattering her legs.

Moira gasped, her head whipping around, as she felt the slithering vicelike grip tightening around her neck and waist, forcing all the air out of her.

She heard a whispered chanting in her left ear, scented a sharp spice she could not identify. She was still trying to scream. But as if in the grip of the darkest nightmare, she found she could not. She tried to open her throat but it was blocked. She began to gag as if her body needed to vomit in order to clear her throat.

She saw no face, no personification of the being who engulfed her. It was as if her own fear, her death wish had magically been given life and now sought to destroy her. And in a blaze of light, powerful in its revelation, Moira saw that she did not want to die. In the grip of death, she battled for life with all her might and soul. She opened her mouth, closed it with great force on the flesh pushed against it. She felt flesh tearing a great hot gout of blood running down her throat that almost choked her.

The strength of determination was in her. The sweetness of drawing breath, of watching a sunrise, of a friend's love, of a child's innocent face, an afternoon's picnic; the parade of days and nights stretching out before her. The pleasure of her own future children's warmth, her grandchildren's excited laughter, the adventure of growing old in the world, of living, of living! All these things and more she now longed for with a passion she never thought possible.

Her head shook back and forth as she bit deeper and deeper into the flesh and at last she was released. She wanted to scream but all she was capable of was a great stentorian wheezing as her hungry lungs drew oxygen out of the air.

Even half-stunned as she was, she felt something coming at her and, instinctively, she raised her arms to protect her face. She heard a soft whistling like an old man calling pigeons in the park.

Moira screamed. She recoiled. It felt as if a bolt of pure energy had smote her. Her wristbone was shattered. Liquid fire blazed along the nerves of her arm with such intensity that the entire limb began to tremble.

Another blow rocked her and she reeled drunkenly, crashed to the floor of the kitchen. Rain struck her but she did not feel it. Blood coursed down her forehead, into her eyes. She blinked, swaying on one knee. The whistling came again, gentle, admonishing just before the side of her head above her ear, seemed to explode outward in a shower of fiery sparks.

Moira's cracked lips opened and closed but all she could do was pant like a dog. The blows came again, in measured cadence, on the top of her head, against her forehead. She toppled backward, one leg under her. She could not move. She stared up at the ceiling. It was alive now with shadows that seemed to be calling her. One of them loomed over her as large as a mountain and she glimpsed through her one remaining good eye a flash of silver. Like the pointed finger of God it flew down at her in a blow. She was deaf to the soft whistle this time, at last anaesthetized to the pain. But she knew she was going, that all the people she wanted to meet, all the things she wanted to do, were beyond her now. A void swept upward to cradle her, to exchange the darkness for the light and, as it did so, she thought of John and the chance she had of seeing him once again.

Khieu stood back, staring at what he had wrought. His mind was filled with the hideous images of war; his country burning, his sister picked up bodily, kicking and screaming, impaled upon the quivering stake of the conqueror. Silence had been Khieu's master then because death had been hovering everywhere around him. To call attention to himself in any way, was to bring down the wrath of the black bird, the Khmer Rouge. He felt their force against his skin like a pressure, smelled their power like a spice clogging his nostrils. It was the scent of hysteria, a conglomerate of the stench of oiled weapons and enforced fear.

Khieu blinked, turned away from the mass of blood and bones on the kitchen floor at his feet. It was all right, his task had been completed here – almost. There were things to smash, small items to be taken with him.

He went into the living room, saw the hearth with its Mercer tile floor. Above it he saw the wooden Buddha and, immediately, got down on his knees on the tiles.

Buddham saranam gacchāmi, Dhammam saranam gacchāmi, Sangham saranam gacchāmi, he prayed. 'I go to the Buddha for refuge.' And, recalling his catechism, he went on: 'Happy are they who do not hate. Let us live happily then, free from hatred among those who hate. Happy are the pure. They are as the bright gods who live on happiness.'

He was peaceful, floating, suffused with harmoniousness, attuned to the eternal pulse of the universe. And, at that moment, with his eyes closed against the blood on his hands, he did not even yearn for the joys of heaven, understanding that, as he had been taught as a child, only in overcoming all his desires and inclinations, would he achieve true happiness.

BOOK TWO
The Call Up

1

July, Present
Bucks County/New York City/Washington

Moira. They did not want to let him see her. He supposed they didn't think he could take it, lose his breakfast all over their spotless floor. But Tracy had taken a lot more than one death. He had been witness to grisly, inhuman incidents that would have given these cops nightmares.

So why did he hesitate to pick up the cloth sheet and look?

The ME looked pointedly at his watch. 'Look,' he said, 'I've got to be in court in twenty minutes.'

Chief Lanfield turned his head. 'It's just down the road, Hank,' he said quietly. 'Take you all of five minutes to get to town. Give the young man his time. He's got a right to look; and you've got a duty to be here.'

The ME shot his cuff, shut his mouth. It was Lanfield who had called Tracy with the news of Moira's death. Lanfield was the Chief of Police for Solebury Township and it was to his office Tracy had first come.

'It's like nothing I've ever seen before,' Lanfield had said. He waited until Martha, the one matron in his complement of five patrolmen, poured them both some coffee.

'But then I haven't had cause to see much since I've been here.' He stirred his coffee while adding Cremora.

'Solebury's a quiet place for the most part.' He licked the coffee off the spoon, put it aside. He had had the good grace to come around from behind the metal desk when Tracy had come in. They sat facing each other on a pair of old spindleback wooden chairs.

'Hell,' Lanfield said, 'the last homicide we had here was eleven years ago and that one was a suicide. I've been here that long and I know.'

His blue eyes watched Tracy carefully. He was a tall man with a lined leathery face and straight brown hair brushed neatly back behind his ears. He was talking now because he didn't know what else to do. This kind of thing was out of his ken and he thanked God for that; he had seen the body or what was left of it. He marked the stony face on Tracy and thought he'd better get on with it.

Lanfield cleared his throat and cursed himself. No one should have to hear this, he thought.

'The reason we didn't call you right away, Mr Richter, is that we thought we'd do an ID first. We had her wallet, of course, but it contained no photographs. We used dental records.' The Chief's eyes slipped away from Tracy's.

'Dental records?' Tracy echoed. He leaned forward. 'Those are only used when –'

Lanfield's face was pained. 'You couldn't identify her, Mr Richter. Her own mother wouldn't be able to do that.'

Tracy was on the edge of his seat. 'What happened to her? All you told me over the phone was that she had been murdered.'

'At that time there seemed no reason to –'

'Tell me.'

Lanfield blinked, steeling himself. 'I resist telling you only for your own good, Mr Richter.' He saw the look on Tracy's face, gave in. 'But, on the other hand, you have a right to know.' He took a deep breath, let it out all at once.

'She was beaten to death, Mr Richter. But a beating like I've never come across before.' He shook his head. 'It was an evil thing, an unbelievable thing that was done to her. Even her face; *especially* her face.'

Tracy felt numb with the unreality of it. 'How bad was it?'

'The ME says he thinks every bone in her body was broken. Some three or four times. Her face is unrecognizable, like I said.' He put his palms on his thighs, rubbed them back and forth against the cotton fabric. It was a quiet Saturday in Solebury, this far from the tourist bloat of New Hope. He could hear Martha typing in a room down the hall. Ed was on the phone with Bill Shirley again. The beer drinking that son of his did was slowly getting him into deep trouble. Upstairs there'd be little enough to occupy those manning the Township Hall.

But down here in his office, the atmosphere had turned ghostly.

'I want to see her,' Tracy said abruptly. He startled Lanfield.

'Now listen here, son.'

'Please arrange it,' Tracy said, getting up.

Lanfield sighed, went over to his desk, slipped off a blank sheet of paper, handed it to Tracy along with a ballpoint pen. 'And while I'm doing that, I'd appreciate it if you'd give me a statement about where you were the night of the murder.'

'I was with someone,' Tracy said.

Lanfield nodded. He put a hand on Tracy's shoulder, squeezed it. 'It's just a formality.'

Tracy leaned forward now, down the basement of Doylestown Hospital, a new and beautiful complex of buildings out in the countryside that had no business being used for disease and death.

'Why don't I do that for you, son,' Lanfield said softly and drew back the coroner's shroud.

Tracy thought he knew what to expect but he was wrong. What confronted him now froze him down to his bones. And Lanfield had been right; there was absolutely nothing to connect this pitiful pile of broken bones and rent flesh with the human being who had once been Moira Monserrat. Whoever had done this to her had managed to reduce her to a thing, no more than the substance of an inexplicable nightmare.

He heard her voice in his ear, *I can't thank you enough for letting me stay here.* 'Thank you, Chief,' he said hoarsely. He'd had enough.

'Just a moment. I'd like to take a look.'

They all turned to see the large figure of Detective Sergeant Thwaite standing in the open doorway.

'What the hell're you doing here?' Tracy said angrily.

Thwaite ignored him, shouldered his way into the small room, peering down at the half-draped slab.

'I'm afraid that was my doing, son,' Chief Lanfield said, looking uncertainly from one to the other. 'Miss Monserrat's name was not unknown to me. I'd read the papers. Last night, after I called you, I notified the commander of the 27th Precinct, her – assuming it *was* her – district precinct.' He nodded in the detective's direction. 'They put me in touch with Detective Sergeant Thwaite here.'

'That was unfortunate.' Tracy moved away from the crowd around Moira's broken body. Thwaite caught up to him in the parking lot.

'Hold on a minute, Johnny-boy.' Thwaite reached out a hand, grabbed Tracy's arm. 'You're not gonna get away with running away from this any more.' His face was red with anger and he seemed to be trembling with a tightly-withheld force. 'You've got some mighty important things to answer for.' He pointed. 'We both saw what the hell was left of a human being back there.' His eyes blazed. 'Meat for the butcher, Johnny-boy. And we both know why. You're such a fucking hard case, you thought you could do it all: stonewall me and take care of the Monserrat woman and the Governor's death. Well, from where I stand, you've messed all over the lot.

'I was just about to get my machine together when I learn you've had the body cremated, then you come along and hang me out to dry with my dick in the wind.'

Something happened to Tracy. Thwaite took an involuntary step backward. It was as if he had been hit by a physical force. He stared hard into Tracy's fierce countenance; opened his mouth but could find no words. He felt as if he had been hurled into a vacuum, his lungs collapsed. Still, he struggled to regain his equilibrium, staggering a little but coming towards Tracy again.

'What d'you want me to say?' Tracy's voice shivered Thwaite's spine, bringing out a line of sweat. 'Confess all my sins to you?'

Thwaite opened and closed his mouth twice. 'Yes,' he finally managed to croak. 'If that'll get us anywhere, that's just what you're gonna haveta do.' The effort cost him and his face went pale.

Tracy knew what he was doing, at least up to a point, though he was aware that he should not be using *kiai* so indiscriminately as a venting of his own inner anger and guilt. But he could not help himself. He knew Thwaite was right. Moira's death was his own responsibility. Inwardly, he berated himself for not interrogating her about the feeling that had overcome her at the moment of John's death. Rationally, he knew she had still been on the verge of hysteria and would have had nothing more to tell him. Perhaps. His rage against Thwaite was anger at himself turned outward.

'What's this John Holmgren crusade you're on, Thwaite? What the hell could he possibly mean to you? He was just another politician, right? And we know how you feel about politicians, don't we.'

Tracy came closer. 'What the hell d'you care if John Holmgren died making love to Moira Monserrat!'

'What?'

'They were in love,' Tracy went on, ignoring the other; there was too much steam to blow off now. 'There was nothing sordid or dirty about it. But d'you believe for an instant that all the good John was able to achieve would've been remembered if that was brought out?'

'Wait a min —'

'Not on your life.' Tracy shook his head. 'The press would've had a field day. They would've dragged his name through the mud, and what a legacy that would be, Thwaite, for the man who was responsible for the budding re-emergence of the State Public Education process; reforms for the elderly; the massive slum clearances in Albany, Buffalo and the South Bronx through luring big business back to the State.

'What's your seeking after the petty vices of one man — this holy quest of yours — in the face of all that.'

But Thwaite's face had changed completely. 'My God,' he said, 'there's more to it than that. I don't give a fuck who the Governor was banging, Johnny-boy. I leave that to the scumbags at Vice. You telling me now that all this setup I was feeling around in was to cover up Holmgren's affair with his assistant?'

'Why else would I do it?'

Thwaite leaned in closer. 'But the Monserrat woman has been murdered, Johnny-boy. And not just by some wino breaking and entering to rip off a coupla bucks. Whoever took her down knew what he was doing and did it in very premeditated fashion. That tells me she knew something she wasn't supposed to know.' He stared hard at Tracy. 'There's one very smart and *very* dangerous monkey out there and if you know anything about it, you'd better spill it all out now.'

He saw the look on Tracy's face and shook his head. 'Don't matter a shit if you pull that thing on me again. I'll just get up off the ground and keep on coming. Think about that, Johnny-boy, while the sight of that busted-up *thing* in there's still fresh in your mind, 'cause she's the one who's screaming now . . . just as loud as she can. We got to find the fucker did that to her. We got to find him fast because by Christ he's a nasty one. I don't know what seeing what he could do did to you but it sure scared the shit outta me.'

Tracy began to see just what kind of a situation he was in. He had been so wrapped up in protecting John's reputation that he had in a very concrete way, aided his friend's killer. And Thwaite had a right to be afraid. Moira's killing was like the atrocities he had witnessed in the jungles of Southeast Asia. Whoever had done it was special, of that he was certain.

He looked at Thwaite and a sudden thought came unbidden: Here stood a man he could trust far more than Kim.

'I can't get Moira out of my mind,' he said softly. 'Something she said the night John died.'

'You mean murdered.' Tracy nodded and Thwaite shook himself a little as if throwing off the last of the effects of the *kidi*.

'Moira told me that she had felt a kind of . . . well, *presence*, for want of a better word, at the moment of John's death.'

'Is that the word she used: *presence*?'

Tracy nodded. 'Yes.'

'She couldn't be clearer? Did you ask her?'

'Yes, but you saw the state she was in that night. She's . . . *was* an extremely bright woman. She was highly emotional especially where John was concerned. Being there when he died . . .' He shook his head. 'It tore her apart.'

Thwaite stared at him. 'I know what you're thinking,' Tracy said. 'I spoke to her several times by phone afterwards; She'd be coherent for several sentences then completely break down again. Under those circumstances, I didn't think she'd be of any help. Now I'm sorry I didn't press her.'

Thwaite did not comment on that. He looked at Tracy. 'There's more, isn't there?'

Tracy took a deep breath. He was about to betray a confidence he had with Kim. Well, to hell with Kim. 'I used to work for a, well, let's call them a security network. I left them rather abruptly. I'd become fed up with that way of life.' He shifted a bit; Thwaite said nothing. 'Recently a field executive I once knew – his name is Kim – approached me. He told me they wanted me back, at least temporarily. When I said no, he told me it concerned John Holmgren. Together, we went back to the brownstone and I had a look around.' He dug in his pocket, produced the handkerchief-swathed bug. 'What I found, very cleverly secreted inside the pear at the bottom of the brandy bottle on the coffee table, was this. An electronic listening device.'

Thwaite looked down as Tracy carefully unwrapped the tiny package. Both were careful not to say a word until the thing had been put away again.

'Christ,' Thwaite whispered. 'What the hell's going on here?'

'I wish I knew.'

'Okay, listen. You'd better give me that thing. I'll have the lab go over it and –'

But Tracy was already shaking his head. 'That's not the way. Think about it. Officially, you're off the case. I'm sorry that happened but now there's nothing either of us can do about it. Besides, whoever put this thing in the pear is a real cutie. I seriously doubt whether your lab boys have seen anything like this, whereas I've got access to an expert.'

The parking lot was baking in the afternoon sun. Reflections spun like slivers of glass off the roofs and hoods of the cars. The two men stood very close but the antagonism that had marked their earlier relationship had disappeared.

'From here on in,' Tracy said, 'we just have to trust each other. I don't think we have a choice.'

Thwaite thrust his hands into his trousers pockets. He looked past Tracy, towards the undulating carpet of the horizon. Because there was a great deal of emotion behind it, his voice was a growl when he spoke.

'The truth is important to me on this, Richter. Very important. One day you wake up after twenty years and realize you've been living in shit all that time. You wonder how the fuck you ever managed to do it. And then you know it's gotta end, that *you've* gotta end it. I mean, these days I look at myself in the mirror and I don't know who I am any more. Is this the same sonuvabitch who's learned how to shake down pimps and numbers runners all over the city I ask myself.'

His head turned and his eyes focused on Tracy. 'What I'm tryin' to say is, I know you got a personal stake in this. I want you to know now, so do I.'

'The fact,' Atherton Gottschalk said, 'that we have increased our Army's manpower by twenty-five thousand over the figure generally given for our 1981 levels should not make us – any one of us – feel in the least bit secure.' He turned his head this way and that, his piercing gaze singling out people throughout the audience of AFL-CIO officers so that their attention would not wander.

'These are perilous times we live in and we should have a firm understanding of the fact that the level of armed forces our former Chiefs of State felt were adequate to protect this country was in reality quite the reverse. We have found them to be inadequate to meet today's greatly expanded needs.

'For, more than ever now, we are a *global* power, with a global power's responsibilities. The expansion of our Rapid Deployment Force in times of emergencies in the Persian Gulf is essential to our present as well as our future welfare. This nation runs on energy and that means, by and large, oil – foreign oil – whether we wish to acknowledge it or not. And those critics who do not clearly see our responsibility to the safe-keeping of stability in those oil producing areas of the world are of no more use than the ostrich who sticks his head in the sand. Problems will not disappear merely because of our failure to acknowledge them!'

Gottschalk paused while the tide of applause washed over

him. It was a good feeling, especially so since this AFL-CIO was traditionally a hard sell.

He took a sip of iced water and continued. 'By 1987, the Army must be able to field a force of at least 900,000. That is the bottom line. But, I might add, this does not include the RDF or my own plan for an élite anti-terrorist unit to handle emergencies that might arise within the borders of the United States itself.

'For years now, we have seen a constantly rising tide of international terrorism. We ourselves have felt at least partially thrust into this arena during the lamentable hostage crisis with Iran. Yet so far we can count ourselves lucky.

'In England, Italy, Germany, time and again we have been witness to the escalation of coordinated terrorists working on an international scale. It is a documented fact that a great majority of these terrorists have been trained either within the Soviet Union or in camps run by the Soviets.

'I pose to you now that there is a clear and present danger to this country from this quarter because I am convinced that the so-called Cold War is taking on an utterly new and frightening dimension.'

He leaned forward on the podium. 'I ask you now – as representatives of this nation – a question of burning import. Should international terrorism come to American shores are we equipped to handle such a volatile and potentially lethal situation? I say we are not. The current Administration is woefully ignorant in this particular quarter.

'At this moment, ladies and gentlemen, America is vulnerable to such an attack. It is imperative to train and maintain a substantial antiterrorist force as well as to begin, now, to increase the size of all our armed forces. This growth will require extraordinary manpower policies to include significant augmentation of the Volunteer Concept. That is a notion whose time has come and gone.'

But with the speech over and the applause only an echo, Gottschalk knew he was not yet through. There were the reporters to be reckoned with and he was counting on that.

'Mr Gottschalk,' Ross from NBC-TV said, 'about these

"extraordinary manpower policies" you spoke of. Are we to take it that you are advocating a return to the Selective Service system of the draft?'

Gottschalk smiled. 'I think it would be safe to say that if our figures called for such a massive increase in the armed forces, I would not be adverse to such a policy.'

'Mr Gottschalk,' Adams of CBS said, 'wouldn't you be putting this country perilously close to a state of war-readiness by such an action? The last time we had the draft was during the Vietnam war. Surely you don't envisage such a nightmare scenario.'

'Of course not,' Gottschalk said in his most reassuring tone. 'Nothing could be further from the truth. What I am advocating is solely for the *defence of this nation*, not to fight another nation's battles.

'These times see the world closing in on us. The Soviet Union has seen fit to take the Cold War onto another and entirely different plateau. Our job now – and it's an imperative one – is to combat the network of international terrorism before it gets out of control completely. This, gentlemen and ladies, is an invasion. A vicious, calculated plan to undermine the world-wide security of the United States. It is something we just cannot allow.' He nodded to them, smiling again through his stern visage. 'Thank you all. Good night.'

Though he knew it served no good purpose to blame himself, that was precisely what Tracy was doing. Because now it was too late. John Holmgren's corpse was gone from the hands of the ME. If he had been murdered, they would never learn it from his body. All that was left was the one tiny artifact Tracy now rolled back and forth within the folds of Kim's handkerchief, the one shred of metal and plastic linking him with John's murderer.

He parked the Audi on Greenwich Avenue. He walked east until he reached Christopher Street, then turned right.

He pushed through a doorway of black enamelled wood and glass. He was in a tiny vestibule with cracked black and white check marble flooring. He pressed an intercom button marked '9F', went through the inner door into the lobby.

An elderly groaning elevator took him up. Thoughts of Moira tried to chase away the ghosts he was approaching. The door at the far end of the hall opened before he got there. A figure stood in the shadows, his features nevertheless clearly defined. He was over seventy and looked it. His hair was yellow-white and thinning markedly over the high domed crown of his head, which was in any case bony and skull-like. His eyes were as dark as Tracy's own, sunken back as if all the flesh between the vital organs and the bone had been dissolved away. A faint tracery of blue veins could be seen down each cheek.

It was a strong face, still, but Tracy was appalled anew by its gauntness, the unhealthy quality of the skin: thin, translucent, brittle-looking. Well, he thought, what else could you expect? But still, still. He never imagined he would see this man this way. Tracy had always thought of him as invulnerable.

'Hello, Dad,' he said, abruptly embracing the man. 'It's good to see you.'

The moment the street light's reflection from the inner door to the house on Christopher Street sparked in reflection behind Tracy's back, a man ostensibly snoozing in his parked car, sat up. He stared at the doorway a moment to make certain Tracy was not about to come back out. Then he stretched and got out of his car, crossing obliquely across the street.

On the corner, he found a pay phone and used it, dialling a special number the Bell System had no record of and could not trace. He listened to it ring on the other end, humming contentedly to himself.

'Yes?'

He did not recognize the voice. 'He's in on the old man.'

The connection was abruptly cut and the man sauntered out across the street. He had been dying for an ice cream cone for over an hour.

'That's my heart you're holding,' Tracy said and his father looked up. With the jeweller's loup strapped to his face he looked like some goggleeyed sea creature.

He studied his son for a moment with the same degree of

intensity with which he had been examining the bug. 'You've a heart like an anvil, Trace. I saw to that.' He turned his head quickly back to his work, hunching down again until his sharp shoulderblades seemed about to pierce the thin flesh covering them.

'Mom saw that coming. She always hated that in me. She wanted me to be one thing and you wanted me to be another. Sometimes I feel as if I've turned out to be a kind of hybrid.'

Fluorescent light streamed down, pulling a dazzling rectangle of glowing illumination that throbbed hard and blue-white out of a field of shadows. 'That was a tragedy, what happened to the Governor.' His head twisted. 'Uhm,' he grunted. He was examining the bug which he held very carefully at the extreme end of a pair of long gleaming tweezers with jaws curved like the fangs of some great asp. His tongue stuck out between his pursed lips and he made that odd high whistling sound Tracy remembered so well from his youth. He saw the cords at the back of his father's neck like sailor's rope pulled hard and fast, anchoring the nodding head to the thinning torso.

Tracy turned his head away, looking out of the window at the blackness of the chestnut tree standing tall and firm in the backyard. How many times had he climbed that tree when he was young? How many times had he heard his mother calling to him to come down, 'It's dangerous, Tracy. Much too dangerous!' The world was too dangerous for her and she wanted him alive and safe and so, for the times when she was watching, Tracy rode his father's back, instead, never suspecting that one would give out before the other.

My father, the invincible, Tracy thought. At his side, his hand clenched the knuckles white as his nails dug crecsent weals into the hard flesh of his palm.

'At least you've the good sense to come in out of the rain.' Tracy knew his father meant the bug. 'You give this thing to some so-called electronics expert off the street, he wouldn't know what he was looking at.' Louis Richter looked up, unstrapped the loup from his head. 'I do.' He was proud of his expertise, Tracy thought. Always had been.

The older Richter lifted the bug high with the tweezer tips.

'This little device,' he said now, 'could pick up a fart in this room – and I mean *anywhere* in the room – and deliver a signal of almost perfect fidelity from 20Hz to 20,000Hkz, the entire theoretical spectrum of human hearing – to its receiver up to fifty miles away.' He was sweating now, a large-dropped unhealthy sweat that worried Tracy. 'Damnit,' he said wonderingly, 'I could've designed this thing ten years ago. Why didn't I?' He waved it around. 'I could still build one, though.'

'We found this inside a bottle of pear brandy,' Tracy said. He did not want his father drifting off like a horse cropping grass. 'Inside the preserved pear at the bottom.'

'Sonuvabitch!' Louis Richter said. 'I've gotta find the bastard who did that.'

'That's what I want,' Tracy said.

'And when,' Louis Richter said proudly, 'haven't I given you what you want?'

When Khieu emerged from the electronic elevator onto the penultimate floor of the building on Gold Street in lower Manhattan, Miss Crawford was on hand to meet him.

With long confident strides she moved across the plush grey carpet, her hand held before her. Khieu took it and, drawing it upward in a graceful arc, kissed the back.

'*Merci beaucoup,*' she murmured. Behind the lenses of her glasses her eyes sparked. She was wearing a tailored suit of a lightweight nubbly material. She smelled lightly, pleasantly of perfume. It was a measure of Khieu's importance here that she met him and not one of the brace of secretaries on this floor.

Miss Crawford, who held several doctorates, was a woman of remarkable talents: chief among them was never interfering in affairs that did not concern her.

Khieu was one of those. Nevertheless, as she said, 'He's waiting for you. Go right on up,' she thought, What I wouldn't give for a couple of hours alone with that body.

Khieu thanked her and ascended the wide spiral staircase set with charcoal grey slate steps. The view from this office that was, in effect, the entire top floor, was wholly in keeping with the decor. North, south and west, the skyscrapers of Manhattan stretched away in clumps and shoots, growth in a gargantuan metallic garden. The World Trade Center, City Hall Park with its stone and mortar arch and, just beyond, One Police Plaza, the Hudson River, New Jersey and even a fair chunk of Staten Island all were on display through the panes of glass that stretched almost from floor to ceiling as if they were part of a collector's jewel-encrusted harvest.

The tall man was already up and pacing behind his massive black onyx desk. Behind him, the world of Wall Street was filled with shadows. He held a Telex flimsy in his hand and there was that odd contrast again: the calloused edges, the highly polished nails gleaming.

In the spill of illumination it was possible to pick out all the distinguishing features: the wide apart blue eyes, the long hardened jaw of one born to command, a sharp nose with pinched nostrils. His immaculately groomed moustache matched in snowy colour his thick hair which had just – during the past three or four years – begun to recede, leaving a narrow swath of freckled flesh in its wake.

He pushed the flimsy at Khieu just as his intercom buzzed.

He stabbed at a hidden stud. 'Yes, Madeleine.'

'Your call to Harlan Esterhaas has been routed, Mr Macomber. He's on three.'

Macomber put it on the speaker-phone. 'Senator! How are you.' His voice was hearty.

'Just fine.'

'I hear you're going to be in town tomorrow. I thought we'd finalize our transaction then.'

'I admire your sources. Even my aides didn't know until about an hour ago.' He laughed. 'Tomorrow'd suit me just fine.'

'Let's say 3.15. at the Museum of Modern Art. Know where it is?'

'No problem. See you then.'

Macomber reached out, broke the connection. He smiled. 'This routing you came up with beats using a pay phone. These calls must remain untraceable.'

Khieu had finished reading the Telex but Macomber could not resist reiterating its contents. 'The *Vampire*'s an unqualified success! It went up for the twenty-seventh time today at Hungry Horse.' He was referring to the company's airfield in a desolate area of northwestern Montana. 'The ceramic engine's working like a charm, even under the most adverse conditions. Imagine' – he came around from behind the desk – 'twentyseven runs in just under eight days! The goddamned thing is one-fourth as light as a cast aluminium engine with no cooling system needed!' His face was radiant as he spoke; Khieu felt his enormous pleasure.

'We were right! We can stuff the fighter with three times the defensive and offensive systems of any other aircraft its size.'

Khieu looked up. He was pleased. 'What about LITLIS?' This was their private acronym for the Light Transmitted Logic System which was really the heart of the *Vampire*'s devastating power. Every electronic circuit locked into the on-board computer – and this meant the advanced night-vision rangefinder and all the offensive weaponry – was handled not by old-fashioned electronic chips but laser-driven chips. This meant that the decision-making time-factor for the computer was not limited to the speed of the electronic pulse through a circuit but now could flash at the speed of light. This made the *Vampire* the most deadly plane aloft because it could out-think, out-manoeuvre and out-fire anything in the skies including ballistic missiles.

'Hungry Horse put up nineteen markers today in the space of three seconds.' Markers was a term used to describe 'dummy' missiles of all types, with all the speed and manoeuvrability but without the explosive payloads of their real counterparts. 'LITLIS blew them away. All of them. I just got off the phone with the pilot. He said he's never seen anything like it in his twenty years of fighter flying. He's beside himself with excitement.' All the Hungry Horse personnel lived on-site; there was no possibility of a security leak there.

'We've done it,' the tall man said. 'On time and still within the high end of the budget guidelines the main computer system predicted.'

Khieu glanced again at the telex before placing it on the onyx desk. 'It's the ceramic engine that did it,' he said. 'Takakura's idea of modifying the NASA design for the shuttle engine was a great risk that paid off. But it was you who set him on his course. You knew we couldn't build a sixth-generation fighter like this with the conventional aluminium engine.'

'No,' Macomber agreed, 'of course not. It was apparent to me once we'd come up with LITLIS, that the computer's lightning signals would be useless in a plane like that – the goddamned engine would overheat within the first few minutes of combat.'

He rubbed his hands together. 'All right. I'm satisfied with the results. We'll pass on the information in a few days and then we'll be rolling.'

'I take it then you'll be accepting the Trilateral Commission's offer.'

Macomber nodded. The commission, a conglomerate of prominent businessmen and a sprinkling of politicians from the New York area, had invited him to accompany them on their forthcoming trip to China. 'For right now, it suits the image for me to help forge a more solid trade relationship with the government of the People's Republic.' He smiled. 'Besides, it makes a perfect cover for what I must do in the East. I'll be in Shanghai the beginning of next week. It will be time to light the fuse.'

Khieu smiled.

'But tonight,' the tall man was saying, 'it's time to celebrate.'

'You'll go out with Joy,' Khieu said hopefully.

'I don't think so.' Macomber had gone to the brass coat-rack in one corner of the room; its hooks were made of polished elk horn. 'Women are not appreciated at the Club – even one's wife – and, in any case, I'm in an expansive mood. Joy constricts me.'

'There's still Findlan,' Khieu pointed out, 'and one or two of the senators to bring into line.'

Macomber paused. 'Khieu, the problem with you is that no matter how hard you try, your reliance on the luxuries afforded us by modern science, is still open to question. You saw what the system did with its selection of a score of representatives. It not only gave us their names, personal affiliations, it was also – after a three day search – able to print out all of their peccadillos. Human nature being what it is, the printouts gave us the key to each of those individuals. The *angka* owns them now, body and soul. The same is true for seven of our crucial senators.'

He slipped on his jacket, a rich muted plaid of lightweight worsted. 'But, yes, that leaves Findlan and two others.' As he moved past the other, he squeezed Khieu's shoulder. 'Have faith. Leave them to the system. It'll give me enough to work with. And don't worry about Findlan. I know what a tough reputation he has. I'll crack that, too.'

'None of them worry me as much as Tracy Richter does,' Khieu said seriously. 'He was the one who found the bug when everyone else failed. Now you've allowed him to take it to his father.'

'Forget about Louis Richter,' the tall man said confidently. 'The man's on his way out. Frankly, I'm surprised Tracy went to him. The old man's been retired for more than five years *and* he's so ill I doubt he can even think straight.'

'I just remember what I heard about him.'

Macomber's raised hand dismissed Khieu's words. 'That was a long time ago. We've nothing to fear from that quarter.'

Khieu was not so certain. 'Still . . .'

'All right,' the tall man said in resignation. 'I've learned to live by your instincts as well. Keep an eye on things. But for Christ's sake be careful around Tracy. I don't want to even give him a hint of your existence. He used to be a goddamned ferret, smelling out the enemy at long range. Don't underestimate him.'

Khieu nodded, satisfied for the moment.

Macomber was about to walk out of the office when the intercom buzzed. He went back to the desk, thumbed a hidden toggle switch. Miss Crawford's voice came thinly but distinctly in the room. 'Sorry to bother you, but your son's here, Mr Macomber.'

'Oh, Christ.' Delmar Davis Macomber looked at his gold watch. 'The boy's only three hours late.' He glanced up. 'I wish he had your sense of responsibility, Khieu. In fact there are a lot of your traits I'd prefer he had.'

Khieu bowed his head. 'He's your son. He does his best.'

'I can't see why you bother to defend him, especially considering the way he's always treated you.'

'He cannot see past his own guilt. That, at least, is quite plain.'

'Guilt?' Macomber almost laughed. 'What the hell has *he* to be guilty about?'

Khieu's voice was quiet as he said, 'Surely you cannot forget that your first wife, Ruth, died delivering Eliott. That is a difficult burden for any child to bear, especially a son. There is a special bond between mother and son. To have it so mercilessly severed as it is forming –'

'Oh, bullshit! I have no patience for all that psychological crap!'

'Interesting,' Khieu murmured, his head still bowed. 'Psychology is one of your chief weapons both in business and in ... the *angka*. Curious that you reject it so out of hand when it concerns your own son.'

Macomber leaned over the desk. 'I only mean,' he said softly, 'that the boy's weak. I cannot abide that in anyone. It's especially galling in my own son.'

Macomber did not move. 'I trust you understand, Khieu, that I would allow no one else the liberties you take.'

Khieu nodded his head. 'Yes.' He was staring very deliberately at the carpeting.

'Because I do not question your loyalty. Your love.'

There was silence in the enormous room. After a time, Macomber closed his eyes and said, 'Take the private elevator down. There's no need for Eliott to see you here.'

Khieu nodded and, without a word, disappeared from the room.

'Mr Macomber? Shall I send Eliott up?'

Macomber shook himself as if from out of a thinning reverie. 'Yes, Madeleine. Do that. Then you and the staff can leave. It's terribly late.'

'Yes, sir. Good night.'

'Oh, Madeleine ...' He could hear footsteps on the spiral stairway, ascending.

'Sir?'

'You did a helluva job collating all the Hungry Horse data. I don't know what I'd've done without you.'

'Thank you. We're all quite proud of the *Vampire*.'

Macomber broke the connection, went across the room to the wet bar. He fixed himself a long gin and tonic. He needed to cool down. Eliott affected him this way.

He turned his back on the figure emerging onto his office level, busying himself with cutting himself a thick slice of lime, squeezing it into the frosted glass.

'Well,' he heard his son's voice floating through the office. 'I'm here. What is it you want?'

Macomber whirled, his face set in hard lines. ' "What is it you want?" ' he mimicked. 'You're three hours late for this appointment and that's what you have to say? No explanation, no apology?'

'I don't owe you either of those things,' Eliott said hotly.

'Oh, yes,' Macomber said quickly, 'yes, you do. This is still a family, even if you choose to ignore my hospitality to remain at home. You have responsibilities . . . to me and to the *angka*.'

'I've got my own life now.'

'And what a life it is!' Macomber swung around the side of his desk, advancing across the room. His drink lay forgotten on the mirrored bartop.

A peculiar flinty look came into Macomber's eyes. 'You're a boy who made dean's list all through your four years at Columbia. You were made valedictorian of your class yet you not only turned it down, you didn't even show up for the graduation ceremony. Can you imagine the embarrassment I felt? What was I to say to all the people who asked where you were? I had no idea. You never told me.

'You spent six months here at Metronics, during which time you showed more potential and initiative than three-quarters of my current staff. Yet you walked away from that as well.' He gestured. 'And for what? To act – and not even very well from all reports.'

'Who told you that? Khieu? Your dog on a leash?'

'Why are you doing this to me?' Macomber was close to his son now. 'What the hell is the matter with you. You've got talent, you've got brains. What are you doing with them? Nothing!' he thundered so that Eliott stumbled backward.

'What makes it so important that I do something with them?' Eliott said. 'It's only *your* idea of life; *your* idea of what's good for me that makes it so.'

'You've got no concept of the value of money, of what it means to work for a living,' Macomber said bitterly. 'In short, you've no idea what it is to be a man. You disgust me.'

Tears welled up behind Eliott's eyes but he willed himself not to break down in front of his father. 'All right! You said it. I don't want your love.' His eyes were open wide, unnaturally bright. 'I don't want to be like Khieu. You love him only because he bows down before you. You're a bastard, d'you know that? A goddamned bastard!'

Macomber broke himself from their ever tightening orbit. 'I won't stand here and trade insults with you, Eliott. My time is far too precious to waste it in that manner. I originally called you here because there is a message for you to deliver.'

'Give it to me, then,' Eliott said, tightmouthed.

Macomber handed him a slip of paper. 'Memorize it.' While his son was doing that, he said, 'Khieu worries about your role within the *angka*, you know.' Eliott's head did not lift to meet his gaze. Macomber waited until he was finished with the text, handed the sheet back.

'He loves you but thinks you're perhaps a touch too unreliable for such delicate and crucial work. Like me, he would prefer it if you were working for Metronics.'

Eliott gave a crooked smile. 'Then I wouldn't be able to do this, would I, Father? Not being connected with Metronics at all makes me quite useful as a go-between.' He put his hands in his pockets. 'But the two of you need have no fear on that score. I know that if I screw up, my only recourse is that job here. I don't want that in the worst way.' He said the last with great force, knowing how much pain it would cause his father.

Macomber merely said, 'You know the procedure.'

'You know I do,' Eliott said to let his father know that this was merely small talk to cover hidden feelings.

For a moment their eyes locked and something, neither of

them could say what, passed unspoken between them. Then Eliott turned away and the connection was broken.

'I'm going to the cemetery on Sunday,' he said, not looking at his father. 'I'd like it if you went, too, sometime.'

'I think you go there far too often,' Macomber said. 'It isn't healthy.'

'It isn't healthy to honour your own mother? How can you even think that?'

'She's gone, Eliott.' Macomber's voice had turned cold. Why did this weakness in his son disturb him so? 'You have to face up to the fact. Joy's my wife now. You get along with her. I know she loves you, though she certainly doesn't see nearly enough of you. Life has to go on.'

'You don't love Mother,' Eliott said hoarsely. 'You never did!' Red rage swept through him.

In one swift stride, Macomber recrossed the room. His hand shot out. He slapped his son across the face. 'If you were younger I'd wash your mouth out with soap.'

'It's true!' Eliott cried, retreating from his father's wrath. 'I know it. It's all true!' He turned and went down the spiral staircase. At the bottom, in the semi-shadows, he looked up at the hole cut in the ceiling. All he could see was a tall black silhouette standing spread-legged at the crest of the staircase.

At that moment, he had the distinct bone-crushing feeling that that magisterial figure could reach out across all that distance and clamp him with a hand of iron. Yes. He believed it with all his heart.

Sobbing, he ran out of there.

Tracy was already at home when Lauren walked through the front door. He was on the phone with Kim, filling him in on the most recent events. He cut the conversation short when he saw her.

Lauren was wrapped in a long trenchcoat. It had apparently begun raining sometime after he had come in for she shook out her lacquered rice paper parasol in the bathroom.

Her spectacularly long legs propelled her across the room

with the natural elevation a dancer has enhanced by the training of her profession.

'How was the performance?'

She smiled. 'Better.' She crossed to the kitchen, poured herself a club soda. 'You want anything?'

'No.'

She emerged, sipping, came and sat next to him on the wheat-coloured sofa near the window. 'I love dancing *The Dreamer*. It's such a relief from the easier parts Martin's had me doing while I've been building up my hip again.' Striped, the streetlight filtering in through the Levolors, threw patterns of dark and light across her like the ripples the wind makes across the desert sands. She cocked her head to one side.

'What are you staring at?'

'You.'

She was about to say something but, seeing the look in his eyes, merely made a tiny sound in the back of her throat. Tracy's arms came up to enfold her and she leaned forward, melting into the warmth and comfort of him, her eyes closed, her lips opening until she felt the brush of his tongue, the press of his lips. All breath left her. She sighed and put her head on his shoulder, turning her lithe body around so that she lay against him, her long legs stretched out on the sofa.

There was silence for a time, punctuated only by the cars hissing by outside the window.

'Just before you dance,' Lauren said at last, her voice soft and floaty, 'your mind begins to wander. The tension of anticipation combines with the inertia of waiting. Once you get out onstage, it's different, of course. It's all concentration and there's no time for anything else. But before . . .' Her head turned against him so that he felt the long train of her unbound hair against the bare skin of his neck. 'Before, the oddest thoughts come to mind . . . Memories.'

'Like what?'

She gripped his hands more tightly to her as if trying to intensify the warmth he was bringing to her. 'I suddenly found myself thinking about . . . Bobby's funeral.' Tracy stirred against her. 'You flew home with him into Dulles. I saw that medal pinned to his casket ... and a folded American flag.'

'I remember,' Tracy said thickly. 'What brought it to mind? That was a long time ago.'

'I think a lot about Bobby,' Lauren whispered. 'Even now.' She did not bother to wipe away the tears rolling down her cheeks. 'Sometimes I miss him so much I want to scream. I mean, he was my baby brother. He died so young. He wasn't even a man.'

'He was almost nineteen.' Tracy was trying not to remember. 'He was a man all right.'

'No. You don't know what I mean. We knew each other mainly as kids ... growing up. We never really' – her voice choked, giving out, and she ducked her head, at last wiped at her eyes with the edge of her hand.

'What's the point in bringing all of this up again?' Tracy said as gently as he could. He was frightened. It was getting too close.

'I remember how you looked when you got off the plane with Bobby's ... casket.' She spoke as if she had not heard him. 'Your face was white. You couldn't look me in the eye. You kept staring away from us ... my parents and me ... towards Virginia.'

Tracy recalled that vividly. The Director had been with him on that first flight home. He had been in the field with Tracy for some time, trying to trace a supposed leak at the Ban Me Thuot base camp. He had found nothing but he had been the one to approve Tracy's promotion to lieutenant for valour on seven hazardous missions.

The Director – a Special Forces Colonel – worked his own shop completely independently. As far as anyone was concerned, the Director headed a SCMU, a special covert missions unit, whose orders came directly from the Pentagon. This was a piece of deliberate disinformation that was for the Major's own good as well as the Director's. The last thing anyone wanted was to confuse the Director's crowd with the bunglers at the CIA.

'We met through Bobby,' Lauren said now. 'Why shouldn't I think of it?'

Tracy wanted to get her off this subject but he couldn't think how. When he dreamed of the jungles of Cambodia, it was often of Bobby's death. There was good reason for that; and good reason why he should never tell Lauren the truth about it.

He pushed her up and off him. He rose, went across the room to turn on the radio. He turned the dial, came in on the opening of Falla's 'Nights in the Gardens of Spain', left it. She watched him as he moved.

'He was a good boy,' Tracy said. 'He fought very hard. It was . . . especially hard to lose him.'

'He cared about you a great deal.' Lauren's voice followed him around the room in his restless search for solace. 'Whenever he found time to write, it was invariably about you.'

'He was quick to find friends there,' Tracy said a bit harshly. 'Too quick.'

Lauren cocked her head. 'What do you mean?'

He turned to face her. 'It was a war, see? No matter *what* they chose to call it back home. A war's no place to make friends. Attachments can be lethal.'

'I think,' she said, staring at her nails picking at the nubbly material beneath her, 'he was happier there than at home.'

Tracy watched her for a moment, surprised by what she had said.

Then her head came up and her eyes met his. 'Can you tell me why you did it?'

He started as if she had jabbed him with a needle. 'What?'

'Went over there, I mean. Were you saving the world from Communism or what?'

He had told her enough over the years so that she knew he had not been in the Army *per se*. He had, of course, never mentioned the foundation by name. But she knew that his work in Southeast Asia was of a highly classified, clandestine nature.

He could not speak of the distant fires that burned in his heart, causing him to seek out – through his father – the foundation.

He stood and stared out the window, into the striped night, while he spoke to her. 'My first leave in Hong Kong is the one I remember most vividly. One day, I drove into the countryside just north of the city – the New Territories. I came across a

Taoist temple. They're interesting people, the Taoists — very attuned to nature and the human spirit; they take care of the city's elderly and infirm.

'The gardens were beautiful, filled with carefully pruned bonsai and sculptures of mythical Chinese creatures meant to bring good health and fortune to visitors.

'Just inside the open doorway to the temple itself, I saw a Chinese woman kneeling before an altar. In her right hand was a round wooden container holding what looked like a bunch of chopsticks, long and square. But each had a row of Chinese characters written down one side.

'It was very still. I remember, I could hear the rustling of the old gnarled trees. Birds were singing, and I could smell the rich scent of incense.' He came towards her, sat down on the other end of the sofa.

'The woman was praying. All the while she was shaking that wooden container in front of her, holding it at such an angle that the sticks were inching their way out. Then one did clatter to the floor.

'She stopped her prayers and took the stick to an old woman who sat behind a rickety desk to one side. The old woman read the stick and, consulting a book of tables, wrote on a small square of paper.

'The woman paid for this and went through an archway, into an alcove where an ancient man sat. I had heard of the Taoist fortune tellers and decided to have mine read.

'I went through the same motions as the woman before me. The old woman showed no surprise when I handed her my stick but the fortune teller himself was another story. He looked up from the slip of paper I had handed him, said, "Soldier. You make war".

'I was curious. I wasn't in uniform. I've told you, we never wore uniforms because of the nature of our ... work.'

Lauren smiled. 'Yes. Cyanide teeth and all that.'

She had meant it as a joke, of course, but unconsciously Tracy's tongue explored his lower left wisdom tooth. Fifteen years ago, it had been hollowed out in the Mines, an artificial crust put on beneath which was a nonsoluble capsule of cyanide.

All he had to do was bite down at a certain angle with enough pressure.

'Something like that,' he said to satisfy them both. ' "War is foreign to me". The old man said it without hostility but with a great deal of sadness. He asked me if I understood the nature of geomancy. *Feng shui*, he called it. I told him no.

' "Natural forces constitute the fabric of the world around us: earth, air, fire, water, wood. One is either aligned with these forces or one works against them. It has been my experience that Westerners understand nothing of importance."

'He stopped here, I think, to see if as he suspected I would take offence and leave. When I didn't, he went on: "*Feng shui* is of the greatest importance. You strike me as a most singular foreigner. The forces emanating from you are strong indeed. That is curious in a Westerner. Tell me, have you come from the jungles?"

'I told him I had.

' "Not the jungles of China, surely. But close."

' "Close enough", I said.

' "You are a leader there. Others defer to your judgement."

' "That's right. Many of the men are afraid of the jungle."

' "But not you," he said. "No. Because I find in you an alignment with wood and earth. You are at home there".'

He had ended up staring out the window again.

'No wonder Bobby trusted you so much,' Lauren said. 'He was sensitive to those kinds of things.'

'Can we, for God's sake, stop talking about your brother?'

Lauren drew her legs up under her. 'It's important for me to know that he made the right choice in . . . leaving home. That he was happy –'

'Happy?' Tracy cut in. 'How the Christ could anyone who was sane be happy in such an environment.' He got up abruptly. 'If you want my opinion he would've been better off at home.'

'Goddamn you!' she cried. 'How can you talk about him that way? He was your friend.'

'Because,' he said as calmly as he could, 'he would still be alive now if –'

'I don't want to hear that!' It was a full-fledged scream and it brought him up short. 'I want to know that he was content! That he wasn't a misfit there. That at least he had a home he could call his own before . . . my God . . . before he was slaughtered!'

'Now, Lauren –'

'Well, that's what he was! Right? Slaughtered!'

'There were no easy deaths over there. I've told you that.'

'But especially' – she had to stop now between enormous sobs – 'especially for Bobby!'

He was holding her now as she wept into his chest, her lean body shuddering in quick convulsive bursts like explosions.

Afterwards, while he was wiping the tear streaks from her face, she said, 'You never answered my question.'

'I think I did,' he said softly. 'Now come to bed.'

Curled up together beneath the sheets, he fell asleep with his chin in the hollow of her shoulder. She stroked his thick hair and watched the patches of light thrown and pulled back across the ceiling as traffic rushed by below them.

Across the room, two stone statues stood on either end of the bookcase. Age had pitted them in spots, smoothed them in others. On the right was a *naga*, as Tracy had explained it, a seven-headed serpent out of Cambodian mythology. On the left was a *garuda*, a man with a bird's head. They were symbols of neither good nor evil but they hated each other just the same. As in so much of Khmer mythology, no one could quite remember the cause of the enmity.

She would never tell Tracy this now but she could barely remember what her brother was like. Oh, yes, as a child, a gawky adolescent there were many memories. But he had died a man and Lauren did not know him at all.

Silent tears coursed down her cheeks and she turned her head away so that they should not touch Tracy and wake him. Perhaps that small movement affected him for he stirred in his sleep, his legs scissoring. She thought he might be dreaming.

Then he arched up out of her embrace and uttered one word quite clearly.

His eyes snapped open and he felt her arms around him, cradling him.

'It's all right,' she whispered close to him. 'It was just a dream.'

'None of it's a dream,' he said without thinking. His voice was still furred. 'Cambodia.'

Running his hands across sleek flesh that was not there, his lips searching for a mouth of air, a female heat that was the sodden drenched atmosphere of Southeast Asia. The jungle, exploding shells and flickering chemical flame, gouting blood and fearful screams, life seeping irretrievably away into the black muddy earth, Bobby's face, pinched and white with pain, the eyes of betrayal, the burning and Mai's admonishing voice, *How much of her do you see in me?* The commandments broken. *Could I be her sister?* The foundation's commandments.

'Tell me now, Tracy.' Lauren's voice. 'Why did you go?'

'I wanted to be there.' So close to sleep there wasn't time to think properly.

'To kill.'

'No.' He shook his head. 'Not to kill.'

'Killing's what war's all about. There's no secret to that.'

'I went because ... there was something I had to prove. To myself.' His eyes were clouded; he stared at nothing. 'My mother was always afraid that I'd die. That fear was very deep in her. I woke up one day and thought, I've been infected by it and I knew I had to combat it so I turned to my father and asked him for his help.'

'And he took you to the place where he worked.'

Tracy nodded.

'And you fell in love with ... I don't know, whatever it was they did there.'

'I wanted to be purged of fear. To do that I had to throw myself into the most dangerous situation I could find.'

'But you weren't vulnerable ... like Bobby.'

'No. I'd've been far more so in the Army. That ... place fortified me well.'

'And now you truly *are* fearless.' He said nothing but he was still breathing hard. 'You spoke in your sleep.'

'What did I say?' A cold tentacle writhed through him.

'You called out a name.'

Oh, God. Not Bobby.

'Who,' she said, 'is Tisah?'

And he lied to her. 'I don't know.'

Khieŭ sat cross-legged on a small rug in the middle of the room, studying the horoscope he had just completed. Though Preah Moha Panditto-might have outwardly denied it, for Khieu the link between his Theraveda Buddhist teachings and the rituals of astrology were strong indeed. Both were a way of life for him, beliefs that went beyond questioning or even conscious thought. They provided a continuity, a quotidian affirmation of the individual's interlocking place among all living things; a seeping in. Home.

Within the heart of the Khmer Rouge, Khieu had had to discard it all. For them, Buddhist monks, prostitutes and astrologers were all lumped together as 'the lice of society'. And while he was with them, he had to believe that, too.

Aspects, retrogrades, the houses themselves ... something seemed curiously out of alignment. But the longer he studied the chart, the further the disturbance seemed from him. It was as if some unseen force were manipulating events. There was only the vaguest hint of that here but if it were indeed true, he would have to take some kind of action on his own.

In all ways but this, Khieu was wedded to Macomber. He obeyed him in all matters. But the world of astrology was another affair entirely. What Macomber could not understand, he could not work.

Khieu set pen and paper aside, closed his eyes. He felt the presence of the house like a living entity around him and, within that, Joy's loneliness like a sharp pain in his heart. She kept the household together yet she and Macomber rarely connected on any level Khieu could fathom. Her inner sadness seemed cruel and unjust to him in much the same manner his own childhood seemed cruel and unjust. His hand began to throb just as it did during the nightmares of Malis that robbed him of sleep. His own *kmoch* rode him hard.

He wore a loose-fitting black cotton blouse and trousers with a simple draw-string top, the end of the legs coming to just above his bare ankles. This was the uniform of the Khmer

Rouge. Though it had been washed many times since, it still retained the stink of those days of fire and death in Cambodia. No amount of modern detergent could rid them of that.

Yet he refused to throw them away. Rather, he chose to wear them on certain occasions. Curiously he seemed to find a certain dark strength from them that kept him going when his days as well as his nights became filled with the shuddering nightmares that stalked his sleeping mind.

At other times, he would open the bottom drawer of his campaign chest and, finding them there, neatly folded and laundered, he was certain they belonged to someone else; it was a struggle to remember what they had once been.

He sat in the precise centre of the floor of the basement. He began the ritual chants: 'I go to the Buddha for refuge', tuning himself into the cosmos as he stared with unblinking eyes at the small bronze Buddha surrounded by twelve thin sticks of incense, slowly burning, their columns of smoke like fingers pointing the Way. He glided down the long snaking corridor in his mind that firmly linked him with the centuries. His mind's eye saw himself: a black crow, the land burning all around him, quaking with thunder falling from the sky, running with blood. He became the fish in the stream, the tiger in the bush, the serpent coiling itself around the rough bole of a tree. And he became the tree itself, the blade of grass entangled in its root, the hot wind soughing through the branches of the forest. And then he became nothing at all, floating free, egoless, a holy man.

It did not last long. *Malis*. His eyes flew open and he rose. He felt heavy as lead as he crossed to a rosewood, altar-topped cabinet. There was a peculiar brass lock in its centre. From around his neck he unfastened a small brass key. This he slid into the side of the lock, snapping it open.

From the darkness inside, he produced a leather-handled steel implement. It was perhaps a foot long. It was round and had a leather thong attached to the handle. Khieu put his hand through it, gripped it. It was like putting on a gauntlet. It calmed him in the way his prayers should have and did not.

Silently he rose, moving across the room like a shadow. There was one overhead light – a bare bulb. There was an old beatup couch along one wall, a TV set from the 1950's with its rounded picture tube, piles of dropclothed odds and ends. And a rawhide covered four-and-a-half foot-heavy punching bag hanging from the ceiling. Its sharklike sides were scored with oblique marks as if some hellish giant cat had been using it to sharpen its claws.

Khieu seemed to look at everything but the bag as he crossed the expanse of the basement. When he came to within two feet of it, his left leg moved with such blurring speed that if anyone had been witnesses he would have thought it a mirage.

But the flat of the sole had landed squarely against the side of the bag, setting it swinging in great arcs, away from Khieu, then back. At the height of its inward arc, Khieu lifted the steel implement up and back, snapping his wrist at the last. With no noise at all, the implement shot out over his head, telescoping to a length of more than three feet.

It made a hard whistling sound as he swung it around so that it slammed into the two-hundred-pound, sand-filled bag. Again and again, Khieu struck it, circling slowly, methodically excoriating the leather. The heavy chain holding the bag jangled and finally hummed with the force of the constant jolts.

Fury was a white-as-ice ember implanted within his heart. It throbbed now like a wound long untended, left to fester, infected, turned black as the depths of an unknown night.

His eyes squeezed shut, his corded muscles jumping as he swung from the soles of his feet, he felt again the heated humid air of Phnom Penh, sitting cross-legged, watching Malis dance, her hair catching the lights, the look of intense concentration in her eyes, the unending, sinuous motions of her hands and arms and then, at last, the fluid, animal sensuality of her whole body as she walked across the floor towards him.

No, no, no, no ... This now was his chant as he swung again and again, the sweat running down his sleek sides, across the arched and ribboned cables of his muscles.

Denied, denied, denied, he thought, and Joy is like that. So sad about us.

A sound came from behind and above him made him whirl. His eyes were black and lost, staring at the figure at the top of the stairs. It stood quite still for a moment as if undecided as to whether or not to make the descent into the basement. Khieu stood with his feet planted wide, the weapon raised high as if about to deliver a blow.

At last the figure came slowly down the steps. Joy Trower saw him only when she was all the way down.

'Oh,' she said. 'I wondered why the light was on down here.'

Khieu continued his practice. His face was shiny with sweat. Behind him Joy made a move to leave, then apparently changing her mind, came towards him. She winced every time the weapon struck the shuddering bag with a loud, thick *thwack*.

'Dinner is ready . . .'

Khieu nodded. He went on with what he was doing, laying it to the leather with even more fervour.

'But if you'd rather . . .' Joy's voice trailed off as she watched him. 'I know you practise' – she winced again as he struck, *thwack*, the leather bag with the steel truncheon – 'every day and I don't like to disturb you.' She came all the way down the stairs into the basement proper; she never took her eyes away from him. 'I feel just the same about your praying. I wouldn't – *thwack, thwack* – 'think of disturbing you then, either.'

Droplets of sweat flew off him now as he worked and he shed his black cotton blouse. His flesh seemed oiled, almost as if it had turned molten.

'I don't know what happened,' Joy went on, apparently oblivious to the fact that he had not answered her, 'but all of a sudden I couldn't bear it being alone up there in the house. I' – *thwack, thwack, thwack* – 'I'm sorry for intruding but I . . . I needed some human companionship.'

Khieu allowed the weapon to rest at his side after the last blow. The red rage still flickered but only intermittently now. The physical release had somehow exorcized for the moment his personal demons. He turned to face her. He was breathing altogether normally.

'Will you think it evil of me if I tell you he doesn't make me happy . . . that he *can't* make me happy anymore?'

Joy could not look at him when she said this. It came out all in one spastic gust, a spent storm's last gasp. All she could see was an image of herself and Macomber endlessly circling one another, searching for a lost element they would never find. She wondered why she didn't just turn around and get out of there. But, she told herself, she could not bear to return upstairs just yet; the oppressive atmosphere had become too much for her. Or was there another reason entirely?

'Won't you please say something,' she said, lifting her eyes to his. 'Anything.' Then all sound fled her. His eyes defeated her mind, her body, her emotions, even, in some awesome, unfathomable way. She *felt* him. His presence was like a white-hot heat fanning her. The force of his personality reached out across the gulf between them and touched her like a phantom hand. She felt the muscles along the insides of her thighs begin to jump.

And yes, Khieu thought now, as he watched her, Macomber has not made her happy. It was not his fault, perhaps. Nature was a beast impossible to tame. Macomber's nature made him the genius he was, made his love for Khieu pure and whole; without it he would not be Macomber and Khieu would, in that event, be dead now, along with Sam and Malis, the rest of his family. Buried beneath the scorched earth of Cambodia.

Khieu felt duty engulf him. In giving Joy pleasure, in dissolving her pain, he was honouring Macomber. He knew how important Joy and her brother were to Macomber. If Joy did not find satisfaction within this house, she might very well seek it elsewhere. That Khieu could not allow.

He had seen her tears, had recognized her pain. That he could accomplish what Macomber could not seemed right and proper to him. Not to allow her access to that part of him was meanspirited.

'You must learn to listen to more than the spoken word. You must learn to hear with your eyes and your heart as well as with your ears.' He was very near her now, near enough to see the trembling of her body, to feel the fluttering of her heart in fear or excitement.

All at once, she sensed the room around her as if it were a breathing, living entity: she became slightly aware of the deep bass thrum of the central air conditioning unit, could feel a slight breeze on her cheek from some hidden crack. She inhaled the rich scent of dampness and sweating walls mingling with some strange spice.

But most of all, she was aware of Khieu's eyes. They seemed as black, glossy and depthless as a bird of prey's. She saw her own image replicated on their convex surface but she could not recognize herself.

She felt abruptly hot, beads of sweat popping out on her broad forehead and upper lip and, before she had time to think, Khieu had come against her, the leather and steel truncheon a bar behind her head, a pressure. She bent her head towards him, felt rather than saw his tongue come out to lovingly lick each drop off her. The gesture was so sensual that she moaned a little, her knees giving way slightly, her head coming back without volition so that she was supported only by the steel bar warming now to her own blood heat. She still felt the bite of the metal but now it did not disturb her.

Rather it seemed to relax her as she stared at Khieu. It was almost, she thought, as if she were seeing him for the first time. She saw how completely hairless he was. This fascinated her and she reached out a hand, smoothing her palm across the sleekly muscled contours of his chest. She gave a little cry. It was like putting her hand in a river of fire that had raced up her arm, through her torso to a pool between her legs. She felt wet and open and vulnerable.

He wanted to come against her once more but she held him off, wanting first to eat him with her eyes. He was the colour of bronze here, copper there in the shadows along his sides. He had a scent that she wanted and when her gaze returned to his eyes, she was dazzled as if she were looking into the sun itself.

She was limp and full of coursing energy, all the solid flesh inside her turned to liquid. Her arms and upper torso felt free of gravity, all her weight pooled in her hips and thighs. Joy had, in fact, the distinct impression that she had been transformed into a creature of someone else's imagination. And, staring into Khieu's hot black eyes, she knew whose it was.

Her lids fluttered down like wings as his lips covered hers with a heat she thought impossible. She felt his encircling arms pulling her slightly forward and then the pressure against her pubic mound, a soft circular stroking. She thought of the Siamese she had had when she was a child and how it fell into an ecstasy of purring when she scratched it behind its long pointed ears. God, she felt the same way now.

She shivered, her arms rising up his body to encircle his neck and now it was she who was pulling him towards her, opening her lips to drink from his mouth in greedy gulps as if, having been starved by Macomber, she could now not get enough.

She felt in the centre of her being, at the fulcrums of their bodies' contact, the hard bar of his manhood but it seemed to her as if his entire body were one enormous sexual organ and she was drunk on it, saying, 'Here, oh here!', lifting the hem of her dress with one hand and feeling the intimate rubbing coming closer to her flesh. She was heated, her vagina swelling. She already felt as if she were in orgasm but her ecstasy continued to climb instead of abating and, for the first time in her life, she used her voice as a sexual instrument to croon to him, plead with him to enter her. She wanted more than anything now to feel that silken intimate stroking, to feel the bump and grind of his pelvic bone against her clitoris. She was wild for it.

And at last, at last she could feel the first brush of his rampant sex against her intimate hair. She cried out and reached for him, stroking him lovingly between her fingers, revelling in the wetness he expelled.

She climbed him then, as blind as a troglodyte, locking her ankles at the small of his back, feeling the hard flesh of his buttocks against her heels and, placing the head of him against the swollen folds, pushed him inside her.

The moment he felt himself engulfed by her heat, Khieu felt a long stab of pain deep inside himself. Thoughts roiled through his mind and his stomach clenched, seeming to double in on itself.

The nerves along the beachfront of his skin registered the pressure of her writhings as if they were mere markings on a scientific graph. Feeling rushed from him, so that he felt numb in the area of his pelvis.

Night surrounded him like the grave, the erotic gyrations

seen within his mind's eye too clear to deny: a bed, an open window, curtains fluttering, the oppressive heat of summer in Chamcar Mon. And Malis touching herself, spreading those magnificent legs, opening her secret folds in the ultimate intimacy of that still and clinging semi-darkness. Stone *chedi* loomed over him and he could scent the rich sweet stench of the cindered dying. His own death seemed very close to him then. He shook while Joy came in a long convulsive burst, a starfish against him, and he was almost unaware of her climbing down from him, until her lips slid over his erection and her tongue began to lave him.

Her cheeks hollowed as she began to suck in earnest, her fingertips finding their way between his damp thighs, into the cleft of his buttocks and over the contours of his scrotum. His connection to her – because she was like him in an important and elemental way – evoked feelings in him now he would prefer not to feel. Death sailed through the night towards him and he saw its billowing sail, the bitter hatchet, its device of pain. The wailings of his *kmoch* were at their height and he whipped his head back and forth to deny the force of pleasure threatening to engulf him.

Joy felt him jerk in her mouth, swelling even more with blood and she moaned a little, moving up and down on him all the faster. Her tongue lifted, laving the underside of his head and then spasm after spasm shook him, the hot viscous jets coming against her working tongue and palate.

And he could no longer contain himself. Malis, Malis, *Malis, oh!*

Around to the side, towards the FDR Drive, Thwaite had seen a pair of ambulances from Bellevue Medical Center, just a few blocks to the south, standing dark and empty. The whole place had the aspect of a graveyard at midnight but he knew from long experience that it was only outwardly that the CME building was not humming with activity. Inside, you were lucky to get a ten-minute interview with the associate ME handling your stiff.

There was a uniform Thwaite did not know at the front desk, a black man with a short afro and splay teeth as big as shovels.

He flipped open his case to the gold detective's shield. 'Here to see Miranda on the Chin snuff.'

The cop nodded, consulted a typed sheet attached to a fibre clipboard on the table in front of him. His wide finger stopped at a printed extension and he dialled it. He spoke in low tones for a moment before cradling the receiver. 'She'll be right up, sir,' he said. He could not have been less interested. Thwaite saw a copy of *Ebony* open on the table beside the clipboard. He was about to reprimand the uniform when he changed his mind. He eased up on his tone. 'You been on this tour long?'

' 'Bout three weeks,' the black cop said. 'Between you and me, it's boring as shit.'

'Pretty dead here, huh?'

'Hell, yeah,' the other said. He made a face. 'Talk about the graveyard shift!'

'Detective Sergeant Thwaite?'

Thwaite turned to see Dr Miranda. She was somewhat of a surprise: a formidable Indian woman somewhere close to forty with skin that looked as if it had been dusted with kohl. She was dressed in the regimental cool green autopsy gown that was standard here. Her gleaming black hair was pulled back from her face in a tight bun.

'You wished to see me?' She had the knack of being able to impale you on the sharpened ends of her clipped words. Thwaite disliked her on sight.

'Yes,' he said evenly. 'About the Chin homicide.'

'Not here,' said Dr Miranda, as if he had uttered a filthy word in front of the children.

She took him upstairs to her office on the third floor. The old-fashioned door had a frosted glass panel at head height. Inside, it was warm and cosy, if you liked Bunsen burners, beakers, vials and thick textbooks on pathology. Thwaite liked none of those things.

Dr Miranda sat in the one slat-backed wooden swivel chair in front of her cluttered desk. She turned to him, put her hands in her pockets. She crossed one leg over the other at the knee and Thwaite saw she was wearing orthopaedic shoes. Flat feet. Served her right, he thought.

'*Now,*' she said with the air of a crotchey professor, 'what do you want? I've got three reports to write before 3 a.m. and I've got to testify in court at ten this morning.'

'Let's start at the beginning,' Thwaite said.

Actually, Thwaite had no interest in the Chin slaying at all. Flaherty had given it to his unit and he'd assigned it to Enders and Borak. A typical Chinatown snuff: a member of the Dragons had been shot to death at close range with a small calibre pistol in the orchestra of the Pagoda movie theatre on East Broadway.

'You're up late, aren't you, Sergeant?' she said now.

'Caught blowing bubble gum on duty,' he said, 'so I'm cruising with the bats. What's your excuse?'

'Dedication,' Dr Miranda said, without a trace of humour. She turned behind her, opened a battered green metal file draw, spun a buff folder across her desk towards him.

'Read it here. This isn't a lending library.'

Thwaite had her number. He reached out a fresh pack of un-filtered Camels, slit the top with his thumb.

She waited until he had one in his mouth and was about to touch the tip with the flame from his lighter. 'I wish you wouldn't do that.'

Thwaite, who had seen the discreet NO SMOKING sign over her desk, ignored her and took a deep drag, hissing the smoke out into the room. The associate ME turned her head away in disgust.

Of course, it was much easier for him to get access to the files at One Police Plaza but in this case it would have done no good. Normally, a police photographer took photos of any death scene even nominally considered not of natural causes.

Such had not been the case with John Holmgren. The associ-ate ME who had responded to the call had, in turn, notified Barlowe, the Chief Medical Examiner who, because of the personage involved, arrived himself. His preliminary verbal report indicated nothing more than a massive MI, brought on, he surmised, by overwork and fatigue. His unit took photos as a matter of course.

By the time Thwaite had given credence to any of his doubts about the nature of the Governor's death, it was too late.

But there remained the set of photos and Thwaite was determined to get a look at them.

Dr Miranda was coughing. Thwaite pretended to peruse the Chin file, ignoring the hostile glare she was throwing his way. The phone on her desk gave a buzz and she grabbed for the receiver as if relieved at the distraction. Thwaite listened.

Dr Miranda said nothing for a moment, then, 'I'll be right down.' She cradled the phone, got up. 'A case's come in,' she said. 'Just leave the folder on my desk when you're through.'

At the door, she gave him a thin smile. 'Don't get too comfy. Officer White has to log you out downstairs and I'll be taking a look at it on my way back.'

'Thanks,' Thwaite said to her retreating back, 'for nothing.' He listened to the soft squeak of her orthopaedic shoes down the tiled hall. He waited five minutes, then took a quick peek out into the hallway. It was deserted. Dr Miranda, besides being one of the four associate medical examiners, was also the librarian.

Thwaite went through the 'H' s twice but could find no file on John Holmgren. He looked around the office. In the far corner, next to the window, was a smaller set of files – one column – all locked. It took him just over two minutes to pop it. He figured he had another three minutes before he had to get out. It wouldn't do for Miranda to see how long he had been alone in her office.

The Holmgren file was there. He quickly skimmed the preliminary autopsy report. Nothing out of the ordinary there. There was Barlowe's scrawled signature at the end of the report. More papers behind: statements by the attending associate ME, the two uniforms who were first on the scene, even a copy of Thwaite's own preliminary statement from the Monserrat woman. All appeared in order. No photos.

He cursed under his breath, went to another drawer of the file. All the photos were in one section and under 'H' he found five of them. He had no more than a minute and a half to look at them. Not enough time. But it was all he had. He could not risk smuggling them out. Not with the ever-suspicious Dr Miranda knowing he'd been alone up here.

His eyes roved the photos. He could detect nothing but these had been taken by the ME's photographer for strictly medical use. A police photographer would've taken a different set entirely.

Thwaite looked at his watch, reluctantly shoved the photos back in place, carefully closing the drawers and locking them. With a handkerchief, he wiped all surfaces he had touched. Then, leaving the Chin file on Dr Miranda's desk, he left the office.

There had to be another way.

He stopped at the desk to sign out. White, who had seen him coming, had put away his issue of *Ebony*.

'All through here, Sergeant?' He hummed sadly. 'Wish I could walk right outa here, know what I mean?'

Thwaite nodded. 'I do, indeed.' He lowered his voice, beckoned for the man to lean closer. 'And I've got your ticket right here with me.' This was the other way.

White smiled, his splay teeth showing. 'Who I gotta ice?'

They both laughed softly and Thwaite knew the pact was cemented. 'You think you can get me a set of photos out of the files?'

'Piece o' cake, m'man.'

'The locked section.'

White raised his eyebrows. 'In that case,' he said softly, 'you're gonna have to give me a reason I can live with.'

Thwaite nodded. 'Fair enough. I'm running a little number, ah, independently of the department.'

'Legit?'

'If it pans out, it's one hundred per cent.'

'And if not, we all get our fannies bounced, that it?'

Thwaite laughed. 'Don't worry. I got you covered. You bring me the goods, you're in on the machine. I've been looking for another good man. What d'you say?'

White smiled, gripped Thwaite's hand. 'I say, get me the hell outa here, man.'

'Okay.' Thwaite scribbled on a slip of paper. 'When're you on the day shift?'

White told him.

'Right. Bring the material to my house.' He handed over the

slip of paper. 'Let's say midnight day after tomorrow. That suit you?'

'M'man, I am at your service.'

Fifteen minutes after Thwaite had departed the building, Dr Miranda returned from the basement morgue where, contrary to what she had told the detective, she had gone for a sweet roll and a cup of freshly brewed espresso. There was something interesting about receiving such a strong jolt of life in among the tiers of the dead. It was as peaceful as bliss down there.

However, this particular night, she had not been alone. The man who had come to her the previous afternoon had been waiting for her, leaning against the gleaming central storage bay. The close proximity to all those stiffs seemed not to affect him at all.

'Which one of them was it?'

For a time, Dr Miranda said nothing. Despite the government shield he had shown her, she resented any intrusion into the world she thought of as her own. Her domain was sacrosanct. Instead, she busied herself with brewing the coffee. She did not ask him if he wanted any.

It was not until she had begun to nibble at her sweet roll and had taken her first sip of the espresso, that she answered him. 'The cop.'

Kim nodded. 'Thwaite.'

Dr Miranda eyed him. He had come around to the front of the gleaming stainless steel bank. He opened a storage bay at random, peering down at the waxy-skinned corpse slowly being revealed. The large T-incision across the chest indicated that the autopsy had already been performed on this one.

'How'd he die?'

Dr Miranda frowned in distaste. She disliked both irreverence and indifference to her charges. They were there, each as a singular puzzle for the staff to unravel, bringing a kind of solace to an otherwise griefstricken family.

'I would have to look at the file,' she said, 'in order to tell you that. Why, do you know him?'

'No,' Kim said. 'Just curious.'

'Curious about death?'

He looked up. 'I know so many ways to inflict it, I'm always on the lookout for new ones.'

'Surely you're joking.'

He pushed the bay closed with a dull clang. 'I must leave, Dr Miranda. Please be assured that the Federal government is in your debt. The photos of John Holmgren will disappear within two or three days.'

'You're very sure of yourself.'

Kim ignored her. 'I want you to know they will be put to good use.'

She shrugged. 'They were gathering dust here. But I don't see why you had to take them for an hour yesterday.'

Kim decided it was time to turn on the charm; this cold war was doing him no good. He smiled widely. 'Dr Miranda, you already know far too much,' he lied. 'To reveal anything further would be to put your own life in jeopardy.'

She put down her half-eaten sweet roll. 'Really?'

Kim nodded. 'Quite. As I've said, you've been most helpful.' As he turned to leave, he said, 'But that all could change drastically if you should tell anyone about this.'

Dr Miranda had got the message. 'It's already forgotten.'

Kim's smile was dazzling. 'Splendid. That's just what I wanted to hear.'

April–May 1967
Battambang, Cambodia

Lost within the darkling jungle, Sokha moved ever northward. The skies turned from dirty grey to brown with the incipience of storms. Often, the ground shook from the sonic wash of low flying planes and once he heard the dull booming of what he at first took to be the storm's onset. But the trees shuddering all around him gave evidence that the sound was something more sinister, man made and lethal.

As if by instinct, he found the growing enclaves of *montagnards*, restless and fearful of Lon Nol's marching troops. They fed him and housed him overnight but the stench of their anxiety, exuding like a sickening perfume, was too much for him to bear for long.

He was a soldier now and during those long hours of march when there was nought else for his mind to do he sought the meagre comfort of the military discipline, steeling himself for whatever was to come.

He had not asked for this war, had, in fact, prayed to the Amida Buddha that it would never come. But it had been made his. He was part of it now for good or ill and he knew that he must be prepared. Death and destruction were all around him like a ghostly pall.

It was already the beginning of the rainy season and Sokha was obliged to make many detours because so much of the lowlands, especially around Tonle Sap, were beginning to flood and footing was treacherous.

Like a Buddhist monk, he subsisted on the meagre food of the folk he passed. At one tiny outpost, two days out from Phnom Penh he first heard the word *Angka*. The organization was already behind the *maquis*. No one knew precisely just what *Angka* was but all seemed to fear and respect its power.

From that time on, he invoked *Angka*'s name at villages where he wished to be fed and encountered no difficulties.

There was rice and, because of his increasing proximity to Cambodia's swollen great lake, always fresh fish. The ancient Khmer gods, he knew, had graced their country with Tonle Sap, a virtually inexhaustible supply of food.

Upon leaving the city he had, of course, discarded his glasses as well as his two-syllable given name. He had been around Sam and René enough to understand the nature – at least outwardly – of the *maquis*. They detested intellectuals and would in all likelihood execute him should they guess his origins. Glasses, quite naturally, were a dead giveaway as would be his name. He became Sok to all who asked.

Once he made the mistake of speaking his classroom-taught French to one of the mountain people who had addressed him in the same language. From the look on the man's face he knew something was wrong and then when the man spoke again, he understood. He would have to remember to bastardize his French with these people in order to fit in. At night, when he camped in the wilderness, tired though he was, he would practise breaking all the rules of grammar he had so painstakingly learned as a child in the *lycée*. Thus he taught himself to speak like an illiterate.

On a day when it had been grey and overcast, raining on and off all the morning so that his progress had been significantly hampered, he collapsed against the sodden bole of an ancient palm. He put his head back against the rough brownish bark and, ignoring the swarm of buzzing insects, closed his eyes.

He had been on the go for more than four days now and he was exhausted. His limbs ached and his head throbbed. Despite the fact of his purporting to be a member of *Angka* he had not had enough to eat during his journey. The peasants were being systematically robbed of their crops and their debts to local moneylenders were becoming unbearable. The twin spectres of abject poverty and starvation were slowly becoming a reality here.

Sok could hardly believe it. Where was the Cambodia of yesterday? Swallowed whole by the mists of revolution, war and political greed. A premonition abruptly washed over him. He had always thought that behind the revolution would come

198

peace. Like a dark cloud that hid the sun, the revolution would roll over them, leaving at last clear skies again. In that moment beneath the palm tree he was chilled with the thought that his Cambodia would find no peace, no solution, no end to the suffering that was tearing it apart.

He began to cry and in that moment he heard stealthy sounds emerging from the background wash of the normal jungle noises. He was instantly alert but he knew enough not to move or even to open his eyes. Whoever was coming, he would let them.

'*Mit mork pee na?*'

'*Mit chumos ey?*' A second voice.

He opened his eyes, saw three men in black shirts and trousers. All three carried old M-1 rifles. They were pointed at him. *Maquis.*

'I come from the south,' he said, answering them. 'From the fields. The rice paddies. Most of my family was killed by Lon Nol's men.

'My name is Sok –'

'*Mit Sok*,' one of the *maquis* corrected.

Sok nodded. 'Yes. *Comrade* Sok, I've come to join the revolution.'

They took him with them but whether as a prisoner or as a comrade he had no way of judging. They walked a circuitous route through the jungle for perhaps thirty kilometres until coming upon a clearing where a number of buildings had been constructed. The largest one was a pagoda with a pale green tiled roof.

One of the *maquis* took him by the arm, led him into a smaller structure across from the pagoda. There was no door.

The interior was musty. Some broken-down furniture existed still in the dim corners of the room. A man sat on the mildewed rattan arm of a couch with no legs. He looked at Sok with spiritless eyes then dropped his gaze to the floor at his feet.

'One of Sihanouk's pigs,' the *maquis* said, jabbing the air with the muzzle of his M-1. 'They seek to wipe us out, the *Prince* and Lon Nol, at Battambang. But we have a surprise for them.'

'He's a prisoner of war then.' Sok was understandably nervous.

The *maquis* turned on him, slamming the butt of his rifle against the side of Sok's face. 'Shut up,' he said angrily. 'You'll speak when you are spoken to directly and no other time.'

Sok put his palm up against his cheek. It felt hot and he could discern a slight seepage of blood. Wisely, he held his tongue. The *maquis* moved away to stand just outside the open doorway.

The day died swiftly as a monk blowing out a candle's flame. Fires appeared and torches carried by *Mitneary*, female soldiers. Sok's hunger deepened but no one came with food or drink. The *maquis* ate within the flickering orange light of the smoking fires, sitting in a rough circle.

The meal over, they sat where they were. Sok could discern no talk. One of the men re-entered the pagoda and returned with a monkey. This creature was common within the jungle but Sok was surprised to see one within a *maquis* encampment.

The monkey was brought to the edge of the circle of men and unceremoniously thrown into the muddy centre. Now Sok could see that it was fettered with a length of hemp around its neck. This cord was held by the man who had brought it out.

The monkey screamed and chittered nervously, jumping this way and that, always jerked back into the perimeter of the circle by his hempen leash.

Sok saw the glint of steel shining redly in the firelight. The men had all drawn knives and as the monkey leaped from one to another they swiped at its long tail with their weapons.

A man made the first cut and the monkey howled. Blood ran as it bared its teeth and chittered madly. Its eyes were wide and staring, the whites showing all around.

Sok could see its face clearly, a small frightened countenance, chillingly human in its range of emotions, the features an odd sorrowful blend of a young child and an old man.

The knifeblades rose and fell, rose and fell. The animal screamed in pain and terror, jumping this way and that in a vain attempt to outrun the torture as its tail was slowly reduced to a useless stump.

Sok felt a movement behind him and turned to see the soldier prisoner standing just behind him, watching the scene outside.

'There,' he said derisively, 'is your new order for a free Cambodia.' And was butt-ended by the *maquis* guard for his effort.

Sok stared, dumbfounded. Is this what he had left the rotting hulk of Phnom Penh for? Which was worse, he wondered, the old or the new? There seemed to be no answer. As in a nightmare, all logic had fled, leaving a void nothing could fill.

Someone had taken pity on the creature out there and had slit its throat. Its mutilated corpse lay grotesquely on the ground, revealed as the circle broke up.

Now five men approached, walking slowly across the compound towards him. He felt the tension come into the frame of the *maquis* guard and knew the cadre's leader was approaching. Indeed, he saw that one of the five had a black leather belt around his waist. Hanging from it along his left hip was a holster and a handgun.

The five stopped in front of the open doorway. The man with the sidearm beckoned Sok out. He moved out from the shelter of the interior of the building, feeling for the first time terribly vulnerable and exposed. His heart raced within his chest and his mouth was cottony with fear.

'Comrade,' the man said, 'I have been told that you have come to join the revolution.'

All Sok could do was nod. Fear had put blinders on him. He saw only the man with the holstered handgun. Then he felt the presence of the *maquis* guard behind him and this somehow put him back into reality. This was no nightmare from which he would awake in a moment, safe in his own bed within the protective walls of his family's villa in Chamcar Mon.

Now he looked from face to face. He recognized two of the men who had come across him in the jungle. There was the leader. And the fifth man, standing behind the others . . . His eyes began to open wide.

Sam!

But Sam was shaking his head slightly back and forth. He pursed his lips, put the end of a forefinger up against them.

The leader cocked his head to one side. 'This is what you have told us,' the leader said, 'but how may we be certain of the truth? You may, in fact, be an infiltrator. You may, in fact, be the brother of that scum in there.' He pointed to the prisoner in the blackness behind Sok's back. 'How may we be sure, uhm?' He took a step towards Sok and said abruptly, 'Are you hungry, Comrade Sok?'

Sok nodded again.

'Well, here you will have to work for your meals as all of us must.' The man stared at him. 'Are you willing to do this, Comrade?'

'Yes,' Sok said, finally finding his voice. 'Of course. That is why I came.'

'Good. I am pleased by your response.' He gave a nod to the guard behind Sok and Sok felt him move away. 'Now I am told of your poor family's murder at the hands of the pig general Lon Nol's forces. Is this so?'

'Yes.'

'Yes, *Comrade*.'

'Yes, Comrade.'

'You must hate the régime, then.' He smiled slyly. 'But of course you must. That is why you are here, no?'

Sok looked at him. Fear flooded into him and his knees felt weak. He tasted bile in his mouth.

As if to confirm his fears, he saw the *maquis* guard bringing the prisoner out into the compound.

'This man has been found to be an enemy of the revolution. He has killed and maimed, raped and pillaged all in the name of the same pig general who ordered your family's death. Does this interest you, Comrade Sok?'

'Yes,' Sok said faintly.

'I can't hear you.'

He cleared his throat, licked his parched lips. He repeated his answer.

'Good,' the man said. 'Now I will give you a signal honour, Comrade. In recognition of the pain you have suffered.' His hand unsnapped the flap of the leather holster and he withdrew his pistol. Its steel side glinted in the firelight.

He jerked his head. 'Mok! Prepare the prisoner for execution.'

The guard grabbed a handful of the soldier's thick hair, dragging him down to his knees in the mud. He held him tightly.

'Now come, Comrade Sok,' the leader said, walking with Sok to where the prisoner knelt on the wet ground. He put the pistol in Sok's open palm. 'Here is the revolution. Bullets are at a premium so place the muzzle of the pistol against the side of his head when you pull the trigger. I do not want to waste precious ammunition.' He stepped away. 'Now do your revolutionary duty, Comrade. For your mother; for your father; for your sisters and your brothers. For all of Cambodia!'

Sok took one involuntary staggering step forward. His head turned and he looked at Sam. There was nothing on his brother's face to give him a clue as to what to do. He was on his own.

He felt the eyes of the *maquis* on him, felt their presence in a kind of supranormal way. This is what he had come so far to do. This was the future of his country.

He took one more step and, stiff-armed, brought the gun to bear on the side of the man's head. He pulled the trigger.

But in that split instant, like a camera-flash captured for all time, he glimpsed the Khmer's face and in it he saw precisely the same expression he had seen on the monkey's wrinkled tortured countenance.

Then the pistol's report exploded into the heavy night, the recoil bringing the muzzle up and away from the man's shattered skull. Bits of flesh and pink bone sprayed Sok's face, making him choke.

The *maquis* guard let go of the head and the man's corpse slumped to the earth as if embarrassed at the mess it had made at the last. Sok became aware of the awful stench of warm faeces and he turned away.

'Comrade,' the leader said, putting his arm around him and taking the pistol from his stiff fingers all at once, 'the revolution is proud of you. The *vinheanakhan* are at peace.' He was speaking of the Khmer ancestral spirits, presumably of Sok's family, though he might have been referring to the broader sense as well. His voice lightened. 'Now it is time for such a hero of the revolution to fill his empty stomach.' He waved a hand. 'Come, *Mit* Chea, *Mit* Ros. Let us have some food for Comrade Sok!'

They put before him a bowl of wet rice. On it were a number of fish heads. Sok did not know whether his hunger had gone or whether he was so famished that he must eat immediately. He looked down at the steaming food. Fish cheeks, a favoured delicacy. How did they know? He was about to reach for the food when something stopped him. A cold dread crept through him.

Fish cheeks were a delicacy of the rich. If he were indeed from the rice paddies to the south, he would not reach for this so eagerly. So, despite his almost painful hunger, he scrabbled in the rice, eating only that.

'Ahah!' the leader cried. 'We see now how to differentiate a true Comrade from the scum that comes creeping up to Battambang to seek to destroy a Cambodia free of paternalism, colonialism and the influx of the ingrate Vietnamese.'

He clapped Sok on the back and, raising his voice, said: '*Mit Swakum mok dal dambon rumdos!*' Comrade Sok, welcome to the liberated zone!

'Welcome to *les Khmer Rouges*!'

2

Delmar Davis Macomber turned his gaze from the granite and glass counting houses on Wall Street to the flickering expanse of his computer terminal. He punched in the 'Eyes Only' access code, then the full name, using the third-generation, dropped-digit code Khieu had devised.

It was a complex and time-consuming process for this reason: Macomber was delighted to use the system for the donkey work that left him free to employ a few high-level technologists, instead of a truckload of assistants. Such logic systems were superb for their data gathering capabilities. But he was all too aware of the ease with which such banks of information could be picked clean by modern-day thieves – he had used several such processes himself to gain key bits of classified data.

Because of the nature of Metronics' business, *every* piece of information in his own system was of a high-security level. This was, of course, trebled in the case of the 'Eyes Only' program. Here was the true heart of Macomber's *angka* begun fourteen years ago within the jungles of Cambodia.

He reached out now and pressed the 'unscramble' code key and the lines of letters resolved themselves on the screen before him. Had he been an intruder attempting to electronically force entry, the program would have immediately shut down, to be reactivated only by his own voice.

What he saw was this:

ESTERHAAS, HARLAN (D–TX), CHMN SENATE ARMED SRVCES
COMM/AGE: 66; MARRIED: BARBARA (NEE) PARKINSON/ AGE: 53
CH: ROBERT/ 33 EDWARD/ 29 AMY/ 18

It would have gone on, detailing places of residence, dates of birth, etc. but Macomber depressed the 'Personal' key, watching the readout carefully to see what the system had come up with in the last week.

The screen delivered up three different pieces of information. It could easily have been programmed to offer optimum scenarios to go along with these but Macomber had drawn the line at this. Electronic assistance was all well and good but there was a danger in becoming overly dependent on it. Besides, devising scenarios was one of the things he enjoyed most. It was what had made him so valuable to the Special Forces people in Ban Me Thuot.

He had forty minutes to his meeting with Senator Esterhaas. Time enough to choose the most effective tie-line into the Senator's soul and work up the proper pattern for entry. Esterhaas was not exactly unknown to Macomber; none of the politicos in the system were. Macomber had used the power and prestige of Vance Trower, Joy's brother, to gain entrance to these rather closed circles. The elder Trower was a senator of no mean importance and his devotion to his baby sister was an aspect of his personality Macomber had first seized on like a pressure point, wringing it for all it was worth. In fact, he thought now, Joy herself had become that much more desirable to him once that fact had surfaced.

He was not a man who made attachments to women easily – not with the ghosts of Ban Me Thuot still haunting him. In his entire life, Macomber had wanted only one woman. Ruth, his first wife, had been boring out of bed . . . and Joy was there for another reason entirely. The *angka*'s network of over a score of key political figures had been slowly built up, screened, approached and processed through her brother. Unwittingly, he was the creator of his own doom. Macomber had wanted to recruit him at once but caution had proved a wiser choice. Vance Trower was incorruptible and, early on, Macomber had decided to steer clear of any hint of extra-legal activity with him.

Perhaps, once, Macomber had been in love with Ruth. Truly, now could not recall. His experience in Ban Me Thuot had reduced much of his previous life to gauzy greyness. All because of one woman: huge almond eyes, lips full of sensuality, a body that, for him, went far beyond mere carnality. Her disappearance had not dimmed his ardour for her. Nothing could. She lived on inside him like a furnace.

She had been part of a violent brawl that he had gone to break up; its racket was disturbing the only peace and quiet he had known in two weeks behind enemy lines. Gunfire, the heavy bone-chattering *thwop-thwop-thwop* of copters' rotors, the distant thunder of bombs detonating still echoed in his mind. He could still feel the hot vibrations of the semi-automatic on his arms and chest, see the spitting orange wake of the death he delivered. But back in Ban Me Thuot he was angry and restless. Peace and quiet: they made him crazy.

A pair of burly Marines were having at it like stags in the forest. Tattooed, crewcut, with biceps bulging out of their rolled-up uniform sleeves, they had progressed from angry and abusive shouting to an alarmingly violent physical display.

Macomber rose from his rattan stool and silently and scientifically, took each of them apart with the thick soles of his boots and the first two knuckles of his right fist. He had been trained well; he knew how to do it with an economy of motion and expenditure of energy.

He used a straight-knee leg kick on the larger of the two, a pair of sword-strikes to the bridge of the man's nose. Then there was his pal. He was smaller but quicker and Macomber feinted with his hand because that's what this man had seen last, then managed to bury his steel-shod boot toe into the Marine's groin.

That left Macomber alone, standing next to the source of the fight. The Oriental girl had been at the heart of it and he could immediately see why.

She was impossibly tall – just under six feet, with a long sleek head and almond eyes that seemed otherworldly. She was slim-hipped and wide-shouldered with large breasts for an Oriental.

'From my mother,' she said later, sliding her palms over them in such a way that Macomber's mouth watered. 'A Cambodian of royal lineage.'

'And your father?' he asked. They were both drinking Scotch at her flat, a one-bedroom affair within walking distance of HQ.

She smiled slightly and Macomber felt his knees go weak. 'He is a South Vietnamese. Very powerful. Very rich.'

She spoke a great deal about her father. She admired him immensely. 'The war goes on,' she said one rainy, lightning-filled night, 'and he makes money.' She moved against him, a magnificent creature who turned the most prosaic motion into fluid grace. 'It's not that he's insensitive; he's merely smarter than all the rest.'

Macomber thought about that as the night shook within the storm. Intermittent, blue light, stuttering like a bad connection, electrified the sides of their naked bodies. Somewhere, shutters were banging in the wind.

'It's not so difficult to amass money,' he said after a time. 'Especially in this kind of situation. The demand for goods and services is at its peak.'

She looked at him sceptically. 'If it's so simple why aren't you doing it?'

'Because I want something more.' The rain began its tattoo again along the slanted tiled roof above their heads. The sound of water was everywhere. 'I want control.'

She was up on her elbow, looking at him from out of the shadows like mountains. 'Over what? People?'

'Destiny.'

She laughed, a rich musical sound, full of warmth. 'I'm afraid the age of empires is too long gone.'

'Perhaps,' he said softly. 'But isn't that what you worship most in your father?'

He had entered into the relationship with the express intention of escaping from it at the time of his choosing. That was his custom in such matters and, in any event, he had assumed this liaison would be no different from any other event here on the other side of the world: impermanent, ephemeral, as distancing in a way as a dream. The war made it so.

But slowly, so subtly that he was never aware of it until the moment of her disappearance, he was being turned around. Lost within the web of disavowed feelings, he began to allow them a power over him he could not understand or control.

Physically she stirred him as no other woman had before or

since. In entering her, his past life seemed to melt away from him into a cloudy pool. It was in those all too brief moments that he found he could release himself into her. He spoke about what he had done, what he had seen done. Some form of guilt at the joy with which he embraced the lawlessness of war surfaced and, in disgorging it, he was exorcised.

To be lost within himself was a new experience for him; it went beyond sex towards an approximation of love he had never before believed himself capable of.

All this came home to him when he returned from his final and most important mission into Cambodia. While he was making the first incision into the unknown fabric of his new life, while he was quite literally giving birth to the *angka*, she had left her flat in Ban Me Thuot.

No one saw her leave – he made certain of that in the ensuing days and nights after his return. But of one thing he was certain: she had not left on her own. Someone had taken her.

The possibilities were endless. She had told him over and over that there were no other men in her life. But there were nights when she couldn't see him, long stretches when he was away sweating in the jungles, wiping the blood of the Khmer Rouge off his Bowie knife. And now the incident of their first meeting replayed itself in his mind like a defective tape that would not stop: the two Marines fighting over her. Had she, after all, been married? Or been sleeping with another of the Special Forces soldiers?

He would never know. In the waning days before he was flown back to the States for the last time, the stories he uncovered piled up in a bewildering heap: she had been a paid informant for the Viet Cong; she was actually full Khmer, ideologically tied to the rebels in Cambodia; she was a double agent working with the Communists, transmitting to them disinformation prepared by Special Forces Intelligence.

Those were bleak days, despite his mounting excitement at the beginning of the *angka*. In his mind, he tried to retrace every intimate conversation he had had with her. How many missions, how much of his private thoughts had he communicated to her? It was impossible for him to say. His love for her made the desire

209

to recall soft and unfocused until he found that it did not matter to him what she had been. She had been his; there was nothing as important as that.

And she was for him the last enigma left in the world.

The Museum of Modern Art was a mess when he arrived there. The sculpture garden was a morass of rock-laced earth and Caterpillar machinery. It was a discouraging sight to many folk, so the museum was much quieter than it normally would be in the afternoon. It was cool inside, the textured grey walls and white stone floors showing the colourful art at its best.

Senator Harlan Esterhaas was a dour-faced man with a thick shock of yellow-white hair, a beefy-cheeked face to go with his rather corpulent body and black-rimmed glasses with half lenses perched near the end of his nose. He was dressed in a dark three-piece suit despite the weather.

Those who did not know the senator all that well, invariably made the mistake of underestimating him. Because he refused to allow the rough edges country life had given him to be eroded by his work in Washington, he had often been considered an easy mark for one scheme or another.

Nothing could be further from the truth. He was canny, experienced in the oftentimes acrimonious senatorial infighting. Striding confidently up to the man now, Macomber vowed to give Esterhaas no room to manoeuvre.

'Senator,' he said, smiling cordially, 'it's good to see you again.' He shook Esterhaas' hand warmly. 'How are things up on the Hill?'

'I don't mind telling you,' Esterhaas said in his wheezy drawl, 'that getting appropriations out of this Congress is like pulling teeth. Hell, it's gotten worse since we last spoke. We need to beef up our armaments, but even more we require *new blood*, like a champion stud to sire us a new approach to defence. The apathy on the Hill is, frankly, very scary; the sheep're taking their cue from the Chief Executive and you know what a goddamned dovecote he is.'

'I'm particularly concerned with the situation in Egypt,' Macomber said. They were walking slowly through the new, temporary gallery. Outside, through smoked glass windows they could see men in hard hats sweating as they worked bright-sparking welding irons.

'We've been, too,' the Senator nodded. 'But I think we've got Mubarak in line now and, in any case, we're dispatching Roger DeWitt — who's having briefings now with the Secretary of State — tomorrow. I don't know whether you know him. He's called a military attaché but he's much more. He's a tremendous negotiator and an even better intelligence gatherer.'

'It's not Mubarak, *per se*, I'm worried about,' Macomber said as they stopped to admire a primary-coloured Calder. 'It's all those secret sects trained in Russian-financed terrorist camps. The whole situation's terribly unstable.'

Esterhaas gave a wry smile. 'I see you stay up nights, too. Well, it'll all settle down now that DeWitt's going in. He's our best man, really.'

'You've got security all mapped out, I assume.'

'That's State's purview; I don't get involved in security.' They moved away from the Calder towards a soaring Brancusi sculpture. 'Anyway, the evidence for Russian involvement on the scale you indicate just isn't there at the moment.'

Macomber grunted. 'Maybe I should fly you into Southern Lebanon to see for yourself.'

The Senator laughed. 'Very amusing.'

Macomber turned towards him. 'I'm perfectly serious,' he said bluntly. 'I can arrange it within two hours. It's up to you.'

Esterhaas had gone ashen. 'What, infiltrate a PLO camp? We'd be shot to death.'

Macomber nodded. 'There's always that possibility.' The sudden deflation of the senator's confidence disgusted him. They were all alike, these politicians. It was so easy to make them back off and once having done that, they were yours.

'But I doubt very much it would happen. I wouldn't let it.' He flexed that calloused hand and Esterhaas' gaze was drawn to it, a snake enrapt by the mongoose. Macomber shrugged. 'My point is this. You refute my contention with reports compiled by agencies to whom funding is far more important than the work they were created to do.

'I back up my views with the real thing. You think the Russians' involvement in international terrorism is minor. If you don't take me up on my offer, you must believe me. What other choice do you have?'

The Senator stared at Macomber. 'You sure are confident,' he said softly.

'I'm certain of my facts. Are you?'

Esterhaas looked away towards the bright fizzing arcs of the welders' torches. 'I thought I was sure until now. But the idea of actually going ...' He turned back to Macomber. 'I don't honestly think I'd be comfortable with that.'

'I want you to remember this moment, Harlan.' Macomber had moved subtly closer to him. 'In everything that follows I want you to remember. You had your chance to experience it for yourself. You chose not to. Well, from now on it will be *my* information you rely on.'

'I see.'

Macomber turned his head like an owl on scent. 'Does that offend some sensibility of yours? You'd do well to be honest about it now.'

Esterhaas shook his head. 'Whatever sensibilities I was born with have been bred out of me by thirty-odd years in politics. There's no room for the thin-skinned.'

Only for the gutless, Macomber thought. This was what the system could not foretell in picking Esterhaas. If the going got rough, as it might at one point or another, Macomber had to be certain he would not cave in under the pressure.

They walked on. Macomber put his hands behind him and this simple gesture transformed him somewhat, giving him more or less a professorial air. 'A tragedy about Senator Burke,' he said in a conversational tone. 'It's terrible to be cut down so senselessly at such an age.'

'Don't play games with me,' Esterhaas said, abruptly angry. 'Roland called me the day before he was murdered. I know what he was about to announce. It stands to reason that he wasn't killed by some intruder as the police in Chicago have convinced themselves.'

'That could be true.'

The Senator stopped walking. 'Listen, I don't cotton to those kinds of tactics and if you think you can scare me by what happened to Burke, you'd better think again. He was stupid enough to dither over his decision instead of going out and acting on it immediately. If he'd done that, he'd still be alive today.'

'If it helps you to believe that,' Macomber said easily, 'be my guest. But the fact is, there was no threat implied, Harlan. Not to you. I don't underestimate you for a moment; you can be as dangerous as you are powerful. I know that. That's why you were picked by me.' Macomber's voice had turned silky, soothing. 'I have nothing but respect for you, Senator.'

Esterhaas nodded. 'That's more like it. You know, I'm a pragmatist. Where this world of ours is concerned, I can see the handwriting on the wall real clear. And from where I sit, you've got the right attitude. This country's been sinking into the international sea for more than ten years now. Hell, I knew about it and I've done my best to fight it. But up to now it's been a losing battle 'cause there hasn't been nearly enough people in the right places who think the same way. Now I think we got a fighting chance. I admire you for givin' this country that chance.' He scratched at his jaw. 'Just so's you know not to cross me. If the saddle you give me to ride begins to chafe my behind, I got a right to change horses. That's how I always do business.'

'And I appreciate that, Harlan.' Macomber's tone had not changed. 'I understand the concerns that prompt you to make such a statement.' They moved on, past a Lictenstein which Macomber loathed. 'How's your family, Harlan?'

'Everyone's fine.' The senator had begun to relax, the last of the deal over with. 'Barbara's gone back to school to get her Ph.D.' He chuckled. 'Can you imagine? At her age.'

'It's never too late to learn,' Macomber said. 'And what about your beautiful daughter, Amy.'

'The light of my life?' Esterhaas smiled in happiness. 'She's top of her class in Stamford. My only complaint is that Barbara and I don't get to see her often enough, what with her being all the way out in California.'

Macomber halted them before his favourite Brancusi. The sinuous lines of the sculpture were breathtakingly sensual. 'Brancusi is a certified genius, Harlan, don't you think?' And then continuing in precisely the same tone of voice. 'I have films of Amy.'

'What?' Esterhaas thought that perhaps he had not heard right. 'Did you say films?'

'Your daughter,' Macomber said, drawing it out, 'your baby, has a female lover. A radical involved in a splinter group of, shall we say, a decidedly revolutionary bent.'

'This is out –!' The Senator could not go on. He staggered a little, red-faced but when Macomber gripped him to steady his stance, he shook the hand off. 'I don't believe any of it.'

Macomber produced a colour snapshot, handed it over. 'It's taken from one of the frames.'

Esterhaas' hand trembled and he held the thing by its extreme edges as if he might be contaminated by it. 'Oh, God,' he moaned, looking down into the face of his fear. 'Oh, my God. Barbara will die if she ever finds out.' He was almost speaking to himself.

'I know that.' Macomber took the photo from the Senator's nerveless fingers and, walking over to a sand–filled standing ash tray, quickly burned the snapshot with the flame from a gold lighter. He came back to where Esterhaas stood. 'And she'll never know, the world will never know. Not from me, at least. I want to make that very clear, Harlan. Not from me.'

'I think I . . .' The senator seemed to be coming slowly out of a trance. 'I understand.' Animation returned to his face. 'You're a despicable sonovabitch.'

'That's very funny, Harlan,' Macomber said as they turned to leave, 'coming from you.'

A stifling humid twilight was descending over Alexandria, steeping Washington and its environs in wet heat.

Gottschalk, still in his dark blue suit trousers, had nevertheless divested himself of his jacket, waistcoat and striped tie. They lay lankly over the back of the lawn chair like discarded flags. He picked a tall iced drink off a pebble-glass-topped wrought-iron table, rolled the beaded side of the glass against his cheek. He sighed.

At his feet, Kathleen lay stretched out on the immaculately groomed lawn, hands pillowing her head. She wore a loose-fitting sleeveless top in a green, brown and grey jungle print not unlike the camouflage jackets Gottschalk had seen the grunts wearing into the dangerous jungles of Southeast Asia. She wore forest-green shorts that exposed a crescent slice of the bottom of her buttocks. She had kicked off her silver European sandals, had crossed one ankle over the other.

Gottschalk had come here for solace, a haven from the incredible pressure of the nomination race. He needed a respite from the seven-day-a-week grind. He had been in every state in the Union at least three times during the past eight months for the primaries as well as spending time with each group of delegates to the forthcoming convention in Dallas. It was an exhausting as well as an exhilarating way of life. He found reserves inside himself he had not been certain would be there. But every so often he needed an escape from everything: pressure, politics, the public face he had so painstakingly fashioned, the strategy planning, the in-fighting, the endless rounds of interviews, addresses, speeches, off-the-cuff remarks, backslapping, hand-grabbing and cigar-chomping. Even Roberta

Kathleen, who provided all this and more for him, was staring over her head at the verdant screen of foilage that backed the bamboo fence that screened the house from the sleepy street. She felt safe here; safe and secure. But even more, she loved the house itself because it was a symbol to her. It was like an arrow pointing her way upward.

She stared at it now. The front had a double stairway guarded by filigree wrought-iron banisters that collapsed in on themselves at an intermediate landing placed directly in front and just below the wide front door. Above the stone and deep red brick façade was a small semicircular balcony of worked limestone, open along its curving side as carved double serpents rose, snaking , to confront each other in an endless aggression, tongues exposed.

It was a fabulous place but Kathleen did not count herself

lucky to be living in it. She knew she earned it every time Gottschalk came over. If she had dug deep enough she might have come to the ultimate conclusion that she did not enjoy being tied to a leash, at his beck and call. However, even then, she would not have found the idea demeaning. It was merely a means to an end, and not an utterly distasteful one, either. She loved her own body, revelled in its sexuality. She had few inhibitions and, in the face of her ambitions, even those disappeared.

Long ago, she had given her heart to a more demanding lover than any one man could ever be. Whatever her body was put through was all right with her; her heart, the inner core of her, remained sacrosanct. In sex, nothing could be asked of her that she could not do. It made no difference to her except that some acts were pleasurable and others not.

Gottschalk was not a pig as some of her former lovers in earlier less prosperous days had been. He was, in his own self-involved way, good to her. But she was certain that he did not fully understand the nature of his involvement with her. She might be similar to a pinball machine he went to in order to forget himself for a time and unwind.

Certainly he was ignorant of the overall picture. This did not disturb her particularly. In fact, it was just the way she wanted it at the moment. His time of revelation would come but only when she chose to raise it in front of his eyes. She smiled slightly at the secret thought. So close to him and thinking such evil thoughts. It gave her a warm, secure glow.

Gottschalk stretched. He had finished his drink. He wiped at his sweating forehead. There were damp crescents darkening his shirt under the arms. 'Christ,' he said, 'you've got to be a masochist to live here during the summer.'

Fluorescent blue streaks coated the dome of the sky high up, reflections of a sun already dropped below the skyline of Washington.

'Well, I expect I can stand it another couple of years.' He laughed, a sound deep down in his throat. 'After that, I'll be spending weekends at Camp David.'

God, but he was confident. Kathleen knew him well enough

to feel that this unshakable certainty could not be wholly his own. Where was it coming from then? It was a question she had been trying to decipher for months now. It was a secret she knew she must unearth.

At that moment, he rose. 'I'm going to work out for a bit,' he said, looking down at her. She was sapphire and amethyst in the darkling shadows of the rustling trees.

She began to lift her head and shoulders off the grass; her hair was like a black cap. 'I'll come in with you.'

His brow creased. 'No, don't bother, I'd rather be alone.' His head swung around and he gave her a vague smile almost as an afterthought. 'Anyway, you look like you're enjoying the evening too much.'

He began to step over her and, looking up, she had the odd prickling sensation that it had hesitated when it got to the centre of her body so that its cool shadow rested across her like the palm of a powerful hand. Then it had moved on and he had stepped across her.

She watched him until the door closed behind him. Then she closed her eyes, counted to sixty slowly. She got up and without a sound went across the lawn. She put her ear to the door, listened for sound or vibration. Hearing none, she turned the knob and when it reached its limit, pushed the door open.

Immediately she heard Gottschalk's voice talking and, she crept across the kitchen floor. She reached up for the wall phone, hesitated. She looked around, saw the glass bowl of fruit on the table. Without hesitating, she took a swipe at it with the back of her hand. It flew off the table, crashed to the floor in splintered shards. At almost the same instant she raised her arm to protect her face, Kathleen picked up the receiver off the wall.

'What the hell was that?' she heard Gottschalk bellow down the hall.

'Just me,' she said, carefully covering the phone with her palm. 'I came in for a drink and knocked the fruit bowl over.'

'Well, for Christ sake make sure you pick up every piece. I don't want to find one in the sole of my foot tonight.'

'All right.' She heard him back on the phone. 'Just someone

mucking around. You tell him I'd like some assurances, that's all.'

'I'm not an idiot,' the voice on the other end of the line said. Kathleen strained to make it out.

'But your heart's not in it,' Gottschalk said. 'That's every bit as dangerous. I cannot understand why he insists on using you.'

'Because I'm his son,' the second, lighter voice replied. 'He doesn't trust anyone else. Would you?'

'I wouldn't even trust my son ... if I had one.' He laughed. 'I don't trust my own wife.'

'Must be some kind of marriage.'

'Don't get so cute with me, sonny,' Gottschalk snapped. 'We'll see how long you're doing this after I talk to Macomber!'

'Jesus!' The other voice came back hushed, filled with an odd kind of fear. 'What're you doing? No names! Jesus Christ! He's my father.'

Kathleen could hear Gottschalk breathing hard into the phone; he was making no effort to disguise it. 'That's what you get for needling me, you little snot nose. Anyway' – his voice had regained its composure – 'this cloak-and-dagger business is a load of manure. Who the hell is going to bug this line without my knowing it, huh? I have it swept twice a week.' He took a breath. 'Just do your job and leave the psychology to the experts. Just get the message straight.' The voice on the other end repeated it and Gottschalk hung up.

In the kitchen, Kathleen carefully replaced the receiver as slowly as she dared. She did not want Gottschalk blundering into her as he came back down the hallway. When she estimated it had gone down far enough in the cradle she let go. It swung there, a wagging yellow finger admonishing her.

Christ, she thought, staring at her hands. They were trembling with excitement. She had stumbled across the secret. She paused to look at it logically but that would not work. Outwardly Gottschalk and Macomber espoused different sides of the political pinwheel. She shook her head. Powerful as Gottschalk was, he could not do it alone; no one could. The image of the President as a lone heroic figure making lonely decisions was one that belonged only to the imagination.

Kathleen had been around Washington all her life and she knew the banal truth: it was everyone else who made your decisions for you and no matter who you were when you were elected, you were a dedicated centrist when you left. It was the office itself that battered you down to size. The good men survived and even prospered beneath the staggering weight. The others came away defeated, old before their time. And Kathleen, fixed as she was towards power, could not understand the lust men had to become President.

She laughed to herself. What was the saying? There are no brilliant Presidents, only providential decisions.

She went back and using a wet towel picked up the broken glass. Then she went out the door. Night had swept in while they had been inside. The crickets droned on as the heat continued unabated.

Damn! She thought. She turned back towards the house as if she could see through the walls. Maybe he *will* be President after all, she thought wonderingly. And it will be me he takes to Camp David. She knew she had just scratched the surface and she had no idea of where it would lead her. But one thing she was quite certain of: the alliance of Atherton Gottschalk and Delmar Davis Macomber was a potent one indeed.

Lauren was at the *barre*, one hand lightly placed on its wooden length, slightly in front of her elbow. 'The *barre*,' Stanilya, her first dance instructor, had said, 'allows you to concentrate on one movement at a time. This is essential because you must *build* them one at a time. But more, it allows you to develop a quiet discipline so that you can explode into motion from a position of absolute motionlessness.' And because under Martin's tutelage, her leaps had become even more spectacular in both their height and their illusion of weightlessness, she never forgot these basics.

She went to the fifth position as soon as she had warmed up because in this position her body's weight was directly over her foot. She had learned long ago not to use the *barre* as a support – a common habit among young students and a difficult one to get out of – and to keep the balance within herself.

She began with *pliés*, working up through the feet, to *battements tendus*, into the knees, *battements frappés*; hips, *grands battements*, to stomach and back, *développés* and stretches. As she did so, she alternated slow and fast, the one for strength and control, the other for execution.

By the time she got to 'turn-out', she was satisfied and she turned her body to the opening steps of the new choreography Martin had created for her. She went neatly through a three-combination into turns on point, sustaining the elevation as the turns became slower and slower.

The section ended with a triple line of *pas de chat*, modified in Martin's brilliant fashion so that the legs crossed in midair and, by tightening the leg muscles up towards the crotch at the height of the arc of the leap, gave the impression of the dancer being suspended in flight.

Several of the younger girls – soloists – paused in their own work to watch her and wonder among themselves when they would be able to perform the *pas de chat* with such precision and *élan*. One of them, a willowy blonde who had not been with the company long enough to work up sufficient inhibitions, approached Lauren then, asking her advice about a stone bruise she had developed from holding fifth position in the extraordinarily tight fashion Martin had dictated so slippage would be to third, not first.

Lauren was happy to help; she felt little of the almost painfully sharp jealousy many of the other principals felt at the rise of younger talented dancers. Perhaps it was only because her memory was better than theirs; she could not forget scenes after auditions at the American Ballet School when frail little girls, crushed by their failures, would curl up in a corner, weeping uncontrollably into their raised hands, their whiplike bodies trembling like lost animals.

In any event, Lauren respected talent; because she recognized her own, she was not frightened of it in others.

Yet when the young blonde left her side, she found herself inexplicably depressed and, staring into the mirrored wall, she recalled the stone bruise she had once had – an ugly thing which Bobby had persisted in making fun of. She wanted so much then to bring to mind the good memories of him but what surfaced was vastly different.

A summer's afternoon filled with pelting rain and blue lightning. There was nothing to do – all of the day's bright plans cancelled: no picnic with the Levitts, no swimming in Water Mill's salty surf, no sandy tunafish sandwiches and Hostess cupcakes, her favourite meal at the time. Instead, she had been pent up in the old rambling beach house with Bobby.

She had been twelve; Bobby was ten-and-a-half. He was introspective and, she thought, dumb. He wanted to read and sit around while she spent her time working at her dance. Already her body was becoming a finely tuned instrument with which, she found, she could do anything she set out to do.

It was not only her technique that thrilled her instructor but her discipline. 'I've never encountered such unflagging diligence in a child of Lauren's age,' she had told Adele one day after class. Lauren had been so very proud of that singing moment. She replayed it again and again in her mind until it became her favourite movie.

Yet she longed for a more normal life with friends and parties to go to, real films to see and sundaes to be consumed. She had to be content with living all of that through Bobby. She could not do it and she could not change herself. So she did the only thing that seemed to make her feel less bad. She tormented him.

She teased him about his reading, the smell of sweat on him, his rumpled clothes and, especially, his body. Lauren was already an expert on bodies and fitness. To her way of thinking, Bobby was a little weasel with his thin, undermuscled white body. She laughed when she saw it and poked the end of her finger into his soft flesh.

She would watch him eating six slices of white toast smeared with melting butter and groan inwardly. If she had done such a thing on the same regular basis he did, she would be a blimp overnight. He ate and ate and never got fat. He demolished calories as if they were pennies.

Yet they had – as almost all siblings do – their moments of quiet and love when Lauren would read to him at bedtime about King Arthur and his Court or *The Adventures of Robin Hood* by

Howard Pyle, or she would come home from practice on her birthday and unexpectedly find a card for her painstakingly handmade by him.

But that stormy summer afternoon with their parents gone for the day and nothing to do, something had happened. Something awful and irretrievable.

Lauren had left Bobby in front of the TV watching *The Dick Van Dyke Show*, Mary Tyler Moore's high thin voice following her out onto the huge screened-in porch. Rain dribbled down the metal mesh and the outdoor furniture felt too damp and sodden to sit on. She stared out at the dismal overcast day and thought about the surf breaking across her chest and the hot sun striking the tops of her shoulders, turning them the colour of toasted almonds. She did some stretching exercises without really thinking about technique, then did a couple of spins. But, off-balance, she was obliged to reach out for a painted porch beam. It was slick with moisture and, wiping her palm down, she abruptly had had enough. She headed back inside to get a diet cola.

Bobby was not in front of the set. A commercial for Pepsodent toothpaste was on. She went into the kitchen, opened the refrigerator. There was no diet cola, no diet soda of any kind. She rummaged through the shelves. She found milk and a pitcher of iced coffee. Two sealed bottles of tonic water.

If she wanted the diet cola, she'd have to go out into the weather for it. But then again, she reasoned, the store was only three short blocks away. She decided to go.

On the TV, the second act of *The Dick Van Dyke Show* was on. Rob was in jail with a stripper. He was attempting to explain how he got there to an angry Laura. Bobby was missing his favourite show.

She went down the hall, crossing the threshold of her room and stopped short. All thought of the money she needed for the diet cola flew out of her mind. She saw Bobby bending over an old wooden dresser. It was the second drawer. The one in which she kept all her underwear. As she watched, he extracted a pair of her panties. She had just graduated to what she thought of as 'grown-up' pants. Bobby stuck his fingers inside the elastic waist band, pulled outward experimentally. He stared at the double inset panel at the crotch.

It struck a spark inside Lauren. She was incensed. She felt simultaneously violated and humiliated. But all she knew at the moment was anger. She strode across the room in three lithe strides, ripped the pants out of Bobby's hands.

He looked up at her, terrified, opened his mouth. 'But –'

Lauren slapped him as hard as she could. Taken unawares, his head snapped around on its thin neck and he staggered against the dresser. His stockinged feet slid along the waxed linoleum and he fell on his hip at her feet. He began to cry.

Oddly, this angered Lauren even more. 'Baby!' she cried, tears of outrage spun from her. 'You're nothing but a baby!' She flung her panties back in their drawer, slammed it closed with the heels of both hands. She loomed over her brother. 'Don't you ever, ever go through my things again, Baby! If you do, you'll be sorry, I promise you!'

She hauled him up to his feet. 'Now get out of here and don't you come in again! Ever! Do you understand me?'

Bobby understood. He never asked her to read to him at bedtime again.

'Then it went well.'

'Exceptionally well. He bowed before the inevitability of his fate. He was humbled by it.'

Khieu smiled. 'That is good.'

Macomber had always felt that the world blossomed when Khieu smiled. There was a peculiar power in that expression he was incapable of defining. Many others were affected by it, he knew, especially women.

'Harlan Esterhaas is an important link for us; he controls the Armed Services Committee. Now we control him. It pleases me that there were no problems.' Khieu moved but made no sound as he did so. The scent of incense perfumed the air; he had just completed his evening prayers.

Macomber turned his head. There was a restlessness in the other. Quietly, almost gently, he said, 'Khieu, what is it?' He followed the other's movements with his eyes.

'I am ashamed,' Khieu said, stopping suddenly. 'Senator Burke's ... unavailability rests on my shoulders.'

'Forget Burke. I don't think I could have done a more forceful selling job than you did. Time was of the essence ... we split our targets. If there is a fault, it lies in the system. It kicked out his name, after all.' He smiled. 'It's worked out for the best anyway. Our replacement will serve the *angka* far better than Burke ever could. Jack Sullivan, the Republican senator who heads the Select Intelligence Committee. The delay has been beneficial – he's ripe for us now.'

'And what about Richter?'

Macomber thought about that for a moment. 'I think his old man's a dead end for him. And where's he got to go after that? There's nothing left for him to go on. We leave him alone for the time being. I mustn't get too close to him and if we have to take him out it must be a one-time affair.'

Their eyes locked. 'I understand.'

Macomber nodded. 'Good.' His long forefinger stroked the impeccable line of his moustache. 'Still that bug is a loose end. Soon, I think, you'll have to devise a way in there to retrieve it.'

'I doubt that will present any special problems.'

'Otherwise, we're on schedule for the *angka*'s timetable.'

'Gottschalk will be pleased to hear that. He's asked us through Eliott for confirmation.'

Macomber grunted. 'Well, have Eliott give him the okay. He's got all the information by now, hasn't he?'

'All of it, yes.'

Macomber had, of course, first asked the system to amass psychological profiles on the politicos he had met who he felt might be presidential material. There were five of them but the system soon reduced that figure to a majority of one: Atherton Gottschalk. Then and only then did he make his offer. He did it slowly, a piece at a time, being careful to use what he had learned about the man, choosing an approach to slide Gottschalk into his current position. Macomber told him only as much as he needed to know in order to make his decision. Just like a tailor-made suit, it made Gottschalk comfortable and, after all, Macomber had learned that comfort was next to pliancy.

During his tour of duty in Southeast Asia Macomber had also learned to cover every angle, even those that seemed remote possibilities at the time. And so he had returned to his investigation, turning up facts here and there, extracting them, placing them in what he called Red Files in a safety deposit box at a midtown Citibank branch. 'Operation Sultan' had made him most cautious.

Not that he really expected there to be problems with Gottschalk; the system would not have picked him, otherwise. But then again, it had chosen Roland Burke. Macomber had to admit that when it came to people he did not fully trust any computer system. They were merely programmed morons; they could not actually think and certainly could not weigh intangibles.

So he had managed to get two reels of Super 8mm film – complete with a highly illuminating soundtrack – depicting Atherton Gottschalk and Kathleen Christian in the midst of some steamy activities that were definitely not presidential in nature.

'Then he knows just what to do with it.'

Macomber stood with one hand on the iron frame of the window, looking down at the joggers circumnavigating Gramercy Park. He did not mind that kind of activity. Fitness was something he understood quite well.

It occurred to him to reward Khieu's intuitiveness but he had to restrain that part of him, knowing that the other would take offence at such a gesture. The fact that Khieu was keeping Joy occupied had not escaped his notice. Far from being angry, he was delighted. His physical attraction towards her had quickly dwindled away. But since he wished to do nothing to anger her brother, he had begun to leave the house more often, throwing the two of them together. He had counted on Khieu's magnetism, fuelled by Joy's loneliness, And of course Khieu's peculiarly Oriental sense of loyalty. Neither had disappointed him and he was satisfied.

'Turn on the TV,' he said, 'it's almost five o'clock.' He was an inveterate early news watcher. The late-breaking items he savoured in detail the morning after via the *New York Times*.

There was Dan Rather, his face looking lined and white and

Macomber said, 'What the hell's going on? Turn up the sound, will you.'

The graphic behind the newscaster was a black-and-white photo of an eagle-faced man in a black-bordered inset.

'... recap,' Rather was saying. 'Lieutenant Colonel Roger DeWitt, the American military attaché, in Cairo for talks with President Mubarak, has been shot dead by unidentified gunmen. Reports are still sketchy as to details but sources indicate at this time that at least three assailants were involved.'

Rather glanced down at the sheaf of papers on the desk in front of him. 'Just moments ago in Beirut, a terrorist group known as the Lebanese Revolutionary Faction, issued a statement apparently claiming responsibility for the assassination.

'In Cairo, President Mubarak has called the killing "dastardly". He went on to call on the mobilization of the Egyptian military in an attempt to find Lieutenant Colonel DeWitt's murderers.

'No official word from the White House as yet, however, Press Secretary Edwin Weeks was quoted as calling the assassination a terrifying sign of the times.

'Presidential hopeful Atherton Gottschalk, long an advocate of stricter security measures for American military and diplomatic personnel both here and abroad, called for the President to put into effect plans for the creation of a select paramilitary unit specializing in anti-terrorist action.

'Mr Gottschalk said he was shocked by the cold-blooded killing of Lieutenant Colonel DeWitt end quote.

'For an up-to-the-minute report on the hunt for the assailants, here's CBS correspondent David Collins in Cairo ...'

Macomber waved a hand. 'I've heard enough.'

Khieu switched off the set. They looked at each other for a moment. Macomber smiled now, a soft Mona Lisa expression that was not truly characteristic of him.

'Isn't it wonderful,' he said softly, 'how life works out.'

Kathleen stepped off the Eastern shuttle at LaGuardia Airport at precisely 10.10 p.m. Only three minutes late despite the rain storm surrounding New York like a blanket.

It was odd to be so high up in the midst of black rolling clouds, howling winds, the frame battered by sleety rain and outside in the airy night, the shifting blue-white electric shocks of the silent lightning.

Kathleen went through the terminal, picked up her luggage from the revolving carousel. She strode out through the Magic Eye doors which parted at her approach and breathed in New York's rank humidity. She sighed. At least it was cooler here than in Washington.

She saw the limo she had ordered through the company and signalled to the driver. He stowed her luggage in the trunk, came around and held the rear door open for her.

'The Parker Meridian.' She settled back in the plush seat.

It had been absurdly easy, Kathleen thought now, to arrange for this to be a business trip through the company. She was head researcher for Brady & Mheerson, one of the finest firms dealing strictly in corporate law in the Washington area. In fact, Mheerson was already in New York, working on the tail-end of the AT&T anti-trust case against the company the government had just settled. He had all but danced a jig when she had suggested she join him in New York to assist him. He was a cheery-faced Dutchman and still Old World enough to insist on the highest order of personal service wherever he went. Kathleen had known he would welcome the request despite the grumbling by some of the lesser partners with whom she had been working lately. They lusted after her; Mheerson did not.

But, in fact, she could not have cared less about the AT&T case and Mheerson; she was aiming much higher than a mid-level position in the field of law. And, she thought wryly, I won't have had to go to boring graduate school for it, either.

She glanced at her gold and diamond wristwatch. Just past a quarter-to-eleven. What was Gottschalk doing now? At home, at work on the business he let slide while he was with her? Or with that cow of a wife of his, fondling her big breasts? Kathleen felt the flame in her cheeks: a proprietary jealousy.

No. More likely, he was giving one of his doom-laden speeches at some fund-raiser. Not that she disbelieved him all that much. Not at all. But if she believed the international scene was going to hell in a handcart at least she would grab everything she could manage as quickly as was possible.

Now, preferably.

Tracy, who had been following Thwaite's dark blue Impala in his own Audi 4000, drew up at the tree-lined kerb of Sixty-ninth Street in Bay Ridge; Thwaite was just behind him.

The night was quiet; it was almost midnight, time for their rendezvous with Ivory White and the ME's photos of John's body. Two of the lights on the block were out and another, at the far corner, was buzzing, blinking fitfully.

Their shoes ground against the gritty concrete. At the top of the steps Thwaite, who was just ahead of Tracy, stopped so suddenly he slammed into Tracy's shoulder and cursed mightily.

Tracy came abreast of the detective, saw the scrawled message spray-painted across Thwaite's front door. HIJO DE PUTA, it read and, just below it, PUERCO SIN COJONES.

'Sonsabitches!' Thwaite growled and shot the key into the lock. At that precise moment, Tracy scented that peculiar sharp resiny odour that brought back missions filled with distant birdcalls, batwings' brushings and great livid blossoms, scars on the night.

'Don't!' he cried out, lunging forward. 'They've —'

But the rest of the words were drowned out. Thwaite had opened the door. The night sky lit up in orange, black and crimson. They felt a shudder as of a subway train thundering by below them, then the heavy fists of the shockwave hit them.

They were blown back off the steps, stumbling, legs and arms flying. Thunder rolled in their ears, deafening them, their eardrums stretched to the pain point.

They lifted their arms reflexively to protect their faces and squeezed-shut eyes, felt the stinging of a hail of tiny missiles ripping open their jackets, the sleeves of their shirts, ribboning their flesh like the bites of insistent rodents.

'No!' Thwaite was screaming. 'Christ, no!' He got to his hands and knees, pulled himself up onto his feet by wrapping his arms around the bole of the stickly plane tree out front. He stumbled forward, unthinking but Tracy, knowing better, tackled him, bringing him down again as the second explosion ripped through the house closer to them, bringing thick chunks of the front wall ballooning out towards him, rolling and skidding, impaling themselves like blades in the lawn.

Choking smoke and the pattering of smaller debris like gentle hail after the holocaust. Blankets of ground glass picking up the highlights of the licking fire, brillianting the night.

Sounds of running feet and the wail of sirens. Shouts and cries from everywhere behind them. They were on their feet now, faces blackened, clothes torn, bleeding from scores of tiny nicks and cuts. Their ears ached, filled with a white rushing.

Thwaite staggered across the blackened, studded lawn towards the remnants of his house, his wife and child. He wanted in; he was certain he could save them. But the fire stopped him with its heat and fury and still he bellowed at it as if it were a living entity, his enemy.

'Let me in!' he screamed. 'Doris, where are you?' His fist raised flinging his impotent energy in all directions. 'Phyllis, my baby. I'm coming!'

But Tracy was behind him. 'You can't go in there,' he said as calmly as he could. Christ, he thought. What a bang.

'Who's gonna stop me?' Thwaite said. He was irrational.

'They're gone, Thwaite.' Tracy secured his hold on the detective. 'Think, man! Look at what's in front of you! Nothing could survive those blasts. You'll kill yourself if you go in there.'

Thwaite spun in Tracy's grip and Tracy was shocked at what he saw. In the livid flickering light of the voracious fire, Thwaite's face was drained of all colour. His skin was tight across his skull, his eyes sunk deep within his face. Tears streamed down his cheeks, leaving clear tracks where they washed the soot away.

'Let go of me,' Thwaite said. His eyes were rolling like a panicked horse but within their depths, Tracy recognized the resolve there. 'Let go or I'll kill you.'

Tracy dropped his arms, said, 'Listen, Thwaite, don't –'

But the big detective was already racing away from him. Not, as Tracy had thought, into the burning house, but out across the lawn away from it.

'It was that bastard Antonio!' Thwaite screamed. He hit the first wave of thronging curiosity-seekers and they split apart like the Red Sea at the the approach of Moses. 'I'm gonna rip his balls off and make him eat them!'

'Wait!' Tracy cried. But Thwaite was fast disappearing up the street. The sirens were close now, the fire engines arriving. Jesus Christ, Tracy thought and left them to it as he lit out after Thwaite.

Block after block of eerily-lit houses ribboned by him, colours odd, stained as if with age or disappearing altogether in the red inconstant light. People's faces white with fear and confusion, whipped by him. One or two tried to shout at him, to ask him what had happened. But most were mute and tight-jawed emerging in robes and hastily-donned trousers turning their inquisitive heads towards the blaze and rubble like photo-tropic plants, as if to view the end of the world.

Off to the right he could see the still treetops of a park. It too somehow reflected the fire, seemed to be on fire. The air, even this far away, was thick with floating ash, chokingly filled with noxious chemical taints.

Tracy saw Thwaite disappear around a corner to the left, followed him down a dank alley overgrown with dandelion and other weeds. Now he was on his own. Where had Thwaite gone?

He slowed down, inspected the alley further along. There were doorways on both sides but no windows below the second storey. Tracy went to the doorway on the right, inspected it carefully. It was old wood, painted over and over during the course of years. It was scarred by knifed graffiti. There was a metal knob, white and blobby in the dim light filtering in from both ends of the alley. He tried the knob. It was locked.

The second door was almost at the alley's far end. Tracy approached it cautiously. This door was composed of pressed tin, riveted in a patchwork of sheets. Someone had spraypainted a rough sine wave across door and jamb.

Tracy inspected the knob and this time he discerned the tiny bright scratches one makes when hurriedly picking a lock. He stood up and, grasping the knob firmly, turned it slowly. It opened without a sound. A hallway gaped blackly.

Tracy crossed the threshold and, closing the door behind him, stood perfectly still, accommodating himself to the new atmosphere. The stink was overpowering. He could hear the building settling around him like a decaying body. Wooden boards groaned in protestation, sawdust patterned from the shadows high up in the rafter, once he caught the *skree skree* of a frightened rat. And that was all.

Tracy inched forward, his senses questing. Water dripped from some place over his head, a steady tattoo, loudening. Light drooled along the floor, thin and yellow as a corpse's skin. And now sounds came to him, muffled and indistinct. Tracy had the fleeting impression of being Orpheus descending into the underworld.

Light strengthened and with it, sound: an arrhythmic thudding such as an engine might make.

'Oh, oh, oh!' Tracy heard. Sounds of pain.

In Virginia they had taught him to do everything all over again as they knew it should be done even before he had set foot in Cambodia. Without their knowledge, they told him he would never come back.

Tracy walked now as he had been taught by Joe Fox – the one Sioux Indian at the Mines – not on the balls or heels of his feet for true balance was lost there, but on his outside edges. There the entire foot had contact with the floor, anchoring you fore and aft. But your footfalls were totally silent.

He made no sound as he moved, half-sliding over the dusty rotting floorboards. A pyramid of dirty light lay in front of him like a holographic projection. He entered it, turning into the open doorway.

It was an apartment such as he had never seen before. Fur throws lay sprawled like indolent relatives over everything: filthy floor, long sunken sofa, a green Naugahyde Barcalounger, even a plank coffee table. On the walls were woven rugs depicting elks at a riverbed, a mountain of ice and snow behind them; cheetahs racing through a crudely rendered African veldt. The evil light came from a pair of standing metal lamps with oiled paper shades which crudely revealed the lit bulbs behind them.

Tracy saw the huge form of the detective. He had his back to the door.

'He's not here . . . Oh oh *oh!*'

It was a female voice, high and bubbling with dread. Now Tracy saw a coffee-coloured leg wave into view, kicking high in the air with an almost reflexive jerk.

'Tell me where he is . . . You know.' It was an almost guttural sound, the syllables bloated with saliva and rage.

There came a high scream as Thwaite's shoulders tensed, his upper arms moving slightly. Tracy thought he knew what Thwaite was up to. He moved so that the detective's bulk would not block his view.

As he suspected, Thwaite's strong hands were at work on the woman's left kneecap, applying principles of isometrics, making the victim's own body work against her.

Snap! snap! Tracy heard the sure scrape of bone against bone just before the woman screamed again. Her face was streaming with sweat, dirtied by the smears of dissolving makeup, her hair a dark mass, gleaming with diamond pinpoints of moisture. But it was her features that had betrayed her, transformed as they were by pain and fright. She knew where Antonio was, all right, but Tracy suspected she was more frightened of him than she was of Thwaite: the detective might put her in the hospital but Antonio would surely put her six feet under if she revealed his whereabouts; even locked away, she knew his arm was long enough to bring her down.

Tracy could see all this clearly but then he had not just lost his family. Thwaite saw this woman as his only link to Antonio.

Tracy was tempted to pry Thwaite away from the woman but he knew no explanation would deflect the detective. He cast his gaze around the rest of the apartment, looking for another way out. It was conceivable that Antonio was already on the run but Tracy was inclined to think otherwise. *He* was an amateur and amateurs always liked to stick around to see how their little tricks worked out.

If his thinking was correct, it meant that Antonio was still there, somewhere. He went across the living room, deafening himself to the woman's cries and whimpers; the only conceivable way he could help her now was to find Antonio.

It did not take him long. He suspected Thwaite would have seen it had he not been half-blinded by bloodlust.

Tracy crouched down now on the opposite side of the room from the one where Thwaite hunched, administering his coercion.

Part of the fur throw was ruffled here, as if recently, hurriedly moved. Tracy bent forward, using the tips of his fingers to gingerly peel back the thick throw. Underneath he saw revealed the oblong outline of what could only be a trap door. Recessed into the floorboards was a ring of iron wide enough to get two fingers through. In the centre of that was what appeared to be a Medeco key lock.

Tracy made the decision immediately. There were only two choices. If the thing was locked it wouldn't matter but if it wasn't it would make all the difference in the world. Time was all that mattered now.

Bracing himself firmly, he grasped the iron ring with two fingers. He breathed in deeply, exhaled completely. He repeated this three times. He cried out from the pit of his stomach as he had been taught, *kiai*, the exercise of one will over another, bringing back drifting scenes of Ban Me Thuot and tiny Yu; some disciplines the people in Virginia just did not know about. At the same instant, he hauled back on the iron ring.

The door in the floorboard flew up with an enormous bang and Tracy was forced to let go of the ring in order not to dislocate his fingers. He was down the hole the instant there was enough room. He found himself in a dirt-floored cubicle no more than six feet on a side. It was perhaps seven feet deep. Echoes of his *kiai* yell were still reverberating.

He dropped into a crouch and immediately saw Antonio. The pimp was huddled in a corner. His liquid brown eyes stared out blinking like an animal's. His flat-planed freckled face was smeared with dirt. His prominent ears stood out well away from his slicked-back hair. His thick lips curled in a snarl.

His silk shirt was torn and bloody and through it Tracy could

233

see a bandage over what must have been a recent wound: blood was still seeping, tingeing the gauze. In his good hand he held a small .22 calibre pistol with mother-of-pearl grips. The gun was cocked.

All this Tracy took in in the first fraction of a second of his descent into the pit beneath the apartment's floor, along with the fecund scents of raw earth, nearby sewage; the wriggle of worms.

In the aftermath of the *kiai*, Antonio crouched, frozen. It had been used since time immemorial, the shout undoubtedly primitive man's initial reaction of mortal danger. The Roman legions had used it, Yu şaid, to strike fear into their enemies while advancing in phalanx. It was, he had insisted, the origin of the English word, 'panic', deriving from the great shouts the Greek god Pan would bellow, indications of his voracious appetites for life and sex.

Tracy shifted his weight onto his left leg, lowering his buttocks in the cramped space, shooting his right leg forward in the process, the sole of his shoe a blurred battering ram, slamming the .22 out of Antonio's trembling grip.

The pimp swung but it was with his bad arm and Tracy ducked under it easily, brought both his fists on rigid-stemmed arms, into Antonio's stomach.

'Oof!' he let out a long breath, folding over like a paper doll, beginning to gag as Tracy drew him up and out of the earthen chamber.

'Thwaite!' he called. 'That's enough now!' It was said sharply, the voice of command and Thwaite looked around, a stupid, inward-directed look in his eyes. They focused slowly, their colour seeming to change, clearing. He threw the woman away from him.

Tracy could hear her whimpering as she curled up onto the sofa, slowly edging into the foetal position. He thought he might have saved her life. He shoved the pimp ahead of him so that he stumbled across the fur-strewn floor. 'Here,' he said.

' 'Tonio.' It was a sound that made the pimp shiver, a voice, a slither of serpents, a whisper devoid of life, of compassion. The colour was leaving Thwaite's face, turning it as white and taut

234

as it had been just after the blast. Tracy thought there was another explosion coming.

'You sonuvabitch 'Tonio,' Thwaite said, crouching. 'Come here, you.' His head seemed to be trembling with the force of his rage. 'You killed my Doris, my little Phyllis.'

Antonio shivered again, touched his left shoulder with his right hand. 'You shouldna come down on me, man. An in fronta the bitches. S'not good for business, man. You know that. They don't listen so good no more, man.'

'That's your problem,' Thwaite said, advancing. His shoulders were hunched, tension ran through him like a hurricane.

The pimp shook his head. '*Our* problem, man. We partners, you muthafucka you, *recuerda*? I had to lock Carla' – he indicated the woman curled up on the sofa – 'in the box.' He shook his head. 'In the fuckin *dark*, man. *Comprende*? *Con los gusanos*. With the worms, man, like she was dead.' His fingers dug deeper at his wounded shoulder. 'Now. *Now* she listens. Now she understands my power.'

'You're gonna die, 'Tonio,' Thwaite grated. 'Sure as I'm standing here.'

The pimp drew back a step. '*Idiota!* It was *you* who did this! You!' But Thwaite was coming on, his mahogany baton in his hand. Tracy saw the look of utter concentration on his face, the fixedness of his eyes that indicated the narrowness of perception.

Tracy took two steps forward, saw the glint of the knifeblade protruding from Antonio's fist as he drew it out of the folds of the bandage where he had been hiding it. Tracy cursed himself for not searching the pimp and began to move.

But Thwaite was already on top of Antonio, his baton whistling downward on a short flat arc. The knifeblade was already on its course and Tracy saw that he do nothing; he was too late.

The blade went in as if slicing butter along Thwaite's right side, high up near the ribs. The pimp twisted the blade and Thwaite cried out, dropping his baton.

Now the knife was out, filthy with the detective's blood. Tracy could hear the wheezing coming from the detective's drooping mouth, his eyes were open wide. He was off-balance, completely vulnerable. And there was the knife, beginning its second strike, a twisted smile of power suffusing Antonio's face.

And there was only time for the *kanashiki*, one of the *atewaza*, the lethal percussions. Tracy judged the distance and, extending the left leg, brought all the centralization of his power up through his pivoting hips, streaking like a current of light into his right shoulder as it swung forward, following the motion of the hips, picking up momentum so that by the time his rigid arms extended, the first two knuckles of his hand leading, all the power was focused, licking like lightning.

He struck Antonio just behind the right ear, high up on his neck, the spot where a professional gunman will shoot his victim. He felt the violent contact only dimly, concentrating on that patch of space directly behind the pimp's head, surging his energy through skin, flesh and bone.

Thwaite, on the other side of Antonio, was startled to see the abrupt transformation of the leering freckled face. One moment it was full of hate and triumph, the next: nothing. All animation, all *life*, fled from his features, leaving him, in the moment before he crumpled to the furred floor, with the appearance of a wax doll.

Thwaite looked beyond the lifeless thing, spread-eagled at his feet, beyond his own consuming pain, at the man now standing in front of him.

'Jesus Christ,' he said softly, then closed his eyes.

June 1967
Angkor Thom, Cambodia

Sok's indoctrination into the Khmer Rouge cadre seemed long and arduous. In fact, only the latter was true. Military discipline and ideological intimidation went hand in hand and was repeated over and over twenty-four hours a day. A breakdown of the normal definitions of time and place were considered essential in re-educating the new recruits.

There was no longer any morning, afternoon or evening. The night was not for sleeping but for work. During the day, the cadre fought. First in the Samlaut rebellion at Battambang and, later, on its own in guerrilla forays against the hated enemy: the old corrupt régime. A new and free Cambodia could not wait for the human condition and so sleep was reduced to the minimum.

The disorientation did its work, of course. The new information slid into place with a minimum of effort and resistance. New recruits were formed out of the naked clay and assigned their patriotic duty in the fight for control of their country.

Fear and intimidation played their part as well, especially among the recalcitrant peasants of the countryside. The smallest offence was punishable by death. Those found siphoning gas from automobiles, for instance, were instantly executed and the disappearance within a village of certain of its members instilled a permanent kind of terror among the remainder of the inhabitants.

And always there was the hammer of the *Angka Leu* – the higher organization – to hold over the heads of all. Sok never found out precisely who or what the *Angka Leu* consisted of or even if it existed at all except in the active imaginations of the cadre leaders.

The nightmare was filled with political cant. Already Khieu Samphan was the Khmer Rouge's god. In Paris in 1959 he had written a thesis entitled, '*L'économie du Cambodge et ses problèmes d'industrialisation*'.

Essentially, it postulated that the French colonial intervention in the Cambodian economy of the 1950's introduced a form of capitalism to the rural sections of the country that undermined the indigenous crafts and thus the entire economic structure. Khmer craftsmen, who found it impossible to compete with foreign-made textiles of better quality that were cheaper to produce, turned from producing themselves to becoming merchants of foreign goods.

Thus the Cambodian economy became more and more dependent on imported goods while its own local ability to produce atrophied. Peasant indebtedness, the key, the thesis argued, for attaining self-sustained industrial growth for Cambodia, increased instead of slowly being eliminated until the country was strangling to death on its post-colonial status.

All this and more, the new recruits learned at night, until they became certain day was night. Sok was not unaffected; this was an impossibility. He was young enough to feel their energy for revolution and intelligent enough to know when they weren't lying. He accepted the fact that the viciousness of their actions was dictated by the evil times in which they were living. Had he not himself felt the weakening of the Amida Buddha's influence? Put the spirit of Buddhism in your back pocket to be brought out sometime in the future.

Except that they abhorred religion and everything it stood for. The meek pacifism of Buddhism was a crossgrain to their purposes of toughness of martial spirit and of bravery in the face of the enemy. But more, the very essence of what religion was about filled them with fear. You were to worship only the *Angka*. The *Angka* would protect you and take care of you always as the old corrupt and weak régime could not; as the Amida Buddha could not.

Yet there was another difference between Sok and the other members of the cadre. He had always in the back of his mind that tinge of knowledge that he was not Sok but Sokha. He was from the upper class, an intellectual, a member of the enemy whom they wished to exterminate as dangerous foes to the revolution. Always he was afraid of forgetting his broken abject French for the perfect form he was more used to.

And he had nightmares about Sam. Because Sam was no longer. He was now known as Cheng and, what was worse, he believed that to be his name.

'I've changed, *Own*,' he had whispered that first night when, at last, they had been alone. 'The revolution's changed me. I have a new name to go with my new purpose.' He smiled then. 'But you made me very proud of you. You passed all their tests.'

Sok had stared at him in the flickering light. He still looked the same. He reached out to touch him. He still felt the same. 'Does that mean,' he said in a small voice, 'that you're no longer my brother?'

Sam's face broke then. 'Oh, little one,' he said, embracing Sok, 'we'll *always* be brothers, no matter what.'

Through his tears, Sok tried to smile. 'It's all so hard,' he whispered almost to himself.

But Sam heard him. 'They're the ones who've brought us to the brink. Now all they want is to wipe us out like so much vermin. Do you understand? We cannot allow that. We cannot allow Cambodia to die.' He held his brother close. 'Yes, it's hard and many of us will die. Who knows, maybe even me. But I'm prepared for it. So should you, *Own*. Cambodia comes first. Its life before ours. Yes?'

Six weeks later, Sam came to him. His shadow falling long and crooked on the ground before him in the early morning light. It had rained all night but the day looked clear.

Sok was preparing to leave. He and his cadre of five were being sent north into Angkor Thom to clear out the ruins for future Khmer Rouge use. He looked up at Sam's sudden arrival. His brother's face was hard, his dark eyes filled with an odd aqueous emotion.

'I must talk to you before you leave, Comrade,' Sam said for the benefit of those others within hearing.

Sok nodded silently and they moved off to the edge of the clearing. Birds filled the morning air with song and a little way off the monkeys chattered loudly, swinging in the trees.

'What is it, *Bawng*? What's happened?'

Sam gripped his arm. 'I've just received some very bad news, Little Brother. The worst, in fact.'

'Will you please tell me?' Sok was shaking; the look in Sam's eyes was enough to turn his legs to fluid.

'There was some kind of an explosion in Chamcar Mon the day before yesterday. A blast of very high intensity. A flash of fire raged. There was nothing left but ashes.'

Fear gripped Sok's heart with an icy grip. He fought for breath. 'What are you saying!'

'*Maman*, Malis . . . everyone. They're all dead, Sok.'

'No!' Sok shivered and tried to jerk away from his brother's grip. 'It can't be!' *Maman*'s soft milky eyes, unseeing. 'It's some kind of a mistake!' Beautiful Malis. 'It must be another villa!' Dancing Malis. 'Not ours!' No one left. 'Not ours!' Little Soryia and Ratha, whom he had hardly known. *Maman*!

They held each other tightly, each knowing that the other was all that was left, each cherishing even more the long blood friendship between them; the iron bond that nothing could break.

They both cried, turned away from the encampment as if they were urinating into the new pale sunlight feathering through the thick foliage of the surrounding jungle. Sok felt the first ray, rising from the horizon, strike his cheek, flaming it with warmth. But all he could think of was the cindered bodies of his family, lying curled, hollow cylinders through which the summer wind now blew unhindered.

Now there was nothing left to do but say goodbye and wish each other well. They would meet again in a month or so when the main cadre rejoined to the east of Angkor Thom for a concerted military thrust against Lon Nol's forces.

They kept to the jungle for most of the way. But the men were proficient in local geography and they made their way unerringly. Sok never once felt that they were lost or wandering and, curiously, this began to make him feel secure within the cadre's midst.

They were under specific orders not to engage the enemy until they reached their objective. It was surmised that since the Prince felt himself to be a direct successor to the line of Khmer kings who had built Angkor Wat and Angkor Thom, he would seek to have Lon Nol's army occupy the ruins for propagandistic as well as strategic purposes. Sok's cadre had been dispatched with that in mind.

The jungle through which they passed seemed ancient, lush, fecund – primaeval, even. It set him thinking about the replicas of life in long-ago Cambodia that had been set into the walls of his family's villa in Chamcar Mon. They too must have been destroyed by the explosion and fire. But his desire to confront the real ruins remained, burning stronger inside his chest. What would he find there? What would he feel upon stepping out into that tangled clearing? He did not know but that did not stop him from anticipating the moment.

During the journey there were many times when he felt alone and infinitely sad. At those times he turned his mind towards Sam. His older brother's presence was strong within him and he realized just how much their continuing closeness in the face of this new life meant to him. What would he ever do without Sam's help and advice? This too he did not know. But it was a question he was reluctant to contemplate.

It took them perhaps four days on the route they had chosen. On that night, they camped near the ruins but out of sight of them. At dawn, Sok was told, they would go cautiously in. There was no fire that night and very little talk. But the cadre was keyed up. They had bypassed two army patrols on the way here and they were disgusted at having to turn their backs and run away. They were thirsting for a fight and no one slept much.

They were all up and prepared before day. An odd brownish light began to filter through the trees, filling their small clearing with faint illumination.

Ros, their leader, signalled directly for them to move out. Sok's heart was beating fast. They all carried old M-1 rifles, the kind used by the Americans during World War II. Ros carried a German Luger as well. He had a check scarf tied around his neck. These two symbols marked him within the Khmer Rouge, as Sihanouk had dubbed them, as an officer.

The emerald foliage parted, whispering at their approach. The morning was quite still. The cicadas droned like beaten brass at fifteen second intervals. Sok bypassed a serpent uncoiling oily in the dense underbrush.

Abruptly the quality of the jungle noises changed and Sok, looking up, saw that they had at last come upon Angkor Thom. The structures were immense. He knew, of course, their actual height and girth from books he had read when he was younger. But being confronted by the three-dimensional reality was something else again. Too, they possessed a presence that transcended mere space. They seemed to him to occupy time as well.

But most of all he was staggered by the carved stone faces in bas-relief staring down at him from the four sides of almost every structure. The same face, passive, benign, regal, knowing. Those stone eyes seemed to follow him wherever he went within the complex.

'Careful now,' he heard Ros whisper. 'Keep your safeties off and your fingers on the trigger.'

Angkor Thom was steeped in slanting sunlight, great chunks of stone gleaming whitely while their nether sides were dusky in the wash of shadows still tinged by night.

He came upon one of the originals that had inspired the contemporary sculptor to copy it for their villa walls. He stopped and stared. What did he feel?

'Over there!' Ros' shout galvanized the cadre and they ran, shouting, through the deserted ruins. Sok followed them. There was no one here, he was certain of that. At least no military presence as they had feared. In a short time he had become adept at scenting out the enemy.

Yet the cadre had captured someone. He came up on the cluster of them, saw in shock that they had captured a Buddhist priest. His orange robes and shaven head were unmistakable. His eyes regarded them impassively. His thin lips were moving slightly so that Sok had the impression he was praying.

'Lice!'

It was Ros' voice, raised again in that semi-hysterical tone that was reserved for ideological cant. As if that was a signal, the cadre reversed their weapons and began to beat the priest with the heavy butts.

He made no sound, did not even lift his arms in order to protect himself. Soon enough he was battered to his knees. The panting of the men was all that could be heard. The birds, the small creatures had all deserted this spot for the moment. The cicadas' din rose and fell like an unseen tidal wave.

Blood and bits of bone rose along the stocks of their rifles, splattered the black cotton of their rough uniforms. Now Sok could no longer see the priest, just the hem of his robe, dark and limp with his fluids.

He was sickened, wanted desperately to turn away or, better, fire his rifle into their midst, killing them as they were killing their priest. But that was too humane an end for them. Anyway, he could never get away with it. He forced himself to watch, feeling now as if he were witnessing in this one intensely vile moment the true death of his country.

At last he did turn away, to look again upon the bas-relief of life in Cambodia long ago that he remembered from home. But on seeing it, he felt nothing at all. There was no sense of continuity, of his place in history.

It was as if he gazed again upon the shining pile of lifeless insect shells and felt only the engulfment of eternity.

On an evening in Washington when the humidity was higher than the temperature, when even the indigenous population was seeking excuses not to venture out into the steambath, Kim opened his mailbox to find two pieces of junk mail, three bills, a letter from his brother, and a folded menu from a Chinese restaurant called Blue Szechuan.

He discarded the first, stuffed the bills back in the box, slipped the letter into his inside jacket pocket and stared at the menu. It looked like any other such circular that appeared from time to time in neighbourhoods in every major city across the country.

Kim took the menu upstairs to his apartment. The first thing he did was burn it, grinding the ashes to powder between his hardened fingertips. Then he went to the hall closet, got down his battered leather suitcase, dark with use and, as he began to pack, dialled Pan Am. He booked a flight to Tokyo, was informed there would be an hour's stopover at San Francisco. He said that would be fine. He finished packing and called a cab.

On the plane, he asked for tea and, when it was brought, settled back in the wide seat and withdrew the letter from Thu. He used a long nail to slit open the envelope.

Thu was all that was left of Kim's family. Mother, father, three brothers and a sister. Incinerated. Only Kim had remained unscathed. Thu's ruined legs had been paralysed as a fiery wooden beam had crashed down on them as he was trying to carry their sister to safety. The beam, one of the three heavy central bars holding up their house, had crushed her skull like an eggshell.

Kim had returned only in time to save Thu whom having been witness to all the terrible carnage, had begged his brother to be allowed to die in peace. Kim did not pay him any attention and in the hospital they had to sedate him heavily during the nights and tie his wrists to the metal framework of the bed by day in order to keep him alive.

Kim did not see Thu for several years after that; his work in the foundation made it impossible. But as soon as he had enough money saved, he had sent for his brother.

For the three months Thu had stayed with Kim, he had loathed Washington. Everything about it reminded him of the war, of home, of his burned family. Their spirits stalked his dreams, he said, like animals on scent. Finally, he told Kim that he must leave him.

He had chosen Seattle, a particularly gloomy place, where the suicide rate was the highest in the States. But since Kim was convinced his brother no longer was leaning in that direction, he had let him go.

Beautiful Thu. The ravages of war and fire had not altered his delicate features. But inside, his heart had blackened and shrivelled, as if that was where the flames had scorched him. He thought only of home . . . and the war.

Kim had made up his mind to go and talk to him when he received a letter. Thu had abruptly returned to Southeast Asia. 'I want,' he had written in his peculiar backward slanting scrawl, 'to return to the site of the holocaust. I'm not really concerned for my own welfare and, after all, who would harm a helpless cripple? I have somehow become the guardian of our past – the family's, I mean. Brother, I must find out what happened that night. Otherwise I will never rest. The enigma eats away at my soul like a disease. Can you understand that?'

Kim could, very well indeed. And, as it turned out, Thu had returned to America having discovered the incredible secret buried in the past of that night. He had come to Kim, saying, 'Brother, if I am the guardian of our family, then surely you must be the instrument of its revenge. I am the pen and you are the sword. Here is all I have been able to unearth about that terrible night.'

That had been more than a year ago and, since then, Kim had been using what free time was available to him tracking down leads. Through his inquiries, he began to make certain key connections, fighting the sickness of spirit that Thu's news had

245

brought him. He knew he had to be certain before he made a move.

So it was, then, that the foundation's own Library had offered up that proof. In the 'Ragman' file. It was all there if one had the outside information, the other facts that Thu had so painstakingly acquired.

Now, with the muted roar of the jets in his ears, Kim unfolded the flimsy sheets of airmail paper and began to read.

In San Francisco he went straight through to the Pan Am desk, handed over his ticket folder.

'I'm ticketed through to Tokyo,' he told the pretty attendant. 'I've just gotten word from my office that my plans have been changed. I need connections to Brussels.'

The attendant consulted tables, then a computer terminal. 'I can get you on a flight that leaves in three hours. I'm afraid that's the soonest —'

'No problem.' Kim smiled genially.

In Brussels, Kim did not leave the airport. Instead, he gathered his luggage, went across the ticket desk and booked a flight to Amsterdam. He made certain that the male clerk was given the impression that that city was his final destination.

In fact it was not. In Amsterdam, he caught a commuter flight to Eindhoven, an industrial city of no great beauty in the southeast corner of the Netherlands.

There he went to the public phone, dialled a seven-digit number. 'I'm here,' was all he said. Within fifteen minutes a black limousine pulled up at the kerb of the arrivals terminal. A liveried chauffeur took his bags.

Kim climbed in, settled himself into the crushed leather back seat. Kim thought idly of Blue Szechuan, the code words for his presence. It was all he had from the man with the lard-white skin. It meant he must be in Einhoven within twenty-four hours.

The summons rarely came. For one thing, Kim's work took him into places where he could not extricate himself on such short notice. For another, more often than not, the man with the white skin was dispatched to speak to Kim personally. Kim had known him for years, had no idea of his real name, had only ever called him by his code name, Tango.

Though Kim did not care much for these people, it never occurred to him that were it not for the financial burden Thu put upon him, he would not have had to supplement his foundation salary with independent work. Duty was synonymous with life.

The limousine slowed to a stop and Kim emerged onto the spotless sidewalk in front of a glass and steel building which took up the entire block. There was no company name on its face, merely the numerals of its address: 666.

Kim went through the reflecting doors, past the uniformed armed guard to the visitors' desk. There, behind a semi-circular cherry wood desk, sat a man with a ramrod back and a long waxed moustache. He nodded at Kim's approach, stood up and pinned a plastic, colour-coded card onto Kim's lapel.

The high-speed machine took Kim racing up the building. There were two cameras high up in the corners of the cubicle, one normal video tape, the other, infra-red.

A chime sounded softly and Kim stepped out onto the top floor. It was carpeted in a dove grey Berber, the walls light cherry wood, hung with paintings. Kim recognized a Vermeer, two Van Goghs and, astoundingly, a Rembrandt.

'Welcome,' Tango came forward, his hard ice blue eyes bright. 'You made good time.'

He ushered Kim down the slightly curving hall, through wood double doors, into a conference room. There were twelve men sitting around the rectangular table. Kim estimated their average age to be perhaps fifty-five or sixty. This was the Panel.

All wore conservative suits in muted brown or blues. They were businessmen all, of that there was no doubt. And although he knew none of their names, or cared to, Kim could discern a great deal about them. The scent of money was about them like a heady perfume. But it was old wealth, family fortunes built up over time, maturing slowly like fine wines, the great art of European management handed down from father to son in an unbroken skein.

These were all shrewd men, in their way, Kim knew. And

though he loathed them in the same impersonal manner with which he loathed all Westerners, he nevertheless did not make the mistake of taking them lightly.

'*Setzen sie bitte,*' Tango said, indicating a chair. '*Mögen sie ein Kaffee oder ein Schnapps trinken?*'

'Have you any tea?' Kim asked in the same language.

'Regrettably, no.'

'Nothing, thank you,' Kim said, straight-faced. Barbarians, he thought.

'Very well.' Tango took his own seat, on Kim's left. German was spoken here at all times in order to simplify matters. These men represented interests indigenous to six European nations. Had not a common language been decided upon, the resulting clamour would sound like a meeting at the tower of Babel.

Surprisingly, the man with the red-gold hair, sitting directly opposite Kim, rose. Usually, Tango did most of the speaking for the Panel.

This man had the low forehead and close-set eyes Kim automatically associated with football players. He was burly in an athletic sort of way, not fat at all. And this muscularity seemed quite at odds with the bush of wild wiry hair sprouting from his head.

'This meeting,' the man with the red-gold hair began, 'has a two-fold purpose.' His voice was guttural, thick with the glottalstops inherent in the language; Kim was certain he was a native German. 'The first is for you to clarify your last status report to Tango.' Though he was addressing Kim, he never once looked at him directly. He flipped open a black crocodile case, glanced down briefly. 'In it, you summed up the death of one of the leading American candidates for the Republican presidential nomination, one, John Holmgren. The demise of this individual, you further reported, apparently opens the way for the eventual nomination next month of Atherton Gottschalk.'

He looked penetratingly from face to face around the room. 'You have, of course, provided us with detailed and up-to-the-minute dossiers on all candidates of both parties, along with critical evaluations of their chances in the coming election.'

He paused for a moment, as if marshalling his thoughts. 'Before I go on to ask the questions that must be answered here today, allow me to digress a moment. We are, by and large, businessmen – all of us here. I say "by and large" because today in Europe we are increasingly seeing the politicization of all fields of endeavour.' He shrugged his broad shoulders. 'Perhaps, as some of us around this table feel, that was inevitable. Or perhaps – as I feel very strongly – we businessmen have been to blame for the erosion of governmental power.

'Increasingly, dissident networks – radical political splinter groups as well as all-out anarchic terrorists – have infiltrated the fabric of societal power structures in all of our countries. This information, I hardly need add, is not new to us. However, what *has* become a pressing concern to us is that several founding members of the Panel have taken, shall we say, overtly hostile countermeasures against these insidious forces quite recently.' The German's fingertips gently stroked the surface of his crocodile case. 'These men are no longer with us. One was blown up in his bathtub; the other broke through the glass windows of his top floor office and fell twenty-three floors to his death.'

The German took a deep breath. 'Within these walls you see a conglomerate worth of over three point four billion dollars, American. Still, we have taken no more action. For all our wealth, we dare not. For to do so would be to enter into a war so devastating as to, at best, cripple us permanently. This we will not risk.'

He nodded in that rather formally cool fashion only the Germans can manage, but to Tango, not to Kim. 'That is where you come in. So far, you have served us admirably. But in a strictly observer manner. Now with the death of John Holmgren, we wish a change in status. That is the purpose of this meeting. Decisions on complex issues must be reached.

'What is your personal opinion of Atherton Gottschalk? We have the dossier on him you provided us, of course. But at this juncture, we feel it prudent to hear about him from you in person.'

Kim thought for a moment. 'Gottschalk is an absolute bar of iron. Before Holmgren died I would've thought the Governor had a slightly better shot at the nomination, primarily because he was better funded. However, given the current international climate, I must rate his chances very highly now. And all of a sudden there's been a great deal of fat-frying on his behalf.'

'Pardon?' the German said. 'Fat-frying?'

'An American political slang term,' Kim said, happy at his superior knowledge. 'A lot of fund-raisers for Gottschalk are sprouting up and the money's coming in for his campaign. I'd have to say the nomination'll be his.'

'And the Democrats?' Tango spoke.

Kim shrugged. 'There're a number of able men, looked at objectively. But ever since Kennedy beat Nixon on TV during the debates, nothing in American politics has been objective. All the front-running Democrats suffer from image problems.'

'Do I understand you to say that should Atherton Gottschalk in fact achieve the Republican nomination, he will be elected President of the United States?' Tango said expectantly.

Kim could almost see him salivating at the prospect. Their telegraphing of intent lost them a great deal of face in his eyes. They certainly deserved the trough at which they ate their daily slop, he thought, this industrial maze of Eindhoven. 'That is the gist of it.'

'And Gottschalk,' the German said. 'Is he really as hard-line as your dossier on him indicates?'

'Absolutely. You've heard what he's said.'

The German nodded. 'But does he have the balls to act on his words. Has he the courage of –' He caught himself.

'A *German*?' Kim said, sardonically.

The colour on the man's face began to match his red-gold hair. 'I meant to say "Has he the courage of a Caesar?"'

'He's not a bag of wind,' Kim said disgustedly. He'd already had enough of these wild animals. Even their smell was getting to him now.

The German gave a curt nod. 'In that event, we come to the second part of this meeting. We wish direct intervention in the theatre to which we have assigned you.'

Kim sat up. 'Meaning what, precisely?'

'We are not politicians, *per se*. However we *are* students of history, for, we have gleaned, all important lessons may be learned there. And history, my dear sir, tells us that we have never fully understood the nature of the American mind. That, if I may sum up such a complex undertaking as the Panel, is the reason for our existence. We thought we knew the Americans when Reagan was running for President. We welcomed his election with open arms. More fools we.

'Now you have provided us with insight before the fact. Thus do we make our future decisions. We cannot handle these fanatic networks ourselves and – left to their own devices – they will eventually swallow us whole.

'Let the new President of the United States, Atherton Gottschalk, deal with these dissident elements for us. Anti-terrorism is his forte. That is well known, even so far away from America as Eindhoven. And to ensure his aid, we will provide him with what we have most to give: money.'

The German spread his sausage fingers on the table; he was hunched over a little with the force of his emotions. 'It will be fed into these – how do you call it? – fat-frying sessions. He is not to know now. But on the eve of his nomination, it must be made clear to him that the, er, European source of this spur to his successful campaign requires a *quid pro quo*.'

Behind his blank façade, Kim contemplated what they were asking him to do. Anti-terrorism was Gottschalk's meat and potatoes. Wouldn't he welcome the opportunity to put into action his word policies? And there was certainly enough money leverage in this room to make it worth Gottschalk's while.

Kim nodded his head slightly. 'I believe with a bit of subtle handling, it can be worked out to your satisfaction.' He paused a moment as if considering. 'Of course I needn't point out that this is a delicate matter. An approach for the situation you have just outlined to me will take some time to formulate. I can guarantee that if it is not accomplished in just the right way, you'll lose him.' Of course, Kim thought to himself, they'll lose him anyway. With the clues I've provided him, Tracy will surely bring Macomber down and, with him, America's newly emerging military superiority that Gottschalk has to be counting on once he gets into office.

'Besides time,' he continued, 'I fear that extra expenses will be incurred.' He spread his hands. 'But that, surely, cannot be counted as a deterrent of any consequence.'

The German was staring at Tango again. 'We are interested only in results, not in expenditures. I take it you want money now.' He nodded. 'That is permissible. We will require you to monitor Gottschalk every step of the way.'

'Fine,' Kim said. 'Now if that's all.'

The German waited until Kim was almost to the door, his timing again perfect. 'Just one more item.' His voice, though not loud, nevertheless cut through the room like a knifeblade. 'In your last report to Tango you mentioned a man, Tracy Richter, I believe his name was, whom you were employing to do much of the legwork for your research for us.'

'That's correct,' Kim said warily. 'What of it?'

The German's blue eyes sparked with fire and a barely-suppressed delight. 'In view of our expansion of scope; our, shall we say, more direct involvement in this matter, it behoves us to eliminate all middlemen rather than turning to hindsight at some later date and asking ourselves why we left an avenue open back to us.'

'What, precisely, are you saying?'

The German stared hard at Tango. 'Simply this. If his usefulness is at an end, dispose of him now. If not, the moment it is, do it. Then you will have earned the full measure of your new fee.'

When the elevator's doors closed, Kim put his head back against the textured wall and breathed deeply and evenly. His eyes were closed but his mind was at work. He thought about Tracy, thought about how important that one man was to him. He was a goddamned genius at penetrating hostile cells, Kim thought. I don't believe that kind of talent can dissipate over the years.

And that was why Kim was running Tracy, why he could not kill him as the Panel had ordered. It was all quite personal. A concept that the barbarians back in the meeting room could never appreciate let alone tolerate. He glanced at his watch. Just about now, Tracy should be getting a full dose of what those death photos of John Holmgren had to offer. Kim had given him a whiff of his quarry and he'd be off like a shot.

Kim thought about Tracy in an entirely different frame of reference. Tracy had been the only person alive to have seen Kim weak and vulnerable. At that moment, deep within the jungles of Cambodia, their relationship had changed for all time. Being witness to Kim's shame, Tracy had become an impossible amalgam in Kim's mind: he was now mortal enemy to whom Kim owed an awesome debt. That was not a thought he could easily live with.

And though his hatred of Tracy Richter glowed like a living thing, Kim knew something else, deep in the very secret heart of him: In all the world he had no friend to whom he could turn for understanding. Save Tracy Richter.

'It was a matter of pride,' he said, lifting his whisky. 'I admit it. Now that 'Tonio's dead, I can see it.'

Privately, Tracy thought Thwaite should have seen it coming. But what he said was, 'We're all afflicted with it. Pride's a very human trait. Without it, we'd all be drones, no man better or worse than another. None of us are totally selfless creatures.'

Thwaite looked at him carefully. The whisky was returning some of the natural colour to his face. Still, it seemed older to Tracy, networks of lines like new scars in the soil of his face, eyes shadowed, darkened around their perimeters by the physical and emotional pain of recent events. 'Yeah, well, we may all be human but you did ... Jesus, something more back there.' He lifted his glass again, drank slowly. 'It keeps going through my head.'

His hands were steady now, though they had trembled somewhat in the hospital. Tracy had called 911 and the cops had come, sirens screaming, guns drawn and flashing. An ambulance for Thwaite, questions for Tracy. They were cursory; no one cared about an animal like Antonio. Whoever wasted him had done society a favour. So the uniforms said.

Thwaite's wound was far less serious than it had at first appeared. There was a lot of blood but really it was superficial.

'His ribs got in the way,' the young Pakistani doctor had said in his singsong voice.

'I think I had you figured all wrong,' Thwaite said. They were on their third drink and his voice was slightly slurred. He had wanted to get out of Bay Ridge and, since it was already late, had suggested they go into Chinatown, where the restaurants and bars are open late into the night.

Tracy took them to a place he knew well on Pell Street, three steps down from street level. It was always dark and cool inside, even at noon on the hottest July day, the only recognizable colour the almost ubiquitous Chinese red lacquer which gleamed and glinted like jade.

They sat at a table far back in the corner. Earlier, there had been quite a few teenagers from New Jersey in, joking and eating up a storm. Now, however, it had cleared out sufficiently for some of the kitchen staff to sit around the one enormous round table, drinking Johnny Walker Red in water glasses, eating whole poached bass with seaweed, flash fried giant prawns, their tiny black marble eyes still on them. The men screamed at each other good-naturedly, gesturing with jabs of their oily chopsticks.

'I thought you were some candy-ass bastard,' Thwaite was saying, 'who had it in for me.' He shook his head as he drank. 'Christ, I hated your guts.' He put the empty glass down, ordered a refill. One of the men from the round table got up to do his bidding. 'And it was all wasted energy.' Tears were in his eyes and he was ashamed, putting his thick hand up as if rubbing at his face.

'Jesus, I can't believe they're gone.' His voice, when he spoke again, was unnaturally high and strained, as if his vocal cords were constricted. 'Just like that' – he snapped his fingers – 'in the blink of an eye.' He took his hand away and Tracy could see that his eyes were reddened. 'I didn't even have a chance to . . . say anything to them, to tell them . . .' He turned away. His chest heaved and for a moment Tracy thought he was going to be sick.

'My own father's dying,' Tracy said. 'I know it; he knows it. There's plenty of time, you see, for us . . . too much time, I sometimes think.' Thwaite was still turned half-away from him, contemplating the nothingness of middle distance. The waiter came with his drink. He did not touch it. 'There's an awful feeling of impotence at a time like this. There's nothing you can do but stand aside and watch it happen.'

Thwaite was shaking his head. 'You don't understand.' The tears were rolling again and this time he made no effort to hide them. 'I was such a rotten husband. Doris loved me. There was no one else for her. And me . . .' He left it hanging in the air but there was no mistaking his meaning. He put his head down, ran his splayed fingers through his damp hair. 'I don't know what I'm going to do now.' He meant the guilt, that was clear, and Tracy felt an odd kind of kinship with this hulking, rage-filled man.

'We all have demons to wrestle,' he said softly. 'It might help if you talk about it.'

Thwaite's head jerked up as if it had been on a leash. His eyes flashed. 'Don't you play shrink with me,' he barked, then blinked and sighed. 'Christ, I don't know what I'm saying anymore.'

Tracy pushed his full glass towards him. 'Here,' he said. 'Take a drink.'

Thwaite did as Tracy bade him, nodded. 'Maybe you're right.' His eyes closed. 'There's this twist . . . a hooker.' His eyes snapped open and he looked Tracy fully in the face. 'A special one.' He waited.

'Go on,' Tracy said without inflection.

But the moment had passed. Thwaite waved a hand. 'Ah, she's just what I said, nothing more. A twist.'

'But you kept going back to her.'

'Yeah, sure. I could . . . do things to her I couldn't with my . . . with Doris.'

'So you cheated on your wife.'

'It was more than that, don't you see?' The whisky was doing its work, deadening his pain, both physical and mental. 'I was leading a double life. I see it now. It took this . . . kind of thing for me to see it. I never even said goodbye this morning.' His face was anguished, his hands trembling again with suppressed emotion.

'Years ago,' Tracy said, lifting a hand to order another round, 'I was in the service, never mind which branch. I was assigned to Southeast Asia and I went. It was during the Vietnam War.

'I had six men under me. One of them was this tall skinny kid. Kind of inept, you know the kind.' He waited for a response from Thwaite and when he got it, went on. 'We were getting all kinds of kids at that time, most of them hastily trained; there was no time, really. They just threw these poor bastards into the front line and expected us to win battles.'

'Mostly blacks and PR's, right?'

Tracy nodded. 'Mostly. But this one guy – Bobby – he was white. He was one of the most gung-ho guys I'd ever met. He looked to me as if he had something to prove.

'Anyway, he fought like a demon and was a quick learner. I began to teach him what he had to know. Only the one bit of advice he wouldn't take from me was don't get close to anyone in a war. He had a mate in our outfit, a real sociopath, a guy with button eyes and a serious penchant for killing. The man had no friends but Bobby. What they saw in one another, I'll never know.'

The drinks came and Tracy waited until the waiter went back to his top-of-the-lungs conversation.

Tracy saw the interest in Thwaite's face. He had turned back to face Tracy and was partially hunched over the table. For the moment at least he had forgotten his own sorrows and that was all Tracy wanted.

'One time we pulled a night patrol, Bobby's friend, the sociopath, had point – that's the way I wanted it. He was like a goddamned bloodhound, sniffing out the VC.' Tracy took a drink. 'But this night, he wasn't so lucky. He stepped into a VC booby-trap and got blown into six different parts.

'Bobby was in shock. I had told him but he hadn't listened. He was a boy who thrived on people. What he was doing in the war, I couldn't say. I knew he hadn't been drafted but had signed up, requesting an assignment in Southeast Asia.

'If only the service'd done the normal thing and snafued – sent him to a nice safe base in Iowa.' Tracy finished his whisky.

'The next morning we had another patrol. We moved out . . .

all of us except Bobby, that is. He refused to leave his friend. We had an important assignment and I was already one man short. I got angry. I screamed at him, slapped him in front of the men, humiliated him into going.' Now it was Tracy's turn to stare fixedly into the middle distance. He was remembering the heat and humidity of the jungle, the call of the birds, the crawling of the outsized insects, the itching of the skin, the sweat and discomfort. And the stink. Death was everywhere like a shroud, hanging tangible in the leaden air.

'And,' Thwaite prompted. 'What happened?'

Now Tracy wondered what his reason was for telling Thwaite. Was it only to take his mind off of what had just happened to him or had he, Tracy, a more selfish reason in mind?

'But I was still so angry with him, I assigned him to point. I never should've done that; he wasn't good at it.'

'What happened?' Thwaite repeated.

'He never came back,' Tracy said dully. 'He hadn't wanted to go; he wasn't careful. I should have anticipated that. I found him, eventually, in the smouldering remnants of a Khmer Rouge camp. They'd beaten him slowly, burned his testicles and penis, rammed crude stakes through him. It was a holy mess. They'd taken their time with him; it was obvious from the expression frozen on his face. And to this day, that's the only way I can remember him, with eyes staring beyond hell.'

'So that was that,' Thwaite said.

'Not quite.' Tracy made wet circles on the Formica with the bottom of his glass. Around and around. 'I went after the bastards.'

'And you found them? Christ, I don't believe it.'

'Him,' Tracy said slowly, 'or someone like him. Anyway, it was important to believe it was one of them.'

'And you killed him.'

'Yes,' Tracy said. 'Eventually.' Around went the empty glass. 'I fashioned a bamboo pole about eight feet in length. On one end was a noose I put around the VC's neck; I held the other. We took him with us and now he was our point. We'd run afoul of no more booby-traps that day.

'I had gagged him but he was able to communicate to us where the lethal points on the trail were. He led us around each of them in turn, terrified that at any moment he would be blown up, spiked or impaled.' Tracy shoved the glass across the table in a violent motion.

The high volume jabber at the Chinese table dissolved into silence. They stared at the two men for the first time as if they were outsiders. Then the conversation blossomed anew as if it had never ceased. A Chinese girl came and demurely cleaned up the shards of broken glass.

'At the end of the mission,' Tracy said, 'I made certain that his fears were not in vain. We took the same trail back; I knew where all the pitfalls were. He had outlived his usefulness. I terminated him.'

Thwaite eyed Tracy carefully. He recognized the pain there. 'I thought,' he said after a time, 'that you had told the kid – Bobby, wasn't it? – not to make friends.' He downed the last of his drink. 'Sounds to me like he really got under your skin. So, how come you didn't take your own advice?'

When Kathleen Christian pushed through the Parker-Meridian doors onto Fifty-sixth Street, she found it not nearly as humid as she was used to in Washington and therefore quite pleasant.

She was wearing a pair of silvery-grey trousers, tied at the ankle, made out of parachute silk, and a teal blue cotton sweater. Lizard-skin high-heeled pumps in the same shade as her sweater and a string of black pearls completed her outfit. She felt strong and confident; ready for what she knew lay ahead. It was going to be, as she was fond of saying, a perilous day. But then Kathleen thrived on perilous days; without them, she would wither and die. She often thought that all human beings were junkies of one sort or another. Her shot was power and so much the better for her.

Kathleen turned left, walked the half block to Sixth Avenue. There she flagged down a cab. 'Third Avenue and Twentieth.'

She rolled down the window, sat back, watching the city drift by. She had grown up here but, curiously, felt no attachment. This was supposed to be the hub of commerce and perhaps that was true. But commerce held no appeal for her. Washington was where the real power was. It was where the country was run from and for her it was like no other city on earth. Paris was the place to vacation; Washington was the place to live.

Fuck you, New York! She hurled her silent insult out the open window in the face of the warm oxygen-poor breeze. Kathleen knew in her soul how deeply Atherton Gottschalk was tied to her. But still she did not want him to desire more. She alone must suffice. He must be made to see that quite clearly and that meant – because men were such obtuse, limited creatures – on his own terms.

The moment she had identified the voice of Eliott on the other end of the line, Kathleen knew what she must do in order to secure her hold on Gottschalk for all time.

And now here she was, in downtown Manhattan, sliding out of a Yellow Cab on grungy Third Avenue. She looked west, saw the perfect jewel of the small park, enclosed by the black iron fence with its sign that read: FOR RESIDENTS' USE ONLY. That was Gramercy Park . . . and Delmar Davis Macomber's house.

It was a four-storey limestone and brick structure. The second or parlour floor window, which ran the width of the building, extended out from the face, supported by four pillars two storeys in height. It was filled with tiny leaded glass squares and surmounted by a semicircular stained glass panel of ruby, emerald and a yellow-orange.

The entire structure was set well back into the block, enclosed by a rather forbidding-looking iron gate. Inside was the wide stone stairway up to the front door, a magnificent slab of honey oak, carved in an interlocking succession of squares.

To one side, an old fashioned lamppost with a horned, glassed top stood. She saw that at night a real gas flame would burn there, fluting and purling light and shadow.

Macomber! Could he really be Gottschalk's fat cat? Kathleen, an astute acolyte of power, knew him well, had followed the rapid rise of Metronics, Inc., and knew that as far as the public was concerned, he was unaligned with any political candidate. If there was any kind of fat frying here it was being kept an absolute secret. That in itself might not be so surprising. There were many millionaire businessmen who preferred to keep their political fat frying behind strictly closed doors. But Kathleen had also heard about the bad blood between the two over Macomber's current wife. She was rapidly becoming fascinated by this puzzle.

She bought a *New York Times* on the corner of Third and began to walk, as if drawn by a powerful magnet, west along Twentieth, slowly, feeling the emanations of power and money sizzle the air about her. But perhaps, she thought, it's only my Machiavellian mind at work and the connection's merely with the junior Macomber. But, again, why? What did Eliott Macomber possess that Gottschalk needed? For she knew well that that would be the only reason Atherton would have any dealings with the young man at all.

Carefully, she chose a doorway at a ninety-degree angle to the front of the Macomber house, and, in its oblique shadows settled down to wait. The more she thought about it, the more Eliott and Gottschalk made no sense. She felt her pulse beating a tiny pattern at the base of her throat as she contemplated again the awesome power of a Gottschalk-Macomber combination. She sighed deeply.

A woman with a pram strolled by, bending forward to arrange the light plaid blanket across her baby's breast; an old man with a doberman lifting its leg to urinate against the mottled trunk of a plane tree; a young man whistling out of key an old Beatles song she recognized.

'Strawberry Fields Forever', she mouthed and glanced down at the front page of the paper. *A powerful explosion*, she read, *ripped through the European Headquarters of the United States Air Force in Ramstein, West Germany today, injuring 30 people including a ranking American general.* Christ, she thought, looking up and checking the entrance of the house. She did that every twenty seconds as she continued to read. She turned to page three. There were two sidebars. One described the State Department's reaction which was basically, *There is no cause for alarm.* Though Ramstein was the largest American air base in Europe, home of the 86th Tactical Fighter Wing and the headquarters of the North Atlantic Treaty Organization air command for central

Europe, the official line out of Washington was that nothing sinister could be read into the attack – if in fact it was an attack. 'Terrorist organizations abound in Western Europe,' a State Department official was quoted as saying. 'If we took them all seriously, we would get nothing else accomplished.'

The second sidebar was a news analysis by a *Times* foreign correspondent, linking the bombing with the ones several weeks back in Peru and with the more recent attack on Lieutenant Colonel DeWitt in Cairo. In its own subtle way, the *Times* was asking, Is America under attack?

It was Kathleen's twelfth check and this time she got a positive. A shadow sliced away from the front of Macomber's building. A young man emerged and for an instant Kathleen thought it was Eliott. She began to move, then froze.

The figure could not be Eliott Macomber, she saw now. He was Oriental, a beautiful young man with a wide sharp-edged face she was certain was not Chinese or Japanese. In the course of her job at Brady & Mheerson she came in contact with a great number of Asians and it was imperative that she be able to distinguish one nationality from another.

Not Burmese surely, she thought. His skin wasn't nearly as dark. No. All things considered, he must be Khmer. He had the dusky skin and a perfectly beautiful face, masculine in a subtle, sculpturally sensual manner – all smoothly flowing lines, rather than the hard chiselled look of a Westerner – she found most apparent in Cambodians.

Seeing him, even from such a distance as this, brought saliva to her mouth. Business before pleasure, she reminded herself. Nevertheless, she watched his straight back as he turned away from her, walking west towards Broadway. Those broad shoulders, the rolling hips and sinewy thighs and – glimpsed for just an instant – those depthless, serene eyes.

Because of him, she almost missed Eliott. He was by no means ugly or even plain-looking. But he suffered greatly by comparison to the Cambodian. He lacked any sign of the magnetism that his father possessed. He held the rebel's rather uncomfortable pose, dressed in faded jeans and a checked short-sleeve shirt with a narrow silk knit tie.

She sighed and thought, why couldn't it have been the Cambodian? But it wasn't. Kathleen was a realist and she knew that Eliott was the one.

She came down the steps, moving off after him as he, too, went west. She stayed a half block behind him and stuck to the opposite side of the street. She watched him by keeping track of his reflection in storefront windows she passed.

She had done just this kind of thing for Bill Brady, the other senior partner of the law firm, many times. Of course, the firm hired a private investigator from time to time but as Brady was fond of telling her, there were times in the life of any specialized organization when going outside the family was not the intelligent course to take. Under the guise of a vacation, he had packed her off to one of the best surveillance schools in the country, just outside Great Falls, Virginia where she had learned all the basics in just under two weeks. She had graduated with the second highest marks in her class.

Eliott took her crosstown, moving with short determined strides. Kathleen had no doubt he had a definite destination in mind. At Seventh Avenue, he turned south, crossing Fourteenth Street into the West Village. A few blocks later, he pushed through the glass door of a bar-restaurant.

Kathleen counted to fifty slowly, then crossed the street against the lights, went in. There were perhaps a half dozen tables in the sidewalk cafe. Through a centre doorway she could see the beginning sweep of the wooden bartop, gleaming with oil. There were few patrons and it was not difficult to pick Eliott out.

He sat with his back to her at an oak booth. Facing him was a blonde girl. Kathleen thought she could be no more than nineteen or twenty. Her hair was short, spiky with a touch of peacock blue to it like a patch of mould along one side. She was wearing black skin-tight pants and a sleeveless tanktop in an exaggerated leopard-skin pattern. Her skin was very white.

Kathleen slipped onto a stool at the bar, ordered a Bloody Mary. The girl was talking heatedly though not angrily. Eliott was calm, deliberate. Kathleen strained but she could not make out any of the words.

She was just deciding what action to take when the conversation at the far booth erupted. The leopard-skin girl snarled and Kathleen came off her stool.

The girl slapped Eliott while Kathleen was halfway towards them. She was looking away from the brawl while keeping the figures in the periphery of her vision.

Snarling again, the girl leaped up, spilling her drink across the table-top. Now Eliott was on his feet, too. He pushed her and she lurched badly, losing her balance. She dived headfirst into Kathleen who, prepared for just such an event, made a show of staggering backwards under the assault. She righted the girl who swung her animal head around, hissed at Kathleen, baring yellow teeth, stalked out of the restaurant.

Kathleen stood very still, staring at Eliott and watching for it all to happen.

'I'm terribly sorry,' he said, concern on his face. 'Are you all right?'

'The question is,' Kathleen said, 'are you?'

She had made him smile; it was an expression she immediately liked. His face was transformed by it and him with it.

'We have this kind of thing all the time.'

'Do you?' she said. 'That must be fun.' She went past him and into the ladies' room. There wasn't anything for her to do there but read the graffiti. *He breaks hearts along the boulevards*, she read. And just below it: *Yeah? What's his number?*

She looked at herself in the smeared mirror and walked out. Eliott stopped her on the way back.

'I don't suppose you'd have a drink with me,' he said.

'Can you give me a good reason why I should?'

'I'd like you to.'

'Well, at least you're honest.' She smiled. 'All right. I imagine you owe me a drink anyway.' She signalled to the bartender who brought over her Bloody Mary.

'Tell me about your lady friend.'

'Oh. Polly –' He laughed – 'she's more interesting to look at than to talk to.'

Kathleen looked at him levelly. 'Then why do you see her? You don't look to me as if you're an underachiever.'

Eliott, who had never in his life been talked to in this way by a woman, was momentarily tongue-tied. 'She was just a joke, that's all.' He looked up hopefully, extended an awkward hand. 'I'm Eliott Macomber.'

She saw his sharp eyes watching her face carefully for the hint of a reaction. It's a test, she thought. He needs to be appreciated just for himself, not for his father's wealth and influence.

She allowed his fingers to enfold hers. 'Kathleen Christian,' she said, her face perfectly composed; it had registered no sign of recognition of the name. 'Now how about taking me to lunch?'

Tracy had taken Thwaite back to his apartment on East Thirtieth Street because there was nowhere else for the detective to go.

'Maybe you want to drop in on Melody,' Tracy had said as they were leaving the restaurant.

'Not a chance.' Thwaite winced a little at the pain. 'I don't want her to see me like this. She's liable to think something happened to me and it'll bring out all her maternal instincts.'

Tracy looked at him. 'Maybe that wouldn't be such a bad idea. You said she was special.'

Thwaite snorted. 'So I lied.' The words came out hard and bitter. He looked away from Tracy, across Third Avenue to the almost Germanic façade of the Manhattan Bridge. 'I suppose it's too late to call White. I want a look at those photos.'

'So do I,' Tracy had said. 'But right now both of us could do with some sleep. It'll keep until morning.'

'Sure it will,' Thwaite had said. He was weaving slightly on the high kerb facing and Tracy had had to take hold of his elbow to stop him from crossing against the light. 'Ah, who'm I kidding?' He was talking to no one in particular, in the manner of many drunks. 'Sure, I'd like to go there.' His head swung around and his eyes tried to focus. 'Her kisser's prettier'n yours. She's cuter, too.' He tried to pull himself together. He sniffed loudly. 'You're a lotta things, Tracy, but you ain't cute.'

Now, the morning after, he arose slowly from the sheeted sofa, groaning a little. Tracy was already in the kitchen. He came into he living room, saw Thwaite with his fingers laced, hands clamped between his knees. He was staring at the carpet, at nothing.

Tracy set a steaming mug in front of him. It sat on the glass coffee table, untouched. Lauren was already out of the apartment. She had early classes all this week and, as Tracy looked around, he realized just how empty the place felt without her. It gave him a slight shiver: the knowledge that he was coming to depend on another person's comfort and presence so strongly.

'C'mon,' he said softly to Thwaite. 'Drink up.'

'Uh.' The other did not move. 'Not thirsty.'

'Got breakfast cooking.'

'So that's the stink I'm smelling. Not hungry, either.'

Tracy looked down at him. 'Just hung over.'

Thwaite couldn't manage a reply. Tracy sipped at his coffee, feeling the heat centring him. Finally Thwaite looked up. His eyes were red-rimmed. 'And what about you?' he managed to croak. 'You drank as much as I did. Maybe more. You should be crawling on your belly like the rest of us. What makes you different?'

Tracy smiled. 'I've got a constitution of iron.' He bent down, offered Thwaite the mug from the table. 'C'mon. I need you wide awake and alert. We've got to pay a call on Ivory White. The photos, remember?'

Thwaite nodded and winced. 'Ow, that was a mistake.' He rubbed his palms across his face, trying to peel away the grimy layer of lassitude the liquor had left him with. 'Yeah, I remember. Only suddenly it don't seem all that important. Not after last night. I –' He hid his face in his hands. 'Oh, God, it's some kind of a nightmare. Tell me it's a nightmare.'

There was silence in the room. Tracy went away into the kitchen, silently ate his breakfast without tasting any of it. For that moment, there was nothing he could do . . . nothing anyone could do save perhaps Melody. But Thwaite had to find his own way in this.

When he was finished, he returned to the living room. Thwaite was sitting up rather more normally. The mug of coffee was between his hands.

'Should I heat that up?'

'No. It's okay as it is.' He lifted his head and Tracy saw a ghost of a smile there. 'You know cops. Get used to drinking anything. If it hasn't got mould growing on the sides of the cup, I can't recognize it.'

'Listen,' Tracy said, 'why don't I go pick up the stuff from White? You stay here and get cleaned up. There're a couple fried eggs in the pan, if you can get them down.'

'That might not be such a bad idea.' Thwaite fumbled in his shirt pocket. 'Got his phone number here, somewhere. Call him and get his address. He'll likely be home; he's got the graveyard shift again.'

Patrolman Ivy 'Everybody calls me Ivory' White lived just across the Fifty-ninth Street Bridge in Sunnyside. He and his slender wife and a squalling infant lived in a one-bedroom garden apartment just south of Forty-seventh Avenue.

'Jesus,' he said as he let Tracy in, 'I didn't know what to think when I got to Thwaite's house. I put in a call to 911 and the Fire Department, then I split.' He shrugged apologetically. 'I mean I didn't have any idea . . .' He peered into Tracy's face. 'Thwaite all right, isn't he?'

'He'll be okay.'

'And his family?'

'They weren't so lucky.' Tracy watched White's wife as she held the bawling infant. She was staring at him wide-eyed. He'd seen that kind of fear before. Now it made him uncomfortable; this man was an accessory to what they were doing. He didn't care for that much.

'Oh, Christ.' White crossed himself.

'Honey, what is it?' The woman's voice was thin and piping with her anxiety.

'Uh, nuthin', babe.' He turned towards her. 'Why don't you take Michael back to the vaporizer? He's coughing his brains out.' He turned back to Tracy. 'The kid's got the croup. Neither of us's had a good night's sleep in a week.' Abruptly he was at a loss for words. He went and got a manila envelope, handed it over.

'Goddamned terrible shame about Thwaite's family. He's

okay, for a white man.' He smiled and Tracy saw his splay teeth.

'Mr Richter – '

'Tracy.'

White nodded. 'Tracy. I got three to think of, now that Michael's here and I gotta get my advancement any way I can. If that means helping Thwaite out, I said to myself, I gotta do it. Jenny, she doesn't understand it. She thinks if you're good at what you do, you get advanced no matter what.

'Maybe that's the way it should be . . . that's the way it is, with white policemen.' He paused for a moment. 'I just hope . . . well, I hope this tragedy, ain't gonna change Thwaite's plans none.'

Tracy smiled. 'We both appreciate what you've done, Ivory. I don't know your deal with Thwaite but I know he'll honour it.' He shook the other's hand. 'Don't worry, okay?'

'Do my best.'

The detective seemed much improved on Tracy's return. He had showered, and shaved and he seemed pink-cheeked. The bright spark had returned to his eyes.

'Listen,' he said the moment Tracy walked through the door, 'I gotta apologize for weeping all over your carpet before.'

'Forget it, Douglas. We're all human.'

Thwaite shot him a peculiar look. ''Cept you, maybe. I been thinking about what you did last night. I don't know why. Maybe to take my mind off of . . . what I gotta do today. Doris's family . . .' He looked away, towards the dusty light of morning filtering through the Levolors. 'They never liked me much, anyway. It's gonna be very hard, man. Very fucking hard.'

He shrugged, turned back. 'Anyway, I've got this mental picture of you . . . what you did last night to 'Tonio. How the hell did you do it?'

'I don't think it can be explained,' Tracy said. 'It's got to be learned.'

'That guy at the *dojo* teach you that?'

Tracy smiled softly. 'No. Higure's my *sensei* now. The man who trained me is dead.' A faraway look came into his eyes. 'He died three years ago on a beautiful farm in Virginia surrounded

267

by rolling, wooded hills, thoroughbred horses and a brace of golden retrievers. All the things he loved.'

'We should all be so lucky,' Thwaite said bitterly. He began to open the envelope. 'You know, while you were talking about it I got the strangest feeling you wanted to go back there.'

'Where?' A sudden cold knot had formed in the pit of Tracy's stomach.

'You know. That farm in Virginia.'

'No,' Tracy said firmly, 'I don't ever want to go back.' But he wondered whether he was lying to Thwaite and to himself. There was an undeniable magnetism about that place: the rolling meadows and pastures, the buzzing woodland, shivering its leaves with the change of the winds, and far off, against the horizon, the hazy blue guardians, the Shenandoahs, marching southward to become the Blue Ridge and, finally, in Tennessee, the vast Smokies. The Mines.

There was never a time when he didn't sweat there, even in bed at night, thinking of the next day's lessons Jinsoku would take him through. Yet there was an odd kind of longing for those days, a particular ache in the heart you feel for your first love. He shook himself.

Thwaite had slid the photos out. 'Let's take a look at these.'

They spread them out on the coffee table, side by side, like playing cards, four black-and-white 8 × 10's. Four faces of death.

The first two showed John Holmgren as Tracy and Moira had left him: on the sofa, one leg draped to the floor, his clothes rumpled and heavily creased. The first was an overall shot, establishing the corpse along with the immediate surroundings. The second took in only the top half of the body, which meant details were more apparent.

Tracy studied the countenance of his dead friend. The expression already seemed unreal, as if he were looking at an artist's rendering of real life. There was nothing for them there. They moved on.

The third shot was a close-up of the lower half of the body and seemed to reveal nothing more than the first two had offered.

'These look pretty standard to me,' Thwaite said. 'This last one just shows him on his stomach.' He belched lightly. 'I think I roped White in for nothing.'

Tracy had picked up the fourth photo. It focused on the upper two-thirds of the corpse. He peered at it intensely while Thwaite got up, began to look around the room.

'You got a magnifying glass or something?'

'In the drawer of the sideboard,' Tracy said, not taking his eyes from the photo.

Thwaite came back and Tracy handed the thing over. Thwaite hunched over, closed one eye as he ran the glass across the top part of the print. He shook his head. 'Don't see nothin'. If this guy was iced I don't know how the hell it was done.' He put the glass down on the table, handed the shot back to Tracy. 'I had a long shot. Thought maybe Holmgren had bought it with a narrow cord – you know, like a piano wire. But there's nothing like that around his neck.'

'You think the ME wouldn't've –' Tracy turned his head. 'Wait a minute. You could see the flesh of his neck?'

Thwaite nodded. 'Yeah, sure. Why?'

His heart racing, Tracy reached for the glass, looked carefully through it. He scrutinized the photo, a centimetre at a time.

Thwaite moved closer on the sofa. 'You find something?'

'Maybe.' Tracy did not look up.

There was silence until Thwaite's irritated voice broke it. 'Well, you gonna let me in on it or what?'

Tracy finally looked up, handed over what he had been holding.

'What'm I looking for?'

Tracy sat back on the sofa and closed his eyes. 'The flesh at the back of John's neck. Just between the two vertical tendons. At the centre of the base.'

Thwaite did as he as he was told. He saw the edge of the Governor's shirt collar and just above it and somewhat darker since Holmgren had been wearing a white shirt, the bare flesh. He missed it the first time and had to refocus. 'It looks like a black spot. Could be anything: a bruise or a speck of dust on the negative even.'

'Or,' Tracy said slowly, 'it could be a puncture wound.'

The detective's head came up. 'Now how in hell could you tell that from a print like this?'

'I said I wasn't certain.' Tracy took a deep breath. 'I'm not. But I've got a feeling.'

Thwaite was about to open his mouth to urge the other on, decided against it. He knew when to shut up.

Because he needed to do something, Thwaite got up and turned on the air conditioner. Peering through the blinds, he saw the street filled with people in shirtsleeves, some with their jackets draped lankly over their shoulders. It was already a bitch of a summer's day. He turned back at the sound of Tracy's voice.

'The first time I saw it done was in Ban Me Thuot. A North Vietnamese. All it took was two fingers, a short needle between them. Kim had brought him in for articulated interrogation –'

'What the hell is that?'

'Articulated interrogation,' he repeated. His eyes were glassy, turned inward. 'It's like all such words: a euphemism. What it really is is five stages of implemented torture.'

Thwaite gave out a nervous guffaw. 'Just like in the movies, right? The Dragon Lady's about to take the burning bamboo shoots to the hero's fingertips.'

There was no smile on Tracy's face. 'In real life, Douglas, there *are* no heroes. This's guaranteed to break *anyone* down. You don't survive it. Not the way we learned it.'

'Jesus.' Thwaite shook out a Camel, lit it. Somehow the pull of the rich smoke into his lungs reassured him.

'Precisely. It all depends on the principal.'

His eyes focused and he looked at Thwaite. 'The articulation stages remain the same regardless; it's the principal – the subject – who determines the area.' He was speaking more quickly now. 'For instance, some people can't stand the pain of having their teeth drilled, for others it's the pain of a knife gouge.

'It's called pain anxiety and it has nothing to do with the physical sensation. Everyone has at least one variety that he or she fears. It's universal. So there's *always* a way in; a starting point. And once you've found it, the rest is merely a form of mechanics that doubles and re-doubles the pain anxiety at irregular intervals until it becomes unbearable.'

Thwaite swallowed hard. 'But what's this got to do with the way in which Holmgren was murdered?'

'Like I said, Kim had this North Vietnamese in for articulated interrogation. The principal went through the first stage.' Tracy's voice had slowed to a crawl. The images were running back at him, bouncing painfully against the insides of his eyelids like the sharp regulated flicks of an unfiled fingernail. His nostrils flared abruptly; he could smell the stench of sweat and fear and urine dribbling down the principal's leg. A boy of barely seventeen.

Tracy did not want to remember. 'Kim turned away for a moment, perhaps to get another implement, I don't know. There was a blur of movement as if the principal were slapping a beetle from the side of his neck. The next moment he had arched forward and was dead.

'We brought a military medic in and he pronounced the man dead of a massive heart attack. But then he hated us. What we did in there sickened him. He was delighted to tell us that.'

Tracy got up; sitting was too difficult for him now. The past was like an explosive barrage detonating inside him, quivering his muscles. 'But of course we knew he must be wrong. We found the needle, we saw the puncture wound. I came up with a forensic genius over there. He was a second-generation Japanese; American but had spent plenty of time in Japan.

'He told us the man had received an infusion of an enormously powerful stimulant that jolts the cardio-vascular system with such force that it brings on almost immediate MI.'

'Even if you're a healthy sonovabitch?'

Tracy nodded. 'It seems to make no difference because the substance is so powerful. The forensic specialist said he found it only because he was looking for it. Unlike manufactured poisons, this stuff builds up no residue in the surrounding muscle or fat tissues. It's apparently flushed out through the endocrine system.

'And because it's a nutmeg derivative he said he'd bet ten out of ten MEs in the States wouldn't pick it up.'

'But there's no way to be sure. I mean –'

'Look, Douglas,' Tracy said, 'even if we still had John's body to work on, I don't think the substance could be found now.'

'But there'd've been a chance.'

Tracy looked at him. 'A chance. Yes.'

There was an electric moment between them when they seemed to be walking at the edge of a precipice. Something dangerous prowled the room, an almost definable rippling of the atmosphere.

Then Thwaite said, 'Ah, what the hell. Does no good to think about "what if's". We gotta go on what we have. Period.' And it was gone. But inside, he still felt the shadow of its invisible presence. He cleared his throat, stubbed out what was left of the Camel. 'Still, I don't see how you can make this connection to Holmgren's death. Just from a black spot on a photo?'

Tracy began to move around, the restlessness growing. 'It's not only that I've been thinking about the way in which Moira was murdered. I've seen this done before. Occasionally, the Viet Cong would do it out of a sadistic desire to "crush" the enemy. The Khmer Rouge did it, also, in their formative days. They had a more practical reason, though. Bullets were at a premium; they were for waging their holy war. Prisoners were often executed by beatings just like that, inflicted by rifle butts or wooden clubs.'

'It's disgusting.'

'Invention is the mother of necessity.' Tracy shrugged. 'But let's take that view for a moment. We have John murdered by an arcane poison, virtually unknown in this country; we have Moira murdered just days after, beaten to death; we have a highly sophisticated electronic listening device I pulled from the Governor's brownstone.' Their eyes locked. 'They may all be links in the thinking of one man – a man who's been, as I have, in Southeast Asia, during the war. Who knows it as well as I do.'

'What about your friend Kim? He's a Vietnamese; he was there; he's a master torturer.'

'It couldn't be Kim,' Tracy said immediately. 'First of all, he got me into this.' He could not, of course, tell Thwaite too much about the foundation; that it had no jurisdiction within the

United States. 'For another, beating's not his style. He likes cleaner work than that. Also he knows next to nothing about electronics. This bug was hand-built by a master. I've got a feeling I'm right about this; John was poisoned, I'm certain of it.'

'You don't mind if I don't take your word for it ... at least not yet. Let's hear what your father has to say first.'

'Fair enough.' Tracy relaxed a bit.

Thwaite got up. 'I gotta get downtown. There's a lot to do today. I appreciate last night's hospitality but three's a crowd. I'll check into a hotel tonight – my insurance company will pick up the tab. I'll let you know which one.' He put on his crumpled jacket. 'Meanwhile you have my number at the precinct.'

He eyed Tracy carefully, hesitated a moment. 'You know,' he said slowly, 'you're a very scary guy. After seeing you in action, I'm just as happy we never tangled. The violence you can whip up ... well, it goes beyond anything I've ever seen and I thought I'd seen it all.'

'I've been trained for it.' Tracy held his voice expressionless. 'I use it when I have to. It's survival.'

Thwaite shook his head, his eyes canny. 'Hu uh. My point is you do it so *well*.' He rolled his tie up into a ball, put it in his jacket pocket. 'It occurs to me that wouldn't be the case unless some part of you enjoyed it.'

Tracy stared at Thwaite, his eyes shadowed. The light from outside was behind him and Thwaite thought it made him appear larger than he actually was. He wondered if that could be an illusion of Tracy's own making.

As for Tracy, he was thinking of the conversation he had had with Higure. *Kokoro*, the *sensei* had said. *The heart of things. To peer into this and to survive is life's only heroic act.*

'I think you're crazy.'

Thwaite smiled. 'Yeah. I guess I am at that.'

There was a surprise awaiting Sok when he and his cadre returned from their mission in Angkor Thom. Someone new had joined the main cadre. He was not a new recruit. He was not, to Sok's way of thinking, a young man. He was not even Khmer.

All during the day the men saw him walking in and out of the encampment and they speculated about who he was. Sam seemed to know. He was now Serei's right-hand man. Serei was the main cadre's leader; the one who had first indoctrinated Sok. But when Sok asked him he just smiled and said, 'Wait until tonight. Then you'll all know at once. I don't want to spoil the surprise.'

After the evening meal, Comrade Serei called them all into a circle and, as Sam had predicted, introduced the man. It turned out he was Japanese. 'This is Mit Musashi Murano,' Serei said. 'He is a teacher who has travelled a long way to aid us in our fight for a free Cambodia. Listen closely to him and when he speaks you will obey him as you would obey *Angka*.'

Murano was a short, heavyset man with iron filings for hair and lines in his face as if scored deep into a granitic core. He was a man who, Sok became convinced, had never learned how to smile. He showed his approval by baring his teeth in somewhat the same expression that Sok had seen on men who had died a hard death.

Murano's eyes were extraordinary: they looked as if they were double-lidded like a lizard's. When he watched you there was the impression of intense almost painful concentration to the exclusion of all else. And when one was in the midst of a lesson he was teaching, those eyes would become almost pale in their milkiness, frightening in their alien cast.

Of all of Murano's Khmer Rouge students, Sok was the only one with the temerity to ask him why his eyes changed so during those times. The Japanese folded his arms across his barrel chest and stared straight at Sok. At that moment, his eyes went pale as if that translucent second lid had been tripped by some inner source.

Sok flinched. It appeared to him as if something hard and flinty had punctured his heart and kept on going into the very core of his soul. It stuck there, squirming like an impaled serpent, until he gasped and shook himself like a dog coming in out of the rain.

When his eyes focused again, he saw that Murano's own eyes were black as night once more. The writhing snake was gone from inside him.

'Now you know,' Murano said softly. 'I enter into the fray. I become one with you as you become one with your body, your mind, your reflexes, the animal core of you. *Kokoro.*'

At first, Sok found this impossible to understand but as he became more and more involved in the lessons Murano taught, the knowledge began to seep into him like the subtly shifting bed of a river being coaxed by a new tide. To an outsider, for instance, it might seem that Murano dealt with the physical side of aggressiveness.

Nothing could be further from the truth and, as Sok eventually discovered, that kind of traditional thinking in an opponent was a blessing, a state to be perpetuated rather than rectified.

'There is no physical,' Murano told him one day in his oddly accented French – he did not, of course, speak Khmer. 'There is no mental. These two distinctions only exist within the artificial framework man has created for himself. These concepts are easy to deal with; the truth is not so.'

He lifted his right arm so that it was vertical from elbow to wrist. He made a fist. 'Now come here,' he said, 'and move my arm.'

Sok did as he was bade but found he could do nothing to budge the raised arm even a millimetre.

'So,' Murano said. 'If I tell you I am stronger than you, that is the truth. But if I say I used the strength in my muscles to defeat your efforts, that would be a lie. Can you tell me what the difference is?'

Sok said that he could not.

'In combat,' Murano said, 'one enters a state that is whole. There is no, no inside. This truth is vast so listen well. If you understand this, you will be able to master everything else that will come after.

'If you see an opponent and you think, "I will move my arm now", you are lost. There is a thing called reactive aggressiveness. It exists in every human being but it is little known and understood even less.' He lifted a finger. 'Let us say you are driving somewhere in a car. You are hit, the car begins to spin, then turn over.' The finger described movements in the air as if Murano were directing an art class. 'The car bursts into flame and now the situation has become lethal. The brain interprets this via the sense. It makes a judgement, then acts on it.

'Your arm lashes out against the locked door with such force that the metal springs open and you leap to safety. Has this happened because you have the muscles of a body builder? Has this happened because you have carefully worked out your escape route?' His head shook back and forth.

'It has happened because the human organism is in immediate danger of extinction. The primitive core is somehow set into motion. Without thought, the being is flooded with super-human power and stamina.

'This is real. It happens every day. Now this is reactive aggressiveness and it is possible to reach down into your soul's heart and extract that strength when you need it.

'This is *kokoro*. Believe me when I tell you there is no one else in the world who can teach you this method of fighting. Elsewhere you may learn many methods from many *sensei*. That is good. I encourage experimentation when one is young.

'But the killing spirit is here. Believe that if you believe nothing else. I ask only for your undivided attention. Time will give the rest to you. Faith has no place in this discipline. You see; you hear; you feel. And you learn directly. This is the only method by which *kokoro* may be taught.

'Now we begin . . .'

To say that from that moment on Sok's life changed would be a misnomer. In fact his life achieved a kind of metamorphosis.

He found within himself – or more accurately Murano put him in touch with – the bedrock animal core. He found it violent and at first frighteningly primitive. In the first days he lived with it inside himself, shaking as if with the ague. It felt like some great lion let loose from its cage to stalk him. He could scent it, could feel its presence in a wholly palpable way.

And, in a frenzy of reaction, he tried to push it away from him.

In the process he almost killed himself. In that one terrifying moment not even Murano could get to him. He was locked in mortal combat with himself and, in the end, it was only Sam's intervention which saved him.

It was Sam who took him away from the makeshift compound in Baray and, off in the jungle with only the birds and the wide-eyed monkeys to watch, broke the inner deadlock within his younger brother.

'*Own,*' he whispered, crooning. '*Own.*' At last he could hold Sok tight. They were both sweating heavily. 'Can you tell me what happened?'

For a long time Sok said nothing. He sat with his back against the bole of a banyan, his black blouse sticking uncomfortably to the damp flesh of his back. He looked out into the chittering emerald world around him and shuddered.

'Murano showed me ... *kokoro,*' he said, finding his voice at last. It seemed to him that it had altered subtly, deepened and steadied. 'The heart of existence.' His head swung around and he looked into his brother's face. 'I think you were right to doubt the teachings of Preah Moha Panditto. Buddhism is not the universe.'

Sam looked sceptical. 'But now you think *kokoro* is.'

'No,' Sok shook his head. 'No, I don't think that at all.' He ran his fingers over his eyes and forehead; he dried his sopping face. 'But he showed me a part of myself I never understood before.' He put his hand in Sam's. 'You know, I used to watch your anger and wonder where it came from. I used to wonder why it was you were so angry. What could have happened to make you feel that way?

'Well I found out that I have the same kind of anger inside

me. I just never could express it as directly as you always seemed to.' His face was sad; he was on the verge of tears. 'I could never explain it but when we were in battle, when I killed that way . . . I don't know, it made me feel good. It distilled my anger into a recognizable shape and allowed it to pass out of me. Can you understand that?'

'Yes.' There was no hesitation in Sam's face. 'Our life is not safe; it's not secure. Looking back on it now, I don't think it ever was. The crisis was always just around the corner, lurking like an evil *kmoch*. Now, in a way, I'm glad it's all out in the open. For me at least it's less frightening because I can actively do something. I was never a talker.'

Sok looked out over the rim of trees. There was nothing but jungle though just beyond he knew there to be terraces of rice paddies, a kind of civilization. 'Sam,' he said softly, 'I've been frightened about what I've become. I've been frightened to say that this part of me is really me.'

'But it *is* you, *Own*. You know that.' He squeezed his brother's hand. 'You're not evil, Sok, if that's what's troubling you. None of us are.'

But he was not convinced of that; he had already been witness to too many atrocities. The priest in Angkor Thom haunted him: a vision of the beating replaying in his mind like a growling dog on a tight leash, ready to spring at his master's command. After the beating, they had erected a crude crucifix and nailed him to it, bloody and torn and already dead. 'As a sign,' Ros had said, 'that this is sovereign territory of *Chet Khmau*.' He had raised his arm, the M-1 filling his hand. '*Here* is our flag!'

No, Sok thought now. This could not be the emblem of the new Cambodia. But try as he might, he could not rid himself of that foul image. That priest could have been Preah Moha Panditto; only by the grace of the Amida Buddha was it someone else. But still a life; a life dedicated to peace and the teaching of peace taken by the sons of the revolution. What manner of beast had Cambodia spawned?

Sok, sitting in the humid jungle, holding hands with his brother, did not know the answer to that question. Nor could he put a name to the creature let loose by Murano who now stalked inside, filled with an unnatural power.

What he could not quite articulate, even to his brother, what was not yet fully formed in his mind was that this let-loose terror was wholly antithetical to what he had absorbed like mother's milk since the time when he could speak sentences: Buddhism. He had eaten it, drunk of it, breathed it for eight years without a second thought as to its significance or place in the world around him.

But the revolution had changed all that. He had many teachers now and all espoused different causes, taught different lessons, brought out different parts of him. Yet he was whole, not fragmented. He lived and as he did so, thought. There was only one Khieu Sokha.

With forceable will he calmed himself. As he had already told himself, this was not the time for the Amida Buddha. Those who turned to him were beaten down and hung up to be flayed away by wind and rain and sun and carrion birds. This was a time to make one's presence felt, to fight for a free Cambodia, as Sam said. And then, when this evil time was over, he would return to the teachings of Preah Moha Panditto . . . at least in his heart. He was still Buddhist but with no desire to forsake the real world for the priesthood.

Feeling much better now, he rose. Sam stood beside him, silently. Together in the great sparkling jungle, surrounded by palms and creepers, flora and fauna.

It was time for the evening meal.

But there were other metamorphoses in store. In battle, he used the knowledge Murano had imparted to him and thus gained the respect of all the cadre. And behind his back he became known as *la machine mortelle*: the killing machine. And he moved up in rank, becoming one of the cadre officers.

As for the Japanese *sensei* he watched Sok's rapid progress and felt that his emigration to Cambodia had been worth the trouble after all. Murano had had two wives in his long lifetime but no progeny. This he meant to rectify. He did not want a baby, of course. He knew he did not have enough years left within him to wait for a baby to grow into the youth from which the proper moulding could be achieved.

Outlawed in his native land, he began to move further east searching for a young man in his early teens with just the right psychological makeup. Physical requirements were less stringent: there had to be no abnormalities or deficiencies. That was all,

In Sok he felt he had found the perfect specimen. Now he could cease his wanderings. It was here in Cambodia where he would die and be buried. Well, that did not matter to him so much. He had never held the soil of Japan in that much reverence. Soil was soil as far as he was concerned. At least here he would be remembered as mentor, as *sensei*; he would be revered as a father of a sort.

That was all he required now for his life to be complete. He had always been a self-sufficient individual. The nature of his life's work made it so. One could not share *kokoro* with wife or aunt or uncle. The intimacy between *sensei* and student was all he had lived off of for more years than he could remember. It was all he had ever known. Orphaned as a boy, he had always wondered if somewhere in Japan lived a blood brother or sister. Now he would never know. Seeing Sok grow before his eyes he thought it no longer mattered. Here was all the family he would ever need. And through him a continuation of *kokoro*.

It did not seem at all odd to him that his true child should be a fleshless, bloodless creature of the mind. *Kokoro*. He had built his life from it and around it. For him it was the only form of existence; it comprised the Ten Commandments of the universe, more potent than either Shinto tenents or Buddhist catechism. It was the only law he acknowledged.

Deep within the second summer of his coming he drew Sok away from the cadre's encampment. Within the deep green bower made by a banyan tree swept around the remnants of an ancient temple, he whispered, 'Sok, my son, I am dying.'

Behind the Japanese Sok could see *apsara*, beautifully carved out of stone, caught frozen in the midst of her celestial dance. 'It cannot be,' he said. 'There are those within *Angka* who claim you're immortal.'

Murano bared his stained teeth. 'In that they are quite correct.' The sun was going down, the last rays filtering through the shifting layers of fronds to illuminate them; the rest of the camp was already dim in indigo shadow. Murano took Sok's calloused hand in his; his eyes seemed serene.

'*You* are my immortality, Sok.'

4

Macomber met Senator Jack Sullivan at the Club. Although it had a much longer name, that was how Macomber always referred to it.

The mansion-like greystone was located just east of Fifth Avenue in the mid-Fifties. There was no plaque on its facade, no insignia on its dove-grey awning – save for the numerals of its address, written out in flowing script of the deepest maroon – nothing at all to give the passerby an inkling of what was housed inside.

There was, beyond the two sets of wide reinforced mahogany doors, a liveried attendant who would politely but firmly deflect the inquisitive individual who now and then ascended the worn marble steps to the Club's vestibule.

There were no blacks allowed as members and, especially, no Jews. There was more than enough money and power here to make certain of that.

A wide staircase gave out on the second storey gallery which it split in two. To the right, was the vast library where most of the members liked to congregate for a drink or a bit of a read before lunch. He turned towards the left. Here three smaller rooms could be reserved for meetings of a more private nature.

A rigid-spined steward named Ben opened the gleaming panelled door to his knock.

'Good afternoon, sir,' His head bent slightly forward. His dark hair was parted and slick, as if it were brilliantined. 'Your guest, Mr Sullivan, has not yet arrived.' He ushered Macomber into the comfortable room.

Macomber, who had made certain to know this fact already, said, 'Quite all right, Ben.' He sat in one of the well-used but spotless wingback leather chairs of outsized proportions. To his left were the high carved mouldings, broken only by the black marble fireplace. Steel engravings hung neatly within each panel described by the mouldings. The room was painted cream and robin's-egg blue. There was a small polished wooden table at his right hand. Across the room were table and chairs.

Macomber stretched out his long legs, crossing one ankle over the other. 'Bring me a dry vodka martini, will you, Ben?'

'Certainly, sir.'

'When Mr Sullivan gets here, bring him a drink if he wishes one, then you can attend to the food. Cracked crabs legs and cold lobster, right? Plenty of salad and I think we'll have Heinekens with that.'

'Very good, Mr Macomber.'

Ben was the only steward Macomber used when he booked one of his private meetings. A generous annual bonus was not necessary to ensure his discretion, Macomber was sure, but nursing homes were expensive and Ben's mother had been in one now for more than five years. He found the extra money indispensable.

Macomber was halfway through his drink by the time Ben ushered Jack Sullivan in. The two men shook hands and the Senator ordered a Glenlivet on the rocks. 'Better make that a triple,' he told Ben. 'I've had one helluva morning.' He sat down heavily opposite Macomber.

Jack Sullivan looked more like his pugilistic namesake than he did any senator Macomber had ever met. He was square-framed and broad-shouldered with a rather large head, given unnatural height by his wild wiry reddish-gold hair which came low down on his forehead. He had long arched eyebrows the same colour and cheeks so red you might think his skin held burst capillaries. He had a heavy square jaw and a nose verging on pug. It was, all things considered, a pure-blood Irish face as Sullivan himself loved to point out. He could name every one of his ancestors all the way back through six generations and once started on the revolution – to his way of thinking there was only one – he could talk and, of course, argue, for seemingly endless hours.

His great muscles bulged out the fabric of the three-piece poplin suit he wore. The collar of his shirt was already damp around the top rim from sweat and he exuded a mild odour.

Macomber made small talk until the other had been served his whisky and Ben had departed. Across the room, the table had already been set with silver and sparkling crystal in the Club's own exclusive pattern designed by Tiffany.

'Jesus,' Sullivan said in his gruff slightly accented voice, 'this Egyptian thing's really fucked us six-ways from Sunday.' He took a long pull at his drink, the ice cubes cracking as they melted. 'Not only is DeWitt slaughtered like a goddamned sacrificial lamb but these bastards managed to penetrate our own security. It's just like what happened today in West Germany.'

'Who set it up?'

'Ah, it was the usual dual thing between the CIA and State.' The senator's bright blue eyes were like chips of stone. 'But do you know that not more than ten days ago my Select Intelligence Committee put a document on the President's desk outlining inadequacies in our intelligence-gathering methodology in both the Middle East and the Latin American countries.'

Sullivan leaned forward and the chair creaked in protest. 'And d'you know what old Lanolin' – the President's name was Lawrence but some wit among the ranking Republicans had applied the moniker during his first hundred days in office – 'told us? "Thank you, gentlemen, for your diligence in this matter",' the senator continued in a scathing parody of the Chief Executive's idiosyncratic speech. ' "Please rest assured that I will consider your recommendations as soon as I have the time. As you know, our primary goal for this year is our own economy. With double-digit inflation and unemployment at nine per cent, I think we all know where our priorities lie".'

'It's too bad that remark wasn't picked up by the press,' Macomber mused, 'in light of what just happened overseas.'

Sullivan grunted. 'Just wish I could leak such a thing.'

Macomber eyed him speculatively. 'Why can't you, Jack?'

'Hell, it ain't the American way, that's why!' He was shouting now, red-faced. 'So a goodly number of my fellow Republican senators have pointed out. "We've got to pull together on this one, Jack," they say. "We've got to rally 'round the White House, Jack," they say. "This's an *American* issue now, Jack, not a party dispute".

'Piss, I say! This Democratic bastard's running us right into the toilet, internationally-speaking. The Oval Office's populated by wimps and nail-biters too scared of the Red Bear to make a move.' His fist hit into his palm. 'And by Christ I've already heard from Europe that unless we track down these sonsabitches who blew DeWitt away, we're gonna be the laughingstock of the international community.

'Del, I tell you America's overseas clout has never been lower in all my days in politics. It makes me sick to my stomach, d'you know that? I'm ashamed to say I'm a senator.'

Sullivan could no longer sit comfortably. He got up and paced back and forth along the tapestried runner spread across the wood parquet floor. 'I'm beginning to think that Gottschalk is on the right track, after all. I mean, you know me, Del. I'm a conservative and damn right proud of it. Sure, I came from liberal stock. My old man worked on a Ford assembly line all his life. Well, what'd it get him besides split fingers, flat feet and emphysema? Oh, yeah, he helped build up his union.

'But I'll tell you something, Del. I'm goddamned glad the old man's not here now to see the end of his dream. It'd break his heart to see how the union's've priced themselves out of the work market. Whatever we do, Japan can and does do it cheaper and – by Christ this hurts me to say it – better. Fucking unions want more money every three years, cost-of-living increases inbetween and all for what amounts to a four-day week. You tell me, Del, how the hell our industry can survive on that kind of diet? We can't, that's how! We're drowning in shit. Detroit's only the front-runner. The big field coming's computer chip manufacturing. And I don't have to tell you – because I know your dealings with the Far East – who's already so far ahead there we can't ever catch up.

'Within five years, we're gonna be up shit's creek with not even a boat under our behinds.'

'Now you're sounding just like Atherton Gottschalk.'

'Goddamn right!' Sullivan said, sitting back down. 'You oughta think about changing your mind about him, Del. He could use a fat cat like you right about now. The way things're leaning these days, all he's gonna need in August is a nice chunk of money and a bit more influence in some of the major cities in the East.'

'We don't get along from way back,' Macomber said. 'You know that, Jack. Just about everyone does.'

'Hell, that was personal. I'm talking political now. So he made a play for Joy Trower while you two were engaged. What the fuck, we're all a buncha animals, anyway.'

'I don't —'

'Listen to me,' Sullivan said, hunching forward. His forefinger tapped at Macomber's knee. 'Got a call from Gottschalk late last night. Know what he suggested the Committee do? Begin an investigation into the security procedures in Cairo for DeWitt's visit. *Now* what d'you think? I know how you feel about this shit's been going down since Lanolin took office. He's a dovenik from way back. Wants to be palsy with the Soviets, believes their peace lines at the recent Malta meetings while they're stabbing us in the neck every chance they get with these fucking terrorist schools they've set up all over Lebanon, Honduras and West Germany. They'd be in Italy, too, if the Red Brigades weren't so intent on ratting on each other.'

He looked hard at Macomber. 'Del, I really think it's time for you and Gottschalk to bury the hatchet. He's got an instinct for the jugular. You do a little fat-frying for him and I think he can do it. I don't say that the convention will be easy but, Jesus, with Holmgren gone — God rest his soul — it won't be nearly as bad as it would've been.

'I mean, after all, the Dems'll have to run Lanolin again — they've got virtually no one else good, except Hickock and nobody's heard of him outside of Illinois.'

Macomber sat back and gave a convincing show of mulling over what Sullivan was suggesting. He tapped his long forefinger against the double ridge of his pursed lips. When he had judged enough time to have gone by, he said, 'Now just assuming that I was interested in such a thing, Jack, I'd want to know some things.'

'Shoot.'

'Could I count on you? At any time?'

'Hell, yes, Absolutely.'

Macomber put his palms against the arms of the chair. He sat perfectly still. 'Let me ask you this, Jack. How good are you at taking direction?'

The senator shrugged. 'Depends on how I feel about it.'

'A reasonable answer.' Macomber's tone had turned silky. 'But what I'm suggesting is something quite different. You get a piece of information and are . . . asked to act on it. You do so.'

'No matter what?'

'Yes.'

Sullivan's heavy brows knit together. 'Christ, I don't know. I've done the party's will when I've had to; I've gone against it when I thought I was right.'

Macomber said nothing. He pressed a hidden button beneath the right arm of the chair and Ben appeared. 'You may serve lunch, now.'

Neither of them said a word until the table had been filled with food. Six bottles of beer had been poked into a pair of chased silver buckets mounded with shaved ice.

'Would you care to eat?'

'Not just yet.' Sullivan smelled a deal here and he wanted to understand its nature before he relaxed.

Macomber went to the table and, standing, took a king crab claw, dipped it in the herb mayonnaise, munched on it. It was fresh and delicious, the tender meat snowy.

'Tell me, Jack,' he said, his voice quite soft, 'how's your financial situation these days?'

'Fine,' Sullivan growled.

'That's not what I hear.' Macomber discarded the reddish shell, picked up another. He dipped. 'You're really in bad shape, Jack. Very bad shape.'

'So I gamble,' the senator said a little too quickly.

'You're not very lucky.'

'I've been in jams before. I always get out.'

'Not from this one, you won't.' Macomber dropped the second crab claw, wiped his fingertips and mouth with a linen napkin embroidered with the Club's name. He turned to face the other. 'You're in too deep this time. Your once-rich wife doesn't have enough to bail you out, you've got three kids in

287

college and one in medical school. It's a heavy load you're carrying, Jack. Too heavy. You've let the thing slide too long.' He looked directly into the senator's eyes. 'Three hundred and thirty thousand's going to break your back.'

'What are you saying?' Sullivan's voice did not rise above a whisper.

'I don't want to see it happen to you, Jack.' He came back across the room. 'That's all I'm saying. You're much too important to me. Just as an example, think of what good you can do if you should decide to convene an investigation on the DeWitt security thing; think, too, of the good you could do if you leaked your conversation with Lawrence to the national press.'

'You mean I should turn my life over to you . . . just like that.'

'I'm proposing nothing of the sort,' Macomber said. He stood by the side of his chair, relaxed and calm. 'Frankly, Jack, I can't imagine my asking you to do anything that would go against your grain; we think alike, after all.'

'And once Gottschalk is inaugurated . . . assuming he will be.'

At last Macomber sat down. 'Look, modern politics has very little to do with the man – the *presidential* man – himself. Policy is made by the people he surrounds himself with. The Democrats're in now so we're back to more Federal government . . . a proliferation of bureaucracy, boondoggle agencies supposedly on the lookout for social welfare. We get more of that environmental crap, solar energy, more anti-big-business policies.

'The fact is, history equates great presidents with those individuals able to sell themselves better than anyone else. It's all *personality*, Jack, now that television's *the* campaign medium. The rest's all done with mirrors . . . and fat-frying.

'Who came up with supply-side economics? Whiz-kid Stockman. It just happened that enough of Reagan's advisors bought the package; then *they* sold the old man on it. It had nothing at all to do with him. Not really.'

'Except it was his ultimate decision to go with it,' Sullivan pointed out.

'But, don't you see, that's exactly what I mean. It's got to be the President who sells himself. Otherwise, his administration will never outlast its mistakes. Christ, JFK was the best example of that in recent memory. We see a man whose administration gave us Vietnam, the assassination of the Ngo brothers and Diem, the Bay of Pigs, and all the while he's banging the greatest sex symbol of the twentieth century on the side.'

He leaned forward. 'D'you honestly think that *any* of those blunders mattered a damn in the long run? We both know better. Because people never stopped believing in the *man*. It was Camelot reborn and the American people bought the fairy tale hook, line and sinker. So Johnson took the heat for 'Nam and was helpless to do anything about it. It wasn't his decision to go in. He gave no command for commitment. King Arthur did it. But policy had already been set. Johnson just never knew how to sell *himself* effectively and he eventually went down the tubes because of it. Carter, as well. Imagine, to have all that power and have absolutely no control over it. Amazing!'

'You're espousing the men–behind–the–presidency theory.' Sullivan said this last thoughtfully. 'But you have no rapport with Gottschalk.'

Macomber smiled. If the senator had only been moved a centimetre, that was proof enough he was on the right track. 'But all this kind of talk is moot anyway, wouldn't you agree? I mean for someone who's on the verge of bankruptcy. The trouble with you, Jack, is you're too much a betting man. It's gotten you nothing but trouble. You're hardluck prone.'

Sullivan stood up. He took off his suit jacket and carefully laid it over the high back of the leather chair. As he moved Macomber watched the play of bulging muscle; there seemed to be no slack in the shirt at all. And if there was any fat on the man, Macomber failed to spot it.

'You're goddamned right, Del. I *am* a gambling man and I'm damn proud of it. It's lineage, history, my heritage.' He sat back down and now his blue eyes glittered cannily. 'I got a sporting proposition to make you. We'll have a little arm wrestle and whoever's the winner, well, that'll decide it.'

Macomber smiled. 'You're joking.'

'I never joke about a wager,' Sullivan said calmly. He began to grin as he watched the play of emotions across the other's face. 'Come on, Del. What's the matter? Your mouth's been doing a lot of spouting off the last half-hour. Let's see what you have to back it up with.' He lifted his massive forearm, flexed his biceps. He laughed. 'The only way you'll get me is to whip me, fair and square.' He reached over with his left hand and pulled the small wooden table at Macomber's elbow so that it now stood directly between them. 'One take-down. No rematches. That's it. Period.' He laughed again. 'C'mon, Del, you've gotta have *some* sporting sense in you.'

'I guess I don't have much choice,' Macomber said, standing up. He took off his jacket. He was well-muscled but in comparison to Sullivan he appeared thin with not nearly enough bulk.

'Get your ass down in that seat, Del,' the senator said in obvious delight. 'This's gonna be a piece of cake.'

Macomber settled himself and, together the two men placed the points of their elbows on the table top. They gripped hands in a perfectly vertical position.

'We should really have a third party in here to give us the countdown,' Sullivan said. 'But, what the hell, you do it, Del.'

Macomber shook his head and called for Ben. 'I want this by the book all the way down the line; that way, when it's over there'll be no cause for griping on either side.'

Sullivan shrugged. 'It's your funeral, you plan it any way you want.'

The steward arrived, evincing no surprise at the request given to him. He gave the count-down crisply and professionally, as if he had been doing it all his life. Then he left them to the struggle.

Sullivan, in the manner of many a professional arm-wrestler, thrust first and hard, in order to achieve an immediate advantage and build upon it throughout the match.

To a large degree, he was successful, though he encountered more resistance that he had imagined he would. His confidence blossomed and he settled in to lay Macomber low as quickly as he could.

The ferocity and lightning quickness of Sullivan's attack had almost caught Macomber by surprise. As he felt the appalling pressure on his wrist and the tendons of his arm, he knew that had it not been for his training, the senator would have pinned him on the first bullet shot. As it was he was already feeling a sharp twinge in his shoulder where the unaccustomed strain was telling. He had never arm wrestled at this level before and it had been years since he had done any at all – not since his time in Ban Me Thuot – and it took him some time to work out the power vectors and leverage points.

When he was quite certain of both, Sullivan already had him more than a third of the way over. That could not have been helped; he had needed the time. He'd just have to compensate. As his aikido *sensei* had told him, *It's not your own strength you'll use for victory, but your opponent's.*

He applied the principles of immobilization, altering them slightly to fit within the rather rigid confines of the arm wrestling game rules. More quickly than he had expected, he felt the answering surge of power and, though Sullivan sweated and strained, their rippling arms were back at the vertical, where they had begun.

Now Macomber switched to the projection techniques he had learned and Sullivan's once smiling face began to take on a serious then a worried look. His muscles knotted and his brow furrowed until his whole body began to tremble as he attempted to block Macomber's unexpected counterattack. He used every strategy he could think of. Nothing worked, as, inexorably, their bound arms slid further and further towards his side of the table until he felt the cool wood brushing against his knuckles and he knew that, despite all the odds, all the muscle, he had lost.

He lurched up from the chair, walked stiff-legged over to the laden table. He was breathing hard.

The senator pulled a bottle of beer out of the ice, opened it, tipped it up to his dry lips. He did not stop swallowing until he had finished it. Then he opened another.

'Hey,' he said over his shoulder, 'let's eat. I'm starved.' He reached out, pulled apart a lobster. He poked the meat into a dish of creamy Cumberland sauce, popped it in his mouth. Macomber had come up beside him and, without bothering to swallow first, he said, 'You know, I won't be content with being a senator after January one.'

Macomber smiled. 'Jack, I never thought you would be.'

*

One of New York's all-news radio stations was on as Thwaite walked through the detectives' room door at One Police Plaza.

'The question,' a sonorous voice Thwaite recognized as Atherton Gottschalk's was saying, 'is whether this country is adequately prepared to deal with the proliferating acts of terrorism against American military and diplomatic personnel and property overseas. Judging by the most recent of tragic events in Egypt and West Germany the answer is clearly, terribly evident. I ask these questions: How could terrorists have infiltrated our *own* security in Cairo as they gunned down one of our most important military advisors; how did the terrorists in Ramstein obtain the blueprints for our military installation there; how long will we allow the American consulate in Lima to be desecrated, scorched and battered before we are willing to stand up and say, "Enough!"

'I call on Senator Jack Sullivan to begin a hearing into the breaches in security abroad at the soonest possible date. I reiterate my call upon President Lawrence to immediately form the élite task force of antiterrorists I have been calling for.

'For if we remain mired in apathy – if we choose to turn our heads in another direction – where will these terrorist attacks end? On American soil itself?'

'Jesus,' Enders said, flipping off the switch, 'you just know it's an election year. I can't turn on the radio or TV anymore without that guy Gottschalk mouthing off.'

'I don't know,' Borak said. 'Personally, I think he's got a helluva point. I don't like to see us being pushed all around Europe and the Middle East. I think it fucking stinks.' He looked up at Thwaite's approach. 'Look what the wind blew in.'

Ted Enders came around from behind his metal desk. 'Hey, Doug, how are you?' There was concern on his face. 'Jesus, we're all sorry as hell about what happened.' He shook his head. 'Christ, what's the world coming to?'

'Just what I've been saying.' Marty Borak gave a twisted smile.

'Hey, Thwaite, that bitch from the ME's office called. What's her name? Miranda, right?' he guffawed. 'Enjoy your evening at the slab factory?' His grin turned into a leer. 'Pork any hot stiffs while you were down there?'

Thwaite lunged at him and Enders leaped between them. 'Okay, okay, that's enough.' He turned to Borak. 'I swear, Marty, one of these days I'm gonna let him make hamburger outa your face.'

Borak was shaking, his face hot with rage. 'Big man.' His voice was thick with emotion. 'Me'n Teddy do all the dirty work and you get the citations.' He glared at Thwaite. 'Now you wanna take over the Chin thing after we've done all the leg work. Uh uh.'

Enders turned to look at Thwaite. 'That true?'

'Nothing like it.' Thwaite was annoyed at having to justify his actions to his own unit. 'I needed access to the ME's office. I figured the Chin thing was as good as any.'

Enders pushed Borak away from him. 'See? How come you can't curb that big mouth of yours?'

Borak said nothing, went back to his work. Thwaite sorted through the accumulated mail on his desk but found he had no interest in any of it.

'Hey, Doug,' Enders said. 'I forgot. Flaherty wants to see you.'

Borak grunted. 'Yeah, he's been practising the hearts and flowers speech all morning.'

They're just schmucks, Thwaite thought, on his way over to the captain's office. Afraid I'll take the Chin murder away from them. That's a laugh. It's just another one of those troop–the–kids–in–for–a–lecture–and–hustle–'em–back–out–on–the–street deals. They didn't have the goods. Chinatown did their own policing when it came to that.

He knocked on the door and it was opened immediately. The freckle-faced countenance of his captain confronted him. 'Thwaite, I was hoping you would stop by, though of course I would've understood if you'd called in sick.' He waved an arm 'Come on in.' He closed the door behind Thwaite's back. 'Christ,' he said, shaking his head, 'it was a shock to all of us. You know, as policemen we all live with the know-ledge that we or our families might one day become targets but, I've found, when that day comes it never prepares you. Never ...'

'Do I sound like Poly?'

Eliott could not take his eyes off her. 'You don't do anything like Poly,' he said huskily and buried his face in her breasts.

Kathleen smiled down at him as a goddess might at a favourite mortal. One arm came up, enfolded his head, stroking. After a time, she pried him gently from her, pushed him back down on the rumpled bed. Her flat palms made circles across his chest, nails flicking at his nipples. Then she reached up and slowly undid the clasp of the string of pearls around her neck. She knew how her raised arms threw her breasts out even more and she kept the pose, feeling the lick of Eliott's hot gaze as if it had a physical presence.

They were in the bedroom of Eliott Macomber's East Sixty-Street apartment. The walls were an ice green, the long low dresser, sleek armoir, wide bookcase all a blued metal that harmonized perfectly. But it was a cold room, like all the rooms in the apartment and Kathleen did not like it much. 'I love it,' she had told him when she had first seen it.

'What are you doing?'

'You'll see,' she said. She took the pearls and put them between her legs so that they made a vertical line bisecting her mons. 'Here,' she said softly, guiding his hands to the ends. 'Pull back and forth.'

Eliott did as he was told, watched with glittering eyes as the beads sank one by one into the furrow of her sex, reappeared at the bottom.

'Keep going,' she whispered, her eyelids fluttering.

'Now he could see the shine of moisture coating the pearls. 'Oh, wow,' he said a little breathlessly. 'Wow, wow, wow.'

'Yes, darling,' she said, her head falling back. 'See how wet they get. Don't they shine in the light?'

'Yes,' he said thickly. He seemed mesmerized by the back and forth movement of the pearls through her slit.

'That's enough,' she said, putting a hand over his. She took the pearls away from him. 'Now lie down, darling.' Putting a palm against his chest, gently compelling him to lie on his back. 'Relax.'

She crawled towards him until she was crouching between his legs. Her head came forward. 'Did your Poly do this to you?' Her lips opened and her tongue flicked out at him, running a line along the velvety length of his erection. 'Or this?' Her opened mouth swooped down over the head, down and down until her lips nizzled the crisp hair at the base.

Eliott groaned, his only answer.

Kathleen set a rhythm and kept to it, knowing from experience that this was what set men off. She was not out to tease him, not this time. She wanted to trigger in him an explosion he would not soon forget.

Every so often she would come up his shaft, working directly on the head with a very fast pull and suck, was gratified to see Eliott's buttocks straining off the shadowed sheets.

When she felt the trembling begin in the muscles on the insides of his thighs, she lifted her head for a moment, said over his sigh of disappointment, 'Now spread your legs wide, darling.'

'What?'

But her lips were back on him and Eliott had no choice but to do as she asked. He felt coolness there as the air seeped in and then a kind of pressure.

Kathleen increased the pressure on his penis and Eliott groaned, helpless. At the same time, she took the pearls, wet with her own sexual secretions, and pushed them one by one through the sphincter muscles. Six or seven went in before she stopped. Eliott was in the final stages and was barely controllable. He gasped and wheezed like as asthmatic. His muscles jumped and twitched as if pierced by a live wire.

Kathleen was happy now, drenched in his pleasure; pleasure she was providing him.

She felt the tightness in his scrotum, the slight but unmistakable quivering of his penis. Eliott gurgled and cried out and as he began to shoot into the depths of her mouth, Kathleen caught hold of the end of the string of pearls, pulling evenly so that pop! pop! pop! they left him along with his semen.

Eliott cried out, his fingers like claws, bunching the sheets into sweaty clumps. Never in his life had he felt so much pleasure at one time. It had a physical presence, a kind of third dimension he had never known existed. 'Ah! Ah! Ah!' with each heartbeat, each pulse of blinding ecstasy.

His breathing was like a bellows for a long time afterwards. His body was bathed in a sweat and, lifeless, he watched Kathleen climbing over his body, licking it off.

At last he rolled over, stroking her. 'Kathy?' His fingers played with her breasts. 'Could we do that again? Now?'

Kathleen laughed and thought, Just like a child; only thinking of himself. What a boring lover. She touched his flaccid penis. 'I think we ought to give it a few minutes to recover, don't you?' She stretched her length out alongside him, touching him everywhere. Eliott shuddered, closed his eyes. She watched his face.

'I want to stay with you, Eliott.'

His arms came up, embraced her. 'Oh, God, yes. There's nothing I want more.' He licked his lips.

She pushed him back, hands on his shoulders. 'But no secrets, Eliott. I can't stand that. I couldn't stay if I knew there was something you were keeping from me.'

The telephone rang and he looked at it. It continued to ring. 'You'd better answer it.'

'I've got a better idea,' he said and reached for her. He brought one of her hands down to his crotch.

Kathleen picked up the receiver off the Plexiglass night table, handed it to him. He took it reluctantly.

'Hullo?' he said sullenly, looking at her. A voice spoke and he sat up. 'Yes, sir.' Looked at her again. 'Of course I'm alone.' He snapped his fingers, pointed to a pad and pencil on the night table. Kathleen got them for him. 'Okay.' He began to write. 'Got it,' he said, nodded unconsciously. 'Yes. Right away. He'll have it in an hour or so.' He hung up.

'What was that?' There was nothing at all to her voice.

'Ah, just business.' He tore off the top sheet, folded it in half. 'Nothing important.' He pushed the pad and pencil away from him. 'Now,' he said grinning, 'for the really important stuff.'

'No,' Kathleen said, moving away from him on the bed. Her

eyes flashed and her voice was steel-edged. 'I told you, Eliott, I will not tolerate secrets. How can we trust each other?'

Eliott looked troubled. 'Listen, Kathy, you don't understand. This isn't something I can't just . . . I mean I hardly know you.'

'Then it *is* important.'

He said nothing, stared at her petulantly.

'All right,' she said. 'You don't think you can trust me yet. I'll show you how wrong you are.' She reached for the pad and pencil. Holding the point at a forty-five degree angle she began to scrub it back and forth lightly over the surface of the top sheet. 'Look at this,' she said, threw the pad over to him.

Eliott caught it on his lap, looked down. 'Jesus!' he breathed, staring at the imprint of his writing Kathleen had exposed. 'It's all here.'

Kathleen nodded. 'I could've read it any time and you would've known nothing about it.'

He put out a hand, clasped hers. 'Christ, Kathy. I'm sorry about this.' He looked down at the pad again, thinking. Then he took it and offered it to her. 'Here,' he said, 'read it. I *do* trust you.'

She smiled at him. 'I don't really care about it, Eliott.'

'No, read it, please. There *is* something . . . I haven't told you.'

Her eyes were liquid, their blue turned dark as the sea. Bars of shadow fell obliquely across her as she sat on her ankles. To Eliott, eternally overshadowed with women by Khieu, she was the embodiment of all he had ever wanted from the female species: sexy and smart and, especially, possessing an innocence belonging to another era.

He was, in short, enchanted so that when she said, 'I can't. You still don't trust me. I can tell,' he read the message to her himself just to prove how wrong she was:

'Holo must be at eleven-thirty hours. August three-one. Patrick's.'

Kathleen looked at him wide-eyed. 'It all sounds so cryptic,' she said in a puzzled tone. 'Like spies.' She leaned forward, took his hands in hers. Her face shone like a playful puppy's, all innocence and light. 'It it something juicy, Eliott? Ooh, I'll bet it is. Please tell me.' She cocked her head.

It was madness, he knew. But it was also a chance to do *some*thing on his own. It was Khieu who could do everything, Khieu and Delmar Davis Macomber. *He* should've been my father's son, not me, Eliott thought bitterly for the thousandth time. But here was a chance to decide for himself.

The more Eliott contemplated it, the more inclined he was to tell her. He felt her fingers moving across his flesh, saw that languid, lustful look in her eyes that made him melt inside.

Involuntarily, he made a sound as her hand encompassed his hardened penis. His mind, unbidden, returned to the galaxy of pleasure she had introduced him to. He wanted to go back there so much that the desire was a physical ache. But even more than that he remembered her spoken words. She thought him a man, not a boy and, thus, he became a man.

Kathleen's sleek head came forward, through bars of shadow and light so that it appeared to undulate like a serpent's uncoiling body.

He saw the pink of her tongue tip, bright and shining as it passed through a swath of light just before it touched him. His eyes closed as he felt the exquisite pleasure as she explored the nerve on the underside of the thickening head. 'Go on,' he said thickly. 'Go on.'

'Tell me,' she whispered just before her lips engulfed him in liquid heat that rushed up his body.

And he did; not, he told himself, because she had asked him to but because he himself wanted to.

'It's my father,' he said through gritted teeth. 'He's got this crazy idea that the President of the United States can be created wholly out of his own mind.' Having said it, he thought it the funniest thing he had ever heard. He began to laugh, tears rolling down his cheeks unchecked. His chest heaved as he spoke. 'He's going ... he's going to –'

But that was as far as he got. There was a noise at the bedroom doorway, a peculiar, frightening sound akin to the growl a large beast makes just before it strikes. It set the small hairs at the back of Eliott's head on end, sent a chill shiver through him as if he had been struck with a bucketful of freezing water.

He felt the passage of air, no more. The kind of rocking one feels in a small car when one is passed by a truck six times the size. His eyes, half-glazed with lust, picked up a dark blur.

For her part, Kathleen heard and saw nothing, concentrating as she was on her task, until she felt her scalp scraped, a violent pull on her hair that jerked her head up and back, stretching her spine unmercifully.

She found herself staring into depthless black eyes she was certain she had seen before but which were so frightening to view at such close range, all coherent thought was flung from her mind.

Tracy got the call at his office and bolted like a sprinter. His father's voice trickled down the line sick and frightened and vulnerable. He had never heard his father sound like that except on the night Tracy's mother died in a godawful smashup on the Long Island Expressway, the Volvo slammed from the rear by an enormous twenty-wheel semi, abruptly blocking out all light like an eclipse as it slewed obliquely across the slick tarmac, its frame shuddering, squealing like a shot animal.

Louis Richter, driving, was protected by the collapsing steering wheel but his wife, his beloved Marjory, was thrown free of her safety belt, the mooring ripped right off the car wall as the high square grill of the semi rudely invaded the Volvo's interior and she was flung headlong through the windscreen. At least part of her. Because of the peculiar gravity well set up by the car's momentum, her legs were jammed like sticks against the dash, imprisoned. Tracy's father awoke inside the wrecked auto with those bloody amputated members for company.

As for the child, Tracy, he had been curled up, fast asleep on the driver's side of the back seat. That was fortunate for the entire right rear end of the car was torn away as if from the bite of a voracious monster.

His head had come up but the momentum of their slide had brought the side of his head into traumatic contact with the edge of the front seat back. He had awakened in a hospital room, knowing nothing of his mother's death until much later.

He wondered now whose experience had been worse, his or his father's. To have been there at the moment of her death and to have been unconscious, seemed to him cruel beyond his understanding. As a child, he had often dreamed of saving her. But then again at the hospital Louis Richter had inexplicably turned his head away from his son and soon after that the nurse came and took him outside into the squeaky hallway, leaden with pathos, sodden with tears.

'Here,' Louis Richter said when he had closed the door behind his son, 'take this.' And had dropped the bug into Tracy's palm.

'What's the matter?'

'I don't want it anymore,' he said. He looked tired and more drawn than the last time Tracy had seen him.

'You're finished already?'

'Don't you listen to me when I talk to you?' his father shouted.

Tracy stood looking at his father for a moment. He tried to summon up some more noble emotion but it was only pity he felt, swirled like oil slicking water's surface.

'I don't want any part of it,' Louis Richter said more softly. He walked away towards the living room, sitting down heavily on the leather sofa. His fingers reached out, picked the gunmetal lighter up off the highly polished driftwood coffee table. He flicked it open and closed while he talked.

Tracy picked an easy chair covered in faded ochre corduroy, sat on its edge. 'Dad?' he moved his head, trying to pick up his father's deeply shadowed eyes.

'I have to go into the hospital soon,' the old man said as if to himself. 'Blood transfusions.' He snorted, the outraged sound a beast makes at the last, before it falls to its knees to die. 'I know why they want me in there.' He took a deep breath. 'It's just a matter of time now.' And laughed thinly. 'It was always a matter of time, after your mother passed away. All that time to think of what I had done to her.'

'Dad,' Tracy said, appalled, 'it wasn't your fault.'

'Oh, yes,' Louis Richter said. 'Yes, it was. I was driving. It was pissing down rain, mist like smoke coming up from the macadam. Cars came in and out of that junk like ghosts riding the wind. I didn't see that semi bearing down on me, didn't know anything until it hit and we went swinging. I tried to gain control but it was impossible. And then your mother began to scream.' The flame went on, off, like a signal to someone unknown. 'And when I wake up at three in the morning – as I always do – that's what I hear: your mother's scream in every whine, creak, siren of the city.'

He looked up at Tracy then. 'I'll tell you something, Trace. For a time, I thought about going after that bastard driver myself. He was doing seventy in that weather. Can you believe it? Seventy! And Drive Safely stickers all over his goddamned machine.' There were tears in his eyes now, clear and reflective. 'You remember when I went away to Corfu, just after?' Tracy nodded wordlessly. 'That's when I made the decision. If I had stayed here another day, I would've built something to blow the sonovabitch up.' He gave a thin smile. 'Imagine that. All my training washed away by one vengeful act. I couldn't do it, Trace, d'you understand?' His fist clenched whitely around the large lighter. It trembled when he spoke. 'So much of me wanted to . . . to do *something* to make amends for what I'd done . . . or failed to do.'

'But, Dad' – Tracy reached out for his father's hand – 'you did everything you could.'

Louis Richter gripped his son's strong hand and hung on. 'Yes,' he whispered. 'Everything. I'm too disciplined a man and . . . well, there was your mother to think of. In Corfu, away from it all, I realized that that act of vengeance was for myself; your mother hated violence. And, well, you know, I always believed in the two of us.' He began to shake and Tracy got up, hugged his father to him. 'That's why it's so damned *hard* now.'

The wail of desperation in his father's voice chilled Tracy and he stroked his thin back. 'I'm here, now, Dad,' he said softly. 'We're together.'

After a time, Louis Richter pulled away. He was in control again. 'This bug,' he said, 'how important is it?'

'I think that whoever planted it murdered John Holmgren. John was my *friend*,' Tracy said, leaning forward. 'I won't leave him to the dogs. I'm going to find whoever killed him.'

'And then?' Louis Richter cocked his head. 'You sound just

like me, Tracy.' He shook his head sadly. 'It's back to the war then.'

'The war was necessary, Dad. So is this.'

'Killing's necessary?' the old man said. 'Is that what you're telling me?'

'That could be funny, coming from you.' Louis Richter put a hand over his eyes and he sank back into the sofa with a deep sigh. 'I'm old, Tracy. I feel worn down, like time was gravity and I'm sinking down into it.'

'You don't want to die, Dad,' Tracy said. 'Don't give me that.'

'To die, no.' Louis Richter smiled. 'But comes this time in life and something changes. You feel closer to' – he shrugged – 'I don't know. Something else.' He put his bony hands together and Tracy saw the thick tracery of blue veins pulsing just beneath the surface. 'God, maybe. Oh, not in the religious sense. You know I never believed. But sometimes I feel near to a kind of life force ... the centre of things.' He shrugged again. 'It's changed my thinking, maybe. I'm certainly not the man who made all those miniaturized explosives for the foundation.'

'You can't expect me to feel the same way.'

The old man took Tracy's hand in his own. He stroked the palm with his fingertips. 'Trace, I realize now that that's all I've ever wanted from you. If God wanted us made in his image, I wanted you made in mine. I saw my immortality in you.' He waved a hand. 'Oh, I know. All fathers must feel the same way. But I wanted it perfect and complete. I wanted you to think, to do the same things I did. And when you inevitably didn't, well, I guess I blamed you.

'It was an unfair thing to do. I tried to live my life as fairly as I knew how.' He paused, looked into his son's eyes. 'I guess I just didn't know enough.'

'That's all over with now, Dad,' Tracy said. He kissed his father on the cheek. It felt cool and dry.

Louis Richter got up slowly, went over to the rosewood hutch, poured them both a drink, brought them back. 'Now about that bug. What can I do?'

Tracy dropped it back into his father's palm. 'Is it possible to get a line back on the receiver?'

Louis Richter smiled as he sipped at his whisky. 'Now you sound just like my son. I can do many things,' he said, pleased. 'But magic unfortunately isn't one of them.'

'Then how do we go about finding out who built it?'

'It's more a matter of who *didn't* build it.' Louis Richter put his glass down. 'Now we know it's not one of the experts. They're all world-renowned, at least in my circle. And all of them have a distinctive style. The bug you gave me doesn't fit anyone I know. There are some Japanese-manufactured parts in it but that only means the person who made it knows what he's about.' He lifted a finger. 'At first I thought Mizo might've been involved because a number of delicate elements are hand-tooled, the way he goes about this kind of stuff. But on closer inspection it turned out not to be his.'

'Then that's a dead end.'

'Not quite.' Louis Richter's eyes were sparkling. 'Mizo is one of the few masters who teach.'

'Are you saying that the bug might've been built by one of Mizo's students?'

His father nodded. 'It's a possibility but I don't know how far that'll take us. Mizo's properly close-mouthed about who he trains and, anyway, this person – if he *was* Mizo's disciple – must've been one some time ago. That bug's no work of a student. The builder's a full-fledged genius. All I can say is I hope he's working for us, otherwise, God help us all.'

'Come on, Dad. It can't be as bad as that.'

'Worse, maybe. This guy's on the verge of revolutionizing the electronic surveillance field. I don't have to tell you what that could mean.'

'No,' Tracy said morosely, 'you don't.' He stood up. 'Where's this Mizo work?'

'Hong Kong,' his father said. 'But it's no good my talking to him. He hates my guts. We were both bidding for the foundation's work once a long time ago and I won.'

'Don't worry about that,' Tracy said. There was a faraway look on his face that his father had seen before.

'I don't think I much care for that expression, Trace. I remember the last time I saw you look like that. You almost blew up this apartment trying to circumvent the three basic laws of electronic surveillance I taught you.'

Tracy nodded. 'Yeah but that was when I was just a kid. Don't worry about it.' He smiled. 'Just make me up one of your Care packages.'

'But Mizo'll never talk to you. I'd better devise something extraordinary for you to take.'

Tracy was no longer listening. He walked over to the window, stood looking blindly out at the city. 'He'll talk,' he said softly. 'And he won't even know he's doing it.'

Khieu had picked up the movement out of the corner of his eye as he had emerged from Macomber's house. He was instantly alert but he did nothing out of the ordinary. He continued his movement, knowing that any deviation would alert the watching figure.

He turned and walked away, in his usual strong stride. All the while his mind was going through the ritual of picking apart the diverse data that his senses were flooding it with. He knew the approximate height of the individual in the shadows some thousand yards away because he was familiar with the doorway and, without thinking, his mind had already calculated the differences in height, had come up with a measurement of five foot-seven inches which was, in fact, less than an inch off.

He did not, however, know whether the watcher was a man or a woman. For one thing, a newspaper blocked most of the head and all of the face. For another, shrubbery partially blocked his view.

He cut across the street. He was already out of sight of the watcher and he began to double back. He saw Eliott emerging from the house and melted back into a doorway. It was a brownstone and he reached behind him, opening the outer door, fading himself inside.

He pushed aside a wedge of the curtains on the outer door just in time to see Eliott pass by on the opposite side of the street.

And, a moment later, a woman passed also, closer because she was on Khieu's side of the street. There was no paper to hide her features this time; he got a good look.

Breath hissed and his hand curled up into a fist. What had gone wrong? he thought. How had Atherton Gottschalk's woman latched on to Eliott?

Khieu followed them as far as the restaurant. He left them there, went down the block to the first pay phone he came to. That one was broken and he had had to cross the street. He phoned Macomber, spoke for some time.

'She's made contact,' he said at length. 'There's no doubt about it.' There was silence on the line. Khieu felt nothing. He was an empty vessel waiting to be filled up. 'I don't like it.' 'Neither do I.' Macomber's voice boomed down the line at him. 'Atherton's obviously made some kind of blunder. For all I know, he had her in the house when he called Eliott. That doesn't concern me right now.'

To take a life – any life – was a sin. So his thought of Malis. To protect himself he began working on the catechism Preah Moha Panditto had instilled in him as instinctively as he had once fed at his mother's breast. His hand ached and he turned his mind away.

'Something will have to be done,' Macomber said. There was no indecision in his voice; nothing at all but firm resolve. 'Our security has been breached and we must assume the worst. Do you agree, Khieu? You are my son, after all.'

'Yes, Father,' Khieu. It was part of the ritual. Khieu would never have thought to disagree with one of his father's dictums. 'Miss Christian obviously knows something. How much, we have no way of knowing unless they get back to his apartment and who knows if they will do that.'

'You have the portable receiver with you?'

'Yes,' Khieu answered. 'No matter where they are in the apartment, I will hear every sound.'

'I'm glad I told you to keep an eye on Eliott,' Macomber said. Khieu thought he could discern some emotion in the voice now. 'I had hoped to be proven wrong.' The voice paused for a moment. 'Why doesn't he love me, Khieu?'

'I don't know, Father.'

'A son should love his father, shouldn't he?'

'It is his duty.'

'I love him. Doesn't he know that? I really love him.'

'I know,' Khieu said, and did not catch the sadness in his own voice. 'He is your only flesh and blood.'

'My flesh and blood, yes. But I can't trust him the way I trust you.'

'Thank you, Father.'

A singing on the line, jumble of ghost voices all talking at once. At last they died away. Silence. 'She must be stopped, Khieu,' Macomber said after a time. 'We have absolutely no choice. Terminate her with extreme prejudice.' He could not or, more likely, would not give up the military term. The first time he had said it, Khieu had had to have it explained to him.

Khieu turned to watch the entrance of the restaurant a block away. 'Yes, Father,' he said and bowed his head.

Kathleen was making a high wailing noise. She was a gibbering idiot, dancing on the end of a string held by the owner of those demonic eyes.

In the long moment when she stared into them, she had time to see impossible things. In their depths, she thought she could see evil, capering nightmares, gleaming skulls, corpses vomiting blood. She saw children burning and mothers hurling themselves into infernos. She saw rape and vicious sadism, the entire panoply of horrors.

She knew now who had hold of her, facts finally overriding the blind animal fright that had invaded, paralysing her mind. It was the Cambodian. There was no mistaking the face, those features. She wondered how she could ever have felt that strong sexual attraction for him. For now she felt only revulsion. It was as if she were staring into the face of death itself.

It was hideous. She shivered and cried out, saw at the corner of her vision, the bright flash of an expanding steel bar as it passed through a glade of sunlight. For an instant it seemed beautiful to her and then the terror came welling up, washing over her in a wave so strong that she began to gag.

Her sphincter muscle gave way and she defecated, the stink unholy. But at least it's me, she thought. I'm still alive.

The bar passed into darkness. Light again like a sun, burning, and then the darkness like an eclipse. It was her entire world now, all her senses contracted to monitor its passage.

It came at last to her flesh and she felt a burning unlike anything she had ever experienced before. It was as if she had been hurled into the heart of the sun.

She gave way, peeling back, then raw flesh and blood gurgling. Her blood. And now her mouth opened and she gave up the nourishment she no longer needed. But still the burning went on and on, increasing in intensity until her mind could no longer accept what was happening to her and one by one it sealed off the synapses of the nerves. Now nothing was left except in a grey floating speck whirling in the vastness of airless pace, away and away, fading with infinite slowness.

Thus did Kathleen give up the life she so coveted, holding on, grasping and fighting until the last instant.

'No!' Eliott was screaming. 'Oh God, no!' He was sobbing, tears rolling down his cheeks. He was backed up against an ice green wall, sweat trickling down the indentation of his spine. His brain felt as if he had been invaded. An army of ants was crawling around inside.

His hands were claws, scraping across his scalp, pulling at his sodden hair. He thought, drunkenly, that he must turn away from the horror being enacted in front of him. But he did not. He could not even get his eyes to blink. It was as if they were stapled open.

This is my punishment, he thought, for going against my father's orders. He never thought to question Khieu's presence let alone his actions. Death made a terrible kind of sense to his half-hysterical mind.

To Eliott it seemed as if Khieu was God's messenger, doing his will. I should be whipped for this, he thought, wildly. *Beaten.* But another part of him felt as if his very soul had been sliced open; that the essence that made him an individual, different from everyone else, was leaching away through his fingers like water. Nothing he had been before Kathleen had walked into his life and nothing was what he was again.

Shrinking away from the fearful act taking its course before him, he felt no anger, no sadness. He understood that nothingness was his lot in life. There was no point in struggling against it. He had tried, this one time, and he had seen the outcome. Death rained across the bedsheets, drowned.

Khieu, arms rigid, knelt on the bed, holding Kathleen upright. He was drenched in blood and bits of skin, gore. The place stank but he was used to that.

Blood dripped like the tick of a clock from somewhere. He looked down. Blood spattered him; blood coated the woman. Her head lay unnaturally on one side, the mouth opened, a black yawning cavity. Khieu smelled the stench of eternity, a wind from the dead depths of the corpse.

But her arms still reached across the gulf between them, her taloned fingers gripping him, seeming to pull at him. She had struggled, clawing him, raking her nails, pounding his hard flesh even as she was dying, as if to take him with her.

Khieu shook his head, pried her stiffening fingers, one by one, from his shirt. Beneath, he saw the tears her sharp nails had made, a small tattoo of crescents, and the pink of his own blood, seeping slowly. He pushed her from him, let out a long slow breath.

Eliott screamed, pressed back against the wall as Kathleen's head fell in his lap. Khieu looked up, lunged out viciously, pulled him across the steaming slippery corpse atop the bed.

'Come here, you!' He took Eliott up by his shoulders. He was frightened by how close his brother had come to blowing the *angka*. 'Do you know what you were doing?' he cried. 'Do you!'

For an instant, a light burned far back in Eliott's. He remembered all the girls Khieu had taken from him; girls who were rightfully his. 'Yes,' he said defiantly. 'I knew just what I was doing. She made me feel alive; she wanted to be with *me*!'

Khieu hit him then, hard across the face. Eliott's head spun and he gurgled in surprise. Khieu's face was a tightly controlled mask, hard and pale as if devoid of blood. 'No. She made you forget your responsibilities. Your duty to the *angka*.' This time a backhand blow. 'You have no respect for your father.' Slap. 'You understand nothing. You are deserving of nothing.'

And Eliott, cowering, crying like an infant, drooling blood, heard that word resounding in his skull, echoing on and on until it seemed devoid, even of thought. *Nothing, nothing, nothing.*

'Yes,' he whispered in a piteous tone. 'I know.'

Three years fighting in the jungles of Cambodia could feel like three centuries. Especially if events surrounding the fighting appeared to have changed not at all.

True, the Khmer Rouge were now a force to be reckoned with in the struggle for liberation. Their numbers had swelled considerably and their supply of weaponry had increased fourfold.

But the Cambodian government was still in power. The hated Sihanouk still reigned though the Khmer Rouge had long ago vowed to destroy him. His prime minister, Lon Nol, had been in a car accident in the countryside, while reviewing firsthand some of the fighting. He had severely injured his shoulder and in 1968 had resigned his post to fly to France for recuperation. But now, a year later, he was back in his old job and it seemed oddly as if they had all been thrown backward in time.

Except for one thing: Musashi Murano had died.

That event, above all others, seemed to mark the passing of time for Sok. The memory of his dead family was already a cold black ember encysted within his heart. He could no longer remember the month of the year of their burning. The jungle and the constant fighting had seared that out of him, leached away into the bloodsoaked earth beneath his feet.

But Murano's death was still fresh in his mind. It had been he who had helped dig the grave, who handed down the corpse, so oddly light in death, he who had shovelled the dirt back over the body with the butt of his M-1, he who had cried in the middle of the night when no one else – not even Sam – could see him.

Sam had neither liked nor understood the *sensei*. That kind of discipline was not for him. He was a man like René Evan: an architect of the revolution's philosphical progress. He fought side by side with the other members of the cadre but all knew he lacked the fervour for it. Rather, he had gradually become one of the élite officers involved in policy and man-oeuvre coordination, at times liaising with other cadres in the Khmer Rouge's long march towards ultimate victory. It was even rumoured throughout the encampment that he had met with members of *Angka Leu*. Though no one could find the courage to ask him directly.

Yet even the death of Murano was pushed to the background by the advent of the cadre's newest assignment. The Chinese were developing an enormously complex pipeline to funnel heroin to the American soldiers in an effort to undermine their war effort.

Angka Leu, it appeared, was in full agreement with this philosophy for Sok's cadre had been chosen to be one link in this pipeline. And two weeks before, the sacks of the drug began trickling into the encampment to be buried until the next link could be contacted. It had been Sam, on one of his trips out of the encampment, who had brought them the news of this very important assignment. A definitive link with the Chinese was important since it brought with it increased military aid to further *Angka*'s cause.

Thus it came as a total shock when one evening, in those few dusky moments before true darkness descended upon the jungle, Sam was remanded into the custody of the higher council.

Immediately this happened, Sok was herded out from the cadre, divested of his sidearm and put into a tent alone. There was a guard at the doorway.

The night passed with interminable slowness until at last a figure filled the opening. Sok moved towards it, saw that it was Ros.

'*Mit* Cheng is on trial,' he said without preamble. 'It has been discovered that he has been secretly working against *Angka*.'

'My friend!' Sok exclaimed incredulously. 'But that's impossible! He is absolutely loyal to the cause. I'd stake my life on it. There must be some mistake.'

'He is on trial now,' Ros said, ignoring Sok's words. 'You will be informed of the revolutionary court's decision.'

'I don't understand any of this. I –' Ros began to turn away.

'*Mit* Ros!' The man turned back. 'I would like to see him.' But Ros had already turned away.

Sok's mind was whirling. What had happened? He concluded that he must be dreaming. But he knew that he was not; the pain he felt inside himself was very real. The flickering torchlight was real. The smells of the jungle were real.

The evening meal came and went. No one brought him food. No one talked to him. From time to time he could see the men walking in small groups of two or three across the compound. Often they glanced off to where the tribunal had gathered to hear the damning evidence.

At length he heard the commotion then and rushed to the opening, trying to draw it aside so that he could see what was happening. The guard barred his way but he could see the tribunal had broken up.

Outside, at the centre of the encampment, a circle was forming, the same kind of circle the men made when a monkey or a wild pig was captured. Only there was no animal this time. There was Sam.

Sok considered killing the guard then. But what could he expect to achieve? He would be shot before he advanced another ten metres. What else was there to do? Think! he berated himself. You've got to save Sam.

Now he could glimpse the top of his brother's head as he was led into the circle. It was going to happen without delay. Oh, Sam! Sam! The judgement had been rendered; the court had found Sam guilty and, as Ros had said, Sok would be informed. The circle of soldiers was his messenger.

If only there was a way to save Sam's life. But he knew that there was nothing he could do. *Angka* had spoken and its voice was law in the jungle. Should he attempt to interfere, he would be summarily executed. What purpose would that serve except that he would not have to endure witnessing his brother's death.

Then he remembered Murano; he remembered his training. The essence of *kokoro* was nonprecipitous action. *Reactive* aggression. It was a discipline only for the patient.

If he could accept what was about to happen, he could turn his thoughts to the aftermath. He knew the men responsible –

those who comprised the tribunal. One by one *kokoro* would take them from this life, hurl them downward to a land filled with serpents. This Sok vowed even as he heard the first blow struck.

The sound of the cudgel was a distinctive one. Some time before they had replaced the rifle butts which *Angka* had decreed were too valuable to trust to crush human bone without sustaining damage.

It was a wet ungodly sound with no analogue in nature: the *thwap* of bloody flesh peeling and splitting, the crunch of bone fracturing. It seemed to go on for a very long time and even though Sok had made up his mind, he put his fists to his ears in a vain attempt to block out the sounds. He bit his lower lip so hard he drew blood, its taste hot and salty, coppery in his mouth.

He thought of the damage he would do to them, one by one, afterwards but with each arrhythmic sound his body jerked as if seized by convulsions and his mind snapped back to the present. Into this nightmare.

At last the sounds slowed, then ceased altogether. Sok let out a long sigh. It was over. The agony that had racked him began to fade. The muscles of his body commenced to tremble in brief rippling clusters.

'*Mit* Sok.'

He turned to confront Ros who stood now in the opening. His face was shadowed, his black uniform stained and struck with blood and gore.

'You are summoned by *Angka*,' Ros said without definable emotion. His dark-flecked cudgel was held at his side. 'You will come outside now.'

5

For Macomber the return to China was as difficult as plunging his fist into a sheet of flame. He had not expected it to be so bad but the memory of his first and only love burned like a living jewel in his heart, the heat rising, the nearer he came.

All the dusty layers of images began to rise like spectral skeletons and it was as if no time had passed since he had last been to this vast Asian shore. Particularly, he felt with the acuteness of pain the enigma of her disappearance. He thought he had successfully laid that to rest but he saw now that he had only been fooling himself. Was she alive or dead? He stared out the train window as it rumbled and rattled up the southeast coast of the mainland on its way to Canton. The Hong Kong New Territories were already far behind to the southwest, their carefully terraced paddies of brilliant emerald, the acres of fish farms a sharp contrast with the newly constructed high-rises in the burgeoning, teeming new suburbs just outside Hong Kong near Sha Tin. The government was doing its best to induce citizens to relocate from fiercely overcrowded Hong Kong to the rapidly expanding suburbs. Macomber had to laugh. The New Territories were on a ninety-nine-year lease from the People's Republic. That lease – which the communist Chinese did not acknowledge in any case – expired in 1997. What would happen then to the New Territories? No one knew but the British government, at least, was banking on the fact the communist Chinese made too much money from Hong Kong ever to overrun it. Besides, what would they do with the eleven-and-a-half million Chinese citizens there who had been brought up in relative freedom?

Macomber would have preferred to fly into Canton but the Chinese government had been insistent. They wanted the commission to see for itself the prosperity of the new China and thus

314

the train ride had been arranged. At least they would fly from Canton to Shanghai.

They had debarked at Lowu, a small village on the northern border of the New Territories. The tracks stretched straight on through a covered bridge spanning the Shum Chun River that only freight trains passed through unhindered.

Up ahead he had seen the concrete and stucco guard posts and outbuildings flying the red flag of Communist China. The delegation was met by a group of Chinese in olive drab uniforms, red stars embroidered on their caps, bands of the same colour on their uniform collars. Guns were much in evidence, 'to discourage any form of incident', they were told through an interpreter. Macomber needed no such interpretation, quite naturally, but he thought it prudent not to mention his facility with the language to anyone present.

The members of the commission were walked across the covered bridge where they boarded another train for the remainder of their journey into Canton. They were all in one car filled with plush seats obviously built for just such an occasion for surely the normal tourist inside the mainland would not receive such red carpet treatment.

A slim young Chinese woman was appointed their guide and she kept up a running commentary, pointing out the pertinent sights the government wished to display. But her expertise was curiously specific. If questions were asked by various members of the committee concerning sights observed about which she had not spoken, she merely went on with the prescribed programme.

Macomber turned her sing-song drone off almost as soon as she had begun; she would, he knew, say nothing he could use. The itinerary of the Trilateral Commission contained ninety-five per cent dross and five per cent real business. In any case, Macomber had other business to attend to; his real reason for accepting a post on the commission. It would take him into China on a perfectly legitimate purpose.

As he stared out the window now at the flowing green and blue of the mainland, he wondered for perhaps the thousandth time what it was that made life so different here. He had the kind of analytical mind that sought logical answers even in the realm of the mystical because the nature of life, as he saw it, was sorting out all the pieces of an incredibly complex jigsaw puzzle. To do it right, he felt, one needed only logic to filter through the facts, assemble them in correct categories, give them specific priorities and then act on the resulting information.

And, in truth, if anything angered him, it was Khieu's misunderstanding of that logic. He possessed a faith in mysticism that was anathema to Macomber. That was one of the reasons Macomber had sent him off to college in Paris. Sound thinking, economic as well as philosophical, he felt, would cause Khieu to realign his thinking. And it had, to a large extent. But Macomber had not counted on the fact that his Cambodian son had no sense of history. Well, how could he? The history, such as it was, of the Khmer lay in the mist-shrouded buildings and temples of Angkor Wat, built by the Khmer king, Suryavarman II from 1130 to 1150 AD.

But the knowledge the ancient Khmer had used to construct these awesome edifices remained a mystery. Macomber counted himself fortunate indeed to have walked through the ruins of that forgotten city before the Khmer Rouge allowed the jungle to creep back, slowly re-engulfing the city.

But what could Khieu or any Khmer for that matter know of Wat? It was as much an enigma to him as it was to Macomber. The Khmer had no heritage, no history and therefore no sense of themselves in the timeline of the world.

What could you do with such people but turn them to your own will? After all, the French had managed to swing the entire country around but so unsuccessfully that the Khmer had begun to turn against one another. But such were the battles of the radical philosophers, too cerebral and too chaste to bring their own fingers to bear on the triggers. They were far too busy calling the foot soldiers to arms to fight for them.

Macomber hated and admired those French radicals all in the same breath. He could not help thinking of them as cowards but the other side of the coin revealed them to be master manipulators. From the moment the first of the Khmer intellectual élite emigrated into their circle, they had politicized the Cambodians to their own polarized point of view. The Khmer were hooked and in Khieu Samphan, the Khmer Rouge at last had found their self-sought saviour. His now famous paper, 'Cambodia's Economy and Industrial Development', became the rebels' bible with which they pointed out the only way for the New Cambodia to survive: to destroy everything and everybody associated with the old, corrupt régime. But by extension the destruction went on and on until the new and 'enlightened' régime became the thought police for the entire country.

That Macomber had taken Khieu out of such an environment had saved the boy's sanity. Cambodia might be his birthplace but the world was his home now. His mind and body had been turned to other, more profitable pursuits by the educating process Macomber had devised for him. The end result was that Khieu was comfortable enough to function in any country.

In many ways, this process had been far more enjoyable for Macomber than siring his own son. He had done his best with Eliott, consulting the best paediatricians, child specialists, teachers, educators. He had steeped himself in their theories, applying the synthesis to his rearing of his son. He was at a loss to understand what had gone wrong. That he loved Eliott made his disappointment that much more difficult to bear.

This incident with the Christian bitch had seemed like the last straw – initially – and Macomber had decided to punish Eliott immediately. Then Khieu had brought him the entire transcript of Eliott's dialogue with the woman and, within that exchange, Macomber had at last begun to sense a way in, a handle, a kind of unconscious power he could wield over his son as he did with everyone else.

How many times had the Christian woman called him a man? A real man. And how Eliott had responded to that. Macomber had immediately understood the intelligence of the woman, knew she was far better off dead. She had found his soft spot and had plunged into it without hesitation. He resolved to take up where she had left off on his return.

Then he turned his thoughts elsewhere, his disquiet returning. It was China: filled with intangibles, abrupt surprises, puzzling multiples. For him there was always a disturbing sense of alien flux occurring just outside his field of vision. He felt he could never rest here but must be continually on the move in order to stay one step ahead of whatever it was he felt dogged his footsteps in the Far East.

Macomber closed his eyes, willing himself to listen to the high-pitched voice of their guide. Soon its insistent buzz had lulled him into sleep.

Outwardly, at least, Shanghai was a city that looked as it always had, dominated by the enormous sweep of the business district along the wide Bund at harbour's edge.

However, that was as far as it went. Once the outlaw capital of the world, where any illegal substance or service could be had at a price, Shanghai was now the trading centre for Communist China. It was less of a tourist attraction to the relatively newly opened mainland than Beijing and some of the more industrial cities to the north.

For one thing Shanghai had always been a foreigner's city, clinging to the mainland as Kowloon did now. Refugees from World War II streamed into the city from Eastern Europe, settling there, hiding within its cosmopolitan clutter.

All that was gone now. But, more than that, the burgeoning variagation that had made such an impression on the teenaged Macomber, had been beaten into the earth. Communism could not tolerate such unchecked individualism.

Now there was one standard, one mode of dress, one way of doing business, one way of obeying the law as well as one standardizing mode of speech. But, as he was about to find out, more than one way of life.

Perhaps because it has always had a history of being China's most open city, the Communist régime understood that there was only so much terraforming that it could do here. Or perhaps it was merely that they were not as omniscient as the mythos they had created made them out to be. Besides, as 'sidestreet news', the unofficial but highly accurate grapevine of the country, said, the government was in desperate need of money to continue the financing of its gargantuan modernization programme. In Shanghai, so it was said, local entrepreneurs were being encouraged to devise their own ways of raising dollars.

At least that was what the Monk told Macomber.

Macomber met the Monk, as prearranged at the Jin Jiang Club. The building, a large, rambling structure with Romanesque overtones, had been the site of the Colonial French Club of Shanghai before the invasion of 1949.

It had been opened in January of 1980 as a kind of playland for foreign businessmen and officials of the government with enough clout to trade in on favours. It housed an Olympic-sized swimming pool, a pinball room, bowling alley, a smoke-filled billiards room, even a place to play mah-jongg, a game the government, at least, frowned upon as being immoral, coming as it did from 'China's decadent feudal' past.

Macomber, in black tie, met the Monk at the French restaurant housed within the many-roomed building. He had been greeted at the door by a tall slim Chinese in a dark Western business suit who bowed as soon as Macomber had handed him the card of invitation.

Soft light of saffron, emerald, sapphire and ruby from Art Deco lamps of coloured glass, illuminated the entranceway, sending gleaming streaks like trembling lacquered nails across a wall composed of imitation Persian mosaic, all deep purple-blue and peacock green.

Macomber was taken past the green-carpeted card room where six Chinese citizens were hunched over their clacking tiles, sweating liquor, creating their own peculiar dialect different even from the off-centre Shanghai variation.

The Monk was sitting at a table for two covered with spotless white linen, gleaming cutlery, sparkling crystal. Behind him, windows overlooked a lush garden in the centre of which were spotlit a pair of green clay tennis courts.

The Monk – it was not his name, of course, but it was the only designation by which Macomber knew him – was a heavy-set man somewhere between fifty and seventy – it was impossible to make a more accurate assessment. He was lithe on his feet and quick to smile. His utterly black eyes were bright and beady. His hair was still black but a natural tonsure had appeared over time at the very top of his skull, thus presenting him with his *nom de guerre*. He was a businessman with no affiliation.

He looked up as Macomber arrived, showing tiny yellow

teeth like ivory antiques, and gestured for the other to sit down. He said nothing, continued to draw blue smoke from a thin, vilely smelling cigarette. A narrow tin with a Victorian design imprinted on it lay open beside his right elbow, displaying perhaps a score more of these instruments of torture.

'Your trip, I trust, was a pleasant one.' The Monk did not look at Macomber when he said it but rather above and a little to the left of him. He wore a wide-lapelled suit that had gone out of style in the 1970's.

'Pleasant but far too long.'

'Ah yes, we have not yet mastered the speed for which you Westerners are so justifiably famous.' His teeth showed again in what might have been a smile in someone else but in the Monk was nothing more than a kind of primitive animal rictus not unlike the baring of one's teeth. 'I want the world and I want it now!' he mimicked in an astonishingly accurate portrayal of an American accent. He looked to Macomber like a gorilla, dressed up, taken out of its cage. 'I like you Mac-omber.' The Monk ground out the failing butt of his cigarette, called the waiter. 'You are not spineless, a fault I find most prevalent among your race.'

'Is that what you consider our major flaw?' He asked for a Scotch on the rocks and the Chinese ordered Stolichnaya.

The Monk considered this question as if it had been put in a perfectly serious way. 'Ah, Mac-omber, faintheartedness is not the quality displayed by a true man. That is so.'

'Yes,' Macomber said. 'I agree with you.'

'Indeed.' The Monk contemplated him for a time. Then he drew out another of his obnoxious cigarettes, lit up. 'Well, perhaps I should not be surprised. After all' – he shrugged – 'you are here with me now. That takes a certain amount of courage.' He bared his teeth again as the drinks came. They lifted their glasses and toasted something – each other, their as yet unconsummated business dealings – in silent communion.

Macomber was surprised at how smooth the liquor was and said so.

'Oh, everything here is imported,' the Monk said. 'Otherwise it would be unpotable.'

'I cannot,' Macomber said, 'understand why you insisted on the meet here.'

'You mean in the Jin Jiang Club?' The Monk ordered another vodka. 'It is the only public place to be in Shanghai. The only truly *civilized* place to meet.' He waved a hand. 'There is the Red House, of course – or Chez Louis, as the older foreigners here still refer to it – but in my humble opinion, the food is not nearly so fine as here.'

'Not what I meant.' Macomber sipped at his whisky, watching the Chinese down the potent vodka with appalling swiftness; the Monk lifted a hand, signed for another. 'Why China at all? There were any number of cities to choose from: Hong Kong, Singapore, Bangkok. All places where we could more easily be lost in the woodwork.'

'More neutral territory, hum?' The Monk accepted his fourth vodka; he had been finishing one when Macomber had come in. 'Well, the fact of the matter is, my dear Mac-omber, I was more concerned with you.' He put a hand up to his chubby chin. 'I blend in in any of those cities.' He chuckled. 'I've got the face for it, you see.'

'But you – you're an American and a well-known American at that. What are you doing in Singapore or Bangkok, hum? In business, so I am given to understand, you deal with the Japanese, primarily. Even Hong Kong is out of the way for you.

'Seen in this light, I found the prospect of the Trilateral Commission's presence here impossible to pass up. In your own country you are publicized as going overseas: your presence here, then, is satisfactorily explained. There is no comment.'

Macomber could find no fault with this analysis. But far from reassuring him, it somehow added to his anxiety. He felt China like the cold fist of an unseen ghost clamping his heart. He thought of how this continent had just swallowed *Tisah* up as if she had been nothing more than the wrapper off a candy bar; as if she had not been a thinking, feeling human being.

Eerie tendrils seemed to enfold him. He did not understand the Chinese; and he did not like them. They made him feel wary because he could never seem to predict what they were thinking or what they were about to do next. They had always been

Tracy Richter's strong suit. He seemed able to get inside these foreign minds; he could think like them. Where the hell had Richter gone when he had dropped out of sight? Then, nine years later, resurfacing as John Holmgren's media advisor.

Well, it didn't matter a damn. Now he was in it and would have to be dealt with.

He had instructed Khieu to get the bug back without causing any kind of disturbance. After he had heard the tape, he had sat and thought for a time. A frontal assault was out of the question. With Richter, subtlety had to be the watchword. Khieu was to retrieve his bug but not until after Richter had passed it on. He had never liked Richter; had always envied him his skills. All Macomber had been able to do in Cambodia was kill. Richter had done much more.

The Monk ordered the Hawaiian cocktail, the *filet mignon Monte Carlo*, a small green salad and, for dessert, the omelete Vesuvius. Macomber, inwardly disgusted by such caloric extravagance, selected the *potage aux langoustes* and the pheasant *en casserole*.

'No sweet?' The Monk's eyes opened wide in astonishment. 'But you must. The head chef is a refugee from a French cruise liner; you refuse his speciality. The soufflé vanilla is superb.'

'I think not,' Macomber said, standing firm. 'I watch my sugar intake carefully.'

A peculiar look crossed the Monk's face as swiftly as a breeze. 'Another round of drinks,' he told the waiter.

Over bitter European coffee, Macomber said, 'About the consignment –'

'Business is not a fit subject for the dining table,' the Monk interrupted. 'I make that a strict point.' He smiled winningly. 'Appearances mean everything here.' He looked at Macomber from beneath his wide brow. 'Surely you are not in a rush?' He giggled lightly. The vodka, Macomber could see, was taking effect. 'Not in China.'

Macomber sat back, relaxed at last. Personally, he disliked this man. He was a boor. But he could easily put his personal feelings on the side. Business was business and the Monk was the only man with a reputation spotless enough for Macomber to go to.

It was not guns his consignment consisted of; not siphoned oil from the Middle East or diamonds smuggled out of South Africa, though he had no doubt that had he a need for any such item, the Monk could supply it within a week's notice. No, his consignment was quite a bit more special than that. The thought built patience within him like a fortress.

At last they were through. The Monk leaned back in his plush chair, stretching. He belched mightily. He noted Macomber's look of obvious distaste.

He called for the bill, paid it with his MasterCard. When the waiter returned, he had with him a plain brown paper shopping bag. The Monk signed the receipt with a flourish, took possession of the bag. With one knuckled fist he pushed himself away from the table.

'Now,' he said, 'it is time for you to see some of our city.'

Though it was after ten when they emerged onto the wide curving steps of the columned entrance, there were still plenty of people about. Macomber followed the Monk's lead as they went down the steps and through the jasmine-scented garden. Close by, he could see the lights of the Jin Jiang's new buildings, making it the city's largest hotel.

They passed a clump of teenagers doing nothing in the semi-darkness. All talk ceased as they approached.

'Do you know the phrase – let me see, how would one put it in English? – ah yes, iron rice bowl?' The shopping bag clacked against the Monk's leg as they walked.

Macomber shook his head.

'The Government has had a change of heart. It now no longer will guarantee a young person a job. It is, instead, encouraging free enterprise. There are just too many people.

They had come out onto Nanjing, one of Shanghai's main roads. Macomber saw poster ads for Sony Walkman cassette players, Pentax 35mm cameras. A battered trolleybus rattled by, nearly empty inside. There were still some pedicabs about.

'Private enterprise,' the Monk said, standing still amid all the motion, 'used to be known as "the tail of capitalism". That was merely three years ago; not much time as these things go.

'They have been used to the security of state work, state medical insurance, and, eventually, a state pension. The iron rice bowl. Take these things away; tell them to go to work for themselves. They do not understand.'

He pointed to a vendor. 'Would you like a Rubik's Cube? My treat.' He laughed throatily. 'No?' He shrugged. 'There are five factories here engaged in making them now. More are sure to start up soon. There are many people in China to feed the craze.'

Macomber was growing impatient. 'Why tell me all this?'

The Monk spread his arms wide, the shopping bag swinging incongruously from one hand. 'All around us there is change. It is in the air, in the food we eat, the liquor we drink.' He turned into the wash of the streetlights, his face looking wider and flatter than it actually was. 'Think of it, Mac-omber, here is yet another potential customer for your wares of war. We are coming of age; we will need the advanced equipment your company designs and manufactures.'

Macomber was taken aback. 'If that's a joke, it's certainly not funny. I sell only to the United States Government and its allies under direct governmental sanction.' He leaned forward, his teeth clenched. 'That excludes all communist countries.'

'Of course,' the Monk said hastily. 'Your politics are well known in our, uhm, community. I was merely making a general point. China *is* in the midst of vast and constant changes. What is true today, falls apart tomorrow. Policy ebbs and flows, eddies and turns back on itself like a dragon's body. We are like the man long blind who finds himself edging into the light. Gradually he begins to observe what is going on all around him. But what is he to make of it all? One day this, the next day that. In the beginning, his progress is slow and not without mistakes. But he goes forward all the same. Because, once having seen the light, he must.'

'I'm not concerned with China,' Macomber snapped. 'And my time is limited. Business calls me home. May we begin now?'

The Monk inclined his head slightly and stepped off the kerb into the midst of the rushing traffic. Before Macomber could react, a beatenup car screeched to a halt. The Monk opened the back door, indicated that Macomber should enter.

Macomber bent his head and sat down; the Monk followed him, slamming the door behind him. He shouted something in incomprehensible Mandarin to the driver who bobbed his head. Gears clashed and the cab took off in herky-jerky fashion.

'Now,' the Monk said beside him, 'we'll get down to business.'

Atherton Gottschalk was ushered into one of the six large conference rooms along the outer perimeter of the Pentagon. Awaiting him in that darkly panelled room with its baffled black acoustic ceiling were the assembled Joint Chiefs of the armed forces of the United States. Behind them was a now quiescent wall video screen flanked on one side by the Stars and Stripes and on the other by the triple flags of the military services.

He took his place behind one angle of the octagonal burl-wood table that had been left vacant for him. Directly in front of him was a set of pens and a metal carafe filled with ice water, a wide-mouthed plain glass. The same, he saw, was true for all the participants present. They sat in high-backed swivel chairs covered in black vinyl. Chrome ashtrays were set into the right arm of each chair. The room was already blue with smoke.

Gottschalk turned to his aide, nodded. The man began to disperse blue-bindered folders to each of the men sitting around the octagonal table.

'Gentlemen,' Gottschalk began, 'what you see being placed before you now is a blueprint for *your* future. A blueprint for the security ... and military superiority of the United States of America in the latter half of the 1980's and the beginning of the nineties.'

He paused here, opening his folder in a silent bid for all of them to do the same. 'Now as I am certain all of you are aware, my nomination for my party's candidacy for President is at a serious stage. I need additional support, I won't deny that. I have not come here to snow you' – Gottschalk smiled almost shyly – 'but to *snowball* you.'

There was a generous amount of chuckling at his small joke. He looked around the room, from formidable face to formidable face, making eye contact with each in turn, giving them the impression that he was speaking intimately to each one alone, imparting a well-kept secret.

'Now most of you know me well. You know that in the past I have fought tooth and nail for military appropriations of a considerable order, especially during these past four trying years in the face of a truculent and, in my opinion, weak-willed Democratic administration. I have fought an at present losing battle against certain dovecote appointees to the National Security Council.'

He paused again, poured himself a glass of water, took a sip. 'The decided détentenik tilt to the present administration is in all ways alarming. The State Department's strained relations with Israel, an ally who even in the best of times – which this certainly is not – is essential to this country's Middle East interests, comes from the mistaken notion that the Saudi princes must be cajoled at all costs.

'But there is another issue that you must face. My Republican competition come August is a man who brings with him all the dangerous baggage of the Republican Establishment détente policies so much in vogue a decade ago. He will weasel diplomatic talks with the Soviets while they cut us down to size in Afghanistan, Poland, and Third World nations I need not itemize here; while their trained minions infiltrate our own bases, murdering such heroes as Lieutenant Colonel DeWitt.'

Applause ringed the room and Gottschalk felt distinctly satisfied. It was a signal that an initial rapport, so vital in this kind of situation, had been secured. He had gained a beachhead; he was no longer the outsider, a poacher on private military territory, a problem every civilian, no matter his politics, faced when entering this sanctum.

'I have seen the monthly intelligence summaries and I, too, am becoming increasingly alarmed at the great strides the Soviet Union in particular has made in its arms development over the past four or five years. The previous Republican administration, as I am certain you are well aware, did its level best to increase

326

military expenditure. But they only scratched the surface before opposition from several quarters scuttled their attempts.'

He glanced down for a moment. 'You will see on this first page, the vital statistics for a totally new, computer-controlled helicopter.' There was the rustle of pages being turned. 'It is fully armour-plated, capable of speeds approximately three times what even today's advanced choppers are capable of . . . either here or in the Soviet Union.

'It is equipped with total "night vision", the operator is computer-assisted, via a revolutionary laser-activated circuit and, best of all, it can carry up to eight cruise missiles. In short, gentlemen, the Vampire is a breakthrough in military technology: it makes us mobile and lethal at the same time.'

The senator took another sip of water. 'The folder before you contains six more militarily advantageous designs to give us the capability edge against our foes. All of them – including the *Vampire* – are not only off the drawing board but are fully operational. Yes you heard me correctly; *Fully operational.*' Gottschalk leaned forward again. 'All that remains is your approval and, of course, the most difficult part, additional appropriations.

'Now, gentlemen, as you can see, all these new weapons systems are the result of one company's efforts: Metronics, Inc. As you may know, the company's founder and president is Delmar Davis Macomber and as you also may know, he and I are not exactly the best of friends.' Chuckles again at the senator's wry smile. He lifted his hands, palms outward. 'Well. All right, I admit, we've had our differences.' His voice was almost boyish; he was confiding secrets again. 'And we continue to have our differences, personally, professionally and, yes, even politically. But' – he lifted a forefinger in warning – 'in one important matter we *do* agree. And that is in our belief that the *Vampire* provides us with an unequalled window of opportunity in determining this country's security from not only worldwide communism but worldwide terrorism.'

Gottschalk was grim again. 'Gentlemen, we have seen all too often in recent years the escalation of incidents of terrorism against the United States of America in Iran, West Germany,

Egypt, and Peru. And these incidents are increasing as we head into the 1990's. We have already seen it spread like a plague from the nations of the Third World into Europe. Such allies as West Germany, Italy, France and England have already succumbed.

'And I say to you now, our time is soon coming. We must be prepared for that occurrence and deal with it swiftly, strongly and surely. For, gentlemen, where will we be then, when the land of the free and the home of the brave is held hostage by forces hostile to our way of life?'

Gottschalk had timed it well, had judged his audience perfectly. Applause rang out again, smiles, head noddings and handshakes. Everyone wanted to congratulate him, and pledge his support in the coming convention and beyond into the election.

Their applause and well wishes echoed in his mind even after he had left them, was safely ensconced in his limousine, being driven back to Alexandria. He turned, stared out of the window. Never had the lights of Washington seemed so clear and crisp to him, never had they seemed so alive and full of promise.

On impulse, he pressed the intercom, told his driver to turn around, take him across the bridge into the city. This was no time for home and Virginia. It was an awesome moment, a quintessentially DC moment.

As they rolled across the Arlington Memorial Bridge, he leaned forward, staring straight ahead at the brilliantly illuminated needle of the Washington Monument just beyond the long reflecting pool. The beams of the spotlights seemed to him ethereal guy wires holding the edifice tall and majestic.

He climbed out of the limo at the Lincoln Memorial, ascending alone up the white marble steps up which so many Americans had come over the years to marvel, just as he was doing now, at the wonder of the lifelike replica of the former President.

For Gottschalk, it was as if he had been born again, as if this night he was seeing the enormous sculpture of Abraham Lincoln for the first time though in reality he could not count the number of times he had gazed at it.

The greatness of the man seemed to suffuse the night and

Gottschalk came closer as if in a trance, feeling the power flooding into him. For that blazing instant Lincoln was again alive bestriding the earth with his energy and convictions.

It was a supreme moment in Gottschalk's life. He tingled with the energy flooding through him, basking in the floodlights as if they were meant for him. And they will be he thought. One day soon.

Only one thing was left to make this night complete and he turned, went quickly down the steps, and into the waiting limo, reaching immediately for the telephone.

Kathleen was in New York, so her office had told his secretary when she had called, and there was little he could do about it. He asked the mobile operator to get him the number of the Parker Meridian Hotel in New York, sat back on the cushions.

Idly he thought about chartering the jet to New York to surprise her, pick her up. Part of him knew how crazy that was but it did not stop another part of him from wanting to do it. Only the thought that it would cause heavy enough waves to perhaps jeopardize his nomination deflected him.

She had not been in when he had called earlier from the fund-raising dinner at the Hilton, still he had to try again. Perhaps it was late enough for her to be in. Christ, but he hated this feeling of impotence and sitting on the phone, listening to an un-answered ring made it all the worse. Angrily, he slammed the receiver into its cradle. No, he did not want to leave a message for Miss Christian. If he did that he might as well call the *Washington Post* with the news of his affair.

Gottschalk growled under his breath, his previous mood of elation punctured like a fragile balloon. His mind raced with thoughts of Kathleen. Who was she out with? Would they come back to her hotel room and make love? Perhaps that was what they were doing now, ignoring the insistent ring of the phone.

With thoughts of Kathleen flooding his mind he willed himself to think about 31 August, noontime in New York, he fresh from his nomination, the campaign for the Presidency in full swing. And then, on the front steps of St Patrick's Cathedral, one of the most revered and beloved edifices in the world, would come Delmar Davis Macomber's master stroke: An élite cadre of international terrorists taking hostages, Gottschalk among them.

His chest puffed out in pride at the thought. What an amazing and audacious strategist Macomber was! How fortunate Gottschalk felt to have allied himself with the man. He was an absolute genius.

Gottschalk saw himself standing tall in the midst of the ensuing chaos at St Pat's, hanging tough, emerging heroic when it was all over, being swept into the White House by the largest plurality since Nixon's first win.

His face glowed. Christ, how I love it! he thought. And he believed in it with all his soul. He could see every moment unfolding in his mind's eye as if it were a slow-motion film: each shot, gesture, expression, photograph, headline. Oh, the headlines! Gottschalk moaned as he allowed himself to revel in the future. The press!

He was getting hard, and he shifted uncomfortably in the seat. Soon the bulge was noticeable even in the semi-darkness of the limo. The hell with Kathleen. He had not wanted her to go to New York anyway. He decided not to phone her again until she returned. He could do without her.

'Home,' he told the driver.

Immediately, an image formed of the swell of Roberta's breasts, the sweep of her legs, the quiver of the soft flesh on the inside of her thigh.

Just another example, he thought, of events overshadowing the importance of one mere individual. It was politics at work.

Tracy called Thwaite just before they were about to leave. It was a bright sunny day and because of Tracy's imminent departure for Hong Kong and the advent of one of Lauren's infrequent days off, they had decided to drive out to the beach.

'It's about time we thought about motive,' the detective said.

'I was going to ask you how you were,' Tracy said, 'but I guess I don't have to now.' Tracy had gone to the double funeral and had stood beside Thwaite. He had seen the look of hatred his in-laws had directed at the detective. They would not speak to Thwaite nor come anywhere near him. He was right. They

330

blamed him and him alone for the deaths of their daughter and granddaughter. The aggression in the air had given the funeral a strange, chilling atmosphere that seemed to negate the reason for its existence in the first place. Thwaite had been stoic throughout, only breaking down at the graveside after everyone else had left, the sun beating down on his head, the wind plucking at his hair like ghostly fingers.

'I'm okay,' Thwaite said quickly. Then, after a small pause, 'It comes and goes like some weird disease I can't get rid of. Work helps. I'm glad something does.'

'You do any more thinking about Melody?' Tracy said into the phone.

'I been thinking, yeah.' He cleared his throat. 'Ever since you phoned me with that Hong Kong angle I've been going through motives. I figured it was either something Holmgren knew that got him iced or maybe something on the political side. You'd know more about that than I would. Had he any enemies?'

'Politicians *all* have enemies,' Tracy said. 'That's part of the territory. But I don't see anyone who'd murder him. Not in the particular way it was done. Who'd have that kind of access to knowledge of that sort? Anyway, I can't see a politician even *thinking* along those lines. It's too complex; too arcane.'

'Okay,' Thwaite said. 'Maybe I'm asking this the wrong way. Who had the most to gain from Holmgren's death?'

'Are you speaking politically now?'

'Yeah. That's right.'

'I'd have to say Atherton Gottschalk. He and John were at loggerheads over the upcoming presidential nomination at the Republican convention next month. It's still going to be a helluva fight but now I think Gottschalk's got the momentum, especially in light of what's been happening overseas lately.'

'Hum. Think he could be behind it? You know I can't get that bug out of my mind. Watergate and all that.'

'I see what you mean. I thought of that right away. I know Gottschalk pretty well. He's tough and he hated John all right. His entire staff did. He wants to be President very badly but then again three or four other candidates do too. I think murder's out of their line.'

'I see.'

'What's on your mind?'

'Maybe nothing. I don't know.' Tracy heard the shuffling of papers. 'Report crossed my desk. I asked the computer to give me a list of all deaths other than from natural causes of politicians for the past six months. It came up with only one. You know a . . . Senator Roland Burke?'

'I knew of him. Never met him. He was a good man. I was frankly surprised when I heard he was thinking of not going up for re-election in September. At the time, I thought that would have been a blow for the Senate and now that he's dead, I know I was right.'

'Says here he was taken out by an intruder. The Chi police are convinced of that.'

'What was the MO?'

'You're gonna love this. Autopsy report shows death by massive cranial bleeding caused by the jamming of his bone cartilage up into his brain.'

There was so much silence on the line after that that Thwaite was forced to say, 'Tracy? Are you there?'

'I think,' Tracy said slowly, 'you ought to go out there.'

'Trail'll be a bit cold by now but I agree it's worth a shot.' He cleared his throat again. 'You think this's our boy?'

'I think it could be.' Tracy's mind was racing. 'Of course, an extremely strong man could do it but the angle has to be –' He broke off. 'Does the report say what shape the cartilage was in?'

'No. I don't see anything here.'

'Okay, I didn't really think it would. When you're down there go see the ME who did the autopsy. He'll know.'

'What'm I looking for?'

'I'd say that if the cartilage was whole we've got a shot. He'd've got the angle right. A strong man without training would've mashed the stuff to paste with the second or third blow.'

'Right,' Thwaite said. 'I'll see what I can dig up.' He laughed. 'Don't stay away too long.'

Tracy knew Thwaite was trying to tell him to be careful. 'Only as long as I have to. I'll see you.'

Lauren was staring at him from across the room. Beside her was the wicker picnic basket they had filled with cold roast chicken, tuna sandwiches, potato salad, olives, fresh fruit and a bottle of white wine.

'What d'you think you're doing?' she said softly. Her long hair was pulled back and braided in a double line at the back of her head so that her cheekbones and lips seemed more pronounced. She wore a red tee shirt emblazoned with NYCB and a pair of white shorts that showed off her spectacular legs. 'I thought that after what happened to Douglas's family,' she rushed on, 'you'd let it alone.'

'I can't,' he said simply. 'I thought you'd understand that.'

'What I understand,' she said angrily, 'is that the two of you may get yourselves killed.'

He looked at her stolidly, aware of the tears glistening in the corners of her eyes.

'Don't you understand,' she said, shaking a little, 'that I can't bear the thought of losing you? Not now. Not after all the garbage we've cleared away. How often in a lifetime does love come, d'you suppose? Once, if you're lucky. More only if you're willing to settle. I'm not.' She moved closer to him. 'You're flying off to the other side of the world to meet God knows who and do God knows what. Did you ever think that you might not come back?'

'Nothing's going to happen to me.'

'Oh, Tracy.'

Her voice broke and he took her in his arms, kissed her softly, lingeringly.

'You're so sure.' Her voice was a whisper. And then, as a small child might, she asked, 'Why must you?'

'Because,' he said, 'I've a duty to John. I have a responsibility to see this through.'

'It has nothing to do with Kim?'

'Something, maybe. Yes.'

'I know where Kim is from. I thought you walked away from there.'

What could he say? He heard again Thwaite's voice . . . *some part of you enjoyed it*. Was that Higure's *kokoro*? Was that what

333

Jinsoku saw in him at the Mines? Was he hero enough to look for himself and find out? He turned his mind away.

'I have Kim under control. He's useful because he gives me access to my former outfit's resources. Don't worry about Kim.'

She pushed away from him a little. 'Don't you see? It's not Kim I'm worried about. It's *you.*'

Perhaps to help assuage her growing anxiety, he took her first to meet his father. That they had never met before was no fault of hers. Rather it was a function of Tracy's past relationship with Louis.

He parked the Audi on Christopher and while Lauren waited in front of the building's front door, he went around the corner to a Greek coffee shop and bought her a package of Hostess cupcakes as a surprise.

The old man was delighted to see her; he had always wanted a daughter and, in fact, Tracy's former reluctance to bring her around had in itself been a sore point with him.

Tracy quite deliberately did not tell her about Louis's illness because he wanted her reaction to him to be genuine and not a function of sadness and, perhaps, pity.

He needn't have worried. She took to Louis right away and he watched in fascination as the old man led her on a tour of the large rambling apartment.

In fact, Tracy could not know the depths to which she responded to the old man. Lauren was utterly charmed by him, feeling his warmth and concern. He was so unlike her own stern, no-nonsense father that she soon discovered a long-held ache within her chest melting like a spring thaw. In the fifteen minutes she had been with him, Louis Richter had asked more about her dancing – her life in general – than her father had in fifteen years. With him she experienced none of the unpleasant echoes of childhood she found deadening whenever she went home to visit her parents. Invariably those visits turned into confrontations.

Driving east on the Long Island Expressway, sometime later, she found she wanted to talk about the past. 'Why do you refer to it as Southeast Asia when you really mean Cambodia?'

Tracy gave her a look, then accelerated past a small red Fiat.

334

'For a long time,' he said slowly, 'nobody was to know what we were up to. Cambodia was ostensibly neutral in the war and therefore off-limits to both sides. That, as we both know, was not the case. Cambodia was harbouring tens of thousands of Viet Cong. Sihanouk made the wrong-headed decision to allow them to infest the border. He felt that by dealing with Vietnam instead of persisting with the traditional policy of distrust and hatred, he could keep Cambodia safe. He thought he could put the Communists into his country's debt and ensure Cambodia's sovereignty for the future. But he failed to understand the ramifications of his actions. He failed to take *us* into account. Looking at the world view was never one of his great virtues.'

'Then he should have shut the North Vietnamese out.'

'I don't know. It's not as simple as that. He felt threatened. It was all he could think of to do. But what his successors, Lon Nol, Pol Pot, Ieng Sary, and the Khmer Rouge proceeded to do was even worse. Their campaign of genocide and race hatred against the Vietnamese alienated them from every civilized nation and eventually resulted in their own defeat in January of 1979. It threw Cambodia totally open to Vietnamese emigrés. The country has lost not only its sovereignty but its national identity. It's all gone now, drowned in rivers of blood and napalm jelly.'

He took the Southampton exit, turning south until he came to Montauk Highway. He continued east. 'In any event,' he went on, 'we were in there clandestinely.' He shrugged. 'Then, later, after I had been inside the country for a time, after I had gotten to know ... well, I think it was my shame at what we had done – not only us Americans but the French, particularly the French, the Vietnamese and the Chinese – to the Khmer, to their beautiful country. We turned them on themselves, turned the country into a nightmare of blood and death.'

Lauren shuddered. They had turned off Montauk Highway just past Water Mill, heading south again to the shoreline and Flying Point Beach. It was far enough out on the Island to be relatively deserted even at this time of the year.

Back in the lee of a high dune, they were sheltered and alone. Far down the beach to the west, past a long curving slice of land, the million-dollar houses began with their cantilevered sides and glass bubble skylights.

Tracy put his hands behind his head; Lauren was beside him with the sun in her eyes. Her long lashes threw tiny shadows into the soft hollows of her face so that she looked as she did onstage.

'It would be so easy, I suppose, to say I went to Southeast Asia because there was a job to be done and I wanted to do it,' he said. 'Oh, sure, I was young enough then to believe that it was as simple as getting the communists out of Vietnam and Cambodia. But they taught us nothing of politics.'

'You were too busy learning how to kill.'

Tracy looked at her. 'First we had to learn how to survive.' He put one hand on her arm, stroked it. 'But you see they thought once we'd passed through the training they could just plunk us down anywhere and let us apply what we'd learned. It wasn't nearly that simple. And what finally drove me out was the knowledge that *they'd* never change. Time after time I saw them applying the same principles – *their* principles – to *every* type of situation and when they failed, as they often did, they were at a complete loss as to explain it.

'I knew what it was, of course, but they didn't want to hear it.' Tracy sighed. 'They made the enormous mistake of treating the Khmer the same way they treated the North Vietnamese. Christ, what idiots! The Vietnamese have a history of warfare and aggression. But Cambodia was a pastoral paradise, filled with Buddhism and peace. That was before the war. Now Cambodia – the old Cambodia – is dead, buried beneath the crumbling ruins of Angkor Wat. And the *new* Cambodia, if you can call it that, is eating itself alive like a rabid dog.'

Lauren was shocked, her face white and pinched. 'But how could that be?' she asked. 'What happened?'

'We were out-politicked not out-fought. As usual, we backed the wrong party. It was clear to me, at least, that Lon Nol was the last person we should have endorsed. But we were attacking what we saw as the problem by rote – not as a separate situation. The Khmer Rouge immediately seized on our support to convince the populace, even down to the Buddhist monks, that they – the Khmer Rouge – were the country's own salvation. But the day after they overthrew Lon Nol, the anti-Vietnamese pogroms began in such force that the Khmer Republicans pleaded with the Saigon government to intervene.

'The Vietnamese army invaded Cambodia, slaughtering as they came. Since then Cambodia has known only war and subjugation.'

'And that's what's been eating at you.'

He looked away. A fishing trawler was coming down the coast, its thick black nets slung like drapery from its forked yellow masts. Briefly they heard the liquid thrumming of its diesels. Tracy longed to tell her. He knew that until he did nothing could be truly right between them. He was holding back a secret part of himself, a part that concerned her in the most intimate way. That he held himself responsible for her brother's death was a chasm he felt yawning between them. He had to span that gulf one day and make it disappear. He *had* to tell her.

'You know, it's funny,' he said at last, 'when I was younger I used to wonder how my mother ever married my father.'

'Are you kidding?' Lauren shaded her eyes. 'He's so wonderful.'

'What I mean is, she knew what he did . . . for whom he worked. She was such a pacifist, you see. I guess she just resigned herself . . . because her love for him was so strong.' He looked at her. 'Can you understand that?'

Lauren nodded. 'Of course.'

A small breeze had sprung up, the green dune grass waving like the tendrils of a sea anemone above their heads along the crest.

She was running handfuls of sand through her fingers, reclining on one elbow, her long legs stretched out, crossed at the ankles. They had both doffed their light street clothes in favour of bathing suits. Lauren's was a maillot the same creamy colour as her skin so that, from a distance, she appeared startlingly nude, beribboned only by the design of obliquely curling pink and mauve flowers at the end of their waving stalks.

'How long will you be gone?' She spoke so softly that Tracy wondered if he had imagined the question.

337

'I don't know.'

She looked up, shading her eyes again. 'Where are you staying? I'll want to call.'

'I don't think that'd be a good idea.'

There was nothing along the beach but the wind and the crash and suck of the surf, moving from left to right like writing on a page, endless and comforting. Wisps of her hair had come undone, fluttering now against the skin of her cheeks in the warm breeze.

'Maybe I'll be able to call you,' he added. But he knew it was far too little. She knew he could not mean it, not where he was going, not with what he had to do. She knew well the meaning of concentration.

But Lauren was only thinking of him in an oblique fashion. Somehow his imminent departure had triggered in her intense memory flashes of Bobby. Of the last time she ever saw him alive, of that moment of seeing him leave the house out of the periphery of her vision while she was in the middle of her morning's ballet exercises. She had been too busy then, concentrating on what she must learn by the afternoon for the audition, to kiss him goodbye. She had not even said a word to him. Perhaps he had called out to her. She did not remember. And that moment was the first thing that popped into her mind, the afternoon she had accompanied her parents out to Dulles International to take possession of the earthly remains of Robert Arthur Marshall. He would have been nineteen in a week and a half.

Concentration. It was what made her great. It was also what had doomed her that one cold grey day when Bobby had dropped out of her life like a stone.

'Tracy, I don't want you to go.' Her voice tightened up and she worked on ignoring the lump in her throat. 'I know I'm being terribly selfish but I don't care. I'm frightened that something awful will happen to you. I'm frightened that you'll get on the plane and I'll never ...' She put her hands up over her face. Her shoulders shook as she wept. 'Oh, God, I'm sorry. I'm just being weepy, I don't know why, I ...'

He took her head in his hands, pushed himself towards her.

He began to brush away her tears so he could see her beautiful eyes unclouded. He thought of how much pleasure the sight gave him.

They kissed long and deep, their tongues exploring as if for the first time. He felt her body strong and supple against his, the ripple of her breathing, the warmth of her breasts and belly. He touched her cheek, the side of her neck, the hollow of her collarbone, the flat planes of her shoulder. He put his lips against her neck and her eyes closed.

'You're in the darkness,' she whispered, 'and I'm in the light.' Her arms came around him, her fingertips pressing at the contours of his muscles, moving slowly, methodically as if she were a blind woman learning the body of her new lover.

In her mind, she saw his face dappled in moonlight, moving from shadow to shadow, the hero he said himself to be. She believed every word that he said, knew that, if anything, he had underplayed his prowess. She understood without him having to explain it to her that by the very nature of what he had once done – what she was now certain he was again engaged in – he could tell her only the bare outlines. She was grateful for that intimacy while at the same time acknowledging her own yearning to know more.

His flesh felt hot as it slid against hers and she whimpered. He began to roll down the top of her maillot, his head lowering and she started to turn her head to see if the beach was still deserted. But the instant his lips closed over nipples, she could think of nothing else.

She cradled his head in her arms while veins of pleasure raced down into her groin. She felt heat suffusing her pelvis and with it a wetness she revelled in.

She cried out when she felt Tracy's long forefinger touch her along the centre crease of her vagina. The outer lips were already swollen and parting and even through the second skin of the bathing suit she could feel him pressing inward. The sensation of the fabric moving to the beat of his finger against her rising clitoris made her suck in her breath.

His mouth was moving, leaving her nipples tingling. Desire clotted her throat making speech next to impossible. Guttural

339

sounds emanated from her instead, a siren's song of lust and love, entwining passion with the emotional bond without which sex soon sours.

Tracy had never been so aroused, even in his early encounter with her. He found that he could not catch his breath and when he panted his exhalations seemed fiery. He had been hard even before he had peeled back Lauren's bathing suit but now he was so large, his own brief suit could not contain him. And when Lauren's fingertips snaked down, enfolding his scrotum, the tip of his penis quivered and jerked as if he were about to come.

'Oh!' The exclamation forced out of her mouth as if with a blow. 'Tracy . . .' A sigh like a cloud riding high on warm wind and sunlight as she traced his long length upward. She gasped again when she encompassed the naked head pushed up above the suit's waistband. 'It's so silky.' Her words a spur, heightening their pleasure.

For Tracy, Lauren's husky voice, deepened by lust, was enough for him to come erect. It was filled with hidden depths, promises of unsaid delights. At that moment he was convinced she could croon him to orgasm.

And no one loved to kiss as much as she did. Her breasts shook with her body's shivers as their lips crushed together. Her taste was like no other, as if it contained some spice unique to her.

She would not allow them to stop the kiss but still her arms moved down him until his bathing suit slipped off and he was naked. He pushed up against her and she cried out, frantic now for the union, the reunion in full, her nails tearing at her maillot, groaning in frustration until he helped her.

He wanted to enter her then but she shook her head, whispered, 'First, first', thickly so that he had no desire to do anything she did not ask.

Her head swooped down, sunlight shining on the hair, burnishing it, lightening it to the unearthly shade of a goddess's and her opened lips engulfed him slowly, slowly and so wetly and he groaned deep in his chest, the vibrations passing back and forth from one to the other. Her mouth rode him, an exquisite silkenness surrounding him, spirals of pleasure swirling with each swipe of her tongue around the head until he was trembling, his buttocks clenched tightly as his hips strained off the blanket.

Her lips lifted and she stared into his face, her eyes huge and liquid with lust. 'Now,' she said to him. 'Oh, now.'

And Tracy, his penis quivering with tension, moved against her, probing and an instant later penetrated her in one long slow heated slide that brought tiny tears to the corners of her eyes.

'Oh,' she sighed. 'Oh, oh, ohhh . . .' And clenched his buttocks fiercely, rhythmically as she slid up against him and back.

Neither of them ever wanted it to end but their desire was soaring, fluttering and unbound with release the only recourse. Tracy stroked faster and faster, his arms around her strongly and tenderly as if he were afraid she might fly off him at any minute.

Lauren had one hand on his buttocks, the other spread wide as a starfish, drinking in the play of muscles along his back. Her open mouth sucked hungrily at the tightened cords of his neck and when she felt the peculiar singing come into his frame – recalled from oh so long ago – like an airplane lifting off, she pushed one long forefinger through the moist crease of his buttocks, further and further, searching until she found the entrance. Nearby, the pull and suck: the friction building to unbearable heights.

She found it and went slowly in, impaling him as he impaled her. He felt his thickly muscled body give a warning shiver. 'Oh, yes, baby,' she whispered hotly into the shell of his ear, 'That's right. Come, baby. Come. Ohhh!'

Lauren lost all sense of time and space, as if her orgasm had thrown her free, displaced and rushing with the wind. The speed of a bullet, in the space of a heartbeat. Travelling past. She was aware of herself and Tracy only, linked by the rising pool of pleasure like ripples in a lake, spreading outward endlessly, the hot lick of the sun against their damp flesh.

For Tracy, the aftermath was very hard. He had the taste of ashes in his mouth as the spectre of Lauren's broken brother rode like a slave-driver, urging him on. Their shared intimacy – that sparked moment when he felt closer to her than he had to anyone else in his life – only exacerbated his guilt until he could no longer bear the burden. It was as if, once having known how close they could really become, he now experienced his withdrawal from her as something obscene, his secret at last too hideous a deformity.

'Lauren,' he whispered hoarsely. 'Lauren . . .'

Close to him, she saw the look on his face and was abruptly terrified. 'Darling, what is it?'

He clutched her to him as he told her all of it. Everything he had vomited up to Thwaite during that long drunken night in Chinatown.

He felt with despair the spasm of her frame when he described the manner of Bobby's death; felt with deadening emotions her pulling away from him as he recounted his belief in his complicity in it.

'Bastard!' she spat out. 'Cold-hearted bastard to have done such an unthinking thing to him!' She had scrambled up on all fours as animals will do when they are surprised and frightened. 'He was a boy! Just a *boy*!' Her body felt cold despite the heat of the sun on her; she was contracting into the same ball she had been in on that day at Dulles when they had wheeled out the wooden casket from the belly of the plane, the sun spinning crazily off the bevelled edges. She stared at Tracy now, shadowed by his own body as the light struck him from behind; he did not seem the same person who had driven out with her to this spot. Her heart felt swollen and old but the hot flame of righteousness burned beside it, imparting to it an unnatural glaze of strength.

'If it hadn't been for you,' she cried wildly, 'he'd be alive today!'

'Lauren, I only wanted to –'

'I don't care what you wanted!' She snatched at her clothes, began to retreat up the sloping bank of the face of the dune. 'I don't know how I ever could have cared!'

She stumbled, on her knees now, facing him, facing the creaming waves, the beautiful crescent shoreline, his beautiful face. But none of those things mattered to her; there was no longer any beauty left in the world. Only the ugliness of her brother's horrendous death, the vileness she found humped inside her like some leprous growth.

He reached out towards her, beseeching. 'Lauren, I did what I could to make amends. I –'

'I see! That's right! You killed again!' She was quite hysterical, her eyes opened so wide he could see the whites shining all around. 'No wonder you couldn't look at me when you got off the plane with Bobby's body! I don't blame you! But if you'd had any decency left in you, you'd've left me alone. But you didn't. You pursued me!' Her voice dropped to a harsh guttural sound. 'For the love of God why?'

'Because I loved you. The way I love you now.'

'Love?' Her laugh was chilling. 'What love?' She was mocking him now. 'You make love to me all the while knowing what you did to my poor Bobby!'

'Lauren, he was my friend. I cared about him.' His voice held a note of desperation he could not control; he could see the situation was already slipping by him. 'He relied on me; we relied on each other. How d'you think I felt when I saw what they'd done to him?'

'I don't think you felt *anything*! You know that? I don't think you're capable of anything approaching human feeling. The war, the war. *That's* why you were there! That's all you thought about. Save the mission! Because war means killing, Tracy, and let me tell you something, you must like it an awful lot because that's what you did there! Kill, kill and then kill some more!'

He reached out again but the space between them seemed far too wide now. 'Give me a chance to explain, at least. Surely you owe me that much.'

She scrambled up, retreating now to the high snaking crest of the dune. Rivulets of sand dribbled down, hissing at his bare feet. 'I don't owe a *murderer* anything! Bastard! Just get me out of here!' She turned her back on him, disappearing towards the car while slowly, as if he were in the middle of a dream, he packed up all the detritus of their picnic.

Tracy held the unopened Hostess cupcakes package in his hand, cupping it tenderly. There were tear strains on it when he packed it away with the other debris.

The Shanghai night was too hot, despite the breeze blowing

in through the taxi's open window. Macomber contorted himself in the back seat, taking off his jacket. Beneath, his white cotton shirt clung to his back like a clammy layer of half-peeled skin.

'A pity the cab is not air-conditioned, eh, Mac-omber?' the Monk said. His head was not turned, the eyes slid sideways in their sockets. 'There, is that better?'

'Even the damn wind's hot.'

The Monk nodded. 'Summer's often difficult here. But one becomes used to such inhospitable circumstances.'

The cab had headed north, out of the old French quarter in which they had dined so sumptuously. Now they were in the northern part of the Old Chinese City.

Along Anren Street the cab screeched to a halt and the Monk handed the driver a handful of *fen*. Macomber did not think he had tipped the old man.

They debarked onto the kerbside. In front of them, beyond a white wall, loomed black trees.

'Yu Garden,' the Monk said. 'Come.' He took Macomber inside. It appeared deserted.

'I feel very conspicuous here.'

'Nonsense.' The Monk led him forward. 'This is the best time to come.' He made a face. 'You would not care for it here during the day, Macomber. So filled with people. Impossible to enjoy the serene calm and beauty here.'

They went through a turning. A white curved wall confronted them. It was surmounted by a dragon's undulating body. The Monk guided them to the left where the wall ended in an intricately carved dragon's head.

'There are over thirty pavilions here,' the Monk said with a touch of pride. 'It was begun in 1537, during the Ming Dynasty.' He turned slowly around. 'Now where would it be best for us to disappear? There are many, many places.' His eyes lit up. 'Ah, there.' He pointed. 'The Bridge of Nine Turnings.' They began to walk. 'There is a famous tea house there but I regret that at this time of night it is closed.' He could not contain another giggle. 'Ah, well, it is the better for us, eh?'

They made themselves comfortable on the stones which were

cool and refreshing to lean against. All around them, trees whispered, turning the city night to pitch.

The Monk scrabbled in the paper shopping bag, extracted a bottle of Stolichnaya, broke the seal. 'Ah, now,' he said. 'This was worth waiting for.' He poured into two waxed paper cups, handed one to Macomber who could see the Chinese had filled his own cup almost to the rim.

'Isn't this a bit premature?' Macomber said sardonically.

The Monk peered at him. 'My dear Mac-omber. You have flown halfway around the world to see me. You wish a consignment I alone can make available. Shall we both walk away from Yu Garden unfulfilled? I think not.' He raised his cup. 'Will you drink with me?'

Macomber was well aware that he had no choice. He sipped while the Monk drowned a third of the contents of his cup.

'Now to business.' The Monk rubbed his palms together as if in anticipation. 'For seven men – Islamic fanatics – the price must be high. I'm certain you understand that.'

'Perfectly.'

'They have to be recruited, segregated and suitably indoctrinated.'

'All in their own language,' Macomber said. 'This is essential. No hint that a foreign power is involved can be leaked to them.'

The Monk nodded sagely. 'I understand. It shall be done ... for a price.' He dug his ample buttocks more comfortably against the cool stones of the bridge's sides. 'Let us say seven million; one for each man.'

'Out of the question.' Macomber twirled his waxed paper cup between his thumb and fingers. 'I am prepared to offer you two million dollars.'

The Monk looked as if Macomber had offended him mortally. An odd animal noise came from between his lips. 'Six million. That's as low as I can possibly go.'

'Three.'

'Five-and-a -half.'

'That's double what they're worth,' Macomber said.

The Monk shrugged, poured himself another cup of vodka. 'Go somewhere else then.'

'I can't pay you more than four million.'

'If you pay me five, you'll have your consignment,' the Monk said. He began to drink.

Macomber thought about it. Five million was more than he had anticipated paying. But on the other hand he did not believe the Monk would go any lower. What other choice did he have? He needed the men ... he was working with a timetable that allowed him little leeway.

He nodded. 'Done. They're to be delivered in two lots – one and then six. You know the dates. August thirtieth and December twenty-third.'

'Done and done!' The Monk cried, downing the rest of his vodka. He immediately poured himself more. He eyed Macomber. 'I'll tell you, I'm glad that's over. Frankly, I don't enjoy negotiating. I'm a doer; I like putting things together. *There's* the challenge.'

'War's the only real challenge,' Macomber said. 'Nothing's left of this country now.' He was half-fearful of offending the Chinese but the liquor he had consumed during the long evening allowed him to voice his real feelings. 'The place gives me the creeps. It's as if the country's just waiting for a war again. There're too many ghosts here.'

The Monk eyed Macomber and nodded his agreement. 'Yes,' he said. 'It's perfectly true. Too many friends are dead; too many families disappeared as if swallowed whole.'

'You've got it,' Macomber said.

The Monk looked bewildered. 'Got what?'

Macomber laughed. 'What I mean is, you're right. I was worried about you for a while.'

The Monk looked politely curious. 'Yes? How so?'

'Thought maybe you were a communist.'

'A free trader has no politics,' the Monk said, his head beginning to nod a bit. 'Can't afford to.'

'But you're loyal to the People's Republic. Surely you're political to that extent.'

The Monk stared out over Macomber's head towards the spreading boughs of an ancient gingko tree. 'It's said that tree's four hundred years old.' He sighed deeply. 'That is how old I feel, Mac-omber, I will tell you truly.'

'I have seen them come and go here. The powerful and the shrewd. They all get sliced up in the end and me along with them.'

'You're still here,' Macomber pointed out. 'Thriving.'

The Monk's head swung around and he looked into Macomber's eyes. There was a glow there. 'But I have no one. Once I had a wife, a precious daughter. All gone now ... China has swallowed them whole.'

'I don't understand.' Macomber leaned over, poured more vodka into the other's cup.

'Once, long ago – or so it seems to me now – I had a brother. He was a wilful man, a violent man. He hated the Americans.' The Monk picked up the paper cup. 'My Government found a use for him. They trained him and put him into the field. He was immediately successful. So successful in fact that they requested he begin recruiting other agents.'

'When was this?' Macomber inquired.

'1967.' The Monk closed his eyes as he took in the liquor. He must be swimming in it by now, Macomber thought. He edged closer. Perhaps the Chinese would let something slip; something incriminating. Macomber liked having information about other people. It ensured they would do as they were told.

'What happened?' he prodded gently.

The Monk's eyes had glazed slightly but Macomber's question brought him back. 'Among the people he found was a woman. A beautiful woman. A half-caste, part Khmer, part Chinese.' Wings brushed through Macomber's mind. 'He trained her and she became his most successful agent. She was cunning, resourceful and utterly amoral.

'You must understand that my brother was a driven man. He was never content with today's success; he was constantly looking ahead. And this woman had given him an idea for a daring coup. He would infiltrate her into the Special Forces compound at Ban Me Thuot.' Macomber heard a startled cry down deep inside the core of him. He held his tongue for fear of breaking the Chinese's train of thought. His heart raced with dread and when he tried to speak his tongue clove to the roof of his mouth. 'What,' he managed to croak out at last. 'What was her name?'

The Monk's eyes crossed in concentration. 'Hideous. It was

hideous I tried to block it out.' He was rambling and Macomber held his breath. 'Tisah, that was it. My brother set her in place, gave her instructions to use all her knowledge to form illicit liaisons with the high-ranking "spook" officers there.'

Liaisons. The plural of the word resounded in Macomber's shocked mind like mortar fire. Tisah, he thought. You were mine. Only mine!

'As I said, she did as she was told and the information she fed my brother was first-rate. He was very pleased.' A shadow seemed to pass across the Monk's countenance. 'Then one day everything changed.'

'What do you mean?' Macomber was appalled to hear that his voice was a hoarse croak.

'Or, more accurately, something changed *her*. She stopped completely giving intelligence. Fearing for her safety my brother went in after her. She was not in her own house.' I know, Macomber thought in an agony of tension. What had happened to his Tisah? Now, after all these long years of not, knowing, he was about to stumble on the truth. In, of all places, an ancient garden in China.

'He knew the names of her contacts – her lovers, to be more to the point – and he went to their billets.' A cold chill crept through Macomber at the thought. He had never known. He had thought at the time that she might have been working for the communists; he did not think he could forgive her. But over the years he saw that he had. Only her, of all people. He could forgive Tisah. She had brought him life in the midst of death. Only she had come to save him.

And now he knew the ultimate truth about himself. If she were indeed a communist agent, it did not matter. He trembled with the force of that revelation. It did not matter! What were all his carefully constructed political building blocks in the face of this one incandescent love?

Love!

If Tisah were indeed alive that was all he cared about. His mind was on fire at the thought that he might, if he was able to manoeuvre the Monk in just the right way, at last be able to discover the truth. *Alive!* The word flared in his mind.

Slowly, he thought, gagging on the rush of questions he longed to ask the Chinese. Go slowly or you'll lose it all now.

'You used a word before,' he said as calmly as he could. ' "Hideous." What was hideous?'

'Why, the aftermath, of course,' the Monk said in a tone of voice that indicated he could not understand why Macomber had asked for an answer to such an obvious question. He appeared very drunk now and inwardly Macomber laughed in secret delight.

'When my brother returned to his base camp, he found a message awaiting him. He had been recalled; his superiors were furious. The last of his information from Tisah had proved false. Men and supplies had been committed to a fictitious offensive; they had been, to a man, destroyed by an ambush. My brother was in disgrace.'

The Monk's voice came to an abrupt halt. A combination, perhaps, of the emotions of his words and the heat of the liquor had burnished his face with sweat. His eyes were hooded and sleepy, his balance slightly askew.

Just when Macomber felt compelled to urge him on, he began again, his voice softer than before. 'In his cell, my brother realized what had happened. Tisah had made special mention of her last contact, an American Special Forces soldier. He was very canny, she had said in one report. Very smart. She thought he might be the most dangerous of all the men at Ban Me Thuot to approach. But the promise he seemed to hold out of secret knowledge far beyond what she had been able to scavenge before, drove her onward.'

His shiny, moon-lit face swayed a little, like flowers in the spice-laden breeze from the east. 'In prison, you see, there is much time to ponder that which has taken but seeming moments to unfold; time enough to return and sift over every tiny detail, remembered now in the utter silence of isolation.

My brother knew that she had been turned by this very dangerous man. Her last contact.

'Well' – the Monk spread his fingers like delicate branches – 'the knowledge did him no good, of course. It was a bad time for our Government, an evil time. They accused my brother of

349

everything including treason; they wished, in the essence of it, to make an example of him. They did just that. They killed him; they killed all of his family. Then they started on mine. 'First my eldest son disappeared, then my middle son was reported missing from school. Then my wife and baby daughter. As a lesson to me. "They will be returned to you," I was told, "when we are satisfied as to your innocence. In the meantime, an enemy of the State has no family".'

The Monk put his fleshy cheek against the heel of his hand. 'Eventually, the men in power were deposed. Others came to take their place. I was vindicated but as for my wife and children . . . no one knew or was willing to tell. No one.'

The Monk rose unsteadily and with the slow and overly careful motions of a drunk leaned against the parapet of the bridge. He appeared to Macomber to be an old man now, the soft wrinkled light striking him in such a way it turned his skin to vellum. 'So here is your definition – is that the correct word? – of hideous, Mac-omber. I want no more part of that.' He spat wetly over the side.

Macomber pulled himself together as he stood up. He watched the Monk carefully, knowing that the moment had at last come. 'And the girl?' he said slowly, easily. 'Tisah.' It was the hardest word for him to say. 'What became of her?'

For a time, there was silence. Macomber heard the soft whine of insects and, below them, in the water, came a dull splash as of a frog jumping in.

The Monk stared down into those black depths, as if he could re-read the past in the streakings of mud lying along the bottom. 'Of course, no one will know now precisely what happened that night. My brother was able to piece together most of it, however.'

'Tisah had begun to balk at her dual duplicity. So much so that her last contact must have come to the conclusion that she was more trouble alive. He came to her flat in the middle of the night.'

'She must have heard him, perhaps only at the last possible instant. In any event, she escaped, fleeing into the jungles of Cambodia.'

Macomber's heart was throbbing so painfully that unconsciously he grabbed at his breast. His eyes seemed to go in and out of focus. *Alive!* his mind screamed. *Tisah's alive!*

He took deep breaths. *Prana*. Even so, he was a while at it. He stared at the pitted, pock-marked cornice of the stone bridge, reminding himself of the immutability of things. After he was certain his voice would not betray him, he said evenly, 'I want you to find her for me.'

The Monk made no move; he continued to contemplate the water just as if Macomber had not spoken. Then his head shook from side to side as if he wished to physically shake off the sorrow that seemed to engulf him. 'This was an evil man who cut her, Mac-omber. Quite an evil one.' He turned slowly. Moonlight silvered his face and, for just an instant, a butterfly flitted past his ear. He did not seem aware of its presence.

'To you, perhaps, this man is a hero, yes?,' he went on. 'But I know him as evil.' His eyes were dark and somehow luminescent. Macomber thought the excess of liquor had made them so. 'Now you say that you want me to find Tisah for you. It is not unknown to me that you were in Ban Me Thuot, Mac-omber. Yes and it has also come to my attention what you were doing there. I would be a most abject fool not to have checked out your background before I agreed to this meeting.' He put his hands together as if praying. 'I know what you are.'

'What I have been,' Macomber corrected.

The Monk shrugged. 'Call it what you want. It occurs to me that I do not know your motivation in this.'

'It's none of your business.'

The Monk's eyes were half-closed, the upper lids floating up and down slightly. 'Allow me to say, Mac-omber, that though we may be business partners in one venture, we are not on the same side of the wall, as you might say.'

'You just spent the better part of a quarter-hour telling me how you hated the PRC's guts.'

The Monk looked downcast. 'Then we both spent that time in vain. Do not confuse politics with loyalty. How I feel about my Government is one thing; my love for China can never be questioned.

'Therefore, when you ask me to find for you a half-Chinese from out of your past – a spy who, for many long months worked against you – I must then ask myself the next logical question. *Why?*'

His head came up and his black eyes glittered in the moonlight with an unnatural force. 'Do you wish to finish what you began fifteen years ago, Mac-omber?'

'What?'

'Will I search through all of Cambodia for you, bring you your Tisah and like your Christian Judas watch while you execute her?'

'What – What are you saying?' Macomber was almost shouting. 'That *I* was her last contact?'

'You're a very dangerous man, Mac-omber. That much I do know.'

'I'll give you five hundred thousand extra if you find her.'

'My dear sir –'

'All right. Another million!'

'What are my assurances that –'

'I wasn't her last contact, damnit!'

'I never said you were,' the Chinese said blandly.

'If I knew who he was, I'd kill him myself!' Macomber said thickly. '*That's* how I feel about him.' In the silence that followed, the eerie hollow sort that rang out after a military bombardment, Macomber looked hard at the Monk. 'Does this mean,' he said softly, 'that you know who her last contact was?'

'In point of fact I do.' He came away from the side of the bridge at last. 'I have carried that knowledge with me for many years. It is my brother's only legacy.'

'I want to know,' Macomber said hoarsely. His mind seemed on fire. The thought that someone at Ban Me Thuot had tried to kill Tisah acted like a painful burr in his heart. 'I want to know that, too.'

'Yes,' the Monk said seriously, 'I see that you do. I see the tiger of revenge inside you; I have distilled the nature of your spirit.'

He toddled sloppily to the apex of the bridge and there turned back to face Macomber. 'So I perceive the true nature of my poor brother's legacy at last. It has a purpose after all.

'Yes I will find this Tisah for you, Mac-omber, for I know that she is still alive.' He raised an arm. 'And as for the other, the information is yours. I need not be burdened with it any longer.

'Before he died I saw my brother. He wept in my arms because he knew what they were going to do with him, though I, in my ignorance and naivety, would not believe him. That is how I have remembered him for all these years. Perhaps now, when I give you the name of the man who traduced Tisah and, through her, him, I will be able to forget.

'His name is Tracy Richter.'

Tracy's flight was at 6.00 p.m. Before heading out to the airport he stopped by his father's to pick up the Care package the old man had prepared for him.

It was not only his own quest which occupied his mind now, it was the overall picture. He tried to fit Roland Burke's death into the scheme of things; he tried to come up with the foundation's angle. Their interest made him curious. He had begun to wonder if there was some kind of foreign security angle. Had John been into something that Tracy hadn't known about? Tracy thought that it was highly unlikely. But, he had to admit to himself, it was still a possibility.

His mind was so involved with these enigmas that he was totally dumbfounded when Lauren opened the door to Louis Richter's apartment.

They stared at each other for a long electric moment. He thought later that perhaps there had been an instant within the time span of the first shock of recognition when, if he had been quick enough about opening his mouth, he would have had a ghost of a chance with her.

In that moment he saw her as others, perhaps, did from the remoteness of the stage, the aura of her profession, an icy mask about her features and, without a word, she stepped back so that he could go on past her.

He heard the echo of the door closing at his back as he went down the entrance hallway. Lauren crossed straight to the kitchen, disappearing.

'What is she doing here?' Tracy asked his father. 'I've been calling her all over trying to track her down.'

Louis Richter put his arm around his son's shoulders. 'I think this is the only place she feels comfortable in at the moment.' He saw the look on his son's face. 'Come on,' he said softly, 'time heals all wounds . . . even hers.'

In his back studio, he said, 'I don't think it's all you. I think it's eating away at her insides.'

'What is?'

'I don't know all of it.' Long ago he had shuttered the window in this room for security as well as safety precautions. He had never bothered reopening it. Now in that absence of light, Tracy could see his face as if it were already a skull, as if it had already been stripped of all flesh and only a thin covering of varnish laid over the bare bone. It angered him to see death hovering so close to his father.

He gripped Louis Richter's shoulder as if by that firm contact he could somehow transfer a part of his own vital energy to the old man.

Louis Richter's eyes were full and he turned away because he did not want his son to see him cry. He cleared his throat. 'It has to do with . . . something in the brother and sister aspect of it . . . I'm not certain.'

'There's so much I want to say to her.'

'I know,' Louis Richter said, turning back. 'And you'll have your time, believe me.' He picked up a grained pigskin toiletries case from the top of his workbench. He pushed it into Tracy's hands.

'Don't open it now,' he said. 'Let the Customs people do that if they want.'

Tracy took the Care package, put it under his arm.

'Tracy . . .'

'I'll be careful, Dad.'

'I know you will,' Louis Richter said.

Tracy leaned forward, kissed his father's cheek. The skin felt as oddly smooth and new as a baby's. Then he turned and went out of the apartment. As he passed, he could hear Lauren working in the kitchen. It seemed hard to open the door. But he found that was not nearly as difficult a task as walking down the hall to the elevator and the waiting street.

Macomber saw he had made a mistake. The Monk must have given the taxi driver a tip, after all, because the hunk of metal was still waiting for them when they emerged from the labyrinthine depths of Yu Garden. Macomber felt satisfied. The deal was set and he had picked up a stray bit of very valuable information in the process. The six million suddenly looked like a small price tag. That bastard Richter, he thought. How I hate him.

The Monk opened the taxi's back door and Macomber climbed in. The door closed behind him and he turned.

'I'll take another route,' the Monk said. He yawned hugely. His eyes had slowed to somnolent slits. 'You'll agree it's wisest that way.'

'Oh, yes. Certainly.' Now that the business was over, Macomber was anxious to be away from this uncouth man, this febrile country. He longed to return to the hotel and make his call.

The Monk folded his arms as support for his chin. Macomber saw with dismay that flecks of dinner's grease still dotted his chin. The sight disgusted him.

'There is,' he said, 'a matter of the payment.'

Macomber tried not to breathe. 'One-third will be deposited into the bank you designated in Hong Kong tomorrow morning, one-third on the date of the first delivery, the final third in December when the bulk of the consignment arrives.'

The Monk nodded. 'The taxi will take you back to your hotel. Do not concern yourself with the fare, Mac-omber.' He smiled. 'The ride is on me.'

He said something in Mandarin, took his arms away from the window-sill. The cab rattled off, Macomber relaxing back in the seat.

The Monk watched the vehicle around the turning of Anren Street at the southern end of Yu Garden. He looked upward, into the night, as if he could see beyond the city's glow into the heart of the stars burning there. He began to whistle a tune no

Westerner would make sense of. He heard a deep throaty roar as of an engine starting up and, moments later, a gleaming roan Mercedes came into view from the north, its great amber headlamps like a tiger's eyes, piercing the dark.

The Mercedes stopped in front of him. The driver who got out, came around the front to open the door for him, was dressed in the uniform of the Army of the People's Republic.

As soon as the Monk was within the roomy confines of the car, he brought out a white silk handkerchief and carefully and methodically wiped his chin.

Vodka, he thought, was an interesting liquor. Not only did it not stain the breath as the American, Canadian and Scotch whiskys did, it could also be easily substituted for. He smiled a secret smile. Who could tell the difference between water and vodka without sipping it?

The management of the Jin Jiang Club had been overjoyed to do their patriotic duty and, on his request, substitute water for the Stolichnaya he had ordered.

Of course, the bottle he had opened in Yu Garden and had shared with Macomber had been real. The Monk stared out the window as the Mercedes slipped through the thick humid night. It seemed a shame to him that the Russians were the ones who made such a fine liquor. He hated and distrusted the Russians. They were liars – belligerent liars at that; clustered around China's borders, itching to inch in. It was a constant problem since their technology was in all ways more advanced.

China still had no heavy industry and, worse, no coherent trade programme to finance it out of the dark ages. The Monk sighed. That, unfortunately, was the course Mao set for them and it had proved to be disastrous.

He leaned forward to tell the driver to slow down; he needed some time to think and he did so best when he was mobile. It seemed ironic but somehow not so odd to him that his country should be following the same path that the Japanese took in the seventeenth century when Isyasu Tokugawa and his successive heirs maintained that country's historic and cultural integrity at the cost of total isolation from the rest of the world.

When the two-hundred-year-old Tokugawa shogunate was finally overthrown and the Meiji Restoration begun, Japan found itself in just the same position China now did: hopelessly backward, starved for cosmopolitan culture and in desperate need to leap a technological and psychological span of many years in a compressed period of time.

The psychological was the most difficult to overcome. The so-called Cultural Revolution in China, the Monk knew, had been a sham, nothing more than a fixing of the lines of power. Now that had all been done away with, the country was in flux. Ministers and officials came and went with appalling swiftness. Policies had no coherence or continuity. Yet the current government knew what had to be done to make China a modern world power.

That was principally why they allowed him to operate as he did. His clandestine dealings brought in enormous revenues for a Government starved for vast amounts of cash. China was still staggering beneath the burden of its population and the strides it found itself needing to take. Heavy industry and modern militarization were just two of the major imperatives. The Monk's business made a great deal of difference to them.

Thus his was a strictly independent situation, unique in all of China. He lived abroad for months out of the year. He came and went as he pleased with very few restrictions. But if it wasn't a state-run business, it was, at its very secret heart, state-controlled. It had to be. This was China, after all. And the Monk had played a great part in its progress.

It was, of course, essential for the Monk's various dealings, that his true affiliation be withheld. His reputation had been built on his pristine independence. Any contradictory information would put him right out of the market.

But that, the Monk knew, would never happen. He was a man who in all respects was dissimilar to Delmar Davis Macomber. He was careful, conservative, patient. He was not greedy, nor was he monomaniacal. He took the long view.

It seemed to him now that Macomber was obsessed with his own position in life. It had been fascinating to finally meet the man after all he had heard about him. He'd give him precisely what he wanted and no strings attached.

He smiled. Well, perhaps there was *one* string.

*

On the Eastern shuttle to Washington, Tracy spent ten futile minutes thinking of what he was going to say to the Director.

Rain spattered against the Perspex window; heavy cloud cover hid both the land and the sky above him. Tracy closed his eyes and thought of other matters, allowing his unconscious to wrestle with the problem.

First thing that morning, he had asked Irene to reroute his flight to Hong Kong via Washington and set it back twenty-four hours. Then he dialled the Director himself on his private line.

The limited access number had not changed but security had. He heard the hollowness on the line as he spoke to the female operator. 'Administration', was all she said; the listening devices were hard to work. Probably, Tracy thought, some of his father's own design.

'I wish to speak to the Director,' he said.

'The Director is in conference at present,' the clipped voice said without inflection. 'May I inquire who is calling?'

'It's Mother,' Tracy said.

'Pardon,' the operator said. 'I did not get that.'

That was the first lie. She got everything, absolutely everything; that was part of her job. Tracy repeated the name the foundation had given him.

'Please hold,' the voice said, 'I have another call coming in.' That was the second lie. The silence on the line echoed hollowly.

'Hello, Mother!' It was a hearty, jovial voice. Male. 'This is Martinson.'

'I don't know any Martinson,' Tracy said evenly.

'Of course you do, Old Son. We went to Princeton together. Surely you remember?'

'I didn't go to Princeton,' Tracy said, following a long established procedure. I graduated the Mines, class of Sixty-eight.'

'I see.' There was a pause. The joviality had gone out of the voice. 'One moment, please.'

Three clicks. He had been transferred again. It was nothing less than he had expected.

'Mother?' This voice was deeper, also male. But the good old boy atmosphere had been replaced by a quiet businesslike attitude. 'Is that you?'

'The one and only,' Tracy said. 'Unless you've given my number to someone else.'

'I don't think the Director would've done that ... do you?'

'I wouldn't put anything past him.' This was all small talk.

'Price here,' the voice said. 'We graduated from the Mines together.'

'The Price I know dropped out after a month; he was administrative material, not for the field.'

'We both trained under Hama,' the voice insisted.

'Jinsoku was the one that year,' Tracy said, 'and every year until his death three years ago.'

'Is that so?'

Tracy had had just about enough. 'Price, you sonovabitch, you almost blew your hand off with the first firearm you drew at the Mines.'

'Christ. Mother, it *is* you!'

'Price, I want to speak to the Director.'

'Yes ... of course. I'll tell him you're on.' There was a pause but he did not switch Tracy to hold. 'Mother ... it's damn good to hear your voice again.'

A moment later, the Director came on. 'I trust you still understand the necessity for all this screening.' His voice was as liquid as an icy stream; thick in the middle-ranges. It went down well with the big boys with whom he was always hanging out. 'One can never be too careful.' There was no question of a more personal greeting.

'Still getting obscene calls?'

The Director snorted. 'Always and forever. Goes with the territory.'

'The reason I called ... I'll be in town tonight. I thought a dinner would be a change of pace for both of us.'

'After ten years out of touch, I would say so.' He sniffed. 'Shall we say eight o'clock at Lion d'Or?'

'No,' Tracy said immediately. 'I'd rather Chez Françoise.'

'Of course,' the Director said amiably. 'How could I forget?

But in my position, one gets used to being a bit more chic. Now where is that place?'

'Outside Great Falls,' Tracy said, knowing the Director had not forgotten the restaurant's location. 'Out along the river.'

'I'll find it,' the Director said and hung up.

The 'Fasten Seat Belts–No Smoking Please' signs had come on as the plane banked, lowering its flaps as it headed down through the soup towards the Washington airport.

He tried to clear his mind for his meeting with the Director but images of Lauren floated through his mind, confounding him. He saw her turning in slow motion, one leg held high, angled sharply at the knee; he saw the sunlight spinning in her hair, his own slightly distorted reflection in the sea green of her eyes. Tears welled there, as if tethered tightly.

He tried not to think of his apartment, so empty and seemingly dead without her presence to animate it. Darkness. And she was not there. Guilt ribboned him as he pictured her face again. *Bobby*.

The 707 landed with two quick bumps, the engines sighing down as they lost power. People were already in the aisle, pulling down their briefcases and weekend bags from the overhead cabinets.

Before leaving the terminal, Tracy checked all his larger bags with the airline he was flying to Hong Kong, keeping with him only his overnight bag and the pigskin courier case within which his father had carefully packed away the goodies. Anyone, including Customs, opening the case for inspection would find such innocuous items as electric razor, travel clock, hairbrush and comb, three bars of Ivory soap and a sterling silver nail clip. None of these items, of course, were what they appeared to be.

Tracy left the terminal, went down the steps to his immediate left, caught the red-and-white Avis shuttle bus. Within ten minutes, he had picked up his rent-a-car, a metallic-coloured Cordoba, and was in the midst of the thick traffic on the outer ring road leading out of the airport.

He eventually got on the Washington Memorial Parkway, crawled along. The Pentagon came up on his left and, just past that, the traffic thinned out as most of the cars went right over the Arlington Memorial Bridge into the downtown area. The Washington Memorial itself stood tall and white in the last of the day's light. As he watched, lights came up, throwing it into brilliant illumination.

The foliage was lush, a testament to the city's constant high humidity as well as government planning. The river turned magenta, then, as darkness swept in, indigo with spirals of gold cast by the city's lights.

Chez Françoise was an unprepossessing restaurant out in the countryside. The Director was already seated when Tracy walked in.

To Tracy, the Director had always looked like a genetic throwback. With his outsized jaw, thick neck and hulking body, he seemed at least outwardly to belong more to the world blooming a million years ago. His brain was another matter entirely. More than once, Tracy had seen the Director outthink a roomful of professional types.

'Sit down,' the Director said. He looked only a bit older than he had the last time Tracy had seen him. 'I've ordered you a Glenlivet on the rocks, though I thoroughly disapprove. You'd do better having it straight up.' His eyes watched Tracy as he sat down. 'Ice inhibits the smoky bouquet.'

'You have it your way,' Tracy said, 'and I'll have it mine.'

The Director smiled. 'You haven't changed, I see.'

'Nor you.'

The Glenlivet came and Tracy sipped at it. The Director waved away the menus. 'Later,' he said. He wrapped his fingers around his bourbon and branch water. No ice rattled in its jewelled depths.

'Washington seems much the same,' Tracy said.

'On the surface, yes.' The Director took out one of his hand-rolled cheroots, black and green and a little crooked. 'The foundation gives me many small pleasures', he had always been fond of saying, 'not the least of which is obtaining Cuban cigars.' 'Obtaining', was the Director's favourite euphemism. 'On the inside, it's another matter entirely.'

He paused while he went through the ritual of lighting up.

361

When he had the thing going to his satisfaction, he continued. 'This goddamned Democratic administration doesn't know its armpit from its asshole.' He glanced at the glowing end of his cheroot. 'They haven't the sense to know what to do with our intelligence or the good grace to let us alone. Lame-brained sonsabitches.' His eyes crept back up to lock with Tracy's. 'I am heartened, however, by this groundswell for Gottschalk. Helluva fine man. Just what we need.' The Director frowned, a formidable expression, since his bristly eyebrows, coming together, threatened to do battle over the bridge of his patrician nose. 'The cities've not seen fit to embrace him wholeheartedly yet. But I expect that'll take a little time. They still remember Reagan.' He heaved his bulk, sighed. 'It's not easy being a Republican.'

The Director's eyes roved and sought, piercing the distance between them. 'Sorry to hear about the Governor. Good friend of yours, I gather.'

'Kim came to see me recently.'

'Really.'

Tracy was instantly alert. There was absolutely no inflection in the Director's voice and his face was a mask. But something in his posture, a minute stiffening, straightening of the spine, a slight turn of his head to the left, bringing his right ear more to bear on the conversation, had sent a warning through Tracy's frame. Reasoning ability was handled by the left side of the brain and that was fed by the right ear, eye, etc.

'It had to do with the Governor's death,' Tracy said casually. 'But I imagine you know all about that. Unless I'm terribly out of date Kim reports directly to you.'

'Nothing that radical has changed inside,' the Director said. 'The majority of our field personnel liaise with Price. But Kim's a special case. Mmmmm. I'm not talking out of school. You know Kim better than almost anyone. He requires ... special care.'

'You mean to make sure he doesn't go off like a mad dog, snuffing people left and right.'

The Director sniffed, the only clue that he had taken offence. 'The results he obtains rather mitigate against any other kind of action on our part.'

'He's a bloody mass murderer,' Tracy said angrily.

'If it comes to that, so are you,' the Director retorted. His voice had remained even but colour had come to his cheeks, points of red like rouge roughly applied. He took the half-smoked cheroot out of his mouth, leaned forward across the table, occluding the tableware with his bulk. 'In the last six months alone he has obtained more information for us on the opposition's overt use of trichothene mycotoxins in Cambodia than State has had in the previous two years. I don't for a moment doubt his enormous value to us.' The Director was hot now. 'The vacation he's currently enjoying is a well-deserved one, I assure you.'

'I'm sure it is,' Tracy murmured as he struggled against showing the enormity of emotion racing through him. Kim was on vacation? Then his coming to Tracy – the Holmgren investigation he had involved Tracy in – was not a foundation assignment. The Director knew nothing about it. Christ, Tracy thought. To calm himself, he took a sip of his Glenlivet. His mind was racing off in ten different directions at once. Immediately, he gained control, slowing himself down.

Prana. He longed to use its centring influence now but deep, controlled breathing in front of the Director was out of the question. He would see and know something was amiss.

'What is it Kim wanted of you?' the Director inquired.

'Merely a condolence call on his way through.' The lie came easily to him. Too easily. And he had to remind himself again that this was the last time, the very last. After he had tracked down John's and Moira's killer, he would be finished with this life forever.

The Director called for the menus and while they were deciding what to eat said, 'There are always situations arising ... which would benefit greatly from your expertise. Now more than ever, in fact.'

'I'm sure there are.'

'I think I'll have the chicken,' the Director said. He closed the menu, placed it flat on the table in front of him. Yes. With a bottle of iced Rhine wine, that sounds just right for a night like this.'

*

'I don't want you to go,' Joy said softly and then, as if sensing that was the wrong tactic to take with him, began again, 'You can't go.'

Khieu was thinking of the last briefing he had had with Macomber just before his China trip.

'Now you know as much about the foundation as I do.'

'Does he know Kim?' Khieu had asked thoughtfully.

'He knows *of* him through Tracy, of course,' Macomber had said. 'But they've never met.'

'He seen a photograph?'

'No. There are none of any of the foundation personnel.'

Khieu recalled how he had bowed before the image of his gilt Buddha, through whose eyes all the universe could be seen and known. 'Then there will be no problems.' Then he had begun to pray, moving slowly and methodically through the Buddhist catechism.

'It's far too dangerous.' Joy's voice pulled him back to the present.

He smiled at her, stroked her soft hair. 'How can you know such a thing?'

Her eyes were liquid. 'Because I'm frightened for you.'

He laughed. 'Nothing can harm me. I'll slip through the new Cambodia like a wraith.'

'And what about your ghosts?' Joy had slept beside him enough for her to have come to fear his nightmares as if they were her own. She did not know their contents; she would not ask him and he, certainly, would not speak of them. It was more than enough to experience the overflow of frightful emotions pouring out of his soul like a torrent of sewage. And she would hold him tightly as he writhed and moaned, talking in endlessly repeating phrases, Khmer words she could not decipher. In those fevered moments he could have been some alien, drifted to earth from ten thousand light years away.

Yet her passion for him, the relief and the solace he brought to her at night bound her to him, would have done so even if they had not been able to communicate verbally.

For he was what kept her in this house on Gramercy Park South. Without him, she would have drowned beneath the seas of this strange marriage she had entered into. Surely she would have left Macomber, returning to her family in Texas. He was so strange, this Khmer, yet she half-suspected it was this very strangeness that was a great part of his attraction for her.

'My ghosts,' Khieu said after a time, 'are within me. In the new Cambodia, too, they cannot harm me.'

'But there is war there,' she breathed.

He stared into her face, his eyes impenetrably dark and utterly depthless. 'I have lived all my life with war. I am a war child, in the most literal sense. Do you think war can destroy me now, after all this time?' He shook his head from side to side. 'Do not fear for me, Joy.' He reached out his open palm. 'Here I am.' He slid her hand over his, gripped it tightly. 'Here I shall always be.'

The doorbell rang and Lauren said, 'I'll get it,' because Louis Richter was busy in the kitchen putting the final touches on their light dinner of roast beef sandwiches and German potato salad. Lauren glanced at her watch. She was tired. It had been a long gruelling morning filled with exercise classes that had, unaccountably, made her irritable in their stresses on the basics. In the afternoon's rehearsals for the new ballets, at least, she could lose herself completely in the steps. Most of the other members of the company were grumbling these days at the double rehearsals Martin was inflicting on them. He would not tell them the reason and, though there was a kind of ill-defined but measurable excitement in the air, the enigma of its source chafed annoyingly at them.

Not so Lauren who, since her breakup with Tracy, wished only to plunge herself deeper into ballet, driving herself and those around her almost as hard as did Martin himself.

On her way to answer the door she thought about Louis Richter. She had had an uncle once who had been warm and loving with her. She remembered sitting on his lap, his long arms around her. She could recall the particular scent of his shirts, a blend of cologne and tobacco; she had loved to put her ear against his great chest and listen to the indefatigable thrum of his heartbeat. He had died when she was eight so it had been a long time since she had felt so comfortable, so secure with a man of Louis Richter's age.

So much so that she had even become interested in what he had to say about Jack Sullivan's sudden public disclosure of the President's knowledge of security problems abroad just prior to the assassination of that military attaché in Cairo recently.

'Oh, yes,' he had said, 'I think old Lawrence's got his ass in a sling on this one all right.'

And she found as often happened with Tracy, the force of his opinions, the scope of his knowledge, were enough to carry her along for a time.

She was adjusting to all this, feeling herself melting into the warmth and comfort it provided when she opened the front door.

The moment Khieu saw her he experienced a sensation akin to dying. He knew precisely what that was like; he had come so close so many times in the jungles of Cambodia.

The charming smile that had been on his face faded into the dark handsome contours of his countenance. Bile seemed to rise up through his oesophagus like molten lava, threatening the choke him. He opened his mouth in reflex and said without thinking: *'Louis Richter nev ptas tay?'*

It was a stifling summer's day, the high palms standing still and calm, sprayed upon the vault of the yellow sky. Dampness like strands of pearls, lying heavy upon his shoulders and forehead. Standing within the perimeter of *Chau Chhaya*, a Thursday afternoon, when they danced, near enough to *Khemarin*, the palace's throne room, to feel the presence of Sihanouk and the lineage of the ancient Khmer kings.

Malis in her *samput chang kbeu*, her knees bent, small bare feet turned outward, the toes gripping the polished marble floor. Only her arms moved. Her hands told a story, expressed emotion, encompassed the gamut of human experience. Her body was silent; her face was a mask as was dictated by the Khmer ballet. Sok was filled with the sight of Malis, her superbly controlled fingers dancing, whispering their poetic tale of vengeful gods, frightful demons and lost love.

He was consumed by a pale fire whose name he must not mention, whose own origins he must never contemplate.

Outside, the orange-robed monks roamed the royal gardens, pastel parasols resting on their shoulders to keep the broiling sun off their bald pates. Above their heads, the navy, red and white trisected Khmer flag with the image of *Angkor Wat* at its centre, flapped and rippled in the sporadic breeze, folding in on itself like Malis' expressive fingers in the periods of stillness.

On this stifling afternoon, he was convinced that Malis was *apsara*, one of the mythic celestial dancers with supernatural powers. It was said that the ancient Khmer kings used *apsara* to speak to God, translating their message of words into the symbols of the ballet.

Sok Khieu's eyes were filled with lust, for as his sister danced, as she told her mythic story of the Khmer past, he was recalling how she danced for him at night. Only for him. A dance of abandon such as could never be tolerated here. A dance only for the pleasure of Malis. But because he had been there as well, a dance for his own pleasure. A shared intimacy, illicit and therefore so much more delicious. Only for him. For him and for her. Together.

Within the blue-green, the changing colours of Lauren's eyes, Khieu now saw Malis resurrected, strong and healthy, gleaming with animal vitality. In the manner in which she held herself, in her long neck, the tilt of her head, the bearing of her shoulders and her hips, in her long legs and, most of all, her dancer's stance, the echoes of Malis seemed to fill him like the rising hoofbeats of an army of horses. His thighs were weak and he blinked, seeing again the hand-carved ruby earrings in the shape of a lotus she wore always.

'What?' she said again, staring at him curiously. 'What did you say?'

It occurred to Khieu then that he had spoken to her in Khmer, precisely as if she *had* been Malis!

'I'm sorry,' he said softly. 'I must learn to speak up.' He cleared his throat. 'Is Louis Richter in? May I see him?'

He said this all by rote; he knew what he had to do. But his head was swimming.

'Of course,' Lauren said, stepping back to allow him to come in. She shut the door behind him. 'May I have your name?'

'Kim,' Khieu said automatically. He saw her turn and regard him now with more curiosity.

'So you're Kim,' she said, smiling. 'My name's Lauren Marshall.' She held out her hand and for a dizzying instant he did not move. He took it then, bringing it up to his lips, pressing them to the back, feeling the soft skin there. His eyes closed and he was engulfed again by the scene at *Chau Chhaya*.

When she turned and walked away from him down the hallway, his dark eyes followed her, as if they could trace her movements in the air, as if they were magic circles through which, indeed, his beloved sister had been conjured up.

He thought wildly, What am I doing here? He knew the moment he saw her he should have excused himself for ringing the wrong doorbell and turned away. Louis Richter should have been alone. He could still do that, he told himself. There was still time to leave.

But the scents of Phnom Penh were too strong, the memories far too overpowering. In Lauren he saw a spectre, a resurrection of the spirit as well as of the flesh. He did not think this a coincidence; such a thing did not exist in his world. He had been fated to meet Lauren Marshall. It was his *karma*. And you could not walk away from *karma*; it was not an alternative that would occur to him.

Besides, in her Khieu saw the first glimmerings of a path for him; a path he had thought never to encounter. For he believed that in Lauren Marshall lay his own exorcism. The atonement for a life of sin unimaginable for any Khmer.

Lauren disappeared around the corner of the hallway and he could hear her voice. 'Louis, someone here to see you.'

Khieu came into the living room just in time to see Tracy's father emerging from the open doorway to the kitchen carrying a black lacquer tray filled with laden plates, silverware and glasses.

He paused when he saw the newcomer. 'Yes?'

'Kim,' was all Khieu said.

Without taking his eyes from the Oriental, Louis Richter set the tray down on the dining room table. 'Lauren,' he said softly, 'I imagine our guest would like something to drink. Tea, perhaps?' And when the other inclined his head in assent, Louis went on, 'Would you mind?'

Lauren was looking from one to the other. 'Not at all.'

'Second cabinet on the right,' the old man said. 'Over your head as you face the sink. That's the Chinese Black. Kettle's already on the stove. I'll have some, too.'

'Louis?'

He turned at the tone of her voice, saw the concern on her face and smiled. 'It's business, honey.'

When she was gone, he said, 'Korean, aren't you?'

'Vietnamese.'

The old man snapped his fingers. 'That's right. An old man's memory's not what it used to be.'

Khieu smiled a little; he had expected this. 'Your memory's fine, Mr Richter, even if your body's not.' He was surprised to feel the enormity of his relief now that Lauren had left the room. 'The Director sends his regards.'

Louis Richter moved to the sofa, indicated that Khieu should do so as well. 'Does he now. The Director of what?'

'A place that never forgets its former employees.'

'In Delaware,' the old man said, sitting down with a sigh.

'DC.' Khieu sat without a sound.

'Oh' – his head cocked – 'you've moved then.'

'We're still at the same location, Mr Richter.'

'Yes. You are at that. How is the old bird? Still fighting budgets as usual?'

Khieu knew he had to be careful. His knowledge of the foundation was limited and patchy. If he did not get the old man off this line, he would be in trouble sooner or later. 'The Director's never had to worry about budgets, you know that as well as I do, Mr Richter. The ... ah, place where we work was granted an annuity at its genesis; a percentage of the Federal budget.' He was tapped out; now he needed to regain the initiative. He sat forward with his bronze hands in the attitude of prayer. 'Now come on, Mr Richter, don't you think we've had enough of this game playing?'

Lauren emerged with the tea, set the tray on the coffee table in front of them. Khieu felt his eyes drawn to her as if he were magnetized. He drank in the way she walked, moved, spoke, searched his face with her wide-apart eyes. His pulse rate was becoming too rapid and he sought disciplines long ago learned to calm himself.

The old man spent the next few minutes pouring the tea. He handed Khieu a cup, took the other himself and sat back. Tendrils of aromatic steam rose before his face as he began to sip.

'Yes,' he said, after a time, 'it's been many years since anyone from my former employers visited me.'

Khieu waited as long as he could. He knew he could not appear anxious but, on the other hand, the longer he stayed with these people the greater the ultimate risk to himself. 'Mr Richter, forgive me if I come to the point. My time is not all my own.'

The old man had risen, walking slowly across to the wall of bookcases. He stopped before them, ran one finger down the spine of first one book then another. 'Tell me,' he said. 'Where is it you were born again?' He turned around to face Khieu. 'My son told me once but I've forgotten.'

Khieu knew the time had come; more than pure guile was needed now. He allowed his anxiety to float away from him; he willed the minutae of daily life to pool at his feet like an unwanted cloak.

Instead, he felt the force of the cosmic clock beating on around him, the white silence of its metronomic pulse matching the rhythm of his heartbeat, the soughing of his breath. He felt the air between them, tasted it, heard it, saw through it. And he said, completely surprising himself, 'Phnom Penh.'

Louis Richter gave a curt nod. 'Yes. That's quite right. Stupid of me to have forgotten.' He came back towards the sofa, rubbing his hands together. 'Now,' he said, his tone crisp and businesslike, 'how can I help?'

'The Director has decided to take a more personal role in this investigation. In fact, I'm here on his orders. I am to remove the electronic listening device you have in your possession and deliver it to him in Washington.'

'I see.' Louis Richter had felt the stirrings as soon as this young man had announced himself. Now the feelings were fullblown. It was like the old days again and he could not believe just how much he missed them. This new excitement almost delivered him from the constant pain enshrouding his world. He felt alive again. Tracy's return had begun the process; he had felt useful again. Now he knew that Kim's appearance had completed the cycle. The foundation needed him one last time. 'This must be important.'

'Extremely,' Khieu said.

'Well, you just hold on,' the old man said, smiling. 'I'll be right back.'

For a time, when they were alone, there was a silence so complete that Lauren was certain she could hear the bars of streetlight clattering against the windowpanes like hail. She blushed hotly beneath Khieu's intense gaze, something she could not remember doing since she was a socially awkward teenager.

She was terribly aware of this man's beauty, although mixed in with it she experienced a wildness, a kind of carefully modulated anarchy puzzling in its seeming contradiction. She felt, when she stared back into those black glossy eyes, as if she were peering down a well of infinite depth into the very heart of chaos, but a well-ordered chaos for all that.

He attracted her at the same time he frightened her. She felt beneath her skin a rippling as of an invisible current, as if he were a lodestone filled with an unquenchable power. There had been times during her on-again, off-again relationship with Tracy when she had been aware of a strength of his very much akin to what she was experiencing now. But since she could not define it, even to herself, she had never articulated it to Tracy. She had even, at one point, been successful at convincing herself that it was all a figment of her imagination.

After all, personal aura was far from unknown to her. All great ballerinas had it, all dancers strove for it. She knew how she affected dancers when they came in contact with her; she knew how the audience responded to her. Too, she had felt that same aura in many of her male partners within the company.

But this was something else altogether, for mixed in with the power she was aware of despair, hatred, fear and, most strangely of all, a blissful kind of peace that she had never before known existed.

Unbidden, she came across the room and sat down on the sofa, facing him. His ebony eyes drilled her. She had seen that look once before on an animal's face and she had never forgotten it. Tracy had taken her hawking one lazy afternoon in Virginia and, just after he had yanked the hood from the creature's head, as its great pinions were spreading to the wind, she had, for one brief instant, stared into its eyes, mesmerized, seeing a kind of cruel eternity fixed there.

'What is it you do for a living?' the young man she knew as Kim said.

'I'm a ballet dancer. Do you know –' She stopped short, staring at the change that had come over his face. He seemed pale beneath the patina of bronze his heritage had given him. His eyes had opened up wide, his thick lips drawn back over his white teeth so that he appeared as if he were about to snarl, to leap upon her like a rabid dog. At the same instant, her system registered an odd kind of shock, as if someone quite close had somehow slipped a probe inside her so that she jumped a little.

Lauren's chest constricted abruptly, disconcertingly and she launched herself up from the sofa, putting its comforting bulk between herself and this strange young man. Her fingers clawed whitely into the foam of the pillows as she fought to regain control of herself.

As for Khieu, he was experiencing something else entirely. As she had uttered those few words, *I'm a ballet dancer*, his shock had been enormous. Something had groaned within his core, had broken away, floating swiftly upwards and he felt the danger so acutely that it made his eyes go wide, his nostrils dilate in fear. But it was not a fear for himself; that was an emotion he could no longer generate. Like many other things, the war had atrophied that.

No, the fear he felt was for *her*. He knew the danger was quite real, causing him to want to reach out and protect her. But from what? He could not say; he could not see the source. His lips were white with the force he was exerting in order to peer beyond the mists that veiled his inner sight.

In the end, Louis Richter saved him.

'Here we are,' the old man said, returning to the room. He carried a small parcel wrapped in brown paper and electrician's tape. He handed it over to Khieu. 'Take good care of it.'

Khieu passed a palm across his face. It came away damp and he rubbed his fingers together, working away the sweat. He managed a thin smile. 'Thank you, Mr Richter.' He still had sense enough to remember there was more he needed to learn from this man. 'I had hoped you wouldn't be reluctant to part with it.'

'Why should I?' Louis Richter said. 'I've no more use for it.'

'Oh?'

He smiled. 'I've gotten all the information I can out of it.'

'What kind of information?' Khieu said casually. 'Is it anything I may be able to use?'

The old man put his arm around Khieu's strong shoulders as he led him down the long foyer hallway. 'Possibly. Just possibly. But Tracy's already running down the lead.'

Khieu's eyes caught Lauren's and that same sense of personal danger to her rose again within him, more powerful this time. For just an instant, he was frantic, seeking the knowledge of its origins.

With a wrenching effort, he brought his attention back into the proper focus. 'Tracy will soon tell me where he's gone.'

The old man laughed. 'Not likely.' He enjoyed having the edge on this man who he had heard so much about. He was feeling good. Energy flowed through him like electricity and for that moment he was whole again, thoughts of the disease slowly eating its way through him dissolved in the happiness and well-being of being born again. He opened the front door for the man he knew as Kim. 'He's already on his way to see Mizo.' So it was a breach of security. So what? He was drunk on the energy flow; he wanted this man to understand that he, Louis Richter, had the information at his fingertips. And how d'you like that, my dear Kim? he said silently, jubilantly.

Khieu almost stumbled over the doorsill. His stomach heaved

precariously, sending bitter bile up into his mouth. In a daze, he turned, shook the old man's outstretched hand. Ah, he thought, Mio. Buddha protect me.

'Be sure to give the Director my regards ... and thanks.'

'Yes,' Khieu said mechanically. 'I will.'

It all seemed to be slipping away from him; the entire fabric of the *angka* his father and he had worked so hard and long to weave. One tiny rent now tearing at speed away from him. He must stop it immediately before it got too big for him to handle.

His gaze slid across Louis Richter's smiling face, to light on Lauren standing halfway in shadow in the foyer hallway. She seemed to be staring at him unflinchingly now as if she felt that with her gaze alone she could flay away his skin and flesh, burrowing into the dread secret locked away like a pale and sightless worm within the marrow of his bones.

Then he had recovered fully. All fear fled him as, silently he recited the prayers of centrism. Feeling returned to his legs, his stomach quieted. He was whole again. Free of fear; free of malice. His mind was perfectly clear. All emotion had been leached away. Free of its interfering dazzle, his resolve returned stronger than ever.

With a flash of insight he recalled the astrological chart he had cast. That moving flux – a hidden force, powerful and deadly. Tracy Richter? He must find out. If it was Richter, he'd have to deal with him. But he must say nothing to his father, taking matters into his own hands, seeking only his own council.

And he looked at them both as if for the last time.

BOOK THREE
The Angka

1

August–September, Present
Hong Kong/Stung Treng/Kenilworth/
New York/Cambodia/Shanghai

It was already Wednesday for Tracy, flying thirty thousand feet in the skies, high over the Pacific. Twenty-five hundred kilometres after crossing the International Date Line, leaving Midway Island far behind them, the 747 ran into a storm filled with blue fire and precipitous air currents as it slid across the Tropic of Cancer.

There had been nothing to see out the window but a sea so far away that it appeared to be a sheet of glass. Once the black silhouette of the freighter was out of sight, there was nothing but a curving horizon, blackening as night swept in more swiftly than it ever could have on the surface.

The plane jumped and dived like an elevator with its cord being controlled by teenage hooligans. Passengers moaned, refusing their fresh shrimp appetizers, preferring to reach for the white paper bags discreetly secreted in the pouch of the seat back in front of them.

Staring out the Perspex window at the shuddering drops of rain holding on for dear life, Tracy thought of the clouds beyond; clouds of the Far East.

He had jumped into those clouds just once, the wind rushing in his ears like sirens, the air split with the sound of gargantuan engines and the misty ground, filled with the new dangers of tangled treetops, coming up faster than he could have imagined.

Then the fierce but reassuring tug of his chute opening and he began drifting over southeastern Cambodia, breaking the heavy cloud cover into a light so perfectly pellucid it took his breath away. For just that instant the war, the killing, the mission itself, passed from the realm of existence and he was merely a tourist regretting the stupendous blunder of leaving his camera at home.

Then he was among the first of the treetops, pulling strings like a master puppeteer just as they had taught him, manoeuvring himself towards the small clearing ahead and to his right. Around him, the four men comprising his unit used the air currents, following him in.

An early mission, that had been the only time Tracy had used a chute, preferring copter transportation because it was more precise and gave him better protection until he could melt into ground cover. It had been the time he had been asked by the organization to use strict Special Forces personnel in infiltrating a specific Khmer Rouge encampment. *Snoop around*, they had told him. *We're getting reports that a renegade Japanese is working with them. If so, we have to know about it*. Tracy had wanted to know why all the fuss. What was one Japanese to the foundation?

The man is purported to be Musashi Murano, they had told him, *and if so he cannot be allowed to function for the insurgents. He is a self-styled martial arts master. If he's there, he's teaching them more than we want them to know. Mother*, they had warned him, *he is a very dangerous man, indeed. Take him out with a fusillade and make certain. Under no circumstances are you or one of your team to approach him one-on-one, hand-to-hand. He'll eat you up alive. Is that clear?* It was very clear.

The mission had not been a total failure. They had, after perhaps ten days – as usual, information was snafued and he had been given the wrong encampment – they had come to the right place, arriving just in time for a funeral of considerable pomp and circumstance. That in itself was unusual and Tracy had ambushed a Khmer Rouge, bringing him back to base camp, working on him for more than half a day before he got what he wanted.

Musashi Murano had indeed been at this camp – as he had been at others over the past two years. Here he had stayed for perhaps eight months, training the Khmer Rouge and Viet Cong in what he knew best: unarmed combat, infiltration and assassination using small-bladed weapons. Tracy did not like the sound of that. It reminded him too much of one training session at the Mines. Ninjutsu was only something they had talked about, giving broad outlines because not even Jinsoku had fathomed its secrets. Though he had joked about it, saying, 'There are so many sub-disciplines of the martial arts. How can you expect me to have mastered them all? That is not the Way,' Tracy had been certain he had seen a sliver of fear distort the *sensei*'s face for just an instant, a wisp of gauzy cloud passing before the face of the moon.

However, all that speculation came to naught, for the stricken Cambodian revealed that the funeral had been for this same Musashi who had recently perished from malaria, drugs being unavailable in the jungle. So that threat was at an end. But still, Tracy had been cautious. Because his services were needed elsewhere, he withdrew all but one of the Special Services team, a hard-as-nails individual who did not mind being on his own. Tracy set him in place for two weeks just to make certain of Murano's death. He had always been a man to doublecheck every story he picked up in Southeast Asia. He had found, through bitter experience, that tales seemed to be automatically distorted in the leaden atmosphere so unutterably alien to the Westerner.

The 747–SP banked crisply and he craned his neck to catch a glimpse of the magnificent sight of Hong Kong, divided by Victoria Bay, as they began their descent.

Bright towers shot from bedrock, climbing in layer upon layer up the steep peaks. Beyond the thick cluster of the Central District on Hong Kong Island, Tracy say the white shoots of the Mid-Levels, groups of high-rise housing sprouting like a forest of bamboo from the slopes of Victoria Peak.

Tracy debarked from the jet liner's air conditioning to the debilitating heat and humidity. A mini-bus was waiting for them, to ferry them to the terminal proper. During the five-minute ride, his thin shirt managed to plaster itself to his damp back. His lungs already felt saturated with moisture.

Kai Tak Airport was on the China coast, the Kowloon side of Hong Kong. The first time Tracy had been here on leave during the war, he had been told that Kowloon, freely translated from the Chinese, meant 'Nine Dragons', referring to the nine hills on which this part of the city had been built. Since then he had learned to speak not only Cantonese, which was the prevalent language here, but also Mandarin, the official language of China *per se*, and the odd Tanka dialect which seemed dissimilar to both tongues.

He passed through Immigration, waited by the creaking carousel for his bags. Customs was no problem at all; they looked at nothing, merely waved him through.

The Princess was one of the oldest hotels in Hong Kong. It was also the best run. In the manner of the Colonial days, it had the feel of the old Empire in its groined and mullioned lobby ceiling, the great width of all its doors which were half again as wide as the typical American one, in the splendour of its thick-walled, wood-panelled rooms and marbled baths.

Though other, more modern and to many an American, more splendid hotels had sprung up over the years, it was to the Princess he would always come. He took a quick shower and, changed into loose, light clothing more suitable to the environment, ventured out.

The Princess had been built in a superb location sixty-odd years ago and, though Hong Kong had been frantically expanding in the interim, it was just as well situated now. Overlooking the bay and Hong Kong Island, it had been, when new just a stone's throw from the railway station. Since then, of course, a new station had been erected to the northwest. Now that old husk with its famed clock tower had been turned into the Star Ferry terminal, the Princess was within walking distance of the city's major public carrier.

After twenty-four hours travelling time and a time difference of eleven hours, he felt lightheaded, his inner clock struggling to adjust.

The short walk helped a bit. Crimson doubledecker buses zipped by him, jammed to the windows. He passed the massive structure of Ocean Terminal with its seemingly limitless arcades filled with countless shops selling antiques, jewellery, fabrics, food, watches and electronics. Just as Las Vegas was built on the concept of non-stop gambling, so this city ran on non-stop buying and selling.

He got change of the HK dollars by buying a Chinese newspaper at the terminal. He paid his forty cents, went through the second-class turnstile. He needed to seep in, to return to the sights, smells and sounds to the Asian shore. He needed to be with the Chinese. Up above, on the *Evening Star*'s first-class deck, the tourists and businessmen sat. Here he was that much closer to the filthy oily water and the real residents of the city.

At the rail he shed thoughts of New York, Washington, of Western impatience. A fisherman in a small boat poled across the bay, staring blindly out across the expanse.

And Tracy, in the middle of Victoria Bay, with the jam of Kowloon behind him, where two-and-a-half-million people resided, with the steeply layered skyscraper-festooned cityscape of Hong Kong Island in front of him, felt alive again. A profound sense of peace drifted over him like a languorous tide. The fingered high-rises were pink in the setting sun, hazed like a master photographer's fine print.

Perhaps, he thought, it was a question of *time*. History itself had no real function here because the Colony was such a complex interweaving of Eastern and Western cultures reacting and resounding one upon the other. Here, there could not be the one without the other. But, oddly, the commingling had not produced anything new, merely a humpbacked hybrid which belonged to neither world yet was an integral part of both. It was as if Hong Kong had become by unspoken tacit agreement a crossroads trading territory, a no man's land full of pleasure and disarray, housing beauties and sharks without discrimination.

Just over eighteen-hundred-foot Victoria Peak loomed up behind the light-smeared towers' faces, like the forbidding backdrop of a doom-laden play. To starboard, Tracy could see the swaybacked outline of Stonecutter's Island, a nineteenth-century prison. Hidden just beyond to the west, he knew, lay the sunken remains of the burnt-out *Queen Elizabeth*, sunk in 1972. But further south, it was impossible to miss the enormous bulk of a US aircraft carrier, anchored out in the deep water channel just north of the Green Island lighthouse.

Hong Kong was approaching fast and Tracy moved down the rail to where a cluster of Chinese were shouting at each other in their normal tone of voice. He wanted, before he set foot on the island, to get used to the speed and inflections of the tongue, so difficult to pick up once you've been out of the environment for any length of time.

A duck had just been purchased, he heard, in honour of Uncle Pei's birthday. What a fine time the family was going to have!

Tracy moved away, wishing them well in the silence of his mind. Low-slung junks with sails furled against the winds of night wallowed in the small wavelets tossed up by the ferry's lugubrious passing. Mahogany-hulled ketches, brass fittings agleam, conglomerate's launches, low-lying cargo vessels, preparing to be off-loaded, one from Brazil, another from France, a third from England. And always, the ubiquitous police and customs patrol boats. Not a day went by in Hong Kong harbour when at least a score of smuggling pipelines were not at work. That law-enforcement battle was never ending and, more often than not, frustrating for those not on the inside.

The brief gurgling clatter of a wallah-wallah, the water taxis powerful businessmen used during the day in lieu of the Star Ferry and which, after the ferry stopped running at eleven, was the only way back and forth across the bay, interrupted his train of thought. Three brush-haired Japanese sat huddled together in the aft section, discussing price futures and godown rentals.

The ferry slowed and the engine died. There came the creak of thick hemp lacing vertical pilings, the squeak of peeling wood against old tyres strung along the dockside. The soft sensual slap of waves against wood and a brief bump, one, two.

Hong Kong.

Up the ramp in the terminal as those making the return journey were let through on the other side. The walls filled with primary-coloured billboards extolling the virtues of Audemars Piguet watches, Daimaru, the Japanese department store, and such diverse films as 'Sex Boat' and 'Shaolin Brothers of Death'.

The Central District was criss-crossed with elevated walkways and Tracy used one of these to the far side of Connaught Road Central and down into the heart of the island. He turned up, heading into the old Western District. Every street was lined with shops, every alleyway filled with clothing stalls and, in the lobbies of office buildings more tiny shops tucked away against a wall, selling carved plastic for ivory, bogus 'Casio' calculators, used Canon cameras for new.

Everywhere one looked, the commerce of the city was in evidence, turning unwary tricks like a ten-dollar whore.

The scents of the Orient came to him, strong and thick on the humid air: a conglomerate of spices that was impossible to unravel. He paralleled Hollywood Street, where some of the best antique bargains could often be found, moving into the produce district with its streets filled with lines of identical shops all selling dried fish products. Skates, octopus, whole squid, prawns and sea scallops as well as garoupa and carp hung from cords at the open entrances.

Old Chinese women bent, pawing through the barrels and wooden cases of sea food to find proper presents to bring to friends' houses. The stench was unbelievable.

Near Jervois Street he came upon the snake shops. This was not their season. In winter, when the serpents were somnolent and slow from the cold, you could pass along here and pick out a likely candidate, then watch as the proprietor held the thing between thumb and forefinger just behind its jaws while he slit its head. The resultant black bile was squeezed in a thin stream into a cup which was then filled with yellow rice wine. The mixture, it was said by herpetologists, was most healthful.

Slowly, he felt engulfed by the inexorable pull of the city. To his left, the hills and houses of Hong Kong rose steeply in a mixture of concrete and raw earth. Dust laced the air; construction was all around him, everywhere the skeletons of the bamboo frameworks within which chrysalid high-rises were beginning their climb. As he watched, Chinese workers scrambled over them like kids on an oversized jungle gym.

At length, he came upon the restaurant he had been seeking far from the gaudy neon-scented tourist traps of Tsim Sha Tsui. He carried no maps, preferring to rely on memory, rusty but working, getting the island's geography set in his mind again.

Beside the restaurant's entrance, an elderly Chinese lady sat, dressed in traditional black trousers and mandarin-collared blouse. Black sandals were on her scarred feet, a single bangle bracelet on her left arm. She wore the large flat-topped hat with its black veil, tied with pink string around her chin that marked her as one of the Hakka, originally from the Northern section of mainland China, emigrating to the New Territories in the sixteenth century. Below, her placid, lined face stared at him, only her eyes moving with his passage. Tracy stopped, bent down, said something to her in Cantonese to make her smile.

Inside the restaurant, Tracy was seated amidst the clamour and, by raising his voice, was able to order. He looked around, saw he was the only Occidental present. He dined on cold 'drunken' chicken, in its pungent yellow rice wine marinade, followed by fish that was brought out raw, cooked at his table by placing it on a sizzling hotplate. All washed down by steaming cups of perfumey jasmine tea. It was as he had remembered it: Shanghai cooking at its best.

Afterward, he wandered the streets, soaking in the jabber of Cantonese, the blaring of horns, snatches of music bursting forth from doorways to nightclubs as he passed or where doors were opened for arriving patrons.

He ducked into one of these, searched out a public telephone in the dimness. He was near the coatcheck room. The girl there smiled at him. He asked information for Mizo's number, committed it to memory before dialling.

A feminine voice answered after the fourth ring.

'Is Mizo there, please?' He said in Cantonese.

'I'm afraid not.' The voice was light, airy, definitely Chinese. 'May I ask who is calling?'

Tracy gave her his name. 'When you speak to Mizo, tell him it's the son following in his father's footsteps.'

'I do not understand.' The feminine voice was guarded now, the lightness gone.

'Perhaps not,' Tracy said. You *will* give Mizo the message.'

'When I see him.' The voice had turned cold with initiative gone. 'I cannot say when that will be.'

'My business is most urgent.'

'That is too bad.'

'Too bad for Mizo. In precisely five days I plan to blow the main vault on the Bank of Shanghai. I'll do it with or without his help but in any event it will be Mizo who will get the publicity ... doubly so if I fail.'

He heard the sharp indrawn breath. 'Will you please hold a moment. There is someone at the door.'

Tracy watched the coatcheck girl. She was a slim, moon-faced Chinese with her glossy blue-blue hair in an elegant bun. She knew how to move. She saw him watching her, put one long-nailed forefinger to her lips, pressing inward for a moment, then turning the finger pad outward, extending it towards him. He saw the faint coral blush of her lipstick smear there.

'Mr Richter, are you still there?'

He said he was.

'My apologies for that delay.' The voice had changed tenor once again, revealing as many colours as a chameleon. Now it had softened, even seemed sensual. 'It happens I was able to take a quick peek at Mr Mizo's appointment book. He does have a bit of time tomorrow. Twelve-thirty. Do you know where the Jockey Club is?'

Tracy said he did, he would be there. They hung up without another word being spoken.

The Royal Hong Kong Jockey Club lay along Stubbs Road, built into the eastern face of Mt Nicolson. The two-building high-rise was flanked by the race course – one of two the club maintained – and by a tarmacked garage. It was not a particularly pretty section of the island as it was surrounded by undistinguished apartment houses almost all the way to the bay.

Here might be the true power in the Colony for, as many knowledgeable residents pointed out, it was the club and its 700 members who controlled all horse racing and the government lotteries, the only legally sanctioned forms of gambling allowed in Hong Kong. All charites here, Tracy knew, were served by income from the club as well as much of the governmental financing, through a betting tax and a healthy cut from the lotteries. His Excellency, the Governor of Hong Kong, might be the titular ruler in the Colony but the Jockey Club was the real power behind the office.

Tracy was driven by jeep further up the mountain. From

there he was directed to the roof of the Jockey Club's stables where he found a pair of fenced-in exercise yards for the club's 400 racehorses. It was not surprising. The Colony's mountainous terrain made flat space difficult to find. Here, rooftops had to suffice.

Tracy emerged into the hot stifling sunshine, moving along the curving walkway to the left. The smell of horse was strong. Barechested handlers led sleek muscled horses in a clockwise direction around the longer outer track as well as the inner one. Across the way was the apartment building reserved for the stables' personnel.

Two people stood against the railing further along. They watched a particular stallion moving in the outer ring. Both were Oriental, the man, who was closer to Tracy, was short and squat with the enormous bunched-muscled shoulders of a wrestler and a head as large as a football, deeper than it was high.

As Tracy approached, he became convinced that the man was not Chinese at all. Hong Kong held many Chinese of different origins: Chiuchows from Swatow on the mainland, Tibetans, Mongols, Chinese Muslims, Turkistanis as well as refugees from Peking and Shantung. All might be considered Chinese in this community though all differed considerably in physical terms as well as philosophical and even religious and cultural. This man was none of these.

He was, Tracy now believed, Japanese. That seemed odd, even singular, and Tracy was at once suspicious. Once, before the onset of World War II, Shanghai had been the wide-open city whose officials asked no questions and interfered in no dealings no matter how nefarious. But the coming of the Communists had changed all that. Now it was Hong Kong which attracted those pariahs who were beyond the law. Tracy thought this man might be one of those.

'Mizo-san,' he said, bowing his head before the squat man. 'It is an honour to meet you.' Except for the address, Tracy had used Cantonese.

The short man turned slowly from his contemplation of the racing stallion, contemplated the newcomer. Without turning his head, he said, 'Jade Princess, is this the one?'

The woman who stood next to him nodded her head, 'I recognize his voice.'

'You address me in an odd manner, Mr Richter,' Mizo said. He had a disconcerting voice, its sing-song tone as high in pitch as a girl's. 'Since you are a Westerner, perhaps new to the Colony, I will take no offence.' He eyed Tracy. 'However, I believe you owe this lady an apology. I'm afraid you gave her quite a fright last night.' His face registered distaste. 'All this talk of banks and safes.' He shook his great distorted head from side to side. 'I cannot imagine what you thought you were about.'

'If you did not know, I hardly think you would have consented to meet me,' Tracy said evenly. 'In any case the lady has my apologies. I meant only to get through her armoured gate.'

Mizo threw up his hands. 'That is the way of the world, I'm afraid. The more one is in demand, the more one must safeguard against unwarranted intrusion.'

'It's a tough life, all right,' Tracy's voice was edged in sarcasm.

'If you show us your ignorance, young man,' Mizo said somewhat stiffly, 'that is loss of face. But I imagine that particular idea holds no interest for you.' He made a sound low in this throat. 'You Westerners are all alike. American, English, French. It's all the same to me.'

He turned away from Tracy, returned to watching the horse. 'You see that stallion, Mr Richter? He cost me as much money as a score of Hong Kong residents will earn in their lifetimes. And do you know something? He is worth every cent of that. He runs like the wind and he finishes first. That is all he knows.' He turned back to Tracy, his black bead eyes, slits under heavy epicanthic folds, shrewd and sharply observing. 'He is a specialist. That is one of the many reasons why I love him. He is perfection at what he does, a moron in all other matters.' His great mountainous shoulders lifted, fell. 'The world contains few real specialists anymore. Now everyone's a dabbler, spending a matter of months like moths going from one discipline to another.' His head shook again from one side to another. 'That is not my way, Mr Richter, but I perceive that it is yours. I think we have nothing more to say to one another.'

Beyond the slow clockwise clip-clop parade of the thoroughbreds, beyond the bland white façades of the municipal housing projects forking up from the island, the rising hills of the Asian continent could be seen, misty, streamlined with low clouds, purpled by industrial haze.

'My father is a specialist,' Tracy said. 'I would do nothing to dishonour him.'

For a moment, Mizo did nothing. His slow breathing was like the workings of an enormous power plant. Beside him, Jade Princess remained aloof, as separated from the conversation as if she were in another part of the roof. But Tracy was not misled. She was drinking in every word; she was a part of this. And he watched her now for any telltale signs. She was a handsome woman of not more than thirty. Her skin was like porcelain, having that pale almost translucent quality so impossible for Western women to achieve. On the other hand, most Oriental women longed for blonde hair.

She was, from her facial structure, Chiu-chow, with a long swan's neck and uptilted eyes. Her lips were wide, her cheekbones so high they seemed to pull the corners of her eyes up with them.

'So,' Mizo said at last, 'we have come to the essential question. I have a service to offer, you have four days to learn what must take no less than a year-and-a-half.' His smile when it came was crooked and altogether unpleasant. 'You begin to understand my point of view. I have only so much time to devote; why should I bother with you?'

'My father –'

'Your father I know,' Mizo interrupted, 'by reputation only. He himself means nothing to me.'

'I may be able to rearrange my schedule.'

'Too little, too late.' Mizo took Jade Princess's arm, nodded. 'Good day to you, Mr Richter. I wish you well in your future endeavours.'

'There is one more thing,' Tracy said casually as the pair began to walk away from him. Mizo paused, let go of the woman's arm, turned back. 'My father is very ill; he can no longer work the way he . . . once could. But the honour he holds within his heart is still as strong as it ever was.' Tracy paused, watching the Japanese. There was nothing there for him. It was like staring at a perfectly blank wall. Even those black button eyes refused to blink. 'He has been working on a project . . . for some time now. I don't know what it is. He wouldn't tell anyone about it . . . even me. But I know that it is something revolutionary in the surveillance field.' Now a great stillness had come over Mizo. And in that calm, a minute tremor.

Tracy hesitated now as if, at the brink of a decision, he was undecided. 'I have the project here with me. I . . . took it from him because he is no longer capable of going on.'

'What is it you wish of me, Mr Richter?' The voice reedy, thin as rice paper.

'I want to show it to you,' Tracy said with some emotion. 'I want you to teach me what you can. I want to complete my father's project.'

Fire burned deep within the recesses of Mizo's slitted eyes. He had glimpsed a doorway opening into treasure. Tracy did not think he could resist.

'And that story about the Bank of Shanghai?'

'I had to find a way to you face to face,' Tracy said.

'You took a dangerous route, Mr Richter,' Mizo came forward, leaving Jade Princess in the growing shadows. 'Perhaps after all there is something I can do for you. To revere one's parents is without doubt the highest virtue. It is not the outlook of a dilettante.'

And Tracy thought, I have him!

On the border, Khieu paused to listen. He heard the bright-plumed birds calling, the brief explosive chatterings of the monkeys. Behind him lay Aranyaprathet. In little more than a day and a night he had come halfway around the world. Before him the layered profusion of the jungle reared like a many-headed beast: mythical, primaeval, unbowed. One could still gaze upon it and not see for miles the scars of war like the rude furrows of a giant's nails scored into the belly of the country: home.

Cambodia.

He walked ahead two paces and he was there.

389

Back again, the prodigal son returned to the delta of his creation. To the cruel crucible of his youth. To the bowl of blood it had now been reduced to.

He did not know whether to laugh or cry.

And in the end, he did neither. Merely began his trek, heading south into the interior of his beloved country. He had no clear idea of his ultimate destination; that would be dictated by the information that would come his way during his journey. But, he knew, his time was severely limited. If Macomber did not know that when he had called from Shanghai and had explained the mission Khieu surely did. The anxiety of leaving New York without fulfilling his duty was a constant ache inside him. His shame burned like a beacon from the centre of his soul. If Macomber had not been so insistent, Khieu would have counselled against such a trip as this. But his father was in no mood to be overridden. Something had happened to him in Shanghai and even Khieu's recounting of Senator Sullivan's disclosure and his decision to open the inquiry into the laxity of security procedures in Cairo had failed to deflect him for long from his desire.

'Khieu,' he had said heatedly, 'you must return to Cambodia now. It's impossible for me to go myself; I have been away from it for far too long.'

'What is it, Father?' he had asked, concern in his voice.

'There is a woman, an Oriental you must find for me. She is in Cambodia, that's all I know.'

'If she is there, I will find her,' Khieu had said. Then he had asked for all the relevant information.

He moved steadily through the jungle, passing beneath swinging creepers, stepping carefully over half-sunken root networks. The black professional Nikon 35 mm camera slung around his neck, along with hard leather cases for two long-focus lenses and a string of perhaps a dozen metal canisters containing what appeared to be rolls of film, was no weight at all.

Three miles south of Aranyaprathet, he had encountered a Thai patrol. He had not considered running from them or hiding. They stopped him, asking for his identification. These documents he produced: an American passport and a laminated ID card. The one showed him as a free-lance photographic journalist, the other said he was currently on assignment for *Newsweek*.

The Thais were used to this kind of thing. Their commander did not ask where he was headed. He had seen too many European and American journalists come this way in the past on just such assignments. Cambodia's eternal suffering seemed to draw them like honey. The held-out promise of the sight of disaster was too strong to ignore. Instead, he silently accepted the money Khieu handed over to him for safe conduct.

'Good luck,' the commander said in the manner the Westerners had taught him. His tone was solemn; how many of them never returned. 'You'll need it.'

The forest itself shielded him from the baking heat of the direct subtropical sunlight but here the humidity was at maximum. That was all right. Heat was something he had been born into. It was far easier to take – even at extreme levels others would find intolerable – than New York's numbing winters which, try as he might, still shivered him each year. They seemed endless to him and he hated them.

At least, he thought, as he made his way south in a snaking line, I was able to warn Mizo. Just after Macomber had called him, he had gone out of the house and used a public pay phone. Long experience with this procedure ensured he had just the right amount of change to make the call station-to-station. If Mizo were not at home, no one would answer that particular number.

It had taken him three attempts. At last, he had got through to Jade Princess. He had had to speak for a long time and once he had to calm her, using his most soothing, persuasive tone of voice, assuring her he was speaking for Macomber as well as for himself. The *angka*, he reminded her, must remain sacrosanct. And in the end he got what he wanted. The business they had built with his father's help could not flourish on stupidity. They knew what had to be done. They were fully security-minded. In Hong Kong that was a way of life.

A subtle lessening of the filtered light told him the day was waning; he needed no man-made instrument to confirm that. He began to search for tubers and fruit. But no animal. He was mindful that he must not build a fire. It was not the Khmer Rouge he was concerned about; he was convinced he could handle them. It was the Vietnamese army he could not afford to be spotted by.

But, in point of fact, he was hoping he would not have to spend this night in the open. He remembered a small village near here. He had been heading towards it for most of the day and, if he was not mistaken, he could not be more than a mile or so from it.

Just before the swift fall of night, when the light within the jungle was deep green heightened by thick black shadows, spreading outward as if from some central source, he came upon the village.

Or what was left of it.

Once, years ago, there had been about a half-dozen huts. A network of families who had been in this area for generations. A society complete with their own Buddhist priest.

Now there was only a glade blackened by fire. The scorched earth cracked as if groaning in protestation at his advance. Jagged shards of bamboo stuck up here and there, seemingly at random, the last remnants of hut poles. There was evidence that animal predators had roamed here in the not too distant past: hardened dung and even some spoor lingering around patches of new growth springing up in its infancy. Only the jungle survived.

In the last few instants of light left in the world, he spotted a pale glimmering. He bent down, unearthed a skull partially sunken into the ground. It was a human skull and, he saw by the thickness of the bones, a female one. It had been shattered in three places, the orbit of one eye so displaced as to be all but unrecognizable.

Two paces beyond, he discovered the remains of another skull, significantly smaller than the woman's: a child had been butchered. He crouched for a long time with the last of the child cupped in his dark palms. It could not have been more than four or five, a threat to no one. The jungle chittered and rustled on around him as if it had no heart, no soul, no remorse left within it for its people. Perhaps that had been burned out of it by the tons of napalm, the endless tramp of foreign troops across its broad fertile back. Now the hated Vietnamese fished in the sacred waters of the Tonle Sap, lake of all the Khmer gods.

Khieu slowly enclosed the thing with his long fingers. So this is where the great struggle for revolution had led. The fanaticism of the Khmer Rouge had brought down upon the nation the scourge of the invading Vietnamese. Once, Khieu had thought that peace between the two peoples was possible, essential for Cambodia to survive. That, at least, had been Sihanouk's stand and, as Sam had more than once pointed out, it was therefore invalid.

It was possible now for Khieu to understand the insidious nature of Sam's indoctrination into radical politics. René had sucked him in, the false promise of a kind of freedom that was, in reality, no freedom at all, had infected them all. Khieu Samphan, Ieng Sary, Pol Pot, none of them were immune. But it was power they lusted after and that lust blinded them to the fact that what they were buying wholesale was a philosophy of negation. To achieve their goals, the entire history of the Khmer needed to be wiped out so completely that it would be as if it had never existed.

How could they? Khieu asked himself now. How could they? Tears dropped from his eyes, seeping down from his clasped fingers onto the dried bones of this unknown Khmer child. See how your dream has ended? The *Yuon* own the land now and they butcher us just as you butchered us before that. Death without end. Life without hope.

He fell asleep, propped up against the bole of a huge tree, without eating the bananas he had found in his foraging. He dreamed of a place filled with dark light. A network of naked animal jaws rose above his head, the long curving yellowed teeth overlaid one upon the other like the profusion of stars on a cloudless night.

The place he dreamed of was bare: a wooden floor, walls he sensed rather than saw. But in its centre was a raised rectangular structure draped in black cotton, the folds of fabric along the sides, rippling like flags in the wind. A bed or an altar, the concepts seemed to merge and fuse.

He became aware of a shape atop the raised structure and, moving closer, he saw that it was a human figure ... a female figure. She was moving and he squinted in order to get a better look. She writhed on the platform, contorting her body this way and that. It seemed to him that she moved in a purely erotic, primeval way.

Malis. It was Malis!

He felt himself growing hard as he saw again the sensual rocking of her hips, the slow spreading of her legs, the passage of her delicate fingertips up along the satiny pale flesh on the insides of her thighs. They moved to the very core of her and then over it, upward over her bent torso to caress her hardened nipples. She pinched them, pulling her breasts upward gently into spouts, moaning slightly with the action. Her tiny pink tongue came out, licked at her lips, wetting them. They parted invitingly.

Then her hands had swept downward, the palms pressing briefly against the hard rounded bowl of her belly. Now she raised her legs and her fingers tangled in the dark rich delta of hair at the base of her thighs. She sighed and her breasts shook in response to the deep caress.

Watching this, he felt again his brain on fire. Now, he thought, now is the time. I can have her all to myself. To take her. To love her, enfold her, plunge into her, to give her pleasure and in her moaning under me release my hot seed into her.

His penis was so painfully hard he had trouble standing upright as he approached and this distraction, perhaps, was what made the shock all the greater.

He was close now, very close. And he saw that he had been mistaken. Completely and utterly mistaken. What he had thought were writhings of pleasure must surely have been the spasms of pain, the hands at her core not a caress but a protective gesture.

For he saw towering over her a great muscled *Yuon*, the hated

Vietnamese invader. He had a grip on her that Malis could not break though she would not give up trying. She clawed and scraped at him until he balled his free hand into a fist and punched her viciously between her thighs so that she gasped and tried to vomit with the shock and pain. But his other hand was clamped over her mouth. She could do nothing but swallow or drown in her own bile.

Now the *Yuon* had a knife in his free hand, the blade black as the core of night. Its darkness was chilling. The blade whooshed down towards Malis and the *Yuon* moved the hand holding her so that he had her around the throat. He leaned into her, savagely jamming the back of her head against the black cotton covering the structure, bringing the lower half of her face up towards him.

The knifeblade swooped down in a swift arc as a predatory bird when it sights its prey. It sliced into her flesh neatly at the side of her jaw, peeling away the skin as if it were the rind of a fresh orange.

Brother and sister leapt upwards at the same time as if both had been cut. Khieu, howling with rage, shot forward and, as he did so, saw the huge *Yuon* begin the backward motion for the second cut. He reached out, ready to tear the arms from the man but there was nothing for him to grip.

Gasping and shaking, the cold sweat dripping off him like rain, he stood there, watching the black blade begin its terrible journey up the hills and valleys of Malis' face. Now there was a double tract of raw pulpy flesh, quivering like jelly as the exposed nerves jumped in unending agony. The skin peeled away in another long strip, joining its sister at the feet of the *Yuon*.

Again and again the Vietnamese soldier sliced into Malis, until Khieu was at a loss to recognize anything human beneath the veil of blood and rent tissue.

Sunk to his knees, crying and beating at himself uncontrollably, he knew there was nothing he could do to save her. He had abandoned her when he had left Phnom Penh to join the Khmer Rouge, to follow Sam's shining example, to join the glorious revolution against the Western capitalist aggressors and the *Yuon* infidels, to build a free Cambodia. Left her to be captured by the Vietnamese, to be tortured, raped repeatedly, killed slowly and lingeringly.

He heard her screaming then, the bare white teeth drawn back in a rictus of terror and agony, her swollen bloody tongue flickering back and forth until the *Yuon* had had enough and, with a thick grunt of satisfaction, took the wet thing between thumb and forefinger, lifting it out as far as it would go, and slicing it off with the honed cutting edge of his knife . . .

Khieu started awake. Had he cried out? He was shaking. The hot night beat on all around him. He heard the stealthy pad of predators, the flurry of nocturnal wings high above his head in the arboreal reaches.

He stood shakily up. The bitter taste of copper was in his mouth. He put one hand against the tree trunk to steady himself. He was sweating profusely and he felt slightly nauseated as if he had been forced to overeat. His breath came loudly and he heard the high-pitched *skree skree* of bats in flight, signalling to each other.

After a time, he sat back down, his soaked back against the bole of the tree to wait for morning. No more sleep for him this long night.

He knew now what he must do before he left Cambodia and the thought filled him with a creeping pervading dread.

Thwaite stopped off to see the police surgeon before he left town. He thought briefly about dropping in on Melody or calling her even but somehow he never got around to it.

The surgeon, a porky jovial man with a balding bullet head and a moustache turned yellow from his constant smoking, expertly redressed the wound. He asked Thwaite if he was feeling much pain and at what times.

Thwaite told him the truth. The thing only bothered him now when he twisted his body sharply and, sometimes, if he had overdone it physically during the day. The surgeon nodded, wrote out a prescription for a mild pain-killer. As soon as he was out of the office, Thwaite threw it away.

That morning he had phoned a friend of his in the Chicago Police Force.

Since he needed an entrée into the Kenilworth police department, Thwaite had decided on Art Silvano. They had worked together more than once but on the last occasion the Chicago Detective Sergeant had had to come to Thwaite for a rather large favour. Together, they had bent the departmental rules a bit and that was a powerful bond between them.

Silvano met him at O'Hare. He had a bit more white hair and the shade of blue in his eyes seemed to have lightened a little but otherwise he seemed the same. He was a man whose wide shoulders allowed him to carry more paunch than he had to without attracting too much attention. He had a tanned, seamed face which always reminded Thwaite of a full-blooded Texan though he knew Silvano was from nearby Cicero.

The two shook hands warmly and Silvano told Thwaite how sorry he was about the death of the other's family.

'I got a connection in Kenilworth,' Silvano said. 'One of the three sergeants, guy name of Rich Pleasent. Not too bad a sort considering where he works. He'll take care of us.' They were passing the urban blight of the city as quickly as was possible. 'Now you'd better fill me in on what you're looking for.'

Twenty minutes later they were at Pleasent's office. 'Thwaite here's been after a fugitive, thinks the bastard may have had something to do with Senator Burke's murder.'

Pleasent shrugged. 'I think you're outta luck, then. I was the one who caught the squeal so I was first on the scene. It was nothing but a B and E. Burke must've caught the perpetrator in the act and tried to attack him. That was a mistake. This guy was a professional. He left nothing.'

Silvano nodded thoughtfully. 'Still, we'd like to take a look at the ME's report. Can you help us out?'

'Sure.' Pleasent swivelled around, pulled open the drawer of a metal file cabinet. He extracted a buff folder, spun it across.

Thwaite opened the folder and went through it carefully. There was no mention of the nose cartilage.

Thwaite found the name of the associate ME who performed the autopsy. 'You know a Dr Wood?'

The sergeant shrugged. 'Don't know any of 'em down there. I mean, why would I hang out with a buncha ghouls? You think I wanna eat my lunch in the cold room with all those stiffs? I got other hobbies.'

Thwaite leaned forward. 'Mind if I make a call?'

Pleasant turned his phone around. 'Help yourself.'

Thwaite dialled the number. When the operator answered, he asked for Dr Wood. He was put on hold, then was told that Dr Wood was currently in court, testifying in a case. Did he want to leave a message? Thwaite said he did not and hung up.

He tapped the cover of the report absently before sliding it back onto the desk. He asked for and got the police photographs of the crime scene. He didn't think he'd learn much from them but it was bad procedure to overlook anything, even the obvious.

'I'd like to see the list of stolen property. The insurance company must've furnished you with one.'

Pleasant shrugged again. 'Why not?' He got the stuff. 'But I still think all of this's a waste of everyone's time.'

Thwaite ran his eye down the list: stereo, a portable TV, two antique clocks, video tape recorder, Intellivision video game, an inlaid gold box. A list of personal jewellery followed: rings, diamond cuff links, a Philippe Patek solid gold watch.

'I'd appreciate it,' Thwaite said carefully, 'if you'd take us out to the Senator's house.'

'Oh, for Christ's sake,' Pleasant said to Silvano,' is this really necessary, Art?'

'I gotta take a look at the place,' Thwaite insisted quietly.

'Ah, shit, okay. C'mon.'

They drove out to Kenilworth. The countryside was spectacular, long, tree-lined streets, well-paved and perfectly clean; large, expensive houses and estates bordered by sculptured hedges and low-growing trees. Sunlight, dappling through the foliage, lit their way.

Pleasant took them into the house. It was hot and stuffy. All the windows were closed and, of course, the air conditioning had not been on in recent days.

The place struck Thwaite as odd immediately. All the black

and white was somehow eerie. He wondered how anyone could've lived here.

Pleasent stood in the centre of the living room, explaining to them just where the body had been found, how they had reconstructed the crime.

'Know how the intruder got in?' Thwaite asked.

'The front door wasn't locked when I came by. I just walked right in. Maybe the perpetrator did the same.'

'Yeah, maybe,' Thwaite said without enthusiasm. He could not buy that. It was a lazy answer and he never trusted lazy answers.

Pleasent stayed where he was, jangling the keys to the house while Thwaite and Silvano made a search of the rest of the rooms.

The master bath was all black including the porcelain fixtures. Thwaite wondered what the senator had thought about while he was in there; it seemed to him more like a crypt.

The bedroom, expansive and airy, was, in contrast, all in white save for a double lowboy dresser that ran the length of one wall.

'Quite a spread,' Silvano said sarcastically. 'So this's what I voted for.'

The den with its rows of bookshelves seemed the most lived-in; it appeared as if no one had slept in the guest bedroom for some time.

'Let's take a look at the grounds,' Thwaite said and Pleasent groaned.

Burke's property extended off to one side and straight out back. To the side, the original wild stands of trees had been cut down by the builder and a professional landscaper had been brought in to do the replanting.

Out back, the original trees had been left. 'How far does this go back?' Thwaite asked.

'Oh, quite a ways,' Pleasent said, not paying much attention.

Thwaite and Silvano took a walk. The sun was lowish, sending oblique rays filled with dancing dust motes through the gaps in the trees. The stand of birch and oak lasted for perhaps a hundred and fifty yards, then broke slowly apart as the land sloped down to the bank of a rather large pond. Swans and a pair of mallard ducks swam contentedly, ruffling their feathers in the summer sun.

Returning to Silvano's car, Thwaite asked the police operator to patch him through to the MEs office. This time, Dr Wood came on the line after a slight pause.

'This's Detective Sergeant Douglas Thwaite from the NYPD,' he said carefully. 'I'm currently out here with the Kenilworth and Chicago police, looking into the murder of Senator Burke. I understand you performed the autopsy.'

'That's correct,' Dr Wood's thin voice came down the line.

'Can you tell me what shape the senator's nose cartilage was in at the time of the autopsy.'

'What?' The pathologist seemed nonplussed.

'The cartilage was, in effect, the agent of death, was it not?'

'Well, yes, but –'

'Doctor, please answer the question.'

Wood thought a moment. 'The nasal cartilage was pretty much intact.'

Thwaite's heart beat harder. 'Pretty much?'

'Well, I mean to say, there were minute chips here and there along the interior end but, other than that, it was in one piece. Quite remarkable.'

'Thank you, Doctor,' Thwaite said excitedly. 'You've been a big help.' He put the mouthpiece back in its cradle.

'Well?' Silvano asked anxiously. He was bending down, peering through the open window. 'What's up?'

Thwaite looked up at his friend. 'This's my bastard, all right, Art. The ME just confirmed it.'

'Yeah, okay,' Silvano said. 'But you're still at a dead-end.'

Thwaite got out of the car. 'Maybe not. I'm thinkin' that he's no B and E man. That means the stolen property was a scam all the way.' He turned his head, looked out at the sun-dappled trees rustling in the warm wind. 'He had no truck to cart off the heavy stuff so what did he do with it? Even if he was as strong as a bull, he couldn't've taken the shit too far.' Then he

400

began to walk back the way they had come. In the stand of birch and oak behind the house, he answered his own question.

'The pond.'

Tracy would have preferred to linger awhile down the hillside in the cool refined atmosphere of the Jockey Club bar on the eighth floor, overlooking the now deserted race track. An iced daquiri would have done him well now in celebration. But he decided that would not be politic. He did not want to rub Mizo's face in it, after all.

He tried not to gloat as he climbed into the taxi he had had them call for him at the stables but it was a difficult task indeed. For the first time, he felt closer to his quarry and the resulting surge of adrenalin almost eliminated his concern.

From the moment he had come away from his dinner with the Director, he had been on guard. That the Director had no knowledge of what Kim was up to told Tracy much. But not nearly enough. For every answer it provided, ten questions had sprung up in its place. For instance, it was now not surprising that Tracy had been unable to contact Kim during the last forty-eight hours. Yet he was still in the dark as to why the Vietnamese had brought him in on this.

Partly to clear his mind of unanswered questions, he told the driver to take him to the Diamond House on Queens Road. On the long flight over, he had had much time to think about Lauren and he had determined that he would not allow Bobby's ghost to come between them. He'd find some way to explain it to her.

It took him two hours — most of that fighting traffic — but he returned to the hotel with a four-carat flawless blue-white stone in a platinum setting. On entering the lobby, he crossed straight to the concierge's desk, requesting the use of the hotel's safe. He gave them the small gift-wrapped parcel from the Diamond House and the concierge, a young Chinese with bad skin and a winning smile, signed the receipt, handing Tracy the original.

'You merely have to present this,' he said helpfully, 'and your parcel will be returned to you, Mr Richter.'

Tracy thanked him, went across the lobby, took a lift up to his room.

In the hallway, he slowed his pace, waiting for the French couple to pass him, take the elevator down to the lobby. When they had gone and the hallway was clear, he knelt in front of his door, inspecting the lock. He was expecting nothing but old habits die hard and he was, after all, on a mission. It was a mistake to become careless.

Satisfied, he put his key in the lock, turned it over. Inside, everything was where he had left it. He went to the bureau, opened the bottom right-hand drawer. Under a pair of Sea Island cotton shirts, he uncovered the case his father had so painstakingly packed for him. He smiled. He did not think he would need any of the contents now.

It had been up to Mizo, of course. Tracy had devised the plan and it was always open to change depending on the current situation. But, in the end, it had to be Mizo's response that everything hung on.

Tracy crossed to the bed, sat down. He slipped off his shoes, one by one. A cool shower would be just the thing before heading back out into the heat and humidity for lunch.

He thought that Mizo must be the key. If John Holmgren *had* been poisoned, as the photos seemed to suggest, Mizo could have that knowledge. Running a school for terrorists could include that kind of training, Mizo's protestations of specialization notwithstanding. Tracy's father had enough knowledge about the man to provide Tracy with that answer. But in any event it was certain that Mizo had trained the man who had constructed the bug.

Then there was the matter of Moira's death. Tracy still had not overcome the intense feeling of guilt. Her words came back to him. *I just felt ... something. Like waking from a nightmare into a nightmare.* Had she somehow felt the presence of John Holmgren's murderer? She had been a perceptive person, highly intuitive. Tracy's fingers closed into a tight fist of frustration. If only he had talked to her more about what she suspected; if only he could talk to her now.

He shook his head, angry with himself. That kind of thinking was counterproductive. He had to concentrate on Mizo. He was the master and soon he would reveal the identity of his pupil.

Bare feet against the wall-to-wall carpeting, Tracy reached for the phone. He calculated the time difference. Night in America. That was all right. His father slept little these days and the nights, he said, were far too long. Anyway, there might be something more he could tell him about Mizo, if Tracy nudged his memory a little.

The receiver left its cradle and his world exploded into red light, a percussive hammerblow, a wind like a typhoon lifting him bodily and then a blackness as deep as death.

Just before noon, Khieu began to see signs that told him he was approaching another village: several intersecting, well-trod paths through the jungle, a kind of garbage dump, a pair of domesticated water buffalo, grazing.

He slowed his pace and kept a wary eye out. In the old days, this kind of thing would have been easy enough. All he would have to do was invoke the name of *Angka* and he would be given any information he desired. Now, it was different.

He had passed as many as six Viet patrols since he had set out at first light. They seemed well-armed and disciplined. Once, in the distance, he could make out the pop-pop-pop of small arms fire, evidence that the Khmer Rouge now, after uncomfortable years in power that did not suit them, returned to their original status as outlaw revolutionaries, were nearby. The new People's Republic of Kampuchea was a figment of the occupying Viet forces' imagination. It was as spurious a representation of the will and desires of the Khmer people as was Pol Pot's hideous reign.

But most depressing of all to Khieu was the enlistment in the Viet-RPK army of many Khmer. The impact of this was never brought home to him as vividly as when, approaching the village from the north, he suddenly saw swarming activity not five hundred yards in front of him. He was near the verge of the jungle. Beyond, a jagged pool-sized bomb crater straddled what was left of an undulating ridge that abutted a flat field scarred with long mounded dark-brown earthen furrows.

There were perhaps forty soldiers at work here, Viets as well as Khmer under their control. They had formed up into two parallel rows. They appeared to have been digging into the earthen furrows for some time.

Khieu, keeping low, crept closer to see what they were up to. He poked his head through a gap in the undergrowth. Now he could see what lay within the furrows: the litter of pale skeletons.

He was situated somewhat near several of the RPK officers and could hear snatches of what they were saying. The first phrase he picked up was 'killing ground'. This field was one of many such 'killing grounds', according to the officer, found scattered throughout every district of Cambodia.

'Many visitors have already come here,' said the one with the pockmarked face, 'so we felt it time to dig it up. It's served one propaganda purpose.'

'Why do we tell the foreigners there are 129 of these?' asked the younger of the two.

'A firm number is always impressive,' said the other one. He turned slightly and Khieu could see that he had a rough black patch over his right eye. 'It gives the impression that all is under control. That is most important, the Soviets have told us.' He turned and pointed to a Khmer soldier. 'You there! Careful with that one. It deserves a place of honour in our new People's Museum.'

The young soldier bent down, lifted up a skull in his cupped hands. The lower jaw was missing; perhaps it had been blown away during the execution. But the blindfold, still russet with dried blood, was tightly bound over its eyes. 'Yes,' the officer with the one eye crooned, 'that's the one.'

He turned back to his pupil. 'The Museum, of course, will serve the same purpose as exposing these "killing grounds", but it will be a more permanent reminder. These are the remains of the New People, we tell visitors: those unfortunate Khmers who lived in the cities or who were otherwise outside the Khmer Rouge control. These are the victims of Pol Pot's maniacal hatred. This aids us in a battle still to be won.'

'Then it is not the truth?' the young Viet asked.

'What is the truth?' the pock-marked officer said. 'It is what we make it. The great revolutionaries tell us history must be remade to capture the zeal of today's proselyte. That is what we do here.'

Sickened, Khieu crawled silently away. Getting to his feet, he carefully skirted the activity, heading towards the village. What *was* the truth? he wondered. Had Pol Pot and his Khmer Rouge, in fact, executed all those people? Or had it been the Vietnamese themselves, in the early days of their occupation? One question he asked himself was how the RPK officers knew of all the 'killing ground' locations. Had they chanced on them? Had their whereabouts been beaten out of dying revolutionaries? Or had they known the locations all along?

In the end, he knew, it did not much matter. Those dead could scarcely be concerned with the identity of their murderer. Dead was dead. And they were still being used. Even the crossing over into death could not save them from that. They were still the focal point of an international power struggle that seemed to have no end.

He flitted through the forest as if he himself were a *kmoch*, a ghost of his country's seemingly distant past. There were many low-hanging branches here and he moved quite carefully, his eyes always roving, on the lookout not only for human predators but for the lethal Hanuman, the all-green serpents who spent all their time lying along the twisted branches, dropping silently down on their prey from above. He could scent the *chhoeu teal* trees, from which Khmer villagers drew oil used in lighting lamps. He was on the verge of real civilization. It struck him strongly how isolating the Cambodian jungle could be. He had not, after all, been within its embrace for fourteen years yet how easy it had been to slip on the mantle, to find his way within its clinging green labyrinth. It was as if all that time in between had never occurred. As if Western civilization had not truly stayed with him but had merely been imprinted temporarily on his brain.

His path to the first outlying hut was clear and he moved towards it with the soundlessness of a cloud. He found women and children, an old man – the absent husband's grandfather.

They were frightened of him, frightened to talk to him. The woman put her two children behind her as if he were some foreigner bent on snatching them. The old man's head drooped and he snored. He shook in his sleep; Khieu could see he was dying of malaria. He had caught sight of the children's unhealthily distended bellies before their mother had swept them from his gaze.

He asked them simple questions: where was he, how far was it to the next village south, had they any food he could buy?

To all of these he received the same reply from the terrified woman: 'My husband, Chey, has joined the army. He has a rifle now. He will shoot you down if you harm us.'

Khieu had no intention of harming them nor had he made any sign, overt or covert, of hostile intent. Still, the wild-eyed woman's fear was palpable, the strongest emanation from the foul-smelling room. He saw a pitiful hoard of thin tubers, hairy with roots, in one corner but his glance made the woman even more afraid. 'I will not take your food,' he said softly, calmly. 'I see that you do not have enough for your own family.'

She repeated her speech and it occurred to him that her husband had made her memorize it and say nothing more to strangers. 'I am searching for someone,' he said, using his hands for emphasis. 'My family . . . the only one left.'

She repeated her speech by rote.

Outside, back within the concealing jungle, he realized his mistake. He was dressed in no known style. His presence could only confuse the woman who must be used to seeing the outfits of the peasant labourer, the RPK army uniforms, or the Khmer Rouge black. He was dressed as none of these. He would have to remedy that situation.

But silence was of paramount importance. There must be no hint of his presence here; he had no desire to become the object of an army manhunt throughout Cambodia.

He returned to the area of low-hanging branches and turned his gaze upward. It took him close to half-an-hour but at length he spotted a Hanuman lying along a green branch. It was not sleeping. He could see one large yellow eye with its tiny vertical pupil.

Mentally marking the spot, Khieu turned right, towards the dirt track leading into the heart of the village. He was too close to the village's perimeter to see the excavation work at the 'killing ground'. Nevertheless, there was a moderate amount of traffic. He must be close to an RPK installation because the majority of people passing by were soldiers.

He crouched down, totally concealed from view by the thick foliage, and scrounged around for a stone of suitable size and shape. He found one several yards away and, gripping it loosely, returned to the spot he had chosen.

He waited patiently, reciting his Buddhist catechism, until he spotted a Viet officer striding into town alone. His arm floated in air, the wrist cocked. With an abrupt blur of movement, he sent the stone whizzing on its way. It struck the officer's leg on the side of the kneecap with enough force to make him wince in pain. He paused, turning towards the source.

Khieu waited a moment, then allowed his body to brush aside some low-lying fern as he moved back. The officer caught sight of the movement and, drawing his handgun, strode into the jungle, parting the foliage ahead of him with one hand.

Khieu, still crouching, ran ahead, allowing the Vietnamese officer a sight only of leaves trembling in his wake. The other man had no idea whether he was tracking man or beast. But either way, Khieu knew, he would want to kill it.

At the place of low-lying branches, he turned and waited. He placed his hands on his Nikon, turned it upside down as if unsure of its workings.

He felt the presence of the other before he actually saw him. He looked up, startled, to see an army officer levelling a pistol at his stomach.

'Pardon me,' he said in English, 'but can you tell me how to load this thing with film?'

Mit mork pee na? the officer said in Khmer. *Mit chumos ey?*

The same question he had been asked by Ros in his first contact with the Khmer Rouge a lifetime ago. Where do you come from? What's your name? The officer jabbed the air between them with the barrel of his pistol. He repeated the questions.

Cowed, Khieu retreated before him. He was still fiddling with the Nikon. 'I can't seem to get this damn camera to work,' he said, moving steadily backward, the irregular network of low-lying branches passing just above his head.

Now the officer was angry. He was used to immediate and obedient answers to his questions. He pursued Khieu, who he saw quite clearly was unarmed, more quickly now. He raised his voice as he asked his terse questions again. 'Who are you? Where do you come from?'

Khieu ignored him, babbling on in English, retreating still until he had the Vietnamese in the proper spot. Then he stopped and said in Khmer: 'I come from Aranyaprathet. At least that's how I entered Cambodia. I have been sent by those sympathetic to your cause to build up photographic evidence that the PRK régime is creating a new Cambodia out of the ashes of the old.'

The officer's eyes opened wide on hearing this political cant. It was certainly not what he had expected from this man.

'Why did you not answer my questions when I asked them?' He had the gun; he had the power. He merely wanted Khieu to understand the nature of this meeting and who had the upper hand.

'I cannot take these pictures unless I can get this camera to work,' Khieu said as he prayed to Hanuman. 'Can you help me, Comrade?'

The officer's thick upper lip curled in contempt. 'I am a captain in the People's Republic of Kampuchea Army. I have better things to do with my time than –'

He corkscrewed on his feet as if pulled by invisible strings. His arms shot out automatically in a desperate attempt to rebalance himself. In the process, the pistol bounced on the jungle floor.

Khieu watched calmly as Hanuman, the green adder, wound itself around the Vietnamese's neck and, arching back its head, bit him in the carotid. It did not take the man long to die but, from all accounts, Khieu knew it must be extremely unpleasant.

He waited until the body's irregular spasming ceased, then

he kicked at the serpent with the toe of his boot, sending the deadly thing spinning high into the treetops.

Then he set about stripping the corpse.

Only one half of Delmar Davis Macomber's office atop the Metronics, Inc. building on Gold Street could be termed a conventional work space. The other half was where he relaxed during the long business day, and thought. The majority of this area was taken over by two spacious rooms. One was a steam bath, which Macomber used during the relatively dry winters; the other was a sauna, which he preferred to use while those outside sweated through the city's notoriously humid summers. He was convinced the Finns were all wrong in their application of the health aid they had made world famous.

Be that as it may, he was comfortably ensconced in the sauna when he heard the knock on the cedar door. He beckoned with his hand at the figure he could just discern through the small double glass panel set into the door.

Eliott entered tentatively. He seemed a far cry from the young man who had reacted with such positive enthusiasm to Kathleen Christian's careful and calculated seduction. His hair was uncombed and there were signs of dark circles beneath his eyes.

'You wanted to see me.' It was not a question.

'You look positively awful,' Macomber said. 'Haven't you been sleeping?'

'Sleeping or eating,' Eliott said tonelessly. He had already begun to sweat in the heated atmosphere. His skin felt terribly tight.

'You have every right to be unhappy, Eliott,' Macomber said judiciously. 'Frankly, I don't blame you a bit.'

Eliott's head twitched and his eyes opened wide. 'For God's sake, you being so *civilized* about it!' He seemed to be a little wild. 'Why aren't you screaming? A tongue-lashing is what I –'

'It's unhealthy to stand around here like that,' Macomber observed. 'Go take off your clothes and then come back.' Eliott had turned to go. 'And don't forget to take a cool shower first. You've got to be wet when you come in here.'

When he was alone again, he sat with his back rigid against the tile wall, his rather large hands clasped loosely, wrists on thighs. He tried hard not to think about Khieu, not to think about Cambodia, not to think about how he might be jeopardizing the entire *angka* by having sent his son back into that hellhole; not to think, above all, about Tisah. Anything but Tisah and the promise her return held out to him.

So when Eliott returned, he said, 'We've really got Lawrence on the run now. The latest Gallup Poll shows his popularity at 38 per cent. That's down 13 per cent. Jack Sullivan's little revelation to the press really torpedoed the President. I hear there's some talk starting in Democratic circles about not running him for re-election in September.'

'It's a little late for that, don't you think?' Eliott said, sitting down at right angles to his father. His head drooped on his neck and he stared at the slats at his feet. He had a white towel draped across his loins. Macomber was totally naked.

'Not if you're desperate.'

He watched his son as the silence built. At last he said in his softest voice, 'I'm sorry it had to end this way, Eliott. Truly I am.' He leaned forward to ease himself from the tension that had come into his frame. His teeth clenched at what he was about to say. But if it brought him back his son, then it would be more than worth it. 'I think I know how you felt about her.'

Eliott looked up instantly. His eyes were sparked with tears. 'Do you? Khieu sure didn't.'

'He was simply thinking about the sanctity of the *angka*. You can't blame him for that.'

'But he's not human,' Eliott protested. 'He doesn't *feel*.'

Macomber had put his head back, stared at the ceiling. After a time, he said, 'She wanted it all, Eliott.' He was speaking of Kathleen now. 'She wanted into the *angka* so that she could blackmail Atherton with what she found out. She was a very dangerous woman.'

'But she made me feel . . . *alive*. No one else's ever done that.'

'I understand that but –'

'No,' Eliott said heatedly, 'I don't think you do.' He stood up and the towel fell to the slatted floor. 'How could you. I had nannies who brought me up; you consulted Dr Spock and I don't know how many other child experts on the proper way to bring me up. You took from them what they believed was right and wrong.'

'I did the best I could,' Macomber said rather stiffly.

'Yes!' Eliott cried. 'Yes! And that's what's so pathetic. Your best was no good at all. You treated me as if I were a chapter from a How-To book. I wasn't a real person to you, not a thinking, breathing human being. You couldn't face that. The responsibility was too much for you. You could manage an empire easily. But raising one son was beyond you.'

'How can you say that?' Macomber said indignantly. 'I got the most expert help –'

'But nothing came from *you*, don't you see that? It was all other people's theories and philosophies.'

He pointed to himself with one long finger. 'I am *me*! An individual, unique unto myself. If you had only been able to respond to me naturally, I truly think we would have been able to enjoy each other. Instead, you pushed me away, distancing yourself while you told yourself what you were doing was giving me the best care available.

'Only my mother would have cared. I know that –' he choked a little before he could go on. 'But she was gone.' He closed his eyes. 'Too soon. Too fucking soon.'

Exhausted by his outburst, he slid back down on the slatted bench, slumping forward, his chest heaving.

Macomber wiped sweat off his forehead, brushed his thin moustache of accumulated moisture. Then he reached up to the wooden-handled chain, pulled it downward. Scalding water vented on the pit of hot rocks to one side, a cloud of steam resulted. The temperature climbed markedly.

He found himself staring at his son's hands. He realized how much like his own they were. He flexed his fingers, watching their workings as if for the first time.

'It's not a father's place to make his son feel like a man.'

'That's the trouble with you,' Eliott said, his head coming up. 'You'll never change. When will you learn that being a father is what you make of it, nothing more, nothing less.' It was said in an even tone. There seemed no more anger left in him.

Macomber cleared his throat. 'I'm sorry that's how you perceived it. It never occurred to me ...' He saw the look his son shot him and decided to begin again. 'Perhaps I'm not so much as a father. But you can't spend all your life blaming me. You've got to get on with your own.'

'I know that.'

'Uhm. Well, sometimes I wonder. You've run away from every responsibility –'

'It runs in the family,' Eliott said archly. Then in a more normal tone of voice, 'You know, very early on, it seemed clear to me that I was somehow fated to follow in your footsteps whether or not I really wanted to.'

He gave a harsh, brittle laugh. 'I think I must've been the only high school kid afraid of his own intellect. But all my courses seemed to goddamned *easy*. I couldn't understand it; I hated it.

'You paid my way through college and, by my senior year, I saw that unconsciously or what, I don't really know, I was fulfilling all the expectations you had for me. I saw quite clearly that the next stop for me was Metronics and that would be the end for me. The beginning and the end. It was like a trap I couldn't see a way out of; I mean, there were even areas within the company that fascinated me.'

'So your not showing up for graduation; your walking away from your six months here, it was all to spite me.'

'No, no,' Eliott said. 'I was frightened, don't you understand? I felt I had no choices in life; that I'd *never* had any choices; that the simple fact of *being your son* had somehow preordained me to be another you.'

'That was what I wanted,' Macomber said almost absently.

'And I knew that,' Eliott said.

Macomber looked down. 'I suppose ... well, I never really thought about what it would be like for you. I never ... I always wanted you to be as successful as I was; to be *more* successful, in fact. I wanted you here with me, by my side. I thought that was a natural place for a son to be.' He looked up. 'Am I so wrong?'

Eliott let out a sigh so deep he might have been holding it in for years. 'The fact is,' he said slowly, 'you aren't. I was never cut out to be an actor. I knew it when I signed up. I think now that that was the main reason I *did* sign up. I wanted to fail at it and to let you see me fail. I thought that'd get you off my back for good.'

'You know,' Macomber said, 'I don't think anything would've done that.'

'Not even my fuck-up with Kathleen?'

Macomber perceived that his son still expected an outburst. 'I blame myself as much as you for that, Eliott. If we hadn't been at such odds, I don't think it ever would've happened.'

Eliott looked away. 'For a long time,' he said softly, 'I was certain you loved Khieu more than you loved me. He has everything that I don't. The looks, the expertise and, especially, that magnetic personality.'

Macomber got up, stretched his back and legs. 'The problem with you is that you always gave too much weight to Khieu's magnetism. I used to get a laugh thinking that you'd imagine him spending hours in front of a mirror working on his charm when nothing could be further from the truth. His ... aura ... is totally natural. He never worked on it consciously, never even would have known he had it were it not for me. I saw it; I brought it out in him.'

'I can't help feeling the way I do about him.'

'That's too bad,' Macomber said. 'He'd be a good friend to you. A very loyal friend.'

'I don't want to talk about him anymore.'

Macomber contemplated his son. 'I want you here at Metronics, Eliott. You know that. Nothing would please me more. And I want you more involved in the *angka*; I can use your opinions. This Sullivan committee investigation, for instance. The Secretary of State's involved; has to be, because his department shared responsibility for the botched security in Cairo. But Findlan's bound to be called in to testify, things may get hot for him for a while: the CIA was in on this, too.

'He's part of the *angka*. I don't believe you were aware of that before. Well, you are now. D'you think he can weather the storm? Our deal with him has not been finalized; we can always sever our relationship. But it must be within the next few days to avoid any ... overt unpleasantness.'

'From what I know of Marcus Findlan he can weather this storm and any other that comes his way,' Eliott said. He stood up, too. 'But before we go on, I have to tell you that I don't know whether I want to know more about the *angka*. I only know bits and pieces now; unrelated factors. I have no clear picture of the overall pattern. For now, I'd rather take it easy and leave it alone. Let me concentrate on Metronics, all right?'

Macomber nodded. 'Whatever you want. But I don't want you to feel slighted when you're excluded from discussions I must have with Khieu on the subject.'

Eliott gave a thin smile. 'I promise.' He bent down to pick up the towel, moved towards the door.

'There's just one thing, Eliott.'

He turned. 'Yes?'

'If Khieu hadn't come in on you and the Christian woman, you'd've realized what she was up to quite soon. I know that; so do you.' He stared hard at Eliott. 'What would you have done about it?'

Eliott's eyes flickered with some emotion. 'I think I loved her, father.' His voive was soft but without a quaver in it. 'Don't ask me to make that choice now.'

There was muck lying unevenly along the upper ridge of the black mask as the diver's head breached the water. Spotlights trained on the surface of the pond sent shards of light streaking in the widening ripple pattern away from his emerging body. His face was opaqued by the angle of reflection.

Thwaite had had to wait a long time for this. It was now well after midnight. Bradford Brady, the Kenilworth Commander, was hard, unfair, and resented bitterly an outsider knowing more about a case so close to home. In fact, at first he was downright intractable.

'I don't want to hear about it; I don't want to know about it,' he said in his odd unpleasant rather high-pitched voice. He was a short man with a small turned-up nose and a ruddy complexion.

There was no way at all to reason with the man so Thwaite let loose with the big guns right away. 'I don't think you'd want this to get as far as the Illinois Attorney-General's office, would you, Commander?'

'What?'

'I'm just asking for a little auxiliary manpower. A couple of divers, a standard rescue light setup. 'That isn't much.'

Bradford Brady turned to Pleasant. 'What's he mean, the Attorney-General's office?'

'It's little enough to ask for, really. Neither Sergeant Silvano or I wants to make any more noise over this than is necessary. It'll be between you and us for the time being.'

'I don't want the goddamned Attorney-General down around my ears,' Brady thundered. 'I've got enough woes already.'

Thwaite shrugged his shoulders.

Bradford Brady squinted. 'What foul-smelling wind brought you my way, Thwaite? That's all I want to know.' Then he gestured to Pleasant, grunted. 'Get him what he wants, Sergeant.'

Thwaite could see now that the diver had something with him. He slipped slightly in the slime of the tilted bottom, went back in up to his shoulderblades. His partner gave him a hand up. Together they brought the thing out of the water.

It was caked in mud and the roots of water lilies and one of the divers went to his knees on the shoreline, scooped handfuls of water over the top of it.

Thwaite came closer. He could see the metallic RCA logo now. The diver went on washing the thing and its black top came clean. It was a video tape recorder. Brady looked on silently.

'You got it?' Thwaite asked, holding out a hand. Silvano put the insurance company list of Senator Burke's missing property into it. Thwaite ran a finger down the list until he found the VTR. It was an RCA. Still, he had to make certain. 'Call off the serial number from the back,' he said to the diver. The man bent, used his electric torch.

'Five four six three one eight, E,' he read.

'Bingo!' Thwaite said. 'It's all going to be down there!'

Back inside the senator's house, he had more questions for Pleasant. It did not matter to him that there was no reason for the Kenilworth police to suspect it was anything but a routine homicide at the time. They had made lazy assumptions, taken the easy way out. He could not forgive them for that.

Thwaite went away from the centre of the room where they had congregated. He made a search of the perimeter, moving a settee or a chair or table away from the wall when he had to. He came to the fireplace, a streaked black-and-white marble affair constructed in a modern, almost futuristic style. Its acute angles made him want to throw up. He crouched down.

Curious. The andirons were blackened with recent soot. He shifted the angle of his sight. 'What's all this stuff doing here?' he asked.

Pleasant came closer for a look. 'I don't know.'

'Was it here the night of the murder?'

'Just a sec.' The sergeant flipped open a flat black pigskin notebook that made Thwaite curl his lips in contempt. Pleasant flipped through pages until he found the place. 'Yeah.'

Thwaite took a Bic pen out of his breast pocket, poked it into the fireplace amid the curls of ashes. They had been difficult to see against the rough-hewn black surface of the fireplace's interior. 'Helluva lot of ashes.'

He took one of the curls up by the barrel of the pen. 'Most of it's ground to powder,' he said slowly.

'Which suggests,' Silvano said, 'that whoever burned it didn't want anyone else to see it.'

'Either Senator Burke or his murderer,' Pleasant said.

'I think we can eliminate the senator,' Thwaite said. 'If he'd done the burning I think some of the sheets would have remained. He'd've done it fast. This material was incinerated, *then* ground to dust.' He looked up at them. 'Why? To ensure that we wouldn't be able to reconstruct anything in the lab.'

The curl of ash fell apart under the strain of gravity and Thwaite put his pen away. He stood up. 'Gentlemen,' he said, 'somewhere in this black and white nightmare is the place these papers were once hidden. Why don't we see what we can dig up.'

It took them three-and-a-half hours. Thwaite and Silvano were in the master bedroom suite and the Chicago cop was once again going through each drawer of the double lowboy dresser just to make certain he hadn't missed anything. They were tired as dogs: it was just past four-thirty in the morning.

Thwaite was standing to one side so that he saw his friend and the black lacquer dresser in profile. 'You're not all the way at the end of the drawer,' he said automatically. 'Don't they teach you anything at the Academy?'

Silvano grunted. 'What're talking about? I can do this with my teeth and blindfolded. Of course I'm at the back of the drawer. What'd'you think I am, a rookie?'

Thwaite got interested. 'Yeah? Well, from where I'm standing you still got about five inches to go.'

Thwaite ran his fingertip along the bottom edge. Nothing. But when he switched to the top, he encountered a slight protrusion. The beam showed a matte black mini-catch.

Moments later, he and Silvano were standing in front of the dresser. Arrayed before them were a set of buff folders, neatly arranged in alphabetical order. There were more than a dozen of them. Not all letters were represented.

They began to read what was inside. Thwaite finally looked up.

'Well, well,' he said. 'It looks as if your Senator Burke was a rather naughty boy.'

'Jesus,' Silvano said. He whistled through his teeth. 'No wonder he was unchallenged. There's enough shit here to indict more than half the officials in Illinois.'

'Outside the state, too,' Thwaite added.

'This's hot stuff,' Silvano said. 'Obviously Burke had something the murderer didn't want known. But now it's gone without a trace and we're back at square one.'

'Maybe not,' Thwaite said. 'I found this taped to the top of the vault.'

He opened his hand, held it out for them all to see. Nestled

417

within his palm was a loop of black electrician's tape. Bound within it was a key.

Now they were truly frightened of him. The fear seeped through the pores of their skin like cold sweat. It was the uniform that terrified them; they no longer even looked at his face.

They had been so conditioned that faces, personalities, all human emotions meant nothing to them.

Now they were afraid not to answer his questions.

None of them, however, had any knowledge of the woman he sought. But late in the afternoon, Khieu stumbled upon an old man. He sat on the stump of a rotted tree while ants crawled between his horny toes. The village lay perhaps a quarter of a kilometre to the east.

He glanced up at Khieu's approach but immediately went back to work. He had an old American Army helmet between his bony knees. He was using a rough file to work the shape to his own ends.

'You at least are not afraid of me, old one,' Khieu said, squatting down beside him.

'And why should I be?' the old Khmer said. 'What more can you do to me? My wife is gone many years. All my sons died in the war. Some were recruited by the Khmer Rouge, others were killed when our village was bombed. I lived more to the south then, near Svay Rieng.' His thin wrinkled fingers continued their work. 'The *Chet Khmau* overran us, their minds on slaughtering. Human beings raping and murdering women and children. They carried the babies' heads on pikes through the villages and consequently met little further resistance. City folk and priests were murdered *en masse* daily.'

His fingers trembled a little, the file wavering in the patches of intense sunlight. 'Then the *Yuon* came, driving out the Khmer Rouge. "We are the saviours of Cambodia", they told the world. "See, we do not slaughter Khmer as their own people do. We treat them better." Then they took the harvest of all our crops, the fruit of our fishermen. My daughters-in-law, my grandchildren died of starvation or of too many diseases to count. There is no honour left in the world.' He went back to his work.

'So, therefore, when I am given an order, I laugh in your faces. What more have I to lose? My life? What is that worth to me now?' He grunted and spat sideways. 'Nowadays, they leave me alone. That is how I know you're new to this area. Go away. There's nothing I can do for you. I'm old and I've seen far more than I ever should have. At night I pray for the array of diseases that strike all those around me to infect me. Yet I remain unscathed. I am yet whole; if you can call it that.'

'I seek nothing from you but information.'

Something in Khieu's tone brought the old man up short. He stared hard into Khieu's face. 'You're not one of them,' he said slowly, wonderingly, 'are you?'

'No.'

'Then the uniform . . .'

'The former occupant no longer required it.'

The old man began to grin, dark gaps between his teeth. 'Yes,' he said, his tone abruptly lighter. 'Yes, I see.' He hunched his thin body forward. 'How can I help you, *Comrade*?' He gave the last word an ironic emphasis.

'I'm looking for a woman. She has apparently been living in the jungle for a long time . . . since 1969 or '70.' Khieu commenced to describe her in detail.

'Uhm,' the old man said at last. He set aside his work. 'I don't know. I heard of someone, maybe like the one you want. She's supposed to have a riverboat or something like that in . . . let me see now . . . yes, in Stung Treng, in the east. Near there on the Mekong. Quite close to Kong Falls, as I remember it told.'

He shook his head back and forth. 'Soldiers tell the stories. They go there, you know, when they can. At least that's what I've been able to pick up. Bits and snatches here and there. My ears're still good, so's my brain. Got the *Yuon* to leave me alone. And our kind joining up with them. It's too shameful to think about for long.' His head shook again, back and forth. 'No honour.'

'About this woman,' Khieu prompted.

The old man shrugged. 'Who knows if she's still there? I don't and I wouldn't advise asking around too much. But they all go to her, those in the high command as well. *Yuon*, Khmer Rouge, even the Soviets, I hear, though I wouldn't put much store in tales like that.

'Still, she must be an impressive whore because none of them can tame her. They're afraid of her, I think. Can't see why, really. A whore's a whore. But then again, they can have more than their fill in any local village they come to. Still they make the journey east to visit her. She has *something*, all right. A goddess, *apsara*, she rides them in her golden chariot until they faint away from exhaustion and a surfeit of pleasure.'

Khieu thanked the old man and left him sitting there, taking up his filing again, turning an instrument of war into something that pleased him.

Khieu thought it was worth the long trip east. This woman sounded very much like Tisah. She had been a whore of sorts when his father had known her and there was no reason for her to have changed. She had been young fourteen years ago; she'd still be young enough now to be desirable, mature enough to have mastered all the arts of love.

He returned to the outskirts of the village briefly, moving clockwise around its perimeter until he found what he was searching for. An army sergeant had left his bicycle unattended, perhaps while he went to deliver a message.

Khieu took it.

He was north of Siem Rap but still he had to cross the very upper part of the fertile district that has the Tonle Sap as its centre and which runs northwest to southeast through Cambodia. The sky, though yellow and cloudy, held no prospect of precipitation.

Though he tried to avoid RPK patrols whenever he could, Khieu no longer felt obliged to duck them every time. After all, he was a captain in their ranks now and few officers had sufficient rank to question his activities.

More than once, he got a ride in a jeep, the bicycle slung across its wide flanks. There were plenty of opportunities to ride by ox-cart but that form of transportation was far slower than his own mode.

As with everything else in Cambodia, he saw the changes the Khmer Rouge had wrought in the country's agriculture. The traditional curved dykes that had served the peasants so well under the Sihanouk regime had, of course, been denounced by the Khmer Rouge as antirevolutionary as soon as they gained power. They had set peasants to work, not on harvesting crops, but on rebuilding the dykes so that they were now straight. As a result, thousands of kilometres of usable land had been flooded on one side of the 'revolutionary dykes'; the other side then became too dry to grow rice. They had gone against the essential nature of the land.

He deliberately skirted *Angkor Wat* but, perhaps unconsciously, he had come close enough to see not only the machine-gun and mortar pockmarks on the great stone heads but the terrible regression the abject neglect of those in power had worked on the sacred city. The jungle was returning to dominance, trees sprouting, taking root within and above the arched passageways, the extending systems worming their way through the stone blocks, acting as wedges to pull the structures apart, to, inch by inch, year by year, destroy the edifices, rotting them from without and within. The long war was inflicting only minor wounds compared to the rapaciousness of the jungle and independent thieves who crept in during the night to saw off the heads of the ancient Khmer gods of *Angkor*.

How many days passed, how many nights he slept fitfully or not at all, he could not say. The chatter of gunfire, now distant, now close at hand, was always with him. At least, the daylight was filled with constant motion and he had a sense of making progress.

In the darkness nightmares flared whether or not he was asleep. Visions of his past stalked him like great bengals, fangs bared, intent on his destruction. Skeletons of his friends danced in the moonlight; the terrifying sight of his catatonic mother, rocking, rocking, singing herself to sleep with songs from her own childhood, surged upward once more with all the stink of regurgitation. And so, too, his guilt at leaving Malis, the young brother and sister he had hardly known, to follow Sam. Sam, who he had looked up to, who he had admired almost as much as Preah Moha Panditto, then more as the onset of the war had showed him the erosion of the power of Buddha. Peace was a concept, then, too dangerous to contemplate. The revolution had stolen in upon him and peace was not a weapon he could use against the hated enemies: Sihanouk, the Americans and the Vietnamese. Burn the old! Burn the old! Burn the old!

So by day, he made progress. But at night he slipped back more and more into the crater of his old terror-streaked life.

On the far side of Preah Vihear lay Stung Treng. The city itself was situated beyond the winding Mekong River, just south of Kong Falls and the beginning of the river of the same name. Khieu did not think he would find the houseboat so near the city. For one thing, there was too much of a concentration of people. For another, it was too far north, too near suspected Khmer Rouge strongholds for the Viets and Soviets to venture that far. Even though the RPK was fond of claiming that most of the population was harboured within the central area of Cambodia, within the fertile district of the Tonle Sap, Khieu knew better. There were many pockets of civilization, either Khmer Rouge or villages not under RPK domination, that remained along the perimeter of the country.

He had never been this far north-east and the terrain itself was unfamiliar. But he had a working knowledge of the geography of the area from his refugee work at Pan Pacifica.

He could hear the falls, now, far upriver, a kind of background wash he experienced more as a pressure than a sound. The jungle was thick as he approached the bank of the Mekong. It was narrow here and he could see a roughly triangular stretch of land that separated this offshoot of the great river from its main body.

Logic told him to cross over and explore the main river southward but instinct urged otherwise. He abandoned the bike, concealing it well in a spot he marked in his memory. Then he began to creep southward along the border of this smaller offshoot.

The current was not so strong here. The muddy water cast uneven reflections of the surrounding jungle in its long single eye. The day was very hot. Insects buzzed, screaming and swarming in the humid air. The sky, where he could make it out through gaps in the foliage, had darkened prematurely to a kind of deep ochre, a sign of imminent rain.

Sure enough, several minutes later, he heard the deep triple rumble of thunder. The still air abruptly stirred and increased in weight as the low front began to move in. Thunder came again, booming against the mountains to the west in Preah Vihear.

The insects were so thick now that Khieu was obliged to put his hands up in front of his face, breathe as shallowly as he could through his nose. He picked up his pace.

The fourth time he peered out into the muddy water, he saw it: a long dark shape rising out of the river. It was not moving, nor had it, it seemed, in some while. Jungle creepers had extended out from the near bank to entwine its snubby bow. He could see the hawser at the fore end looped into the foliage.

As he approached closer, he saw a narrow plank dock, lying close to the shore. No one seemed about. He went as close as he dared and hunkered down to observe. He watched the boat, the dock and the immediate vicinity. He heard monkeys chattering amiably and, once, the stealthy pad of a large predator, probably a large cat. Three red and yellow birds took flight from the treetops on the near bank, swooping low down over the water, then up again, disappearing among the thick foliage on the far bank.

That was all.

Still, it was close to forty-five minutes before Khieu moved. And when he did, it was like the unwinding of a serpent. Silently, he regained his feet, parting the rampant undergrowth until he reached the plank dock.

In two long effortless strides, he was on board. It was large enough to be a houseboat with less deck space than would otherwise be normal on a craft of this length. He ducked his head, went belowdecks.

The stench greeted him. He went quickly down the companionway, through the narrow wood-panelled corridor. Perhaps, when it was first built, the boat had had a larger number of bedrooms. Now it only had one. There was a parlour, galley, head, even a library. But the one bedroom was vast. It had undoubtedly been beautiful once, opulent even. Now it was merely covered in blood.

Three bodies lay tangled half-in, half-out of the wide bed. Silk sheets were clutched in their whitened fists. All were quite naked.

There were two men and one woman. On a settee to one side, Khieu found the two uniforms. Both bore the dull brown and red piping of the Red Army. He sniffed at their firearms. They had not been used recently. Hadn't there been guards for these two? In any event, they wouldn't have come here alone; they would have been driven.

The woman had been a beauty: rich copper-coloured skin, dusky and smooth. Khieu judged her to be in her early thirties. That fitted with the information he had on Tisah. One of the Russians lay across her opened thighs, the other still clutched at her breast.

There was no way, of course, to determine if she truly was the woman Macomber sought so desperately. Khieu was looking at headless torsos.

He made a quick search of the room but found no personal writings, no diaries, nothing that might give him a hint of the woman's true identity.

At last he could stand the stink no longer and he went back up on deck. He took a quick tour around the deck. On the river side of the boat, perhaps two-thirds of the way towards the bow, he came across a thin bamboo fishing rod. A rather taut line ran down from its tip into the muddy water.

Khieu took up the rod, pulled tentatively on the line. Whatever was hooked on there was heavy. He drew it up.

What arose from the depths was at first an amorphous muddy blob but as he dipped it back slightly several times, the configuration began to come clear.

First the tip of one brown ear, then lanky strands of brown hair tangled with long black clots. The protrusion of a nose, the highlight of a cheek, then another, and another until he was certain of what he held at the end of the line: the three severed heads of the lovers below.

'How d'you like our handiwork?'

The French was rough patois, the tone somehow familiar. Khieu whirled, saw a broad figure dressed in the black cotton of the Khmer Rouge. He had a bright-coloured scarf tied around his neck and, instead of the normal Thompson rifle, an American memento from World War II, the man held a Soviet-made AK–47 on him.

The eyes were bright as beetles in the broad face. A crooked grin spread across his dirty thick lips. 'Khmer traitor! They sent you here, your Soviet masters, to see what had become of their strategists.' Laughed like the bark of a dog. 'Well, there they are.' He cocked his head and Khieu could see the cast in one eye, making it slightly milky. 'I'll tell you they were not *fighters*. They did not know how to defend themselves properly; they did not know how to die. But then I'm a demon from out of the mists of the north. They couldn't stand against me.'

He made a curt gesture. 'Your name? *Quickly!*

'Sok.'

'*Mit* sok. I am Tol. In the days ahead, we will become very intimate, you and I. More than lovers, more, even, then brother and brother.' He nodded sagely. 'See the heads twist in the wind, *Mit Sok*. Study them well so that you may come to know the nature of your miserable death before I begin on you. It's going to take some damn *long* time before you die. And days before, I can promise you, you'll beg me to post your own head on a pointed stick.'

Khieu slid the line to his right, set the grisly bundle down on the deck at his feet. There was no more blood, of course. Consequently, the heads looked as white as wax, the skin bloated by the immersion. Water flowed from their half-open mouths, seeping in serpentine curls across the wooden planks of the deck.

'This whore was *kbat*. A traitor just like you, *Mit Sok*. She bedded us but she also bedded the *Yuon* and their masters, the Soviets.' He spat wetly, the yellow globule spattering the heads. 'Pol Pot determined that she must die. Now we'll take her head and those of her lovers back south, to display whenever visitors come to Phnom Penh and're told *Yuon* lies about the Khmer Rouge, about how under control the "new" Cambodia is.

'*Nothing's* under control. This is total war. They know it, the *Yuon*, and they're afraid. Even with the Soviets' help they're afraid. I can't blame them.'

'So here is the great liberator of Cambodia,' Khieu said with as much contempt in his voice as he felt. 'He creeps up on unsuspecting soldiers, naked and unarmed and, killing them with ease, crows about his prowess.' He shook his head. 'It disgusts me to think you still believe Pol Pot is any better than the *Yuon*. Well, the truth is, you're both the same; both murderers, both bent on the utter annihilation of our past. We have no past; our present is no better. What then of our future? Who among you – Khmer Rouge or *Yuon* – cares for the people? You exploit them, use them. You have no feeling for them whatsoever.'

Tol spat again. 'D'you really think the common peasant is smart enough to know what he wants? Bah! He's concerned with his crops, with feeding his family. And in the old days which you extol so glowingly, he sat when he should have been working, corrupted by the lice who espoused the "glory" of Buddha. Well, at least *they've* been exterminated.'

'Along with all the intellectuals, any core who could –'

'*Silence!*' Tol roared. 'Why should I even speak to you? Look at you! You've joined the *Yuon* against your own country!' He jerked the barrel of the AK-47. 'Now, come on, *kbat*, shoulder your load! The heads are yours to carry back to the spot I have in mind. Where no one will hear your screams of agony, your pleadings for mercy, where the stink of your own piss and shit will offend no one, no one but the river and the jungle and they don't care about you at all.'

Khieu bent, picking up the line. As he did so, the heads twisted slowly in the air, the female rotating towards him. And then his whole being seemed to burst into cold flame. He heard a roaring in his ears, Tol shouting to him as if from the far end of a long torturous tunnel.

For he saw that piercing the lobes of her ears were the lotus flower design ruby earrings his sister wore. Each specially-cut facet seemed to sear across his memory like the slash of a knife: size and shape were identical; the workmanship unmistakable. And at last he knew the truth, the terrible incomprehensible truth. This was not Tisah's head he held in front of him, swinging back and forth like a frog-eyed totem.

It was the head of Malis.

The first time Khieu saw Macomber he was coming down out of a sky filled with fire.

Khieu watched him descend from his place of concealment. Macomber swung like a pendulum; hard sound beat like rage against Khieu's eardrums as the air erupted in pinpoint fire-storms, followed by harsh gusts of searing wind that bent the plumed tops of the high palms to its will. The world consisted only of bone-shaking vibration punctuated by the lethal flowering of explosions.

Red filaments flew past Macomber's hard, grim face, streaking like lasers, trip-firing livid reflections along the edge of his nose. Khieu thought he seemed larger than life, black-clothed, firing quick accurate bursts towards the Khmer Rouge encampment as he came within range. Four other parachutists were with him.

It seemed strange to Khieu even many years later after he had learned the whole story to see five Caucasians he recognized immediately as Americans descending onto Cambodian soil dressed as Khmer Rouge. He found it eerie.

Ros had taken command of the cadre after Sam's execution and he was directing the men now. He called to Khieu over the horrendous noise of the enormous choppers, hovering. Above their bloated black bellies the ochre sky was dark, lowering with the unloading under-carriages of the 'Arclight' B-52s.

Macomber and his unit hit the ground, rolling, their broad shoulders taking the brunt of the impact. Thunder followed him as if it were his own personal servant. The stink of the explosions was everywhere, their fireball heat carrying far down the valley.

The trumpets of war were howling as they had been over this area of the country for a month now.

Khieu turned his head reluctantly away from the invaders; Ros' screaming commands had become too insistent. 'The shipment!' he called out to Khieu. 'They've come to take the shipment! Remember our orders, *Mit Sok*! Defend the shipment with our lives!'

Ros moved out with three members of the cadre; there were just over a dozen in all. Khieu could see three already dead from the American unit's precise fire. He wondered briefly how they could shoot so accurately hanging by threads, swinging in air filled with fire. He could admire that; Musashi Murano certainly would.

Dimly, he heard Ros' distinctive voice: 'The revolution calls us, comrades. Let us not be found wanting.'

He was an idiot, Khieu thought now. He had no real knowledge of tactical warfare. Rather, he was a master of butchery; his bloodlust for what he perceived as the aims of the revolution held no bounds.

Once, Khieu thought now, he had been the same way. Musashi Murano had told him so. 'These people are fools,' the Japanese had said to him just before he died. 'They fight for a cause they cannot understand. If they did, they would surely know how badly they are being duped by their leaders.' He shook his head sadly. 'I am afraid, *Mit Sok*, that there can be no peace in Cambodia. There are far too many factions ... and all are fanatic in their own way. I know. I come from a nation of fanatics. Because there is no possibility of compromise here, there can never be peace.'

Now, at last, after all that had occurred, all the deaths he himself had been party to, Khieu understood his mentor's words. 'Now I die happy,' Murano had said in a voice filled with an ineffable peace. His body lay in Khieu's warm arms. 'You will – you *must* – carry on my tradition. But first, you must escape this country of madness or surely you will perish before your time.'

The revolution. What did it mean to him now. It was nothing. A lie, a deceit. They had been betrayed – all been betrayed – just as Murano had said.

The American unit was coming on now, killing as it advanced. The Khmer Rouge's Thompsons, aged and not in the best of condition, were no match for the sleek AK-47s the

Americans were employing, shiny with oil, spitting orange death as they chattered over the deafening thunder from the metallic skies.

Two more Khmer Rouge went down before the first of the Americans was hit. He was a tall man with blond hair and blue eyes. He clutched at his throat as blood gouted through his fingers and he arched back, pitching sideways into the undergrowth. A second American followed him soon after but by that time fully half of the cadre had been taken out.

Still the Americans advanced. Khieu found his heart held no delight to see the foreigners' death. Nor did he participate at all in the defence of the cadre's perimeter.

He was an observer, totally neutral.

Flames rose, seething, to obscure the rumbling, cloud-filled sky. Mean huts burst into bright light, fragments raining, as the shelling continued onward north by northeast up the valley towards Sre Khtum. The heavy moisture-laden air hummed with the *whut-whut-whut* of the copters as they began to veer off in the wake of the B-52s. Cindrous smoke drifted upward in charcoal-grey petals only to be pressed down again by the beat of the rotors. The stink of ash and kerosene almost managed to mask the stench of running blood and faeces. And fear.

Macomber had taken temporary refuge behind a sagging wall creaking in the wind fanning the firestorm. Off to Khieu's right, he could detect movement now as the remaining two Americans scuttled from one clump of cover to another. The rapidly spreading fire was hampering the Khmer Rouge defence; they were nonplussed by having guerrilla tactics used against them. Khieu could see that the Americans were both very smart and well-trained. His heart leaped to witness this beautiful assault.

Ros and the remaining members of the cadre had picked up the advance of the two Americans now and they moved to cover themselves. There was a murderous look in Ros' eyes.

The cadre began their fire against the advancing American duo. At that moment, Macomber darted out from behind the half-collapsed wall, zig-zagged along the cadre's left flank. He held his fire, wanting to get as close as he could to maximize the shock.

It would have worked to perfection, too, had one of the American duo not inadvertently stepped on one of the concealed mines.

The soldier, broken in half, was hurled high in the air. The hellish cumulus of the raging firestorm took him and he was gone. His companion had been hit as well, but not fatally. Blood drooled down his left leg where the thin cloth and much of his skin had been stripped away. He fell to one knee, firing his AK-47. Then a fusillade riddled him and his corpse was flung away.

Macomber began to fire. A Khmer Rouge spun, clutched at his shredded chest, his mouth full of blood. Macomber never ceased his short-burst fire. Three more of the cadre staggered back and fell to the ground, seeping blood. Only Ros and one other was left and in the swirl of smoke and fire, on the increase, Khieu lost sight of Ros.

The last member of the cadre had leapt at Macomber and now they were grappling along the ground. Khieu emerged from his place of concealment. He found that he did not want this American to die; rather, it was his former Khmer comrades for whom he wished death. For what they had done to his country; for what they had done to Sam.

The Khmer Rouge – it was Mok, Khieu could see now – had his knife out. Khieu saw the flash of the blade as it arched in towards the American's face. He began to run, unsnapping the holster at his side that housed his prized .38 pistol.

He had just set himself to aim when he saw Macomber extend his left elbow in a blur of movement. Mok screamed as the American applied enormous pressure to the other's eye socket. Then Macomber's right hand was free and he had torn the knife from Mok's weakened grasp, slashing in a long deep horizontal strike from one side of his neck to another.

He was up in a moment, having thrown the corpse from him. But now Khieu spotted Ros, half-hidden behind the low shelter of a crumbling stone wall. He was taking aim at Macomber.

'No!' Khieu cried and as Ros turned in reflex towards the sound of his voice, Khieu shot him twice. Ros went down as if pole-axed.

Then, calmly, carefully, Khieu walked over to the American,

stepping over the mounds of the dead. Glowing cinders rolled along the ground like evil eyes and smoke plumed the air in gasps.

Macomber had sunk to his knees and Khieu could see that he was bleeding slightly from several superficial wounds. He stood over him now and, pointing the .38 Smith & Wesson at Macomber's head, said in perfect French, 'Well, well. What have we here?'

Orange skies and the peeling blackened bark of a charred palm. Those were all Khieu was aware of. His heart beat so fast he thought it must burst his ribs, the bars of its cage.

But first, you must escape this country of madness.

He thought now that Musashi Murano had been right; he could stay in Cambodia no longer.

'Êtes-vous blessé?'

The American stared at him uncomprehendingly and Khieu thought, Buddha, how could they send him in here ignorant of French? He repeated the question, this time a bit more slowly.

'Are you hurt?'

He knelt in front of the American and, holstering the .38, picked apart the open front of the black blouse that clung, sticky with blood, to the American's flesh.

'Not so bad,' the American said in fairly good idiomatic French.

'Good,' Khieu said, 'you speak the language. My English is not so good.' He looked into Macomber's sweat- and dirt-streaked face. 'I'm sorry about your men. There was nothing I could do about them. If I hadn't waited to help you, they'd've shot me instantly.'

'I thank you for your help,' the American said, struggling to get up. He introduced himself then. 'Lieutenant Delmar Davis Macomber.'

'I am Khieu Sokha,' he said, extending his hand. Unconsciously he had used the Eastern form: last name first.

Macomber had taken his hand in his own. 'Good to meet you, Khieu.'

Khieu had never corrected him. He was about to when he realized the import of what had just occurred. That reversal of his name came to represent to him his break with his past.

'I thought you were going to kill me back there,' Macomber was saying. 'Why didn't you?'

'You came to destroy the Khmer Rouge,' Khieu said.

Macomber nodded. 'Yes. This camp was our objective.'

'I want to destroy the Khmer Rouge.'

'But you *are* Khmer Rouge.'

Khieu shook his head. 'I want no more of the Black Heart. They destroyed my brother. Now you have destroyed them.' He lifted his prized .38 and put it firmly in Macomber's open hand. 'Though this is my only possession worth anything, it is but a token.' He bowed his head in front of the American. 'I owe you a debt I can never repay.'

'I'm not interested in that, Khieu,' Macomber said softly. He put his free hand on Khieu's shoulder. 'I have a mission to complete and now there's only me to see it through.'

'I will help,' Khieu said. 'You must allow this.'

Macomber smiled, squeezed Khieu's shoulder. 'All right.' His face clouded. 'But I've got to warn you. If you *do* help me, it'll be very dangerous for you here in your own country.'

Khieu looked up at him. The thunder had at last ceased. 'The war devours Cambodia like a great tiger. It has left me nothing, not even my own life. I go where you go.'

'All the way back to America?'

'All the way,' Khieu said, nodding.

2

The day was filled with drifting clouds, grey and puffy, no rain dancing in their midst. Just a diffuseness of light ever changing, shifting, banding and breaking, apart.

Music played deep within their celestial depths, dark reverberating chords, spinning down corridors, rich tapestries of melody and counterpoint harmonies. The choir of the ages sang, full-throated and angelic.

Then the first rumblings of war shattered its perfect peace. A line of palms flew skyward, shrieking in gold and crimson flame. A serpent of oily smoke blossomed and plumed, smudging the sky, hanging thickly in the heavy humid air. The stink of cordite, the awful cloying stench of human flesh frying.

Tracy awoke with his nostrils full of war, jerking up and crying out. Soft hands held him, murmured words sounded, softening the bursts of exploding shells in his mind. He breathed and slowly the stink of crisped flesh transmuted itself into the antiseptic scent of a hospital. His eyes fluttered closed and he was gently laid back to bed.

'Doctor . . .'

And his mind, tired, sinking back into drugged sleep, picking up the word, throwing it back and forth like a ball in his drifting mind.

Doctor, Doctor, Doctor . . . sent him drowsing, burrowing down again into the darkness from which he had been briefly pulled.

Lauren tried the triple *pas de chat* for the fifth time. This time she was not alone. Her partner, a tall Dane named Steven, was at this rehearsal, along with the sixteen members of the corps: eight boys and eight girls.

The first two times, she was slightly behind, after that, over-compensating so that she was a full beat ahead. The Stravinsky score, a work she particularly loved, just did not seem to mesh inside her head. Melody existed apart from tempo which, of course, was disastrous for a dancer. She had begun to respond to the changing tone of the notes rather than the metric four-four measures Martin had mapped out for them.

She fell into Steven's arms in the middle of the second jump and almost injured them both. Martin broke off the music immediately and the girls in the corps began to whisper among themselves. The boys stared in curiosity.

Martin came away from the wall against which he had been observing them. He clapped his hands sharply several times and the large room emptied quickly until only he and Lauren stood within it.

The long line of mirrors which covered one wall was behind him, opening up the space, increasing Lauren's sense of isolation. Martin did not approach her. Instead, he crossed his burly forearms over his chest. He wore a white shirt, sleeves rolled up slightly old-fashioned black trousers. Ballet slipper were on his feet.

'Lauren,' he said, after a time, 'how many years have you been dancing now?'

She looked at him. 'Since I was five-and-a-half. All my life.'

Martin began to walk along the *barre*, fingertips against its polished wooden length. 'Did you ever consider being anything else but a ballet dancer during that time?'

'No. Never.'

He turned towards her. 'Why do you think that was?' His handsome Russian head was held perfectly erect. The tic in one eye was barely noticeable at this distance. Still, the ice blue of the irises projected across the space between them.

'I wanted to dance. Always.'

'And you wanted to dance with me. With Vlasky. Always.'

Lauren nodded. 'Yes. The New York company's the best in the world. I always aspired to be the best.'

'And that's why you're here now!' Martin said with some force. 'The best are here ... and not just to *dance*. One can *dance* in the Royal, the San Francisco, American Ballet Theater. You are here to *learn*, to expand yourself as a dancer. To become

435

something more!' There was a kind of cool fervour in his eyes if not his voice. Martin never proselytized to dancers as he did to the press and the members of the Guild. The two were absolutely distinct: one was dance, the other publicity and funding. As Martin was fond of saying, one could not occur without the other. No, dancers came to him.

He came across the expanse of the room towards her now. 'You are something more, Lauren. Yet you are also what you always have been. A professional. Whatever is troubling you, I want it erased from your mind. It distances you from the music. I create the steps; you bring them to life. If your concentration is broken, you cannot do that.'

'I don't know what's the matter with me,' she said miserably.

'It doesn't matter,' Martin snapped. 'The consequences are what concern me.' He was close to her now and she could feel his presence, his calmness of spirit like a soothing hand across her brow. 'If you are a professional, you will dance. Period. We must have this ballet ready within the week.'

'Why? What's so important that this all has to be rushed.'

Now Martin's eyes were sparkling. 'The season is over,' he said, 'but we will not go to Saratoga. We have been invited to be the first Western ballet company to perform in China.'

'China!' Lauren breathed.

Martin nodded. 'Delicate negotiations have been going on during these past three weeks. I have said nothing because I was told by our State Department that at any moment the deal could fall through. The Chinese are apparently unpredictable that way. But this morning the call came from Washington. We'll be on our way in several days.

'I planned to make the announcement at this afternoon's rehearsal. But, in this case, I thought it might do you good to know beforehand.' He turned away from her and moved easily across the room. His arm moved outward from his side, floating. 'The music awaits,' he said simply and disappeared out the doorway.

In a moment, Steven reappeared. Lauren smiled at him and went to turn on the Stravinsky. As she did so, she fought to clear her mind, to again become the professional she had studied so long to be. She willed her thoughts of Tracy away, pushed the anger and whatever other emotional baggage that was tenaciously holding on, into a dark corner of her mind.

The music returned and, with it, the joyous tempo of the ballet. She flung herself into Steven's arms and out again, leaping away, one, two, three. The *pas de chat*.

It took them a day-and-a-half to find it, principally because it wasn't at O'Hare. The key bound in black electricians' tape opened a small locker at the Greyhound Bus terminal on Clark and Randolph Streets in downtown Chicago.

The team, including Brady, had taken most of the next morning off to sleep off the effects of the long night before. It took a lot of convincing on Thwaite's part to get the Kenilworth Police commander to relinquish the piece of physical evidence over to Art Silvano and his hot-shot Chicago PD squad.

'By all rights,' Brady said when they had reconvened in his office just after noon the day after they had cracked Senator Burke's private files, 'we should be bringing the FBI into this. The case has taken on distinct interstate characteristics and procedure is unwavering in this regard.' He was staring directly at Thwaite.

'I hate those sonsabitches,' Thwaite said. 'They think we're cretins because we haven't been to Washington. They're infected with Fed fever.'

Brady had grinned. Thwaite found the man almost looked human that way. 'If I remember correctly, Thwaite, you once said something about keeping this between us roosters. Still feel that way?'

'More than ever.'

Brady nodded. 'Then let's keep everything as small as possible. I don't want to move this case out of Kenilworth.'

'I appreciate that, Commander,' Thwaite said gently.

'Look, Commander,' Silvano broke in, 'no one wants to horn in on what is essentially a Kenilworth PD operation. But I gotta tell you, the facilities in town're gonna get us home. I gotta connection into a locksmith who can smell out anything. There's no number on this thing . . . it's been filed off. But worse still we don't know what *kind* of lock it fits. Is it a house? A car? Safety deposit box? What? This guy I know'll be able to clue us in if anyone can. But other than him, I can guarantee no one at my precinct'll know shit about this op.'

Art Silvano was as good as his word. The locksmith, a studious looking young man, took the key from them. Along one wall of his laboratory he had perhaps a hundred locks of every conceivable type.

'It's a locker key,' he told them after an examination that took no more than fifteen minutes. 'The kind you find in terminals ... airports. That sort of thing.'

The locksmith took the key over to a setup with empty glass beakers. He donned thick rubber gloves and bade them to stay back.

'See, the guy who had this, he filed off the number. Probably had it memorized.' He took down a glass bottle.

He unstopped the bottle, carefully poured an amount of the clear liquid into a beaker. he added water from the tap in a slow steady stream, keeping his head away from the mouth of the beaker. Thwaite began to scent a faint but distinct acrid smell.

The locksmith took the key up by a pair of tongs. 'This is acid,' he said, indicating the contents of the beaker. 'It may just be possible that it'll run through whatever's left of the etched numerals and recreate the pattern. Can't guarantee anything but it's worth a try.'

He lowered the key into the dilute acid, holding it beneath the surface for several seconds. Then he ran it under cold water for a minute or so. He took a look.

They held their breath. 'What I got for you,' he said, looking up at them, 'is one number: Nine. The only other thing I can tell you is that it's the middle numeral of three.'

'Well,' Thwaite said, 'It's better than starting blind. Thanks.'

Now the four of them, Thwaite, Silvano, Brady and Pleasent, were grouped around the square locker in the fourth row inside the bus terminal. The number of the locker read: 793.

Thwaite put the key in the lock, turned it quickly to the right and pulled. The small metal door swung out towards them. The lighting inside the terminal was all overheads, throwing thick shadows down every vertical surface. Consequently, none of them could see anything within the tunnel of darkness.

Pleasent took out his pencil flash, snapped it on, trained the beam directly into the locker.

Thwaite said it for all of them: 'Shit!' His voice was filled with frustration and suppressed rage. 'Not a goddamn thing!'

Rain sleeted down, turning the world to a grey-green blur, pelting them both. Khieu on his knees.

Tol sniffed, as if he had just developed sensibilities. 'You just sit there,' he said, laughing, 'while this downpour washes the vomit of your trousers.'

Between Khieu's spread knees, the tangle of matted hair and bloated flesh. The eye sockets of one of the Soviet heads were empty; in the short time the bundle had been over the houseboat's side, half-buried in the silt at the river bottom, scavengers had already been at work. Sharp nips here and there on cheek or neck where ribbons of skin dangled.

Malis, *apsara*, danced in his mind, her dextrous fingers weaving a silent story to the soundless music, echoing. His mother, nodding her head, sightlessly singing nursery rhymes to ward off the overpowering pressure of the outside world. And of his tiny brother and sister? His mind shut down that avenue of thought, shrinking back in abject horror from the myriad possibilities.

'Look at you,' Tol jeered. He touched the muzzle of the AK-47 to the strap holding Khieu's Nikon around his neck. 'I no longer know what you are.' He was heartened by Khieu's physical and mental collapse. He did not know what had caused it, did not particularly care, merely gloated at the result. 'Are you a soldier or a spy? What were you going to take pictures of?'

He grunted. The rain sizzled along the deck, pinged loudly against the metal fixtures, ran in rivulets out the gunwales. The surface of the river was gunmetal grey, stippled as if by an impressionist's stiff brush. The treetops bowed and swayed beneath the assault.

Tol jabbed Khieu in the Adam's apple with the automatic

weapon to get his attention. 'Your hand gun,' he said, almost shouting to be heard over the clatter of the storm. 'Give it to me.'

As if he were sleepwalking, Khieu unsnapped the leather holster at his left hip, lifted the pistol out.

Apsara danced, sending her message to the gods. Sometimes she was dressed in her traditional outfit; sometimes she was naked, her body oiled and glistening, flaming braziers sending flickering tongues of light shooting across the erotic planes of her thighs, her hard breasts lifting and falling rhythmically to her controlled breathing. And sometimes she was pale and headless, a jerking grotesque thing, whose spastic dancing was but a parody of the beautiful and delicate Khmer ballet.

Khieu was trembling, his eyelids flickering in arrhythmic spasm. His hair was plastered to his head and he felt the pain of the hard-driving rain against his skull as acutely as if each drop were a needle piercing his flesh.

'Get up, now,' Tol said. 'You've had enough of a rest.' He jabbed Khieu viciously in the ribs. 'Just think. It'll be the last rest you'll ever have.' He laughed harshly. 'In *this* life, anyway.'

Khieu stood up, his head still filled with his roiling vision. Clothed, naked, acephalous. Love, lust, horror. They mixed now in an inexorable swirl.

'Take up your burden, *Mit Sok*,' Tol commanded.

Khieu carried the three heads before him as he moved along the deck, Tol just behind him. They went slowly around the stern and off onto the tiny plank dock.

Twenty metres into the jungle, Tol bade him stop. 'Over there, *Mit Sok*,' he said triumphantly. 'You of all people should appreciate that sight.'

Khieu swung his gaze dully in the direction Tol indicated. Beneath a tangle of low-lying trees, he could make out the brown uniforms with the red star insignia. There were three of them, three more soldiers in the same uniform he was wearing: RPK.

'They could not save their officers,' Tol said. 'They did not know how to fight.' He prodded Khieu again. 'Get over there now with your burden, *Mit Sok*. I have just had an idea that gives me immense pleasure.'

Khieu stumbled over a half-buried tree root, righted himself before he fell to his knees. His dripping bundle scraped against the ground. He lifted it up, carefully wiped mud from Malis' chewed cheek.

'Stand by those men,' Tol directed. The rain was already lessening, the driving hiss of the downpour being slowly replaced by the dolorous drip of moisture sliding from myriad leaves. When it had abated entirely, Tol came over to where Khieu stood and took the heads away from him. He made a grab for Malis' head and Tol slammed the backs of his hands with the barrel of his weapon.

'Go over there,' he directed. He held up the heads, put one booted foot on the back of one of the Soviet corpses. He bent quickly, detaching a red star from the uniform, pinning it over his heart. 'There. Now. Be a good comrade and take my picture ... Wait, not yet.' He twisted the bundle of heads around. 'I want this one facing the camera. He was a colonel, after all.' He chuckled. 'He deserves the place of honour by my side.' In fact he was holding the trio of heads in front of him, roughly at the centre of his chest. 'Besides,' he added, 'we need him very recognizable for propaganda purposes.' His voice rose. 'Think of the good you will do by taking this one photograph, *Mit Sok*. Think of how you will advance the cause of the Black Heart.'

Khieu stepped back until Tol was just over three metres away. He snapped off the camera case and took aim. He set aperture and speed and, finding Tol centred, pressed the shutter stud.

Blue-white flame like a demon's tongue licked out of the centre of the lens as the miniature impact-explosive projectile blurred towards Tol.

The man just had time to open his eyes wide in alarm and shock before the thing embedded itself and detonated. He rocked back, thrown against the bole of the tree. He slid down it partway, then righted himself. The trio of heads had taken most of the impact of the explosion. Blood seeped from one shoulder but otherwise he was unharmed.

Tol made a dive for the rifle which had been whipped out

of his grasp by the percussion of the blast but Khieu was already upon him.

The purpose of most disciplines, Musashi Murano had told him, *lies first in immobilization of the opponent. This presupposes that there is an amount of time during the encounter – however minuscule that may be; remember we speak here not of seconds or even tenths-of-seconds but hundredths or, in the case of the most adept professional assassin, thousandths-of-a-second – when your opponent will have an opportunity to kill you.*

This we cannot allow. If you seek to immobilize, you may die; if you seek to maim, you may die; if you think to yourself, A hundredth-of-a-second cannot possibly be lethal, you may die; if you underestimate your opponent, you may die.

Remember kokoro.

Khieu remembered. He could not do otherwise. *Kokoro* was imprinted within him as strongly as Buddhism. In the hierarchy of the known universe it, too, was a celestial body. His training had not been like school. With Preah Moha Panditto, he had not attended classes: the training he had received from *Lok Kru* had been his life – *all* of his life, bound up in tradition, family, responsibility, the worth of being Khmer. It was not merely religious, as a Westerner perhaps enters a monastery to be ordained. It was social, anthropological, political and historical – *especially* historical, which was why the Khmer Rouge hated and feared the Buddhist priests so virulently.

So, too, with *kokoro*. Musashi Murano, Khieu's *sensei*, had encompassed his life. For without believing, *kokoro* was nothing.

In Japanese, Musashi Murano had said, kokoro *means 'the heart of things'. But as in many other languages, Japanese gives multiple meanings to words. For me – and not for you – kokoro means the interior ... the heart of my discipline: the void. The nothingness that fills you fuller than all things of this world: the emptiness that brings you a strength out of time.*

Khieu employed *kokoro*.

With it, he used the stiffened tips of his fingers, slightly curved so that anyone with sufficient knowledge would have recognized in them the precise angle of the Japanese *katana*, as projectiles fully as lethal as the ones with which his bogus Nikon was loaded to puncture Tol's diaphragm. He ruptured spleen, pancreas and liver within the space of a single heartbeat then, rising, as the mist at dawn will reach for the cloudless sky, took up his camera and, with Tol's head resting against the puffed chest of his Russian quarry, with the last breaths of life rattling from his half-open tremulous jaw, took a final shot.

And left one more headless corpse to add to the pile.

Kim was summoned to Seattle.

It was Thu, of course. He saw his crippled brother rarely, but now Kim was glad to be coming to see him. Over the last months, Thu had been even more withdrawn and uncommunicative in his letters and in the back of his mind, Kim had suspected that his brother was slipping back into his earlier morose pattern of behaviour. In fact, he regretted not coming out here sooner; it had been more than a year since he had broken the heavy cloud-cover here, as he was now, disembarking from the plane at Sea-Tac International Airport. The ultramodern three-stop underground took him to the main gate.

Thu lived high up in a building fronting Puget Sound. The apartment had a balcony that overlooked the water and, just to one side, a concrete marina where Thu had a 35-foot sloop berthed. Kim knew all of this because it was his money that paid for the various accoutrements of Thu's new life in the West.

It was his brother's fondest pleasure to take the sloop north up the sound past Port Townsend, then west beyond Victoria, in British Columbia, up the Strait of Juan de Fuca to Waada Island at the very Western tip of Washington. There, he would rendezvous with Makah from nearby Tatoosh or the Indian reservation across the water on the mainland.

In the years since he had come to Seattle, the Makah remained his only friends. Kim often wondered what they had in common with his brother, save that they were both outcasts, misfits, deformed each in his own way, uncomfortable in society.

Thu taught them how to read their futures in the stars and they in turn taught him how to drink. Or, at any rate, that was how it seemed to Kim. The suicide rate on almost all Indian reservations was six or seven times the average for the rest of the country. The Indians seemed to like it better than peyote mainly because it had no religious overtones.

But it was not Thu who met him at the door to the apartment this time but a young woman he had never seen before.

She smiled on seeing him. 'You must be Kim.' She reached out and effortlessly and quite efficiently took his overnight case from him. She closed the door behind him and he followed her into the living room. She wore white shorts and a striped Izod shirt.

She was tall with the kind of full-bodied figure Eastern women could not – indeed did not aspire to – attain. Her large breasts had just enough of a curve along their upper slopes for Kim to know they were real. Her legs were long and firm. Her blonde hair was naturally curly. She wore it like a thick mane, down to her shoulders. She looked as if she had stepped out of some magazine.

'Pardon me,' he said, 'but you are ... ?'

She laughed goodnaturedly and unaffectedly. 'God, I'm sorry.' She extended a hand and Kim thought, This one's American, *very* American. 'I'm Emma. Emma Poe.' Her voice was light and airy. Her cornflower blue eyes watched him with some humour. 'No relation, if that's what you're thinking. My family – all nine of us – comes from Minnesota.'

'Have you been ... with my brother long, Miss Poe?' Kim asked.

'Emma,' she corrected him. 'Absolutely no one calls me *Miss Poe*. About six months, Kim.' She had very direct eyes.

'Now,' she continued briskly, 'Thu is waiting for you out on the balcony. Why don't you join him? Meanwhile, I'll put your bag in the guest bedroom. Can I get you a drink?'

'Tea, thank you.'

'Hot, not iced, yes?'

Kim took another look at her. He nodded.

'I went out this morning and bought China Black for you.' Her eyes were smiling, too.

Kim tried to ignore that. 'Thu drinks China Black.'

'Oh, not for some time now. We both enjoy an espresso now and then. Decaffeinated, of course.'

'Of course,' Kim parroted, inwardly appalled.

The living room had been repainted he saw as he went quickly through it: pastel blue walls, eggshell ceiling. Decorative moulding, a feature unheard of in modern apartments, had been added sometime since his last visit.

He went through the sliding glass doors, out onto the balcony. This, too, had changed. Outdoor carpeting covered the concrete. Thu sat on an aluminium lawn chair, his useless atrophied legs stretched out before him. Kim looked around. There was no sign of his wheelchair.

Thu's head turned as Kim crossed the threshold. He wore mirrored sunglasses. He was dressed in a dark green Izod shirt and a pair of jeans. What was left of his feet were bare. A smile split his face when he saw his brother.

'Kim,' he said, 'it's good to see you again.' His voice was low and furred. That was its natural state since the holocaust, the permanent tattoo of smoke inhalation.

Kim went past his brother, stood with his stiff arms against the metal railing. He looked out at the sound and across it. He could make out houses in Winslow and Creosote. And he thought again, This is a hell of a place to live.

'I see there've been a lot of changes since I was last here.'

'You ought to get out more often,' Thu said. 'You've never liked surprises. But I didn't want to write; I wanted you to meet her.'

Kim noticed that his brother's hair was longer, lying thick and black like an animal's pelt along the nape of his neck. It made him seem somehow younger.

'I never anticipate anything,' Kim said, 'so I'm never surprised.'

Emma stepped out onto the terrace. She set a black lacquer tray down on a pebble-glass-topped table. There was a small rose-coloured porcelain pot and one handleless cup.

'It needs to steep several minutes more,' she said, then took a frosted highball glass off the tray, handed it to Thu.

Kim watched the darkness of the open doorway through which she had just gone. 'Where did you meet her?'

'The marina.' Thu put his head back, sipped at his iced drink. 'I was having difficulty with the aft hawser. She gave me a hand.'

'She gave you a hand.'

'Yes. Is that a crime?'

'Had you seen her around before that?'

'Jesus, I think I'd've remembered if I had.' Thu squinted up at his brother. 'Wouldn't you?'

'I remember everyone I meet,' Kim said somewhat stiffly.

'Not really your type, is she, Kim?'

'She's got too much of everything.'

'Oh, yes. Including brains. You like your women under a hundred pounds and three steps behind you with their heads down.'

'I want to know more about her.'

'Oh, don't be so goddamned suspicious. Every event in life isn't full of sinister shadows.'

'What are you drinking?' Kim asked suddenly.

'Perrier.' Thu held out his glass. 'Here, want to sniff?'

Kim turned away from him, contemplated the beaten brass of the sunlight on the water.

'I don't drink anymore,' Thu said. 'At least not the way I used to. A Margarita once in a while, or some champagne to celebrate.' He sat up straighter in the chair. 'I don't get drunk anymore . . .'

'You don't do a lot of things you used to do.' Kim poured himself some tea. 'You don't drink China Black anymore; you dress like an American, you talk like an American, you have an American woman living with you. You've forsaken tradition. Don't you think about your family anymore?'

'I'll tell you what I don't do, Kim,' Thu said. 'I don't wake up in the middle of the night covered in cold sweat; I don't sit and think about what might have been if that burning beam hadn't crushed my legs; I don't pull my hair and wail for all the death that night; I don't try to run away from my present by passing out stinking drunk every night.

'And I'll tell you something, brother, Emma's been a good part of that. I'm happy now. I think about the present; I'm content with it. And every once in a while I catch myself dreaming about the future. That's something I haven't done since I was twelve.'

'We sail, we fish, we go for walks. We even make love together. We do what every couple who are in love do with their time.' He stared hard at Kim. 'Tell me this is what you disapprove of.'

'I disapprove,' Kim said slowly and carefully, 'of you abandoning all that makes us unique in the world.' He gestured. 'Look at you now, with your designer jeans, your Izod shirt, sipping your Perrier water. Buddha, you're so Americanized even our own mother wouldn't recognize you.'

'But I'm happy,' Thu said leaning forward. 'I'm happy, Kim, and you're not. You'd better face it. You're a dinosaur. You and your kind have outlived your usefulness.

'I know you can't see it but I'm free now. Free of the past, free of the guilt that still weighs you down like a lead cocoon.'

'And what of our revenge . . . what of the time you spent in Phnom Penh tracking down the murderer of our family . . . what of all the time and effort I've put in to setting our revenge in motion.'

'It's the way of death,' Thu said, 'don't you see that? Our life isn't for revenge. It's for us to *live* to the fullest.'

'And what of honour?' Kim said. 'Are we to forget about that? Wave away centuries with the careless sweep of one hand? We have a duty to our family. Their spirits will not rest.'

He put down the cup of now-cold tea, knelt beside his brother. 'Don't you see that without honour, without duty, we are nothing?'

Thu sighed, put his hand over Kim's wrist. 'It's a beautiful day. Clear and clean. On days like this Emma and I take the sloop up north to see the sunset. We eat dinner on board. Won't you come with us today?'

Kim looked at the black reflective glasses covering his brother's eyes for a long time. Then he carefully slid his arm from beneath Thu's embrace, rose and walked back into the apartment.

Emma stood in the middle of the living room, smiling slightly. 'He's right, you know.' Her voice was soft, kind. 'There's time for us all now to be together.'

'You understand nothing,' Kim said. 'You're an American.'

'I know I have him to sleep beside me at night,' she said simply, 'to comfort me and to give comfort to. To talk to. To make love to.

'Tell me, Kim, what do you have at night to give you comfort? You have your nightmares of the past. And, when those fail you, there is only your hate.'

He wanted to know if there had been any calls for him, the moment he awoke, forgetting where he was.

The nurse with the smiling sympathetic face said, 'No, but there was a young lady here about an hour ago inquiring about how you were doing.' There was a secret twinkle in her eye.

She got up and went to the door. 'I told her there was no use in her waiting.'

'But –'

'Now you just relax.' The nurse waved away his words. 'I told her to come back and I'm sure she will. Now I've got to get the doctor. He said to ring him the moment you awoke.'

'But I don't know any woman,' Tracy said to the door as it sighed shut. He was alone in the white antiseptic room. A window to his right was dusty with sunlight streaming in. Morning or late afternoon? Morning, he judged, by the tone of the light.

The doctor was a bald Chinese as round as a beach ball. He waddled in, the open ends of his white coat flapping ludicrously like the useless wings of a penguin.

'Well, well, well.' He chortled. 'Awake at last.' His fingers probed at Tracy's scalp. He smiled. 'Better, better.' Then his wide yellow face clouded over and his tongue clucked against the roof of his mouth. 'What kind of mischief have you been getting yourself into, my boy.' He shook his head and answered his own question. 'Nothing good, I can see that.'

He hooked the earpiece of his stethoscope into place, began to listen to Tracy's heart, never stopping his train of talk. 'The police are most anxious to speak with you, by boy. As you can imagine – cough –they are most anxious – again – to find out your side of what – and again – happened.'

He began using his fingers again, his probing touch remarkably gentle.

'How long have I been here?'

The doctor looked up towards the ceiling; he was feeling for something specific along one of the major meridians. 'A bit over forty-eight hours. That was a very nasty blast.' He opened up his bag, dug out a long thin glass case. Inside, Tracy could see perhaps a half-dozen sterilized acupuncture needles. 'If that heavy-framed bed hadn't been between you and the detonation ...' The doctor clucked his tongue against the roof of his mouth. 'Now roll over, please. No, on your left side. Yes,' – he put one hand on Tracy's arm, positioning him – 'that's good.' He snapped open the case, withdrew one of the long needles.

'Now there is no sign of a clinical concussion and that is good but it has been my experience in these kinds of cases that some form of residual dizziness or slight motor disfunction might, for some brief periods, occur.' He positioned the needle, using the fingers of his free hand to trace the meridian he was seeking. 'Oh, nothing permanent, mind you. Oh, no. But as a precaution' – he slid the needle in, reached for another – 'I find this small treatment, combined with twenty minutes of Shiatsu, will eliminate any discomfort.'

After the treatments, the doctor said, 'The police have asked me to notify them the moment you are conscious and coherent.'

'I'd appreciate some time,' Tracy said. He felt enormously refreshed.

'Since they left it up to my judgement, let's just say this conversation will take place sometime tomorrow morning, humm? Nine o'clock do you?'

'That would be fine,' Tracy said. 'Thanks, Doctor.'

'Think nothing of it.' He paused with the door half open. 'You may doze for a while; that'll be good for you. Remember, there's still a lot of repair work your body's got to do and only time can help. Treat you left arm gingerly for a while.'

Tracy nodded and the doctor went out. The nurse was about to follow when Tracy stopped her. 'That woman who was asking for me, did she give you her name?'

'No, she didn't,' the nurse said.

'What'd she look like?'

The nurse thought. 'Tall, slender, very hot dresser. Chinese ... Chiu-chow.' Her expression was puzzled. 'Isn't she your girlfriend?'

'Uh, yes,' Tracy said. He put his hand up to his forehead to cover his confusion. 'Yes. I just wanted to make sure.' He thought a moment. 'She say when she'd be back?'

The nurse shook her head. 'But she was very concerned. I'm sure she'll be here soon.' She pointed. 'If you want, you can phone her.'

'No, thanks.' He sank back into the pillows.

The nurse smiled. 'If you want anything, just ring.' And showed him where the buzzer was.

'What time is it?'

'Just past dinner time,' she said. 'Five-thirty. Are you hungry?'

Tracy shook his head. So much for his judgement.

'I'll be in at eight to give you your shot.'

'What for?'

'The pain, so you can sleep.'

'I don't want a shot.'

She smiled again. 'Doctor's orders, Mr Richter. You heard what he said. You need your sleep.'

Tracy felt too tired to argue. After she left, he allowed his mind to wander. He wanted to go over every detail, wanting to make certain his memory was clear.

He tried for older memories first: his father, mother, childhood. Then further up the line, the foundation, the Director, Kim. He remembered his flight into Hong Kong, his call, his meeting earlier today – no! – he caught himself – *three* days ago with Mizo and Jade Princess. It was all there, intact. He breathed a sigh of relief.

Now for the more difficult part. He had bought the diamond

solitaire for Lauren, had it put in the hotel vault. In the hallway he had checked the lock for tampering, had found none.

That blast. He closed his eyes. He should be dead now, he knew and he must reason out why he was not. The blast, he knew instinctively, had been strong enough. How had he escaped with just the ghost of a concussion and a bruised arm? He had to remember details.

He was sitting on the bed. He had picked up the receiver, about to call his father. What had happened then? The detonation, of course.

Tracy sighed, a long slow exhalation of air. Naturally it was hard. The organism knew how close it had come to extinction and it was struggling to suppress the memory. It did not want to know; it just wanted to get away, to ensure its survival. Because abruptly, Hong Kong had become a red sector.

It was the weight. Something had transmitted itself to his brain as he had lifted the receiver from its cradle. It had only taken a ten-thousandth of a second. The thing had been too heavy and while his conscious brain was still trying to switch over from what it was going to say to Louis Richter, the instinctive organism, so highly trained, had leapt into action.

Tracy remembered now his frantic roll across the top of the bed as he hurled himself towards the relative safety of the floor beyond. The blast had hit him, of course, before he had made it. But he had been in midflight, his left side towards the concussion wave and it had pushed him further along so that the brunt of the explosion was taken by the heavy steel-and-wood-framed king-size bed.

Luck, his mind screamed at him. *You were lucky.* But Tracy knew better. The foundation – or, more specifically, its training – had saved his life once again. This was not the first time he had thought that but it was the first time he considered the fact that he would not need that training were he not doing this kind of work.

That brought him to what the nurse had said. *There was a young lady here about an hour ago. Chinese. Chiu-chow.* Jade Princess. He began to sweat. He did not think she had come to speed his recovery. There was no doubt in his mind that Mizo had been responsible for the explosive. But why? What had gone wrong with Tracy's plan?

He spent a futile half hour running down every conceivable area and came up with a blank. Christ, he thought, it was bad enough when you screwed up and knew it. This was far worse. A wheel had come loose somewhere and he had no idea where.

He thought again, concluded that his approach had been correct. He judged Mizo's reaction at the Jockey Club, conjuring up his face again, his stance, the minute movements of his body. It all fitted, it felt right. Damnit, he *had* been on the hook.

That meant that the wheel had come off *after* his interview with Mizo and Jade Princess. Something out of his control; something he knew nothing about. That worried him. What could it be? What was so important that Mizo had been instructed to eliminate him?

Tracy first thought of the identity of John and Moira's killer. But no one knew that was what he was after. Certainly Mizo and Jade Princess could not. It was absolutely impossible. Who was giving Mizo his orders? Still that was not enough. The question of Why? continued to plague him.

He lay back with a sigh, drifting. He was tired and he knew instinctively that the doctor was correct. He *did* need rest.

Once, in the Mines, when he had come down with a rather virulent flu, they had sent him to an old Japanese who had no name. He had used acupuncture on Tracy. It had not hurt much at the time but perhaps an hour later he had collapsed onto his bed. His entire body seemed wracked with an odd kind of inner pain.

The next morning he had awoken not only completely free of the virus that doctors said needed six or seven days to run its course, but totally refreshed. He felt as if he'd been asleep for a week. Jinsoku had explained it: *Your body was full of poisons; the pain comes when they flow through the system on their way to being excreted.*

Tracy's eyes fluttered closed, his pulse rate slowed. He slept.

And awoke into nighttime. He started awake as if from a nightmare but he could remember no dream. His throat was dry and he reached for the aluminium carafe on the side table, saw in the process the luminous digital face of the room's clock: 8.13, it read.

That seemed odd to him and he thought about it while he slaked his thirst but nothing came to mind.

The organism begged for attention and he gave himself over to a current inventory. He was holding the cup of water in his left hand and the arm ached a bit. But it was building, so he transferred the cup into his right hand.

He had a very slight headache which had manifested itself when he sat up sharply to get the water. He felt vaguely dizzy. He put the plastic cup down and the time appeared in his field of vision again. 8.15.

And then he remembered the nurse had said she would give him a shot at eight. She had not come or perhaps she had found him sleeping, did not wish to wake him. Well, he would tell her that he was awake now. He reached for the buzzer but with his thumb on the protrusion he froze. It was hospital policy – every hospital – to give its patients their medicine, meals and tests, precisely to its schedule. Sleep was no deterrent to procedure.

Slowly Tracy sat back on the bed. He was very still for a moment, gathering information from his five senses and perhaps a sixth. The animal's sharply honed instinct for survival, they had told him in the Mines, is present in all of us to one degree or another. The layers of civilization have blunted its effectiveness for the most part but in a red sector one lives the life of an animal and the instinct returns. *Think of it as a true sixth sense*, Jinsoku had said. *Trust it as you would any of your other training because there is little doubt it will prove your most important resource.*

When Tracy had asked why, Jinsoku had smiled his secret smile, said, *I will, over the course of your stay here, teach you how to kill or disable an opponent in many ways ... do not bother to count the number. Even how to dispatch several opponents. But this is only for specific circumstances. This knowledge does not make you invincible, nothing will except your own judgement, if it's fine-tuned well enough. What I teach you here will not protect you from the long gun, for instance. Nor will it help in the face of overwhelming odds.*

It is your sixth sense that you must nurture, give reign to, allow to guide you out and away from those situations without a blow being delivered.

This was what he felt developing now: a situation that would soon become untenable for him even with all his skills.

Carefully, he swept the covers off him, put his legs over the side. He felt the cold linoleum of the flooring against his warm soles. He let the change in temperature seep in, revitalizing him. Then slowly he got out of bed. His legs felt strange and he put one palm flat on the mattress to support himself. There was some vertigo but it was manageable.

The closet with his clothes in it was across the expanse of the room. Not more than ten feet but it seemed like three times the distance. He stuck his outstretched arm into the darkness of the closet. He put on his clothes, aware of the need for speed. He knew that this whole situation was shut-ended and his time was rapidly running out.

If, as he believed, Mizo's people had arrived at the hospital to take him out, they were working against a strict timetable. They had taken the nurse off the floor – that was the only possible explanation why she had not arrived at eight o'clock with Tracy's pain-killing shot.

He looked at the clock. It was now 8.18 and they would only have minutes to perform what they had come for. Strictly shut-ended. So there was the impulse to hurry and that sent as yet unneeded adrenalin pumping through his system which in these moments of enforced stillness only led to more pain between his temples.

He crept cautiously to the corridor, trying to ignore that part of his mind screaming at him to for God's sake get out of there! He took three deep breaths. *Prana.* Calmed himself.

A millimetre at a time he edged the door open, saw at last a thin slice of corridor and the blur of movement coming his way. Too late!

He allowed the door to swing back under its own momentum. That escape route was now effectively blocked. He had by rough reckoning perhaps fifteen seconds.

He went to the window, looked down. He was on the fifth or sixth floor as best he could tell, with a sheer drop to a cement courtyard below. He was high enough to break his neck if he went that way. He looked longingly at the carefully landscaped garden in the centre of the courtyard with its high trees too far away for him to use.

Sound in the corridor, just outside his room: the slither of a starched uniform against the static-filled surface of stockings. The nurse? Had he been wrong after all? Had the concussion affected his judgement?

Tracy turned abruptly from the window, climbed back into bed, pulling the covers up over him to hide his street clothes. He closed his eyes to slits as the door opened inward, spilling a widening slice of lemon light across the floor.

For an instant a silhouette was thrown into sharp relief and Tracy reviewed what he had seen. A female figure without doubt. The familiar nurse's cap. Then he *had* been wrong. She had merely been delayed, by a recalcitrant patient down the hall perhaps. Still ...

He heard her moving in the room, quick, efficient steps and her murmured voice, 'Mr Richter? Are you awake?'

She was coming closer but he did not answer. In the half-light, a jigsaw jumble of shades of grey and blue seeping through the window from the conglomerate glow of the city outside, he could just make out the dull gleam of the small metal tray she carried and, lifted off its surface, the loaded hypodermic. The needle turned upwards, liquid burst from its open end.

'Time for your shot.'

The bedsheets were being drawn back and Tracy tensed. Something about that silhouette limned still in his mind. Something not quite right. What was it?

The needle was coming down, describing its short flat arc. He felt trapped in a fog of inaction. All the adrenalin he had not been able to suppress in the minutes before the door had opened, was pooling, running off like excess energy and he felt abruptly deflated. Perhaps it was all right, after all, his nerves merely showing.

The nurse bent over, searching for his arm and Tracy felt the powerful bar of her forearm jammed suddenly across his clavical. It began to dig into his windpipe, cutting off his air supply.

'What's this? You're dressed?'

Tracy began to struggle but the weight of her entire body was now brought to bear on pinioning him. She could not, he knew, keep that up for long – he was far heavier and stronger and, after a time, the leverage would not be enough. But she would ensure that time never came. She needed only enough to administer the injection. He was quite certain now that it did not contain the pain-killer the doctor had prescribed but a poison meant to complete the job the bomb had failed to do.

Height. That was the out-of-place element. He had realized it too late, at the moment she had bent over the bed, clamped him. The nurse – his *real* nurse – had not been more than five-four in height. That was what his mind had been trying to work out. Her silhouette had reached higher up the surrounding doorframe than it should have. This woman must be six feet.

What air was left in his lungs was fast diminishing. His internal pain was combining with her well-directed pressure. He had to do something fast. He tried a sword-strike but she saw it coming, knocked his hand away with the heel of her hand holding the syringe. He had absolutely no leverage and weakened as he was, he was no match for her.

His mind raced; pain flared, radiating, suffusing him. Oxygen-starved muscles were filling with a creeping lassitude and, above his head, the hypo filled with death, was descending for the last time.

Think! He berated himself. So he used his mind instead of his body. He did the last thing she would expect.

He used the *kidi*, the vibratory sound to strike terror, knowing instinctively that this was his last shot, the energy it required would deplete him. If it did not work . . .

'*Jade Princess!*'

It was a war shout, a battle cry, but it was her name and she was immediately startled; she had not expected him to know who she was.

He saw the whites of her eyes all around as her lids opened wide in shock. And, for just that instant, while the percussive blow of his voice echoed around the small room, her grip on him eased up.

Tracy reacted with lightning swiftness, moving an elbow inside her right arm, driving it up and in, connecting with a resounding whoosh with her ribcage.

Her forearm lifted and Tracy rolled to his left, towards her. He wanted in, not away from her where she could manoeuvre or disappear. She was his now and he moved to claim her.

Still she recovered far faster than he could have imagined possible. She met his liver-strike with the prescribed defence, deflecting him, putting him on the defensive. He covered up, allowing her blows to rain painfully on his right side as he protected his left. He could afford no damage there. She might not know of his wound but he dared not make that assumption.

He opened up after her flurry with a double-feint as if moving in on her off side. Confused, she turned slightly to meet him and he used one of the more lethal *ate-waza*, the percussions, switching from karate, which she was using too, to judo to further confound her.

She cried out as one side of her clavical cracked beneath the force of the strike. He wanted to let up there; he wanted to question her. But she would not allow that. She threw the syringe away from them in a clatter, attacking him with her good side and he was forced because of her strength, to abandon the *osae-waza*, the immobilization techniques he would have preferred to use.

She hissed at him, spitting like a cat, beginning to hurt him with a vicelike clamp and he had no choice, bringing the shortened blade of his fingertips blurring forward, striking her just beneath the sternum, forcing them in and up like a shot of steel.

Jade Princess' body arched back. Cords in her neck stood out like rope and her teeth clacked together threateningly. Then she slumped forward into his waiting arms.

Tracy took her to the bed, threw her onto it. He lifted the blanket over her. He slowed his breathing, wiped the sweat from his face. He felt hot and drained and his head throbbed fiercely.

He moved towards the door, grabbed himself abruptly beneath his left armpit. His breath was a hot wheeze and he cursed himself silently. He had moved too suddenly, twisted without thinking, a perfectly natural movement ... for a healthy man. He was not. He would have to remember that. The doctor's words reverberated in his mind. *Remember, there's still a lot of repair work got to do and only time will help ...*

Tracy gritted his teeth, a grimace of a laugh. Well, yes, Doctor, perhaps just a *bit* of strenuous activity to keep my hand in.

He leaned against the door, sweating. Christ, but he hurt.

He opened the door. At least, he thought, the worst is over with.

Shadows in the corridor, moving, and he thought, Oh, God, there's more of them. He turned back into the room, his eyes alighting on the syringe Jade Princess had thrown down. It was one of the new disposable kind. Made of plastic. It hadn't shattered. And it was still full of death.

Tracy retrieved it. Not exactly the weapon he would choose in these circumstances but it would have to do.

In the corridor the night lights were on, cool and burning low. A buzzer set into the console at the nurses' station sounded as loud as a game of Pong. An insistent patient. Where were they?

He saw no one, marvelling at the job they had done in clearing the floor, but he felt their presence and then he was throwing himself face first to the cool polished floor, sliding obliquely from left to right, the hair along the top of his head ruffled as if by a gentle summer breeze. The sound of someone spitting, a second soft *phutt!*, an exclamatory admonition, and he had fetched up hard against the corridor wall, rolling away as soon as he had made contact, seeing a long funnel-shaped slice of painted plaster tear itself away just where his shoulder had been.

His head was pounding as he threw himself behind the door of a utility closet and he immediately began to work on himself. The headache was impairing his capability and he had to do something about it at once. He knew he could not successfully make the break in his present physical condition.

Using the thumb of his opposing hand, he dug into the fleshy wedge of his hands where the base of the thumb met the first knuckle of the forefinger until he found the muscle there. He pressed hard, holding it for as long as he dared, then switched hands. It was one of the major acupuncture meridians, Large Intestine Four, and the pressure he was exerting there gave him immediate relief; the pounding receded to a dull ache.

Distance. That was his most lethal enemy now. When he was being fired upon, he had glimpsed two of them. But they had silenced weapons and it was to their advantage to keep well clear of him. He could only be effective in close quarters. He had to make them come to him. And he had to cut them in two.

He did not like it. He had not been in this kind of situation since the war. It had been what, thirteen years? But then again he had never stopped his classes and he was grateful for that.

He leaned backwards, kicked out the door with his straightened leg, raced out into the corridor. He was too late to hear the sound of the silenced weapon being fired but he saw the scarred crease in the gleaming light wood of the door, deeper at one end.

He headed in the opposite direction, towards the source of the bullet. He felt terribly vulnerable. They would, of course, have changed their positions while he had been temporarily holed up. Because of his last manoeuvre, he now knew where one of them was. But the second man's location was still a mystery. The short hairs at the back of Tracy's neck bristled and he tried not to think of the whistling death that might be at his back.

He caught a glimpse of the black top of a head, saw simultaneously, the gaping hole of the silencer-extended barrel pointed at him and, taking a long gliding stride forward, launched himself into the air. He leaped upwards over the second of the nurses' stations, skidding through papers, pencils, metal files, his right arm leading, knocking the gun from the surprised man's grasp. The man grunted, brought his knee up. It connected with Tracy's left side and Tracy felt all the strength going out of him. He gritted his teeth, determined not to groan, give up the secret of his disability. *Advantages*, Jinsoku had impressed upon him, *are sometimes all that stand between you and defeat. Never give up anything.*

Tracy countered with a liver-strike that bent the man in two, his animal grunt giving Tracy some satisfaction. But he was no pushover and he recovered enough to lash out with the toe of his shoe. It caught Tracy on the tip of his right cheekbone, rocked his head so that he knew he had to end this quickly. Said, To hell with it, and jabbed the man in the thigh with the syringe.

The man struggled, gasping, his eyes bulging out with fear. He grabbed at his leg instead of at Tracy. His chest heaved as if with laboured breathing. His skin went white.

His eyes, as round as they would ever get, stared up at Tracy. Clear bubbles of foam appeared at the corners of his working mouth, began to fleck his cheeks as if he were rabid.

Muscular crampings began soon afterwards. The man looked like a contortionist. He tried to speak but his throat, now a tightly banded shell of cartilage, merely convulsed.

Tracy turned away at last. This was, after all, the death that had been planned for him. He looked around, saw what they had done to the nurses. Three of them were bound hand and foot. That was good. It meant they were still alive. But they were unconscious and of no use to him.

He was breathing harder than he liked and he had used up his one weapon as well as much of his strength. *Prana*. He must regain his inner strength if he were to have a chance to survive this ordeal. The man's gun! Tracy turned, searching for it. He had knocked it away down the corridor and now he went after it, saw it finally perhaps a dozen feet away, part way around the curving of the corridor.

He crouched down, contemplated the weapon. It was tempting indeed, lying as it was so clear and in the open. And that was precisely what concerned Tracy now.

He took a chance, one he did not relish taking. But everything was a risk now with only fractions of a second to attempt to determine the odds. This was what he had been trained for, after all, and all his instincts cried out that the weapon was too good to be true. He backed away from it and, removing his shoes, ran crouched, down the corridor. He was in G wing, the casualty ward. Each floor of the hospital described an almost perfect rectangle with two branch hallways, one at either end, leading off into the smaller wings of the building that housed the special wards such as intensive care, cardiac and the burn centre.

Three-quarters of the way around, he slowed, placed his shoes back on his feet, crept forward, and at last found his instincts rewarded. For there in front of him was the second man, down on one knee behind a pillar, in the classic sharpshooter's position, his pistol aimed at the gleam of his fallen compatriot's weapon clearly in view on the floor. Had Tracy made a move towards it, he would have been dead now.

Tracy came forward. He cursed silently as the man spun. He was large and bulky, his girth belying his speed. He sighted, closing one eye.

Tracy was already committed, on his way, his leg kicking out, the impact of his steel-shod heel connecting with a satisfying crunch on the point of the man's fat chin.

His arms flew out at his sides as the momentum of Tracy's blow and following weight spun him backwards. He hit the outer wall, bounced back. The gun was still in his hand and he used it now as a club, bringing it down in a wicked blow onto the top of Tracy's right shoulder.

Tracy cried out, used his own toppling downward momentum to sweep the fat man off his feet with a swift pull and twist of his forearm. It was Tracy's left arm however and the manoeuvre cost him in recovery time and energy.

The fat man was on him like a mongoose on a snake. He was very adept, using the bulk and momentum of his own weight to keep Tracy off-balance while he struck once, twice, a third time with blows to Tracy's liver and spleen.

Tracy was flat on his back. He lifted a knee but was blocked. The fat man bore down, raining blows as Tracy tried to cover up on his pain-filled left side. His heart was racing and the breath was leaving his lungs too quickly for enough oxygen to be absorbed. Much more of this, he knew, and he would be finished. He knew how he could defeat this man. Jinsoko had taught him that. *You cannot defeat an opponent unless you first determine his style of hand-to-hand fighting. Once you begin to think like him, all the rest will follow.* The key to this man was his enormous weight. He had learned to use it to his own advantage, therefore he relied on it. As a result, Tracy believed it could be used against him.

At the end of another flurry of blows he allowed his grunts of pain to louden – he did not have to put on much of an act. His body slumped slightly – a fraction was all his opponent would need. He raised up to finish Tracy off and Tracy gambled once again.

He used his left elbow, praying as he did so that the bone at the top of his shoulder would not be dislodged from its socket by the resulting impact, bringing it in and upwards in a percussive blow to the man's sternum. The solar plexus, as Tracy knew full well, was only vulnerable in an out-of-shape person. Professionals trained too well and too hard, building many protective layers of fibrous muscle that made the solar plexus impervious to any but the most massive of percussive blows.

But the sternum was another matter. It was relatively close to the surface of the body and no amount of conditioning could protect it because muscles just did not form in that area.

The outer point of his elbow smashed into the fat man and Tracy clamped his hands together, fingers laced, now bringing his own weight to bear, levering himself up while jamming his elbow downwards against the bone.

The fat man let out a scream and tumbled away from Tracy, on his hands and knees, away from the burning pain. He gasped and coughed and Tracy was on him.

The fat man's head was shaking, sweat dripping down from his forehead. Tracy crooked his arm, extending his body forward in a low crouch. He slipped his wrist behind the fat man's left calf and heaved mightily, sending him tumbling forward towards Tracy so that the back of his neck was extended and exposed.

And in that instant, Tracy clamped him with thumb and fingers of his right hand, pressing inward, gaining access to the fat man's sub-occipital nerves, which fed the head through the openings in the very top of the spine.

With a pincerlike motion, he jammed them against the intervening bone of the fat man's spine. The man's entire body jerked spasmodically and was still.

Tracy, gasping, rocked back on his haunches. He pulled in oxygen like a drowning man, concerning now only with his own well-being. Nothing strenuous, the doctor had said. He wanted to laugh but found himself too exhausted.

He got up at last, walked away from the fat man's bulk, looking for the fire stairs. His left shoulder felt dowsed in fire. The concrete stairs were wide and open. The place seemed not to have been washed in decades.

At the landing he had to hold on tightly to the metal banister, red-painted like an arrow descending into hell, as vertigo hit him, this time harder than when he had first got out of bed. What I really need, he thought, is eighteen hours of uninterrupted sleep. But there was much he still had to do before he could rest.

He glanced at his watch, surprised to find it only 8.25. It had been just seven minutes since he had moved out into the corridor. It seemed like seven days. He began to move cautiously down the staircase, mindful of all his aches and pains. And almost tripped over the two policemen, lying along the stairwell, trussed like birds ready for the oven.

Tracy bent down – too fast – and felt the vertigo return. His stomach seemed to rebel, rising up into his throat. He took three deep breaths as he examined the cops, touching the sides of their necks, the insides of their wrists. Alive but unconscious. He had wondered that the police, wanting to question him in connection with the explosion, had not seen fit to post guards near his room. Now he saw that they had . . . and what had happened to them.

It was within his power to bring them around but he hesitated. He had to get to Mizo because only Mizo now knew the Why of all this. Jade Princess might have had the knowledge but she would never tell anyone now. So he had to have his mobility. The police, of course, would not understand that. He decided to leave them sleeping where they were. In a few hours, they would come to with only brief headaches and aches and pains.

Tracy climbed carefully over them. Down and down he went in the silence of the hospital staircase. On the last landing, he rested a moment, regaining his wind. Just ahead and below him he could see the long front hallway and beyond, the soft Hong Kong night. Somewhere people in fancy dress were undoubtedly stepping out of hired cars, laughing, ready for dinner, dancing and perhaps a stage show or two. Carefree and happy. A relaxed evening out on the town. Hong Kong was a city for tourists.

Tracy went down the stairs, froze immediately. Pain rushed into his lower back.

'Be a good fellow,' the deep voice said in lilting Cantonese, 'and take your hand out of your pocket.'

The muzzle of the snug-nosed .38 was ground into Tracy's coccyx. 'By all the gods stay like that,' the voice said, 'I want to remember you just the way you are before I kill you.'

'Ladies and gentlemen!...'

It was a night of rushing energy for Atherton Gottschalk. A night of great purpose.

'... Delegates to the Republican National Convention!...'

A night when he and everyone else packed into this great barn of an auditorium, millions watching on television, listening on radio felt the first culmination of the groundswell.

'... Please join me in welcoming...'

He saw the Secret Service much in evidence, gathered around him, near him like a living network, speaking in low monosyllables into their tiny walkie-talkies, shifting the pattern minutely, glancing from face to face every ten seconds as they had been trained. His chest swelled with pride at the thought that he required them now.

'... the next President of the United States of America!...'

The roar that had begun a moment ago, swelled, shaking the auditorium until he felt surrounded by thunder.

'... Atherton Gottschalk!'

And, straightening his tie, filled with elation, he moved onto the centre of the stage, into the bright hot spotlight of the world where one hundred million eyes watched.

Atherton Gottschalk welcomed that scrutiny, knew the kind of physical appearance he gave. What the heartland had learned in the months of his campaign for the nomination, the big cities would soon acquiesce in. Macomber had been correct all along in his assessment of the country's mood.

When he was President, Gottschalk thought now, he would see that Macomber was amply rewarded. What could he want? A military advisorship? An ambassadorial post? Appropriations for the weaponry Metronics, Inc. developed, certainly. Well, that would be easy. Gottschalk believed in every one of those weapons.

Atherton Gottschalk lifted up his arms in a great V of triumph, acknowledging the crowd's standing ovation. He turned from one television camera to another, smiling broadly, confidently. He radiated poise, control, enthusiasm and the power of, as he thought of it, the big mo. Momentum. One would never guess from the attitude he struck that – as Macomber had told him – were the elections to be held today, 25 August, Gottschalk would most likely lose. Because of the goddamned big cities, Gottschalk thought, smiling away.

He turned this way and that, marvelling at the unity of strength within the party. The goddamned holdout liberals who shied away from the aggressive stance that he knew with a deep and abiding certainty America must take in the world in order to survive the rest of the eighties intact.

Erosion of the democratic way of life was already on the rise throughout the world. Communist propaganda was taking an even more devastating toll now than it had in the sixties. The disinformation they were so cleverly providing their mouthpieces in the Third World was subtly undermining American prestige. It seemed incredible to Gottschalk that the Soviet propaganda was so successful that even ranking members of the current administration refused to believe in the USSR's creation of a unified network of terrorists.

Well, all that would change when he became President. As soon as he was installed in office, he would move to counter those threats. His smile widened now as he thought of 31 August and Macomber's plan. Because of that, there would be no opposition to him at all. By then America would have had its first taste of a terrorist assault on its home soil and it would mobilize.

Gottschalk rejoiced, not only for himself but for the entire country. It was just like the days before America entered World War II: it took great hardship and some loss of life for the sleeping giant to be awakened. But once aroused, Gottschalk knew, no nation on earth could stand before her. Let the terrorists beware. As of this night, their days are numbered. Attacked on its own soil, America could then send out its strike forces into the Middle East, the oil-rich nations of the Gulf, the obliteration of the known terrorist camps, the destruction of already shaky Islamic governments. Oil for the cities of America and, with it, an end to the Soviet Union's stranglehold on much of the world.

Atherton Gottschalk stepped up to the microphone and bowed his head, quietening the crowd, the electronic eye of the country's surrogate audience.

'Delegates,' he began in his deep rumbling baritone, a calming voice filled with the security of confidence, 'dedicated Republicans, fellow citizens of America' – he lifted his head, looking directly out into the sea of shining celebrating faces – 'and fellow citizens of the world! No more for us the chains of a depressed economy! No more for us the heavy weight of 9 per cent-plus unemployment! No more for us the designation of second-class power! Tonight sees the beginning of America's long march towards prosperity and the security in this increasingly difficult world that is . . . *must* be . . . rightfully hers!'

As one, the audience rose to its feet, roaring its approval and its support. Receiving that vast bow wave of energy, basking in its warmth, Gottschalk thought of the spirit of President Lincoln, gigantic and spotlit, shining out across the Potomac to enfold the entire nation. He thought he knew at last what greatness was, and, gratefully, he accepted its glowing mantle.

Hollow sounds filled the ruins of his heart. The harsh cry of jungle birds, the *skreek, skreek* of large-eared bats, the soft pad of great stealthy predators, stalking clearings' edges, lungs like bellows, panting.

And the AK-47 pressed hard against his burning body, its

own sleekly shining flesh growing hotter as he fired in rapid accurate bursts. The air screaming as frightened birds lifted from the treetops and the brown blurs of the monkeys turning tail, scrambling away, swinging, swinging.

How many of Tol's cadre he killed that afternoon, Khieu would never remember. Even on the 747-SP, his legs up, a light blanket draped over him, carefully put there by a female flight attendant who could not take her green eyes from his beautiful and haunted face, dreaming he was still back in Cambodia, numbers were irrelevant. They flew past his fever-bright eyes like sparking tracers from low-running fighter jets until the mathematics of it became an abstract, fading into the background of distant dream.

Even when he returned to the house on Gramercy Park South and made his laconic, frozen-faced report to his anxious father, he could not recall how many men he had driven to the ground. How many Khmer Rouge. How many of the Black Heart.

Chet Khmau.

For all he had not done for his family, they paid. For what his sister had become, they paid. For the terrible catatonia of his mother, the disappearance of his tiny brother and sister, they paid. And for the hideous death of Malis, they paid.

Yet the killing had not expunged the flame of guilt growing within him like the wild spread of some unknown disease. In his mind, *apsara* performed her celestial dance, headless as a demon, even the bright pumping of human blood denied her, blue-white and bloated, dancing on, deft fingers telling the story of her lucrative whoredom.

It was raining when he reached Christopher Street, a soft, dismal pattering that, in the countryside, at least, would have a happier aspect, releasing the fragrant scents of clover and newly-mown grass. But here in the city, it merely turned grimy pavements muddy, soaked garbage in the gutters and streaked unwashed windows.

Khieu stood watching the dark paths form and merge on the flat surface of the front door glass panel. He pushed and, entering the dim, stifling vestibule, pressed the bell of the apartment on the ninth floor. He waited fifteen seconds, depressed the stud again. When there was no acknowledgement, he went to the inside door and spent twenty seconds working on the lock. Because it was after seven in the evening and dinner time, he did not expect much traffic going in or out of the building.

The sharp click of the lock opening resounded just as he heard the door to the street opening behind him. He turned the knob, putting his left hand into his trouser pocket to jangle the keys there as he leaned on the inner door, entering the lobby.

In true New York fashion, he allowed the door to swing shut without looking back at who had entered the vestibule after him. He did not want anyone to see his face; he could bear to be thought of as rude by one person.

He strode quickly past the elevator, took the staircase so that the person behind him would assume he was going to one of the lower floors.

Khieu climbed the stairs slowly, listening for sounds. He heard the soft whine as the elevator started up. He went on, ascending.

He came to the ninth floor landing. One hall light was out, sending a pool of deep shadow across one-third of the floor. He turned to his left, went all the way to the end of the hall and, leaning against the heavy door he found there, began to manipulate the lock until it opened. Khieu stepped into the still hallway, closing the door behind him without a sound. He stood very still, listening. The apartment was empty. Time to go to work.

While Khieu had been gaining entrance, Louis Richter had turned off the hot water and slid gratefully into the steaming water of the bath. He had left the door of the bathroom slightly open as had been his habit even when his wife was alive. He detested cutting himself off so completely from everyone and everything.

He lay back, feeling his muscles slowly unknotting. At times like these the pain was almost bearable. Even the thought of his own end did not tear at him fearfully. It was like a cloudlike dream drifting closer over time. But, Louis Richter wondered, as the philosopher said, Which one is the dream? In times like these, he only understood with some anticipation that he would soon know.

But first, he thought, he wanted to know what it was Tracy had learned in Hong Kong. In truth, he was concerned. He had expected to hear from his son before now. It had been almost a week since he had gone.

He closed his eyes and in the theatre of his mind flickered scenes in his life filled with vibrancy and singing emotion. He wondered what it was he had wanted from life when he had set out to find it as a young man. Certainly it had been nothing grand; he had never been desirous of amassing great wealth or power. But expertise; that had been it.

And in the world of miniaturized high explosives, small though that might be, he had been the dominant force for over thirty years. No one could touch his innovation, he knew that. Even now. Not Pappandrasseu in Athens, Mintter in Munich, Ohlstad in Antwerp, Tynes in Paraná or Mizo in Hong Kong. In one way or another they had all looked to him to create the prototype and build from there, adding clever little fillips of their own.

It was why the foundation had approached him in the first place. Over the years, as Louis Richter had come to know the Director – if anyone could say he knew him – he had realized what a special man this was. The excellence of performance, not only physical but intellectual as well, he demanded simply could not be achieved in any normal government agency overseen by committees, bureaucracies and political jealousies.

That was why it had been created. The Director reported to only one man, the foundation the long arm of the President. That it existed at all – that it had survived the troubled test of time – was a marvel to Louis Richter. He knew full well what its job was and how it went about doing it. The CIA took all the heat, all the press, all the brow-beating from Capitol Hill. That was what it was there for, after all. The foundation, by its very design, was small and compact. The fewer people involved, the better. To Louis Richter's knowledge he was the only man employed by them who did not work out of its headquarters in Washington. It was partly his choice – he had wanted to remain in New York; partly the fact that it was impractical. The building it was housed in simply could not accommodate the kind of equipment and testing he required.

And there was never a day in his life when he regretted bringing Tracy to the attention of the Director. He knew his wife would never have approved, had never been comfortable with what he did. But he could forgive her her pacifist view of the world, unrealistic as he knew it to be. He did not think, however, that she would have been able to forgive him for acquiescing to Tracy's wishes.

It was perhaps a measure of Louis Richter's life that the majority of episodes he chose to remember now involved his work. That did not bother him, rather suffused him with a warm glow.

He opened his eyes, reached for the bar of soap. As he did so he thought he caught a blurred shadow out of the corner of his right eye. He turned his head, saw the door, the small slice of the hallway and beyond that the living room he could glimpse through the opening. There was nothing there. He waited, sitting straight up, his head cocked for sound as well as sight. He saw nothing; heard nothing. A dust mote, perhaps, catching for an instant the light from the lamp in the hall.

He shrugged, took the soap from its dish, began to rub it between his palms. The movements caused the water to splash and at that moment he was certain he heard a sound from beyond the partly opened door. That was something he was not used to in this apartment. It was in an old building with excellent construction. The walls were thick enough so that he never heard a neighbour.

The sound came again and he thought, Christ, there's someone in the house! He was very calm. He looked carefully around the bathroom. What was readily available for him to use to defend himself? He looked to the medicine cabinet. Too bad, he thought, I don't shave with a straight razor; a Remington electric will do me no good. But there was his spray deodorant.

He dropped the soap into the bathwater, rinsing his hands thoroughly. Then he stood up and very gingerly put one bare leg over the side of the tub. He was in this position, one leg in and one leg out, when the lamp in the hallway went out. He did not even hear the click, felt instead the explosion of darkness. Night had fallen and the illumination was dim indeed, as dappled as in deep forest.

He stood frozen for a moment, listening to the booming thunder of his pulse in his inner ear. Warm water dripped from his white flesh, leaving his skin goosebumped and chilled. He shivered. He could not be in a more vulnerable position. That decided him. He took one long stride, lunging for the metal-bound mirrored door to the medicine cabinet.

His wet fingertips scrabbled for a hold, slipped on the steamy glass as he came up inches short. He extended himself, reaching further, curling the tips around the metal edge, pulled. Like a shot from a pistol, the bathroom door flew open.

In the absolute cessation of motion, Tracy was able to hear the magnified beating of his heart as if it were large enough to contain the world. So near the ending of life, that was perfectly understandable.

'I will take all due time devising your death,' the voice said. The muzzle of the .38, feeling as large as the mouth of a cannon, jammed again into the base of his spine. 'Not the heart for the quick, clean kill. You are down here and that means there are three left on the fifth floor. There can be nothing easy for you now. Into the juncture of your spine and pelvis will the first shot be pumped so that you may enjoy the many splendours afforded to the life of a cripple.'

It sounded odd in the high sing-song of Cantonese, and somehow wrong. Put it down to the organism rejecting the concept of death. Make it alien; make it incomprehensible. Make it go away.

He got hold of himself, turning his concentration towards the *tone* of the voice, rather than the content. Only that might save him.

Loudmouths were the same the world over. Give one mastery of another via a mechanical weapon such as a pistol and he would be filled with arrogance.

It gave them diarrhoea of the mouth. Tracy had witnessed it

even in the depths of the Cambodian jungle. The urge to gloat, to extend the time of one's complete mastery over another human being was irresistible.

'Eventually, the other joints will follow: wrists, elbows, shoulders, knee and then, yes, it will be time to look forward to the bullet in the neck.' The Chinese shrugged as if it were of no importance to him. 'You may die of that wound or again you may linger for some time more, slowly bleeding to death.'

Tracy listened carefully, evaluating. The voice was slow, deliberate ... calm and collected. That was dangerous for it meant clear, rational thinking; the suppression of emotion. And what Tracy needed more than anything else now was the heat of raw emotion.

'Three bodies up there. I cannot imagine the joss that allowed you to do it but I must congratulate my employer on his farsightedness. With my older brother in, I had thought this lobby watch superfluous. Because he is fat, he is constantly underestimated; it is his great value, yes. Because of his great prowess as a fighter.'

Tracy saw the key instantly and used it. 'Not so very great,' he said in Cantonese. 'I defeated him easily and I am still weak from my wounds.'

'All gods know you are a liar. It is a notorious trait among *quailoh*.'

'Upstairs lies the truth,' Tracy said. 'Come take a look at his fat corpse.' Let the hard emotion come.

'Incapacitated, yes,' the Chinese said. 'But dead, no.'

But the tone had changed and Tracy noted it. The words did not come as leisurely, the one pitched a half-note higher as the atmosphere of euphoria was dissipated. The man no longer in total control. Tracy knew something he did not; something about his brother. Turn the screws a notch tighter.

'I pinched off the suboccipital nerves.' An abrupt change in tone, his voice harsh and nasty. 'He died an idiot.'

'You lie!' the Chinese screamed. The lid was coming off fast. The pressure-point combined with the severe time shortage the man was working under – how soon would the bodies be noticed? – to rapidly break down his normal stone façade. 'Damn you and all *quailoh*!'

Tracy felt the movement of the muzzle against his spine, the pressure lifting away as the heat of the emotions dissipated rational thought, called for immediate retaliatory measures.

As the pistol came away but just as he was about to make the first strike, he felt a hand at the nape of his neck. The nerve juncture was impinged upon and blackness overwhelmed him. The world formed again in splotches of pale green and grey-blue. The patterns shifted and so did he. His eyelids fluttered as he focused. Trees speeding by outside the window. The big sky. Rocking and bumping. Wind through an aperture.

They had trussed him well, using metal flex that burned his wrists, his ankles even through his socks. He opened his eyes again just to slits and took inventory. Besides the young Chinese on the back seat next to him, there were two others in front.

'He's awake.' Quick, sharp Cantonese.

The one next to him was the Chinese on the stairs. He had his .38 drawn, the muzzle pointing directly at Tracy's head. He was looking for an excuse to fire it. First concern: don't give him one. His brother was lying dead back on the fifth floor of Queen Elizabeth Hospital. He would want to exact a heavy toll for that.

The thin Chinese on the passenger's side in front turned around. He wore a felt hat but Tracy could see that beneath it his head was shaved. He reached out an arm and a tattoo of a dragon clutching a sword was revealed etched to the skin across the back of his hand.

His fingers opened like the petals of a flower. Inside was a gravity knife, the blade tucked away. In an instant, it had swung out. He had wanted to show Tracy the swiftness of his reflexes. Noted.

'I prevented Kau from killing you.' It was odd; his nostrils flared when he spoke. 'That was not an easy task. He hates you for what you've done to his brother.' He swung the point of the blade past Tracy's eyes. 'There must be no trace of you, we have been told.' He laughed. 'At the bottom of East Lamma Bay you can use your prowess to kill fish.' He laughed again as the

473

knifeblade made complex patterns in the air. 'You can sing your last lullaby to the sharks.'

But Tracy's second concern, namely to find out where he was, made movement imperative. Location would give him a fairly accurate estimate of the time he had left when compared with the car's speed.

Very carefully, he began to pull himself up on the seat. He had to do it fast to get Kau's attention in time, slowly enough not to alarm him. Several times he allowed his eyes to lose focus.

He willed his body to relax, letting the bumps in the road move him seemingly at their will. In fact, he was moving to face Kau, sinking back to his left so that his crossed wrists were against the door handle. It was a four-door Mercedes.

The doors were locked, of course, but he could overcome that. He glanced out the window, estimating their speed to be up around a hundred kilometres per hour. With his hands and feet tied he could not put his chance of survival out there at more than five per cent and he discounted it.

Instead, he worked clandestinely at the flex binding his wrists. One end was sticking out slightly and he bent it down, using the door handle as a lever. It was slow work, principally because of Kau's scrutiny and he did not think he could make an appreciable dent in their work by the time they reached Aberdeen.

For the time being, he contented himself with observing the three men. Tracy had seen Kau's type: a fanatic about his body and his control over his reflexes. Yet he used a gun. That was something he could use: no matter how well-trained the body was, after prolonged use of a firearm, the reflexes lost a fraction of their honed speed. It was inevitable and had nothing at all to do with the physical. It was a strictly psychological thing, dependence on a mechanical object.

Of the three, it was Kau Tracy was most concerned with. He was the one a hairs-breadth away from shooting. The other two would not present such problems: one was driving and had to be concerned first with the proper handling of over two tons of complex machinery hurtling along at 100 k.p.h.; the other was physically removed by the barrier of the front seat back.

474

It was essential at this point for all of them to be assured that they had nothing to fear from their prisoner. His shoulders slumped minutely and his head lolled on his neck as if he were continually drifting off to sleep.

The man on the passenger's side in front turned briefly. His hard black eyes analysed positions, attitudes, Tracy's physical condition. He turned back, satisfied.

All the time, Kau stared at Tracy. Tracy lowered his head; he did not want to make eye contact. If the man was as good as Tracy thought he might see in Tracy's eyes what was about to happen.

There was nothing more to do now but wait for the right moment. It was totally out of his hands, dependent on the driver's reflexes and the whims of the Island's roads. They were already in Aberdeen, the water not far away.

There was some talk as the man with the gravity knife directed the driver to the location of the boat. There was a spare anchor on board, the man with the gravity knife said. It would do well.

The turn almost took Tracy by surprise. A squeal of tyres, a shifting of bodies as centrifugal force came into play, disrupting gravity.

It was a turn to the left, sharp enough to jam Kau back into his corner of the seat. Therefore Tracy's own movement towards him did not initially alarm him since, in his mind, it was nothing more than a natural result of the car's turning.

He did not fully comprehend the force behind it until Tracy's bound feet slammed into his chest with sufficient force to drive all the wind out of him. His eyes opened wide and his mouth tried to work but nothing came out.

Tracy braced himself against the door, lifting his wrists and the binding flex sharply upwards as he did so, felt the lock button give as he drove his feet at the man's exposed neck, coming down. He heard a crack as if a branch had been snapped by the sedan's passage.

Now timing was all important. The Chinese with the gravity knife was turning his head. Tracy slid himself over the seat, positioning himself so that he was directly behind the driver. He

475

pushed himself down so that his entire back was braced against the seat. He drew his knees up against his chest as the man in front began to twist his body around. The knife flicked into life.

Tracy drew breath into his lungs, bunching his muscles, kicked out viciously with all his strength as he exhaled, shouting in *kiai* as he did so. The soles of his shoes tore through the velour fabric of the front seat, fetched up against the bracing. As that happened he followed through, ramming still with all his might.

The seat creaked, snapped and was jolted forward, the driver flung headlong out through the windscreen.

There was a high screaming, a shatter of glass and the gravity knife now withdrew as the third Chinese redirected his attention towards the control of the Mercedes now careening down the quay. In a frenzy, he tore at his compatriot in an effort to get at the brakes, his hat falling into his lap.

They were speeding along the old section of the pier, white staring faces in a blur of colour and then they were on the outer quay, the railroad-track effect of the junks at anchor unmistakable.

Tracy fought to return to the left side of the sedan. Kau's body blocked the right side door. This should have been the easiest part of the manoeuvre but the car would not stabilize and the centrifugal force was now working against him, flinging him away from the door as the sedan spun.

Driven to his knees in the well of the back seat, he stumbled across Kau's unnaturally crossed legs. He extended his bound arms, hooking the flex over the handle. He pulled downwards, heard the sharp click and, as the car reached the opposite apex of its spin, was hurled out the opening door like a sack of wheat.

The Mercedes was in midair, sailing side first towards the choppy oily water. Tracy went in, smacking the back of his head while, a moment later, the heavy sedan struck on its left side, the door slamming shut on the Chinese scrabbling over the back of his seat to get out. The weight of the water pressure sealed him in. Tracy had one breathless glimpse of the powerful balled fist smashing through the window, glass shattering outwards, thwarted tattooed dragon between white knuckles, then a torrent of water pouring in through the rent windscreen adding its additional weight and the car sank with a belch of upwards seeking air.

The stinging chill of the water partially revived Tracy. His head ached. With his wrists and ankles bound he had no way of swimming and unless he was able to rise and breach the surface he would quickly drown.

Blackness all around him, a throbbing in his left side, his lungs struggling to extract all the oxygen from the air he had inhaled on his way out of the doomed sedan. Waves of dizziness washed over him, the blow from the water's surface awakening his recent injuries.

But worse still he had lost all sense of direction. He seemed to be sinking and he abandoned himself to instinct, trusting the organism to find its own way, knowing that it viewed its survival as paramount.

He swallowed foul water, choking, was buffeted by mean currents, struck out silently with whatever parts of his body still functioned. Grey bubbles trailed from between his clenched lips as if with each one another bit of his life was failing.

Then abruptly, unexpectedly, he breached the surface, gasping in surprise because somehow he had not seen the lightening of the water, assumed that his eyes had been shut and began to worry in earnest. He could not remember closing his eyes; they *should not* have been closed because he needed all of his senses alert if he was going to make it. If instinct was being impaired then he truly was in serious trouble.

He went under heavily again but with enough oxygen this time and kicked out as best he could with his legs in concert, straining to remain near the surface.

Water rolled off his hair and into his eyes. He was wheezing from lack of oxygen, his mouth opened wide, blinking incessantly in order to see clearly. The crest of a wave slammed into him, filling his mouth and throat with salt water so that he gagged, swallowed reflexively, then vomited up the vile stuff immediately. He lost orientation in the process.

Pain flooded him and, simultaneously, a weakness suffusing his muscles and he thought, None of it was worth anything, not all the planning or the execution because I'm going to die anyway, far from home and Lauren.

At that moment, his left shoulder struck something hard and he struggled to turn towards it, awkward still, but orienting instinctively. *Side*, he thought. This is on my side. He turned again. So *this* way must be up.

Rough barnacles scraped his flesh, flailing off the material of his shirt. Salt water invaded, stinging and that pain, sharp and external and, above all, *new*, brushed the cobwebs from his mind.

He reached upwards along the hard, curving flank of the obstruction, felt himself being pulled upwards from his watery grave. He groaned as his already taxed muscles were stretched. Then he was out of the water, being drawn aboard the ancient junk. A jabbering in his ears. Not Cantonese, not Mandarin but intelligible still. But he was too exhausted to think, to even make a reply. Peering faces, open and concerned. A dimly-remembered, confused trip across the slippery deck, the sharp pungency of fish innards.

Then he was bundled below, into warmth, the incredible softness of a straw mattress and sleep. Blessed sleep.

Louis Richter felt a breeze on his bare back, as chill as death, got his hand around the barrel of the deodorant can. Then he felt fingers like iron spikes gripping him, throwing him away from the open cabinet.

He cried out, his balance gone, his heels skidding across the damp tile floor and he was crashing backwards. He thought, for that instant airborne, that he would surely break his back on the hard floor. Then he slammed into the bathtub, the water breaking his momentum.

There was a shadow above him, looming spectrally down from the ceiling as if larger than life. He lifted his arms as if to feebly ward off a blow. But all the while he was fumbling off the can's cap. The shadow came closer, bending down and Louis Richter knew that this was his one chance.

He depressed the stud, heard the whoosh of the chemical spray. There was a soft grunt and the grip on him eased. He scrambled up and was delivered a blow to the point of his chin which drove all coherent thought from his brain.

Dazed, he sat heavily back in the water, his head lolling. The world was composed of shades of grey, all colour gone. Wallowing in the warm water, he no longer could distinguish up from down, right from left. It was if he were floating in space, disoriented and disintegrating.

He thrashed irrationally like a baby seal about to be clubbed. His swollen tongue crept out from between his lips. His eyes rolled wildly in their sockets and his breathing was stertorous.

Then one thing penetrated the haze closing down his mind, a beacon in the fog: it was one lone note, singing. He wondered where it came from until he saw the glint directly in front of his eyes, a thin horizontal thread, moving inexorably towards him. What was it?

He lifted his head higher and his gaze found a slight crescent of the face looming over him. Silvered high cheekbone, the straight, handsome brow, the shadowed eye. It was Kim, the Director's emissary.

And abruptly, the sight galvanized him, the mists clearing. He could think again, knew, instinctively, all of it. And the knowledge of the terrible danger he had placed Tracy in was sufficient to light in him one last flame of life. Though the disease ravaging him depleted his strength, though he had no weapons but his body and his mind, Louis Richter fought back.

His hands came up, the fingers curling around the horizontal glint. He cried out with the pain as he tried to bring it down and away from his throat. It was steel piano wire and it bit into the flesh of his palms like a surgeon's scalpel.

But Khieu had had enough. His eyes were still stinging from the noxious chemicals of the spray and he allowed the old man to grip the wire, brought the ends around in a loop, trapping the hands within a circle. And now he entwined the strand ends, pulled mightily so that the singing increased as steel scraped against steel climbing inwards, cutting off the old man's circulation.

Khieu grunted with the effort and Louis Richter screamed from the depths of his being as the steel wire bit through his skin, lacerating the raw bleeding flesh beneath. But still he held on, knowing that to let go would seal his death.

Sweat rimmed Khieu's beautiful brow as the hot salty blood drooled down Louis Richter's wrists, running in rivulets across his arms to expand like dark clouds in the bathwater.

The wire sang a high keening note. It was at the bone now, sawing back and forth and the old man gathered himself. Pain ribboned him, shaking his shoulders, turning his arms to lead weights. He brought his feet up under him and launched himself upwards, screaming.

But Khieu was ready for him, whipping the wire away from the bloody pulp that had once been one of nature's great wonders, wrapping the wet wire around the old man's neck. He jerked once, twice.

Louis Richter heard the singing once more but now the one note had turned into many. And then the violence of the dream ended, all pain died and everything was as it had been . . . once upon a time.

3

'A goddamned piece of tinfoil!'

'All that elaborate secrecy,' Commander Brady said, 'and we find nothing but a crumpled-up gum wrapper.'

They were back in Silvano's office, grouped around the table as Thwaite carefully unwrapped the layers. The Juicyfruit wrapper came away, revealing the inner shell of tin foil. It had been stuck at the back of the locker.

Silvano handed Thwaite a pair of jeweller's tweezers and he pried apart the edges. They all stared at what the foil contained.

Thwaite said, 'Who wants to call the lab?'

'Fold it up and I'll take it down to Maurice.' Silvano grinned. 'I'll persuade him that our, ah, project has priority.'

'How'll you do that?' Thwaite asked.

'I'll take him out to dinner.'

'Christ,' Brady said, 'he's an easy bastard.'

Silvano laughed, taking up the sphere of foil with the tweezers and heading for the door. 'It ain't the food so much, Commander,' he said. 'It's the twins I know out near the lake I take him to see afterwards.'

Silvano returned in just over forty minutes. He had in tow a rail of a man with a long beaked nose and tufted eyebrows. His thin jowls were blue-black with stubble.

Silvano carefully closed the door behind them before he made the introductions. 'I think you'd better give them all of it, Maurice.'

The chemist nodded. 'Right.' His brown eyes were large, slightly exophthalmic so that he looked as if he had corrective lenses on. 'The white powder Art here asked me to identify is heroin. Pure heroin.' He looked at them in turn. 'Now I'm talking about the one hundred per cent straight uncut stuff. Frankly, I've rarely come across such super horse.'

'You think it's new?' Thwaite said.

'You mean just in from the Gold Triangle?' Maurice shrugged. 'If you want my opinion, I'd say it's been untouched by American hands or chemicals.'

'Okay,' Brady said, 'so it's choice quality stuff. Where does that leave us?'

'You've only heard half of it,' Silvano said. 'Maurice?'

'Very interesting,' the chemist said. 'There was some writing on the inside of the foil. The horse was covering it and I had to use a couple of this and that to get it up to full readability.' He produced a small notebook, flipped up pages until he came to the right spot. He consulted his notes. 'I got a name and a street for you guys. No town; no address.'

'Let's have it,' Thwaite said.

'I got an Antonio Mogales,' Maurice said, looking up. 'I got a Mackay Place. Either of those ring a bell?'

And Thwaite thought, good Christ, that's Bay Ridge! 'Tonio, you sonovabitch!

There was a quality about the Cloisters that never failed to move Macomber. Perhaps it was the sense of great antiquity, the milieu of European history, of power direct and uncompromising. The thunder of hooves to battle, the darkening of plains with the blood of infidels. The Crusades . . . a holy quest. Victory for God and country.

The thick stone walls, the cool echoes, the stillness of the air itself, as if it held the weight and solemnity of that European millennium, all these and more bound him to this place.

He arrived forty-five minutes early so that he might be able to savour this atmosphere before his appointment. Consequently, he was in good humour, having calmed himself sufficiently from the aftermath of Khieu's puzzling report. It was disconcerting enough to hear that he had not been able to locate Tisah but to witness the manner of that report was even more disturbing. At least, as far as Tisah was concerned, there was always the Monk though Macomber disliked having to rely on him.

But as for Khieu, Macomber was at a loss to explain his son's inward bent since his return. Now, in some subtle way,

Macomber found himself sorry that he had ever sent Khieu back to Cambodia. He should have seen that such a trip might prove difficult, even traumatic for him. But Macomber had been blinded by his awakened love for Tisah – to see her again, to hold her, to take her in his arms – it was too much for him to think about for long. He burned for her, even now after seeing the consequences of Khieu's return.

What had happened to him there to cause such inwardness? He had provided no details and Macomber's probings had been useless. But much of his regret, he knew, stemmed from Khieu's failure to uncover Tisah's whereabouts. Macomber thought about her constantly now . . . he could not wait for the Monk's message, Tisah's arrival.

He turned a corner and saw Marcus Findlan standing in the small courtyard, hands hanging loosely at his sides, looking at that tree with seven sculptured branches like the arms of a Jewish menorah.

Marcus Findlan was well over six feet tall, slim-hipped, with ruddy leathery skin. His lined face, clear light eyes that seemed to reflect the sky and wide-shouldered bearing made him seem like a marshal from out of the old West. Not especially surprising since in his youth Findlan had been sheriff of his native town of Galveston.

Since that time, he had lost only a bit of his Texas drawl. In fact, Macomber was of the opinion that Findlan cultivated that accent. In the midst of the grey power bureaucracy of Washington it gave him an immediately recognizable character . . . one that fitted perfectly his hard law-and-order image.

He had first come to the attention of the local FBI unit during his stint in Galveston which, being on the Gulf of Mexico, was the next logical off-loading point for marijuana after the Fed crackdowns in Rio Hondo and Port Isabel to the south.

Findlan and his deputy burned about a ton and a half of the stuff, chased the smugglers down the gulf all the way to Matamoros, just over the Mexican border, where Findlan shot three of them dead before they wounded his deputy severely enough to make him pull out.

The FBI liked that but he didn't like them much. They were

too straight-laced for his style of warring against criminals and, in any case, he thought Hoover a dangerous maniac.

As it turned out, the CIA was more his style and his advancement within the organization was nothing short of meteoric. He possessed the innate instincts for getting out of tight scrapes. Time and again they used Findlan on operations they thought unsalvageable, where broken bones of those operatives who had gone before littered the shadowed ground.

Then some bright spark called him in to find a deeply entrenched mole and so began one of the company's most infamous non-publicized purges. The resultant carnage left Findlan within arm's length of the top and, inside of three years, he had become the head of the CIA.

'Marcus,' Macomber said. 'It's a treat to see you away from Washington.' He did not extend his hand; one did not do that with this man.

Marcus Findlan turned, nodded. 'Del. It's good to see you.' They began to walk. Meetings with Findlan were always peripatetic; he felt safer that way. 'Good to be out of that madhouse by the Potomac for a while. Griffiths's been raked over the coals so many times now by Sullivan's committee, he doesn't know whether he's coming or going.' He meant the Secretary of State.

'That was his problem before the hearings,' Macomber said. 'And how're you making out under all that scrutiny.'

Marcus Findlan gave a lopsided smile, the result of a bullet graze during his youth in Galveston. 'Just about as well as you would in the same situation, Del. I've movin', makin' way for the other guy. Hell, it was Griffiths' fault all the way. You know how State likes to think they run us. My only mistake was in giving Griffiths his head in Cairo. It didn't make it any easier when I paid my respects to Billie Jean DeWitt. She and Roger were friends of mine. But, shit, there's just so long I can cry *mea culpa*. There's a lot of that going around these days, anyway, what with the President owning up to his idiotic comment to Sullivan. I'll be happy to let Griffiths take his share.'

There was a young woman on a stone bench, her head tilted back. In her lap was an artist's pad with an unfinished pencil sketch in a sure-handed architectural style.

Macomber led Findlan past. 'Do you think he'll go down?'

'Personally, I think he's finished as of yesterday. I heard part of the testimony and there's was more to come this afternoon. By tonight I don't think Lawrence will have any choice. He's been wounded once already; he'll have to ask for Griffiths' resignation or risk certain defeat in November.'

'November's why we're both here,' Macomber said.

They turned a corner, came out onto a balcony overlooking the steep wooded hillside down to the Hudson.

'How're things shaping up?'

'You tell me.'

Findlan gave a short laugh. 'I'm not omniscient, Del, despite the slings and arrows of my critics.'

'I have no secrets from you, Marcus. That was your stipulation. I've filled you in far more than I have any of the others. But then you're far more important to me than any senator or representative could be.'

'The palace guard.'

Macomber knew he was being tested; the mine field of lies and truths he was feeding Findlan was a more complex matter with each meeting. 'Not in the least.' He knew that Findlan could not bear to think of the company in that light. Ever since Nixon, he was a very wary fellow on that score.

A young couple appeared in the archway on their right. Macomber listened to their idle chatter while he waited for them to leave.

At last, he said, 'You're much too distrustful of politicians, Marcus. Where's your faith?'

'I was born without it, Del. When people talk to me of faith, I tune into another channel. It's a damn poor substitute for power.' They began to walk again as Findlan became restless.

'All right. What we – Atherton and I – want from the CIA is, I think, precisely what you want now and cannot get from this administration. Increased appropriations and leeway.'

'And the *quid pro quo*,' Findlan said bluntly, 'is that the company washes your dirty linen before the public can smell it.'

Macomber stopped. 'Neither Atherton or I,' he said coldly, 'plan to *have* any dirty linen.'

'I appreciate that, Del.' They continued their walk. 'Nothing a Texas boy like myself appreciates more than his freedom. Hell, what I *need*'s leeway, just like you said. Then I can build the company back into the first rank.' He fell silent as they passed a pair of girls with their mother. When they were alone again, he said, 'But I'm still not sure of things. You and Gottschalk're so hellbent on foreign policy, I get stitches in my side sometimes thinking about how he's gonna handle domestic issues like the economy. It's in a helluva mess now . . . has been for some years. You don't just flush a thing like that away in two years time. It's maybe a decade in the making. Now your boy's gonna be saddled with the stink come January. Everybody I know on the Hill's screaming about the GNP.'

'GNP, hell,' Macomber said. 'The economy's not in such bad shape.'

'Yeah?' Findlan looked at him sceptically. 'What d'you know that no one else does, huh?'

'It's a matter of re-education, that's one side of it. That's what Gottschalk will begin to stress as soon as he gets into office. Let me tell you something, Marcus, the GNP looks like shit only when you study it as if we were an *industrial* nation.'

'You mean we aren't?'

'Hell, no. That kind of thinking's outmoded. We've gone *beyond* industrialization. Today, we're basically a service-oriented nation.'

'What, you mean like doormen and waiters? What the fuck is that?'

'You'll pardon me for saying this, Marcus, but that's precisely the kind of wrong-headed thinking we're going to have to do away with.

'Look, I'm in the service business.'

'You? You're a manufacturer.'

'Yes. Metronics builds armaments, puts things together. But I don't *manufacture*. I *buy* my raw materials from manufacturers like US Steel, Teledyne. Even our silicon chips come from other service companies, not manufacturers. You see the difference? The entire entertainment field is service-oriented. But the GNP's not biased towards that; it's biased towards manufacturing. Of course, it looks like shit. But it's not giving us a true picture of the strength we have today.'

Macomber reached into his pocket, produced a sheaf of computer readouts. 'Take a look at these, Marcus. They show an un-biased reading of our current GNP. You judge for yourself.'

Even while he was reading, Findlan did not stop walking. He merely glanced up every three or four seconds; it was ingrained in him. Macomber could imagine him making love to his wife, looking up every three or four seconds.

Findlan whistled lightly. 'You certain of these figures, Del?'

'Absolutely.' He was not lying.

'But this is incredible. It shows a full forty per cent difference. We that better off than we're being told?'

Macomber nodded. 'Yes. But it's going to take some time to reeducate government and the public. While that's going on, though, our second phase will be initiated.

'Gottschalk's learned from the past. He doesn't want to be constantly at odds with Capitol Hill. That's why he's going to let them in on every major decision he's going to make three to six months *before* he makes it public. The members of our *angka* will be spreading the policies, talking them up slowly so that we'll have support already built-in when we go public. No member of the Hill enjoys being surprised by Administration policy; that gets their back up and I don't blame them a bit.'

Findlan gave the computer read-out back to Macomber. 'All of that's positive . . . very positive. But even you've got to admit that we've got weak points in our economy. Automotive manufacturing is at the top of the list. We used to be *numero uno* until we allowed the Japs to get the upper hand. Christ, even the Swedes make better cars than we do now. Can you imagine? The goddamned *Swedes*!'

'As far as Detroit is concerned,' Macomber said, 'I think it's already gone too far. They've made their bed of nails, now they've got to lie down in it and bleed a little.

'Anyway, Detroit's not the future of America – that's *manufacturing* philosophy. The future now is in miniature computer chips and we're already beginning to lose that race to the

487

Japanese again. What we've got to do is beat them at their own game.

'The *Vampire*, which you've seen in action, uses a laser-initiated computer system that, right now, is unique. I got the idea but I'm not about to trumpet my own horn. I'm no engineer. I went to Japan two years ago and hired away one of their top brains. There were certain things he wanted; I gave them to him.

'Now I'm the first to admit that kind of thing's not easy. Those bastards're fiercely loyal to the company they work for. Usually, they're there literally for life. That's how things go in Japan; that's one of the ways they beat us blind. What the fuck do they know from unions? Not a thing. Their company is their second family; it's secure as hell. And I'll bet there're a helluva lot of unemployed auto workers hanging around Detroit these days who'd give their eye teeth now for a set-up like that.'

They came out of a cool arched hallway, into the hot sunlight again. Macomber saw the menorah tree; they were back where they had started from.

'But my point is that the chip market now is where autos was just at the point when the Japanese were beginning to come up. There's where we've got to concentrate our business efforts, otherwise we're going to end up a second-rate power by the end of the 1990's.'

Findlan stopped in front of the tree, looked at it for some time just as he had when Macomber had first spotted him. 'Well,' he said in his slow drawl, 'I always knew the team you were putting together was strong enough, Del. I just wondered about the overall philosophy behind it. Now I have no doubts. None at all.'

He turned towards Macomber. 'I'll see you,' he said, 'come January one.'

Macomber nodded. 'Welcome to the *angka*, Marcus.'

For long stretches of time, Khieu wished to avoid buildings now. He was returning from lunch to his office at Pan Pacifica when, as he ascended in the elevator, he was quite certain a

488

bamboo pike, hardened and blackened on its pointed end, was being hurled downwards to split the top of his skull.

He had shivered like a great sigh amid the agglomeration of businessmen and women, had got off on the next floor and had walked down to the lobby, crossing quickly to the glass doors and out onto the street. Blindly, he crossed Madison Avenue, went west into Central Park.

In the heat of the day, children played near the watchful eyes of their mothers; ice cream vendors sold their wares.

Once, off to his right, hidden behind thick foliage, he heard odd, tinkling music and, moving towards it as if in a trance, he came upon a round structure within which painted wooden horses moved up and down as they circled to the music.

He stopped and stared, fascinated by a sight he had never before witnessed. Then he found himself digging in his pocket, paying his fare and climbing on a cream-coloured palomino with flying mane and a red-tongued open mouth.

The music started up and the world began to spin. He moved up and down astride the palomino, gripping the central pole that ran up into the ceiling with sweating hands, while the children with whom he rode watched him cry.

When at last his horse slowed and finally stopped, when the music faded into silence, the children all around him began to dismount or, as with the younger ones, were helped off.

Khieu stayed on, staring at the trees before him, hearing the sharp bird calls, the monkeys' chattering, insects' buzzing like beaten brass. Blood flowed along the ground, first winding serpentine through the underbrush, then gushing as if through a burst dam.

'Hey, Mister.'

A tugging at his leg, as if from far away.

'Mister?'

His head swung away from the trees dancing in the wind, downwards to a small face peering up at him. A child no more than six, his hair and eyes light. He was dressed in jeans and a tee shirt that said AC-DC on it, a musician in red and black holding an electric guitar like a machine-gun.

'You all right?' the child said. 'I saw you crying.'

489

'I'm all right,' Khieu said, holding on, still.

'I thought you might've lost your kid or something, the way you were so sad.'

Khieu smiled, shook his head.

'Bobby, you come away from there now.' A woman called from the sunshine, shading her eyes from the glare even though she wore dark glasses. 'I told you one ride and that's all. Now come on.'

The boy smiled at Khieu. 'I hope you stop crying,' he said. Then he had leaped from the edge of the revolving stage and was gone, a brilliant white mote in the glaze of afternoon light.

A fat man with a cigar stuck in the corner of his mouth was making the rounds of the horses, picking up litter. 'You staying on for another ride?' he wanted to know.

Khieu shook his head, climbed down at last and went away from there, wondering where the boy had gone to.

Sometime later, he found himself on Broadway, across the street from Lincoln Center. He could not imagine why he had come. He felt hungry or empty, he could not decide which. After a time, he was convinced it must be empty because the thought of food was entirely unappealing.

He stared across Broadway and the nexus of Amsterdam and Columbus Avenues which met each other at Sixty-fifth Street. Down a block, he began to see young men and women emerging from the entrance to one of the Lincoln Center buildings that was below street level.

They all had the same look to them but he could not quite make out what it was. They waited in a small group for the light to change, then crossed east, turned north towards him.

Then, as they came closer, he understood. They were dancers. Ballet dancers from Lauren's company. He took a deep, shuddering breath. Was that why he had come here? Was it to see Lauren? He did not know. But one way to find out was to leave now. He scanned the group coming towards him, saw that she was not among them.

He could not leave.

It was as if the soles of his feet had grown roots, anchoring him to this spot. The group of dancers went past, talking animatedly among themselves.

Now he could not stare directly at that underground entrance but could only look at its reflection in a store window.

That was the first time Malis appeared to him, dancing, a real-life, acephalous corpse, resurrected. Her bloody fingers weaved the story of her life since he had abandoned her. And those fingers accused him. Not in an angry way but gently, so gently that the tears flooded through him, running down his face, dropping one by one between his rooted feet.

He could have gone farther in Cambodia . . . should have gone all the way back to Phnom Penh. But he could not. After the slaughter in the jungle to the north, he could not bear to be within the borders of his home anymore. He had dropped the AK-47 and had fled back across the border into Thailand. He did not care anymore whether or not he had located this Tisah; even his duty to his father could not survive the horror he had discovered aboard the houseboat on the Mekong tributary.

He could not yet say what, but something was ascending within him, something cold and relentless gaining hold with each new breath he took. In his mind, thoughts seemed to shake themselves apart and fragment like an ice floe breaking apart in warmer water. Precisely what was happening to him he could not say.

Lauren.

He saw first her head, then her shoulders, then the rest of her emerging from the depths. She moved along the pavement with the liquid roll of the tide. Coming towards him.

He saw her hair shining, pulled back from her face like a polished helmet. He saw her eyes, their colour subtly like the earth rich and running with spilled blood, a hint of dark red, in their depth motes like splintered chips of stone. And in their depths he recognized the motivation for his being here and he sobbed out loud.

As he breathed, as he ate, as he slept though fitfully, he must destroy Lauren. Now that Louis Richter was gone, she alone could link him with the apartment; she alone could tell them Kim had been there; Kim the Vietnamese, and they would soon find out that it had not been Kim. Kim had been elsewhere at that time; she had not seen a Vietnamese at all but another kind of Oriental entirely: a Khmer.

She was the trail back through which Tracy Richter would come to him and, through him, to Macomber. The *angka*'s security would be breached. But Richter was being taken care of a half a world away in Hong Kong; he would not return to these shores.

But if he did?

Thus Lauren must die for without her eyewitness account there was no one, no one to link Khieu with Louis Richter's murder. The *angka* would be safe.

A wind was rising and a coldness he could not tolerate. Winter chilled his bones, congealed his blood. *Apsara* was coming like an avenging angel, a pristine virgin, dancing, dancing on the wings of an icy wind, coming down the street, through the pane of glass against which he stood.

He ran.

Tracy awoke to the creaking of timbers and the smell of stir-fried vegetables cooking. He turned his head and groaned. Gingerly, he put two fingertips up alongside his head, pushing through the thick hair to get at the scalp. He winced, the breath whistling out through his clenched teeth.

He tried to sit up, his stomach immediately beginning to turn over and he lay back down. But his own sodden stale smell assaulted him, drove him up again. He gripped a wooden post with both hands, pulled himself shakily to his feet. He leaned hard against the post, trying to breathe normally.

Then he fell, crashing into a pile of pots and pans.

'Shit!' he breathed, holding his head in his hands. If only it would stop pounding. He felt as if he had a triphammer going off inside it. As for the rest of him, he did not even want to take inventory. The boat rocked and his stomach rebelled. He willed the nausea down.

He heard sounds above and behind him, tried to turn while still on the deck. Pots and pans scattered again and he held his ears to shut out the din.

'Oh, God!' he groaned.

'Are you all right?' A soft voice in the Tanka dialect.

'Yes,' he answered automatically. 'No . . . I don't know.'

Strong hands gripped him, drew him gently to his feet. 'Over here,' the voice said, guiding him to the berth from which he had just arisen.

'Uh, no,' Tracy said. 'If you don't mind, I think I'd rather go above-decks.'

'I don't mind. If you can tolerate it, I'll help you get there.'

Tracy peered into the dim light, saw a wide flat face, seamed with a network of lines that appeared to have no beginning and no end. Wide-apart black eyes, a flat typically Chinese nose. It was a face that contained wisdom, friendliness, contentment.

'Where am I?' Tracy asked as the man guided him over to the stairs.

'On my junk,' the man said. 'We are anchored off Aberdeen. We picked you out of the water like a fish.' He laughed softly, almost a sigh. They began to climb the steps slowly. 'My little granddaughter wanted to know if we were going to eat you for dinner.'

'And what did you tell her?'

'I said, No, you had no fins, no tail, no scales. I showed her.' That sighing laugh again. 'She was disappointed.'

'I'll try to make it up to her,' Tracy said, feeling the wind ruffling his hair, then caressing his cheeks. He stopped, halfway out of the hatchway, taking deep breaths. He looked around, saw a great many faces staring at him from the deck.

'We are Tanka,' the old man said. 'There are many of us.'

And then Tracy remembered. Aberdeen Harbour was just one of a number of berths around the Colony where the Tanka, the boat people who fish for their subsistence, had their floating communities. They worked perhaps fifteen hours a day, beginning in the very early hours of morning, returning with – more often than not – just enough to keep the large family alive. They were the true indigenous people of Hong Kong. It was his luck that he had been pitched into water thick with their junks and sampans.

Half out of the hatch, Tracy held on to the thick oily canvas.

He saw at least twelve faces. The old man, who had introduced himself as Ping Po, went around the circle, introducing his family. Tracy bowed to all of them in turn as he came up fully on deck. All around, yellow lights like fireflies bobbed across the water, evidence of the surrounding floating city. Far away, it seemed, the distance no doubt increased by the night, he saw the green-tinged lights of Aberdeen itself.

He put his hand up to his head. 'How long have I been here?'

'Let me see,' Ping Po said, squinting into the darkness. 'The coming morning will bring two days. Yes,' he nodded to himself, 'that is correct, because yesterday we had an exceptional catch, double what we usually bring in.' He smiled. 'You have been lucky for us.'

He turned, picked up a small bundle onto his hip, wrapping it in his arms. 'And here is my little flower, Li, my grand-daughter.'

Tracy leaned towards her, saw her face, round and perfect and beautiful in the flickering lamplight. 'I am sorry you could not eat me,' he said. 'Will you forgive my bad manners?'

The little girl giggled, turning her head away from him and, clinging with tiny tight fists to her grandfather's cotton shirt, buried her face in the crook of his shoulder.

Tracy reached out, stroked her back gently. 'May I?' he inquired of Ping Po.

The old man nodded, delivering up the child to Tracy's embrace. Everyone else on the junk was still and silent, watching expectantly.

Tracy took Li, who gave up a tiny cry at being separated from her grandfather. But once in Tracy's arms, she put one finger in her mouth, her large eyes staring at him inquisitively.

'I have never seen anyone as beautiful as you,' Tracy whispered to her, taking her across the deck to the railing of the junk. Li was delighted, squirming in his arms to free one hand so she could point to the criss-crossing wakes of the man-powered sampans, pale and faintly phosphorescent.

She told him how her father went to work, how he fished, how she waited for him to come out and Tracy sighed, holding

494

her weight against him, feeling her small heart beat and some-how gaining strength from its passion and newness.

'You're nice,' Li said after a time. 'I'm glad we didn't eat you.' Tracy laughed and the child put her thin arms around his neck. As if that were a signal, the family sprang to life and, minutes later, they were all belowdecks, sitting crosslegged on mats with the matriarch, Ping Po's wife, serving them all.

Slivers of fish were interspersed throughout bowls of fresh vegetables stir-fried in sesame and hot chilli oils, and steaming rice. Tracy brought the bowl up to his face and, in true Chinese fashion, shovelled the food into his mouth with quick, economical flicks of his chopsticks. He smacked his lips loudly while he ate, belched gently at the end of the meal to let his hosts know he had appreciated the food. And indeed he judged it to be the best meal he'd ever had.

Afterwards, he went up on deck again, needing the salt breeze to cleanse him. He sensed movement behind him, had the good manners not to turn around.

'Thank you,' he said, 'most humbly for the food and the sanctuary.'

'You are safe,' Ping Po said, 'as long as you are with us. No one can know where you are.' He was silent for a moment, moving closer to the rail, looking out at the myriad bobbing lights. The stench of fish was strong in the air. But it was a clean smell, a natural smell. 'I saw you go into the bay. I unwound your bonds.'

Tracy understood what the old man was saying. 'I'll be all right now,' he said. 'No cause for concern.'

'You are our good luck charm,' the old man said diplo-matically. 'It would be unseemly, not to say ungracious, for us to abandon you so precipitously.'

Tracy smiled. 'I thank you again, Ping Po. But I must get back to the mainland. You cannot aid me in that.'

'On the contrary,' Ping Po said. 'We have transportation.' He tapped the junk's wooden rail. 'It is certainly safer for you to be with us than to fend for yourself on the island. I do not know what trouble you are in, nor do I wish to know. But you came to us like a gift from the sea. Because of you our larder is full. That bounty must be repaid.'

Tracy could have argued then. He could have told the old man that he did not wish to bring them into jeopardy; that he did not want them to lose a precious fishing day. But those were the actions of a Westerner. By doing that he could only offend this man and that he would not do. A repayment had been offered. It was his turn to be gracious; he must accept.

Antonio's apartment itself was not locked; the door had been ripped off its bolts by the police. The hallway stank of urine and rats. It was dark as death, the rain from the previous night infecting the rotting timbers like a termite's touch.

Now, returning to the scene, Thwaite felt a renewed strength flowing through him. He had been cleared of all charges in Antonio's death, given a clean bill with the department and, best of all, the enforced vacation Captain Flaherty had been threatening to hang around his neck had been rescinded. Thwaite thought he might have genuine cause to be thankful for that before the night was up.

His stomach was tight as a knot as he prowled the semi-darkness of Antonio's apartment. The thought of how the pimp had made a fool of him burned in his mind. Christ, Thwaite thought, a goddamned horse distributor! And I was helping him stay in business!

He berated himself for not being more careful; his venality stuck in his throat like a cracked bone. If 'Tonio had been there, Thwaite knew with a white-hot certainty, he'd kill him all over again ... and this time do it himself, not just stand by while ...

The thought of Tracy calmed him down and he took a minute to actively slow his pulse rate. This kind of emotionalism would do him no good now, he knew. He'd need all his wits about him if he were to uncover the whereabouts of 'Tonio's secret hoard.

He went to work, first in the two bedrooms then, afterwards, in the bathroom and the kitchen. Everything that was against a wall, he drew back, looking for false backs, testing the walls themselves with the butt end of his aluminium flashlight. He found nothing. And forty minutes later he found himself back where he had started, in the centre of the living room. He kicked disgustedly at the tatty rug, then stopped immediately.

... *Con los gusanos*. With the worms ...

The phrase 'Tonio had used came back to him like the sound of rolling thunder. The earthen pit he had used to punish his girls. Excited now he bent down, flicked the rug back, opened the trap door. Using his flashlight as guide, he lowered himself into the musty interior. It had, as he remembered, a packed earthen floor. The walls, which were brick, rose to a height just over his head.

He played the bright beam of light over first one brick face, then another. They all appeared to be the same, roughly constructed, bare, some patches of mould here and there, blackened areas as if heat had been brought to bear on them. Thwaite had a brief image of the pit as a torture room and he shuddered inwardly.

He turned once more, the flashlight's beam running over the third wall. Had he been standing on the floor of the apartment itself, he would be facing the front door. He took a step forward, peering more closely. His eye had picked up an abstract pattern, his brain giving it meaning: a rough rectangle.

His heart beat fast as he traced the outline, seeing here and there a very slight erosion at the edges of the bricks as if beaten by the weather: or the repeated scrape of nails as the bricks were taken out and put back again.

Within fifteen minutes he had unearthed a compartment thirty inches high by forty inches wide. It was impossible at this point to tell how deep it was.

He moved the beam slowly back and forth, cursed softly. It appeared as if 'Tonio was a good deal smarter than Thwaite had ever given him credit for. He was smart enough to kill your wife and child, a voice in his mind said vindictively. Shut up! he told himself. Just shut up about that and concentrate!

What the illumination showed him were stacks of clear plastic bags. He took one out, hefted it, judging it to be approximately a half-kilo in weight. He took out a pocket knife, made a neat incision in the plastic wrap, took up some of the white powder on the pad of his finger, tasted it.

Good Christ Almighty! he thought. This's the same high-grade uncut shit that we had analysed in Chicago. Quickly he put the marked bag aside, began to dig through the piles. They seemed to go on for a depth of more than three feet. He did a rapid calculation. He had counted fifty bags alone in the first tier. There looked to be at least twelve tiers. That made . . .

'Jesus Christ,' he breathed. At least three hundred kilos of the shit. When cut, that would be a flood. That made the late unlamented Antonio Mogales the largest wholesaler on the East Coast. It was no good thinking that if Thwaite had put him away – as he damn well should have long ago – another would've come to take his place. The fact is, Thwaite thought now, I helped him. He wanted police protection and I gave it to him. Jesus, but that makes me one of time's great fools.

The question was: What to do about it now? It was clear to him that whoever had killed Senator Burke might – make that a bit more definite – be involved in all this traffic. Maybe he was the importer and that of course meant he was very high up indeed. There was more to Burke's death, Thwaite was certain of it. The discovery of the senator's blackmail files proved it. But the clincher was the ground ashes they had found in his fireplace. He had had no foreknowledge of his imminent demise otherwise he would have activated a piece of his evidence in his files – that was one reason for the amassed secrets in the first place.

Therefore, Thwaite was now more certain than ever that Burke's murderer and not Burke himself had burned the incriminating evidence.

Yet he had overlooked one very vital piece: the heroin in the locker with 'Tonio's name and address on it. Because of how supremely careful Burke had been with it, Thwaite understood the level of its import. It had been his doomsday fallback. That it had done him no good in the end, chilled Thwaite. It said much about the nature of Burke's – and by extension – Thwaite's own adversaries.

Thwaite stared at the bags of white death and he felt a hideous kind of nausea overtaking him with the speed and force of an express train. The result of all his feverish labours over the last several days lay before him like the bleached skull of a child, revealed by his own clever police work. And this was what raced through him now, soaking him in acrid sweat: that he had helped 'Tonio stay in business — a business Thwaite had thought was a relatively harmless stable of whores — but which, at its core, was founded on this infinitely more lucrative trade.

God in heaven, he thought now, tears of rage and remorse running hotly down his face, if there is a God, cruel and uncaring. Oh no, no, no! I couldn't be a party to this! *I couldn't*! This kind of nightmare is just not possible!

He was shaking now so that he could barely stand, sinking down into this obscene treasure trove.

Then, abruptly, spasmodically, he was vomiting up the plasticized breakfast they had served him on the shuttle in from Chicago, spewing it all out onto the cache like a fountain of vitriol.

He had time to think while he was recovering as slowly the terrible emotions ebbed and flowed through him. He knew that in the morning he'd be downtown, getting his own unit together to handle this entire affair.

Of course Toad Tinelli, Narc's almost infamous Captain, could present a problem. No commander, least of all the Toad, liked poaching on his own preserve. And Thwaite was, after all, Homicide. Thwaite knew that Flaherty could be counted on only up to a certain point. The moment the Toad began to croak, he knew, Flaherty would run for cover.

That meant Thwaite would have to take care of it on his own. It was no good being up front with the Toad and he sighed, knowing what he would have to do to pull this group together. When in Rome, he thought sourly.

This shit was all he had to negotiate with but presenting that kind of bargain to the Toad was dangerous. He was sure to threaten Thwaite with dismissal from the Force. But Thwaite was used to threats and, further, he knew the Toad well. He knew that his weakness was his unending desire to make that next big score.

The lure of this load — an all time high even by the Toad's standards — would be too luscious for the Toad to ignore; he'd do anything to ensure its successful completion. He'd even given over partial control to Thwaite. He'd have no choice.

Satisfied, Thwaite stooped to return the slit plastic bag to its proper place. With the thing sagging limply in his hands, he stiffened, saw what he had failed to see before. It was stuck into one lower corner of the cache, between a bag and the inner wall.

He reached out a hand, picked it from its hiding place: a small roll of soft blotched paper, short lengths of bamboo at each end. It was bound in red ribbon.

He undid the ribbon, allowed gravity to unspool the paper partially. And saw that it was covered with the angular sticklike characters that were unmistakably Chinese.

He stared at the face of the paper for a long time, not even daring to breathe. He knew he was running away from it still. Just as his jumping on the first plane to Chicago had a meaning for him other than the strictly business one. It had put him away from New York, away from Melody.

He knew what he was looking at was Chinese, strictly because of Melody. He had leafed through some Chinese books on her shelves one day and, coming up behind him, she had begun to read softly in his ear as a mother does to her child drifting off to sleep, tracing the characters on the page with the tip of her finger so that he could follow her.

And he understood at last why he was sweating now. His plans had been abruptly changed by the discovery of this scroll. He could tell no one yet about what he had discovered, not until he knew what this paper contained. To take it to someone at the precinct could be a fatal mistake. What if the location of the shipment was contained within it or some other piece of vital information that might conceivably help him in his confrontation with the Toad? He could not take the chance. And that meant only one thing.

He'd have to go see Melody.

Khieu was praying but the well of his soul was empty; he could not connect with the Void. He felt betrayed but by whom he could not say. He beat his bare thighs with fists of iron, bringing bruises, he lit incense and a multitude of candles, praying to the *vinheanakhan* of his mother, who must protect him from harm. He foreswore meat as any good Buddhist should and promised her to abstain from any kind of sexual activity if only she could explain to him what was happening inside him.

At Pan Pacifica, he buried his mind in the mass of paperwork confronting him, the conglomerate misery of the constant flow of immigrants arriving from the eternal war in Cambodia. He listened to each of their separate tales of terror with the kind of supra-normal attention one often finds in dreams, able to grasp the repetitions of violence, burning and horror as if he were constructing a vast tapestry out of the cloth of their words.

It was as if their personal histories had come to affect him in a new and entirely different way. He saw the crimson of open wounds, the grey of smoke, the orange of fire, the yellow-white of pulsating disease. But most of all he felt engulfed by the black of deceit. The French had deceived the Khmer, the Communists had deceived the Khmer, the Americans had deceived the Khmer, the Vietnamese had deceived the Khmer and, finally, the Khmer had deceived themselves.

He had once thought that working at Pan Pacifica would bring him closer to his beloved land. Now he was aware that it had had the opposite effect. He felt distanced from Cambodia because he could no longer rationally put the war in its proper place. It had gone beyond devastation. That was awful enough. Now he saw it as a way of life.

He floated through the day as if he were the spirit and not his mother. He spoke to her, prayed to her silently but she did not answer. At home he prayed again but found no solace.

And he began to doubt the power of the Way. The concepts espoused by the Buddha seemed to become insubstantial before his eyes. Perhaps his father was correct. Reality had no place in it for religion. It was a refuge for people frightened of life. Isn't that how he had put it? For the first time, Khieu understood what his father meant and he was frightened by the knowledge.

But not nearly as frightened as he was of Lauren. She stalked his thoughts like a tigress. When he worked out, which was twice daily, his body would sheen with sweat, his muscles jumping responsively. And his loins would ache. An erection would form that was so hard, it was painful. Shamed, he would work all the harder and it would begin to tremble. His mind burned with images of Lauren and he would stare down at himself, seeing her with hair unbound, sweeping across one cool cheek, her eyes coating him with expressive emotion.

He would feel an extreme breath of pleasure ringing the tip of his erection. He would gasp and try to maintain his concentration on his movements but she would not leave him alone. It was as if she had reached out to gently enfold his penis. She would not let go, maintaining the pressure until he was in agony of desire.

Yet he would not touch himself nor visit any of the females with whom he had liaisons. It was as if she had bound him securely to her, as if she were his only release and, after a time, Khieu became convinced that whatever it was he felt for her — it could not merely be lust for all of his body and mind was involved — was his salvation.

And for the first time in his life he felt terrified of what he knew he had to do. As he became more and more obsessed with her, he suspected that by destroying Lauren, he would be taking his own life. For if a man must kill that which is his only salvation then surely he is doomed for all time.

Again Khieu was appalled by his lack of faith. If, as he had been taught from birth, his salvation lay along the Path of the Amida Buddha, then he had nothing at all to fear. That his faith had been eroded was clear now; America had altered him. And fear at the chaos of the unknown had crept in, infecting him. He trembled in impotent fury, keeping his hands away from his unassuaged penis. It would defile Lauren and himself if he came now.

And at last he made a decision to see for himself. To touch her now, to be near her once again would be enough to know whether what he felt for her was real and whether he could bring himself to kill her.

Lauren spent the first twenty minutes in the cab out to Kennedy Airport oblivious to the world outside. She felt as if being at the top of her form — being back, more or less, where she had been before hurting her hip — was not enough.

There was great excitement of course at the renewed strength she felt flowing through her like a powerful current when she peeled off her leg-warmers and spun away from the *barre*. The feeling that had plagued her at first – that at the first hard contact of a particularly difficult jump her leg would betray her and she would be injured all over again – had passed and now, in many ways, she felt stronger than ever.

She had always thought that that would have been enough to fill her up and, until now, it had. It was not that she no longer loved dancing; she could not imagine a time when that would happen. But she was beginning to recognize that dancing could not be her entire life anymore. When you are nineteen, the fire dancing ballet built inside you was so all-consuming, it was easy not to think of anything else.

Like a thoroughbred, she had been trained for one thing – with the exclusion of all else. But Tracy had changed all that. It occurred to Lauren now that there was more to life than dancing. She stared sightlessly out the window of the speeding taxi and wondered what it was Tracy was doing in Hong Kong.

The truth of the matter was she wanted to be there with him. She wished desperately now that she had not brought up the subject of her brother's death with him. What had been the point? It was long gone now and nothing Tracy could say would bring Bobby back.

She concentrated, conjuring up Tracy's face again, the glint of the sun like spun gold off the wave tops behind him. A light salt breeze had feathered his hair, bright light throwing his face into prominence, showing her the hurt there. She understood now the burden of guilt he carried around with him. Certainly he felt that Bobby's death had been his fault, something that she had accused him of.

Stupid. He had told her the whole story but she had not been listening, hearing instead Bobby's call of pain. Only later when she had recognized the bitter taste of cold ashes in her mouth, felt as the source of it the pain of emptiness inside her, that she remembered what he had said.

That was why she had gone to Louis Richter's. If she could not be close to Tracy then being with his father made her feel better. Briefly then the cloud that was Kim passed like a cold shade through her thoughts. A beautiful man, on the outside. But the brief glimpse she had got into those eyes had frightened her inexplicably. Thinking of him now made her shiver.

That was a soul in torment, she thought, not really understanding why. And abruptly she felt sorry for him. Such a burden of agony should not be borne by any one person. What alien torture must he have suffered to have obtained those eyes? She could not imagine. But just the thought of it drove all fear of him away. She wanted to wrap her arms around him, crooning, rock him to a safe, deep sleep.

The airport was crowded with members of the company and attendant personnel. There was still an hour before they could board and nothing to do but talk with other dancers. It bored her and, inexplicably, she found herself looking around the departure lounge as if she suspected she would see someone she knew.

This peculiar feeling grew until she became nervous with its weight. She scanned the clouds of people passing by with their hand luggage, pausing to buy paperback books or a newspaper to help pass the time.

Her earlier feeling of fear returned and at last she was forced away from her friends, their confines too restricting. She walked to the news-stand, searching the racks for something thick she could read to fill up the long flight hours. She chose a recent Robert Ludlum novel, reading the last page as she stood in line waiting to pay for it. She could not bear to be surprised, wanting instead to feel safe within the structure of the prose. She paid for the book, returned to the area of the company.

Not long after, their flight was called and, forming a single line, their boarding passes extended, they trouped onto the 747 SP.

Khieu took a deep breath, exhaled it slowly. He felt like a condemned criminal who had been given a last-minute reprieve. His hands were trembling from the force of emotion coursing through him.

He stood now in one corner of the crowded news-stand where

504

he had been for the last several minutes and stared at the empty departure lounge. Well, it was done now. She was gone. Perhaps she would never know how close she had come to death.

At the moment she had joined the line to pay for her book, Khieu had slipped in behind her. He wore an unlined and therefore lightweight Burberry trenchcoat in regulation tan. Perhaps hundreds of people in the terminal were similarly dressed. Hands in the enormous pockets that were open at the top of the inside, he had thought of a half-a-dozen ways in which to terminate Lauren without the slightest attention being drawn to him. He felt the warmth of elation he had once experienced after his first beheading as a Khmer Rouge. Like the gilt on his wooden Buddha, the civilized veneer had been scoured away by one atavistic act; he – all of them in the Khmer Rouge – had slipped back in time thousands of years.

'In this, we cut ourselves off from the bonds of our past,' they had chanted as their brown arms had lifted, a second shining stand of trees, bending swiftly in the gust of wind coming from inside themselves, their butchers' blades falling like scythes against the vulnerable backs of their enemies' necks.

Enemies.

They had been priests, teachers, artists: the free thinkers of Cambodge. Not *Kampuchea*. But the old, the French, the colonial Cambodge.

Away, away, away.

How the black birds had lifted from their perches in the treetops at the quick, silver movement in concert, the bright crimson spurting of blood. Enemies' blood. The earth muddy with it as the stakes went up and the heads jammed atop their pointed ends like a line of modern lights along the jungle road as a reminder for all those who passed of the power of *Angka*, the inexorability of Cambodia's future.

Death and its implementation. He ran through the list again, part of him still reeling beneath the force of his memories. It would be so easy to do; he knew that he *must* do it. For the sake of his father, for the sake of the *angka*, everything they had both worked for for fourteen years.

Accordingly, he chose the correct method, moving towards her as smoke drifts through a summer's day. Unnoticed.

He was in position, he meant to do it. His brain sent the proper messages, the synapses moving in galvanic response. All his senses were directed at the soft nape of her neck, exposed above her clothing. Her hair was swept up, pulled tight at the top of her head. All he needed was one square millimetre, exposed. He had that. It was about to happen.

Malis Malis Malis!

The shrieking inside his head battered him like the swift and awful descent of a fighter chopper. He gasped and almost stumbled against her. Only his lightning-like reflexes prevented this.

But he must terminate her. He must! What was he thinking about? Why was he hesitating. Do it! he screamed silently at himself. *Do it!*

But he could not; something inside him would not allow it. The ramifications stunned him, making him feel nauseated and weak and he backed off, never taking his eyes from the back of her neck.

And then he knew with an absolute certainty the reason why he could not do it. The moment he reached his hand out across the gulf of space that separated them, the connection would be made: he would be touching Malis!

And even as this terrifying revelation washed over him, he saw *apsara*, celestial in the awesome precision of her dance, separate herself from the corpus of Lauren, turning as she did so, her fingers undulating like serpents, aimed at him. She stepped towards him as her twin, Lauren, began to move away in the opposite direction.

Softly, seductively, she came towards him, making him remember his Buddhist vows of celibacy. She writhed in front of him and now her motions were overtly erotic, her hips rocking, the muscles along her inner thighs rippling as if in anticipation.

And despite himself Khieu experienced the old familiar tightening in his groin. Was there ever a time he could resist Malis? His penis began to swell and at that moment, he felt a shivering of the air as of some element unseen and when he looked at Malis again she was headless, bloodless, her limbs blue-white and bloated, mud from the river's bottom left behind her like a slug's glistening trail of slime.

Vinheanakhan. Her spirit pursued him.

Even at night the humidity was appalling. Tracy awoke out of the kind of deep, almost drugged sleep one experiences at the very end of endurance. He climbed to his feet. The extended battle in the hospital had taken more out of him than it should have.

I'm out of shape, he thought angrily. Or the blast was still having its effect on him. Either way, he did not like it. He shrugged his shoulders. Joss. It was what they would have said here in this teeming city. Fate without quite being the Western term; or *karma*, as the Japanese would put it. There is no controlling it, so better put your mind on something useful, he told himself as he stooped, walking past a couple of the daughters, huddled together on a reed berth. He went up the companionway.

The running lights were on but that was all. Pinpoints of yellow, red and green surrounded him, piercing the shroud of night and it seemed to Tracy that they rode the back of the many-eyed great dragon which, according to ancient *feng shui*, guarded all of Hong Kong.

Along the rail, getting his bearings, he saw they were just rolling past Round Island, then changing course at Wong Ma Kok, the most southerly projection of Hong Kong Island, tacking into the wind, now heading northeast. In a little while he was able to make out Lo Chau off the starboard side. Up ahead, he knew, was Cape D'Aguilar, where they would change course again, due north into Tahong Channel. He'd know that point because he'd be able to see Bigwave Bay on the port side and the great black bulk of Tung Lung Island.

The wind did nothing to dispel the humidity and Tracy settled down against the gunwale of the junk, listening to the steady, comforting creak of the fittings, the soft, concealing night with its jewel-like pinspots of lights floating by him. The slow swells rocked the junk and, dimly, he could make out the churning of the water.

And slowly the night began to permeate his mind, cutting through the barrier of time, sending him tumbling backwards into the pit of his memories. He was recalling with vivid clarity the first mission he had gone on in Cambodia. He had just arrived, fresh from his graduation from the Mines.

Now you know a thousand different ways to kill, Jinsoku had told him before he had left Virginia's rolling verdant hills. *But you have not yet killed. Be forewarned. Remember all I have taught you and kill without thought.*

That first mission might have been the toughest: only Tracy had been left to make the final approach to the objective: a Khmer Rouge cadre leader. The three other men in his unit had been killed on the way in: Twilley had stepped on a land mine, Dicks had taken a poisoned bamboo stake in the groin, Timothy had bought it in the outset of the final run, carbine fire stitching itself across his barrel chest with indecent finality.

By that time there had been only Tracy and the objective left alive within that area of the jungle. They had come together like two animals, instinctively aware of the fight to the death.

There had been little problem. At hand-to-hand the Khmer Rouge was no match for Tracy and he had gone down beneath Tracy's first powerful onslaught. Jinsoku – one master of death – had been forced out along Tracy's working muscles, his training to the forefront and at last the lethal blow was on its way.

But in that split second, Tracy thought about what he was doing, thought about the taking of life, the snuffing of that divine spark that only God or, at least, nature could create. In the space of the blink of an eye, he was taking it away.

In that moment, his mind turned not towards politics or philosophies or differing rhetorics but to the sheer *humanity* of the situation. Thus, he hesitated.

And almost died.

The objective seized upon that instant when all motion ceased, turning the inertia around, reversing the momentum, rising up like a spirit from the grave, a spectral whirlwind clothed in the blackness of the night. He was very quick, even more so now because he was mortally frightened and was ready to do anything to save himself.

He did what he had to do and he hurt Tracy badly, taking him to the point of death. Then Tracy's own shock was replaced by an accurate assessment of the mortal moment about to encompass him and he reached out blindly, without thinking, allowing the organism to work on its own, to save itself.

On the brink of death, he used what Jinsoku had taught him, jamming the heavily calloused heel of his hand into the point of the objective's nose with an awesome amount of force.

The other's head snapped back with Tracy's vicious follow-through, the eyes rolling back in the head, rolling with fear at the screamed *kiai* so close upon him. Then they clouded over as the nose cartilage broke free of its ligamental moorings, a lethal missile penetrating the soft grey matter of the brain.

For some time after that Tracy did nothing. The weight of the objective slumped upon him was heavy, numbing. Then with a grunt of pain, he threw the corpse off him, staggered to his feet.

It had dawned on him then just what he had done: the process and, just as important, the feelings that went along with it. The enormous intensity of those feelings had rocked him; the power that flowed through him in that moment . . . he felt as if he could power a city with the energy rolling through him like waves, thunderclaps, sheaves of sparks glittering the night.

He knew this feeling set him apart from all the rest of the people around him. And because of it he knew he would not die here: he had entered into the ultimate phase of the training Jinsoku had so painstakingly taken him through. Now he was wedded to it, one with it. For good or ill, this was the whole of his being now and, as he had turned away from his first corpse that dense humid night, he had known that life as he had come to know it would never again be the same.

He looked up now in the huge darkness, saw Bigwave Bay and Tung Lung. It would not be long now. He stared into the northeast searching the night for High Junk Peak. Too soon yet, he knew. Yet his eyes continued to pierce the night, searching for the first signs of it.

He went across the deck, suddenly chill, despite the heat and humidity. He saw a dark shape, small in the lee of the black curl of the aft hawser. Li. At first he thought she was asleep but as he approached he saw her eyes opened, watching him.

He sat down beside her, his back against the hull and said in dialect, 'What's the matter, Little Sister, can't you sleep?'

She stared at him, shook her head back and forth.

He reached out for her and she climbed into his lap. He enfolded her, needing her warmth as much as she needed his. He kissed the side of her head and she sighed, falling immediately to sleep. Then Tracy, too, dozed for a time.

He was awoken by a voice calling softly near him. He opened his eyes without moving a muscle. Li lay curled in his arms, one small hand grasping his elbow in sleep.

Ping Po's face watched him from out of the darkness. 'You've slept well, Younger Brother.' He nodded. 'You bring peace to my little one.'

Tracy was alert now, looking closely at the other. He knew Ping Po had not awakened him to idly pass the time of day.

'I feel much refreshed,' was all he said.

Ping Po's head dipped. 'Good.' He looked up. 'A still night. Very still. We wager on the moment the new day's wind will arise.' He looked cannily at Tracy. 'Have you a good bet?'

'In half-an-hour,' said Tracy immediately without consulting his watch. He knew a quick response was what was required of him. The Chinese lust for gambling was all but insatiable; they'd bet on anything that moved, spoke, lifted or fell. Any hesitation would have marked him as a true *quai loh*, the foreign devil the civilized Chinese felt all Westerners to be.

'Yaaa!' Ping Po breathed softly. His eyes opened wide. 'That will be late. Very late.' His head bobbed. 'One hundred HK.'

'All right.'

Ping Po smiled, his hands rubbed together. 'Yes. Soon we will see.' He spat deftly over the side of his junk. His eyes were half-lidded, the running lights reflected off the curve of the

510

whites, turning the pupils black. 'Until then, perhaps you should know Mizo has many names.'

Now it was Tracy's turn to be surprised and, for face, he allowed it to show only in his eyes: that would make Ping Po happy and he would not lose face. 'Yaaa! How could you know such a thing?'

'I am but a poor fisherman,' Ping Po said, meaning none of it. 'But am I a blind, dead and dumb son of a sea snake as well? If I did not know things I would be ignorant of the tides and the times best suited for running the fish into this unworthy junk. I would not be able to provide for my prodigious family.'

'That kind of knowledge is not the same,' Tracy said. 'It could be dangerous.'

'Aaaa! Do you not think manoeuvring this junk through the byways of Hong Kong is not dangerous? Pah!' He spat over the side again. 'I believe in only two things: gambling and that all banks must fail. They are *quai loh* inventions and therefore not to be trusted. But gold, ah, gold is a friend that cannot fail. Don't you agree.'

'Indeed.'

'Then listen well, my friend, for as I have already said this Mizo, this slippery mother's turd of a Japanese, is known by many names. Sun Ma Sun. White Powder Sun for one business he is in, Backblast Sun, for the other.' Ping Po squinted at him. 'Do you understand all of this?'

'Yes.'

The old man nodded. 'Good. Perhaps it will help.' He yawned and stretched, pointing over Tracy's shoulder. 'High Junk.'

Tracy turned carefully to avoid waking Li, saw the thin string of lights along Cape Collinson and, further away and slightly to the northeast, High Junk Peak, its dark bulk rearing up over eleven hundred feet into the air and rejoiced. High Junk Peak was on the mainland. They were almost there.

Now the junk headed northwest into the Lei Yue-Mun Channel. Directly ahead Tracy saw the blue-violet and deep yellow runway lights at Kai Tak Airport extending out into the water like a long pointing finger.

Their destination was the Kwun Tong district of New Kowloon. It was as close as Ping Po dared take the junk without attracting the attention of the harbour police. Any further in towards Tsim Sha Tsui and their passage would begin to intersect the well-travelled ferry and pleasure boat routes.

Dawn was coming, tingeing the east with pink mother-of-pearl along the undersides of the low-lying clouds. Perhaps today it will rain, Tracy thought, and ease the water shortage.

Across Victoria Harbour, the clusters of high-rise spires on the forefront of the north side of the island were being gilded by the rising sun, the myriad windowpanes being set on fire, burning their way down floor by floor as more of the sun's bulk crept above the horizon. The hard shell of the sky was wholly pink for a time, the first flat rays of the new day turning the water ahead of them to spangled gold, the troughs dark and mysterious with the last vestiges of the dying night.

Up until a moment ago, Violet Hill and Mt Cameron had hidden most of the layered man-made structures of Wanchai and beyond the massed Central District. Then, abruptly, they had been revealed, almost all at once as the junk breasted the point.

Tracy was thinking furiously about what Ping Po had said. The Chinese had many names, ones they picked up during their lifetime, not just the one they were given at birth. These later names were dictated by personal quirks or disfigurements . . . or by what they did. Backblast Sun obviously referred to Mizo's school of miniature explosive and listening devices. But White Powder Sun? In Hong Kong parlance that could only mean one thing: narcotics smuggling. If that were so, Tracy knew he might be in far worse trouble than he had imagined.

Narcotics, and gold smuggling out of Macao were such lucrative businesses in Hong Kong that one needed assurances that one would be left alone to pursue these fortunes unmolested. That meant greasing many palms, most notably within the tong-riddled police force. Here, as almost anywhere else in the world, the police were as honest or as corrupt as you could want.

Tracy now believed that if he went to the police and told the truth the chances of his being detained were excellent. Someone, somewhere along the line of authority, would surely be in Mizo's employ.

Li was stirring within his arms, stretching. He put her gently on the deck. They were near land now, just a few yards and he would be on his own again. He felt a savage pang in his chest at the thought of leaving his new-found family. They had saved his life, fed him and, most importantly, accepted him. He did not leave them lightly.

Ping Po stood up, lifted his head. 'Wind's still not here.'

Tracy glanced at his watch, shrugged, produced one hundred HK, handed the bill over. 'Joss, eh?'

Ping Po laughed. 'Yes. Joss.'

The younger members of the Ping family were steering the junk towards the pilings. Ping Po's Number Three Son jumped onto the dock with the hawser, hauled in on it. There was no one about. The side of the junk scraped against the old wood and slashed tyres hanging against the side, rocking in the swell.

'*Kung Hei Fat Choy,*' he said.

'*Kung Hei Fat Choy,*' the old man answered, smiling.

Tracy was about to step off the junk. He turned back, saw Li awake, sitting on her haunches, staring at him, her dark eyes huge. He thought at that moment that he had never seen such a pure and innocent human being. He reached into his pocket, took out a roll of HK dollars. He folded them carefully, put them in to her small fist. He leaned towards her, kissed her forehead. 'A gift from the sea,' he whispered. 'From the fish who got away.'

She giggled up at him and the family around her sighed.

'Fresh Wind Po,' Tracy said and the old man nodded, delighted.

'Another one,' he said. 'Yes. I think I will use that name when the time is ripe. Oh yes I will.'

Tracy went off the rocking junk, nodded to Number Three Son, saw him leap back onto the deck, hawser in hand. The junk immediately began to back away from the pilings, manoeuvring around the way it had come, heading southeast towards the channel and Aberdeen. Home.

He watched it out of sight. He could not bring himself to move until they had disappeared into the growing haze. Then he turned, walking rapidly off the quay.

There were still few people about and he quickened his pace. His mind was ticking over furiously. There was only one place within the Colony where Mizo's people could hope to pick him up again. The hotel. It was the one place left in the city that was a strict red sector and therefore should be avoided at all costs.

The hotel was where he headed now, taking a No. 11 bus, crimson with the posted admonition FIGHT CRIME emblazoned across it side down through the crushing jumble of a Kowloon morning. The doubledecker careered around corners, its metal frame shivering. He transferred twice before it got too crowded, checking and checking again, even though he was certain no one was following him.

Mizo had foxed him once, using a far larger team than Tracy had imagined. How many people did Mizo own? Tracy had no way of knowing but if the Japanese was truly White Powder Sun then he must have many. It would take only one of them cruising the packed, coruscating streets of Kowloon to identify Tracy and tag him.

On the third bus, he put his head back against the cool metal wall, watching the riot of colour and jostling movement drift past him like artificial clouds. The buzz and jabber of dialects: Cantonese, Shanghaiese, Chiu Chow, Yunnan, even Hakka washed over him like rough surf, the controlled cursing that was such an integral part of the language when Chinese spoke to Chinese, a constant stream of inventive invective.

As in all of Asia, eventually time ceased to exist, light melting into dark, sun into moon, Ying into Yang.

He got off the bus five blocks from the Princess, and insinuated himself into the throngs of people, adopting the rather rapid, short-strided walk of the Chinese.

Still, when he caught his first sight of the hotel's beautiful Colonial white stone façade his scalp began to itch. He gritted his teeth and got on with it because this was his only hope and if they already had a long gun waiting for him here there was precious little he could do about it but, oh, Christ, he could almost hear the brief whine of the bullet's speeding passage, the brilliant flare of pain as it embedded itself in his brain, the last of life flickering by like a chaotically unspooling film.

Christ sake, he berated himself, get a grip on yourself! Time was running out. The thought of going to ground for another twenty-four hours was inviting indeed until he began to grapple with the reality of the police.

They would have crawled all over Queen Elizabeth Hospital long ago, raising an unholy stink. The Hong Kong Police Department was quite fussy about blood and corpses strewn all over their bailiwick and Tracy did not blame them one bit. It was bad enough that Mizo wanted him dead; to have the police on his tail, too, within this compact warren was just too much to overcome indefinitely. He was *quai loh*, after all. If he had been Chinese, it would be a different matter entirely. Over ninety per cent of the population here would be with him.

Across the street, in front of the Princess's great front portico with its enormous white stone Foo Dogs flanking the glass-doored entrance, three black Rolls stood poised and purring.

As Tracy watched from the shadows of the newly-built Space Museum doorway, a tall Caucasian in tropical business suit ushered his female companion through the glass doors opened for them by young liveried Chinese boys. The driver of the leading Rolls opened the kerbside car door as the couple emerged, ducking their heads at the bottom of the stairs as first the woman, then the man climbed into the car. It drove off in a throaty roar.

Tracy waited. There was plenty of activity in and out of the hotel even at this fairly early hour: the Princess's second floor dining room was a favoured place for Chinese and Westerner alike to talk business over breakfast.

No one emerged to claim the other two Rolls. At night, that might not be so odd but this time of the day it was. One of the hotel's liveried attendants came down the front steps; he was quite a bit older than the boys manning the doors themselves and he moved with a great deal of assurance.

The man began to talk to one of the remaining drivers. Soon the chauffeur of the second Rolls had sauntered over, a Chinese in sunglasses. There ensued a heated discussion during which the hotel employee emphatically pointed towards the front entrance again and again. The first chauffeur shook his head and, when the other began to gesture a call of help, the driver extracted a roll of bills from his hip pocket, peeled off several for the other to see.

The gesticulations ceased immediately, calm was restored as the money changed hands. The hotel employee nodded once, curtly. He had lost interest in the two drivers.

Tracy moved with the crowds around the hotel to the rear, entering through the kitchen. He thought about what he had seen. No ordinary drivers, those, otherwise there would have been no need for the argument followed by a sliding of the fragrant grease; all of that would have been prearranged in a weekly amount. They were not waiting for patrons, might not in fact be chauffeurs at all. It certainly had the look of one of Mizo's setups. It was very smooth. Tracy was beginning to know his adversary. Who would suspect limo drivers waiting outside Hong Kong's best hotel? They were part of the background scenery, as invisible as the potted palms in the lobby because one *expected* their presence.

Threading his way through the crowded din of the kitchen, he chose a bellboy to his specifications: young with quick, enterprising eyes, handsome. The kind of man who would understand the meaning of five hundred HK and who, more importantly, would respond to Tracy's story about wanting to ditch his current girlfriend in order to slip away with a Chinese girl he had met aboard *Jumbo*, the largest of the gaudy floating restaurants in Aberdeen harbour.

The young man caught Tracy's air of conspiracy at once and, guided by Tracy's explicit instructions and his folding money, grinned hugely, hurrying to comply. And within ten minutes he had returned with everything Tracy had requested: a change of clothes including a jacket and his case of 'shaving and grooming' gear.

'Some girl,' the bellboy said in Cantonese, grinning as he handed Tracy all the items. 'Aaaa! Is her slit horizontal instead of vertical? Is her appetite insatiable? I ask these questions, sir, because it seems to me that it would take quite a female individual – such as you have told me you have met – to create the uproar both in and out of the hotel she seems to have kicked up.'

Of course he would say no more until – usurious entrepreneur that his father had taught him to be – he had extracted another five hundred HK from Tracy. Then he told Tracy that the management of the hotel had moved all of Tracy's belongings to another room to await his return. 'The police are not so certain of your reappearance,' the bellboy said. 'They have only two officers here and both are horse turds. They scratch themselves like monkeys and think their commanding officer a fool for assigning them to this post.' Apparently the police had not seen fit to impound his clothes. Yet.

Tracy thanked the bellboy, took his gear into the men's toilet where he washed, shaved and donned his new clothes. He checked the case to make certain nothing had been tampered with then stuffed his old smelly clothes in one of the trash cans in the kitchen. His wallet and passport, with him the whole time, were nestled safe in his jacket's inner pocket.

He stole out the way he had come. Along Nathan Road, Tsim Sha Tsui's major thoroughfare, he stopped beneath one of the brilliantly coloured signs, neon at night, so huge they overhung the entire width of the sidewalk, turned into the *White Peony*.

He asked for a table against one wall, took the chair that faced the restaurant's door. The place was enormous, filled in its centre by round tables seating twelve or long ones seating more. The room was brightly lit not only by the six hundred separate bulbs set in the balcony's overhang but by a central chandelier as large as any of the circular tables beneath it.

Tracy dined on *tsung-yu ping*, onion cakes fried in oil and *Chengtu paichieh jou*, thinly sliced pork strips inundated with chillies, vinegar, garlic and the inevitable soy sauce and immediately he tasted the food he was certain he had lucked into a restaurant with a *Ta Shih Fu*, one of the Great Master chefs of Hong Kong.

Movement at the rear of the room, caught his eye. His heart

began to pound in his chest. It was the chauffeur he had seen handing over the money in front of the Princess.

Tracy turned his head slightly, made out the form of a Mongol on the move towards him. It was a pincer movement and he cursed out loud.

There would be no bloodshed here, no guns visibly drawn, certainly no shooting. The men would merely converge on Tracy's table. One would no doubt sit down in the empty chair opposite and using the cover of the table draw his pistol in order to induce Tracy to leave the restaurant with them.

There was little time. They were halfway to the table, threading their way through the narrow aisles, having to stop now and then for waiters, shouting and gesticulating, with laden trays. They were intent now, closing in.

Tracy flagged down his waiter. The old Chinese, obviously harried and overworked in the throng, was necessarily abrupt.

'This is outrageous,' Tracy said in Cantonese. He gestured at the food. 'This stuff's not worth feeding to the hogs.'

'I beg your pardon, sir?'

'This *food*,' Tracy said menacingly. The Mongol was in the lead. He had been forced to take the long way around a round table of celebrating Chinese but he was very close. 'What d'you take me for, a *tourist*?' Tracy deliberately used a disrespectful inflection and the waiter winced.

'Sir, there must be some mistake. You cannot mean —'

'Mistake!' Tracy howled. He leapt to his feet. 'There's no mistake! This food's slop! I demand to see the manager!'

'Sir, this food is among the finest in all Hong Kong.'

'I won't pay a penny, I tell you!' Tracy saw his time had run out. The Mongol was two tables away, the chauffeur not far behind.

'You have no manners, sir!' The waiter had raised his voice now, offended more by the inflection Tracy used in his speech than by what he actually said. His cheeks were flushed. You could get away with a lot in Chinese if you know how to say it.

Tracy leaned forward, summoning up all the anger he felt at Mizo and his plight here, bellowed, *'Wu ku pu fen!'*

The waiter recoiled as if he had been physically struck. He flailed out, cursing. Tracy had delivered to him one of the worst insults one can hand a Chinese. 'You can't distinguish the five grains!' Wheat, rice, sesame, barley and beans. These were the staples of any Chinese's life. To tell him that he cannot tell one from the other was to mortally offend the man.

And under cover of the screaming, lunging scuffle, Tracy got out. Amid the tables jammed with rising customers, straining to see what all the commotion was about, the waiters converging on the spot, the managers hurrying from their posts near the raised entranceway, Tracy slid, veering and skidding in an attempt to lose himself in the throng.

The floor of the restaurant was now flooded with people, all moving and shouting at once. The aisles lost their boundaries, and chairs, pushed backwards by curious patrons as they stood, created a jigsaw puzzle of extreme complexity.

Out the front door he flew, turning right on instinct, then right again to get away from the bright glow of the main street that would point him out to his pursuers. He was on Cornwall Avenue, a narrow street jammed with mean storefronts topped by dark apartments on the upper floors. Above, the sky was blotted out by the criss-crossing lines of wash hung out to dry. He pounded down the street, came out onto Mody Road. To his right, he knew, was the Holiday Inn, to his left Hanoi Road was coming up – no place for *quai loh* to hide. Ahead he saw the crossing of Chatham Road and, beyond, the railway station and he thought, I've had enough of this. It's time to see Golden Dragon, the *feng shui* man.

Macomber was peering into the flickering lambent-green heart of FIRST when Khieu walked into his second-floor study on Gramercy Park South. Macomber did not hear his son's approach at first, primarily because part of his mind was on the current printout displayed on the computer monitor, the auxiliary of the main terminal in his office at Metronics, Inc. Another part was halfway across the world, thinking of the Monk and his promise to find Tisah, to bring her back to Macomber. He itched to pick up the phone and call the prearranged business drop number the Monk had given him at the outset of their dealings; he longed to dash off a telex under their mutual code name: OPAL FIRE, but of course he could not. Where the hell is she, you bastard! his mind raged silently. What's taking you so long?

Briefly, he felt again the chill press of the despair he had first experienced when Khieu had returned from Cambodia, without her. Then a tiny sound from behind made him whirl around and, seeing Khieu standing there, he immediately depressed a stud along the console that wiped the printout off the monitor.

FIRST was another of his in-house acronyms. It meant Flexible Information and Retrieval System and it referred to the vast Metronics computer linkup. That Macomber and Khieu referred to it only as the system was a measure of its incompleteness. Until the laser-activated circuitry that powered LITLIS was fully tested and modified into the system, Macomber had vowed not to use the full acronym.

'Don't just stand there, Khieu,' he said, standing up and stretching, 'come on in.' He made the windows in two strides. He looked out, saw a slice of the park. 'I was just checking the system for last-minute changes against the event-horizon on the Thirty-first.'

'That's three days from now,' Khieu said calmly. 'How did your meeting with Findlan go?'

'Ah, yes, Findlan,' Macomber said, turning. He was desperately thinking of a way to introduce Cambodia into their discussion. What in Christ's name, he thought, happened to him over there? 'Findlan presents no real problem.' He was looking covertly at Khieu. 'However, that may change. He's an ambitious man, our Marcus Findlan, and very clever to boot. I think there will come a time when he won't be satisfied with the throne on which he currently sits.'

'Where would he go next?' There seemed very little animation from Khieu and Macomber's senses quested for emanations.

'Where else?' he said. 'He will seek Gottschalk's position.'

'Would that be so bad?' Khieu sat on a cane-backed chair.

'I think yes,' Macomber said seriously, 'and the system backs me up. It's in Findlan's past history. He's a violent man by nature. Men like him can only go so long before giving in to what has become so natural for them.' He regarded the other levelly. 'We both understand the inevitability of such urges, Khieu, do we not?'

'*Oui*,' Khieu said, shuddering.

Macomber was taken aback. 'Are you all right? Since you returned from Cambodia I've . . . become concerned with your health. Perhaps you picked up some kind of bug there.'

Yes, Khieu thought, but not in the way you mean. 'I'm fine, Father,' he said softly. 'My sleep has been . . . erratic of late.'

Macomber's concern deepened. 'Have they come back again? The nightmares?' He recalled the nightmares Khieu was prone to getting early on after he had been taken back to the States. Macomber had taken him to the doctor who, after an intensive examination, had reported nothing physically amiss. He had prescribed rest and relaxation. After that the nightmares had slowly faded away.

Khieu smiled. What would his father think if he knew that they had never really gone away, he wondered. 'No, of course not. It's just . . . the jet lag. It . . . it was hard going back.' Khieu had not meant to let that last come out.

'Harder than you had imagined?' Macomber asked, probing.

But Khieu had a tight rein now. 'I hadn't thought about it one way or another.' With an effort, he kept his voice level. 'It's not my home anymore, after all. They're all dead . . . my family.'

His voice drifted off and Macomber dived into the breach. 'All that slaughter. I knew in '69 that it was already over for us. The way we went in . . . the way we went about it . . . was all wrong. And now there's still war.' There was no response from Khieu and he thought, I can't push it.

'I think I've judged the mood of the country correctly. They're still wary of the Republicans after Reagan but there's no real confidence in this Democratic administration. Not after what happened in West Germany and Egypt.' He watched the lamplight play off his son's beautiful dark features making him look like a sculpture in a museum. 'Still they need to be convinced and, as should be expected after Sullivan's subcommittee gets through reaming out State, they'll be fed up with words. I think Gottschalk's gone as far as he can go with the normal amount of fat-frying we've been providing him with. He's got the nomination but now what, eh? This's far too big to pin our hopes on probabilities.

'No,' he said easily, 'the day after tomorrow we'll hand Atherton Gottschalk the presidency, won't we, Khieu?'

Khieu stood up. It was a long time before he spoke. He had turned so that from his vantage point across the room Macomber could not see into his eyes. 'Indeed,' Khieu said finally, 'we will.' He ran long fingers through his thick black hair. 'Do you need me now, Father?'

'No, I don't think so.' Even now Macomber was straining all his senses in a supreme effort to find out what was on his son's mind.

'I need some air,' Khieu said in almost a whisper. 'I'll be out for a while.'

'Take your time,' Macomber said carefully, watching him out the door. Then he returned to his desk and, pressing a stud, reactivated the inner program so that the same data that had been on the monitor when Khieu had come into the study reappeared. But sitting immobile, lost in thought, he did not see the program. What has happened to Khieu he thought. Is it major or minor? And, most importantly of all, can I trust him now?

He closed his eyes and in the inner darkness arranged all his options like the cards in a poker hand. He went from one to the next, assessing the strong and weak points of each. Then he selected the best one.

Immediately he picked up the phone, dialled a number. 'Eliott?' he said warmly. 'How are you? ... Good. Have you been given everything you need at Metronics? ... Splendid.' He waited just the right amount of time. 'I think it's time we had lunch together. A real business lunch. Would you like that? Ah, I thought you would. How about Lutece.' He chuckled. 'Yes, my table. All right, we'll go together from the office ... No, tomorrow's no good,' he lied. 'But the day after's clear. Yes, that's right, the Thirty-first.'

Macomber replaced the phone softly, thinking, Perhaps Eliott can accomplish what I cannot.

4

When Thwaite heard the raspy squeal of the police lock being withdrawn his stomach lurched sickeningly. It seemed so long since he had seen her, so long: another lifetime. He thought wildly that he would not even recognize her, that someone would come to the slowly opening door and he would say to himself, Now who the hell is that?

He saw the wing of long black hair, lustrous and curly through the slice of the door, then her pale face and the large dark eyes staring at him. As if in a dream he saw her eyes opening wide, heard her gasp, 'Oh, my God!'

The look on her face as he came inside tore at his heart, 'Doug, I never expected —'

'I've a favour to ask of you.' Better to get it over with and get out, he thought.

Her head was to one side as she gave him a puzzled look. 'You know you don't have to ask. It's part of our d —'

'That's over with,' he said quickly. Even talking about it left a vile taste in his mouth. 'Whatever we had before is dead.'

He saw the shock forming behind her eyes and only then did he understand the dual nature of his remark. Did I really mean that? he asked himself.

'I see.' Nothing showed on her face but he saw that she was pale beneath her minimum of makeup.

'I don't understand,' he said innocently. 'I thought you'd be happy. It means you're free.'

'Free enough to refuse you your favour?' she said archly.

'If that's your wish.'

'It is.' She turned away from him. Her arms were stiff and he saw a muscle jumping near her wrist.

'Then —' Unaccountably his throat seized up and he had to wait a moment, begin all over again. 'Then this's the last time you'll see me.'

Her head went down just as if he struck her a physical blow. He thought she said something then but he could not be sure. He took a step towards her.

'What did you say?'

When she spoke again it was very slowly and he knew she was keeping her emotions in check. 'That's entirely up to you.'

He felt exasperated, as if he were in a situation whose nature he did not comprehend. 'What d'you want me to say to that?'

She whirled on him then and he saw the high colour in her cheeks, the diamond tears quivering at the corners of her flashing eyes. 'I don't for the love of God care as long as it's the truth!'

'You want the truth?' Thwaite said. 'All right. Here it is. I was having an affair with you — with a whore — while I was married. I ignored my wife, didn't spend nearly enough time with my kid and now they're both gone in a flash of fire and smoke and I have nothing. Nothing, d'you understand that?' He was shaking her, he realized only dimly, his strong fingers digging into the flesh of her arms. Their faces were very close; he could feel the heat from her body filling the space between them; he ignored that, spilling it all out, everything he had been bottling up since he had stared dry-eyed at the caskets and could find nothing of them left inside himself.

'And the truth is that every time I think of you, every time I look at you, every time I speak to you I'm reminded of what I've done and I can't stand that!'

'Take your hands off me,' Melody said coolly and calmly and he did that, taking an involuntary step back. 'I thought about you all these long days and nights; I thought I loved you.' She laughed harshly. 'That's right! And I was sure of it the moment I saw you again, standing outside my door. But I thought, I know what he's just gone through. This isn't the time.' Her eyes flashed. 'But I see I was wrong, Doug. Just as you're wrong when you say you're left with nothing because you're filled up, all right. Filled up with self-pity. You're disgusting like this. I don't want any part of you or your favours!'

'I see how it is now,' he said, nodding. His mind was like ice now and he saw what he must do. 'All right. Just as I said, we *are* quits. You don't want to do me the favour, well, okay. But there was a *quid pro quo*. I got some information for your old pimp friends. I mean,' he said nastily, 'that was what you wanted in the beginning. Keep the old pals out of trouble with a little inside info from me. Well, you better tell them that there's a bust due to come down, day after tomorrow. A big one. They got everyone pinpointed. Two, three people you know and love. Now you got it all; what you do with it and the rest of your life's strictly your concern.'

He left her there, staring at him and was glad to be out of that apartment.

Melody went into her bedroom the moment Thwaite had left, tossing off her slipper and donning shoes. She was weeping and avoiding looking at herself in the mirror. She wished she could just pick up the phone and call her friends but they had enjoined her from ever doing that. Phone taps, legal and illegal, they told her, were constantly floating around.

She picked up her handbag, made sure she had her keys and enough money, anything to keep her thoughts away from Thwaite. The tears would not die. She wanted with all her heart to be able to hate him but she could not.

She popped a Kleenex out of its box, dabbed at her eyes. Christ, she thought. All I need is for them to see me like this. Let's, for God's sake, not get sentimental. You have a job to do.

Thwaite picked her up as she was crossing Broadway to hail a cab. He was being very careful. He knew how smart she was, saw her look carefully around before she ducked into the taxi. Sure, he thought, she's smart. But I'm a lot smarter.

There was no way she could make him, slouched as he was in his car, sunlight streaking his windscreen. The ignition was already on. All he had to do was step on the gas.

She took him downtown which was somewhat of a surprise. He had had in mind some posh Park Avenue penthouse. But the tenement the cab dropped her off at was a far cry from the opulence of that twenty-four carat avenue.

Coenties Slip had a history all its own, filled with fishermen and whalers at the turn of the century. Herman Melville had walked these same slick cobblestones, drank his cold beers at the ancient seafarers bar on the corner, its wood dark and gleaming with age, rubbed smooth by hands calloused by prickly rope and the salt wind.

The buildings here were much as they had been a hundred years ago, now slightly ramshackle, leaning a bit as if with the weight of years. Thwaite got out of his car, walked across the broad street, smelling the salt tang, the oily stench of fish flesh and blood from the wholesalers lining South Street a half-block away.

He entered the building he had seen Melody walk into. He had waited five long minutes sitting behind the wheel of his car, tapping his fingers on the top of the padded dash.

He drew his gun the moment he stepped across the threshold. The hallway appeared clean enough. A cat stared at him from out of the shadows, its yellow panther eyes quick with an incomprehensible intelligence.

He went past it, his .38 at the ready. It was not going to be easy, he saw. He counted no less than six doors on the first floor. He had counted storeys during his wait in the car, knew there were five. Thirty apartments and Melody in one of them.

It would, of course, have been easy if he had been able to follow her right in, observe into which apartment she had gone. But one look at the building had convinced him of the impossibility of that. No elevator and one staircase. How could she fail to hear him under those circumstances.

His only choice now was to wait until she came out. Halfway up the stairs he paused to think. If he were holing up in a dump like this his first concern would be security. And here, security meant a quick escape. That meant the ground floor, out the back way or the top floor, across the maze of roofs. Any floor in between was a certain trap.

He went back downstairs to the ground floor, searched around. The rest of the hallway proved to him that if there had ever been a rear exit, it had been boarded up and painted over in the ensuing years.

That left the top floor. He went silently up the staircase, his ears alert for any sound. He was midway between the fourth and fifth floor landings when he heard sound coming from above him. A bolt being drawn back.

He launched himself up the remainder of the stairs, saw Melody emerging from a partly opened door. She was still turned away from him, saying something to someone inside and Thwaite did not break stride, hurled himself across the landing, lowering his shoulder as his high school football coach had taught him, sending Melody flying back into the apartment with a scream, the door swinging wildly backwards to slam against the wall behind it.

'What the fuck –!'

'Okay, freeze! Police!' he cried, taking the classic marksman's stance, his feet well spread, in a semi-crouch, both hands wrapped around the butt of his .38. He caught a fleeting glimpse of three rather grim faces: dark greased hair, well-dressed, pock marks on the cheeks of one.

'You goddamned lying slut! You brought the heat with you!'

A blur of movement to his left and he swivelled. One of the men had drawn a snub-nosed .45. It was a gun with a lot of stopping power.

'Drop it!' Thwaite said. 'Now!'

The man said something in a guttural tongue Thwaite did not understand. His arm came up straight, aiming at Melody.

Thwaite squeezed off a shot, saw the man fly backwards, the .45 exploding from his outflung hand. He hit the floor hard, his back cracking against the leg of a chair, splintering it. He began to drool blood.

'Who's next?' Thwaite growled, swivelling back.

'Not me, man.' The man closest to him, the one with the pock marks, lifting his hands over his head. He began to move. 'We don't want no trouble, brother. You got no cause to bust us. We're just sittin' around here shootin' the breeze.'

He droned on and now the third man, the one behind him with the greasy hair was out of Thwaite's view.

Thwaite waved the muzzle of his gun. 'Get outta there, Johnny-boy. Move away nice and slow so I can –' He saw the movement then and hit the floor, rolling. The shot echoed in his ears.

The room had exploded into movement. The two men were heading for the open window. Beyond, Thwaite could see the black iron grid of the fire escape and the crests of the rooftops to the south.

'Freeze, both of you!' he shouted, scrambling behind an overstuffed chair. The answering roar of the .45 made him duck as wood splintered and stuffing flew through the air like snow.

Thwaite ducked sideways, aiming, shot them down one at a time, carefully and coolly without a care in the world because that was his job and it was all he had now.

He got up slowly, kicked the .45 away. The place was wallpapered, filled with odds and ends of furniture. He gave the sofa a push backwards. He counted the number of plastic bags: twenty. Only the corner of one had shown; his unexpected entry had given them inadequate time to hide their business.

Thwaite looked down at the narcotics, spat wetly. Then he turned away, went over to where Melody was curled in a corner. He saw she was staring at the crumpled bodies of her friends.

He looked at her, saw how beautiful she was, how thick and gleaming her hair was as it fell, shadowing half her face. He brought one of the packets back to her and, bending, took a handful of her hair and forced her to look at the contents.

'Here you go. Take a look at what your friends're *really* into! That's death staring you in the face, Melody.' He took a more savage grip on her hair. 'No, don't turn away. I want you to have a real good look. Here! And here! Needles for the arms of little boys and little girls ... just like my Phyllis. I –'

He looked down, became aware that Melody's right arm had snaked out from behind her back. There was a gun in it. Somehow she had managed to get it when his back was turned.

'You killed my friends,' she said softly. 'Just burst in here, using me to lead you –'

'For Christ's sake!' he cried. 'Listen to what you're saying! Look at what your friends were. My God, they –'

'They put me through school,' she said. 'They looked after me when my father wouldn't and my mother couldn't. If it hadn't been for them, I wouldn't've had an education. We had no money.'

'And in return what did they want, huh? Don't tell me they invested all that money in you out of the goodness of their hearts.'

'Yes,' she said defiantly. 'They did!'

'You're a goddamn liar!'

She cocked the pistol, the hammer going back with a pronounced click. 'You'll never know now, will you?'

Thwaite, staring at the muzzle of the pistol, felt something hard and unpleasant go out of him and he said, 'I don't want to die, Melody.'

She wavered. 'I ought to kill you, you bastard, fucking up my mind, fucking up my whole life . . . just you.'

It was he who cried first now. He slipped down onto his knees in front of her. 'The sonovabitch who killed my family was into this same kind of shit, Melody.' He threw the packet of heroin from them. 'A goddamn wholesaler. And I kept him in business. I thought he was just another pimp, you see?' His face was red now. 'Just like Lovely Leonard, Joe the Wasp and all the rest on my graft list. Only he wasn't like them at all. He was just like your friends, peddling this unholy death to kids! D'you know what I've felt like all this time since I found out?'

The gun was no longer with her. Her open hands had come out, sliding over his shoulders so that when he leaned forward into her she cradled his head, kissing him, caressing him, whispering, 'Oh, Doug, now I'm really broken from my past. There's nothing of it left and I'm very frightened because I don't know what's in store.'

Her warmth suffused him and he saw that she had been right about him. Wallowing in self-pity was no place for him to be. As for what he felt for her, he did not want to think beyond today, did not want to think beyond the comfort she and only she could give him now.

It took them a long time to get back to her apartment and even longer before they were willing to break apart the peace that engulfed them.

At last, he placed the bound scroll in her hands. She sat up in bed and undid the red silk string. 'This the favour you wanted from me?'

Thwaite nodded. 'I'd like you to translate it for me.'

She opened the scroll, did not ask why he hadn't taken it directly to the precinct for translation; she was far too savvy for that. Her large eyes moved up and down the columns of characters.

'Jesus!' she said, after a time. 'Did you really find 350 kilos of uncut heroin.'

'It's real, all right.' He sat up next to her, admiring the play of light along her pale flesh. 'What else does it say?'

She looked at him. 'You ever hear of something called the Mauritious Company?'

Thwaite shook his head. 'No, should I?'

'It's the company that ordered the consignment.' She glanced down at the scroll again. 'Doug, this looks like one of many. Is it possible that so much horse could be imported without being detected?'

'This batch certainly was.' He pointed to the scroll. 'You got an address for this Mauritious place?'

'Yes.'

'Well, then. Let's go.'

Golden Dragon had his offices in a part of one of Hong Kōng's three thousand toy factories. An odd place for a *feng shui* man to hang his hat, as it were, but it was said that the factory was owned by Golden Dragon's brother.

In any event, it was the place where Tracy went now. Because he was a *feng shui* man, Golden Dragon was one of the most powerful men in the Colony. Not all *feng shui* men were thus blessed, he was enamoured of saying. He was the best.

People put up with him because it was true. He was a geomancer, purportedly able to read the fate of men from the twists of the wind, the winding currents of streams, the colour of the daylight. Too, he was in intimate communion with the myriad spirits, ghosts and demons said by the Chinese to inhabit the world. So it was to him that the Chinese went before embarking on any serious endeavour whether it be in the business field or the area of matrimony.

The factory shifts had long gone for the night but the place was open, half-lit as if with a pathway of lemon light. Sounds were eerily magnified by the vast open space, echoes thrown back in rhythmic patterns. The place was filled with shadows that seemed to shift at Tracy's approach as if setting themselves for his visit.

He passed bins of toy parts: dolls heads in clear plastic bags so that no dust or oils could mar the perfect nylon waves of their hairdos; muscled arms of warriors awaiting assembly; thousands of plastic motorcycles; curved train tracks; and, most bizarrely of all, wigless dolls' heads with perfect features, their nylon lashes six inches long, waiting for the assembly-line blade to shear them down.

Golden Dragon's office was in the back, in the left-hand corner which he had determined was the most propitious spot to attract the good spirits and repel the evil ones. It was all red and gold and long before Tracy arrived at its doorway, he scented pungent incense burning with exotic languor.

There was a young Chinese woman in with Golden Dragon and Tracy was obliged to wait until she left.

Illumination was soft and wavering, provided by a pair of brass-based lamps and perhaps a dozen long red candles surrounding a small shrine piled with offerings of fresh fruit and rice. The walls to Golden Dragon's right were covered with enormous silk screens of the Buddha and, to his left, a gold and emerald green dragon chasing its tail. In front of him and across the room, stood a pottery jar glazed in a deep brownish-red. It was two-and-a-half feet deep with a domed top. It stood on mossed stones arranged as if in nature, and slips of paper, 'spirit money', decorated its lid.

This was, Tracy knew, a Golden Pagoda, a Grandfather's Bones Jar. It was the traditional vessel, the religious yet supremely pragmatic Chinese used to house the polished bones of their ancestors. Because space was so at a premium in the Colony and because tradition dictated that the revered ancestors must be treated in the proper manner, the Chinese had reached a perfectly understandable compromise. A permanent grave was beyond their means so they rented one for a period of six years after which they had the bones exhumed, polished and placed in their proper order in a Golden Pagoda. Often they consulted a *feng shui* man to determine the proper placement of the jar within the home or on a nearby hillside.

In this particular Grandfather's Bones Jar no doubt lay Golden Dragon's ancestor.

'*Kung Hey Fat Choy,*' the *feng shui* man said. Rejoice and grow rich. His hands moved. 'We are closed for the day and in any case we require appointments.'

Tracy turned towards the Golden Pagoda, bowed towards it. Then he faced the *feng shui* man, said, '*Kung Hei Fat Fuk.*' Congratulations, I see you have prospered.

'Indeed.'

'I have travelled a very long way in order to see you,' Tracy continued in Cantonese.

'How long?'

'All my life.'

Golden Dragon cocked his head. 'Approach us.'

He was a thin man, far taller than the typical Chinese with a drawn-out skull, polished at its very top. He had sharp eyes, a wide mouth and a receding chin. He wore a black quilted Mandarin jacket with gold and green dragons embroidered across the breasts. His only affectation was a pair of tiny gold pince-nez sitting on the bridge of his blunt nose.

'You know much about our customs.' His voice held a kind of mesmerizing quality. 'What is your name?' he said. Tracy told him. 'And your birth date?' Tracy told him that, too.

Golden Dragon gestured. 'Sit.'

Tracy took an ebony chair before the carved ebony table behind which the *feng shui* man sat, watched as the other made a number of notations. There were a myriad of books by his left elbow. Tracy recognized one of them as a Chinese calendar which he now consulted in order to convert the date Tracy had given him. To his right was a wooden box within which was a circle divided up into twelve segments, marked with the signs

533

of the Chinese Zodiac. At its centre was a free-floating brass pointer such as one finds in a compass.

Golden Dragon looked up, studying Tracy's face. A peculiar look suffused his face and he seemed paler. 'Do you know what *Kan-hsiang* is, Mr Richter?'

Tracy shook his head. 'No.'

'It is an ability — one which we possess, we might add — to read one's fate by studying his face. Have you heard of this?'

'No.'

'Can you say whether you believe in it?'

'I'm afraid I do not have enough knowledge to answer that.'

Golden Dragon nodded. 'You are a wise man.' His hands spread, showing the three-inch-long nails, polished and gleaming. 'Nevertheless, we must ask you to leave now.'

'It is most important —' He stopped in midsentence at the *feng shui* man's raised palm.

'Please. Words are useless. We divine that you have come here not for yourself but to obtain information about another.'

'That is true. But —'

'Then we cannot help you.'

'But you do not even know about whom I wish information.'

'He is a client of ours. A very powerful client.' Golden Dragon sat back. 'What do you suppose would happen to us if we should be so, er, indelicate as to divulge any information concerning him. We would have no business left; our reputation ruined.'

'You know what kind of man this is.'

'We cannot judge here, Mr Richter. It is enough that we see the fates, that we are in touch with all the myriad spirits.'

'I beg you,' Tracy said. 'It is a matter of the utmost urgency.'

'That we can see.' Golden Dragon nodded. 'Still.'

'Then just do my horoscope,' Tracy said desperately. 'Tell me nothing if you deem it not fit.'

The *feng shui* man contemplated him for a time. The utter silence from the deserted factory was deafening. At length, he glanced down at his notes and for the next twenty minutes was absorbed in his work. At the end of that time, he put down his pen. He did not look up but continued to study that which he had written. He consulted the box horoscope but this only seemed to confirm what he had already discovered.

When he at last looked up at Tracy, his face seemed changed. 'We will tell you what you want to know.'

Tracy was stunned. 'Why? What happened?'

Golden Dragon tapped his papers with a nail, the sound like the clicking of an insect's mandibles.

Tracy took a deep breath. 'Where is Mizo now?'

Golden Dragon blinked, moistened his dry lips with the tip of his tongue. 'We knew,' he whispered. His eyes seemed to go out of focus and in a louder voice, said, 'He is at *Loongshan*.'

'Dragon Mountain? Where is that?'

'It is the name of his mistress's house.'

'Jade Princess is dead.'

Golden Dragon did not even blink. 'Yes. We suspected as much. But Jade Princess was not his mistress. She lived with Mizo at his own house.'

'He has two.'

'Perhaps more. Is that significant?'

'I suppose not. Merely interesting.'

'*Loongshan* is a mansion on Victoria Peak.' Golden Dragon wrote swiftly, pushed the paper across the face of his gleaming table. 'This is the address.'

'You know what may happen,' he said.

The *feng shui* man closed his eyes. 'Trafficking in drugs brings evil joss. We warned Mizo of this and he laughed in our face.' His eyes sprang open and now they were filled with an odd impersonal hate. 'He does not believe in *feng shui*; he is not Chinese, after all. He comes to see us merely to placate Jade Princess.'

Tracy had not believed Fresh Wind Po's information to be false but always in Hong Kong, he knew, it was good practice to obtain corroborating evidence.

'Her demise was not an easy one,' Tracy said. 'If you knew her well, I'm sorry.'

'We will say a prayer tonight for her spirit.'

It was time to go, Tracy realized. He rose. But still he hesitated. He must ask one more question. 'Golden Dragon,' he said, 'please tell me what it was you saw in my horoscope that made you change your mind.'

The *feng shui* man looked up at him with a kind of ineffable sadness in his face. 'Death, Mr Richter. We saw death there.'

The late August sun struck the newly steam-cleaned façade of St Patrick's Cathedral, burnishing it white as bone; it splashed across the broad stone steps, the thrown-open doors into the arched coolness of the interior.

Television news cameras had been set up, reporters beginning to talk portentously into their handheld microphones as their carefully cosmetized eyes made contact with the centre of the lens and their watching audience.

It was a national election year, time for political analyses, cinéma vérité coverages and hot one-on-one interviews with the major candidates. It was enough to make you proud to be in the television business.

Crowds were forming, extending south to Saks Fifth Avenue and north to Roberta diCamerino, out into Fifth Avenue itself. Blue uniformed policemen roamed through the throng, their polished nightsticks much in evidence, gripping black walkie-talkies, pressing them against their cheeks as they spoke softly into the mouthpieces.

High-stepping mounted police pranced on snorting horses, their riot helmets splattering blinding sun reflections to and fro.

It was time. A caravan of three black limousines emerged onto the avenue, sliding south until they slowed to a stop in front of the cathedral. It was now possible to discern certain plainclothesmen, hard of eye, stern of visage who, lockjawed, strode through the crowds, superior and supremely confident.

These plainclothesmen were linked by a sophisticated electronic network that allowed them to be on the move at all times like floating cells from one individual being. And as such, they thought alike, reacted alike, spoke alike. Therefore, they were easy enough to neutralize.

So thought the angular young man who knelt like a penitent beside an open window on the tenth floor of a building on the west side of Fifth Avenue that directly overlooked the cathedral.

536

His quick sharp eyes picked them out, one, two, three . . . sixteen in all in a block-and-a-half radius. He assumed there were more out of his range of vision: on the west side of the avenue, inside the cathedral itself, along the Madison Avenue side of the block. But they did not interest him; he would never go anywhere near them. It was these sixteen he studied now, through × 12 Zeiss compact field glasses.

He watched the movement back and forth of the sixteen, observing them circulate, getting to know their patterns. He had memorized the six-page treatise on American security procedures which had been sent to him care of a post office box drop, along with his specific instructions. Both had been in Arabic which had been a godsend. The young man could speak and read a modicum of English, a fair amount of French and, of course, Russian. But in Arabic there was no chance of a misunderstanding. This specific room had been rented for him, too. He had been sent a set of keys along with the documents, which he had already disposed of.

The Russians were rarely so personally accommodating but since he assumed they were directing this operation, he felt warmed by the thought that finally they were beginning to show their appreciation for their Islamic revolutionary brothers. Arms and rhetoric were all well and good, he thought. But equality was another matter entirely; that only came after the long hard struggle that tinged all Islamic life with bitterness.

The young man heard the loudening of massed voices below. Six men were emerging from the newly arrived limousine. They were all dark-suited, sleekly dressed, elegantly coiffed. Their faces were shining. Instantly the young man singled out one of them. The photograph he had been supplied had been quite accurate.

Placing the Zeiss glasses on the windowsill, the young man bent towards a tattered cloth case. As he did so, he glanced at his watch. Three minutes past noon. Dead on time. He smiled at the Anglo phrase he had picked up; it was particularly apt in this case.

He pulled a chamois cloth out of the bag, then withdrew the freshly oiled parts one by one, snapping them into place as he did so. From time to time he wiped the excess oil from his fingertips onto the chamois cloth. He did not hurry; he knew from the written briefing that he had plenty of time. Atherton Gottschalk was scheduled to speak on the steps of the cathedral for twenty minutes before entering the house of worship for a special memorial mass for the former Governor of the state.

The young man had no trouble. How many times had he been pulled from a deep sleep in the early hours of the southern Libyan morning, blindfolded and required to pull apart and reassemble a Soviet-made AK-47 rifle within three minutes? Too many to count. But he viewed the training as necessary; it would not have occurred to him to complain or balk. He had chosen the path of his life and righteousness pumped in his veins like a powerful stimulant.

The young man clicked the last metal part in place and the AK-47 was fully operational. He dug into the bag, loaded the weapon. He began to hear the first squeals of an amplified sound system starting up and, moments later, the opening remarks of Atherton Gottschalk, candidate for President of the United States.

The young man was honoured that he had been chosen, out of all the others, for this operation. It filled him with a fierce pride; to be so instrumental in the furtherance of the cause of the Islamic fundamentalist revolution.

Grinning, he brought the AK-47 up to shoulder height. He closed his off eye, concentrated all of his mind through his open right eye. He brought the 'scope's crosshairs to bear on the crowd, moving idly from plainclothesman to plainclothesman until, in his mind, he had shot them all. His grin grew larger and the long gun swung in its shallow arc until it pointed directly down at the head of Atherton Gottschalk.

The young man had half a mind to squeeze the trigger right then but he restrained himself. After all, he was a professional and he had his specific orders. *At precisely twelve-fifteen shoot at the heart.*

It was true, he thought. The skull was an odd and difficult target at this range. Heavy bone could deflect, even bend or flatten a bullet. Death could not always be assured. But rupture the heart and there could be no doubt whatsoever: the body ceased to function.

The young man glanced at his watch. Thirty-five seconds to go. He settled his cheek back against the cool stock of the AK-47, counting off in his mind. The crosshairs wavered, moving downwards to Atherton Gottschalk's exposed chest. His finger tightened on the trigger, beginning to squeeze.

Macomber took great pride in ushering Eliott to his special table at Lutece. At dinnertime, Macomber much preferred the darkly European elegance of the upstairs dining rooms. But for lunch, the light airy feeling of the ground floor garden room suited him perfectly.

As he sat down, Macomber took a long hard objective look at his son. It seemed ages since he had seen him with suit and tie, a proper haircut. He was a handsome boy, Macomber thought now, the clothes from Paul Stuart doing him justice.

As the waiter filled their water glasses, handed out the menus and the wine list, Macomber said, 'Shimada gave me the most glowing report on your progress with some of the additional FIRST elements we've been kicking around for some time; you know, no one's been able to make much headway with them until you came aboard.'

Eliott ducked his head. 'I guess I ought to thank him but I think he's a bit premature. We still have a ways to go yet before we can integrate the new circuits.'

'How d'you like LITLIS?'

'I think it's goddamned amazing.' Eliott had come animated. 'The speed at which the laser-powered network performs is ... well, it's awesome. It's something you only dream about. I sure as hell would like to see the *Vampire* in operation.'

'I'll authorize a trip to Hungry Horse then,' Macomber said. 'But in a couple of weeks. What you're doing here with FIRST is far too important for me to pull you off it now.'

'I'd like that,' Eliott said. He looked around. A waiter was hovering just behind his father's shoulder. He picked up the wine list, held it out to his father. 'Shall we order wine?'

'Why don't you do it,' Macomber said easily as he perused the menu.

Curiously, with a growing sense of pleasure, Eliott opened the red leather book as if it were the Holy Grail. 'I'd like a red,' he said. 'Do you mind?'

'Not at all.'

Eliott looked up. 'This St Emilion, I think.' He pointed to the wine. '1966.'

The waiter, who had discreetly glided to a spot just behind Eliott's shoulder, nodded. '*Oui, Monsieur.*' And, taking the list from him, departed.

Macomber, having decided what to eat, put his menu aside. He was willing to wait for his son to take the lead.

Eliott fiddled with his silverware for some time, then looked across the table at his father. 'I guess you can see the dark circles under my eyes.'

'Frankly, I hadn't noticed,' Macomber lied. 'I was thinking how good you look.'

'You mean in my new suit.' There was an edge to Eliott's voice.

'No,' Macomber said softly. 'I meant sitting here with me at Lutece.'

Eliott was quiet for a moment. He was thinking that after all the years of struggling with all his mind and soul against this, now that it had actually happened, it wasn't so bad. In fact, it felt distinctly good to him. The relaxed, refined atmosphere of this very European restaurant, the soft voices, the ting of fine crystal, the garlands of flowers against the wall, the filtered sunlight putting a singular glow on everything and everyone in the room, all of it quickened his heart. He found that the heaviness that had been a part of him for so many years was gone and only when his thoughts turned to Kathleen did he feel a slight twinge in the pit of his stomach.

'The truth is,' he said slowly, 'I'm still having trouble sleeping.' He paused as the waiter arrived, presented him the bottle, then proceeded to uncork it. He poured some into a glass. He stared at it; the three of them waited.

'Aren't you going to taste it? You always do.'

'This is *your* choice, Eliott.' Macomber's voice was gentle. 'It has nothing to do with me. It's for you to accept or reject.'

Eliott found himself trembling inwardly at his father's words. *It's for you to accept or reject.* Yes. It's what I want to do, he said to himself, grasping the stem of the glass, first inhaling the ruby wine's bouquet, then tasting tentatively. It was rich and dry, crinkling his palate. 'It's delicious!' he blurted and Macomber laughed at his delight.

'Good, good.'

The waiter poured, then took their lunch order. Macomber ordered the *confit de canéton*, as he often did here at lunch because it was so exceptional. Eliott chose the veal special. They both began with Belon oysters.

'What I was saying,' Eliott continued when they were alone, 'was that I've been thinking a lot since we had our ... discussion.'

Macomber's face did not change; he listened attentively, waiting his turn.

'That day I came up to see you I was so angry I was about to spit in your face. But afterwards, well, I don't know what happened ... maybe we cleared the air or something.' He fiddled with the silverware again. 'I didn't ... mean some of the things I said. I know you did the best for me that you knew how. I didn't mean it was pathetic. It wasn't.'

'Thank you,' Macomber said, meaning it.

Now for the hard part, Eliott thought. 'About Kathleen ...'

He left it hanging so long, Macomber was forced to interject. 'What about her?'

'You were right, of course. I played back the time we spent together. I ... Well, I see now what she was up to. It wasn't me at all. But I believed ... you see, I *wanted* to believe ...'

'She saw that in you, Eliott. I told you she was very, very sharp. If she could fool Gottschalk, she was something.'

'Take it from me,' Eliott said. 'She was.' He saw his father smiling across the spotless table at him, found that he was smiling, too.

The waiter returned with their oysters, fresh baked bread and a large dish of yellow butter.

'I don't know about you,' Macomber said, squeezing fresh lemon juice onto the chilled, cringing flesh, 'but for me it feels good to finally have us both on the same side.'

Eliott said nothing, picked up his tiny oyster fork. It was impossible for him to say just what he was feeling; the swirls of unaccustomed emotions were threatening to drown him. That Kathleen's presence in his life, as well as her death, had marked him permanently he had no doubt. Part of him felt brittle at her betrayal. He had sat up in bed last night, quite suddenly, cold sweat breaking out on him, thinking not of her death but of how close she had led him into betraying the *angka*. And he knew that his hatred of his father had blinded him completely, making him vulnerable to just such an attack. And what was that hatred, after all, but a childhood figment of his imagination. His father was just a man, nothing more: not a monster with the power of a god. Macomber was Macomber and Eliott was Eliott and the twain would never meet *unless Eliott chose that it be so*.

I choose, Eliott thought now. *Yes*.

His head came up and he said, 'I feel the same way.'

'Good,' Macomber said. He lifted his glass in toast and Eliott followed suit.

'*Salud!*' he said as their glasses clinked together.

'*Salud y pesetas!*'

Macomber glanced at his watch. 'Excuse me a moment,' he said, pushing his chair back.

Atherton Gottschalk was concerned. He was more than three-quarters through his speech and nothing had happened yet. When would Macomber's plan begin to roll? At this late hour there would be no way Macomber could inform him of a hitch. His mind went through the variations on a miscue. There were far too many. His stomach lurched, turning over. First Kathleen disappears and now this.

'The inexcusable incidents in Cairo and Germany – premeditated attacks on American military and diplomatic personnel by international terrorists are merely two examples that characterize the increasingly unstable international environment.' His voice was strong, assured, with just the right amount of fervour to engender conviction without the stigma of fanaticism. The outward semblance of a political centrist containing the underlying military fist of iron.

'It is now clear that it has been left up to us – the American people – to deal with the small section of nations who are and have been indulging in policies of murder.'

The crowd reaction was encouraging, Gottschalk thought, looking out over that sea of shining faces like an archbishop in benediction. But where the hell was the show?

'It is not enough to shift our Army combat forces in West Germany to new bases closer to the Eastern European border. It is not enough to crack down on these so-called American mercenaries fighting *against their own country* in the paid service of the armed forces of Libya, Chad and Syria. It is not enough to seek out and destroy Soviet-equipped shock units in Cambodia and Laos who are unleashing lethal mycotoxins of the trichothecene group on the populace there. It is not enough to pad our silos with cruise missiles and MX's to encounter the Soviet Union's SS-20's.

'All these have a place in our systemic approach to up-grading America's status on the international stage. But *none* of them constitutes the *first step*. This must be a programme to inform the public of the nature and sources of inter-national terrorism. We must be prepared to –' Gottschalk faltered as a searing pain erupted in the left side of his chest. '– to –' His hands came up, flat-palmed, clasping his chest. They felt wet and sticky. He heard screams in his ears like the terrible roar of a surf about to engulf him.

The hot summer day turned brassy, broke up into distinct fragments, spurts of movement surrounding him. He felt strong hands supporting him as he began to go down, the erratic stuttering of his heart as if he had been kicked there by a mule. He began to gasp as if the air had turned to jelly and his labouring lungs could no longer get oxygen. He wondered what in Christ's name had happened until he heard a shout above the din and confusion swirling across his plane of vision. 'Shot!' the unidentified voice said. 'The candidate's been shot!' And Atherton Gottschalk thought in some wonder and not a little fear, That's me!

Detective Sergeant Marty Borak was picking his nose when the call came in. He was doing that to save himself from going mad with boredom. Enders was at the St Pat's thing with just about every other ablebodied detective in the precinct. Borak had been given a pass because he was running a stake-out ops over in the meat-packing district on the far West Side of Manhattan.

He'd been working on the pinch for over two months now and it was getting to him. Slow work always did. Borak was the kind of cop who was unhappy unless he was getting instant gratification from his job. And a stake-out was not it.

At 1.14, he had just begun his base shift. That meant, if he got a communication from the stake-out team, he had to organize the mobilization of the back-up units. It was a thankless job and, frankly, Borak hated it.

So when the phone shrilled at his elbow, it was not surprising that he growled a nasty and unprofessional, 'Yeah,' into the receiver. His finger was still stuck up his nostril, exploring.

'Police?'

'You got it, pal.'

'I want to report a shooting.'

'Yah? What kind?' Borak could care less. 'You see someone nip a dog with a B-B gun?'

'This is no joke,' the voice said. 'Atherton Gottschalk, the Republican candidate for President, has been shot on the steps of St Patrick's Cathedral.'

'Who is this?' Borak wiped his finger on the bottom of his scarred desk.

'The man you want,' the voice went on, 'is on the tenth floor of Fifty Rockefeller Center. Room 1101.'

Borak was scribbling as fast as he could manage. 'How d'you know all of this?'

'For Christ's sake hurry. You'll miss him.'

'Hey,' Borak screamed into the phone, 'wait a goddamned

minute –!' But he was shouting at dead air. He saw that he was gripping the phone with white knuckles. He jiggled the pips, got off a priority call, patched in to Enders' walkie-talkie. '... That's right,' he concluded. 'Room 1101. Get your ass up there!'

He put down the phone and cursed. What the hell was going on? he wondered. It had been less than thirty seconds since the candidate had been shot.

Detective Sergeant Teddy Enders raced along the corridor of the tenth floor at 50 Rockefeller Center. Three uniforms were behind him. He wondered how in hell Borak had known about the shooting, let alone got a tip on the assassin. His gun was out, so were the others'.

Fifty yards down the corridor a door opened from the right side and a young man with a tattered cloth suitcase emerged. He looked back at the oncoming policemen just as Enders called out, 'Halt! Police officers! Stand your ground!'

The young man ducked back inside the door, slamming it shut behind him. It was part wood, its upper half, frosted glass.

Enders and his makeshift squad came abreast of the door, their shadows following across the glass and Enders, seeing the risk, stopped short, putting his arm out behind him. 'Back!' he cried. 'Get the hell away from there!' just as the pane shattered outward in a hail of shards and bullets.

This was not the way to do it, he knew. But he'd be goddamned if he'd allow this bastard to get away. He was still half in shock at what this sonovabitch had done. An assassination. And on the steps of St Pat's. It made Enders' blood boil.

'All right, boys,' he said softly. 'That's the way he wants it, that's the way he's gonna get it.' He coordinated them quietly and quickly and they came through the door in a fusillade of bullets, firing and firing again, all four of them, until their weapons were empty.

Silence, echoing, booming away as white noise in the eardrums. The acrid stink of cordite. Enders dispatched one of the uniforms to keep away the curious who had emerged from their offices.

Then he took the rest of them in. The young man lay curled up beneath the open window. The tattered cloth bag was clutched against his chest. An old World War II Luger beside him. He was a mass of blood and ripped flesh. He had been hit in the neck, arms, chest, abdomen, foot. One bullet had sheared away most of his nose.

One of the young men took one look at the mess and vomited up his breakfast.

'Shit,' Enders said. He knew what one moment of white hot rage had cost him. He'd got his man, all right. But that was all. He came close to corpse, looked out the open window. 'This is the place, all right,' he said. 'Call them.' He gestured to one of the uniforms, handing him his walkie-talkie. 'An ambulance, photog and print men right away. Tell them to notify the ME's office.' He was still staring at the young man curled up like a baby. 'And for Christ's sake don't touch anything. And I mean *anything*.'

He reached inside his jacket, produced the pair of surgeon's gloves he always carried with him. He holstered his pistol, snapped on the gloves. Then he knelt down, went to work on the corpse.

'Jesus Christ,' one of the uniforms said as he pried the cloth bag away from the deathgrip. A wave of pent-up blood gushed out, running across Enders' polished shoetops.

He ignored that, pulled open the bag. 'Oh, God,' he whispered, recognizing the pieces of the Soviet-made AK-47. Carefully, he closed the bag, put it back against the corpse's chest. Then he stood up, stripped off his bloody gloves. Turning them inside out, he stuffed them back inside his jacket.

Then he turned, stared out the window at the milling chaos around St Pat's, waiting for the Secret Service. There was nothing else to do now.

Macomber returned to his icy oysters, devouring the remainder with great relish. He used three drops of Tabasco sauce on each.

Still his expression was not placid and Eliott waited until the dishes had been cleared before asking his father what was troubling him. 'Believe it or not,' Macomber said, 'it's Khieu.'

'That's nonsense. Khieu, as you have always been so fond of telling me, possesses perfect loyalty, perfect intelligence, perfect physical prowess. It's why you brought him back from Cambodia, after all, isn't it?'

'You know why I brought him back,' Macomber said a bit more sharply than he had intended. 'He was an orphan. His life was a nightmare.'

'Oh, come off it, Father.' Eliott leaned forward. 'He's a machine. Nothing more. You use him now because you know he'll blindly move in whatever direction you point your finger.'

'Yes,' Macomber nodded. 'In a sense, you're right. But the motivation is different from what you suspect. You don't understand the Cambodian mind. I executed the people who butchered Khieu's older brother. He was family, a person Khieu still reveres above all others save his parents. In his mind, he owes me a debt he can never fully repay, though he tries. What I tell him to do, he *wants* to do.'

That frown came over Macomber's face again. 'But now something's happening to him that I cannot fathom.'

That made Eliott smile. 'You mean he's not the perfect child you thought you had raised.'

'No one is perfect,' Macomber said, feeling that he had regained the initiative. 'Even Khieu. And that's where you can help me.'

The entrées came and they both waited until they were done again.

'I don't see that I can do anything,' Eliott said.

Macomber shrugged. He did not want to make this too easy for his son. He had to be made to feel it was his own decision. 'Perhaps not. But the fact is I must take some form of action.'

Eliott forked up a bite of veal. It was in a rich, burnished brown sauce. 'Why don't you just ask him?'

'Unfortunately, that's no longer possible.' Macomber pushed his *canéton* around with the tip of his knife. 'I ask him questions and either get no reply or evasions.'

'Surely there's a portion of his life that must remain private,' Eliott said reasonably.

'You're a goddamned fool to talk like that,' Macomber said hotly. His cheeks were pink and a tiny vein was pulsing in one eyelid. 'The entire *angka* is at stake. Fifteen years of work. And you talk of privacy. There's nothing private in the *angka*.'

Eliott wondered what his father was leading up to. He obviously wanted something and Eliott was angry at himself for not being able to see what it was.

'Maybe this part of Khieu's life has nothing to do with the *angka*.'

Macomber gave Eliott a look that made him cringe. 'Khieu *has* no life outside the *angka*. Without it, he does not exist.'

Eliott was appalled by his father's appraisal. Where were all the outward signs of love and affection he had lavished on Khieu for so many years? Had it all suddenly changed?

'If he won't listen to me,' Macomber said, pushing back his plate, 'perhaps you can talk to him.'

'Me?' Eliott had to laugh. 'Khieu hates me just as much as I hate him. You should know that. You saw to it.'

Macomber ignored that. 'What you fail to realize, Eliott, is that Khieu's reaction to you is just that. You see the mirror you have placed up in front of your face. He responds only to your anger.'

'You mean he doesn't hate me?'

'No.'

'Then he's a better man than I am.'

Macomber said nothing, merely regarded his son.

After a time, Eliott broke down, said, 'You really want me to talk to him?'

'I want,' Macomber said, 'to know what the hell is up with him. It's extremely important.'

Eliott considered that. Now it seemed to him that the tables had been turned, the favourite cast out. If he took his father up on his request, he'd be in the driver's seat.

'All right,' he said slowly. 'I'll see what I can do.'

'I appreciate that Eliott,' Macomber said, smiling. 'Really I do.'

5

Even in the dark, *Loongshan* was not difficult to find. Tracy stepped out of the taxi a thousand metres from the jewelled blaze of light. Crickets crackled in the night like fireworks, the hard buzz of the cicadas evident.

He turned, watching the vehicle as it would back down Victoria Peak towards the Central District, its taillights crimson dragon's eyes searching out his destination. It was easy to believe in such things in Hong Kong. Tracy thought of Golden Dragon and his art of geomancy. Such mystical expertise would no doubt be scoffed at in the West. But Tracy had spent too much time in Southeast Asia to discount such phenomena.

He turned and looked at the blue-white diamond of *Loongshan* and thought of Golden Dragon's words. *Death, Mr Richter. We saw death there.* Was it Mizo's death or Tracy's he was predicting?

To his right, the mountainside swept away like the hem of an elegant gown. The air was filled with the scents of orange and cardamom, the off-shore breeze shivering the black leaves of the trees. All of Hong Kong lay in a great glittering crescent, the curving blade of a scimitar encrusted with gemstones. It was possible here to forget the squalor of the filthy backstreets, the swaying boats of the Tanka, sloshing in the oily waters off Aberdeen. For the people inside *Loongshan*, perhaps, but not for Tracy. The jungles of Cambodia and Laos were too well branded, hissing in his mind like the mordant cries of a people lost even to themselves.

He came up on it, a two-storey, L-shaped structure with what looked like a tennis court on the roof of the longer section. Wide white pillars at the rear gave out on a half-moon-shaped pool, a sapphire slice of some exotic fruit. Here was the sign of ultimate wealth for how rare was water on the rocky terrain on which the Colony had sprung up.

Tracy crept closer, the small leather case beneath his jacket and shirt. He heard a bird call shrilly somewhere above his head and froze in midstep. He listened for movement outside the house but the music emanating from inside made soft-sound detection difficult.

He chose to enter the back of the house. There was a great deal of glass here but that would serve him as well as increase the danger. If he could be seen from within, so too could he see the movements of those inside the house.

He crept carefully around the pool, keeping its mirror face to his right as he flitted from shadow to shadow. There was sufficient shrubbery to within one hundred feet of the house itself to provide relatively good cover.

At the inner edge of the fringe of bushes, he paused, swung slowly in a 360° arc. He listened to the night and found a change there. Some quality had altered subtly and he fought to define it, knowing that he had no time at all. A decrease in the singing of the crickets.

The knowledge and the sound came simultaneously and he went down on one knee, swivelling at the last instant as he felt the weight of the shadow above him, blotting out the constellations of stars. He lashed out with his right leg, centralizing the weight of his torso and head, bending the knee of the extended leg in midair, jackknifing his foot out at the last possible instant, unfolding it into the man's middle section.

Flash of dark face as it blurred by, the body careening. Enough to recognize the Mongol's face.

The man's teeth snapped shut on nothing and air whistled out through his wide clenched lips. Then he bounced onto the grass beside Tracy, lifting himself up almost in the same motion.

Tracy hooked his still lifted right foot, scrabbling for a hold. The Mongol whipped his leg away, cursing in an unending stream, his hands like claws, racing for Tracy's throat.

Tracy rolled, fetched abruptly, sickening up against a

sharp outcropping of rock and the Mongol was on him, his strength enormous, the momentum with him. Desperately, Tracy searched blindly with his foot for contact, found it behind the other's slightly bent – and thus vulnerable knee – jerking in and up with all his strength.

'Eh?' the Mongol cried and his arms flew out for support, his torso angling back and away from Tracy, twisting unnaturally. Tracy heard the crack as sharp as a rifle shot and knew the Mongol's leg was broken.

He relaxed a bit then, trying to regain his feet, and narrowly missed having his larynx crushed. He felt, rather than saw, the lightning approach of the other's hand. It came on edge first and Tracy sensed the awesome power behind him, knew that if he allowed it to strike, he would never get off the turf.

Moved two ways at once, his head and torso forward, his left wrist upward obliquely so that it crossed in front of his throat, deflecting the lethal blow, turning its intrinsic energy back on itself as he continued to move forward, using the power in his entire body behind the kite that crashed into the Mongol's heaving chest, shattering bone, cartilage and flesh.

Tracy crouched on one knee, allowing his rigid-fingered hands to relax, his breathing slowly return to normal. He opened his ears, concerned lest any small noises he or the Mongol had made during their struggle had been heard. He quartered the grounds surrounding him, could detect no other presence.

The cicadas whirred, working. Time, too, for him.

He turned until he was facing the sliding glass doors at the back of the mansion, opalescent green light streaked the right side of his face, glowing off the still surface of the swimming pool.

He took the last hundred metres to the doors in one blurred sprint. There was a simple lock on the outside but it was unlatched. Carefully, Tracy slid open one of the doors and stepped inside. He stood stock still, directly behind pale ivory raw silk floor-length curtains. There was no wind to speak of and the silk was still. He reached inside his sticky shirt, unzipped the small leather case, drew out the can of shaving cream that was not filled with shaving cream – he had had to use soap in the Princess's public men's room. He held this in the palm of his left hand as he began to part the curtains with his right.

Just a sliver of the room was revealed to one eye, then more as he moved slightly. He was alone. He stepped through, finding himself in the dining area. It was dominated by a glass-topped table whose pedestal was carved in the shape of an enormous gilt, red and green dragon. It was surrounded by twelve chairs whose legs were similarly carved. On its centre was a porcelain vase, obviously antique, of translucent thinness.

To his right was the enormous living room with a wrought-iron staircase at its extreme right end leading up to the upper storey and, presumably, the bedrooms. To his left was a short passageway to the kitchens and probably the garage.

He went immediately to his right, past a length of aqua silk curtains, drawn back partially that separated the dining room from the main living area. He could not know there was a door just behind it, could not, therefore, have known that anyone would be emerging just as he moved past the curtains.

In that instant, electric as a violent storm, there was absolutely nothing to do but stop and stare. He was face to face with a slender Chinese woman. She was a good deal shorter than Jade Princess. Hers was a Shanghaiese face, cunning and hard, dark and proud with none of the softness, the liquid sensuality that seemed an integral part of Jade Princess's countenance. Yet Tracy reacted to another kind of sensuality that was at once more disturbing and more enticing.

Her tilted eyes opened wide with shock and her mouth formed an O. For just an instant, a bolt of sheer, animalistic hostility impaled them both on the same stake, then as quickly was gone. She began to cry out just as Tracy lunged forward, grabbing her wrist and pulling, so that she was whirling around in front of him. He pressed himself against her back, feeling the soft warmth of her buttocks intruding.

There was movement at the far end of the living room. Two Chinese ran in. Both brandished pistols. They stood far enough apart so that if Tracy had been holding a gun, he would not have been able to shoot both before he himself was hit. They were pros and he marked that. Carefully, he kept the woman between himself and the bodyguards.

There was movement from above and Tracy, without diverting his attention, saw Mizo appear on the balcony overlooking the living room. 'Mr Richter,' the Japanese said slowly, 'you have caused me a great deal of discomfort.' He was wearing a black cotton tunic and trousers. 'But the time has come for us to abandon this game. How it is you come here I cannot imagine. But, even you must admit now that your race has been run. Give it up or my men will shoot you down.'

'If you wanted that, it already would have happened,' Tracy pointed out.

Mizo frowned. A forefinger plucked at his moustache. 'Yes. That is true. I wish Little Dragon no harm. But you, Mr Richter, must be eliminated.'

'Who gave you that order?'

Mizo smiled. 'At last there is something you do not know.' His face went deadpan. 'I admit it puzzles me. You obviously know of my narcotics network yet you do not know the connections. Curious. I wonder, then, how you got to me in the first place.' He came forward, one hand on the wrought-iron railing.

'I am quite well insulated and I would dearly like to know the source of the leak.'

'Then we have information to exchange.'

The smile came again, quickly fading. 'Alas, no. You, Mr Richter, are certainly in no position to bargain. While we have been talking, two of my men have made their way around the house. They are behind you now and will kill you if you make a move to harm Little Dragon.'

'Even if I believed you,' Tracy said, 'there is another surprise I have for you.' He brought out his left hand so that Mizo could see what was in it.

'A shaving can?' Mizo's voice was contemptuous.

'The present from my father.' Tracy stared up at Mizo, judging the Japanese's face. 'Remember? It will blow us all to the four winds.'

'In a shaving can?'

'How d'you think I got it through Customs?'

Mizo's face had gone grey. He stood now as still as a statue. A tiny tremor seemed to have been triggered along the side of his face. 'I see that I have underestimated you again,' he said softly. 'Well, I promise you it will be the last time.'

He came down the staircase in slippered feet, waved at the two gunmen. They put away their weapons, disappeared. 'Perhaps it is truly time to end the game,' Mizo said. His voice was filled with a world-weariness. He came slowly towards Tracy, hands clasped behind his back. 'You have done much damage to me already. I do not wish more. I have been here in Hong Kong for almost twenty years. I have done everything I have wanted to.' He shrugged his shoulders. 'What more is there, after all?' He nodded. 'There is Little Dragon and an endless parade of days.'

He was quite close now, his soft eyes regarded Tracy ruefully as if to say, I'm sorry I lost but I respect you for having beaten me. Tracy felt a tiredness suffusing him; his eyelids flickered and at that moment he knew something was wrong. *Too close*, part of his mind screamed at him. *You're letting him tooo close*.

But Mizo's hands had already unclasped behind his back, blurred outward, jerking Little Dragon from Tracy's weakened grip. He lunged down and forward, his right hand as straight as a swordblade.

He almost got through but the fear Tracy registered sent a great spurt of adrenalin coursing through him and his response was off by only a fraction. Still, Mizo hurt him before Tracy took the oncoming wrist in both his hands, lifted up and to his right, ducking under, using Mizo's own body as the fulcrum for stretching out his arms painfully.

Tracy brought the arm down hard enough for Mizo to cry out. Then, still holding on, he bent down, retrieved the fallen can.

'Count yourself lucky,' Tracy whispered into the other's ear. 'And if you're smart as well as very lucky, you'll be able to spend the rest of your lifetime with Little Dragon. If not' – he jerked on Mizo's right arm again – 'you'll die right here. Think it over.'

Mizo's eyes were watering and he was having trouble breathing. 'All right,' he managed to get out. 'Enough. I will tell you what you want to know. Just let me go. You're killing me.'

'Not good enough,' Tracy said. 'I have no reason to trust you.'

'Then I'll give you one,' Mizo's face was red with the strain and the agony Tracy was inflicting.

'I doubt that you can.'

'Give me the chance at least. I know you're wrong. I can prove how trustworthy I am with two words.'

Tracy was curious. 'What are they?'

'Operation Sultan,' Mizo said.

The Mauritious Company was located on West Twenty-seventh Street. It was an area of import–export companies, small warehouses, wholesale businesses bounded on Sixth Avenue by the flower district and on Eighth Avenue by middle-income housing projects.

Thwaite nosed the Chevvy into an illegal parking space, flipped down the sun guard on the passenger's side to which was clipped his POLICE BUSINESS card.

'Okay,' he said to Melody. 'Let's go.'

It was a red stone building, crusty and dulled by a century of New York's increasing grime. The dark, gloomy hallway was narrow, painted a drab institutional green. It smelled of cardboard and twine from a business on the ground floor.

A small directory, its glass spiderwebbed with cracks, told them the Mauritious Company was on the second floor.

Thwaite took hold of Melody with his left hand, drew his

.38 with his right. They headed up the stairs. On the landing, he paused, getting his bearings. It was dusty and dark, illumination coming from one bare bulb high up, hanging from a bare wire from the cracked and peeling ceiling.

Thwaite could find nothing to feel confident about. The hallway had about it an unmistakable air of disuse. Melody opened her mouth to say something and he squeezed her wrist hard, shaking his head back and forth.

The Mauritious Company had its offices halfway down the hall. Thwaite directed Melody to stand against the right-hand wall. He put his lips very close to her ear, whispered, 'Don't move until I call for you. If you don't hear my voice within sixty seconds, turn around and run like hell.'

She looked at him, her eyes large and clear. 'What d'you expect to find in there?'

'I don't know.' He was watching her, knew he should be watching his back. 'Maybe nothing. Maybe everything.'

'More guns. More death.'

'Your friends.'

She bared her teeth at him.

He turned away from her then, crossed to the other side of the door so that it was now between them. He tried the knob with his left hand. He turned it slowly as far as it would go, pushed gently in. Nothing. It was locked. Well, that was to be expected.

He got out his picks, went to work while Melody looked on, wide-eyed. He was close to the lock, heard the soft click. He did not wait to take the pick out, pushed hard on the door, moving quickly inside in a half-crouch, his .38 levelled before him.

The room was fully carpeted in a lush champagne-coloured pile. Mahogany desk and chairs dominated the room, though there was also a leather sofa. A wall unit to his left contained a well-stocked bar. There were three steel engravings on the walls, all of China clippers of the 1800's.

Thwaite went over to the desk, saw a calendar, pads and pencils, a brass letter opener and scissors set, a white onyx paperweight and a brass oversized paper clip standing on its end on an ebony base. And that was all. It was quite odd, he thought. Where was the phone?

There were filing cabinets in the corner behind the desk. Thwaite opened the top drawer, pulled out a sheet of cream-coloured stationery. At its top was printed in coffee-brown letters: 'The Mauritious Company', and just below it: 'Founded 1969'.

There was nothing else on the sheet. Thwaite folded it twice, tucked it into his jacket pocket. He went through the other drawers, found nothing but dust. It was a drop, all right, he thought.

There was a noise from outside and he turned. 'Melody?'

'Who's Melody?' said a harsh male voice.

Thwaite lifted his .38 at the same time hearing a loud *crack*! and he spun away from the bullet's impact. He grunted and his teeth clacked together.

From his position on the thick carpet, he saw a scar-faced man pointing a long-barrelled pistol at him.

'*Sayonara*, buddy,' the scar-faced man said, and smiled.

Thwaite let out a long sigh. His fingers were numb and he watched the shape of his own gun on the carpet in front of him.

He winced at the next shot but, oddly, felt no more pain. He felt his heart beating strongly, heard the bellows of his lungs working unimpaired. He opened his eyes.

The scar-faced man was crumpled on the doorsill, one arm stretched before him, the long-barrelled gun a pointing finger. His scarred face was turned towards Thwaite, the brown eyes gummy and staring. There was a rough ovoid of black and red in the centre of his forehead, a bullet's tearing exit hole. The back of his skull seemed somehow mashed, as if a bolted foot had slammed into it. His hair was singed.

Thwaite blinked, uncomprehending. His mouth flopped open. Then he sensed movement in the doorway behind the corpse. He saw Melody appear, a .45 in her hand. She looked from the ridge-backed mountain of the scar-faced man to him. Her lips opened stickily and he saw a thin line of crimson trickling from a cut up near her hairline. Her face was very pale.

'There was another one,' she breathed softly. 'I didn't want any more killing.' Huge tears welled up in her eyes, spilling over, and the gun slid from her long slender fingers, making a dull thud on the thick carpet. Her head shook back and forth. She could not take her eyes off him. 'Now look what you've made me do.'

She stepped over the corpse, then she was running across the room towards him, her face full of anguish but suffused with another emotion as well. She knelt in front of Thwaite, put an arm around his shoulder. He winced because that was where he had hit the floor.

He put his head back against the wall and she ran her hand down his cheek.

'Sorry,' he said. 'I'm sorry for everything.'

She was very close to him. 'Lie back,' she said. 'Relax now.'

'I said –'

'I know what you said.' Quick, clipped tones.

He saw that she was regarding him steadily and though she was still crying she seemed changed, as if a great burden had been lifted from her shoulders.

His voice was thick, his throat and lips dry. 'You did a helluva thing just now.'

'No,' she whispered. 'I'm going to do a helluva thing now.' Her head came towards his. 'I'm going to kiss you and you're going to turn into a prince.'

Just before her opened lips met his, he was certain he saw the ghost of a smile playing there.

The conditions were crude by New York City standards: the rehearsal rooms were inadequate and so uninsulated against the beastly heat that the dancers dripped sweat almost from the moment they began their exercises. The stage itself was too small and there was a hurried and uncomfortable conference with the principals in order to modify as best they could the choreography at such short notice. Martin was superb at that but still it unnerved the dancers.

But by far the worst of the problems was not actually faced until they went on the stage and then it was too late. Instead of the springy wooden flooring they were used to which aided their leaps and forgave their falls, they were faced with thinly covered concrete.

'It is impossible!' Martin exclaimed. And Lauren had to agree. Still they performed as best they could because that was what they had been trained to do. They would have done the same in the middle of a muddy clearing in the jungle.

The company was superb, the response enthusiastic. Ballet was one of the Western art forms long banned in China and everyone knew the Chinese were starved for culture.

But for Lauren the triumph was somewhat tempered by the muscle pull in her left leg. It happened at the very tail end of her solo, which made it that much more maddening.

She would never know precisely how it happened. She suspected that her partner, Steven, who was impeccably reliable, let her down off her last leap too suddenly. But she could not discount the fact that the unusually hard dancing surface had brought back worries about her newly healed hip and perhaps she was leaning off-centre just a bit. Whatever the case, she came down on the outside of her foot instead of down the centre and the momentum combined with her weight was enough to damage a muscle. She thought she heard a pop and Steven, realizing instantly what had happened, carried her off.

She barely heard the great wave of applause, did not want to go out to receive her curtain call but was carried anyway by the Dane.

Back in the dressing rooms she was sweating and cursing, the company's doctor dressing the leg in ice. Martin came up, his face a worried mask.

'How is it?' he wanted to know.

The doctor shrugged. 'I cannot tell for certain before twenty-four hours. But I don't believe there's a tear.'

'Lauren?'

'It hurts like hell,' she said angrily. 'God *damn* it!'

Martin put his arm around her. 'We have a day off tomorrow before we go in to Beijing.'

'Great,' Lauren said. 'I can spend it flat on my back.'

She rubbed a towel across her sweating face and Martin shot a quick glance at the doctor. He looked up, shook his head.

'Nonsense,' Martin said to Lauren, sitting down beside her. He was smiling now. 'This is a once-in-a-lifetime opportunity for all of us and I won't let it go to waste. You'll come with me tomorrow in the private car the People's Government has so graciously provided me.'

Lauren looked up. A chance to spend the day with Martin. 'Yes,' she said. Her eyes glowed. 'I'd like that very much.'

'Good,' Martin said, patting her good leg. 'Now I'd like you to say a few kind words to one of the cultural ministers, Lauren. He's been waiting since the performance ended to meet you. He is most chagrined at the injury you suffered. Apparently he's taken it quite personally and wants to offer you his apologies in person. We did not meet him on arrival; he was away from the city.'

Lauren was about to protest; she was still steaming but Martin interrupted her. 'This is very important to us, Lauren. Important for the success of the whole tour. Cordial relations are, after all, why we chose to accept the government's invitation to perform here.' Martin got up, smiled down at her. 'And he *does* seem to be a kindly man.'

Martin went off through the chaos, bringing back a heavyset Chinese.

'Lauren Marshall,' Martin said, almost bowing in that endearing Old World Russian manner of his that was peculiarly formal, 'may I present Dong Zhing, Shanghai's minister of culture for the People's Republic.'

Lauren held out her hand and Dong Zhing took it, bowing slightly. He was smiling and Lauren could see his small yellow teeth like perfect pieces of aged ivory, polished to a high sheen.

'I am delighted to meet you, Miss Marshall,' he said in a singsong English that was nevertheless quite good. 'I enjoyed your dancing immensely. A breath of fresh air to this ancient continent, if I may say so.'

'Thank you.'

'I must take this opportunity to apologize most profusely for

561

the unfortunate accident that befell you.' He paused, smiling and when he spoke again, his tone had changed, become more intimate as if he were doffing his official rank. 'I'm most terribly afraid that it was a bit of a screw-up on my part, not being familiar enough with the company's needs.'

Lauren's reserve melted. The man *was* rather charming. She smiled the special smile she reserved for her best audiences, said, 'I'm sure you can be forgiven.'

Dong Zhing bowed his head. 'You are most gracious, Miss Marshall. As an honourable – and tangible – way of making amends I would invite you to have supper with me this evening.' He pointed to her leg and his face fell. 'But I see that your injuries would prevent –'

Lauren had seen Martin's expression, his hands clasped in an exaggerated gesture of prayer. 'Nonsense. I am not that badly hurt. I'd be delighted to accept your invitation. And please call me Lauren.'

The Chinese minister was delighted, his face beaming. 'Capital!' he exclaimed, then clapped one palm over his mouth, giggling. 'Pun intended.' All three of them laughed.

He extended his hand and Lauren took it, allowed him to draw her to her feet. She tested the leg, found only a slight twinge of pain.

'Now, Lauren,' the Chinese minister said, putting his hand over hers, as they linked arms, 'I shall show you Shanghai's night life. Such as it is.' He giggled again and Lauren thought she might indeed have a fine time with this odd but endearing man. At least, she thought, he was not bent on spouting communist propaganda at her; that she could not tolerate.

He opened the door for her, ushering her out to his waiting car. 'And please,' he said, 'you must call me the Monk. Everyone does.'

'What's the matter?' Her delicate fingers travelled up his arm, along his side, with the deftness of a blind man's.

'It is nothing; nothing at all.'

Joy's soft eyes stared up into his, and she began to peel off his black shirt. 'What's happening. Khieu? Please tell me.'

'I saw someone get hurt,' he called down the corridors of time. I saw my sister get hurt. I saw the degradation she had slipped into, whoring for the *Yuon* and their Soviet masters. In order to survive amid the remnants of what once was my beloved Cambodia, peaceful, beautiful. Yes, I saw someone get hurt, all right. I saw how she was repaid by the patriots of her country. I was witness to what she has become: headless, bloated, spewing dank and muddy water from her permanently open mouth.

Oh, Buddha! *Apsara* dances only for me now, pursuing me, her fingers presenting me with a message. *Apsara* tells me what I must do now. But what is it? Becoming an American I have forgotten the meaning of chorus and verse; I can no longer decipher the celestial dances; for is it not true thât only our gods, the gods of the Khmer, may know the messages of their servants, *apsara*?

Stripped to the waist, he found himself being led by the hand down the hall, into Joy and Macomber's bedroom – a place his father no longer seemed to come to. Into the plum and cream tiled bathroom to sit on the closed seat of the toilet while, kneeling, Joy ran the bath.

Soon he scented lilac and evergreen, salts wafting up with the steam. Then Joy had returned to him, helping him to slip off the rest of his clothes.

Apsara came creeping towards him on her disfigured belly as he lay soaking in the hot bath, engulfed in incense with Joy's infinitely gentle hands. *Apsara* spoke to him with her fingers, webs of information he could not absorb or understand. Yet still she came, seeking . . . what?

Khieu shuddered, his hard flesh quivering, and Joy, in her concern for him, whispered over and over, 'It's all right, it's all right now.'

I was right in begging him not to go back, she thought, watching his face, the rolling of his eyes beneath the closed lids as if he were asleep and dreaming in rapid-fire sequence.

It's Del who's driving him to this, she thought, hating her husband in a quite tangible sense for the first time. Del and his goddamned obsessions. What was it this time, she wondered.

Who or what was it he wanted you to seek out in Cambodia? The answer did not really matter to her.

But whatever it was this time she knew it was tearing Khieu apart, and this she could not understand. Her heart broke for him as she held him in the water, the dampness plastering her dress to her skin. She did not care; she felt him and only him close to her.

Thwaite was in the emergency room at Bellevue when they brought Atherton Gottschalk in on a gurney. The attendant pandemonium caused him to look up. He was watching an intern working on Melody's temple.

'Jesus,' the young doctor said. 'You must've been on some tear.'

'Just get it done, Doc,' Thwaite growled.

'I'll have to call the cops,' the young intern said as he dressed the wound. 'It has to be reported.'

'That's already been taken care of,' Thwaite said, flashing his badge. He had called the precinct from the paper wholesaler's phone on the ground floor.

An intern burst through the doors just ahead of the gurney. He was followed by a resident, a half-a-dozen uniforms and as many plainclothesmen. During the brief time the doors were open to the corridor, Thwaite could see the jam up of patients, visitors, more cops, plainclothesmen manning walkie-talkies and three or four men who were obviously aides.

'Who brought him in?' the resident wanted to know. 'Paramedics?'

'No,' one of the cops said. 'Squad car. It was the fastest way.'

'Who was with him?' The resident was helping the intern transfer the body onto a table.

'One of the Secret Service guys,' the uniform said. 'Bronstein, I think his name is.'

'Get him,' the resident said. 'And for Christ's sake, tell your men to back everyone out of the corridor.'

He was very good, Thwaite said. No panic in him, just quick economical movements. He began directing the nurses. 'Get Dr Weingaard down here, will you?' One of the nurses hurried out to do his bidding. Tumult from the packed hallway intruded once again.

The uniform returned with a tall, lanky man with dark hair. 'You Bronstein?'

The man nodded.

'Talk to me,' the resident commanded. 'I'm too busy to look at you.' He was working on Gottschalk, putting in the IV lines. 'Plasma, stat,' he said to one of the nurses. 'And run a blood check right away. We'll need his type if he requires whole blood.'

'I'm Bronstein.'

'You come in with the candidate?'

'I had his head in my lap.'

The resident was having difficulty getting Gottschalk out of his suit. He picked up a scalpel. 'How was his breathing?'

'He was having difficulty –'

'Uh huh. Could you hear it?'

'Like a bellows.'

'Lotta blood, huh? This looks like a chest wound.'

'Right over his heart,' Bronstein said. 'But there wasn't much blood.'

'The hole is over the heart, all right.' The resident bent lower. 'But it must've missed. Puncture the heart and you'll get a fountain of blood. Get the portable EKG unit over here.'

'I saw him get hit,' Bronstein insisted. 'It was the heart, all right.'

'Well, if you're right, I'll go back to my rounds. He'll be dead.'

He used the scalpel, swiftly, lightly to shred back Gottschalk's clothes. Layer by layer it came apart. 'Gotta see if it's beating,' he said almost to himself. He lifted his stethoscope into place. 'Get X-ray ready,' he said to the intern.

Another resident came in, followed by the nurse. Dr Weingaard. He was an older man, his well-clipped beard shot through with grey. 'What've we got here?'

'Atherton Gottschalk,' the resident said. 'Just been shot. This one says through the heart but it can't be, he's still breathing.'

'Let me see it,' Dr Weingaard said.

'Just let me get this last bit of – Jesus Christ!'

'What is it?'

The first resident looked up. His young face was spattered with blood. His dark curling hair was already matted with sweat. 'Take a look at this.' He stepped away so that his colleague could get a clear view. 'This man's been shot in the heart and he's not dead.'

Dr Weingaard shook his head. 'Not possible.'

'It is,' the young resident said, 'if you happen to be wearing a bullet-proof vest.'

'Give me one of their guns,' Tracy said.

'What for?'

'Just do as I say!' Using the slightest bit of *kiai* to ensure immediate compliance.

Mizo's twisted body jerked a little and, using his free hand, he snapped his fingers. One of the young Chinese appeared at the top of the stairs.

'I want the other one in view, too,' Tracy said.

He snapped his fingers again and the second man appeared beside the first. Mizo made a motion with his fingers and the first Chinese came carefully down the staircase. At no time did his eyes leave Tracy's face and Tracy could read the almost palpable hatred there. Hatred for the foreign devil; a more personal hatred. Perhaps he had been related to one of the men who had gone into Aberdeen Harbour; Dragon Tattoo, for instance. Tracy made a note of it.

The young Chinese stopped about ten metres from where Mizo stood and Little Dragon lay, half-dazed. He snaked a hand inside his jacket, produced a .33 Airweight, began to hand it over to Mizo.

'No,' Tracy said sharply in Cantonese, startling the other. 'Grip it by the barrel, slide it along the floor over to me.'

The young Chinese looked from Tracy to Mizo. He got the nod and complied, a sour look on his face.

Tracy knelt slowly down, taking his hostage with him, picked up the pistol. He clicked open the chamber, glanced down, then looked up quickly, grinning. 'It would be nice, you illegitimate son of a pus-ridden sea snake, if you'd give me a loaded weapon.'

There was no expression on the young Chinese's face but Tracy became aware of Mizo smiling. The Japanese shrugged as if to say, you can't blame me for trying. He snapped his fingers again and the man rolled six cartridges along the floor.

Tracy made Mizo lie face down on the floor next to his mistress while he loaded the gun. Then he bent down, placed the muzzle of the enormous pistol just behind Mizo's right ear. 'I don't suppose,' he said softly, 'I have to test this.'

Mizo, whose head was turned to one side, his lower cheek pressed uncomfortably against the polished wooden floor, a break in the Chinese carpets, blanched. 'No, no, no,' he said quickly. 'Everything is in order, I assure you.'

'Yes. Indeed it is. I can tell blanks from live ammo.'

As Mizo twisted his head around further to see him better, Tracy abruptly let the Japanese go, took a firm hold on Little Dragon.

Mizo immediately scrambled up and the young Chinese, perhaps not seeing clearly what Tracy was up to, began to dart forward.

Tracy cocked the hammer of the .38, aimed it at the back of Little Dragon's neck.

'Back away, you dung-infested, lice-ridden offspring of a whore!' Mizo screamed. 'Can't you see he'll shoot her if you move against him.'

The young Chinese backed away immediately, the tension in his shoulders dying reluctantly and Tracy was gratified to see proved his theory that Mizo would be more reliable with Little Dragon under the gun.

Tracy pulled her slowly up and Mizo said shakily, 'I'm going to tell them to move backward out of the room.'

'Don't do that,' Tracy said immediately. 'I want them right where they are; otherwise, they're liable to go elsewhere and plot something nasty.'

Mizo said nothing but Tracy knew he had lost that round and face at the same time.

'Just so we're quite clear,' Tracy said. 'If you or they do

anything I construe as hostile, Little Dragon's brains will end up all over this room.'

Mizo was white-faced. 'There's no need for that kind of reminder,' he said, rubbing his arm where Tracy had twisted it back. 'We have a truce.'

Tracy jerked Little Dragon to her feet. She was wearing a blue-green Shantung silk dress slit up both sides, revealing long lean legs. The mandarin collar framed her neck where gleamed a choker in diamonds and emeralds in alternating vertical bands. She kept her body and head very still, as if awaiting his command but her tilted almond eyes were dark with hate and a power held tightly in check. She was a woman used to getting her own way; she would not take kindly to such treatment. Too bad, he thought.

Mizo lifted an arm, pointing. 'May we at least sit down and conduct this, er, meeting like civilized people.'

Tracy thought that comment amusing in light of the deadly maze Mizo had been leading him through over the last few days but he said nothing.

To his right was a snakebacked sofa of clear-lacquered bamboo frame and Burmese jade-coloured silk cushions. Beside it was a small wicker table from Bali on which was a porcelain lamp. Beyond that, was a traditional Chinese dragon, a triple-s curve rising vertically from the floor, hammered out of brass, painted in gaudy crimson, bottle green and brilliant blue, its long sword-like tongue reaching upward towards the ceiling.

On the opposite side of the room was a matching sofa and a pair of leather easy chairs, incongruous amid the other Eastern-flavoured furniture. A three-fold antique Japanese screen depicting herons in flight over a marsh or river mouth stood behind the far sofa. Scattered about were various artifacts, all obviously old and just as obviously worth a fortune, of bronze, wood and stone: remnants of civilizations either dead or dying out.

'Take that chair there,' Tracy said, indicating one of the leather easy chairs. Mizo went obediently towards it while Tracy took Little Dragon to the bamboo and silk sofa facing it, sat down. The two Chinese looked on impassively, as if they had been turned to stone.

'You are quite a bit more formidable than I had been led to believe,' the Japanese's voice held a note of regret. 'But then my information was spotty.'

Tracy was instantly alert. 'It would be,' he said easily now. 'No one knows much about me.'

Mizo's face fixed in a frown. 'Just who the hell are you, anyway? What do you want from me?'

The more Mizo spoke, the more information Tracy could glean. The trick would be in keeping him talking without making him suspicious. 'I told you why I came here. My father –'

'Oh, please! Let's drop that lie, at least.'

Time to take a stab in the dark. 'I want in on the business.'

Mizo was impassive. 'What business?'

'*Your* business, White Powder Sun.'

This time Little Dragon shivered. Out of the corner of his eye, Tracy was aware that she was staring at him, wide-eyed.

'You know about my, er, school,' Mizo said carefully. 'You know me as White Powder Sun. Tell me, do you even know Louis Richter?'

'As I told you, he's my father.'

'What's a power-ratio resistor?'

Tracy told him.

'A d-Appline micro capacitor?'

Tracy answered that as well.

'Then it is possible,' Mizo said softly. 'You could be the son.'

Tracy wanted to get on with it; his shoulder was paining him; it had been a long day. 'It's "Operation Sultan" I'm interested in.'

'If you really are Louis Richter's son,' Mizo said, 'I'm not surprised.' His eyes were somnolent, the one leg crossed over his knee swinging back and forth in time with some interior rhythm he was setting up. 'It is not unknown to me that his son, Tracy, if you are, indeed, Tracy Richter, was part of the Special Forces while they were in, er, South Vietnam during the years 1969–1970.'

As Mizo's expressionless voice sing-songed on, Tracy felt exhaustion creeping back into his bones and overworked muscles, fraying the edges of his consciousness. With a visible start, he snapped back. Mizo seemed to be smiling slightly. Watch it! Tracy admonished himself. This is just what he wants. He knows what a race you've run; he's been the maze-keeper.

Tracy clicked back the hammer on the .38, enjoying the effect the startlingly loud sound made in the room, jammed it painfully into Little Dragon's ribcage so that she jumped, reaching vainly out with her left hand so that he could see the white jade ring with its surround of small, faceted diamonds on her finger. She cried out softly and Mizo went very still.

'There's no need for that.' His tongue came out, wet his lips.

'Mizo,' Tracy said, leaning forward, 'or White Powder Sun or Backblast Sun or Sun Ma Sun, whatever you want to call yourself, let me make this very plain. I have no time for games. If you don't come across with the information I want right now, I'm going to kill her while you watch. Is that what you want?'

'No,' Mizo said, abruptly switching to English. He sighed. 'Calm yourself, young Richter, and do not harm my Little Dragon.'

Tracy nodded at him and to his hostage, he said, 'Sit back and relax.' He glanced at her, thinking she reminded him of someone but he could not determine who it was.

Mizo settled his buttocks more comfortably against the cushions, then began:

'In the early months of 1969, units of the American Special Forces under the control of Major Michael Eiland of the Daniel Boone operations, began to cross the border of South Vietnam from their semi-permanent base in Ban Me Thuot into Cambodia – a neutral nation. Their objective was to destroy COSVN HQ, the US Army acronym for "Central Office for South Vietnam"; that is, the secret base of the North Vietnamese and the Viet Cong.'

The Japanese paused to determine whether or not he was boring the man sitting across from him. Satisfied, he went on. 'Since 17 March of that year, US "Arclight" B'52s had been daily engaged in "Operation Menu", a clandestine bombing mission, approved by your President Nixon, to accomplish just that: the destruction of COSVN HQ.

'But MACV, General Creighton Abrams' Military Assistance Command, Vietnam, had identified no less than fifteen COSVN strongholds along the eastern border of Cambodia.

'The first of the sites to be hit was Base Area 353, designated "Breakfast" by the Army. That was followed by the bombing of Base Area 352, "Lunch", and then, 350, "Dessert".'

Mizo's head turned a little, his black, slitted eyes catching the light for a moment, turning them opaque. He was watching Tracy very carefully. 'It is this last, Area 350, that should concern us now.' His hands were still and his leg had ceased its swinging.

'There was a certain lieutenant – his name is of no import to us – who led a particular Special Forces unit within the Daniel Boone operational structure. In reality, however, he and his hand-picked men were completely autonomous of Major Eiland or anyone else in the Daniel Boone Ops HQ.' Mizo smiled. 'Does this surprise you?'

'Nothing surprises me in a war,' Tracy said, thinking, I have to be very careful now. Slowly, slowly; it's obvious he's setting traps for me. Does he know? Quickly he shoved the question aside, trusting in time and his own joss to reveal the answers.

Mizo was nodding. 'Just so.' His expression was unreadable. 'Well, this lieutenant did not know the ultimate source of his command, only knew that whatever he requisitioned was immediately provided him, no questions or the usual Army red tape or snafus. He knew, too, that as secret as the Daniel Boone operations were from the prying eyes of the world, so were his own orders from all personnel around him and his men.

'As far as those few privy to the "Eyes Only" and "Top Secret" memos that directed the "Menu" operations were concerned, the lieutenant's unit was, as all the other Daniel Boone units, concerned with the destruction of COSVN HQ.

'Only the lieutenant and his four men knew the truth. Their mission also had a code name: "Operation Sultan".'

In the utter silence that ensued, Tracy said, 'Tell me Sultan's objective.'

Mizo nodded, his eyes closing for a moment. When his head came up again, he said, ' "Operation Sultan" was an ultrasensitive counter-intelligence mission mounted in April of 1969 by ... well, here my sources are slightly vague but the prevailing opinion is that the operation was CIA-financed.'

Tracy wondered if there was any way he could determine if Mizo was telling the truth.

'It was meant as a strike against the Viet-Khmer subterranean network set up and financed, there is little doubt, by the PRC – the People's Republic of China – to flood the American-held sectors of the war with readily available heroin. A narcotic which, in Beijing's estimation, could devastate the US military effort by turning soldiers into addicts. This is correct.' He stared straight into Tracy's eyes. It was not a question.

'Go on.'

'The operation field leader was hand-picked. A lieutenant well known for his brutality as well as for his cleverness in running such missions. This also is correct.'

'You're drawing this out unnecessarily,' Tracy said, fatigue sweeping in on him again. 'Get to the point.'

'As you wish.' Mizo settled himself more comfortably in his perch. 'It is my information – and I know it to be quite correct – that "Operation Sultan" went down on the US intelligence books as a total success.'

'What of it?'

'It's not true,' Mizo said. His eyes watched Tracy's face for a reaction.

'The Khmer Rouge encampment in Area 350 was destroyed as ordered,' Tracy said. '*That's* a fact. There was independent cross-corroboration of that. A back-up team was sent in; that's what they found. They also reported finding the ash remnants of a fire. The narcotics were burned.'

Mizo shrugged. 'Oh, perhaps a kilo was sacrificed on that altar. For just such a purpose. To fool a mop-up.' He shook his head. 'But believe me, my friend, the bulk of that shipment destined for American arms was diverted, not destroyed.'

'And I suppose you have proof of that?'

Mizo spread his arms wide. 'How do you suppose I had this mansion built and three others as well?'

Tracy fought to breathe evenly. *Prana*. 'What are you saying?'

'Simply this. I became the middleman for that shipment of heroin. And all the other subsequent shipments.' He put his hands together. 'You see, the pipeline was never terminated as had been reported. It was merely turned. It still functions to this day.' Mizo smiled. 'I ought to know. I run it.'

Tracy felt dizzy with new knowledge. It seemed incredible but he had no reason to doubt the Japanese. After all, how else could he have got such an intimate working knowledge of a highly classified foundation mission? There could be no other answer. Mizo's smile broadened. 'You look white, my friend. As if you'd just seen a *kami*. A spirit. I cannot blame you. After all, Sultan was surely a mission you would have been assigned had you not dropped out of sight.'

At least, Tracy thought, he does not know all of it.

'Who do you work for?' he said.

'The Mauritious Company,' Mizo said unhesitatingly. 'Do you know it?'

'No.'

'You should. It's owned – oh, three or four times removed, of course; there's absolutely no danger in it – by a former agent, the lieutenant who ran Sultan in the field. Delmar Davis Macomber.' He let one hand drop to his side. He was very relaxed. 'You may have even worked with him; Ban Me Thuot was a small enough enclave.'

Tracy was busy dealing with the flood of information Mizo was shovelling at him. Perhaps at another time it would have been all right. But as it was, without sleep, banged around considerably more than he had been in ten years, the strain of eluding the police while trying to outthink Mizo, it was all too much. He could not even begin to assimilate the ramifications of what he had just heard.

But Mizo seemed oblivious to his plight. 'Oh, yes, Macomber. A very smart man. He used his profits well, funnelling the money into the legitimate business he set up, Metronics, Inc. But I find it fascinating that he still sells death, in whatever form.' He leaned forward. 'Confidentially, I think the man is addicted to it. He lives on the edge, continually walking a tightrope.' The hand at his side twitched like a dog's paw in sleep. 'It is how he thrives.'

Fighting against fatigue and shock Tracy said, 'Why are you telling me all this?'

Mizo smiled like a shark. 'Because you asked me to. I don't want to see Little Dragon harmed. I can live without the narcotics business now but, alas, I cannot survive without her.'

Through the haze, Tracy recognized that something was askew. Yes, what Mizo said was true enough; it was how Tracy had set it up. But it had all come out too quickly, too easily. During the long day and longer night, he had come to know Mizo like an intimate. It was another day now but the man was the same, a Chinese puzzle of a personality. Macomber might, as Mizo said, thrive on death but the Japanese thrived on deviousness. Tracy did not believe for an instant that he was willing to let the narcotics network self-destruct around him without putting up a hell of a fight.

Tracy stared hard at Mizo. It was there, he knew, facing him. The answer to his question lay eight feet away. If he could only find it in time.

'Either you're lying –'

'My friend, you know I am not lying. My facts are perfect; the truth itself is incontrovertible.' The hand flicked again. 'Logic must tell you that I have not lied.'

'Then why –'

In that moment, he knew. As his right shoulder and arm went numb. He whirled but his reflexes were down. Little Dragon, on Mizo's hand signals, had moved on him. He had been concentrating so much on the Japanese, exhaustion and pain had done the rest, fogging out his peripheral vision, his normally clear thought processes.

The first two knuckles of Little Dragon's left fist slammed into the bridge of his nose. The shock blinded him and he felt the gun being wrenched out of his nerveless fingers as the adamantine facets of the outer circle of diamonds on her ring slashed across his face, blinding him momentarily and bringing blood and pain bubbling up through the rent skin.

He cried out, jerking back, using his ears as well as his brain, reaching back behind him for the can of shaving cream, his thumb depressing the hidden stud only he and his father knew about as he heard the movement of the Chinese coming down off the staircase to join his compatriot.

Tracy marked the sounds, calculating distances without the use of his eyes as Jinsoku had taught him, saying *Darkness is their special friend; make it yours also. You must learn to move in it, hear in it, see in it, fight in it so that you will live in it and others will die. And first you must learn not to fear it – an instinctual thing within the species, though you may not even be aware of it.*

He threw the can in an underhand toss, lifting the thing high in the air to attract the maximum attention, to take concentration off himself. He moved at the same time, up and back.

The percussion of the blast blew out the windows at the back of the house, shattering the glass outward in a fierce shower of multi-coloured sparks. White light that was no light at all suffused the room and the ground seemed to slide and shudder as if from an earthquake. Someone was screaming in a high-pitched hysterical fashion and there was a great deal of grey smoke, at first ballooning outward on the rushing winds of the blast, then in the unholy silence that immediately followed, drifting lazily like summer clouds.

Dust filled the air, filtering down again in an inconstant patter like rain on a rooftop. The sofa behind which Tracy had jumped had been slammed backward, its far edge now jammed partway through the ruined floor-to-ceiling windows.

The top half of the antique screen had been sheared away, disintegrating in the first outward thrust of the blast. Of the two Chinese gunmen, there was little left. But the walls behind the spot where they had been standing glistened pinkly.

Tracy came up for air, took a further inventory. Little Dragon was on her knees, behind the sprawled junk of the Balinese table and remnants of the porcelain lamp. Her Shantung dress was torn away from her along one side as if by a vicious hand. Her flesh was reddened and beginning to swell; spots of high colour caused by slowly seeping blood began to grow in a thin spiderweb network. She was rocking back and forth on her haunches, her white fists clamped to her ears, her eyes squeezed shut.

Tracy searched for Mizo. He could not see him through the pall. He felt rather than saw the tiger about to climb his back. He spun and dropped at the same time, saw Mizo's shape hurtling towards him, one leg stretched rigid, the foot held at the proper angle so that Tracy thought, *Karate* and, moving his torso obliquely to the right to take his head out of danger, lifted his left forearm, making contact just behind the lethal hammer of the incoming calloused heel, exploding his arm upward just after contact.

Jinsoku would have wanted him to go for the kill at that moment when Mizo was off-balance and vulnerable but Tracy did not have enough time to set his defence. All he had time for was the preliminary rejection of aggressive force and then Mizo was by him, recovering quickly and turning, scrambling over the bent and twisted frame of the sofa, returning with elbows and sword-strikes.

Tracy fell back beneath the rapid-fire assault. Even though he had been entirely shielded this time, he had just withstood his second explosion in four days; this one had taken more out of him than he had suspected. Though he had slept at the hospital and on board the Tanka junk, he now understood that his body required a deeper more lasting rest and he thought, the twenty-four hour flight home would do me just right.

Three sword-strikes had penetrated his defence, falling with heavy impact on his weakened shoulder, sending sheets of pain rippling through him, before he realized that his concentration was wavering.

He brought the flat of his hand up, ramming it against Mizo's chest, giving himself a momentary respite. He was breathing hard and the sweat was rolling freely off him so that his clothes clung to him clammily. He had three more of his father's miniaturized devices in the case plastered against his breastbone but in his current condition he dared not employ them. His ears were ringing and his head swam; just the thought of enduring another percussion sent his flesh quivering, his teeth grinding.

He looked up. Mizo had broken off the attack and an interior alarm was sounding. He caught a glimpse of the Japanese scrambling over the broken back of the sofa. He wondered where the other was headed and then, abruptly, he knew and, steeling himself, took one enormous stride, vaulting over the sofa and Mizo in one blurred movement.

He hit the carpet on his off-side shoulder, grunting involuntarily with the impact, curling himself into a ball, rolling. He felt a pain in his side, scrabbled to his knees, fell back as the pain came again.

He turned back, away from the Airweight lying on the carpet, the object of Mizo's search. The Japanese screamed as he ground one heel down towards Tracy's face.

Tracy rolled, felt part of the appalling force as the man drove his leg down and, jackknifing his lower body to provide the momentum, struck upward and over with the edge of his right hand. Mizo doubled over and, in a rage, used three of the most complex and lethal *kansetsuwaza* – the techniques of dislocation – as he came down on Tracy.

Had there been sufficient room to manoeuvre or had Tracy's energy been at capacity it would have been all right. *Kansetsu-waza* appear frightening and, indeed, are quite dangerous. But Jinsoku had taught him how to handle them. However, neither was the case and with the third, only partially deflected as he twisted and squirmed beneath the vicious assault, Tracy knew that his bad shoulder was about to give out. If Mizo in fact managed to dislocate that joint he knew he would be finished. In his current state of fatigue, he could not overcome such an opponent and the burst of pain inside him at the same time.

He rolled and kept rolling, seeking time and Mizo, a canny enemy, would give him none. He rolled with Tracy, raining blows on him, working over his body, seeking again a way into that reinjured shoulder, knowing as well that that was the key to his victory and, ultimately, Tracy's death.

Then Tracy's back fetched up against something hard and all the wind went out of him as sharp prongs dug painfully into his ribs. Mizo was upon him, the configuration of his torso and arms indicating that he was about to use what had already worked so well for him, the *kansetsu-waza*.

577

Tracy knew time was short – the ending of his life could be measured now in tenths-of-seconds. He reached around behind him, desperately scrabbling for a controlling grip on the object against which he had been forced. He brought his back away, his torso forward towards Mizo and, simultaneously brought the object around and up. It was tremendously heavy and he gritted his teeth, putting the thing in motion as Mizo began his last assault, moving in so that there was just a breath of air between them, just that small space between life and death, the beating of a heart and the stilled breath, the glazed eyes, the end of all things.

Tracy felt the balance of the thing, thrust it forward with all the strength remaining inside of him, exhaustion giving way at just this extraordinary moment as the organism fuelled itself on the release of adrenaline, the adrenals and then, because of the serious depletion of whole energy, the pancreas absorbing the shock of the almost overpowering stress.

The object flew forward in a blur; Mizo was already a blur. He had turned himself into a missile of destruction and nothing could now deter him from his planned course of action: the space between them far too small, the complexity of the tactics and attack would take him in to his target before a change could be affected. If he had wanted to. Mizo did not.

At the moment of attack, the senses narrow down to a pinpoint: the small area of objective. In a final attack when the enemy is presumed hurt and the kill is to be effected, this is even more so.

Mizo did not even see the object coming at him until it was far too late. Tracy was aware of his changing expression, the fierce warrior's countenance on the brink of victory being supplanted by a combination of emotions: confusion and disbelief chief among them.

Tracy had fetched up against the hammered brass dragon and this was what he used now against the Japanese, its sword-like tongue, barbed with mythical fire, penetrating Mizo's ribcage at heart level.

He twisted upward, trying vainly to counter his heavy momentum forward, to get away from the piercing pain that was already engulfing him. He could not. And Tracy rose up, straining all the harder, panting and swearing as he pushed inward. The entire length of the brass tongue had twisted its way into the flesh and now the gaping jaws tore through Mizo's skin so that he screamed and convulsed. One of his ribs broke under the pressure of the attack, deflecting the point so that it just missed the heart. But it ripped into the lung, and blood from the massive internal bleeding began to pour into the rent.

Tracy saw Mizo was choking to death on his own fluids and broke off the assault. The great dragon was too well embedded within the Japanese's flesh, the twisting tongue too barbed, for him to be able to pull it out.

Mizo lay back amid the rubble of his house. His breathing was stentorian and he coughed wetly with every other exhalation. His face was ashen but his eyes were very clear.

Tracy was aware that he was trying to say something and he bent down, putting one hand behind the other's neck to elevate the head.

'... Dragon ...' It was a dry rattle and Tracy thought for a moment he was talking about the instrument of his death. Then he began again. 'Little Dragon ...' He broke off, coughing worse than before. Tracy judged he had little time. Mizo looked up at him. 'Take her ... take ...' A fit of coughing overtook him, racking his body and covering him with blood. He, too, knew it was time. 'Take her to ... Golden Dragon.'

'To the *feng shui* man? Why?'

Mizo's eyes were fluttering closed; there was no colour left in his face. All his blood was racing away from him, pooling in the torn cavity that had been his chest. His lungs fought to work, failed. His mouth opened one last time. 'Her father,' Mizo breathed, 'loves her ... very much. Return her ... to him ...'

Tracy looked up from the dead man, towards the young woman still closed within herself, rocking gently back and forth, oblivious to them both. He was more tired than he could ever remember being but the knowledge that Mizo had given him fuelled him.

On leaden legs, he rose and walked stiffly through the rubble, through the returning quiet of the Peak, towards Little Dragon. The cicadas were whirring madly as he took her out of there, into the blackness of the steamy Hong Kong night.

6

Kim was holed up in a sleazy downtown Dallas hotel, waiting. He sat on the single bed, his back against the faded wallpaper. A day-old newspaper, obviously well-thumbed, lay folded beside him. He stared at nothing.

Somewhere outside his locked door, he knew, death lay waiting for him, slowly closing in. He was content to wait.

The one window was to his right. He was seven floors up and if he leaned out and twisted his head all the way to the left, he could just make out the leading edge of the grassy knoll where President John Fitzgerald Kennedy had been shot in the failing days of 1963.

Kim felt no remorse now when he thought of that day just as, had he been old enough at the time of the killing, he would have felt no remorse. He had never been subject to the Kennedy mystique that had so inexplicably – in his opinion – gripped almost all of America.

He had been talked into committing American military advisors and personnel to a South Vietnamese régime that could not possibly survive. He had been foolhardy enough to swallow what Kim was certain was Soviet disinformation about the strategic importance of Vietnam without reading his history to find out how useless a modern military effort was in Vietnam's difficult terrain.

And, of course, he had been responsible for the assassination of the Ngo brothers. For that alone Kim could never forgive him.

But the ghost of John Fitzgerald Kennedy was far from Kim's mind now. He had been there several days ago, perhaps, when Kim had first booked into the hotel and made his usual survey of entrances, exits, vulnerable points in security.

Since then, other things, far more important to Kim himself, had occupied him.

It had begun on the night of Atherton Gottschalk's nomination. As he had been ordered, Kim had been in Dallas, had got himself a VIP pass to the convention, security access to the candidates, in order to give the Panel's message to Gottschalk.

Kim had never got that far.

There was bedlam directly after the candidate's victory speech, of course, and Kim knew that was the best time for him to move in. This he had done, insinuating himself within the jostling, festive crowd, showing his various passes when security guards or uniforms from the Dallas PD requested them. He was in sight of Gottschalk when he paused, the crowd taking him a step or two forward in its amorphous exuberance.

Quickly he ducked down, beneath a waving, gesticulating tree of arms and stared straight ahead. At first, he could see nothing amiss but a tight tingling had suffused the back of his neck, warning him. Something was wrong.

The crowd was getting near to out of control in its frenzy after a long, gruelling week of internecine warfare among party members. Now was the time to let loose and celebrate.

Kim looked at the candidate, shaking hands and being congratulated in the full flood of the television cameras' spotlights but all his senses were directed towards Gottschalk's periphery. For it was there his sixth sense told him the danger resided.

They saw each other at the same instant and Kim was careful to watch the man only from the corner of his eye. Kim was among the handful of the élite assassins of the world. He knew that, as in any other profession, there were certain levels of expertise and he judged this one to be somewhere within the middle range. Kim had smelled him out at once.

Now Kim began to withdraw, slowly enough so that the man would have no trouble following him. He turned, made his circuitous way out of the enormous jammed auditorium complex. He left by one of the side doors and, skirting the long ragged line of police sawhorses used for crowd control, walked the short distance to where he had left his rented car in the parking lot.

He got in immediately and quickly depressed the gas, flooding the engine. Then he tried to start the car. He was unsuccessful. Using his side mirror, he watched the man's progress as he emerged from the same doorway Kim himself had used. Kim tried starting the car again and got nowhere. He just hoped the man was smart enough to have come here by car.

Kim turned over the ignition once more, orienting the man, then as he saw the figure dart forward and get into a dark late-model Dodge, he turned the ignition again and the engine started up. He pulled out of the lot and into the hideous jam of traffic surrounding the convention site. For fifty minutes he and his pursuer crawled forward hesitantly amid chrome and heated metal until they were both sufficiently outside the perimeter to break free of the traffic.

During that time Kim had plenty of time to work out what had happened. No one – absolutely no one knew where he was going to be and, more importantly, *what he was going to do*, except the members of the Panel.

Accept for the moment the premise that they wanted him killed. Why? There was absolutely no reason. They had hired him, all they had to do was fire him if they wished a termination of his services. The fact was they did not; on the contrary they *needed* his services. What then was the answer?

He rolled that over for a time, working on all the possible permutations. Within fifteen minutes he had gone through them all. Then he went back to the beginning and started all over again. He came up with three more and dismissed them. All but one.

What if – he posed this question to himself – one member of the Panel was not what he seemed? What if, to put not too fine a point on it, the Panel had been infiltrated by the Soviets? That was just their style and they had the expertise for such a manoeuvre.

What would it get them? The answer was obvious and frightening: a European-based window on the intimate workings of current *and future* American political manoeuvring. Kim was abruptly aghast at the incalculable advantage such an opportunity would afford the Soviets. They could plan and weigh future thrusts with a working knowledge of how America would react.

And his own termination? Again, if he was correct, the answer seemed obvious: the threat of Gottschalk's election to the Presidency far outweighed the mole's continued presence within the Panel. Without the money being funnelled in from Europe, the candidate's election was put into that much more doubt.

Still, Kim thought, this is all conjecture on my part. But there is one sure way of finding out. He glanced in the rear-view mirror; his tick was still with him. First things first, he told himself, a cold fury overtaking him.

Now, when the door to his room burst open, Kim appeared dead. His breathing, which over the minutes he had reduced to an absolute minimum, appeared to anyone but a highly trained observer to have ceased altogether. His eyes were open, staring glassily into the middle distance. He was very pale from the slowing of his circulation.

The man, who was Dutch and superbly trained, hesitated a fraction: this was not at all what he had been expecting. He stood just within the open doorway, his finger on the trigger of the blunt-nosed miniature automatic.

In that instant, Kim was off the bed, crossing the room like a wraith. He slammed against the Dutchman, staggering him, twisting the machine pistol out and up and delivered a stunning blow to the side of the man's head.

For four hours after that Kim worked on the man in articulated interrogation. He could certainly have gone on but at that point he knew he had got all the man had to give. It was not much and in disgust he used the leading edge of his hand in a sword-strike that collapsed the Dutchman's cricoid cartilage in his throat, killing him. It was quick and humane; diametrically opposed to what Kim had done to him previously.

Immediately, Kim checked the room for any signs that he had been there; of course he had not used his real name when checking in. He spent ten minutes carefully wiping off all surfaces even though he had been quite careful about touching a minimum of those that would retain his prints. Then he left, walking over a mile before he picked up a cab. He took it crosstown to the plush Hilton where he booked a suite under his own name. Before he went up to the top-floor rooms he sent a short telex to Eindhoven.

VALKERIE: YOUR INFILTRATION OF PANEL COMPROMISED. MEET DALLAS SOONEST OR DETAILS TELEXED TANGO. TIME AND VENUE FOLLOW . . .

He signed it 'Blue Szechuan'. He read it over again then, satisfied, he handed it over at the front desk to be sent.

Yes, he thought on the way up, this is the only way to draw out the mole.

Then he turned his mind to other matters. Thu, for one. An image formed in his mind of his brother in his designer jeans and American tee shirt, sunglasses wrapped across his eyes. And his American mistress, big-breasted, blonde, as huge as a cow.

The ways of the Vietnamese were fast disappearing and this Kim could not abide. The American mistress was meaningless. But Thu was not. Thu was his brother. Outwardly, nothing would change. But inwardly, it was another matter entirely. Now Kim was totally cut off from everyone and everything he once held dear.

'I look into your face,' the Monk said, 'and it tells me that you are unhappy.' He called for the waiter. 'Is there something you wish for?'

Lauren smiled at that, shook her head. 'No.' Her smile was rueful. 'I don't think there's anything you can do.'

The Monk frowned, dismissed the waiter. They were at the Jin Jiang Club, sitting like a pair of celebrities amid hushed conversations and covert glances. It was, Lauren thought, almost like being at home.

'I think you do me a disservice, Miss Marshall,' the Monk said. He stroked his moustache. 'I am known here as somewhat of a magician.' He smiled, leaned across the table. 'Now how can I help you?'

Lauren smiled. 'Another bullshot.'

'Indeed.' The Monk inclined his head and her empty glass was whisked away. A moment later, a new one had taken its place.

She picked it up, sampled it. 'How do they know to make these so well?'

The Monk grinned. 'I myself have been to many foreign lands.' He drew himself up. 'How many gin mills have I stepped into? I've lost count.'

Lauren laughed, feeling at ease with the Chinese's good-natured bantering. 'I must admit you're not exactly what I had envisioned.'

'Oh?' The Monk cocked his head, drew his eyebrows together in a scowl. 'Perhaps this is more like the fierce xenophobic Oriental you had in mind.'

'Exactly,' Lauren laughed. 'You've captured a certain . . .'

'*Je ne sais quoi?*'

'I should take a picture.'

'Oh, no, don't!' He cried in mock alarm. 'No one would recognize me.'

Their dinner came and they ate slowly, comfortable with each other.

The Monk shook his head. 'I meant what I said before, Miss Marshall.'

'I asked you to call me Lauren.'

The Monk nodded. 'I admire what you do, Lauren. I have great respect for total commitment, concentration, a controlled centrism of energy. That's very Chinese, you know.'

'Now I don't know whether you're teasing me again.'

'About the compliment, certainly not.' The Monk wiped his lips with delicacy. 'As for the other . . .' He waved his hand back and forth like a bird on the wing. 'The grace inherent in such a controlled form reminds me somewhat of a number of our gymnastic experts but really what *you* do is so much different. The expression of interpretation.' He looked sad now. 'That is what I miss most when I am here, in my official capacity.'

Lauren was intrigued. 'You mean you have another one?'

'Certainly. Man cannot live by bureaucracy alone.' He poured more wine for them both. 'My soul would wither and die under such harsh circumstances.'

'I was under the impression that your government, well, frowned on any kind of deviation.'

'My government has in recent years come to a kind of self-realization.' The Monk leaned forward again, took her fingers in the palm of his hand. It was firm and dry; a hand to trust. 'It cannot continue to exist and grow in the vacuum it has created for itself since the advent of the revolution. Up until now, you see, it has been rather a baby about such things; its own infancy, its vulnerability, if you will, caused a kind of hysteria – the xenophobia you have heard so much about.

'But now' – he smiled again – 'time and tide have reshaped thinking. Reality has set in and co-existence with the rest of the world has become an important goal. However, the government found itself at a distinct disadvantage in this quarter since, by its own ordination, it had forbidden contact. It knew next to nothing about the world outside. Officially, it was far too early to show its hand; the Oriental mind cannot be rushed.

'I was one of a handful sent out, in a strictly, uhm, shall we say, free-lance entrepreneurial capacity to, er, get the lay of the land.'

'But now that China is opening itself up there's no need for that any more.'

Thinking that this was a sharp cookie indeed, the Monk said, 'Ordinarily, you would be right. However, my business generates so much income for my government, it would be foolish of me to discontinue my efforts in that quarter.'

'So you're not free-lance after all. The government takes a slice. That's very capitalistic of them.'

The Monk threw his head back and laughed deeply and heartily. 'Yes, indeed. In some respects, we learn quite quickly. Free-lance was perhaps a poor choice of words. Unofficial is more accurate.' He squeezed her hand before letting it go. 'I trust my secret is safe with you.'

Lauren shrugged. 'Who've I got to tell? I haven't any friends in the State Department.' She pushed her glass towards him. 'More wine, please.'

'I wish,' the Monk said, pouring for her, 'you'd tell me what's troubling you.'

Lauren stared into his open alien face for a moment, considering. 'Well, why not?' she said at last. 'A fresh point of view couldn't hurt, I suppose.' And she told him about Tracy, her brother, Bobby, and what had happened between them. She did not use anyone's name.

'I love him,' she concluded. 'And I don't know why I did my best to drive him away from me.'

The Monk thought about this for a time. 'You take an action that is diametrically opposed to how you feel.'

'That's not true,' she argued. 'At the moment I found out he'd been responsible for my brother's death I hated him.'

'Yet you tell me now that you love him. Which am I to believe? That you love him or that you hate him?'

'I can do both.'

The Monk nodded. 'Yes, indeed. The human being is a most complex creature, capable of multiple feelings.' He held up one hand. 'Yet you think of him still; you want him. I cannot believe that is motivated by hate.' When Lauren said nothing, he continued.

'Yet you drove him away. Interesting. Why do you think you did that?'

'I just told you, I don't know.'

'Yes.' He looked at her in quiet contemplation. 'I don't believe you.'

'You got some helluva nerve!' she flared. Then remembering Martin's admonition, gasped, turned away. 'Sorry,' she muttered, thinking, Oh, God, now I've offended him.

The Monk smiled. 'Come, come.' He patted the back of her hand reassuringly. 'I am not as thin-skinned as you perceive me to be. In any case, this is a difficult nut for you to crack.'

She smiled at that. 'I *am* sorry. I shouldn't've yelled like that.'

'Perfectly understandable,' the Monk said. 'When a dentist hits a nerve, you jump, do you not?'

She nodded.

'You know,' the Monk said contemplatively, '*I* had a brother, once. Seven sisters in my family and only two brothers.' He shook his head. 'He was a real hothead, my brother. The revolution still seethed in his soul and he trained hard to go out and defeat the enemy.' The Monk's keen eyes had turned inward. 'I, on the other hand, was a more placid individual. Thinking was my forte.

'I think my brother was always somewhat insecure with that. He'd often deride me about it. That was all right. I was older and stronger than he was; the fights we were often in ended up one way: with him flat on his back, me over him.

'He always loved to practise; I did not. And it irked him so that it all came so easy for me and he had to work like a dog to get 'his, er, practical lessons right. Anyway, one day I was scheduled for grenade practice only I had no eyes for it. He took my place. The second grenade he was given was faulty. He pulled the pin and it went off beside his head.'

Lauren's stomach turned over as she listened to the end of the Monk's story. She was horrified but the physical reaction she was suffering through was more than that. Her mind was filled with Bobby. Not as he had been when he went off to the Special Forces, not when he had returned in a casket. But rather as a boy, carefree and happy, plucking apples off a tree and she underneath, lifting her skirt in her hands, a net for the falling fruit, stealing away with her girlfriends, giggling and pointing, leaving Bobby up the tree.

Yet it wasn't only that one incident but many, piled one upon the other. What am I thinking of? she wondered. All older sisters torture their younger brothers. It's human nature.

'I cried at my brother's funeral,' the Monk was saying now. 'In just the same way my parents cried, my seven sisters cried; my aunts, uncles, cousins.' He looked up at her now and his eyes were focused. 'But then I did something no one else did. I went home and sheared off all my hair. I wore it that way for three years and during that time I wore only black, I foresook my contemplation of the world and threw myself into the pursuit of physical action just the way my brother would have done. And Lauren,' he said gently, 'I did this all not because I wanted to do it. In fact, I hated it. I *had* to do it. The guilt I felt dictated this.'

Guilt, Lauren thought. That was her secret; her burden. It was not Tracy she hated. She knew he had not killed Bobby; the war had. She hated herself. Because, rightly or wrongly, she was convinced that Bobby had run away to the Special Forces because he could not stand where he was. And she had been a big part of it. More than she had been willing to admit. If anyone was responsible for Bobby's death, it was *she*.

'Oh, now, Làuren,' the Monk said quietly. 'Oh, now.' Because she was crying, great tears gleaming like stars in the corners of her eyes, growing until they spilled over, running swiftly down her cheeks to drop on the spotless white tablecloth.

The Monk took her hand, holding it gently, happy inside. There had been no dead brother. His brother, older than he was by two years, was alive and well, highly placed in the People's Government. But guilt was what he surmised was trapping this American woman whom he so admired. He was no psychiatrist but, among his various expertises, he knew he was a more than fair psychologist. One had to be in order to break POW's as he had done during the Vietnamese war. It had not been enough merely to run missions, according to his government. Parallel situations, he knew, could potentially be very useful at opening people up. The Monk had found over the years that the indirect route most often led towards success. That was one of the reasons he was so good at what he did.

Lauren picked up the linen handkerchief the Monk put on the table in front of her, blew her nose. She looked up at him from beneath jewelled lashes. 'Thank you,' she said. Then took his hand and squeezed it. 'I'm so sorry about your brother.'

'It was a long time ago,' the Monk said, making it easy for her. 'These wounds tend to heal slowly. But I assure you they *do* heal.'

'You were right all along,' Lauren said. 'I *don't* hate him.'

'You know,' he said slowly, 'war has a peculiar way of twisting people. Reality changes and you find yourself committing acts you never thought yourself capable of. You survive.'

'It wasn't his fault. I see that now. He did nothing wrong. My brother –' She stopped herself. This was almost a stranger sitting across the table from her. But sometimes, as now, she knew, it was far easier to talk to someone you did not know well.

On the other side of the table, the Monk was thinking the

same thing. He almost told her all of it then. For weeks, he had been planning to find someone trustworthy, to get it all out in one long purgative rush, settle his rebellious conscience. But as Lauren could go no further at this moment, so he too backed off.

Sweat trickled uncomfortably down his sides and he took a deep breath, collecting himself. He was no longer certain that what he had planned to do was the right course of action. Always before this he had been sure of what to do. If he believed in any gods he knew he should pray to them now. But he did not know how; he believed in nothing but the immutability of China. That was what made his decision so difficult. He could not bear to think of himself as a traitor.

'Well . . . it took some doing getting in to see you.'

Atherton Gottschalk sat up in his hospital bed, three goose-down pillows he had specifically requested plumped up behind his back. He was allergic to foam. His eyes opened wide.

'Christ. Macomber. What a surprise.'

Macomber peered at him, standing at the foot of the bed. There was no one else in the room. The air conditioning hummed peacefully. 'Jesus, Atherton, you look like hell.'

Gottschalk's face darkened. 'Just what the fuck d'you *expect* me to look like, you bastard? I could've been dead!'

Macomber smiled, drawing it out as long as he could. It really serves this sonuvabitch right, he thought. Let him twist in the wind and see how he likes it; he gave me quite a start with his foolishness over the Christian woman. 'I see the waistcoat I sent you was the right size.'

'Of course it was the right size.' Gottschalk's head came forward. 'What the hell happened to your plan?'

'Why are you lowering your voice?' Macomber wanted to know. 'The room bugged?'

'Answer me, damnit!'

Macomber came around to the side of the bed, stood over the other, hands folded. 'This *was* the plan, Atherton.'

'*What?*' Whatever colour had been in Gottschalk's face had drained away.

'By the way, I saw your lovely wife, Roberta, just outside, talking to a couple of television reporters. She looks like the First Lady already.'

'Never mind that. I want to know what the hell is going on.'

'And so you shall,' Macomber said in a soothing tone of voice. 'Why do you think I'm here?' He sat down, leaning in closer. 'I hired this Islamic fanatic through a third party of course. *He* thought his country was behind it but to hell with what he thought.'

'Christ Jesus!' Gottschalk almost strangled on the words. 'For the love of God, why? I could've been killed!'

Macomber nodded. 'Yes, that's quite true, you *could have* been. But the risk factor was low. I made sure the man was a professional. He had orders to fire at your heart. And that was where you were protected.'

Gottschalk shuddered. 'He might have missed!'

'But,' Macomber said calmly, 'the fact of the matter is he didn't.' He stood up. 'And as to why.' He pointed to the litter of newspapers and national magazines spread over Gottschalk's lap. '*That* is precisely why.'

'The press?'

'You're a goddamned twenty-four carat hero, Atherton. Your words alone – your platform, along with the advertising dollars the Party's going to spend on you – might've persuaded enough voters. *Might've*. But now I've turned your words into *tangible fact*. You see the difference? I've turned theory into visceral reality. And it's hit the public in the solar plexus. First they're outraged by what's happened to you, then they begin to realize the immediacy of the situation. Now they *know* that something has to be done; they want to do it ... they *need* to do it. And *you're* that something, Atherton.'

'Christ,' Gottschalk said, absorbing Macomber's words, 'at least you could've *told* me what you had planned. I could've prepared –'

'And that preparation would've spoiled everything. Don't you see? It all had to be *absolutely real*.'

'But, damnit, man this's my *life* you're playing with!'

Macomber shrugged. 'High stakes, Atherton. The highest.

You agreed to play by those rules when you joined the *angka*.'

Reddened anger still tinged Gottschalk's cheeks. 'I don't want this kind of thing happening again, d'you understand? What the hell kind've insurance do I have that you won't pull the same kind of crazy stunt on Inauguration Day.'

'You have my *assurance*, Atherton. In January, while you are taking your oath of office, while the entire country looks to that ceremony, the terrorist cadre will already be within the New York environs. The nuclear waste at a shielded site they will believe is secure. But I will know the location and so will you. So when they send their demands, when they threaten this country, *you* will be able to act. You will be able to deploy the mobile anti-terrorist unit against them. They will be destroyed and you will be able to do anything. We'll be able to move against our enemies ... subtly at first, you and I have no desire to be part of a nuclear conflagration.' He laughed. 'We're not madmen, after all. But to stem the flux of European submission to the Russians; the slide of the Third World ... To right the geopolitical tilt ... to ensure America's security ...'

'I want more than your assurances,' Gottschalk said. He still had not recovered from the whine in his ear, the pinwheel of agony in his chest like a white-hot poker. His heart, *his heart*! Nausea built up in him at the thought of what the shock of the assassin's bullet might have done to his fluttering heart. Cardiac arrest. White as a fish like John Holmgren. Breath stilled and unseeing eyes.

Gottschalk knew deep down that Macomber had had something to do with the Governor's sudden death. Usually, when that thought crept up on him, he sealed it away in his own lead-lined bunker. Whatever Macomber had been up to, he did not want to know. That kind of knowledge was lethal, like a virus infecting the system, spreading until it ate away life itself. He wanted no part of the dirt. Just give me the Presidency, he thought.

'I want a guarantee,' he said now, clenching his fist. What good the Presidency if his heart burst in the process, flooding him?

'Atherton,' Macomber said softly, 'let me remind you that you're in no position to demand anything.'

'No?' Gottschalk's eyes flashed. 'And what d'you think you'll have without me?'

'You're not going to give up your one chance for the Presidency. I know you too well. You're too power-conscious.'

'Goddamnit!' Gottschalk cried. 'I want a renegotiation!'

Macomber swooped down on him without warning, leaning very close, pulling the man's gown up between his fisted fingers. 'I'll give you a renegotiation, you sonuvabitch! The same one I offered your former mistress, Miss Christian.'

'Kathleen?' Gottschalk's voice was faint, his eyes wide. 'What do you know about Kathleen? Have they found her?'

'No,' Macomber said. 'And they never will. She's at the bottom of the Hudson River.'

'Dead?' Gottschalk whispered. 'She's dead? What –?' His face was filled with sudden terror.

'That's right. *Morte*. Gone to her final reward which, in her case, can't be much. You were stupid enough to allow her to overhear a conversation with Eliott.'

'What're you saying?'

'She knew *the date*, you moron. She knew about 31 August. She came to New York to infiltrate the *angka*. My thought is she was going to use whatever she learned to control you. To lever Roberta out and her in. Lucky for all of us I found out about it.'

'You!' Gottschalk choked. 'Christ, you killed her!'

Macomber put his lips against Gottschalk's ear. 'That was her renegotiation and I can arrange the same terms for you, Atherton. Just say the word.'

Atherton Gottschalk was trembling in fury and fear. He did not open his mouth, stared straight ahead at the blank white wall.

Thwaite had put off getting the unit together until he returned to the precinct but he might as well not have bothered. Ivory White was at his desk when he checked in. The man was holding a light-green folder, identifying it as an active Homicide case.

'What d'you have there?'

'Welcome back,' White said. 'We all –'

'Yeah, yeah,' Thwaite interrupted, uncomfortable with all the fuss his presence had already aroused downstairs. 'Save the hearts and flowers for someone else.'

'Yessir,' White said somewhat stiffly. 'It's just that everything's been an unholy mess around here without you. What with the Republican candidate being shot, Borak and Enders coming up with the assassin so quick.'

Thwaite saw the two of them getting off the elevator, coming over to where he and White stood. 'I know all about it,' he said. The *Times* had done an uncharacteristically blistering editorial denouncing the act and deploring the country's lack of effectiveness against international terrorist strategy and the next day the *Washington Post* followed suit, citing in particular the presence of the Soviet-made AK-47 rifle. Both *Time* and *Newsweek* devoted entire pull-out sections to the incident along with an up-to-date summary of the worldwide 'pandemic', as they called it, of terrorist attacks. Last night, *60 Minutes* had scrapped their entire show to spend an uncharacteristic sixty minutes exploring the rising tide of international terrorism culminating in the attack on the life of Atherton Gottschalk.

In fact, within eight hours of the shooting, Atherton Gottschalk's name had been on everyone's tongue across the nation and seemed to stay there. The latest *CBS-NY Times* poll showed Gottschalk's political stock to have skyrocketed. Over 76 per cent of the American public now seemed to agree with his views and the incoming Gallup Poll indicated that figure was rising.

'Well, well, well,' Borak said, grinning, 'you came back just in time to miss all the excitement.'

'How you feeling, Doug?' Enders asked.

'Okay,' Thwaite said, though it was far from the truth.

'Christ,' Borak went on, ignoring them both, 'that fuckin' Gottschalk's become a saviour. And why not? The bastard's been right all along. Everything he said might happen is already happening, for Chrissakes. I tell you, he'll be a damn sight better at running this country than that schmuck who's trying to do it now.'

'If I remember right,' Enders said, 'you voted for Lawrence.'

'So what?' Borak said aggressively. 'The bastard looked good then; a lotta things did.' He pointed a finger. 'Thing is this sonuvabitch seemed to know the hit was going down *as it was happening*.' He shook his head.

Thwaite was instantly alert. He knew Borak had switched topics in mid-stream, that he was talking about their tip-off to the assassination attempt.

'You didn't by any chance have a tape running at the time,' Thwaite asked.

Borak shook his head, still thinking about the call. 'Damnedest thing I ever heard.'

'Naw, I guess not,' Thwaite said. 'That would call for some kind of rudimentary intelligence.'

Borak came out of his reverie. His pig eyes flashed. 'What'd you say, fucker?'

'Just that you should've had it recorded.'

Borak's face twisted up. 'I'd've had to've been psychic for that, smart guy. How did I know what was about to come in?'

'It was redirected here from 911, wasn't it?' Thwaite said calmly. 'All 911 calls are recorded. Or had you forgotten that, too?'

Borak leaped and Enders put himself between the cop and Thwaite. 'Asshole!' Borak shouted. 'Shows how much you don't know.' He sneered. 'That anonymous call came in direct through the precinct switchboard. Now what d'you think of that?'

Thwaite was thoughtful for a moment. He looked at them both. 'Did either of you wonder about that?' he said. 'I would. A *real* anonymous call would've come in to the 911 operator. Who the hell would know to call here and get you? Some anonymous civilian? The hell he would.'

He left them standing there, staring after him.

White came along with him. 'What the hell is going on?'

'I wish I knew.' Thwaite looked at him, saw again the light green folder. 'You never did answer my question.'

White stopped them. They were near one of the fortress-like windows that overlooked City Hall and the arch of the municipal building. People were down there, walking, eating al fresco, making the best of being in the city in the summer.

Reluctantly, White handed him the folder. 'Not the best of times for you to see this, I know. But, all the same, I think you better have a look.'

Thwaite looked from White's pinched face to the cover of the folder. He opened it and immediately said, 'Oh, Jesus fucking Christ!'

White winced when he said it but stood stoically while Thwaite read the report through, then start all over again.

'When did this come in?' Thwaite breathed.

'Early yesterday.' White shifted uncomfortably from one foot to another. 'Wouldn't've found him yet but for the water. He lives alone, had very few visitors, apparently. It was the bath.'

'Yeah.'

'Overflowed and seeped down into the apartment underneath. The neighbour called the super who eventually used his passkey to get in and found the body.'

'Bastards,' Thwaite said. He felt helpless and, for the first time since he joined the Force, incompetent. 'I see you're on it,' he said handing the folder back. 'Well, stay on it. I want every —'

'*Was* is more like it, m'man.'

Thwaite swung around. '*What?*'

White nodded. 'Pulled off an hour ago. Some Fed system blitzed us. Just came in and took the whole thing outa our hands. Copies of the authorization're in the folder if you want to take a look. It's all legal. I think the guy used to be one of theirs.'

Thwaite turned away and thought, Tracy's father. Now what in the name of hell is happening?

Outside, a mother and child walked hand in hand. A little girl and a big girl. Together. Doris. Phyllis, Thwaite thought. I'll never see you again. And Tracy will never see his father. Jesus. He shivered inwardly.

I think we're in over our heads.

The telex came in at midnight, New York time; that made it one in the afternoon, the day before, Shanghai time.

Macomber had just returned from a long, leisurely dinner at the Club, hosting one of his monthly affairs in the Club's private dining room. As usual, it was a mixture of business and pleasure. Two or three deals, at the least, were always consummated at one of his gatherings, the informal yet competitive atmosphere contributing to the incentive of having one's associates as well as rivals all together in the same room.

This particular night had been inordinately successful for Macomber himself. Metronics was beginning to ride the crest of what everyone now believed was Atherton Gottschalk's imminent election. These were men who prided themselves in the extent of their forward thinking and all felt certain that Metronics' new groundbreaking projects were about to skyrocket in production and profits, given the climate of the times and the bent of the incoming administration.

Macomber was offered six deals, two of which – added microchip manufacturing and rare metals mining – he sewed up immediately. One other, – the building of a movable oil rig – he had commenced negotiation on.

He had good reason to be joyful on his way home; even the spectre of Khieu's strangeness could not overshadow his elation. He had done what he could about it and he set his mind at rest, allowing the soft rolling of the limo's shocks as he rode downtown to lull him further into the wine-enhanced euphoria he had been feeling.

Yet all that and more evaporated when the telex came. It was delivered to his office at Metronics – as had been previously agreed upon – which was open twenty-four hours a day. Lately he had taken to sleeping there, during this long wait for Tisah, the house on Gramercy Park South reminding him too much now of those lonely days just after he had returned from the war, with money and Khieu but no one else – nothing but his ambition and his sharp and omnipresent memories of Tisah. It was obvious to him now why he could not care for Joy or for any other female for that matter. It was Tisah and Tisah only who had captured him.

He took the thin pale yellow envelope with a trembling hand. For a moment, alone in the thrumming dark heart of Metronics, he debated with himself. Either way – whatever news this telex contained – he suspected he would be far better off sending it into his document shredder unread.

But he knew just as well that that was impossible. There was too much feeling driving him on to open it.

He used a bone letter opener, catching it somewhere on the inside and swearing mightily, using his finger, hooked, to tear the recalcitrant paper.

He was conscious of a long cool line of sweat tickling him as it snaked its way down his spine. He looked down and, unfolding the paper, read the telex:

REGRET TO INFORM CONSIGNMENT SPOILED — REPEAT COMPLETELY SPOILED. CROP OVER FOR SEASON. DID ALL HUMANLY POSSIBLE. CONDOLENCES.

OPAL LIGHT

Dead.

The word hung in his mind, suspended like a pall. *Dead.* Until it began to lose its shape and meaning, until he could no longer understand it as part of the English language.

'Dead.'

He said it aloud as if that might help but still it ceased to mean anything at all.

'Tisah is dead.' And then it all fell into place, her name lending meaning to the phrase.

Macomber crushed the telegram in his fist. He was shaking now with a rage such as he had not felt since the war. For a time, Tisah had been revived. During all those long years he had always believed that she was alive, somewhere. The Monk's words had merely added to that belief, making it a virtual certainty. Until this telex. Consignment spoiled meant that she was dead. Crop over for the season meant that she had been dead for some time and that, given what the Monk had told him, meant only one thing: Tracy Richter had killed her. He had been her last contact; he had stumbled upon her duplicity – had tried to knife her.

Well, Macomber thought now, so he succeeded after all. At this moment his anger seemed limitless. Just as his despair at the abrupt loss of Tisah seemed limitless. It seemed inordinately cruel to him to have her offered to him – so close – only to find out that she was no longer alive.

His mind was very clear as he stared out at the winking lights of Manhattan's moneyed towers. It was cool in the darkened office, blue light playing in on him from the nighttime halo of the city agglomerate illumination against the heavens. The sweat had dried along his back. A decision had to be made and he was the one to make it. Just one of a thousand such he made during the course of a long day. A business decision. Yes. That was it.

All the long years of wanting, of suppressing that want, the renewed hunger at a chance to regain the past, the utter desolation in the aftermath of the dashing of those hopes, all now combined inside him, swirling around the central core of his memories, his eternal love for Tisah.

He walked purposefully to his desk, sat down in the high-backed swivel chair behind it. Reaching down to one of the bottom drawers, he produced a key and unlocked it. Inside was a well-oiled, long-barrelled Magnum .357 and half a dozen cardboard cartridge boxes. He tore one open, saw the tiny cross sawed into the blunt end of each bullet. These were steel-jacketed, their tips made of a softer metal amalgam than the store-bought variety. One of his own plants manufactured this bullet specially for him. It was his own variation on the dum-dum principle, the soft tip, the sawed cross expanding outward on impact, ripping through flesh, organ and bone. No man now walking the earth could survive a shot from this gun. Even a mis-hit in a limb would tear the appendage right off the torso.

Macomber, a strange yellow light in his eyes, began to calmly and methodically load the Magnum, thinking all the while of Tracy, the pulsing of his hatred for the man, and how good it would feel to level the .357 at his head or heart. Head or heart. That was his only decision now. Which would he go for when that delicious moment came? For a moment he allowed himself to fantasize about that moment. He sighted, went for the head. He sighted, went for the heart. He imagined the resulting carnage and knew the spot for which he would aim.

Then, with the gun half-loaded, he stopped stock still as if listening to a sound only he could hear. He was aware of the trip beat of his heart, the rushing of his blood through his veins and arteries, the accelerated pulse. He stared down at the weapon he could never use now.

He had the *angka* to think about, fourteen years of intricate planning to achieve the absolutely ultimate aim a man could hope to achieve: manipulation of America's national policies and through them, a degree of control of the world undreamed of for millennia.

What was his own petty revenge when compared to that pinnacle? It was less than nothing. He put the Magnum away in its chamois holster, locking the drawer. He could not afford to involve himself directly. Not now; not when he was so close to his goal he could scent its magnetic pull on him.

Yet he burned with a fire that required venting. His eyes were alight as he picked up the phone, dialled a local number. When he heard the voice at the other end answer, he said, 'Khieu, there is something very important you must do to ensure the safety of the *angka*; something very important you must do for me.

'Kill Tracy Richter.'

He cradled the receiver without knowing it, swivelling around to stare out at all the winking lights of Wall Street. He was breathing hard, there in the darkness, the filtered blue light like the reflection of massed diamonds bathing him in tenuous shadow.

Lauren glanced at her watch. 'I think I'd better be getting back to my hotel.'

The Monk smiled and stood up from the table. He took her hand, began to lead her out of the Jin Jiang Club's restaurant. 'You have been such delightful company all evening . . . I almost hesitate to ask this favour of you.'

'What is it?'

The Monk's broad face turned towards her and for the first time Lauren became aware of the lines there. And it seemed to her now that each one of the many represented one deliberate blow that life had dealt him. This man intrigued her, in much the same way Tracy and Louis did. It was almost as if these men all belonged to a worldwide secret society, far-reaching in its aims, hidden from the normal people walking the streets. There was, she thought now, nothing mundane about these men.

'If it's in my power to help you,' she added, 'I'll be happy to.'

The smile returned to the Monk's face and, as if they had never existed, the lines of fatigue and concern disappeared.

'There is someone who would like very much to meet you. She could not, unfortunately, attend the performance tonight, could not meet us for our most enjoyable and enlightening dinner. Nevertheless, she is a devoted fan of yours.'

Involuntarily, Lauren glanced at her watch again and, noting her gesture, he added, 'I have sought and obtained permission from your Mr Vlasky. He has been most co-operative. I am grateful to him.' He shrugged his shoulders. 'But it is up to you. If you are fatigued . . .'

'No, no,' Lauren protested, though she *was* tired. The thought of sleep seemed faraway to her now. 'It will be my pleasure. Really.'

The Monk's face lit up. 'Splendid!' He clapped his hands in delight. 'I am most grateful.' He gestured with his open hand. 'This way, if you please.'

He swept her out into the stifling night. The roan Mercedes waited patiently for them, its powerful engine thrumming. They went silently through the streets, the city seemingly ghostly and deserted through the tinted glass.

At length, they drew up at Seven East Lake Road, a monstrous red brick mansion in the Edwardian style. It was surrounded by a high cement wall. An iron gate opened silently at their approach, closed again after the car had gone through.

'This seems an odd place for China,' Lauren said.

The Monk was smiling slightly. 'Do not forget the foreign influence in Shanghai. Westerners were here for many years before the Cultural Revolution.'

The mansion loomed out of the night, spotlit by the Mercedes' amber headlights, gabled, surrounded by trees and shrubbery, all immaculately manicured. The area enclosed by the wall seemed enormous.

'Six acres,' the Monk said in response to her question.

Lauren knew enough about life in China to realize that was an awesome amount of space for any one man to possess.

'Impressive, yes?' the Monk said, helping her out. 'Do you

602

know the name Wang Hongwen? No? He was one of the "gang of four". This was his house, once upon a time.' He led her towards the front door. 'Now it is mine.'

The interior of the house was entirely in keeping with its Western façade: marble flooring, an enormous walk-in fireplace. The living room was high-ceilinged; a curving staircase filled the hallway to the left.

Regency sofas and chairs upholstered in pale gold and pink raw silk shared the cavernous space rather uncomfortably with a rather superb French Provincial desk. There was a chair to match and, behind it, an overly carved ornamental sideboard.

The Monk crossed the living room, moving with a rather delicate grace over an antique Persian rug in dusky reds and golds. He stopped beside the sofa faced towards the fireplace and, with a slight start, Lauren realized there was a woman sitting there. But now she rose and turned towards them.

She was a shapely woman with breasts larger than was normal for an Oriental. But it was her face which drew Lauren's attention. It was sleek and sensual with much of the – for want of a better term – animal in it. Yet it was a face filled with a most unusual kind of intelligence. Lauren was certain that this must be the Monk's mistress.

She came towards them, smiling, and that expression alone told Lauren just how unutterably miserable this woman was, despite her red silk embroidered Mandarin gown, the diamond bracelet around her slim left wrist, the emerald stud earrings.

'Miss Lauren Marshall,' the Monk said from beside her, 'I'd like you to meet Tisah. My daughter.'

Lauren almost faltered when he said that but recovered in time to extend her hand. The other woman took it briefly.

'It's an honour to meet you, misss Marshall.'

'Please. It's Lauren.'

There was an awkward moment when the two women stared into each other's eyes. Lauren thought she caught a hint of some emotion swimming darkly up to the surface in Tisah's black eyes, something long buried, something best left forgotten. Then it was gone.

'Tisah, my darling, won't you get us drinks?' the Monk said, rubbing his hands together. He turned to Lauren. 'What would you like? A brandy, perhaps?'

'Just a Perrier, if you have it, thank you.'

'Please sit down,' he said but he did not take his own advice, walking back and forth behind the sofa. He seemed slightly on edge.

'Is there something . . . ?' Lauren began.

'This man you were talking to me about earlier this evening,' the Monk said slowly as if he were reluctantly squeezing out each word. 'The one whom you thought had been responsible for your brother's untimely death . . .'

'What about him?' Lauren had twisted around on the couch in order to keep him in view.

The Monk looked at her, stopped his pacing and squared his shoulders as if coming to a decision. 'I believe I know him.'

Lauren felt her stomach doing flip-flops. 'Do you?' Her voice was very faint.

'His name is Tracy Richter?'

She nodded numbly, accepted the iced glass of Perrier from the returning Tisah. Something screamed inside her.

Tisah came around the couch, handed her father a drink. He put his arm around her waist. 'We *both* know him, Lauren.'

'I don't think I want to hear this,' she said, getting up.

'Please!' The Monk took a step forward. 'What I have to tell you is of the utmost importance. You must listen; you *must* stay.'

With the intuition of the present lover, Lauren glanced at Tisah. 'She's the one, isn't she? The one Tracy dreams of?'

Tisah's mouth was trembling, her eyes enlarged by incipient tears. Lauren had the impression that she was holding herself together with a supreme effort of will.

'I will ask you a question,' the Monk said earnestly. 'Do you love Tracy? *Really* love him?'

'Yes.' She answered without conscious thought because it was the truth.

'Then you are the answer,' he said, sighing. Tension went out of him and it seemed a great weight had been lifted from his shoulders. 'The time has indeed come to repay the debt.' He turned to his daughter. 'Yes?'

For an instant, Tisah was as still as a statue. Her eyes raked over Lauren's features, probing, seeking ... what? There was hate there and anger, envy and that peculiar kind of misery Lauren had never before seen in anyone. Then the bubble seemed to burst and all those seething heated emotions melted away. The face was calm again. Beautiful and calm. Tisah nodded her head once in acquiescence.

The Monk stretched out a hand. 'Please,' he said. 'Sit.'

As if in a fog, Lauren complied.

'Years ago,' the Monk began, 'my daughter, Tisah, worked for me. She is, as you may have observed, of varied nationality. I have never married. But I have had many ... liaisons.' He stopped for a moment as if considering how best to continue. 'Of all those liaisons, Tisah has been the only issue. That makes her all the more precious to me.'

He came around from behind the couch, sat down nervously at right angles to Lauren. Tisah, standing behind him, put one hand lightly on his shoulder. 'In those days, the danger was very great – much more than now. The war in Vietnam and Cambodia was in full flame. My country called on me to perform certain, ah, duties. I complied.'

He put his palms together, rubbing them back and forth. 'I ran clandestine missions into Southeast Asia. Tisah, being part Cambodian, was perfectly suited for work there. I sent her; she went. She was put in place in Ban Me Thuot.' He looked at Lauren. 'Does that name mean anything to you?'

'It was the Special Forces encampment,' Lauren said. 'Where Tracy and my brother Bobby were stationed for a time.'

The Monk nodded. 'Quite correct. Her objective was to infiltrate the encampment, relay back whatever information on US missions into Cambodia she could.'

'Is that what happened to Tracy?' Lauren said wide-eyed. 'Did she trap him –'

'Calm yourself, Lauren,' the Monk said leaning forward. He put the tips of his fingers on her knee for just a moment. 'You are jumping ahead.'

'But –'

'I assure you there is no cause for alarm.' He saw her glance up at his daughter. 'Believe me.'

Lauren stared at him. 'Go on.'

605

The Monk nodded. 'Towards that end, she contrived to meet one of the key men there. They entered into a liaison.'

Lauren felt as if she were strangling; there seemed to be no oxygen in the air around her for her lungs to extract. She was suffocating in an alien atmosphere. She put her hand up to her throat. 'Who was that ... key man?' She closed her eyes; part of her still did not want to know.

'A lieutenant named Macomber.'

'Thank God.' Lauren's voice was a sigh of relief. Her eyes were wide and very bright. 'For a moment I thought you were going to tell me Tisah had been sent in to ... spy on Tracy.'

The Monk smiled in avuncular fashion, nodded understandingly.

'But as for Macomber ... I've never heard of him.'

The Monk sat very still. His eyes were glittering, as wary as an animal's. 'Yes?' He was able, within the one syllable of that word, to convey many things: Curiosity; bewilderment; concern; interest. 'Can this really be so? A man so prominent in the business world of, er, armaments? Your Tracy has never mentioned him to you?'

She shook her head. 'No. Never.'

'Indeed.' The Monk glanced up and back over his shoulder at Tisah. 'You see, my dear,' he said to her, 'we are doing the right thing after all.'

'I'm sorry,' Lauren said, 'but I don't understand any of this.'

The Monk smiled thinly. 'When I am finished you shall, never fear.' He squirmed on the sofa as if he were uncomfortable and Tisah went to refill his drink.

'You see,' he said, 'in the time I have been speaking of – 1969 to be precise – a man found Tisah out. This man was your Tracy. For a time, he allowed the liaison between my daughter and Macomber to continue. But there was a crucial difference.

'She had fallen in love with him as Macomber had fallen in love with her. He was able to turn her. Now he fed her disinformation ... do you know the meaning of this word?'

'I read the *New York Times*.'

He smiled. 'Yes. Your country is so different from mine. So you know. Good. This is what she began to relay back to me.'

He sighed. 'And for a time, I was fooled. I passed on the information to the, er, appropriate apparatus. But there came a time when I began to perceive the seams in this otherwise flawless quilt of lies. From that I determined what had occurred.'

He leaned towards her, his voice lowered. 'But now what was I to do? If I no longer passed on information, my superiors would question what had become of my operative. I could not tell them she had been turned; they would have ordered her summary execution. I tried to recall her without success. She would not leave Ban Me Thuot; she would not leave Tracy.

'So I was caught in a dangerous bind. I was forced into passing along her false information. My only hope was that my superiors, being less familiar with the situation there than I, would not become aware that they were being fed disinformation.

'Perhaps you cannot imagine the life of fear I lived for those long months. I could not sleep, I rarely ate and, at last, I resolved to go to Ban Me Thuot myself and pull her out by force.'

He accepted the full glass from Tisah, continued. 'It would have been a suicide mission, as you can readily understand – as I myself understand now. But at the time, I was beside myself with worry for her. I was not thinking very clearly. However I was spared that indignity.' He took a sip of his drink.

'Somehow, the Americans got wind of her presence, of what she really was. Now she was in danger from *both* sides.' He put his glass down, took Lauren's hands in his own. 'And it was Tracy who saved her. He took her out of Ban Me Thuot, spirited her away and in her place left a trail of false rumours. Stories circulated that she had been murdered, no one knew for certain by whom but several supposedly reliable witnesses swore it was a Special Forces soldier.'

Lauren was having difficulty absorbing all this new information. Her head was whirling and to the Monk's credit he waited patiently until she caught up with him. 'What did he really do with her?' she asked a little breathlessly.

'He could have killed her,' the Monk said. 'Strictly speaking, it was the correct action to take. After all, she *had* been an enemy agent. But your Mr Richter is a rather remarkable man. He cared for Tisah . . . a great deal. He sent her through a network he knew of, back through Cambodia, through the Khmer Rouge. They made certain I knew of her whereabouts and she returned here.'

The Monk's face fell and Lauren saw those lines appearing again. 'But by that time, some bright spark – and aide to one of my superiors, as it turned out – had analysed the last of her information and had determined its falseness.' He took a deep breath. 'So Tisah did not return to Beijing in triumph but in disgrace.

'Because of my rank and power in the People's Government, it was determined that she would not be executed. But she is a virtual prisoner here. They do not want her seen in public; she can attend no functions, cultural or otherwise. And bringing you here was a great risk to us because she is forbidden any contact with foreigners.'

'And that's why she could not see the performance tonight.' Lauren got up. She felt a heaviness in her heart. She went around the sofa, stood in front of Tisah. Their eyes met but now the other woman had erected a wall; none of the raw emotion Lauren had at first seen there was present.

'Oh, Tisah,' she said softly, embracing the other woman. 'I'm so sorry. So very sorry.' Beneath her palm, she felt the trembling of flesh, the sobbing breaths, and she felt hot tears on her bare neck. She stroked Tisah's hair as the other woman wept. 'A prisoner,' she whispered. 'My God, how cruel life can be.' And she was crying herself.

The Monk rose, walked away from them towards the bleak darkness of the enormous fireplace. He put one hand up against the cool marble, running his fingers over the beautiful surface.

He did not want any part of their emotionalism. Crying was foreign to him but he had done his years of grieving for his daughter's plight as well as his daily prayers to the Amida Buddha for the sparing of her life.

He had known at the moment of her return to him, safe and alive, the enormity of the debt he owed his enemy. Tracy Richter. Yet he knew this moment would one day come, for what is a debt that cannot be repaid? Nothing. Less than the wind. And that was not how the Monk lived his life. Ideology, after all, was nothing in the face of human emotions.

For at the moment he had caught sight of Tisah as she had emerged from the plane on her return from Southeast Asia, he had understood the nature of humanity. He had understood then how a part of him had withered and died at the thought that he would never again see her. Only then had he understood her importance to him for had she died out there he would never have been the same. And, crippled in that most basic of ways, he never could have gone on with his own life. She was all he had, all he held dear. He was no traitor to China. Yet his debt must be repaid; his very life demanded it.

After a time he turned back to them, saw that they were standing together, holding hands. The sight made his heart sing; lightening considerably the task before him.

'There is more, I'm afraid.' He addressed Lauren but it was clear he was including them both. 'I have learned much about Macomber recently.' His face was pained. 'Now recent events have afforded me an insight into what he is striving for.'

'Then you're still in the same . . . business you were in in 1969,' Lauren said.

The Monk smiled, a slow, spreading smile that seemed to suffuse his entire face and give it the glow of a marvellous sunset. 'Ah, my dear Lauren, I like you so much. Really I do!' He made a deprecating gesture with his open hands. 'Perhaps it is that the Chinese often do not show their real age but the fact is that I am far too elderly to still be in such an, er, energetic business.' He waved a hand. 'No, no, I still dabble in affairs of state from time to time. But merely in an advisory – a strictly non-participant – role.' He lifted a chubby forefinger. 'But my sources, ah, they are still alive and active.' He shrugged. 'I am content now to be their conduit once in a great while when the occasion warrants.'

'As it does now,' Lauren said, sensing she was on the verge of being privy to some electrifying knowledge; everything that had happened this night pointed to such an ending.

'Yes,' the Monk nodded sagely. 'As it does now.' He sat forward and Lauren could feel the tension filling him, flowing outward to engulf her so that her pulse began to race and her heart beat hard within her chest. 'While you have been here I have no doubt that you have been out of touch with events transpiring back home. Atherton Gottschalk, the Republican Party candidate for President, was shot as he was making a speech calling for increased vigilance against worldwide terrorism outside St Patrick's Cathedral in New York City this past week.'

'What?' Lauren was aghast.

'Miraculously he was not seriously injured; it happened he was wearing a bulletproof vest. A short stay in the hospital to recuperate and Mr Gottschalk is back on the campaign trail.' He lifted a finger. 'Only now he has become a hero, a victim of just the sort of terrorism he has been warning the populace of the United States about. *And* he has survived! Now he is virtually assured of winning the coming election.' He paused, staring hard at her.

'Yes?' Lauren was struggling hard to see where this was leading. It all seemed like a tremendous once-in-a-lifetime break for Gottschalk; tragedy turned into triumph. Under those circumstances she felt certain she'd vote for the man herself. 'I don't see . . .'

The Monk's shoulders were hunched as if he were a football player about to plunge through the enemy's line. 'Of course you don't,' he said easily. 'No one does yet . . . because they haven't all the information available to them. But just suppose that my sources have told me that six weeks ago Mr Macomber was in Southeast Asia in a country not all that far from where we are now closing a business deal that would bring an Islamic assassin to the United States *under his own control*.'

'What . . .' Lauren's mind was reeling. 'Wait a minute now. Are you telling me that Macomber planned to kill a candidate for the presidency of the United States?'

'I am implying nothing of the kind, my dear Lauren. Instead, I say this: the assassination attempt was meant to fail all the time. It was no coincidence that the man shot Gottschalk in precisely the spot which was best protected.' The Monk smiled again. 'Who do you think gave the candidate the vest in the first place?'

Lauren's mind was reeling so she let him answer his own question. 'Why the same man who is the sole power behind Mr Atherton Gottschalk. Because it is my contention that despite the public disclaimers – the disinformation – Mr Macomber and Mr Gottschalk are and have been for some time acting in total concert.'

In the shocked silence that followed, Lauren's hoarse voice sounded small indeed. 'Why are you telling me all this?'

The Monk stood up, came towards her. He abruptly seemed very imposing indeed standing over her and Lauren thought she would not want this man as an enemy. 'I have a great debt to repay Tracy Richter; it is a debt which, I regret, can never be repaid in full. He gave me back my daughter just as he gave her back her life. I cannot tell you how precious that is to me.'

He leaned down and, gripping Lauren's arm, drew her to her feet. She could feel the rippling of energy inside him and she wondered just how old he was. 'Now you will be the messenger of that repayment.' His voice had become reedy almost as if it had been split in two by his high emotions.

'What you obviously do not know, what Mr Macomber is also ignorant of, is that Mr Richter was his blackout control on an extremely hazardous mission. A blackout control is one where the man in the field is ignorant of the person controlling him and the mission. They knew each other in Ban Me Thuot – obviously. But in "Operation Sultan" they came together.

'But, my dear Lauren, Mr Macomber is well aware of Mr Richter; he is well aware that in the whole of the country Mr Richter is perhaps the only one who can prevent his plan from coming to fruition. And he cannot allow that to happen, can he?'

Staring into those dark, liquid eyes Lauren abruptly felt a cold terror grip her vitals as if a bottomless abyss had opened up at her feet and she was slipping over the verge. 'If you've meant to terrify me, you've succeeded completely,' she whispered.

'Good!' the Monk cried. 'Oh, very good! You tell Mr Richter all that you have heard here.'

'What kind of proof can I give him?'

The Monk looked at her pityingly. 'My darling girl, do you

expect me now to trot out the microfilm of lists, facts and figures? Please do not be naive. Mr Macomber is far too clever a chap to have his secrets so accessible, even to sources such as mine.'

He took her hand, patted its back. 'No, you tell Mr Richter the source of your information, that should suffice. He'll understand the urgency. Because should Atherton Gottschalk indeed become President of the United States, Macomber will, you can be most certain, be dictating policy. You may not know what that means but I and Tracy Richter surely do.'

His obsidian eyes burrowed into her brain as if to link his mind with hers, to impress upon her the force behind his words. 'So you must forget your dancing, Lauren,' he said softly. 'Return home as quickly as you can. Find Mr Richter and tell him all of it. For if what I have said comes to pass, heaven help us all.'

BOOK FOUR

Chet Khmau

1

September, Present
Washington/Dallas/New York City

Tracy deplaned at Washington International Airport in the midst of a driving rainstorm. There was a hurricane off the Atlantic coast of Florida, hovering like the trembling finger of God.

It was barely 5.30 in the morning, a thin seepage of grey gauzy light illuminating the yellow-slickened ground crews scurrying from plane to plane outside the huge-paned windows of the arrival lounge. Tracy was reminded of the face of Golden Dragon, lined and worn, happy-sad, his eyes full of tears as he gratefully accepted the gift of his wayward daughter.

He was first into the lounge the last to leave; he had a number of calls to make. His first was to Thwaite's hotel room. There was no answer. He called the precinct, got a duty sergeant on the night shift. No, he could not tell Tracy where Detective Sergeant Thwaite currently was but Yes, he would make certain the sergeant knew that Mr Richter had called.

Tracy suspected Thwaite might be at Melody's but he knew neither her last name nor her address so he gave it up for the moment. He had had the airline wire ahead to the Four Seasons Hotel in Georgetown and he asked the duty sergeant to have Thwaite call him there as soon as he could.

Next Tracy dialled a local number. The phone burred somewhere across town and the exchange operator came on the line. Tracy recited to her a three-digit number.

'Yes?'

'It's Mother.'

'Welcome home,' the Director said.

'It's full flags,' Tracy said, thinking of the good joss that had brought him home safe and sound: the generosity and love of Fresh Po wind and his enormous family. He had been merely a fisherman? Tracy suspected not but it was something he'd never know for sure.

'Come in under heavy weather,' the Director said without hesitation. And hung up.

Tracy turned away from the phone, satisfied. Heavy weather was a method of access into the foundation that cut through all the red tape. It also meant the Director would meet Tracy at the access point to eliminate any possibility of a slow-down through misunderstanding by staff.

It was the proper response to Tracy's code. Full flags was an urgent request for full facilities. It was generally used at the end phases of a broken mission and only in times of serious emergency.

He had no luggage, still he had to wait almost twenty minutes for a taxi. A combination of the foul weather and the ungodly early hour.

The air was full of mist, Washington's lush foliage appearing pale and ghostly, the monuments all but invisible until he was almost upon them.

He had the taxi drop him on Seventeenth Street near the DAR Building. On his right was the Ellipse. It was 6.15; the streets were nearly deserted. He waited until the cab had turned the corner, disappearing into E Street, then crossed Seventeenth, away from the DAR Building.

He walked north, towards the White House. Just past New York Avenue, he came up on the Executive Offices and saw his first real signs of life.

He went straight up Seventeenth Street to H Street, checking for ticks though he could not imagine how he could be followed – no one, not even his enemies, could have known when he was leaving Hong Kong or what city was to be his destination.

At H Street, he turned right one block to Connecticut Avenue, heading north again on that, changing sides of the street, using the oblique facings of shop and building windows as mirrors to scan both sides of the street behind him.

He found nothing of significance and soon emerged onto I Street and the back end of the small Farragut Square. He made a left onto I, went three-quarters of the way down the block. Here he used the back and side windows of the parked cars to cover his rear.

He waited for the light to change, huddled in the doorway of an office building, watching the rain, ostensibly fuming like any other pedes-trian out at that hour without an umbrella. The light went from red to amber to green, the traffic started up and Tracy ducked out of his temporary shelter, racing out into the street between the slowly moving cars and gaining the far sidewalk. The manoeuvre had taken just under ten seconds and was simple enough. But had anyone been following him he would have been lost or flushed. There was no one.

Tracy went immediately to an iron gate, put his hand through the black glistening bars, slid back a bolt. He went quickly through the gate, closing it behind him.

He was in a small courtyard that to the casual observer appeared to belong to the First Episcopal Church, the nearby edifice. And, in fact, it was maintained by the church staff.

It belonged, however, to the foundation and was its back entrance. Rain hissed through the trees, bent the carefully planted flower stalks back and forth. Tracy went under a lemon tree, wiped water off his face.

Just ten yards away a figure stepped out from the shadows of a building, a black umbrella over its head. Tracy waited, watching.

The figure stopped, surrounded by rain. 'Mother.'

Tracy stepped out from the protection of the lemon tree, walked beneath the umbrella.

'Well,' the Director said, staring straight into Tracy's eyes, 'I hear you've had a rather bumpy ride.'

Tracy wondered just how much the Director really knew. He would not ask; that, he had learned long ago, was a game he could not win.

The Director took him through a pair of smoked glass and chrome swinging doors. Very innocuous; they could have been entering a newly built branch of the public library. Execpt that these doors were bullet and bomb proof.

They were in a glazed-brick vestibule without windows. Tracy was curious. This had obviously been built since he had left the foundation. The only egress point seemed to be to the left, into a small circular room with brilliantly white-painted walls. The lighting was soft and subdued. There was no furniture, nothing on the walls but a small niche at head height into which had been fitted an outsized pair of black rubber goggles.

The Director crossed immediately to the niche, beckoned Tracy to follow him. 'Take a look in there.'

Tracy put his head in the niche, his face up against the pliant rubber. Immediately there was a reddish flare of light that made him blink in reflex, then darkness. He took his head away, made room as the Director bent into the goggles in turn.

The Director stood up. 'We've found,' he said with just a trace of pride, 'that the art of security has not run its course when it comes to identification. It used to be – in your time – that fingerprints were sufficient. Now there are plastic surgeons who can alter fingerprints through microsurgery. Similarly, voiceprints can be duplicated.

'Recently, though, we've found that by registering the pattern of blood vessels on each individual's retina, we can bring security back to one-hundred per cent.' Part of the circular wall rolled back. 'It seems that each person's vascular branching pattern is unique unto himself. With a special lens, the camera logs the patterns via a numerical code. Now you're part of the databank.'

In the hallway, they took the silent elevator up to the Director's office. Tracy accepted gratefully the towel the Director threw at him from the doorway of his private bath.

'I'm having some clothing sent up from Wardrobe,' he said as Tracy began to dry himself. 'You can dress in here.' He pointed at the bath. He walked slowly over to his desk. 'They still have all your sizes; they're rather an efficient bunch. At least they never let their files go out of date.'

'Meaning,' Tracy said, 'that others do.'

'Meaning precisely that.' The Director sat down behind his desk. It was composed of fillips, curlicues and do-dads and, to Tracy's way of thinking, fitting the personality of the man sitting at it. He steepled his fingers, elbows squarely on the desk top. 'Yours, for instance. You've forgotten us over the years, Mother. You never should've left us.'

'I had no choice,' Tracy said, wrapping the thick towel around his waist. 'You know that.'

'You talked yourself into it,' the Director snapped. 'Or, in this case, *out* of it. You put yourself above the rest of us, Mother. Thought of yourself as something special. Something *more*. Isn't that right?'

Tracy shrugged. 'I've become something more. I'm more human.'

The Director smiled now. '*And* more vulnerable. They almost had you for good in that steel trap of a car.'

'You know about that?'

'Forwarding and Receiving has been on twenty-four hour alert, monitoring your trips and falls all over the Colony. I've been in signals all night with HK staff.'

'You knew it all,' Tracy said, 'but you gave me no help.'

The Director spread his hands. 'Why should we? You are no longer a member of the family. And we're not, after all, a charity firm.'

'Then why were you monitoring my movements?'

There was a knock on the door.

'Come,' the Director said.

A thin young man entered carrying a large cardboard box. The Director nodded and the thin young man put the box on the corner of the filigreed desk. Then he left.

'Come get your clothes,' the Director said. 'You'll catch your death of cold sitting around like that.' He swivelled his chair around to stare out the window behind him at the grey misted buildings, all definition washed away by the rain.

Tracy got up, went across the Astroturf, opened the box. Inside he found underwear, a pair of slate grey linen trousers, black socks, a shining pair of black hand-stitched loafers, a narrow alligator belt of the same colour. The light blue shirt had been so recently pressed it was still warm. There was even a shoe-horn, stick deodorant and a small plastic bottle of talcum powder. He began to dress.

'This must've put a dent in next year's budget. Accounts'll have a heart attack.'

'Don't concern yourself with the clothes you were forced to

leave behind in Hong Kong,' the Director said, pointedly ignoring Tracy's comment. 'Staff have got that all sorted out. It's being shipped back on tonight's Pan Am flight.'

'And the police?'

'Forget the Hong Kong police.'

'What d'you want in return?' Tracy said. Now that he was dressed he felt a bit more like a human being.

The Director swivelled around, levelled a cold stare at him. 'What the hell's that supposed to mean?'

'You know perfectly well,' Tracy said. 'You wouldn't've concerned yourself at all unless you had a *quid pro quo* in mind.'

'You've got it all wrong, Mother. What I did for you *is* the *quid pro quo*.'

'For what?'

The Director sat back, ran a finger down the side of his face. 'Much as it pains me to admit it, you were right about Kim. He's become a far more dangerous boy than I gave him credit for. His enterprising mind has led him astray and he has – spiritually at least – left the fold.'

Tracy sat down, crossed his legs. 'I said one thing at the time he made his application. That was, what? in 1970?'

The director nodded. 'Close enough, yes. But that's not all you did. You gave me a clue to what Kim is up to now during the course of our dinner at Chez Françoise. You were too interested in his vacation plans and it set me thinking.

'With anyone else, I might have dismissed it. But not with you. You still have the mind of a ferret.'

So that was why the Director had been so testy, Tracy thought. He detested being wrong; prided himself on his record. And he had given Kim a great deal of freedom.

'I discovered he's been working for a European combine. All old-line industrialists with headquarters in Eindhoven.'

'Eindhoven?'

'The Netherlands.' The Director shuffled some papers on his desk. 'There's not a Communist in the lot. In fact, quite the opposite. Militant right-wingers.'

Tracy nodded. 'That fits the pattern all right. You know as well as I do how fanatically anti-Communist Kim is.'

The Director's ice-blue eyes bore into Tracy's. 'Then kindly tell me what the hell he's doing for them?'

Tracy got up, began to walk around the room. 'I'm not certain – yet.' He turned on his former boss. 'You know Macomber?'

'Delmar Davis? Sure. His military hardware's the best in the world. Got this *Vampire* helicopter that's tremendous. I went to a demonstration he gave the Joint Chiefs. It boggled their minds.'

'He worked for me when we were stationed in Ban Me Thuot together.'

The Director frowned. 'I don't believe I remember.'

'That's not surprising. He was seconded to us out of Special Forces; wanted to join the foundation but I turned him down. He was a brilliant infiltrator with the mind of a Machiavellian disciple.'

'What was the matter with him?'

'He was unstable. He *enjoyed* what he was doing.'

'So did Kim.'

'Yes but there's a difference. Kim has ideological commitments that run to the very core of him. Kim is dangerous, yes, but he's controllable because you can always work out his motivation. Macomber had no such stability. He might have been committed to something – in fact I'm certain of it, judging by the concentration with which he carried out his missions – but I'll be damned if I know what it is.'

'Why did you bring up his name in the first place?'

'I need the "Sultan" files.'

The Director said nothing for a time. Then he turned to his intercom, activated it. He said something to his adjutant, let go of the toggle. 'What's "Sultan" got to do with Macomber?'

'They're one and the same,' Tracy said. 'That's what I learned from Mizo in Hong Kong.' He told the Director the bad news.

'Christ, you mean that entire munitions empire he's built up over the last twelve years – a company from which the United States Government will almost certainly be committed to purchasing five hundred million dollars worth of international deterrence – came from his profits off "Sultan"?'

Tracy nodded. 'Basically, yes. Oh, he was helped along by a number of shrewd investments. But the money for those investments came from the diverted "Sultan" pipeline.'

'Christ Jesus, Mother.' For the first time since Tracy had known him, The Director seemed shaken. He looked up at Tracy. 'We need those *Vampires*, the *Darkside* long-capacity bombers, those *Bat* computer-controlled laser fighters he's developing. I'm convinced of that.'

'We're talking about the *man*, not the product,' Tracy said.

'I don't believe there can be the one without the other.'

'That's nonsense,' Tracy said. 'Macomber's company must employ *thousands* of men, many of them the engineers who came up with the designs for those systems.'

'You don't understand,' the Director said. 'None of that would ever have been done without Macomber's unique vision. Yes, there are men there who designed and built the *Vampire* and the others but what they did was *translate* Macomber's images onto the drawing board. Yes, they made those images conceivable as steel and aluminium reality. But it was Macomber who made it all possible.'

'Take first things first. Worry about whether Gottschalk will get the nomination. Without him as President, Metronics, Inc. is dead in the water as far as the government's concerned.'

'You're a little out of date, Mother.' The Director sat back down. 'Gottschalk's already the Republican nominee. It's September already. And, after the assassination attempt on him, he's a shoe-in for President.'

'Someone tried to assassinate Atherton Gottschalk?' It was Tracy's turn to be stunned.

'A Muslim fundamentalist.' The Director picked up a brass letter opener, its hilt the seal of the Joint Chiefs of Staff. 'It happened almost precisely as Gottschalk had predicted it might. An assault within the precincts of America; an invasion, if you will. He'd been warning against it for many months but for some those were words without substance. The physical attempt changed all that; it changed many people's way of thinking. Now I don't think there's a power in the nation that can stop

622

him from being elected.'

'How badly was he wounded?'

The tip of the letter opener shone in the overhead lights as the Director turned it over. 'It was relatively minor. Just a blow to the heart, a bruise.' He waved a hand. 'Nothing at all. This guy's got God on his side. He was wearing a new phantom-weight bulletproof waistcoat he had made just a couple of days before the assassination attempt.'

The Director threw the letter opener aside, got up from behind the desk as another knock on the door sounded. 'I for one was unsure of Gottschalk before this incident. Too much talk and would he have the balls to back it up if he got into the Oval Office? Now I believe I have my answer. He has my vote.' He turned his head. 'Come.'

The door opened and the thin young adjutant entered carrying a black calfskin attaché case. It was bound by a steel-wire mesh cord wrapped around his waist. The attaché case appeared to be just like any other but Tracy knew that beneath the calfskin was a sheet of molybdenum-steel alloy and, below that, a lead shield so that neither X-rays nor a detonation could penetrate the case against the carrier's will.

The adjutant placed the case top up on the Director's desk. He took out one key and the Director withdrew one from his trouser pocket. Together they inserted the keys in the case's double lock, opened it.

The Director removed the file and the adjutant closed the case, left the room closing the door behind him. The file was in a deep red binder, a black stripe imprinted on its cover starting at the lower left, rising obliquely to the upper right. The colour of the file signified it as an original; the black stripe bespoke its 'Eyes Only' status.

The Director did not open it but rather handed it over to Tracy. 'The "Sultan" file.'

Tracy took it, went back to his chair to read through it. He saw his own words again, in reports, daily logs, cipher telexes. The quotidian progress of what he had thought of then as his crowning achievement, his last hurrah. But, as with Bobby Marshall, he had been too arrogant, too sure of himself. He had been content to run 'Sultan' from a cosy little armchair in an office right down this hall. And in both cases, he had paid the price.

Whatever it was he was hoping to find within the files was not there. He was, instead, confronted with ashes, text now rendered meaningless by subsequent information. 'Sultan' really was dead now.

He closed the folder, looked up at the Director. Their eyes met and for an instant Tracy felt the crackle of contact. Then he came across the room, handed the Director the folder.

'Thanks,' he said. 'There's nothing I can use.'

'I wish I knew what you were getting at.'

Tracy passed a hand across his tired eyes. 'So do I.'

'Excuse me a moment. I've got to get this back to the Library and, as you know, procedure demands that the officer requesting a file accompany the adjutant on its return.' He made a sweeping gesture. 'Relax until I get back. You look like you could use it.'

The door closed, leaving Tracy alone in the enormous room. He went slowly, idly around behind the Director's filigreed desk, sat down in the stippled leather swivel chair. He closed his eyes, began to take deep breaths. *Prana.*

Macomber. Macomber was behind it all. But the murders? John and Moira. Had he committed those? ... *I don't know. I just felt ... something.* Moira's words floated up through the forest of his memory, pale bubbles on the murky earth. *It isn't something I can ... put into words.*

But what *was* it?

Was it Macomber she had seen? Tracy knew that Macomber was capable of murder; he had been witness to the man's innate barbarity numerous times enfolded within the rank bloody jungles of Cambodia. Had he slipped the needle into the base of John's neck? What did Macomber know of Japanese methods of assassination? And Moira's horrendous beating. Oh, yes, Macomber had seen such murder victims more times than he could count, political examples left by the Khmer Rouge to intimidate and terrify its enemies.

No, Tracy decided now, it was not the murders themselves

but their *methods* that he returned to. What was it about them? What was he missing? *Think, damnit!* he commanded himself. But nothing came.

On impulse, he reached for the phone, dialled interior information.

'Operator.'

'This is Mother.'

'Mother!' The voice rose in pitch, excitement. 'Is it really you? Back in the fold?'

'Stein?'

'In the flesh.'

'What're you doing holding down the fort?'

'I retired from active field work two years ago. It was either this or work down at the Mines. I didn't want to leave DC.'

'It's good to hear your voice after all these years.' Tracy remembered Stein well. A powerful man with a sharp mind, he graduated from the Mines in the same class as Tracy though he was twenty years older. He was shipped into Ban Me Thuot in the same month and they had run a number of clandestine missions into the Cambodian interior together. Stein proved to be one of the bravest men Tracy had ever met. 'Drinks sometime.'

'I'd like that. Uh. I was gonna write to you in New York but now I've got you on the line, I'll give you my condolences in person. I'm really sorry, Mother.'

Tracy's stomach contracted, turned over. 'Sorry for what?'

There was silence on the line. He could hear the other's breathing.

'Stein? What the hell are you talking about?'

'Christ, Mother. I saw you come in with the Director and I just assumed that, well, that you knew.'

'Knew *what*?' Tracy was sitting up straight, his knuckles white where he gripped the phone. 'For Christ's sake tell me what's going on.'

'I'm sorry, Mother,' Stein repeated. 'Your father was murdered four days ago.'

*

The soft burring of the telephone broke through the spider's mesh of memories that had been filling Kim's mind. The high curtains in the hotel suite were closed, darkness creeping in like a woman's sigh, relaxing him. He had been back in Phnom Penh with Thu and the rest of his doomed family, reliving once again the night that turned into day . . .

He reached for the phone, spoke into the receiver. 'Yes?'

'This is Valkerie.'

'I don't know you.'

'You know Blue Szechuan.'

Kim sat up in bed, swung his legs over the side. 'The restaurant in Chinatown?'

'No. Eindhoven.'

Kim wondered which one of them it was. Over the phone, he could not distinguish his voice and the KGB Dutchman had not been able to provide a physical description.

'I have been waiting for you,' he said now.

'I've just now arrived. We should talk immediately.'

It was the first bit of real dialogue they had exchanged. All that had gone before was prearranged code.

'If you're near here,' Kim said, trying a probe, 'you can come right up to the room.'

'No,' Valkerie said after a moment's hesitation, 'I do not think that would be prudent.' Kim heard a brief rustle as of clothes. 'Meet me in the street level bar at the Ile St Marie. Do you know it?'

'Yes.' Kim was very familiar with that hotel, old world and luxurious. He had once tracked a Korean there, a hideous, scarred leader of the communist secret police, responsible for the murder of thousands. 'I've heard of it,' Kim lied. There was no point in giving away information.

'Fifteen minutes, then.'

'Will that give me enough time to get there?' he said, adding to the illusion.

'It will be sufficient,' the voice said neutrally. 'If you start now.' The phone went dead.

Valkerie, the man with the red-gold hair who had taken over

the meeting in Einhoven, put down the Hilton house phone and turned to two thickset dark-haired men. *'On pridyot,'* he said. He's coming.

'Pyotr,' he said, still speaking in Russian, 'you wait here and shadow him. I want to know how well he obeys instructions.' He began to move, a bear of a man. 'Grekov, you come with me,' striding confidently through the hotel's lobby and out into the steaming raining night. Grekov got their car and Valkerie got in and they drove off towards the Ile St Marie.

Though Valkerie was known as Helmut Mannheim to the members of the Panel, indeed, to everyone with whom he had come in contact for the past fifteen years, his real name was Mikhail Ivanovich Fyodorov. As a very young man he had distinguished himself in the army and had come to the attention of certain far-thinking men within the KGB. They had recruited him easily; Fyodorov jumped at the chance to serve mother Russia. And because of his physical appearance, they sent him to a camp – one of many seeded throughout the USSR – first to learn terrorist techniques, then to change himself into a German. Within three years, they had judged him ready. Then they put him into West Berlin. That was in 1968.

February, Valkerie remembered now. It was dull and bleak in the west and within a month he found himself yearning inside for one more glimpse of his beloved Urals, clean and snow-covered, the hunting pelts strapped around him and the breath like a many barbed lance coming out of his half-open mouth as he moved effortlessly up the elevations.

There had been a girl, too, during those last two weeks he had been given leave before the commencement of his long assign-ment, a young Georgian with black hair and green eyes. So young, so fresh, Valkerie thought now. And unknown to him, also a KGB agent, used as a last loyalty test for Mikhail Ivanovich Fyodorov.

That was so long ago, Valkerie thought now. So long. Why, I have even forgotten her name. But not the moment, no, I could never forget that moment.

Since then, his superiors, according to well-established form, tested him – without his knowledge of course – once every two years, even though the information he relayed to them was never less than first class. There was nothing personal in it; none of them for an instant believed Valkerie would betray the USSR. But they believed in caution and precise thinking.

The man with the red-gold hair was thinking now about his rank as colonel in the KGB. He was thinking how fortunate he was to have been born a Russian, in the first place, and to have been in superb physical condition all his life, in the second place. Unconsciously, he put his palm against the slight curve of his lower belly as he sat. Well, not as flat as it had once been, perhaps, but then he was not as young as he once had been. And schnitzel, wurst and lager were a far cry from borscht, pilmeny and vodka. He sighed deeply now, as they rolled through the Dallas night. There was much sadness inherent in being away from the motherland for so many years. Yet, as he looked around him at one of the new industrial hearts of America, he was gladdened at the immensely important part he had been chosen to play in the destruction of the West. Yes, he thought now, happy for the moment, all the sacrifice is worthwhile. Then he wrenched his mind away from the past and began to focus on the problem just ahead.

Kim took the elevator down to the Hilton's glittering lobby, conscious of the essence of America all around him. He had never before been so aware of the multitude of irritating cross-currents swirling about him. He longed for the company of his own kind and mourned that in today's world such a desire was impossible to fulfil.

The Dallas night was like Mardi Gras in the aftermath of the highly successful Republican National Convention. The city was alight with elation — the kind of euphoric release one rarely sees. Crowds danced in the streets, oblivious of the rain, waving miniature American flags, wearing the cardboard and plastic straw hats given out at the convention. Multi-coloured confetti filled the air, bands played on street corners, competing with the shouts of the thronging pedestrians. And it seemed that even before his election, Gottschalk's promised new day dawning for America was already here.

Kim had to wait for a cab. That was just as well. It gave him sufficient time to make the man who had been on a house phone when he had come through the lobby a moment ago. Stupid for the man to put down the receiver just as Kim was passing him by. Even more foolish to move after him immediately. But then Kim was an altogether different kind of quarry than this man was used to dealing with. Who could he havé come in contact with before, Kim mused idly, bumbling Americans or Englishmen? Kim spat into the gutter as he climbed into the taxi.

This one was not so different from the Dutchman who had trailed Kim to the other side of town. Dzerzhinsky Square. No doubt this formidable bastion of neolithic thinking was where he had been trained, Dutch descent or no Dutch descent, Kim thought now. They trained their men well; they were especially resistant to most forms of torture.

But then Kim was a master of the art, the uncrowned doge. Others felt certain that he performed miracles in this dark realm but Kim knew it to be far simpler than that – though he chose to feed the myth because it was to his benefit. It all boiled down to basics. Psychological basics. Tracy Richter was the only other man Kim had encountered who understood that concept. And it was Tracy, too, who, Kim was certain, had the capacity to become a master of Kim's expertise. Kim had seen more than enough during their time together during the war to convince him of it. Yet some innate weakness – for that was how Kim viewed it – always intervened to make Tracy back off, to turn away from the power that came with such a total mastery of one human being over another.

Kim had had much time to reflect on this once again as he had worked on the Dutchman. He had been stunned by the revelation that he had unknowingly divulged potentially damaging information to the KGB. He would never have gone near the Panel were it not for his need to support Thu. And that instant he hated family, duty, life itself.

The atmosphere outside the Ile St Marie was a bit calmer, owing to its location in posh Turtle Creek and the long-standing reputation of the hotel itself. The limestone façade seemed to exude quiet and stately wealth, an old world oasis in a decidedly new world city.

Kim went straight through the cut-glass and polished mahogany revolving door. He remembered the layout of the lobby well: concierge and check-out desks to the left, salon, barber and gift shops through an arcade to the right. Straight ahead, across an expanse of blue-green area rugs, was the gilt-doored bank of elevators with their row of old-fashioned clock-type floor indicators above. Further down to the left, through a palm lined archway were the bar, the florist's and the very fine restaurant.

Without hesitation, Kim walked through the lobby, directly into one of the elevators. He waited as the car filled up, one eye on the floor buttons pressed. He saw his tick come in through the revolving doors, look around and, spotting Kim, make for the elevator. The doors began to close and, reaching out, Kim pressed the 'Door Open' button. Someone murmured irritably. Then the dark-haired man was in and the doors slid shut. They went up.

Kim pressed 'five', a floor no one else was getting off at. It would just be him and his tick.

If his memory was correct, the hotel floors were laid out in roughly the shape of a capital H. A lateral hallway led off right and left to turnings for the somewhat shorter hallways set at right angles to the central one.

Kim took an immediate right, heading purposefully down the richly appointed corridor. The thing was to do everything very quickly. The man obviously had orders to shadow Kim and he would do that to the letter. But if Kim hesitated for just a moment, the man might break it off and return to his control.

Just past the corner to the shorter hallway, Kim stopped, pressing himself against the wall. There was very little sound here, the acoustics excellent, bespeaking the quality of the hotel. He heard quiet padding and began to breathe deeply in preparation.

The Russian rounded the corner cautiously but because of the low light and the streaked shadows he failed to see Kim.

Kim reached out and, almost without moving his torso,

encircled the Russian's neck with his arms, the edge of his left forearm hard against the two middle atlas vertebrae, the heel of his right hand rushing inward towards the throat, snapping the neck cleanly so that the man dangled and danced in autonomous spasm before he slid to the floor, dead.

Partway down the corridor, Kim located a service door and dragged the corpse over. He deftly picked the lock and, once inside, stuffed the body into a linen cart, covering it with dirty sheets.

Downstairs, in the lobby, he turned to his right and went through the arch, the palms whispering gently. The bar was just past the florist shop, a dim rather masculine, clubby atmosphere with gas lamps, leather padding on the outward curve of the carved blond wood bar.

He saw Valkerie first in the etched mirror behind the bar, his great bush of wiry red-gold hair visible between the bottles of brandy.

Kim evinced no surprise as he drew up an empty leather-cushioned stool next to Valkerie. He ordered a Stolichaya with a twist and Valkerie gave a thin smile; he was drinking dark German beer.

They took their drinks to a booth. Kim allowed the other man to choose it, knowing that according to KGB principle it would be in sight of another agent. He wanted to set them all in his memory. Valkerie sat first, taking the left-hand seat. That meant Kim would be facing the other agent, somewhere else in the room.

The bar was not crowded at this time of the night and there was no one near them. Still, they kept their voices low.

'It was quite an inconvenience my coming here,' Valkerie said in his thick guttural German.

'I'd prefer that we both speak English,' Kim said easily. 'Foreign languages are noted in this city; this isn't Washington, after all.'

The other man nodded. 'As you wish.'

Kim looked across the small table. He had not liked this man as a German, now he hated him as a Russian.

'How high up are you?' he said abruptly.

631

'What?' The great bear head turned in his direction.

Kim was patient. 'Judging by your age and the . . . importance of the Panel, I would think you couldn't be less than a colonel.'

'What colonel?' Valkerie said irritably. 'I'm a businessman. I run –'

'Then why are you here?' Kim said sharply.

'As I said, I am a business man. I came here to conclude a deal.' Valkerie had regained his composure. This Oriental made him nervous. Never mind that he was Vietnamese; he reminded Fyodorov too much of the Chinese and he, like all Russians, had a pathological fear and hatred of the Chinese that bordered on the xeonophobic.

'What kind of deal?'

The meaty shoulders shrugged. 'You'll have to tell me.'

'Excuse me,' Kim said, rising, 'I must relieve my bladder.' As he went out of the room, he caught that wiry halo of red-gold hair bobbing and, in response, a thick dark-haired man rise from across the room.

Kim went straight across the hall to the men's room. He was at the row of basins, washing, when he heard the door opening. There was a sliver of mirror in front of him that revealed the body of the third Russian.

The man came in and, looking under all the partitions to see if anyone was sitting in the cubicles, came up to Kim and drew out a silenced pistol.

Kim slammed his heel down onto the Russian's instep while swivelling his hips, bringing his right shoulder forward, increasing the momentum he would need for the killing blow.

The man was better prepared than Kim imagined and he managed to block the lethal kite. His wrist broke beneath the impact and his face went white for an instant. Then he had recovered fully and was attacking, the clumsy gun forgotten.

Kim enjoyed the physical contact, reveling in the flex and pressure he was putting his body to. He also savoured the knowledge of his ultimate victory, using the ends of his fingers in concert at last, plunging them into the man's hard flesh just below his sternum.

There was enough force behind it to lift the man right off his feet. His dark eyes opened wide and his mouth yawned in a comic 'O' as he felt skin and ligaments ripped, then blood vessels and organs.

Kim jerked his hand upward, touching the heart, twisting it, and the man died on his feet, collapsing back onto the row of porcelain sinks.

Kim took him quickly into one of the empty cubicles, propping him up on the toilet. There had been a good deal of initial bleeding and he was careful about keeping it off his clothes. When he was satisfied that the Russian's position would not attract attention, he returned to the basin, using towels to mop up. While he was washing, a pair of slightly drunk Texans entered in the middle of telling a smutty joke. Kim resisted spitting at their feet and, with a last look at himself in the mirror as a check, went out.

He slid back into the seat opposite Valkerie and said, 'I'll tell you what the deal is,' ignoring the other's raised eyebrows. 'I've neutralized your cell here so now you're on your own. That should be a new feeling for you. Soviet secret police thrive on being surrounded by underlings and subverted informants.' He smiled with his lips but there was no humour in his eyes. 'Here's a chance to see how the other half lives.'

'You're very clever,' Valkerie said icily, 'but the small calibre pistol I'm aiming at your stomach under the table will neutralize that I've no doubt.'

'What? Shoot me here in this public place?'

'With the air-cooled silencer I have you will think I've farted. Nothing more.' Valkerie was very calm but inwardly he wanted to get it over with. The faster he put an end to the Vietnamese's life, the better he'd feel. 'And as for your head hitting the table, well, everyone knows what can happen if you drink too much. Especially to an Oriental drinking Russian vodka.' He shook his head back and forth. 'You should never have tried such fiery liquor.'

The smile was still etched on his face as the sliver of polished steel, blued on its needle end with a synthetic curare derivative, entered the soft flesh of his underbelly. Because that area is thick with nerve bundles branching out into the entire body, he did not even have time to pull the trigger. The fast-acting poison froze his reflexes. The heart lost the ability to pump and Mikhail Ivanovich Fyodorov ceased to exist.

Kim reloaded the powerful spring-driven tube that ran along the inside of his left wrist, paid for the drinks and left the bar at a normal pace.

Once back at the Hilton, he phoned the Dallas PD and told them where they could find a high-ranking officer of the Soviet KGB dead as a herring. He used just that phrase, liking its aptness. He did not, of course, give his name.

Then he came out of the public phone in the lobby and went up to his suite to sleep; tomorrow was time enough for him to fly out. He lay atop the king-size bed with his hands laced behind his head and stared sightlessly at the ceiling, his naked flesh gleaming in the light.

How he wished Thu had turned out differently. There was no one else left of the family. He felt a gulf between them, as if Thu were no longer his brother but an aquaintance for whom one could feel sadness but nothing deeper. That was good, he thought. It left him alone. Because now he was the sole instrument of his family's revenge. His thoughts flew back to that hot humid night in Phnom Penh when he had been out drinking with a girl. He had returned home to Chamcar Mon to find his family's beautiful villa in flames.

This black smoke curled upwards, blocking out the pinprick diamond stars and ash rained down on the palm and banyan trees, settling like moths surrounding the conflagration.

They had all been in there: his father, Nguyan Van Chinh, his mother, Duan, his six brothers and Diep, his one sister, Diep who he had beaten twice because of her clandestine liaison with the Cambodian up the road. He had found her out some six months before and had threatened to tell their father. Diep had wept, imploring him to keep her secret, swearing to him that she would not see the boy.

Kim had accepted her word but a week later, she had begun again. Perhaps she truly could not stay away from him or, again, she was just being perverse. Kim did not know; and the fire made certain that he never would.

Diep died in the fierce blaze, along with their parents and five of the brothers. Only Thu, who had tried to save her, had lived, broken but alive. And it had been Thu who had been obsessed about that night, who had returned to Phnom Penh, searching for clues.

It had been Thu who on returning from his final trip back home had told Kim that, finally he had discovered the truth. Diep's Khmer boyfriend, the one she could not give up, had been the one to set the blaze. On his way to join the *maquis* he had turned his hate on the family who would destroy him if they knew of his involvement with one of their own.

His name was Khieu Samnang and in the 'Ragman' file Kim had found the key to his revenge. Delmar Davis Macomber's adopted son was Khieu Samnang's brother, his only living relative.

'My ... *father?*' Tracy felt cold, disorientation gaining hold. He had been preparing himself for a while for his father's death. But murdered? No! It couldn't be. 'There must be some mistake. How could –'

'No mistake.' Stein's voice conveyed his sadness. 'Nobody knows who or why. We picked it up from NYPD and the Director ordered us in immediately. They're waiting downstairs now. That's why I thought –'

'They?' Tracy said bewilderedly. 'Who're they?' There was no answer so he swivelled the chair around to look out the window. It faced onto K Street and he stared directly down, saw the line of gleaming black limousines, their tops beaded with rain. There were four cars, the first one in the line longer somehow than the others.

Tracy squinted through the rain, saw the differing configuration at the lead car's sloping rear. A hearse! My God, Stein had been telling the truth.

That was what the Director had been watching as Tracy dressed. He had turned away, looking out the window. Watching the cortège setting up. Oh, you bastard! Tracy thought hotly. You goddamned bastard! Of course there was a *quid pro quo*. Why else had the Director failed to mention Louis Richter's death? Why had he waited? What did he want?

Something from Tracy. Something big.

But *what*?

'Mother?' Stein's voice was hesitant. 'You all right?'

'What?' Tracy brought himself back.

'I said —'

'Yes. I just . . . needed a minute.'

'I understand. I lost my father early. I know what it's like, especially if you're close.'

'We were close,' Tracy whispered, realizing for the first time that what he said was the truth. 'We were very close.' He felt hot tears behind his eyes, searing him. He put his trembling hand up, covering his eyes. The light seemed to pierce directly into his brain, hurting. He fought for breath. *Prana.* But peace would not come this time and his chest continued to heave. He heard a tiny voice crying *Daddy! Daddy*, the sounds of a child's running feet, climbing up into a large warm lap, putting his sleepy head against a comforting chest, hearing the rumble, a physical sense of his father's voice, lulling him to sleep, as he was told a story of faraway kingdoms, fair maidens and brave and gallant knights.

'Mother.' Stein's voice was gentle in his ear. 'You were calling me about something.'

Riding his father's shoulders at Rye Playland, dripping ice cream from a cone onto his thick dark hair.

'What did you want?'

All gone now. In the space of a heartbeat.

'Mother — ?'

But he of all people should know how swiftly death can strike; much of his life had been spent on learning the ways of stealth and murder. His father had understood that; even approved. The defence of America.

Tracy wiped at his eyes. What was it Stein was asking? Why *had* he called?

'I got a guy in mind,' Tracy said thickly. 'I used him for an "Eyes Only" ops in Cambodia. Seconded out of Special Forces. I need some info on him.'

'If he was with us at all, I can get you a tie-in.'

'Listen,' Tracy said, 'I'm not going to mislead you. I'm not coming back. I'm just here, now.'

'What time period you interested in?' Stein said as if Tracy had not said a word.

'You listening to me? I don't want to dump you into hot water.'

'Forget it. Just call it a welcome home present. Now give.'

' '69–'70.'

'Got your man,' Stein said. 'Don't go away.'

He put Tracy on hold. Tracy looked at his watch. The Director had been gone six minutes. He estimated he had five more. One of those was burned while Stein made the connections.

He came back on. 'Okay. Your man's O'Day.'

'What department's he with?'

'None of your business, Mother. But he's not with us.'

'Got it. Put him on. And Stein –'

'Yeah?'

'Thanks.'

'Just don't you forget that drink.' He clicked off and there was dead space for a few seconds. Tracy's watch told him he had three minutes to get the job done. If the Director came in before that he would have to hang up. This call was strictly hush.

'O'Day here.' The voice sounded light. Bit of a Virginia accent.

'This is Mother.'

'What can I do for you?'

'I need some information dating back to 1969 on a man seconded out of the Special Forces – Daniel Boone Ops in Ban Me Thuot.'

'Name?'

'Macomber comma Delmar, middle initial D.'

'Let's see,' the voice said in his ear, 'what the records show. It's all in the computer. What exactly are you looking for?'

I wish I knew, Tracy thought desperately. He had so little time. 'Have you got his return to the States?'

'Last time or between tours of duty?'

'Last time.'

'Coming right up.' There was a small silence during which Tracy tried not to look at his watch. He knew he was not going to make it. 'He returned on a Lockheed L-57 military transport carrying 107 passengers and a crew of five.'

Tracy thought a moment. Was the culmination of Sultan the only reason Macomber had opted to return home just then? He took a stab in the dark. 'What was the makeup of the passenger manifest?'

'Military personnel,' O'Day said immediately. Then, 'No, wait a minute. Records show 106 military persons of various rank and one local.'

'One *what*?' Tracy sat up straight, his heart beginning to pound painfully in his chest.'

'You know. A slope.'

'What nationality?'

'How the hell do I know?' O'Day's voice was annoyed. 'Name's Khieu Sokha. That's all I got.'

Oh, Christ, Tracy thought. I think this might be it. But what he had in his mind was so incredible he dared not run it too far ... yet. He knew he was taking a great leap of faith but there was no other choice. It was no good asking O'Day what the Cambodian national – for there was no doubt in Tracy's mind that Khieu Sokha was Khmer – was doing on a military transport bound for the United States, the same plane that Macomber had been on. He remembered the manner of Senator Burke's death in Kenilworth and found himself anxious to speak to Thwaite to see what progress the detective had made.

'Now we go back to the States,' he told O'Day quickly. 'Same time frame: 1969–70. I need to know if the same subject applied for sponsorship of a foreign national during that time.'

'Okay. Hold on.'

That was just what Tracy could not afford to do. Sixty seconds and he was in a definite red sector. He swivelled his chair around, faced the closed door. He concentrated on the knob. The moment it turned, he would have to cradle the receiver. Come on, O'Day, he mouthed silently.

'Mother?' He was back on the line.

'Yes.' Thirty seconds. His body was tense, leaning forward as he concentrated on the doorknob.

'The computer's down for a moment. Don't go away.'

'Hey!' But Tracy realized he was on hold again. He cursed softly. The seconds slipped by. Five-four-three-two-one. The second hand slid across the six. The Director was now overdue. Tracy knew as well as anyone in the foundation how long it took to get down to the Library, sign in to hand in a file and return. The receiver was slippery with sweat under his fingers and he was about to drop it back into its cradle when he heard O'Day's voice in his ear like a bee buzz.

'We're back in business. Just take a sec now.'

But the doorknob was turning, the door itself opening inward. Tracy could hear the Director's low voice. He was saying something to his adjutant. He came into view now, one hand on the knob, about to enter.

'I'm sorry. It doesn't show anything.'

Disappointment threaded him and all he could say was, 'Are you sure?'

'Of course I'm sure,' O'Day's voice was testy again. 'I'm paid to be sure.'

Tracy's heart sank. The door was opening further. He had been so certain that he was on the right track. Now, as the Director dismissed his adjutant, as the two voices rose slightly as they moved apart, Tracy said, 'Thank you for your time, Mr O'Day.'

'Sorry I couldn't've been more help. That's what these masses've information're for.'

Tracy had cradled the phone by the time the Director walked into the room. What does he want from me? Tracy asked himself. I should see it; it's right there in front of me. But he had so much new data being thrown at him in such a concentrated period of time he could not think straight. He knew he would just have to allow the Director to play out the scene in his own fashion.

'I've been thinking about what you said concerning Macomber.' The Director crossed his arms over his chest. 'What evidence against him do you have, really? The word of a known drug dealer in Hong Kong?'

'You weren't there,' Tracy said doggedly. 'You didn't see his face or hear the words as he spoke them. He wasn't lying. He was fully expecting my death within the hour.'

'They all lie, Mother, all those Hong Kong bastards. It's a way of life for them, they wouldn't know how to stop.'

Tracy privately thought that amusing seeing where the thought came from. 'Mizo wasn't,' he said. 'He was boasting. He had no reason to lie. He *wanted* me to know before he killed me.'

'Or he was misleading you entirely on the assumption you might escape.'

Tracy shook his head. 'You're wrong and the bomb in my hotel room proves it. He was terrified of me *before* I even opened my mouth about what I wanted. He had already broken through my cover story within hours of my landing in Hong Kong. And he *assumed* I was after a piece of the smuggling business. Why would he do that if he were lying about it?'

The Director looked steadily at Tracy. 'I've just had another signal from HK staff. The police've found the mess you made of Mizo. That's the only thing that's mollifying them. As you can imagine, they didn't like him much – except, of course, for the people he was greasing every month.'

When Tracy said nothing, he went on. 'Then all we have is what you've told me.'

'And the murders.'

The Director's head turned so quickly, Tracy heard his neck crack.

'Murders? What murders?'

'John Holmgren's, Moira Monserrat's, Roland Burke's.'

'I don't see the relevance.'

'I don't either. Not yet. But it's there.'

'What you're talking about . . .' The Director came across the room, stood with his thighs against the wood filigree of the desk edge. 'What you are implying to me is a very dangerous course of action in regards the future of this country. He unfolded his arms, pressed his knuckled fists down onto the desk, his arms rigid as iron bars. 'I want to make my – the foundation's – point of view quite clear to you. In my opinion, Delmar Davis Macomber is far too valuable to the future security of this country to be tampered with.'

'Damnit!' Abruptly Tracy had had enough. He stood face to face with his former boss. 'He turned a mission! He lied to us; stole us blind. He fooled us completely!'

'And look what he's done with that money.' The Director's voice was maddeningly calm. 'Ploughed it back into America. I'll tell you truly Mother I don't give a damn how much he's lined his pockets with. That's not my concern. I work for America and that's what comes first. Always and forever. I won't have him touched.'

'Jesus!' Tracy said. 'He's laughing up his sleeve at us.'

'Let him. We need him. I forgive him his sins.'

'But I don't! I can't!'

'I know,' the Director said gently. '"Sultan" was *your* mission. Your last great bit of machinery built for us, as it turned out. I can understand your anger, your need for revenge.'

The Director's head came forward. 'But you were a professional, once. The best kind of professional: sure, confident, controlled. Your personal feelings have no place here. Put them away. Go on with your life. Forget about Macomber. Whatever he's done is in the past. It no longer concerns you.'

It was then that Tracy almost blurted out the connection he saw between Macomber and the two murders. But he had nothing but theory and, given the Director's current bent, he'd just laugh. Tracy saw then just how far he'd come from his immersion in this life. It was true what the Director said. He wasn't family anymore. And never would be again.

Abruptly, he wanted only one item back from his Hong Kong trip: the diamond ring he had bought for Lauren.

'Now that that's out of the way, I'm afraid I've got some bad news for you.' The Director's voice seemed to float in the air. 'I wouldn't have waited to tell you, of course, but I wasn't sure of your state of mind when you came in. Signals informed me what kind of a gauntlet you were required to run for the past four days.'

'Get to the point, will you?'

'Of course.' The Director's eyes locked with his. 'Your father has expired. Rather mysteriously, I might add.'

'What?' Tracy made himself sit up straight.

'To put it quite bluntly, he was murdered four days ago.'

The Director put his hands behind the small of his back, clasping them. 'It happened in his apartment. He was apparently taking a bath; he was found naked in the bath. He was strangled with what we suspect was a length of metal wire. A cord of any kind is out, the PM found no traces of fibre in the surrounding flesh; ditto any threads of material. The nature of the wound suggests a thin metal strand.' The Director broke away from the front of the desk. 'He put up quite a battle.'

'He was dying, you know.'

'I didn't.'

'He had maybe six months left.'

The Director said nothing.

'That was taken away from him, too.'

The Director noted the bitterness in Tracy's voice, said, 'I've had everything arranged. Naturally we took him. He was family. We've been waiting for you to return. The moment you called, I had the cortège drawn up. They're waiting for us out front. We've a spot ready at Arlington National.'

Tracy looked at him.

'The adjutant has your jacket hanging in the outer office.' The Director lifted an arm. 'Shall we go?'

As Thwaite had surmised, Flaherty, his own captain, was no problem. Thwaite outlined the case to him in the most general terms and Flaherty gave him the go ahead. Thwaite had worked for him for over six years and had brought him nothing but first class busts and a raft of commendations from the commissioner. Flaherty liked that; it made him feel secure.

Thwaite emerged from his office, preparing himself to beard Toad Tinelli, the Prince of Narco, in his den, when White told him to call Melody.

'I don't know what's up,' the black cop said, 'but it must be something big. She's called three times within the last fifteen minutes.'

Thwaite went to his desk, dialled her number.

'Doug,' she said, 'I finally had some time to go over that scroll you brought me.'

'I thought you'd already read it.'

'Well, I had . . . in a way. I read it quickly to give you an idea of what was in it. But Chinese is a peculiar language. Ideograms have a number of meanings and contexts when juxtaposed with –'

'Mel,' he broke in as patiently as he could, 'what're trying to tell me?'

There was a pause. When Melody's voice came again it seemed very small indeed. 'Doug,' she said quietly, 'just what are you mixed up in?'

'Why d'you ask?' he said suspiciously.

'Because there's a shipment coming in on the seventh. That's tomorrow.' He heard her take a deep shuddering breath.

'What the hell is it, Mel?' She was beginning to frighten him.

'It's a shipment of military armament.'

The silence was so long, so intense that at last she was compelled to say, 'Doug? Are you still there?'

Thwaite's mind was racing. Murders of a governor, a senator, among others, the largest dope smuggling operation he or anyone else downtown had ever stumbled across and now an illegal arms shipment. What in Christ's name did it all mean? he asked himself. All three were intertwined, of that he was sure. But how? And who stood in the centre of this, manipulating them all? Again, he felt that chill creep over him, entering his bones and he wondered where Tracy was. He had phoned him repeatedly at the Four Seasons Hotel since he had picked up the message when he had come in this morning. Whatever we're into, he thought, is very goddamned big and I don't like it one bit.

'You're sure.' His voice seemed hoarse and raw.

'Four Uzi submachine guns; four AK-47s; twenty-four PC-11 grenades; two Frankes high-velocity mortars equipped with Nitesights; a half-dozen Rheinsböck rocket launchers; a case of Seitran Fintwist missiles; eight gas masks; fifteen canisters of CN gas.'

'Christ Jesus,' he whispered. 'I'll be right over.' All thought of Toad Tinelli was gone from his mind.

There was a hole in the earth into which Louis Richter was descending, step by step, as if down an invisible staircase. Rain, beading across the polished, convex surface of the mahogany casket, ran like tears, disappearing into the bottom of the hole.

The prayers had been said, the handful of muddy dirt dropped in a spatter, washed quickly away by the force of the rain. Not far away, a stylishly dressed woman knelt along the elbow of Sherman Drive, placing blue and yellow lilies before a monument. A uniformed driver held a wide black umbrella above her head, protecting her. A young boy, no more than eight or nine, stood by the driver's side, holding his hand. He was dressed in a dark suit, the wind brushing his sandy hair into his eyes.

Behind the woman's small veiled head, Tracy could just make out the sightseers on their pilgrimage to the Tomb of the Unknown Soldier. He shivered, feeling chill despite the Burberry raincoat the adjutant had handed him along with his jacket.

With a last creak of the winch, the casket came to rest at the bottom of the open grave. Two men stood by, their burly bare arms crossed over the handles of their shovels. They watched the middle distance with unseeing eyes.

'Well,' the Director said softly. 'That's that.'

Tracy turned to go but the other put a hand on his arm. 'Let the others go first. They'll wait for us in the cars.'

Tracy looked at the Director, then beyond him. The stylishly dressed woman was on her feet. She had taken one lily off the grave and now turned, handing it to the young boy. Then the woman took him by the shoulders, moving him gently forward. She whispered into his ear. He dropped the single lily onto the others. He stood there for a moment, staring at what he had done, then he turned around and rejoined his mother. She was, Tracy saw now, quite young. Far too young to be a widow.

Tracy turned his gaze away. That woman's husband should not be dead; just as Louis Richter should not be dead. He only had six months to live. At the very least he could have been granted all of that. But he had not. Life was not neat and predictable. It preferred to come up and kick you in the stomach while your attention was elsewhere.

'There is a final matter we must discuss.' The Director turned a bit to face Tracy. 'One more mission to perform.'

'As you said, I am no longer family. I no longer belong.'

'Yet you were one of us, once. Just as your father was. He kept his faith in us all through the years. He believed in us; in the service we render this country. He understood our importance.'

'Meaning I don't.'

'We are not individuals here, Mother. You knew that once. We are many-headed but we have only one corpus.' The Director's eyes were bright despite the thick lowering light. 'And when one of those heads becomes diseased, when it threatens that corpus, it must be disposed of immediately.' Tracy looked into those eyes. 'I am speaking of Kim. He is a renegade now; we are finished with him.'

'I thought you said you were letting him run.'

The Director nodded his outsized head. 'And so I have. That phase is at an end; Kim has gone beyond the pale. He must be eliminated. But I will not jeopardize the foundation in the process.' He turned his shoulder into the wind, keeping the rain for the moment at bay. 'That is why you must terminate him for us; you are no longer family.'

'You're out of your mind.' Tracy lurched a step backward as if the muddy ground had given way beneath his weight. A moment ago it had been quite firm. 'I'm no hired killer. Get away from me.'

'All right,' the Director said. 'I'll do that. But I'll say just one thing in the process. By killing your father, Kim went beyond the pale. Your abrupt faintheartedness will not – *cannot* – save him. He has murdered one of the family; that cannot be tolerated.'

'Kim?' Tracy said in a whisper. '*Kim* killed my father? But why?'

'I don't know and I have no interest in finding out. Only the act concerns me.'

'The truth!' Tracy cried. 'I want to know the truth.'

'The truth is Kim murdered your father. Brutally, maliciously, almost sadistically.' The Director came across the muddy lawn, pursuing Tracy. 'He roped you into something. I don't know what it is but the results have been devastating. They must be stopped now!'

The Director was shaking slightly, his face in high colour. 'I've given you the best reason in the world to take him down. What do you say now? Still want to save him? What for? Let me remind you, that you yourself were the one who dissented on his application to join us. You knew more about him than I do now. I freely admit that. But I'm trying to rectify *my* mistake. What are *you* doing?'

So this was the favour, Tracy thought, the *quid pro quo* for which the Director had worked so hard. 'What proof have you it was him?'

'An Asian was seen by a tenant entering your father's building within the time span the ME gave us of his death.'

'That's all? You would condemn a man on *that*?'

The Director blinked. 'That's *not* all, Mother. Do you remember an incident in Ban Me Thuot early in 1969? There was an infiltration of Kim's unit. A Vietnamese who had been turned by Charlie; someone Kim had trusted, who had once been trustworthy. He did quite a bit of damage before we found out. Three members of Kim's unit butchered in the night like cattle, secrets extracted from them by extreme measures.' The Director paused and when he spoke again, his voice was thick. He had come out from beneath his umbrella's ring of protection and now the rain slid down his face, beading it like a painted mask. 'Do you remember?'

'Yes. I remember it well. I was the officer in charge. Retribution was up to me.'

'And what did you recommend?'

'Kim came to me. He was practically on his knees, begging me to allow him to be the one.'

They were standing toe to toe now, heads thrust forward like a pair of rams about to crash horns. '*What did you recommend?*' the Director spat out.

Tracy closed his eyes for a moment. 'That Kim be the one.'

'That Kim be the one,' the Director echoed. 'And he was. He took the traitor down, he put him through articulated interrogation that lasted seventy-two hours without surcease. And at the end of that time, we had all our answers. How much of the unit had been compromised; how many missions; how much information had been passed on before he was picked up.'

'I remember all that. Kim did it better than anyone else. He had a taste for it.'

'That he did,' the Director agreed. He stepped back into the protection of his umbrella. 'And do you know how he finally disposed of the traitor?'

'I don't remember.'

'Think!' the Director hissed into the wind.

Tracy had been there when Kim did it, having taken down on tape all that the traitor had to give. 'He strangled the man slowly with a piece of wire flex, squeezing until the loop sides met at the top of the spinal cord.'

The Director heaved a great sigh. 'Good,' he whispered. 'Oh, good. You *do* remember.' He leaned forward. 'Then think on this. That was precisely the method of your father's death.'

Tracy seemed to stop breathing. His hands were whitened fists at his sides.

The Director continued to watch him with the intense scrutiny of a hawk.

'There's something I want you to do,' Tracy said.

'Anything.' The Director was preparing to leave.

'When HK staff picks up my belongings at the Princess, make certain they bring back a small package I put in the safety deposit box there.'

'Gladly.' The Director smiled. 'Take your time. I'll wait for you in the car.'

It was only after the Director had left, fading into the mist and rain, only when he was all alone with his thoughts, his memories of his father, the knowledge of what he was going to do, that he noticed the plot next to his father's grave was vacant, awaiting its permanent tenant.

Joy Trower Macomber had just finished reading it – the dark despicable heart of her husband's past, the last burning leaf of his soul – when she scented the powerful, magnetizing maleness enter her room, moving within it towards her.

Her hands were trembling and her mind was in shock, recoiling from the monstrous description on the six sheets of yellowed paper she held. She had inadvertently come upon this mini-journal through a most banal turn of events. She had somehow misplaced her lint brush and, recalling that her husband kept an antique silver-backed clothes brush in the upper drawer of his dresser, had gone there to find it. As she had picked it up it had slid out of her hands and the resultant drop had caused the back to slip slightly.

At first she was terrified, thinking of Macomber's wrath when he saw what she had done. Only then, on second look, did she see the corners of the journal sticking out and, twisting the back even further had discovered that it was on a latch-locked swivel. The fall had obviously dislodged the latch.

She had hesitated but a moment. She had come this far, she reasoned. How could she stop halfway? Now she almost wished she had. The words still burned their way through her mind like a hideous fire. It was beyond belief, she told herself. No one could be that cruel. Her head had turned, and she had stared at the bed where for so long she and Macomber had slept side by side. She had shuddered. Not for some time, however, and she was grateful for small favours. For the first time she fully welcomed the fact that he no longer slept here or even came here very often; she knew she could no longer bear to touch him. Not after discovering what he had done.

Quickly now, she began to stuff the papers back into their hiding place. But she had failed to re-fold them correctly and they would not fit in quite the same way. In a panic now, she left them, began to close the drawer.

Then she felt his presence directly behind her and she had run out of time. She turned and put her arms around him. Her gaze went to his haunted face and seeing the obvious pain there – knowing what she now did – her heart broke and she began to cry.

'Oh, Khieu,' she whispered. 'Khieu.'

She was filled up with love for him; love and pity and remorse and, yes, guilt, too, because no matter how unwittingly she had been a part of this unholy scheme. With all her soul she longed to tell him the truth, even opened her lips to do so but then her eyes locked onto his and she thought, doesn't he have enough pain to bear already; and before she could think again she had pressed her mouth against his, pushing her warm body against his, wanting to give him her warmth, her passion, her love of life.

He was barechested and she ran her delicate fingers over the hard outlines of his gleaming copper muscles and she began to burn with passion for him. She felt her nipples harden through the thin négligé and, shrugging, felt the shoulder straps drop down her arms, baring her firm breasts. Her hands snaked down between their bodies, unzipping his trousers, feeling inside for his hardening length. The heat there made her gasp as both hands converged on him, urging him, teasing him, one stroking the tip while the other moved inward to cup his balls.

Khieu's eyes closed and he shuddered. His half-opened lips began to move as if in silent prayer.

Joy moved one hand, freeing him from his trousers, then pushing her négligé all the way down. She spread her legs and moved in on him, bringing him upward so that her heated mons came in contact with the tip of his erection.

Slowly, tantalizingly, she moved him in a circular motion through her pubic hair, feeling herself getting wet, rubbing him in it, the moist secret folds of her opening up like the petals of a fragrant flower. And now she heard him groan deeply as his penis entered her slowly, just the head disappearing inside her before she pulled away. Then pushed up. And away. Again and again, teasing him, arousing him to the point where he shuddered and, closing his eyes, reached for her, drawing her to him fully.

This was what she had wanted, why she had teased him, wanting to break down the strange barrier that had somehow come between them during the past few weeks, missing terribly that intimacy that had made some sense of her life here on Gramercy Park South. For without him, without the pleasure he provided her body and her soul what business had she being here? It would be back to Texas for her, a return to the moneyed, boring life she had led before Macomber had appeared to woo her away.

Khieu flexed his muscles, lifting her off her feet. And Joy dangled there, exquisitely impaled, breathless, her heart hammering, an indescribable heat suffusing her loins, waiting. He made her so hot she could scarcely stand it. Drugged with lust she was only aware that when he began to stroke inside her, her head went back, her eyelids fluttering and she lost all control.

It felt to her as if his heart had been torn loose from its moorings and through the motions of sex had contrived to enter her most intimate parts. The core of the sun burst inside her bringing her joy beyond description. She laughed with it, elation and ecstasy combining, filling her with life.

He had backed her against the wall in the movement of their passion and now she climbed it, up and back, as his heart moved within her, roaming.

And, as it did so, she felt the gathering storm within his thighs. His bull-like thrusts were coming more rapidly now, ragged as he approached the end. Still she sensed him holding back, even through the veil of her own unending passion, and she began a rhythmic squeezing of her inner muscles, stroking him fiercely as he drove in and out.

'No, no, no!' he seemed to be saying.

'Yes, yes, yes,' she replied, wanting him to come with an intensity she never thought possible, and she reached down beneath them, held his balls in the palm of her hand, squeezing gently in concert with his thrusts. Then, using the pad of her thumb, she stroking the line of soft skin just above his prostrate.

It was too much for him. He cried out and Joy felt his balls draw up and squeezed harder as his deeply buried erection began to tremble and spurt hotly.

'Ohhh, yes. Yes!' She cried triumphantly, the feeling and the knowledge of his coming, that she had made him come warming her, bringing her to another, higher brink and, feeling him gushing hotly inside her, she writhed and groaned, coming again.

And, as she did so, his right forearm whipped up, the muscles bunching powerfully, and he smashed it against her exposed throat so hard she jumped, her fluttering eyelids snapping open, pupils focusing on him. Confusion clouded her face and she said, once, 'Khieu . . .'

'Khieu,' he said. His voice seemed thick and strange. 'Who is Khieu?' His face was full of fire, his intestines burning as if with streaking napalm. 'I am . . . *Chet Khmau*.' The moving sea of the Black Heart pulsed within him, all the years in Europe and America burned away from him in one cleansing flash of brilliant scorching heat.

Lust had overtaken him, despite his sacred vows of abstinence. He had failed *Lok Kru*, Preah Moha Panditto; he had failed the Way; he had failed Buddha.

Apsara had come crawling on her bloated belly as he had been rutting like a sweaty animal, her headless neck white and scarred with dried blood and cauterized arteries. But her fingers had danced for him and slowly he had come to understand their message. Then all at once as the incendiary spark had ignited the firestorm within him, burning away the dross, he had come to understand fully.

His years away from his home, his years of Westernization had made *apsara*'s message to him indecipherable.

But now he had returned; now he was Black Heart. And *Chet Khmau* could translate freely the signs to the gods. Kill her, *apsara*'s dancing fingers had sung to him. She has caused you to break your vows; she has seduced you. She must die. For you must remain pure for me, for Lauren, for me, for Lauren for me for Lauren for me . . .

Slipping down, *Chet Khmau* slept.

2

Macomber awoke near dawn and checked the system. They were still green-lighted all across the board. Wiping the sleep from the corners of his eyes, he went across his vast office to the shower. Stripping off his sweat-stiffened clothes he stepped into the scalding needle spray, lifting his head upward to ease the ache at the back of his neck.

He was very pleased at the precautions he had taken, especially now that he had had the report of the non-delivery of the last shipment Mizo had imported into New York. If he had waited to move until this moment he felt certain he would have been too late.

The moment the report of the breaching of the Mauritious Company's security had reached him, he had radioed the captain of the *Jade Princess* then two days out from New York, and had ordered him to dump his cargo of four wooden crates designated 'Clockwork Orange' in the system's *angka* program.

He was not concerned with cost. Built into the program was the expense of a second, backup shipment that was at this moment as he soaped himself thoroughly being offloaded at the Newark rail terminal. Macomber knew it would be safe there.

As for the birdcages of nuclear waste, the seeds of his élite corps of terrorists the Monk was providing him with would be spreading all across Manhattan during the waning hours of New Year's Eve, part of a lost shipment bound for burial somewhere in the heartland of America, were being transshipped now.

Come Inauguration Day, the terrorists would make their demands. Macomber glowed at the thought of the final fruition of the *angka*. He would provide the necessary information to Gottschalk, spoon feeding the new President every heart grinding step of the way until New York would be saved from nuclear contamination and Gottschalk's power so consolidated he could do virtually what he wished with foreign policy. For, after all these heroics, who would stand in his way? Not Congress. And certainly not the people of the United States.

So, Macomber thought now, as he stepped out of the shower and began to towel off, it did not matter who breached the Mauritious offices, it did not even matter if that same someone had found the shipment of heroin with its damnable scroll. As of yesterday, the *Jade Princess*'s arms shipment was no more, lying rotting on the rocky bottom of the Atlantic.

Macomber opened a gleaming armoir set into one wall of the corridor between the bathroom and his office, began to dress in fresh clothes; lightweight midnight blue slacks, a comfortable white Sea Island cotton shirt, a patterned club tie. He combed his hair methodically, loving the thickness of it, its silver-grey sheen. He groomed his white moustache carefully, stared into the cool blue eyes regarding him in reflection in the mirror.

This was a good dawn, he thought, as his gaze moved to one of the windows. A pink glow like the inside of a sea shell had begun to suffuse the office.

The only cloud in the day was the fact that sometime soon he must return to his house on Gramercy Park South to retrieve some important papers.

He shrugged, putting that thought aside for the moment and, crossing the thick carpeting, sat down behind his desk and began to make the first raft of overseas calls.

Tracy did not for a moment believe what the Director had told him. Kim had not killed his father, of that he was certain. Kim was incapable of such an act. Even had Tracy somehow managed to offend Kim in some basic way in the present, the revenge he might undertake would involve Tracy alone.

Honour thy ancestors above all others.

How many times had Tracy seen Kim halt at the beginning of each mission, kneel by the roots of a banana or banyan tree, implant a small stick of incense into the spongy earth, light it with great reverence and begin his prayers. He prayed to his parents and their parents before them, asking them to imbue him with courage so that he could honour their name and their memory.

Tracy was neither angry nor particularly surprised at the ploy the Director had employed. It was he who had gone back to the foundation, after all. If he wanted their help he knew he would have to play by their rules.

He still needed the foundation's facilities. To reject the *quid pro quo* on the spot would have been stupid because he would have been instantly cut off. He could not afford that now. He could not precisely say why – something floating around in his memory, some connection with Macomber and ... Who? Damnit, but he could not say. Yet. Give it time and concentrate on other matters.

Kim for instance. It had begun to dawn on Tracy during his long flight back to the States that Kim's involvement was of a totally personal nature. If that were so, there seemed little doubt that he had deliberately finessed Tracy into the chase. It was not inconceivable that he knew who had killed John Holmgren, that he had known all along.

Tracy began to burn, remembering his old nickname: the ferret. They could give him just one whiff of the enemy and he was off. Was that what Kim had done to him here? Then *why*?

He knew how much Kim hated him. Yet their mutual animosity ran on a specific level. That Kim was a master torturer Tracy could neither understand nor tolerate. But that Kim was brilliant he had no doubt. He was also fiercely courageous. On their shared missions of extreme hazard, when life could be expunged within the space of the next indrawn breath, they had become closer than brothers ever could.

In situations that were life-threatening time becomes compressed or elongated, emotions strung quiveringly taut by almost unbearable tension. Within that time skein, they had viewed each other's naked souls.

It was imperative now, he knew, to locate Kim. Tracy was convinced that the Vietnamese knew enough to bring all the disparate pieces together.

On to other fields. He had been so certain that the 'Sultan' file would provide him with the information he needed. But there had been nothing there. Not in the formation of the unit: Macomber, Devine, Lewis, Perilli; not in the raft of codes and cyphers; not in the location of the Khmer Rouge camp: Area 350; not in the progress reports; not in the windup.

The windup. In that the Director had been right. Tracy was furious that Macomber had been able to pull off such a stupendous feat right under his nose, turning Tracy's last victory within the foundation into bitter ash. And worse: a mockery of the original objective.

Something . . . something swimming up . . .

Sleep.

The sound of the phone waking him at dawn, pulling him up through the layers from delta to beta reluctantly, the intense fatigue not yet fully dissipated even by this full night's un-interrupted sleep.

Echoes inside his head and he almost had it . . . Now.

Reached for the phone and Thwaite's voice brought him fully awake. 'Hey, Tracy, is that really you?'

'Thwaite. It's good to hear your voice.'

'I've been trying to get you since yesterday. Doesn't that hotel believe in giving messages?'

Tracy cursed. He had returned late, his mind full of swirling cross-currents. He had forgotten to ask for messages. 'Sorry,' he said, 'I'm still recovering from the rough time in Hong Kong.'

'Hey, you okay?'

He heard the genuine concern in his friend's voice and thought, I'ts nice to be back among real people. 'Yeah, sure. Couple more night's sleep and it'll be like nothing ever happened.'

'Listen,' Thwaite said, the note of concern still there, 'I'm real sorry about your father. I figured the Feds coming and claiming the body and all you being in DC that they'd told you.'

'We buried him yesterday.'

'Christ, Tracy, I was out of town when it happened. I'm awfully sorry. I don't know what else there is to say.'

'Nothing. But I appreciate you saying it.' Tracy sat up, rubbed at his dark hair. 'Now listen, we've got some business to discuss. First of all, what happened out in Kenilworth? How did Burke die?'

'I got to the ME,' Thwaite said. 'It was just like you had suspected. The nasal cartilage was intact.'

'That means our man did it. It's all tied in somehow.'

'You bet it is,' Thwaite said. 'But that's not all.'

'Hold it.' Tracy thought a minute. 'This's an open line. I think we've both got a lot of information to exchange. Where're you now, Melody's?'

He heard the slight hesitation. 'No, the office. I'm not . . . I'm still sleeping at the hotel.'

'Okay. I've got some business to finish up here but I think I'll be through by this evening. Can you meet the 8 am shuttle tomorrow morning?'

'If I can't, I'll have a mobile unit pick you up. All of a sudden things're beginning to pop. But like you said, we'll talk about it tomorrow.'

'Yeah,' Tracy said. 'I'll see you then.'

He got up and padded into the shower, turning on the taps. It was then that it hit him – the linkup. He stared at the racing water and said, 'Three-fifty. I'll be goddamned.'

He was showered, shaved and dressed within twenty minutes. But out within the Washington morning crush it took him forty minutes to reach the foundation.

Lauren stared out the Perspex at the blue and grey layered clouds drifting far below her. She was cold and the thin, recirculated air was bothering her sinuses. A muscle on the inside of her left thigh hurt from her recent fall. But consciously she felt none of those physical discomforts.

She was filled with elation and with terror. Tracy had not after all been responsible for Bobby's death, that she saw quite clearly now just as she knew that should she give him the Monk's message she would be placing him in grave danger. And the one made the other more difficult to bear.

That Macomber was Tracy's enemy she had no doubt now. After what she had learned about their past relationships with Tisah, it was obvious. And at the time she suspected Tracy needed the most support she had blown everything apart – just as she had done a year ago. Now she berated herself for that, even knowing how much emotionalism she brought to the subject of her brother.

It was *she* who had accused him; *she* who had screamed at him hysterically; *she* who had not given him a chance to explain fully the circumstances. But then she had been in no mood for explanations or reason. She had seen red because she herself felt responsible for Bobby's death by driving him out of the house and into the Army.

That knowledge made her skin crawl and she sat now with her arms wrapped around herself so that the flight attendant came over, asked if she'd like a blanket. She accepted gratefully.

Once, she thought now, staring out the window at rippling clouds, folding and unfolding, recreating abstract patterns, once she had been in control of her life and the lives of those around her. But slowly, so imperceptibly that she had not felt its tidal pull, ballet's fierce concentrations had turned her inward and she had drifted from first Bobby and then her parents. She saw that quite clearly now just as she saw that Bobby's enlistment was directed at her.

He wanted desperately to show her what he was made of; he needed her to see his courage, a courage she was certain had been there all the time if she had only taken the time to see it.

There were so many other ways Bobby could have escaped his home environment: marriage, graduate school, a job, even, in another city. But he had done none of those. He had chosen the Army.

Her problem now lay with Tracy. Should she tell him the Monk's message or should she keep it to herself? Her heart told her to say nothing; to return home, go see him and use all her powers to make things right between them, lastingly right. Nothing else was important.

For a moment she trembled on that edge. But then an image of Bobby's face formed in the clouds below and she knew it was time to put away forever the selfish part of her that had dominated her life for so long. She was no longer a sheltered child; she knew something momentous was happening, that she was a part of it.

There was a debt the Monk owed Tracy and in the short but intense time she had been with him she had begun to understand the importance of such a debt. The Monk had entrusted her with the vital information. She had become the link between them and, so, too, she had a duty. She had failed Tracy twice; she would not do so again.

Duty. The Monk and Tisah, his daughter, had taught her the meaning of that word. She felt it now, burning like a lantern in her heart, leading her onwards and she thought, how strange! To come halfway around the world to learn such an elementary lesson!

She put her head back against the seat rest, closed her eyes. Tracy was just eight hours away, concentrate on that, she told herself. Hold that to you, remember always how precious he is to you.

She could scent the salt tang in the air, feel the soft wet wind on her face, sending strands of her unbound hair fluttering against her cheek. The warmth of the sun on her bare back; Tracy's own warmth pressing against her belly and her breasts, the quivering of the muscles in her thighs. Involuntarily she sighed and the small, quiet sound from the depths of her soul startled her, even as it brought the image of him into such supra-real proximity that she began to weep, the tears hot and salty trickling slowly down cheeks burnished brown by the Chinese sun.

And the ache for him became so physical that she put her hands between her legs beneath the thin blanket, warming them. She rocked slowly in her seat and, after a time, she slept and dreamt of home.

Khieu awoke with a violent start, not knowing where he was. He felt lightheaded, his mind suffused with a peculiar clarity he automatically associated with his days with Preah Moha Panditto. He recalled *Lok Kru* reciting to him a small section from the Buddhist text, *Cakkavattisīhanāda Sutta*, which is concerned with the eventual evolution of mankind: decline and disaster leading to a Just Society with a change of heart and a change of system:

Among such humans there will arise a war lasting seven days, during which they will look on each other as wild beasts; dangerous weapons will fall into their hands and they, thinking 'this is a wild beast', 'that is a wild beast', will with these weapons deprive each other of life.

He arose and walked out of the room – he was not conscious of precisely what room he was in – down the hall and into his own room where, passing by the image of Buddha, he went into the bathroom and took a long cold shower.

When he was finished, he dressed in black cotton trousers and loose-fitting shirt and sat in the lotus position before Buddha. Now he spoke another of *Lok Kru*'s lessons, taken from the *Dhammapada*:

> By ourselves is evil done,
> By ourselves we pain endure,
> By ourselves we cease from wrong,
> By ourselves we become pure.
> No one saves us but ourselves,
> No one can and no one may,
> We ourselves must tread the path;
> Buddhas only show the way.

Khieu knew this to be absolute and true. Was it not Lord Buddha himself who said, *'Anicca vata sankāra'*. All things, both animate and inanimate must rise and then die away. This is true of all beings in the world. The everyday experience of the instability of life is an education. No being lives for ever and ever, nothing will remain for ever and ever without being decayed. Why do people wage war? Because they do not know what they are. Contemplation on the body, internally and externally, with Right Effort, Right Mindfulness and Right Concentration will enlighten them that the body is transient, disintegrating into its basic components: Earth, Air, Fire, Water.

Concentration.

To begin, Khieu used *ānāpānasati*, the awareness of breathing in and out and within several minutes had reached the proper state where his *Citta* – his consciousness – was bright, cool, calm and happy. Then, as Preah Moha Panditto had taught him, he moved on to *kammatthāna*, passing through all forty subjects in the Path of Purification.

It was a return to the Noble Eight Fold Path and its three major components: *Sila*, a code of ethics, *Samādhi*, insight, and *Pannā*, wisdom. It was the only path to *Nirvāna*, the absolute reality: selflessness.

And as he proceeded with his meditation Khieu became subtly aware of that memory of Preah Moha Panditto that had never left him, even when he was *Chet Khmau*, that bright light, the energy field that surrounded the priest. How Khieu Sokha, the boy, had wondered at it. How Khieu, the adult, still felt that same sense of pure wonder. That at least had not changed.

Then, as he was finishing the one analysis of the four elements that was part of the *kammatthāna*, he abruptly felt the black swirl of an unaccountable darkness sweeping up from a hidden corner of his soul and the torrent of the war began to suffuse him.

He stood, recalling with unusual clarity the mission he had been ordered to perform; kill Tracy Richter.

Without a glance back at the gilt Buddha, without another thought towards meditation, he went silently out of his room and down the hall of the darkened house. He was aware of the ticking of the clock from downstairs on the first floor.

Without quite understanding why, he made his way to the master bedroom at the far end of the hall and, stepping across the threshold, beheld the twisted corpse of Joy Trower Macomber.

There was a music recital going on at the foundation when Tracy arrived and he went in the main entrance along with clots of others sauntering in. But instead of heading straight ahead towards the ground floor auditorium, he turned to his right, walking down a short well-lighted corridor. The walls were blank but behind them he knew were an awesome array of detection and identification equipment so that by the time he got to the Oreo door, they knew just who he was. They called it the Oreo door because sandwiched between the seemingly normal looking dark wood was a six-inch thick piece of white vanadium-alloy steel plate, making the entrance virtually impregnable.

The door opened as he touched the knob just as if it hadn't been locked.

'Mother!' Stein was up from behind his great sculptured communications console. He shook Tracy's hand with a great smile on his face. He was rather short and stocky with a decided Mediterranean cast to his face. His brown eyes danced. 'Say, I've been trying to scare you up since late yesterday but no one knew where you were staying.'

Tracy was trying to get away, his thoughts locked on the secrets he might find in the Library. 'What is it?'

'O'Day called back very late yesterday.' Tracy was instantly alert. 'Said he'd thought of something and wanted to talk to you. He sounded pretty excited.'

'Can you get him for me now?'

Stein nodded, donning his headset. 'Sure. Just a sec.' He pointed. 'You can use that phone there.' He spoke into his mouthpiece. He nodded and Tracy picked up the receiver.

'O'Day, it's Mother. I understand you wanted to speak to me.' He was aware of Stein breaking his own connection, turning to other business.

'That's right. I'm glad you called back. After I got off the line with you yesterday I began to roll that little problem you gave me around in my mind.'

'Do you mean there *is* another way for Macomber to have sponsored a foreign national.'

'Well, er, yes there is.' O'Day's voice was apologetic. 'I don't know why it didn't occur to me right away. Although it's hardly ever done you could – I mean if you deliberately wanted to circumvent channels and leave no public trace of it – you could, if you had a friend on the proper Senate subcommittee, get it done almost immediately.' O'Day laughed, a high horse's whinny. 'But I mean why would anyone want to do that?'

Tracy was holding his breath; suddenly he was back on line again. 'Did you check that possibility?'

'Well, yes. Of course I did, Mother. I pride myself on my level of efficiency. That's why I rang Stein back. I do have an answer for you: one Delmar Davis Macomber is on record as sponsoring a young Cambodian male.' There was triumph in O'Day's voice.

'What's his name?' Tracy said quickly.

'Khieu Sok.'

'Mr O'Day,' Tracy said excitedly, 'thanks very much for your work on this.'

'It was a pleasure. Anything out of the ordinary is a treat, I assure you.'

Tracy went down to the Library and asked for the 'Ragman' file. It had occurred to him that Area 350 in Cambodia where the 'Sultan' mission took place was also the location of the 'Ragman' operation, the one meant to destroy the Japanese terrorist, Musashi Murano. That was a mission both he and Macomber had been on together, the one Macomber had volunteered to remain on after they had found out that Murano had just died.

Tracy took the file from the Librarian and, signing for it, went across the room to a hard-backed chair. He placed the file on the trestle table and opened it up. He read quickly through the background sections on Murano's birth, growing up in the south of Japan, on Kyushu. He read about an ageing father who had gone mad during World War II when his wife had been incinerated in the awful fire bombing of Tokyo six months before the atomics were loosed on Hiroshima and Nagasaki; the intense martial spirit of the family of the uncle who had taken the young Murano in; the subsequent mastery of numerous forms of *bujutsu*, mostly hand-to-hand. It was said Murano felt disdainful of such weaponry as swords or pistols, preferring to inflict death with his hands.

Tracy skipped over his military service. But he paused at the next entry, fascinated. Murano's politics were radical. He was a hard-line militarist who eventually broke with his own countrymen in order to keep faith with his ideals.

Murano left Japan – or was forced out – moving from Burma and Thailand into Cambodia, offering his expertise to the Khmer Rouge, whose radical philosophies and intense antagonism towards the West were compatible with his own. He was reported working with six encampments starting in 1967 near Battambang. It was said he had a guiding hand in the Samlaut Rebellion which really galvanized the new Khmer Rouge cause and took them out of the minor role they were playing as rural bandits or *maquis*, giving them a distinct political skew.

From there he moved on to Baray, Damber, Prey Veng, on and on.

Tracy paused, curious. Even though he had been in charge of the 'Ragman' unit, this full intelligence brief had not been passed on to him. He had been given the broad outlines of Murano's strength and his potential danger. That was all.

He read on. He had come to the final paragraphs, an entry dealing with the Khmer rumours regarding Murano. These were generally disregarded as a matter of course by the American military command as continuing leaves in the Eastern book of terrorist propaganda.

Here Musashi Murano grew to superhuman proportions, his prowess greatly inflated. All sorts of highly improbable and, in some cases, impossible deeds were attributed to him. There were also reports that he was training a disciple to take over for him because he knew he was going to die. Intelligence had ignored these, putting them down to a fictitious support for the immortality of the revolution.

But Tracy read on, excited. It seemed as if these particular reports were coming out of only one section of the country: Area 350. After Murano's death, reports of a living disciple persisted for perhaps four months and then slowly petered out.

His heart was hammering hard in his chest and he thought, it all fits together now. Macomber never saw Murano; he was already dead. But during that week of surveillance in Area 350, he observed Khieu. Murano's disciple. And if that's true ... He thought of all the deaths: John's, Moira's, Roland Burke's, his own father's. That had to be the answer. Murano had created the most potent fighting machine man could devise and somehow Macomber had found a way to harness him.

But how? What could Macomber have said or done to create such undying loyalty in a Khmer?

That was a question for another day, he knew. As he got up and returned the file, signing out, he knew he had one more call to make. Who had been on that Senate subcommittee? Who had been so close a friend of Macomber's that he would go out on a limb for that semi-illegal sponsorship?

And what was Macomber really up to? Suddenly Tracy felt the weight of all these questions. The enormity of this operation's scope was made clear to him at last and all the breath went out of him.

'I liked her,' Tisah said, after Lauren had left in the chauffeured car. She crossed the living room to the bar, at last drew herself an iced Tsing-Tao vodka on the rocks. She cut a sliver of lemon peel, twisted it onto the ice cubes, took a tentative sip. 'At one point, I was tempted to tell her the truth.'

'I *told* her the truth,' the Monk said indignantly.

Tisah turned towards him, smiling. 'As much of it as you saw fit.' She walked towards him in confident, though somewhat off-balance strides. Without company, she was completely unselfconscious about the limp. She had been injured during her flight from Ban Me Thuot after Tracy had delivered her over to the conduit.

'My dear, you mind is too pure.' The Monk watched her carefully. 'You were my one and only mistake. I should have known you did not have the temperament for this kind of work.' He frowned. 'I never understood how you could have allowed yourself to enter into it in the first place.'

Tisah gazed at him from over the rim of her frost-rimmed glass. 'It was only to please you,' she whispered. 'I wanted so much for you to be proud of me. I knew what you required of me.'

The Monk said nothing. His eyes dropped to the toes of his polished shoes. He was thinking of his meeting with Macomber. Of how, in the story he had told the industrialist, he had seemingly been helping Macomber with an obstacle in his path, Tracy Richter, while trying to achieve the opposite. The Monk had enough faith in Richter's ability to believe that, once he was made aware of Macomber's involvement, he would find a way

664

to stop him. He looked at his daughter now. For purely personal reasons, he wanted Macomber stopped ... permanently. 'It is most fortunate that you did not tell Lauren all of it,' he said. 'That would have been a serious error.'

'Why? I know you hold no love for this man Macomber.'

'Not personal love, no,' the Monk acknowledged. 'But the government wishes to see his plans played out. They believe it could be advantageous to us.'

'And you concur?'

'It is irrelevant *what* I think in this particular matter. I am but an arm of China.'

'Surely you –' But she stopped, halted by her father's emphatic gesture. He had put his forefinger in a vertical position up against his closed lips.

'I grow restless,' he said, 'cooped up inside all evening. First the performance and then dinner; most recently the interview here. Come' – he reached out a hand, took hers – 'let us take a stroll in the moonlight.'

Together they went down the hallway and out the front door. They took the winding gravel driveway as far to the left as they could, then went into the mown grass of the lawn. Dwarf orange trees and jasmine rose spectrally about them, the rough bark slightly luminescent in the cool blue-white light.

They went deeper into the garden which had fallen into disrepair before the Monk had come to live here. It was the first of many renovations he had had instituted since his arrival. There was a gentle breeze blowing, just enough to ruffle the leaves of the foliage. Still it was hot, the nocturnal insects somnolently in evidence.

'First and foremost,' he said, 'came my obligation for the debt I owed Mr Richter. I could not proceed any further without having fulfilled that.'

He turned and the moonlight silvered half his face, bringing bright points to life on the convex surfaces of his obsidian eyes. Tisah thought she had never seen eyes so full of wisdom.

'I chose very carefully the amount of information I gave to Lauren. Is it more than enough to help Tracy, of that I have no doubt.'

'But by doing so you've placed him in a great deal of danger.'

The Monk saw the concern on his daughter's face and sighed inwardly. He reached out, touched her glorious hair. 'My dear,' he said, his voice matter-of-fact, 'firstly, I have full confidence in Mr Richter's capabilities. Don't forget I know what he's made of as well as you do. Secondly, he was always in danger. His relationship to Macomber' – his feigned difficulty in pronouncing that name had been dropped along with his role of simple Chinese businessman – 'put him in jeopardy from the beginning. Your Mr Richter was in the centre of this maelstrom all the time. I have merely given him the edge to extricate himself.'

'Do you know what he plans to do?' Tisah meant Macomber.

'No. I do not. That is for Tracy to discover for himself.'

For a long while the Monk said nothing. He appeared to be listening to the sounds of nature all around him: the crickets' song, the cicadas' chittering, the leaves' rustle as the warm night wind fanned them. An owl hooted not far away and there was a brief flurry of feathered wings above their heads. A shadow swooped across the face of the pale moon and was gone, accelerating downward, skimming the vast expanse of ploughed fields beyond the western wall.

Just as he had lied to Lauren about his current status within the CPR intelligence network so he had lied to his daughter now. It was for their own good. Tisah must never know the gravity of the situation Tracy was now in; for if she should the Monk feared that even he could not control her. She would insist on flying to him to tell him all – and in the process she would unwittingly cause her own father's execution.

The fact was that the Chinese People's Republic had decided to allow Macomber's plan, articulated to them by the Monk, to succeed. They felt that its fruition would bring the full resources of the United States to bear on the Soviet Union, China's number one enemy.

'Why not allow the United States to do for us what we are as yet incapable of accomplishing?' His superiors had said to him rhetorically.

Yet he feared that his superior's intense hatred of the Soviets had blinded them to the terrible ramifications of Atherton Gottschalk's rise to power. For the Monk feared the collapse of nuclear containment. He knew the ultimate power that Gottschalk and Macomber craved was not so easy to control. And if it flew out of hand? In a nuclear holocaust they would all die: Soviets and Chinese alike. There would be absolutely no difference.

So, clandestinely, he had decided to leak just enough information to Tracy Richter. He could not openly defy the wishes of this country. But in this subtle manner he could rid himself of the awesome debt he owed the American and, at the same time, perhaps defeat Macomber. If he had not overestimated Richter's ability.

The Monk looked into the distance, into the moonlight. He thought of the unutterable beauty only nature could give birth to; what human being could recreate such exquisitely delicate illumination?

Then his gaze fell on Tisah and his heart skipped a beat. Her beauty brought tears to his eyes, made him believe in the importance of life, of living. Did not even politics pall in comparison to the form and grace of this ineffable architecture?

'Do not be afraid,' he said softly, taking her hand. They began to walk beside the western wall. He felt keenly her vitality and warmth stealing over him. 'Fear makes one weak; fear diminishes the soul; fear causes the wheel of life to creak to a halt.'

Tisah turned her head, smiling at him and it was if the sun had risen to overtake the cold light of the moon.

Tracy came through the Magic Eye doors of the Eastern Airlines shuttle arrival lounge and saw a black cop with splay teeth walking towards him.

He smiled as he approached Tracy, held out his hand. 'Mr Richter,' he said, pumping Tracy's hand enthusiastically. 'I'm Patrolman Ivy White. Thwaite sent me.'

'Glad to meet you.'

'Here,' White said, taking the strap of Tracy's carry-on bag, 'let me have this. Thwaite told me to give you the *de luxe* service.'

They walked side by side out into the New York atmosphere. It was slightly less humid than Washington but, it seemed to Tracy, just as warm even this early in the morning. The leather weekend bag that White was now carrying had been waiting for Tracy at the concierge's desk when he had come down earlier this morning to pay his bill. That had already been taken care of.

On the way out to the airport, he had opened the bag, delved inside. All the belongings he had left so hastily in Hong Kong were there, including the small black velvet box from the Diamond House. Slowly, almost nostalgically, he opened the top, stared at the perfect blue-white stone in its platinum setting. What had possessed him to buy it? He barely understood the impulse now. Hong Kong was a wonderfully romantic city and he put it down to that. In the reality of Washington, DC and the anticipation of New York, he wondered if he would ever see Lauren again, let alone have a chance to give her the ring. Her anger had been absolute, unshakable.

White led him to a black Chrysler. 'Climb in,' White said. He went around to the driver's side as Tracy slid in and they took off at high speed, White squealing the siren in short bursts where he had to get past small clumps of traffic.

'I'll take you right to Thwaite.'

Tracy had thought about that all during the fifty-minute flight into La Guardia. 'If you don't mind, I'd like to make a stop first.'

'Sure. Where to?'

'Christopher Street,' Tracy said. 'I want to go to my father's apartment.'

White kept his eyes studiously on the road. 'Right. No problem. I know where it is.' It was out before he realized it.

'You do?'

He turned his head for a moment and Tracy caught the sad look in his eyes. 'Yeah, well, I tried to get a handle on the case for Thwaite before the Feds crept in. I don't know why they were interested.'

'He worked for them.'

'Uh huh. Well, that makes sense. Guys who picked up the

squeal found a lotta strange stuff in, I guess it was, his workroom. They couldn't seem to make heads or tails of it.'

'He was the world's best at miniaturized explosives devices,' Tracy said.

'Christ, that a fact.' White nodded. 'No wonder the boys were stumped. Out of their league.'

'He was out of everyone's league.'

'Like you said.' White made the turn for the Midtown Tunnel.

Tracy took a look at him. 'You find anything else out ... before the Feds came?'

'Only that it was someone good who did it. A professional for sure. There were no prints but even so, the – I'm sorry about this – the way it was done, with the piano wire and all, was slick all the way. The guy knew what he was doing.' White cleared his throat. 'No offence intended, Mr Richter, but you sure you wanta go up there? I mean the place hasn't been cleared up or anything and it's a mess. A lotta ... well, you know, blood and all. Your father put up quite a fight. There's ... I mean the bathroom's crusty with it.'

'It's all right, Patrolman. I've seen plenty of blood in my time.'

'I sure would feel a whole lot easier if you'd call me Ivory. Everyone else does' – he grinned – 'even my wife.'

'Okay,' Tracy said, grateful for the man's ease at lightening the atmosphere. 'Ivory it is.'

'Great,' White said, putting on speed. 'Here we go.'

They went careening around a turn and up ahead Tracy could see the clogged steel grey skyline of Manhattan. It set his heart hammering.

When they arrived in front of the building, White killed the ignition. 'If you don't mind, I'd like to catch a bite of breakfast while you're upstairs.'

'I don't mind at all.' Tracy smiled. White was first-rate all right. He knew Tracy wanted to be alone, chose the most gracious way of arranging it.

'Don't worry. I'll be right here when you come back down. I'm only going down the block.' He pointed to a bar and grill.

Tracy got out of the car. 'Here,' White said, throwing a pair of keys across the roof of the Chrysler. 'You'll need these to get in.'

Tracy looked at him as he caught them and White shrugged. 'Thwaite thought they might come in handy.'

Tracy went into the vestibule, using the first key to open the locked inner door. He noticed they had put ivory-white curtains up on the inside to cover the panes of wired glass.

The elevator creaked as it ascended. It smelled of damp feet and roses. He got off at his father's floor, stepped out into the corridor. For no good reason he could think of, he went not towards his father's apartment but rather in the opposite direction.

He stopped in front of the stairway door, then put out a flat palm, pushed it open. There was no lock; the painted-over brass knob did not even work. He took one step inside, peered around in the gloom. He did not know what he expected to find but he understood one fact: whoever murdered his father would not have been stupid enough to use the elevator all the way to this floor. Therefore, he had to have been approximately where Tracy was standing now.

He *had* been here and Tracy wanted to smell him, feel his presence, sink into his soul. He wanted to know him; know him so that he could destroy him. Because that was what this was all about now. It was very personal. And he recognized that it had been from the very beginning. From the moment he had picked up the telephone in the dead of night and heard Moira's voice in his ear, *Oh, God! He's dead! I really think he's dead!*

Oh, Christ, how had it got so out of hand? How had he let it? He leaned against the dingy hallway wall, the lights of the corridor seeming far away indeed now. He was back in that stinking jungle ten million miles away from civilization. More. It was just a word. The kind one says all one's life and then pronounces one day only to find it has lost its meaning. *Civ-i-li-za-tion.* He mouthed it syllable by syllable as if that might help him to understand the concept again.

But monsters did not live within the confines of the civilized world. They were enough chameleon to be able to fool those around them for a length of time. But how could they be expected to live within the confines of something they did not understand?

And this is what we have here, Tracy thought now. An elemental monster.

He went down the corridor, past closed doors, their mirrored peep-holes staring at him like accusatory eyes. How could you have allowed this to happen? They seemed to be saying to him. And he answered them, how could I have prevented it?

He fumbled with the key, opened the front door. He allowed it to swing all the way back before he stepped across the threshold. The barrenness of the place, caused by the absence of human life, struck him immediately and, for an instant, he wanted to turn around and get out of there.

But the feeling passed and he knew he could not do that. This had not been his father's house and he wanted to be here now, to feel its warmth as he had felt the chill in the stairwell.

He went slowly through the living room, noting as he did so, that nothing appeared out of place, nothing was missing, overturned or slit. No evidence of robbery, certainly. He went to his left, poked his head in the kitchen. He saw three or four cockroaches. There was a plate on the sideboard next to the old-fashioned sink. Two slices of rye bread lay overlapping the curving edge, opened as if to receive their filling. They were quite stale now.

Tracy threw them in the garbage, put the empty plate into the sink. Then he took the Black Flag from the cabinet beneath the sink and sprayed along all the baseboard edges and in the cabinet cracks.

He returned to the empty living room, went down the long hall. On the sideboard there, he saw that the lamp cord had been pulled out of the wall socket. He bent down, inserted the plug. The lamp burned mutely, offering mellow illumination.

Three steps forward and he came to the open doorway to the bathroom. He stopped on the sill, one hand on the doorframe.

Ivory White's words rang in his ears: *I mean the bathroom's crusty with it.*

Yes, he had seen a lot of it in his time. But it had never been his father's. He took a deep breath, went in. His nostrils flared. The small room reeked with the thick, metallic stench of blood. White had been right. The place was covered with it.

The water had been drained from the bath but the porcelain was rimmed with dark brownish-red sediment. The tiles coated with it, the walls against which the bathtub abutted, painted with it. The shower curtain was as stiff as wood with it.

Tracy knew precisely how much blood the human body contained and, seeing this, it seemed to him that his father had expended it all in his fight for life. Christ, Tracy thought, he hadn't wanted to die. He had wanted those six precious months but someone had made certain he would not get them.

Deep within the fetid jungles of Cambodia Tracy had experienced great evil, had been witness to many things he did not wish to remember because he suspected that he could not live with himself if he did. But he felt now that *this* evil encompassed something more.

He blinked, his eyes burning. Dad, he cried silently, why did it have to end for you here?

It was not an idle question. He knew it was one which he would have to find an answer for. He knew he would. He would find whoever did this and he would get his answers.

But for now he had had enough of this and he backed out, turning, retracing his steps back into the living room, going through it into the vestibule. And saw that it was filled.

Someone stood there, the elongated shadow rising up the vestibule's right-hand wall, thin and eerie. It was just a silhouette, the corridor light shimmering in around the outline, far brighter than the dimness of the apartment's vestibule.

'Tracy!' It was an indrawn gasp. 'Oh, my God! Tracy!'

It was Lauren's voice, thin and anxious. Tracy began to say something but the words became a jumble, sticking in his mouth like a ball of cotton.

She took a step towards him and checked, rocking on her feet. 'What – ?' Her head moved in the darkness. 'It's so quiet . . .'

And then with a woman's intuition, 'Where's Louis? What's happened to your father?'

'He's dead,' Tracy said softly, hearing her answering cry, sensing her beginning to move, heading her off. 'Don't go in there.' They were very close. He could feel the heaving of her breasts.

'Why not?' Her voice broke and he could feel her beginning to tremble. 'For God's sake tell me what's happened?'

'He was murdered,' he heard himself saying. 'I don't want you to go in there.'

'You don't want me to go –?' Her face was turned up towards him but he could see no feature, only smell her slight scent, see pinpoint reflections along the curve of her corneas. 'Damnit!' She struggled, pushing him aside. 'He was my friend!' She was past him now. 'He treated me –' He saw her rush through the living room, her head turning wildly this way and that. 'I want to see . . . !' Disappearing down the hall, her footsteps stopping at the open door to the bathroom as if by instinct. Or perhaps she smelled that long last exhalation of blood.

And now Tracy went after her, hearing the long wail of her scream, 'Ahhhhhhhh!' cutting through him like a surgeon's scalpel, paining his heart.

He careened through the hall, stepping into the abattoir, found her collapsed and curled by the side of the lacquered bathtub, staring into it as if she saw the body still there, floating in the cooling sea of its own life force.

He scooped her up, bringing her to the toilet in time for her to vomit there, the convulsive heaving of her abdomen coinciding with her sobs. He held her close, his body pressed against her back, feeling her taut muscles contract in spasm.

He took her away to the sink, splashing cold water onto her, cupping it in his palm so that she could wash the taste of bile out of her mouth. He dried her face off with a towel, then took her out of there, through the silent, breathless living room.

He pulled the front door closed behind them, carefully locking it. They were silent all through the juddering elevator ride and when someone got in on a lower floor, Lauren turned away, staring sightlessly at his shoulder. Her fingers were clawed and white as she held onto him and he could hear her breathing.

The elderly woman who shared the elevator had blue-white hair and carried her handbag clutched protectively in both hands. She stared at them, half-hostile, half-frightened, recognizing them as strangers and therefore dangerous.

Out in the street it had begun to rain again. Neither of them had an umbrella.

'Tracy —' Lauren's voice was thick with rage and she could not go on, merely shook her head, turning west towards the river. She took a deep, shuddering breath. 'It's so goddamned *unfair*,' she whispered. 'I came back here hoping to find you. There was no answer at home; your office didn't know when to expect you.' Her head swung around and he saw the light in her eyes, that slight parting of her lips he loved so much when there was something on her mind and she was working out the best way to say it. 'And, you know, for a moment I panicked. I was certain something dreadful had happened to you. Something irrevocable and you'd sunk like a stone.' She lifted her head as if sure at last. '*We'd* sunk like a stone.'

'Lauren —'

She shook her head to stop him. 'No. Let me finish. That day at the beach I acted like a spoiled child. I wasn't willing to listen. I heard Bobby's name, I knew it was about his death and . . . I'd . . . like us both to forget that ever happened.'

Now that they were together again, now that she felt him so near her, she could no longer stem the tide of her emotions. The shock of Louis's death had deflected her for a time but now, out of the apartment, all the force of her love for him that she had kept hidden from herself since the moment of her spark of anger burst its bonds.

She reached up for him, her eyes full of tears and she sighed as she felt him come against her, felt his strength surge through her like a current of electricity. 'Tracy. Oh, Tracy . . . I missed you so. I love you so.' She didn't care anymore, did not want to hold back or hide anything from him. Her meeting with the Monk and Tisah had shown her how much a prison life could be and she knew she never would want that for herself. Her own personal freedom lay in the truth, she knew that now, too. Her awful spite-filled adolescence was dead. It had been unnaturally prolonged by the nature of the life she lived: so highly prolonged by the nature of the life she lived: so highly specialized, so rabidly insulated, so full of tiny fears and pleasures that had nothing at all to do with the complex workings of the outside world.

'I thought I'd never get to see you again,' Tracy said in her ear. 'Never get to talk to you. I thought —'

'Quiet,' she said and opened her lips to his. They kissed, long and passionately, their mouths open, tongues duelling, speaking their hearts' desires and they were lost within themselves.

Eventually he broke away from her. 'I have to say this . . . just this much.'

Lauren studied him quietly.

'I was harder on your brother because I liked him so much. The first rule you live by in a combat situation is don't make friends. It's a cliché, I suppose, but for a very good reason.

'After his friend's death, Bobby lost a lot of his spark. I had to do something to shock him out of it. He had become a liability to himself and to the unit.'

He gripped her hard. 'Lauren, I want you to know I thought what I did was the right thing for him. Looking back on it, I think I was wrong. Bobby was a strange kid. I think if I'd taken more time I —'

She put a finger across his lips. 'Don't,' she whispered.

'I have to,' he said desperately. 'Don't you see? I've been carrying this guilt around with me since it happened. I could've prevented his death.'

She looked at him. Her eyes were very clear. 'You don't know that. No one does. Whatever Bobby's destiny was . . . he found it. You were part of it, that's all. So was I. So was everybody who knew him. There shouldn't be any blame.' She dropped her eyes for a moment. 'It's taken me a long time to come to that conclusion and I know it's right. You should, too.'

Something eased within his chest and he realized just how true her words were. They seemed suspended in time, old wounds healing.

Then the heavy black-painted door to the building opened at their backs and they had to move to let someone pass. The moment was at an end.

Tracy saw Ivory White sitting patiently behind the wheel of the Chrysler and was reminded of what was waiting for him.

'I don't want to go but I've got a meeting with Thwaite.' He could not continue, could not find it in himself to explicate the ending of the process that he had begun so long ago. Not now; not after what they had both witnessed in the apartment above. The idea was somehow obscene.

'It's business, isn't it?'

He nodded.

'Then I think I'd better go along.'

'What? I don't think —'

'I met someone in Shanghai.' She watched his eyes very closely. 'Someone you know and who knows you.'

'What are you —'

'I also met Tisah.'

Her words stunned him into immobility. *Tisah.* Lauren had met Tisah. The unimaginable had occurred. How? 'How is she?' he said softly.

'She's fine.' What did she see in those eyes of his? Did he still love her? Certainly she had seen for herself that he dreamed about her. 'She's a prisoner ... of what she has done. The last POW. I think she's lucky to be alive.' She took his arm. 'But it's not Tisah I have to talk with you about.'

Then he made the connection and he started just as if she had touched him with a live wire. 'The Monk? You met the Monk? But how?'

'It was his doing. He took me to meet Tisah; she loves ballet but was not allowed to go to the performance. It was the most he could do for her.'

'But Lauren —'

'Listen to me, Tracy.' Her voice turned urgent. 'Tisah is his daughter. She told him what you did for her, how you saved her life. He owes you a debt. He —'

'Tisah is the Monk's *daughter*?' Tracy stared at her and as he did so, he began to laugh.

Lauren frowned. 'I don't see what's so funny.'

Tracy wiped the tears from his eyes, heaved a sigh almost of relief. 'No,' he said. 'I wouldn't expect you to. I was thinking of Macomber.' He began to laugh all over again.

'I don't understand you.'

Tracy took her in his arms. 'Back in Ban Me Thuot, Macomber was having an affair with Tisah; he was in love with her.'

'I know,' Lauren said. 'Just like she was in love with you.' She stared hard at him. 'I think she still is.' She waited for a breathless moment, seeking an alternative to asking the question she knew she must put to him now. 'Does that mean anything to you?'

'Lauren,' he said gently, 'that was another lifetime. I have no desire to return to the life I led in Ban Me Thuot or any part of it. And that includes Tisah.' He felt a strung tension leaching away from her, an exhalation of a long-held breath. 'But I still think about her; I had hoped she was happy. It saddens me that she's not. She was very important to me once. She was my only lifeline out of the sewer I was in. Can you understand that?'

'I liked her,' Lauren said by way of answer.

'You've known how I felt about you ever since that moment when we kissed under the streetlight. It was always you who backed away.'

'I know,' she whispered. 'But after all that's happened to both of us I guess I needed to hear you say it again. I needed to know that one thing in my life hadn't turned upside down.'

'Now tell me why you want to come to this meeting.'

Her eyes were clear and sparkling as she stared up at him. She had begun to tremble again. 'It's Macomber, isn't it?' she said. 'Macomber's your enemy.'

'Is that what the Monk told you?'

'I worked it out for myself. But the information he gave me concerns Macomber and –'

He gripped her, his face turned into a mask. 'What do you know about Macomber?'

'Everything,' she said. 'I think I know everything.'

Eliott Macomber found Joy's blood as he was searching for

Khieu. Upstairs, the house was dark and still. Eliott wanted to call out but something he could not explain restrained him.

He went through the main floor, room by room. He found only traces of Khieu and Joy and this disturbed him for it was as if his father had already abandoned the place.

Upstairs, he went first to Khieu's room. The door was ajar and he could see by the sliver revealed to him that the light was not on. He reached out a hand, pushing the door inward without a sound.

Inside, he saw Khieu's pallet on the floor, his desk, all the furnishings he was familiar with. None seemed out of place. But there was no bedding and patches here and there on the mattress were darkened by stains.

Eliott found himself inexplicably frightened. There was nothing there that should make him so yet he felt the pulse in his throat throbbing as if it were an open wound. His whole body seemed to shiver with the heavy beat of his heart.

He backed out of there, his hands leaving dark stains of sweat on the doorframe. Turning in the hall, he looked into the bathroom there before moving on to the room that had been his own when he had lived here. Nothing. Silence; shadows lying heavily along the spotless furniture as if they were blankets thrown here and there to dampen all sound.

Each moment he stayed inside the house he felt his anxiety rising. Continuing down the hallway to the far end, he pushed inward on the half-open door to his father's and Joy's bedroom. For a moment he stood poised on the threshhold, his eyes roving the semi-darkness. Not once had he called out Khieu's name; his voice box seemed frozen.

He took one step into the room and his anxiety welled to such proportions that he was obliged to reached his hand out, scrabble for the light switch.

Illuminations flooded the room and he saw Joy's blood.

It lay in long brownish-red streaks along the wall opposite the bed. It was quite impossible to say how Eliott knew these were stains from the outpouring of Joy's rent body . . . but he did.

He began to have trouble breathing and with a conscious effort of will he jerked his gaze away. He saw the king-size bed turned down as if for sleep, undisturbed. He saw a half-open drawer in his father's dresser. He saw a print on the wall, lying askew. He went to the dresser to put back a white handkerchief that was lying along the open edge of the drawer. He picked it up, folded it carefully and put it back on the pile.

That's when his fingers touched the edges of the badly folded diary pages Joy had failed to return to their hiding place. Eliott stared at them dumbly for a moment. Then he picked them up, opening the sheets and began to read.

He went back twice, rereading the scrawled writing he recognized as his father's. Then he very carefully folded the pages along their original creases. It took him a while his hands were shaking so badly. He could hear his own breathing sawing in and out of his throat as if he had a wheeze. His mind was still stumbling over the information, thoughts coming in quick bright bursts, bewildering him and abruptly he began to cry, large hot tears rolling down, dripping onto the fabric of his trousers just above the knees.

He lurched to his feet and, with a convulsive gesture, pocketed the papers. There was only one place he had not yet searched, having already made his rounds of the first and second floors.

The stairway down leered at him with hostile grimness. He gripped the railing and began his descent, his ears cocked. He heard the clock ticking, its sound somehow magnified in the absolute stillness.

On shaky legs he left the staircase on the first floor, went through the living room to the door leading down to the basement.

He was shaking so much he grabbed hold of the cool brass knob with all his strength, leaning on it until he could regain a semblance of calm. Then he opened the door.

The staircase down to the cellar yawned at him and he froze. A lamp was on. And now that he was standing quite still he could hear a thick sound almost like panting. It was as rhythmic as an engine and as alien to him as a beast's cry, sending a cold shudder through him and he almost stopped right there. The urge to go no farther, to turn around, walk out of the house and

679

never return was strong within him. But stronger still was his determination to find Khieu. So many long-standing feelings were shifting inside him, changing as the new knowledge he had just gained seeping through him like a fiery liquor. Everything he had felt toward his adopted brother ... wrong! All his hate ... misplaced. Oh, God forgive all my hate, he thought. In a terrible way, he had been very like Khieu, part of his father's gargantuan plan; a human part, doing what it was told and no more, knowing what it was given and seeking no more.

No more! his mind roared silently as he tottered at the top of the steps. For so long – oh, it seemed like an eternity to him now! – he had declined to face what was really happening, what was shaping his life. He could no longer turn away. For now he was no longer an outsider. He had penetrated to the core of the *angka*; to its very inception. And so utterly monstrous was it that he knew he had been wrong at Lutece. His father was not just a man; he was everything Eliott had once feared him to be. He was the scheming spider sitting at the centre of a hideous web. He was, truly, the god of war.

So it was with renewed confidence that Eliott began his descent into the basement thinking that at last the chaos of the outside world would be banished forever, that he could at last make his peace with Khieu and at the same time strike a blow for truth and against his father.

Pale light rose towards him as he descended, giving him an odd sensation, skewing for a moment his perceptions of perspective. He heard the stentorian sounds as if he were approaching a smoking smithy. His heart beat fast, his throat was thick with an unknown pressure.

His feet touched the cement floor and he turned slowly wondering what it was making the noise and what it was he was going to see. His eyes focused and he gave a yelp, tiny and strangled. His eyes bulged in their sockets and he fell back against a damp wall, his arms across his roiling stomach.

He tried to turn away from the sight but he could not. He felt pinned to the stone like a fly in amber, compelled to drink in the unimaginable sight before him. There was a prickling behind his eyes; ants crawled through his brain; a silent howling filled him and he had the vertiginous sensation that all sanity had abruptly fled the world; that he had entered a madhouse and he possessed no means of escape.

He fell to his knees, all the strength sapped from his legs and swayed there, drooling. There was no place left on earth for him. No place to run; no place to hide. It was finished for him.

Before him, across the expanse of the basement's width Khieu was on his knees, his back hunched over. To one side there was a hole in the brick facing of the wall, a black hole gaping beyond. But it was the thing he was working on that drew Eliott's attention like a magnet, that imparted to him the chill winds of chaos. Propped up against the dirty brick was what had once been a human being. It was white and yellow with drained blood and congealed fat tissue, dark purple bruises wealed the otherwise pale flesh and here and there brownish welts rose.

It was Joy Macomber's corpse Khieu was bent over.

But what *was* he doing? Khieu reached inside a perfectly straight incision down the centre of her chest, plucked out her heart; Eliott pulled at his own flesh. Khieu extracted her liver; Eliott scored his skin with his nails, drawing blood, whimpering. Khieu pulled out a handful of squirming intestines and Eliott collapsed, his fingers tearing at his hair.

'Stop,' he sobbed, tears rolling freely down his cheeks. 'Oh, please stop.' His voice was soft and infantile, lacking an adult's force of will. 'For the love of God, stop!'

Now Khieu became aware that there was someone else in the room. His senses had been so fine-tuned to the accomplishment of his task that he had missed the minute sounds of approach he would otherwise have picked up.

He swung around and Eliott said his name aloud like an involuntary gasp: 'Khieu!'

'Who is Khieu?' the man before him said. 'I am *Chet Khmau*.' His handsome features were distorted by inner forces, demonic emotions which scoured him like fierce winds. His face appeared ravaged as if he had come off the line in a guerrilla war without beginning, without end.

'*Chet Khmau*,' Eliott whispered through dry, cracked lips. His mind, still partially frozen in shock, was frantically trying to

681

remember when and where he had heard the term before. 'What does it mean?'

Khieu crept towards him as a lizard might and Eliott pressed his body back against the wall, flattening himself as much as possible. 'There were many names for us . . . in those days.' Khieu's voice set the short hairs at the back of Eliott's neck on end; a stiff-bristled broom scraping over a rough sidewalk. 'The crow, Khmer Rouge . . . and *Chet Khmau*, the Black Heart. That is who I am.'

Eliott fought to hold back the terrified scream that was firing his throat, threatening to burst out. He gasped and coughed. 'What . . . what are you doing with Joy?' Eliott's eyes were opened wide and he would not seem to look at Khieu in the face for very long as if he felt burned with every contact.

The Cambodian was very close to him now and he almost choked at the cloying stench of death swirling about him. Khieu's eyes had darkened. Always black, they now seemed to be open pits, depthless and glossy, mirroring a soul so twisted that no man should be exposed to its hideous writhing.

But Eliott was and his muscles trembled at the force of it. He scrabbled along the wall, seeking a corner, seeking distance for he felt seared by the proximity to his adopted brother.

And now those alien depthless eyes bored into Eliott's, shrivelling him, making him choke and wheeze. '. . . There has arisen a war,' Khieu said. 'We look on each other as wild beasts; dangerous weapons have fallen into our hands and we, thinking, "this is a wild beast", "that is a wild beast", with these weapons deprive each other of life.' Those obsidian eyes blazed just as Murano's had long ago.

'She is a prisoner of war,' Khieu hissed. 'Prisoners must be exterminated in the prescribed manner so that the populace comes to understand the inevitability of the new order. The new order must be installed as quickly as possible so that all traces of the old, corrupt, decadent way of life may be eradicated from their memory. The old way was strangling Cambodia. Colonialism and capitalism; hand in hand they worked to destroy the Khmer people. This can no longer be tolerated.'

Eliott gasped. This was a person before him whom he did not

know; the tone, the phrasing unnatural, as if Khieu had had this speech ground into him by rote. Did he believe what he had said?

Eliott could not say. The sheets of the mini-journal seemed to be burning his thigh where they rested in his trousers' pocket. Surely what had been done to Khieu, he thought, could explain everything, every bizarre action. He shook his head, knew he wasn't thinking clearly; Khieu did not know what had been done to him so long ago. So why this . . .

Eliott saw now the absolute madness on Khieu's face and, in a flash of realization, he understood why. A Buddhist, trained in the peaceful ways of the Amida yet also trained as a hardened killer. How many times had Eliott passed by Khieu's room when he was living at home and heard the prayers. From his Oriental studies in comparative religions at school, he knew the substance of those prayers. Yet he had been witness to this man's professional killing techniques.

Now he asked himself how the two personalities could co-exist within one mind. The answer was obvious. With a great degree of interior stress. And at some point that stress would become too great for even the Eastern control and compart-mentalization to handle. Now he knew what no one else in the world knew: that moment had arrived within Khieu; the last defensive wall had crumbled, given way to the chaos of a mind pulled in two disparate directions. The tear had fused, creating . . . what?

And it had all been his father's doing. As if on a motion picture screen, Eliott saw it all laid out before him, one scene sliding seamlessly into another. The true nature of the *angka*. And the terror he felt for the creature not a foot away from him was dwarfed by the anger and rage he felt towards his father for perpetrating this obscenity.

He saw the mutilated corpse of the woman who had, for a time, tried to be his mother; he saw the tortured face of his adopted brother and the rage mixed with a kind of compassion. For the first time since Khieu had been dropped unexpectedly and unwanted into his life, he felt a love for him that transcended deed or consequence. And while that awesome feeling still suffused him he told Khieu the story of the Cambodian's second birth because it was his right to know.

'It's all been a lie,' he said. 'What you've been taught; what you've been told. Your origins. How the man who you call your father came upon you.' He held out the papers and they were taken from him.

Khieu cocked his head to one side; his breathing slowed. 'Tell me,' he commanded. 'Tell me all of it.'

And Eliott did because he thought it the right thing to do. He told his adopted brother how Macomber had been part of a mission to seek out and eliminate a certain renegade Japanese expert in death named Musashi Murano. How the unit reached the Khmer Rouge encampment just in time to find that Murano had already died but that their commander, being a cautious man, had stationed one man from the unit to spy on the encampment for ten days in order to be assured they were not being misled by Khmer Rouge disinformation. That man was Delmar Davis Macomber.

'That was how our father learned of your existence,' Eliott said. 'He did not come upon you by happenstance as he had you believe all these years. As the young acolyte of Murano's, he thought he had a use for you – a future use. And he sought out a way to trap you, turn you and use you for his own ends.'

'And he did just that. He set up your older brother himself by planting rumours he knew would eventually be picked up by the Khmer Rouge. Your brother was no traitor; he was killed by the Khmer Rouge because they believed the lies our father started. They weren't nearly clever enough for him.

'He rode in on the wings of an American "Arclight" bombing raid, took the encampment, killed the ones who had executed your brother. And in the process, won your undying loyalty.

'I'm sorry,' he said, meaning it. 'There is no justice, no solid ground on which to walk. It's all a mine field, hidden beneath the surface. It's never the way you thought it was going to be. And in the end, there's no one to help you get through it all.'

Eliott stared hard at Khieu, wanting desperately to know what effect his words would have. He wanted so much to believe that in some way the truth would be of some help to the Cambodian; that he had at last stood up, made a decision on his own and acted on it. After seeing what was occurring down here he knew he could not live with the knowledge he possessed inside him one minute more. It was not his, anyway. He saw now that he had merely been the temporary caretaker of it until such time as he judged to be right to give it back to its rightful owner. *He* judged. Eliott liked the sound of that; there was importance to it; a definite sense that events would have taken another course had he not intervened.

As for Khieu, he did not for a moment doubt a word of what Eliott said. Though it went against all he had believed in for fourteen years, still he could recognize the ring of truth when it was presented to him. And he understood, too, the nature of what Eliott had done for him.

There was a blackness inside of him he knew he would soon not be able to control; a singing like live wires, tingling his insides. The orange and black blossoms of napalm detonations filled the void behind his eyes. He heard the screams of the Khmer burning, the stench of roasting human meat, the thud-thud-thud of the clubs of his compatriots as they beat Sam and then, that most awful of moments, still and endless, when they all turned to him, when Ros offered him his filthy cudgel, pointing to the crumpled, bloodied body lying in the mud of the clearing and said to him, 'Come. Prove your worth to the cause. Come prove your undying loyalty to the new order. Come and take this club. Finish what we have begun. Kill this dog, this lackey of colonialism, of those who sought to put a stranglehold on the Khmer people.'

And how many times in his nightmare had Khieu retraced those stiff-legged steps he took then, holding out his trembling hand, and feeling the weight of the cudgel in his hand, the rough wood grain as his fingers curled around the haft, the birds that sprang away from their treetop perches as he raised the weapon over his head.

And the terrible silent scream echoing on and on inside himself as he brought the club whistling down with a grunt on the back of his beloved brother's head. *Bawng!*

'Go on,' he said now in a shivery voice filled with phlegm and bile. 'Get out.'

'But —'

His eyes leapt with dark flame. 'Now!' he cried. 'Get out *now*!'

Tracy had been expecting to be taken downtown to One Police Plaza but, instead White stopped in front of a rough stone building on Eleventh Street just west of Fourth Avenue.

'Sixth floor,' he said. He did not turn off the engine.

Tracy and Lauren got out and he bent back down, peered through the window. 'Aren't you coming up?'

'Nah. I got other business.' He grinned. 'Besides, meetings bore the shit outta me.'

Tracy nodded. 'Okay.' He extended his hand. 'Thanks, Ivory . . . for everything.'

White shook his hand. 'Like the man said: the *de luxe* treatment.' He pointed to the doorway. 'Just press the button marked "Six" and tell 'em your name. See ya.'

The door buzzed and they took the oversized elevator up.

'There's something you've got to promise me,' Tracy said seriously, 'or, information or no information, I'll send you back down to the street.'

Lauren said, 'What's that?' already knowing the answer; she steeled herself.

'Whatever is decided up there, you'll say nothing. You'll go along with it.'

She knew he was not talking about police business; it was far more personal than that. So she suprised him. 'When I met the Monk I understood instinctively that he was an honourable man. I know you understand me when I use the term "an honourable man". Just as I knew why the Monk had selected me to be his messenger: he knew I would not fail him.'

Lauren took a deep breath, thinking this was the most difficult task she had ever to accomplish in her life. 'I understand that whatever happens up there, whatever decisions are made, it's a matter of honour with you. I think I always knew that deep down; that's why I came back at the moment I did.'

Tension returned to her frame. 'I won't stop you but I *will* tell you one thing. If I think I'm losing, no one – not Thwaite or you or anyone else – *no one will* be able to stop me. I'll come after whoever is hurting you.'

'Lauren, you can't –'

'Yes,' she said fiercely. 'I can! That's *our* bargain.'

He was about to say something but, seeing the determination written across her face, he thought better of it. He took a deep breath. 'I don't want anything happening to you.'

'Can't you see that I feel exactly the same way about you?'

He relaxed. The fact was he *could* see it. He took one last shot. 'I don't have an alternative?'

'No.'

He pressed his lips against hers. 'Then it's our bargain.' But privately he vowed that he'd never let it come to that.

The elevator had come to a halt, the accordion iron gates pushed back. Tracy turned, saw Thwaite standing there. He was grinning.

'Hey,' he said. 'I thought you were never coming home.'

Tracy took his hand, stepped off the elevator. 'What the hell happened to you? You look like a truck ran over you.'

'Nothing that heavy.' He pointed out. 'This Lauren?'

Tracy nodded, introduced them. As Thwaite led them inside, he said, 'I like your taste in offices but what does the department think of it?'

Thwaite laughed. 'It's Melody's place. I thought we'd have a bit more privacy here. She'll be out for a couple of hours so we have plenty of time to get caught up.'

Tracy saw him take another look at Lauren, said, 'She's got some information on Macomber.'

'You mean Delmar Davis Macomber, the industrialist? What's he got to do with it?'

'You ever come across a firm called the Mauritious Company during the course of your investigations?'

Thwaite turned, stood as still as a statue. 'Jesus Christ!' he said. 'You're not leaving me shit to tell you. I've been to the Mauritious offices. It's nothing but a blind.' He told them what had happened, beginning with the lead at Senator Burke's house.

'Look no further,' Tracy said. 'The Mauritious Company's owned and run by Macomber.'

'Not any more,' Thwaite said. 'As of three days ago the Mauritious Company's out of business for good. And their most recent shipment of horse's stashed away safe and sound, out of Macomber's reach.'

'That isn't all he's involved in,' Lauren said. They both turned to look at her. 'I think it's time I deliver that debt to you, Tracy.' He was grateful she had had the good sense not to use the Monk's name in front of Thwaite.

He nodded. 'All right. Go ahead.'

'A couple of months ago Macomber was in Shanghai.'

'Yeah,' Thwaite said. 'I read about that. Trilateral Commission. He's on it.'

'While he was, he met with our friend.'

'Our friend?' Thwaite said, puzzled.

'Let's just say a procurer,' Tracy said. 'A free-lance.'

'He negotiated for and got the services of a terrorist,' Lauren continued. 'One of his conditions was that the man be an Islamic fundamentalist.'

'Wait a minute!' Thwaite cried. 'Are you saying – are you trying to say that the man who tried to gun down Atherton Gottschalk was hired by *Macomber*?'

Lauren nodded her head.

'But that's crazy! The man's a super-patriot. He may be a criminal but I can't believe he's trying to sell out his country.' He shook his head. 'Uh uh. I can't buy it.'

Tracy was silent, staring at the middle distance between Thwaite and Lauren. He had heard a tiny click inside his head, as of pieces of a puzzle coming together. Pieces that had seemed to have no obvious connection. What was it the Director had said? *The physical attempt changed many people's way of thinking. Now I don't think there's a power in the nation that can stop him from being elected. He's got my vote.*

Gottschalk and Macomber.

Now it was clear to him. Of course! 'No,' he said excitedly. 'Lauren's quite right, Douglas. It *was* Macomber's doing.'

'Then he's a dangerous madman.'

'Dangerous, yes. But a madman? I don't think so. Tell me, what's happened to Gottschalk's chances of being elected.'

'Couple of months ago, it was iffy,' Thwaite said. 'Now he's become the saviour of America; everyone sees that he was right all along. The people love him.'

'Well?'

'But that's just coincidence,' Thwaite protested. 'I mean it was blind luck that Gottschalk was wearing that bulletproof vest. Otherwise he would have been killed for sure. Macomber couldn't take such an enormous risk. What would've happened if the assassin had aimed for his head instead of for his heart?'

'Consider,' Tracy said, 'that the man who shot Gottschalk was a trained professional. As such, he would follow his orders to the letter. What if his orders were to *shoot for the heart*?'

'The call!' Thwaite snapped his fingers.

'What?' Tracy and Lauren said at the same time.

'I knew there was something about it, something wrong.' Thwaite looked at them. 'A buddy of mine got a call about the shooting just at the time it was happening. That's how they were able to get the guy.'

'An alert bystander calling 911,' Tracy said. 'What's so strange about that?'

'The call wasn't to 911,' Thwaite said. 'It was to One Police Plaza. To the man on duty who was linked directly into the security cordon surrounding the candidate. That same call into 911 would have not delivered the same results. By the time that relay had been made the assassin would have been long gone.'

'Macomber,' Tracy said. 'If he set it up he'd be the only one in position to make that call.' He looked at them both. 'My God, do either of you understand the implications of all this?' He hunched his body forward. 'Look, John Holmgren was in a position to seriously threaten Gottschalk's nomination – they must've known everything we were planning; I found the bug they planted in his office. So Macomber had John murdered, making it look like a heart attack –'

'Hold on,' Thwaite said. 'You telling me you know who did –'

'I'll get to that in a minute, Doug. Let me finish. Moira's

murder has an obvious motive – she saw something; they picked that up from the bug, too.'

'And Senator Burke?'

'That's where it gets interesting,' Tracy said. 'And very, very frightening. We already know that Macomber and Gottschalk are working together. 'But think a minute. D'you believe it's enough, in this day and age, with the way our political system's set up, to control only the President?'

'You mean this senator was in on it?' Lauren asked.

'Him and a whole lot more. I'm willing to wager a hundred to one on it. It's the only way the whole thing makes sense. A real and terrifying consolidation of power.'

'My God!' Thwaite said. 'It's ... well, I mean, that kind of thing's unimaginable.'

'You'd better think again, Doug.'

'But it's such a subversion of ... everything.'

There was silence for a time while all of them digested the enormity of what they had been pursuing. Thwaite broke it. He cleared his throat and reached into his jacket pocket. His face was very white.

'In light of what we've just been talking about, I think you'd better take a look at this.' He handed Tracy a list of the arms delineated in the scroll.

'Christ,' Tracy said. 'This's enough to –' He looked up at Thwaite. 'You saying you found this stuff?'

Thwaite shook his head. 'And that scares the shit outa me. I took my unit down to the docks this morning – that's why I had White meet you. We searched this ship – the *Jade Princess* out of Hong Kong, Singapore and Macao. She was as clean as a whistle.'

'That's bad,' Tracy said, thinking furiously. 'Very bad indeed.'

'I know what you mean,' Thwaite nodded.

Lauren looked from one to the other. 'But I don't,' she said. 'Would someone kindly explain?'

Tracy turned to her. 'It means Macomber must still be at least one step ahead of us. He's had the contraband dumped.'

'But what's it for?' Lauren asked.

There was a long silence. 'I think,' Tracy said after a time, 'we're going to have to ask Macomber that. But just from looking at this list I can tell you they're armaments consistent with the kind of military action both he and I are intimately familiar with.'

'Meaning?' Thwaite urged. During the last several minutes he had experienced a returning of the peculiar spinal tingling he had felt when he had thought of the enormity of the hole he and Tracy had fallen into. His heart was racing not only because he knew they were so close to their quarry but because he recognized the stakes involved and knew they were even more vast than he had suspected. Because of Macomber the entire world could shake itself apart.

'Meaning,' Tracy said slowly, 'that this shipment's been expressly hand-picked for a small terrorist cadre. Where they are at this moment or what their mission is I can't say. We've got to get to Macomber for that. But I do know his mind. Back then he was a fanatic about using rogue tactics and if they were successful, repeating them.'

They stared at him. 'I'm thinking about what he pulled with the Gottschalk "assassination", What if he uses this cadre to pull off the same kind of terrorist action – *after Gottschalk is President*? Can you envision the kind of national acclaim the man would receive at successfully capturing such a crew? And, believe me, if Macomber's behind the cadre, Gottschalk will know how to defuse them at the last minute – but only after he milks the most out of the media attention.'

'Christ,' Thwaite said, awed despite himself. 'He could do anything he wants after that.'

'Especially if, as we suspect, the Legislature's seeded with subverted senators and congressmen willing to support him.' Tracy thought of all the planning, all the time, all the money and energy needed to support such an incredible operation. The thought that he – his 'Operation Sultan' – had been subverted and used to fund this international nightmare filled him with loathing for the system that had spawned such a creation as the foundation in the first place.

Secrets, he knew, were always dangerously explosive. And a

secret entity like the foundation multiplied that danger many times over. For the deeper the secrecy went, the less real control there had to be. And that meant more chance for something to go seriously wrong. Witness what had happened in March of 1969 in Area 350.

And there was a great deal of fear inside him, too. He had known Macomber was clever back then but he saw now that he had not suspected the half of it. The scheme was so brilliant and so dark with evil intent that Tracy knew with all his soul that Macomber had to be stopped immediately. The police could not do that: there was no hard evidence. He turned it over in his mind again, knowing instinctively what he had to do and what he might have to give up in the process.

Covertly, he looked at Lauren and felt his heart melt at the line of her cheek, the colour of her eyes, the sheen of her hair. He drank all this in as if it was for the last time.

Then he began it as he had planned. They both stared at him as he told them what he had discovered in the foundation's files.

'This Murano was very special,' he concluded. 'The reports about him struck us all as highly exaggerated. That was then. Now I'm inclined to believe them.' He ran his fingers through his thick hair. 'Thwaite, you and I have seen first hand the kind of incredible damage this man, Khieu, can do. There's no doubt in my mind that he's Murano's disciple. I was even able to get a description of him: rather tall for an Oriental, thin, well-built, thin face, wide lips and very, very handsome. He –'

'Wait a minute,' Lauren interrupted. 'I think you've got it wrong. That sounds like a perfect description of Kim.'

Tracy felt his stomach lurch and he said, 'Where the hell did you meet Kim?' with so much force that Lauren winced and took an involuntary step backward.

'At . . . at L – your father's apartment. He showed up the evening you left for Hong Kong. He came for the electronic bug. Your father gave it to him – he seemed to know quite a bit about the . . . place where you and Louis used to work.' She seemed panic-stricken at Tracy's anger. 'He . . . he was very strange, Tracy. His eyes . . . they showed something; something

I can't quite explain. They made you want to reach out and take hold of him, comfort him. He seemed very sad.'

'Did he have a scar running down the side of his neck?' Tracy asked quickly. But he already knew the answer to that one.

Lauren shook her head. 'No.'

'She's met Khieu,' he said softly. 'Then Khieu killed my father. But *why*? Because he had seen him? Then he would have come after you, as well, Lauren.' He took her arm. 'What else was said?'

'I don't know.' She was becoming increasingly frightened despite her vow to herself to help Tracy all she could. First the arms shipment for a small cadre, then news of this monstrous killer. The Monk had not said anything about these things. What was she involved in?

'Think!' Tracy cried. 'Come on!'

'I can't! I –'

'Come on, Tracy.' Thwaite's calming voice cut in on her roiling thoughts. 'Give her a chance, that's all.'

Tracy looked from one to the other. 'It's very important, Lauren.' His tone was more normal now. '*Very* important.'

She was thinking furiously. 'Well . . . all I can think of is that Louis said something about –'

Tracy made a connection. 'About where I went?'

'No.' She shook her head, still trying to recall it clearly. 'No, he wouldn't do that.' She looked up into his face. 'But he did mention a name. Mizo. He –'

'Oh my God,' Tracy said. 'It's the same damn thing!' Now he knew how Mizo had got on to him so quickly. Khieu. And for just the same reason Khieu had killed his father.

Lauren saw his stricken face. 'Tracy, I'm sorry. He didn't know – neither of us could have.'

Tracy was at last aware of all the elements, of how they fell into place, one by one. And he was stunned by the awesome complexity of it all, just as he was stunned by the force of evil behind it.

'First and foremost we have to neutralize Khieu,' he said. 'He's more dangerous than either of you can guess because we're not just dealing with a simple human being here. It's become much more than that. I think the important thing to understand about him is that he's been programmed. He would not have done any of these acts without being directed; he'd have no reason to.'

'It's Macomber,' Lauren said, turning around at last.

But she was looking at Thwaite, a desperate expression on her face. 'You can see that. The evidence all runs back to him. You can arrest him now.'

Thwaite smiled thinly. 'Unfortunately, I can't. All we have here is a load of talk. We don't have one solid piece of evidence I can take to the DA.'

'But if you went to him,' Lauren pleaded, 'laid all of this out for him. Surely he'd see —'

'He'd laugh in my face,' Thwaite said. 'The DA isn't interested in theories; neither are the courts.' He shook his head. 'No, we just have to wait and hope for a break. There's no way I can make a move against either one of them yet.' He stood up. 'We'll watch and wait.'

Lauren turned her head, stared hard at Tracy. 'That won't be enough for him.'

'What's she talking about?' Thwaite said.

'You're right, Douglas.' Tracy put his hands in his pockets. 'There's nothing you can do now but wait.' He looked at his friend. 'But I'm not bound by that.'

'Now wait a minute. If you think I'm going to let you —'

'You've no say in it,' Tracy said. 'He's tried to kill me once in Hong Kong. D'you think he's going to stop now?'

Thwaite was quiet for a time, contemplating Tracy. 'Just what the hell you going to do?' His voice was soft but there was a warning edge to it.

'I'm going in,' Tracy said. 'Right to the centre, where either of them can get at me. It's the only way.'

'The only way to commit suicide,' Thwaite snorted. 'Forget it.'

'Look, Douglas,' Tracy said doggedly, 'you already know just how dangerous they both are. For the time being your hands are tied. But we know from the arms cache you intercepted that there's another piece of the puzzle we haven't worked through. It's a time bomb in our pocket and the fuse has already been lit. Whatever it is, it's *already running*.

'I know Macomber well enough to believe he's got a back-up running somewhere. Your interception hasn't stopped him; it'd be a serious mistake to think so. We've merely breached his security.

'But time's now an element against us. Who are those arms for and when will they be used? *When?* Tomorrow, next week . . . or tonight? We don't know. And we can't afford to wait.'

There was silence in the room.

'Goddamn it!' Lauren screamed at Thwaite. 'Aren't you going to say anything. Aren't you going to stop him?'

'How can I? He's right.'

'Bastard!' she cried. 'You're both bastards!'

Tracy took a step towards her. 'Lauren, I warned you –'

'Don't expect me to be bound by anything I said before. I didn't know I was talking to a madman.'

He took another step towards her and she turned away, her arms folded across her breasts.

'She's got a point, Tracy,' Thwaite said. 'I'm not going to allow you to go in alone.'

'No one's coming with me. That *would* be suicide.'

'I'm talking about a bug. I want you wired for sound. I'll have my unit out of sight across the street; you get what we need on tape and we'll come in and get you so fast nobody'll know what hit them.'

Tracy smiled softly. 'You're dreaming, Douglas. It'll never happen that way.'

'Have faith.'

'It's not you. I know Macomber; I think I've come to know Khieu as well. They've both got something you'll never understand. You weren't over there in the jungles. It's a different world. A different logic applies.'

'I don't care about any of that bullshit.' Thwaite said. 'And neither should you right now. Concentrate on this. You won't leave this apartment unless you're wired.'

It was typical policeman's thinking and Tracy did not blame Thwaite for it. He was only reacting out of his own training.

'Lauren –' he began.

'I've got nothing to say to you.' She turned away.

Tracy went to his bag, opened it. There, on top of the pile of his clothes, was the black velvet case from the Diamond House. Queens Road, steaming and jammed with tourists, seemed like another world now.

He plucked out the case, went and stood behind Lauren. He felt her start slightly at his touch, twist her head. Her hair brushed against his cheek, setting off memories like a string of fireworks in his mind. He did not want to lose her; did not want to contemplate the possibility that he would never see her again.

On stiff fingers, he held out the velvet case, extending his arm until the case was in front of her. She was still for some time and at first he thought she was looking deliberately away. He waited.

'What's that?' she said in a small voice.

'I went shopping in Hong Kong,' he said. 'I bought this for you even though I didn't know whether you'd ever speak to me again.'

She whirled. 'Oh, Tracy, how could you have thought that?' She reached up, touched his cheek, pressing her palm and long fingers against his flesh. 'It feels like I've loved you forever. That somewhere inside of me I always knew you'd come for me.'

'Then why did you resist so long?' His eyes searched hers for the answer.

And she gave it to him even though she suspected he might not understand it. 'Because I've been a child all my life. That's what ballet is all about. At forty-five you're dead. As long as you're young, you can dance. I didn't want to grow up. And to love you, I had to. I knew that all along. Just as I knew I loved you from the moment we first kissed. But the thought of growing up terrified me. I thought I'd lose the dance. And where would I be without ballet?'

'And now?'

'Now I have you. I have myself. And I'll have ballet for as many more years as I can dance well. Somehow that's not so difficult to accept now; not so terribly frightening because I don't have to face it all alone.'

She looked down at the black velvet box. 'What's inside?' Her voice had become small again, like a child on Christmas morning.

'Open it.'

The blue-white diamond ring in its platinum setting winked up at her. Sparks of colour – red, green, blue, yellow, purple, shone in its facets.

'Oh, Tracy.' Her voice was a whisper. She took it out of the case. 'It's so beautiful.' She placed it on her finger. Abruptly the smile left her face and her head came up, her eyes locked onto his. 'But why have you given it to me now.'

'Because,' he said, 'I'm coming back.'

Khieu felt the elemental changes working their magic inside him. He had sent Eliott away, knowing that if he did not, the next minute he would have leapt upon him, plunging his stiffened thumbs into his eyes. It was not something he wanted to do yet the compulsion was there, sitting like a spider at the bottom of a night-dark pit.

His nostrils flared; the heavy sweet scent of blood was strong in the air of the basement, the rich fecund smell of rotting human flesh. They reminded him of home, of so many things.

Macomber, his father, his mentor, the man to whom he owed a debt he could never fully repay; he was a liar, a supreme manipulator. Khieu felt as if someone had stolen silently inside him, scooping out his guts – his very soul – slipped away into the shadows before he could do anything to prevent it.

Everything he knew, everything he had been taught or told, a lie! His entire perception of the world, its workings, mechanisms, clockwork tickings – all wrong, all false!

He felt bereft, a child again, thrust back into the hell of Phnom Penh with his father dead, his mother catatonic and Samnang suddenly vanished into thin air.

Go! the command had erupted from somewhere deep inside him. *Follow Samnang! Follow your brother!* And Khieu had done its bidding, turning his back on the old colonial life he had known in Sihanouk's court, bicycling out of the city, following his instincts, plunging into the reeking, screaming jungle, into the arms of *Chet Khmau*.

Life as he had known it had ceased to exist. He had been born again, as if in another incarnation. Yet he could not fully forget his former life, the lessons so painstakingly taught him. And so, he had superimposed one upon the other, two layers of tissue overlapping, the one colouring the other, though he struggled mightily to compartmentalize them. He had been only partially successful.

And then he had met Macomber, the man who had executed Sam's murderers. How could Khieu ever repay that enormous debt? He had tried, over the years, bowing to Macomber's wishes. Could he do any less?

The training of Musashi Murano had been brought out, *Chet Khmau* reigning supreme. But what of his other side? His childhood training? The bright light he had once seen emanating from the master had never faded from his memory, the electricity of his touch, his gaze. And all the while, he had struggled to keep up with Preah Moha Panditto's lessons because he believed in him. He believed Musashi Murano. He believed Macomber.

He was sweating mightily, his muscles bunched and jumping with his inner tension. Where was he now? What was he to do? Who could he believe? Perhaps they were *all* liars. He seemed rooted to the spot, unable even to breathe.

Then he knew. Like a rush of wind in his ears, he was buffeted by currents he had only barely glimpsed before. Now the floodgates had opened and he felt on the brink of a revelation. An instant in time that burned forever, imprinted on his brain like a physical convulsion. The instant he had seen the bright light surrounding Preah Moha Panditto; the first instant of his touch; his first kill; the first time he and Musashi Murano had locked gazes; the moment he had held the loaded pistol, pointing it at Macomber's face; the anticipation before opening Malis' door; the first time he had gazed into Lauren's eyes.

A revelation just like those. *Identical.*

His body shuddered and danced to its rhythm.

He would acquiesce. He would do as Macomber ordered.

After all, he owed his father a debt he could never fully repay. Sam's murder revenged. *Apsara* ordered it with her sinuous dancing fingers.

And then he would destroy Macomber, slowly, a piece at a time, chipping away at his sanity, taking from him that which he held most dear, rending it before his wide-open eyes. Khieu wanted his father to know what was happening to him even as it was occurring, so that he could imagine for himself what the end would be like: to burn and burn with *apsara* tearing at his flesh.

The end of all things.

He felt something coming. It was close, close. It was almost here. Not yet. Not quite yet. Khieu turned his head this way and that to look. What was it?

Eliott Macomber sat on the edge of his bed, shivering. It was still daylight out but because his bedroom window faced north, the light was already quite dim and far away, as if viewed from the end of a tunnel. Even the patter of the rain on the window ledge seemed remote, part of another world.

He looked bleakly around his own apartment. He had not turned on the light. Shrouded in shadow, palms pressed between his knees, he rocked slightly back and forth as he used to when he was a child, unable or unwilling to go to sleep. That was a time when he wanted to cry out but he knew it would only summon his nanny and what he had really wanted was his mother. She was dead and he knew it; that was why he rocked and bit his lip instead of opening his mouth to call out. It was unthinkable that his father would come. Even on the off chance that he was home, he was always too busy or too preoccupied with his own world. As he grew into adolescence Eliott more than once had the sensation that his father had never been a child himself but had leapt directly into adulthood.

Eliott stared sightlessly at the carpet in front of his feet. What he really saw was the mutilated corpse of Joy Macomber; he saw Khieu, scooping, scooping, his curved fingers black with her essences; saw Khieu's haunted eyes, filled with death and suffering beyond comprehension; saw Joy's dead eyes, filmy and dark as if blue gauze had been stretched over hollowed-out sockets. These images were more real to him than his present surroundings.

Yet it was not Khieu he hated now, though he had envied the Cambodian for years, though Khieu had been the one who killed Kathleen. It was not Khieu's fault; he saw that clearly now, as clearly as he saw the other images.

He had grown up with the feeling that the outside world was evil, filled with a turmoil and chaos too complex for him to be able to handle. And now he was coming to see that it was not that way at all. He was beginning to understand the true nature of evil and it chilled him to the bone, shivering him with its implications.

He had grown up with a certain view of life. Where had it come from? Not from his mother; she had died when he was too young, he barely remembered her. Not from the teachers at his school. Where then?

Khieu was taught to act a certain way in this country. He had been manipulated and used; he had been lied to. Had the same thing been done to Eliott?

Certainly Eliott knew that had he not been so terrified of doing it, he would have struck off on his own years ago – at the time he had gained his legal majority. He had in fact brought it up several times.

'Go ahead,' Delmar Davis Macomber had said. 'Leave this all behind if you want. I won't stop you.'

He had been serious, even going so far as to transfer ten thousand dollars into Eliott's account to tide him over until he relocated, settled down and found a decent job.

But Eliott had never gone. He had packed his bags once, then sat staring at his plane ticket to San Francisco as the sun went down and the time of his flight came and went. And, at last, had ripped the ticket in two; his tears had already made the writing on it illegible.

Now he suspected that his father had known all along that he would not board the flight. The acquiescence, the transfer of money had all been a sham. Delmar Davis Macomber had trained his son too well. He would not leave his father; he would not leave the business that someday he would inherit and run. There was too much for him to learn. The stage, his father had said many times, is no place to learn anything except deceit. 'And since you obviously can't even pick up *that*, there's no use in your pursuing a career in acting.'

Each remembered word was a blow he felt in a physical sense, wincing as they echoed in his mind.

There was the nature of true evil. The spectre of his father loomed like a great coiled serpent just beyond his shoulder, ready to strike if he moved a centimetre out of line. It wasn't the world he should fear, Eliott saw now. It was his father. It had been his father all along.

He groaned, held his stomach. He felt ill. Joy's white bloated face floated through his mind's eye like a spear embedded in his brain. He had lost her but he could not lose that image. He groaned again, heard the knock at the door.

'Go away,' he whispered. 'Leave me alone.'

But the sound came again, more insistently this time and he lurched to his feet, walking unsteadily to the front door if only to stop the noise. It was giving him a headache.

He opened the door. Khieu!

*

Kim had returned to New York. He had no more interest in the Panel's absurd demands; just as he had no more interest in working for the foundation. Such matters seemed pointless now. He had his own, more personal demands to fulfil.

He thought he had gauged it well. Tracy had had ample time to pick the way through the minefield of subtle clues Kim had artfully provided for him; with Tracy's kind of talent only a few had been needed to set him running in the right direction; those photos showing how his friend Holmgren had been murdered might have been enough.

Now was the time to return to close proximity to the ferret, to shadow him every step of the way so that Kim, the instrument of his family's revenge, could be there when Tracy closed in. So that Kim himself could deal with Khieu Sokha in his own particular way. As for Macomber, he was Tracy's prize. Kim felt no desire to handle him himself; even a ferret deserved a prize at the end of his run. Whatever Macomber had been up to was entirely irrelevant to Kim; he had certainly known part of it, otherwise he would never have been in on John Holmgren's murder so swiftly.

Time seemed to escalate, decelerating to an entirely interior point. Kim felt keenly the enormity of the weight he carried; the weight of his family, the combined strength of their spirits, who cried out for bloody vengeance.

Kim shivered slightly in anticipation as the taxi dodged traffic heading into Manhattan from LaGuardia. His eyes glowed. Now was the time of sweet vengeance.

'May I come in?'

Eliott stared at his adopted brother as if he were a ghost fresh from his graveyard haunt. He stood numbly, not knowing what to do or even what to think.

Khieu was again his normal self: beautiful, well-dressed, supremely confident and self-composed. His face was freshly scrubbed, his black eyes bright and clear, his manner relaxed so that Eilott had difficulty connecting this Khieu with the horror-driven creature down in the depths of his father's basement. Perhaps, he thought feverishly, it had never happened. Maybe I dreamed it all.

'Eliott?'

He took a deep shuddering breath, his head nodding spasmodically like an ill-worked marionette.

'Sure.'

He closed the door and together they went into the living room. Khieu sat down.

'Would you like a drink?' Eliott asked, heading for the kitchen.

'Just a beer if you have it.'

Eliott came back in a moment with Kirens for both of them. 'I hope you don't mind drinking out of the bottle.'

Khieu lifted a hand, waved Eliott's words away. He took a sip of the beer, set the bottle down on a side table. 'I don't have much time but I wanted to stop by and thank you.'

'Thank you?' Eliott parroted stupidly.

'For telling me.' Khieu leaned forward, touched Eliott on the knee. A siren screamed by outside, diminishing. Eliott had not bothered to close the windows and turn on the air conditioning when he had come home. The sounds of Indian summer in the city were strong, a solid reminder of the seasons changing; the abrupt slide into autumn was not far off. 'I wanted you to know how much I appreciate it.'

This calm, cool Khieu in the face of the knowledge he had been provided, set the fright off in Eliott again. He began to say something, choked on it. He swallowed hard, tried again. 'What . . . are you going to do about it?'

'Do about it?' Khieu looked around the room as if he had never seen it before. 'Nothing.'

'But don't you want to?' Eliott stared hard at him trying to understand him. 'You must. I know enough –'

'No, you don't.' Khieu's eyes lighted on Eliott's. 'And perhaps it's time that you did.' His voice, though softer, lower than Eliott's, nevertheless cut through his adopted brother's strident tones. 'You should hear what even our father doesn't know. You've earned it, after all.' He rose, went silently across the carpet to stand behind the chair in which Eliott sat. 'He knows and you know that my older brother, Samnang, was murdered by the Khmer Rouge; as you told me, our father initiated the lies which caused the murder. But neither of you knows how it happened.'

'Khieu –' Eliott said, fidgeting. He was becoming extremely uncomfortable.

'Quiet,' Khieu whispered. He put a hand on Eliott's shoulder, squeezing. 'You may not know this but the Khmer Rouge's favourite method of execution, when they weren't crucifying people and hanging them from trees along well-trod paths in the jungle, was to beat someone to death. Traitors and the like. They did this as tradition because in the early days when they were forming they could not afford to waste ammunition.

'This is what they did to Sam. They beat him until they knew he was dying. Then they called me out and thrust a club into my hand.' He leaned down so that Eliott felt his lips brush against his ear and tried to shy away. But Khieu had a firm grip on him and would not let him go. 'Can you guess what happened then, brother? Can you picture what they made me do?'

Eliott's mouth was dry and he was trembling. He nodded over and over again. Yes, oh, yes! he could imagine. The *Chet Khmau* had forced Khieu to kill his own brother. His eyes squeezed shut but he could not stop the flow of tears. My God! How could he have done it? How could he *not*? What alternative did Khieu have but to take up the club and use it? If he did not, they would kill him *and* kill Samnang. But still. But still. Oh, God!

'I'm sorry,' he whispered over and over again. 'I'm sorry.'

'Are you?' Khieu came around from behind the chair, knelt at Eliott's feet, his depthless black eyes staring up into Eliott's, magnified by the tears. 'Yes,' he said, wonderment in his voice, 'I really think you mean it.' His hands closed over his adopted brother's. 'Now we're close,' he said gently. 'Finally there is something we can share. A secret only the two of us know. There's a bond now. Yes. Nothing can disturb that. It's ours, alone.'

He rose, drew Eliott up, their hands still clasped tightly. Khieu put his arm around his brother. 'Now come on,' he said softly. 'Let's go back home. Together.'

And they went, *apsara* licking at Khieu's heels all the way, her bloated belly sliding grindingly along the asphalt just outside the taxi that rattled them downtown. And when he looked into the rearview mirror, he saw her headless form dancing there. And when he glanced behind them, he saw her image once again, twisted and distorted into ten-thousand tiny fragments by the rain drops clinging tenaciously to the rear window.

The wipers made a sad soughing sound like the wind through the high Cambodian palms. When the fast-moving thunderheads turned the sky yellow and purple from the bruises of the lightning.

Father is coming tonight to pick up his papers on the Australian combine merger. He glanced at his watch and *apsara* signed him the time: 7.40. He began to count it down. Thirty more minutes until Macomber's world exploded into chaos.

He paid off the driver and they got out. Up the limestone steps. Through the darkened, silent house. The French clock ticking on, counting down the minutes. Just twenty.

'Are you hungry?' Khieu said and, when Eliott shook his head, no, said, 'I haven't been hungry in three days.'

Their shoe soles made no sound at all on the thick pile carpet. They might have been wraiths without any substance had it not been for the flitting of their reflections in hanging mirrors, the lick of their thin shadows on the walls.

'Let's go upstairs.' Khieu's voice hung eerily, inundating the silence, in turn being dissipated.

Eliott looked at him. Ever since he had crept down the basement stairs and found Khieu hunched over Joy's corpse, he had felt oddly disconnected. He barely felt the movement of his legs now and certainly could not discern any life in his feet. It was as if he were floating, adrift like a balloon, his movements totally at the whim of the surrounding currents.

It was as if, in vomiting up his father's secrets to Khieu, he had expended the amount of initiative given to him and now, bankrupt, he was helpless, incapable of determining his own fate. He was returning to the long twilight of his adolescence when the misery of confusion every day overwhelmed him when, virtually friendless, the barrenness of his present caused him to fear the future.

The same fear of the future rode his shoulders now like a death shroud, weighing him down. What would happen to him? He felt as if Khieu were the only person in the world who understood him. His father was motivated only by manipulation; when he required Eliott to jump through one of his difficultly placed hoops, he turned on the charm. Whereas Khieu's power was laced with a kind of compassion towards Eliott. As Khieu had said, they shared secrets, torn pasts ... and they had been manipulated and lied to in precisely the same manner.

And Khieu's closeness, his arms around him, made Eliott feel safe, secure, warm; emotions alien to him, too beautiful to ever let go of.

They reached the top of the stairs and went down the dimly lit hallway. They reached the threshold of Eliott's old bedroom.

'You remember your old room,' he said softly in Eliott's ear as they crossed over the threshold.

Eliott looked around. 'Everything's the same. It's as if I never left.'

'That's the way your father wanted it,' Khieu whispered. 'He wants you back, Eliott. He never liked the fact of your leaving. To him it meant you were slipping out from under his thumb.'

'I was,' Elliott said, dazed. 'I *had* to.' He turned to face Khieu. 'You of all people should understand that.' He could see Khieu's eyes shining, their dark centres very alive.

'Oh, I do. I do.' Khieu kept his arm around Eliott's waist. 'I was proud of you when you made the move. I wish –' his eyes dipped for a moment – 'well, I wish I could have been able to do that.'

'But you still can!' Some animation came into Eliott's voice. 'I'll help you. We'll do it together.'

Khieu's eyes were sad and he gripped Eliott all the harder. 'Unfortunately, it's far too late for me.'

'What do you mean?'

'I can't ...' He stopped, turned away. 'This is very difficult for me to say ... to anyone. Even you.'

Eliott reached out, touched his arm. 'What is it, Khieu?' His voice was soft, concerned. 'Can't I help you? I want to. I want to make up for all ... for how I've treated you all these years. That will make me happy.'

Khieu turned in the semi-darkness. His face was streaked with shadow as if he were some creature emerging into a deep forest's clearing. His eyes were steady and Eliott knew he had made up his mind. Khieu would tell him. The ultimate secret shared between just these two. He shivered in anticipation.

When Khieu spoke again, his voice had changed pitch. It was lower, filled with basso rumblings, heavy vibrations that caught in Eliott's ear, stuck there, running round and round. His voice was a whisper but urgent and somehow totally free of sibilants.

'I have spent many years in the kind of hell I thought I was leaving when ... our father brought me here to America ... away from the war, the Khmer Rouge, my blasted family.

'I was grateful to him; more grateful than you could ever know. He knew my psychology and used that. In showing me how he had destroyed the murderers of my brother, he knew the situation he put me in. He trained me and then he set me loose like a dog on a tightly-held leash to do his bidding.'

Khieu leaned forward and streaks of light silvered his cheeks. For a moment his depthless eyes were thrust into an illusion of such prominence Eliott gasped, starting.

'I killed for him. I did things I never thought I'd do again. I did them all for love; to honour the memory of Samnang and my ancestors. I had no other choice.'

Khieu took Eliott's arm, swung him around away from the light. The ensuing darkness seemed suffocating in its density. 'Now I don't expect you to understand all this; just to believe it.

'Honour binds me. I should kill our father for what he has done ... but I can't.'

Eliott blinked rapidly as if he had caught a dancing mote beneath his lid. Sweat prickled his face like the soft scrape of thorns.

'As I said, honour binds me. And now I am without it.' He gripped Eliott's shoulders. 'I cannot live without it. He has stripped me of the most precious thing in my life ... the only thing that matters.'

Eliott tried to pull away. His eyes were wide, the whites showing all around the edges. His lower lip trembled and he sought to find his buried voice. He coughed and choked. 'What ... are you going to do?' His voice sounded like the whisper of the wind.

Khieu's eyes burned. 'I am going to cease to exist.' His grip on Eliott had become painful. 'And you must help me.'

'No!'

'You *must*!' Khieu's voice turned pleading. 'I cannot do it myself. I *need* you, Eliott.'

'But this –!' Eliott's head shook back and forth. 'No. I cannot allow this. I cannot!'

'Yes, yes yes,' Khieu crooned. 'You said you wanted to help me. This is the only way!'

'I didn't mean –' Eliott turned his head away at last, his eyes squeezed shut. 'Ask me anything but that. Anything!'

'Yes, that's your way, isn't it?' Khieu's voice pursued him relentlessly. 'You'll help. But only on your terms. You'll only do something *you* think's right and proper. But you're a

708

Westerner, Eliott. You don't *know*.' He cupped his adopted brother's cheeks in his hands. They felt hot and wet, stretched taut as if under pressure. 'Look at me. *Look* at me, please!' Eliott's eyes opened slowly, reluctantly.

'You must do this. It's what I ask. And you *promised*.' One hand went behind him, came back with a dark shape. Eliott's nostrils flared, scenting oil and an odd, sharp odour he could not place.

'Give me your hand,' Khieu said softly. 'Give me your hand, Eliott.'

Without even being fully aware of it, Eliott did as he was told. He saw only Khieu's mesmerizing eyes. But he felt the hard cool weight of metal in his palm.

'Close your fingers over it,' Khieu said. He never took his gaze from Eliott's eyes. 'Put your forefinger through the trigger guard.' He felt with his own hand. 'Very good.' He turned Eliott so that he faced the open doorway.

'All right now,' Khieu whispered. 'You stand there. Yes, right there. You don't have to move, just lift your right arm and squeeze the trigger. That's all there is to it. And my burden will be released. Do you understand?'

Eliott did not. But he knew with a quivering certainty that he would do what Khieu asked. He had to. They shared secrets; they knew things others did not. They were linked together by more than blood. They were, indeed, closer than brothers. He must do it. There was no question. He knew better than anyone else alive the extent of Khieu's suffering; he felt it himself as if it were part of his own; he felt that it was. He would do what he must to expunge that suffering at last.

'Yes,' he said, though he did not understand. It did not matter that he never would.

'All right,' Khieu said. 'I must go to my room and prepare. There are rituals to perform; prayers to be recited. I must make myself ready. When you hear the prayers stop, I will come. I will stand framed in the doorway. I'll put a light on behind, in the hall so that all you'll see is a silhouette. I know that will make it easier for you, not to have to see my face. 'Just raise your arm and squeeze the trigger. That's all. There's nothing to it. A roar and then it'll be over.' Khieu let go of Eliott at last, backed away to the sill of the open doorway. He stopped when he heard Eliott's strained voice. 'Yes?'

'Good-bye, Khieu.'

'Good-bye, *mon vieux.*'

The chanting began some time after than. Eliott could hear it clearly, curling down the hallway, drifting in the twilight of the room, the twilight of his life. He was saddened by Khieu's parting but he was also gladdened by what he had been assigned to do. It made him feel important and full of worth. Of all the people in the world, Khieu had chosen him. Because they were closer than brothers. Eliott had always wanted a brother; and never considered Khieu one. Now he knew what it was like to have a sibling. It filled him with unnamed emotions, made him want to cry with joy and sorrow at the same time.

He felt alive.

The chanting went on and on and Eliott thought he could smell the intense odour of the incense. How he had once hated that smell. How he loved it now. He could picture Khieu, naked, on his knees in front of the Buddha.

The loaded pistol was heavy in his hand and he could feel a slight film of sweat building between his palm and the warming metal. He wanted to take his hand away, wipe the grip down but he was terrified that in that moment, the chanting would come to an end and he would see Khieu's shadow like a spectre rearing up before him, filling the open doorway with its harsh spill of light, and he would be unready to perform the task given to him. He could not chance that. This moment was too important for him.

His eyes burned with tears or perhaps the mist of incense wafting to him from down the hall. He blinked constantly to clear his vision. The night seemed calm and still around him. But alive and sentient, hovering expectantly. He did not feel alone. Khieu was with him now, standing still at his side, giving him strength and guidance. Eliott ached with his brother's pain. My brother, he thought. *My brother.*

The chanting stopped.

*

Penetration. It was what they said he was best at when he came to them seeking a job. Because his father was Louis Richter, they took him in. They put him through a six-day battery of tests and this they determined was his speciality.

It had been confirmed thirteen months later by Jinsoku himself, on the day he had graduated from the Mines. 'You, my friend,' the old man had said, 'have the mind of a ferret. They'll set you loose and you'll go down the hole for them. You'll find whatever it is they want you to find; you'll do it in cases where others have failed.

'But it's a heavy burden you'll carry. The better you are, the more they'll come to rely on you. The more missions they'll shove at you. Physically, that's no problem at all. It's the emotional side that concerns me. This is between us . . . not for their ears.

'You'll be under pressure. Listen to me now and don't interrupt. I don't expect you to understand this. Just remember it when the time comes. Get out before the overload. I have no desire to see you end up in a padded room. I've put too many hours of myself into you.' He knew it was the closest the old man could come to acknowledging the friendship that had developed between them at the Mines. So he remembered.

It was what was going through Tracy's mind now as he began the penetration. The one thing he did best. Or had done. He had taken Jinsoku's advice and had got out. Now he knew he must do it one last time and he wondered.

Gramercy Park South – those two blocks on East Twentieth Street – was quieter than the rest of the surrounding area. It was how its residents wanted it. The black iron-fenced park itself was dark, locked tight. Few vehicles passed by. A few couples walked hand in hand, enjoying the respite from the vice-jawed pace of the city.

Tracy, in dark-coloured clothes, was inconspicuous as he moved at a leisurely pace behind two lovers, their pressed shoulders affording him an excellent screen from anyone chancing to look east from a window vantage point.

Half a block in, the couple moved to their right, crossing the street towards the leafy park. He waited for a moment, watching a dog root around in the gutter until its owner lost patience, jerking at the leash. Tracy sauntered along behind her for perhaps a hundred yards, until his shadow stretched out in front of her as they passed a streetlight. She started, turned her head partly around to look at him. He quickened his pace slightly, ignoring her as he went past and her interest waned.

Tracy found himself three doors east of the Macomber residence. He watched the thin traffic as well as the pedestrians, turning his head and moving as he scanned the faces so that he looked perfectly natural, a stroller interested in this section of the city. Fixity in anything was to be avoided, Jinsoku had impressed on him. Fluidity to be strived for. The thing was to *sink in* with the surroundings, to blend in to such an extent that you became part of the place.

The sky was cloudless overhead, just the trace of sere nimbostratus over to the west near the tops of the low buildings. The atmosphere was light and clean, almost as if the recent storms had scrubbed the air. There was no carbon monoxide to make the breath short.

Two cars came towards him, one light, the other dark, and he turned his head away as a matter of course, stopping to casually scan the buildings' architecture.

Bells, missing a beat or two here and there, sounded in the air, clear and sharp, hanging for an instant like puffs of smoke before dissipating. St George's Church was just on the far side of the park, on Gramercy Park North. He saw several people walking up its steps, push through its doors. He glanced at his watch: 8 p.m.

His head was down as the limo pulled up in front of Macomber's house. Without missing a step, he turned in at the house just east of it, hid himself in shadows.

He could see the gleaming front grill, reflecting the streetlights, leopard spots on its shiny flanks. The license plate read: MAC 1.

The driver got out, came around in front of the grill, stooped to open the near-side passenger door. Tracy saw Delmar Davis Macomber emerge from the limo's depths. Though he had not seen the man in almost fourteen years, he could not have missed him. The tall frame, the wide square shoulders, the straight back, the fluid motion of the hips. No, he did not even have to see the face to know it was Macomber. But he did catch a flash of burnished cheek, a line of moustache, before the other turned to go up the front steps of his house.

Tracy saw the ornate wrought-iron gates, the spiked gas lamps burning real flame, the short square balcony emerging from just below the second storey leaded glass window. Macomber had already gone inside but he saw that a frontal approach was out of the question. There was far more illumination for one thing. For another, there was a space of perhaps ten feet just inside the gate when he would have been totally without protection.

He knew there to be only one other possibility and he searched for it now. Macomber's house was one of many built at the turn of the century. Times and customs were entirely different then. Many of the wealthy had stables behind their houses and while over the years these had been either razed or turned into a second, smaller dwelling, their narrow entrances had been kept principally because of their quaint, old-fashioned look.

Tracy found this entrance on the easterly border of the house, a brick and masonry arch perhaps three feet wide closed off by a custom-made mahogany and iron door. It was locked, of course, but that was no problem.

Penetration.

He searched for an alarm, found none. It took Tracy a little over forty seconds to snap the lock. During that time only three people passed: a couple and one old man, hands in his pockets, his head down, deep in contemplation. None of them noticed him.

He stepped quickly through, closed the narrow door behind him. He found himself in a cramped courtyard. Directly ahead was where the stables had been. A well-tended garden grew there now, filled with trees and shrubbery.

He stayed close to the side of the building, moving cautiously until he encountered the concrete edge he had been searching for: a side entrance to the basement.

A flight of six steep concrete stairs plunged precipitously down into the earth. The door was padlocked. He felt around the edges of the frame until he found the concealed wires. There were two of them, entwined. He knew if he cut one, the alarm would sound. If he cut the other, he would deactivate it. His father had taught him that.

He ran his fingertips along the wires until they parted company. One went up, the other straight down to what he was sure was the activating box. If he cut that one, the alarm would sound. He retraced his steps, picked up the wire that went up. He cut it.

A siren sounding from Third Avenue where Cabrini Medical Center stood. Cicadas buzz-sawed, shimmering the air with sound. Otherwise silence.

He went to work on the lock and went through the door. He closed it behind him, was about to move, when he scented something, stood stock still. His heart beat fast and his breathing came hot. He felt the electronic bug like a knuckled fist directly on his breastbone. He resisted an urge to paw beneath the buttons of his shirt, rip it from its taped resting spot.

He used a pencil flash in the darkness confronting him, the ribbon of light seeming almost solid as it wove its way through the blackness.

It lit up exercise material: mats, a heavy punch bag, a length of thick rope hanging from a hook in the ceiling. Free weights, wooden bars, two pieces of wooden stick.

Tracy walked over to these. He donned a surgeon's glove – gift from Thwaite – rolled each over. There were no stains, though the sides were dented here and there. They had obviously been used but on Moira? Tracy thought not. Unless wax had been used, it would have been impossible to get the bloodstains off before they seeped into the porous wood.

But now that he had crossed the basement, that smell was stronger and he played the beam of light in a shallow arc, moving slowly. The narrowness of the beam made identification difficult, especially from a distance.

He saw a pile of bricks and, above them, a dark space in the

714

wall. Shine of light like a coin. A reflection. And he moved closer. He moved the pinpoint beam a fraction of an inch at a time until the entire area had been exposed to him. The stench was very strong now.

Tracy went down on his haunches. He slid the beam up again to the face. Who was she? The features were bloated and mutilated beyond their normal configuration. Whoever she had been, he thought, she had died horribly.

But what was she doing lying here, decomposing in Macomber's house? That was a question he could not begin to answer. 'Thwaite,' he whispered, 'there's a corpse in the cellar. Female, Caucasian. In her late thirties, I'd say, though it's hard to tell. Five-seven or -eight. No idea who she is.'

Macomber and Khieu had been so careful until now. He looked above his head. What was going on up there? He went away from the stinking corpse, moving cautiously towards the wooden staircase. He ascended, weighting each step carefully in case the old wooden boards creaked.

He came to the top of the stairway, reached forward until his fingertips encountered the knob. he gripped it, turning it slowly. He pushed the door outward, breathing in the clearer air of the house itself. He smelled wood polish and tobacco.

The lights were off downstairs except for one lamp on a table off to his left in the entrance hall. In its partial glow, he began to take in the character of the place.

It was still. He could make out the sound of a clock ticking somewhere not far off. He stopped where he was, holding his breath. What was that just beneath the clock's ticking? It sounded to him like chanting. A Buddhist's prayer.

Then nothing. He began to move. He could hear voices above his head, muffled and indistinct. An abrupt shout and the thunderous sound of a pistol shot, caught by the interior walls, thrown back upon itself, echoing down the narrow corridors, expanding.

Tracy sprinted for the staircase to the upper storey.

When Macomber walked into his house, he had the impression that something was amiss. He stood silhouetted by the street lights in the open doorway, his keys in one hand and knew that an aspect of the house had been subtly altered.

The first thing he thought of was Tracy Richter but then the sixth sense that had served him so well in the jungles of Cambodia took full hold and he knew better.

He closed the door behind him, walked softly, slowly through his possession, searching for a break in the known and time-worn pattern. While most other people would have instinctively called out, Macomber did precisely the opposite. Whatever was amiss inside his house, he wanted to pinpoint its location, identify it and neutralize it. To do that he knew he had to maintain an absolute silence. If he was not there, it could not harm him. And it did wish him harm, of that he was quite certain.

One lamp was on in the hallway, otherwise the house seemed dark. He was about to canvass the ground floor when he passed by the staircase leading to the upper floors. He heard the Buddhist prayers, his thin lips repeating soundlessly the litany he had heard so often.

He put one hand on the shiny banister. Halfway up, he saw that the hall light was on, its illumination slinking down the steps, brightening them one by one as he ascended.

He did not like being in the light but there was nothing he could do about it. He moved more quickly now, making only a minimum of sound. He was glad that Khieu was home where he could keep an eye on him. It meant, too, that Tracy had not yet returned from Hong Kong. Macomber had no doubt that Khieu would carry out his instructions.

He was on the landing now, about to turn towards Khieu's room, when he noticed that the door to Eliott's old room was open. It was not supposed to be open. Khieu was not in there, he knew. The chanting was coming from the other end of the hallway.

Macomber walked swiftly down the hall, his shadow falling back behind him like a finger pointing towards the room where Khieu sat praying. He reached the doorsill, began to reach in for the knob when silence descended. The chanting had abruptly ceased.

716

In that instant of stillness, Macomber could sense movement in front of him. Someone or something was in Eliott's room. He squinted but the lack of light made it impossible to discern even shadows. But he felt a ripple of air, a current of movement and the short hairs at the back of his neck rose. He was moving as Eliott squeezed the trigger of the loaded pistol, his eyes tightly shut as if to block out the aftermath of the deed.

The pistol's report was deafening but Macomber had shut all sound out. He moved now purely by instinct. It was how he had survived in the jungle.

His left arm was fully extended, the fingers scraping the wallpaper for the light switch, while his right hand had snaked beneath his suit jacket for the knife he always carried with him. Burst of illumination and his target was sighted all within the space of a fraction of a second. Recognition would come later. The balance of the knife was slipping through his extended fingers, the muscles of his arm guiding its flight. A brief whistle and it dived on a line.

Eliott opened his eyes expecting to find Khieu's outstretched form sliding across the doorsill. Instead he saw his father, his face oddly blurred. He opened his mouth to shout but the blur had expanded to fill his vision. Pain and concussion rocked him simultaneously and he lost his balance, spinning around so that he faced the wall where a print of Robert DeNiro had hung until the day he had moved out. Now only a light rectangle remained, as if a void had sprung up and now he seemed to be pitching headfirst through that void. Vision faded and it seemed as if he was crying crimson tears.

He felt nothing. He was a feather, lighter than air. He floated off the floor. His heart stuttered and his thoughts, tangled and confused, slid down through the thoroughfares of his brain to mesh with that primaeval pulse. Soon, that, too, ceased to exist.

Macomber cried out wildly just as the knife left his fingertips. Recognition had followed response, stepping on its coattails and Macomber made a futile, off-balance lunge towards his target as if he thought, absurdly, that he could catch up with and deflect the flight of the thrown weapon.

He could do no such thing, of course, and the lunge merely brought him three steps closer to the result of his action.

'Eliott,' he whispered, confused. He saw the pistol slide from his son's limp fingers, gasped at the gout of blood the entering knife made in Eliott's face. There had been no time to think, to judge, to determine. Just a sense of danger, blossoming. Perhaps he had scented the light film of oil on the gun. That combined with the blind movement he had sensed had been more than enough. Somewhere in the pit of his mind, where the organism struggles to maintain life, he had *known* he was about to be shot at. He had acted in the only manner he was capable of. He had protected the organism, ceding volition and control to that instinctive part of him that did not care *who* was threatening it.

It did not matter that he might be dead now had he not ceded control. He only knew that he had killed his son. He was on his knees, cradling Eliott's limp form, flinging the knife away from him, across the room, hearing its metallic skitter and shuddering at the sound.

Eliott's eyes were open and he was still breathing but there was no recognition there. He saw but what it was he saw, Macomber could not say. He had seen that gaze many times in his past and he knew what it foretold. There was no hope, no time. Nothing was left of his son, his one and only beloved treasure who he had once thought to forge into his own image. Now he would have settled for life and life only. It was too large a request. And for the first time in his life, he felt totally powerless.

He was weeping and he did not know it, would not perhaps have believed it had anyone told him what he was doing. He grieved for Eliott but he thought it was an internal process only. Nothing could affect his exterior. Nothing.

He sensed movement behind him, paid no attention to it for a moment. Then he swivelled around.

'Father?' Khieu's voice was soft. He was clothed but barefoot. He moved one step into the room, two, using the edges of his soles. He made no sound. 'I heard the shot of a pistol.'

'It was Eliott,' Macomber said, still unbelieving. 'Eliott tried to shoot me!'

'Is that so?' Khieu's voice was like velvet. 'I'm so very sorry.'

Macomber's head came up and his eyes were bleak; all the colour draining out of them. 'How can it be?' he asked. 'All the careful planning, the meticulous failsafe mechanisms built into the *angka*. None of it's worth a damn now. How did it happen, Khieu?'

'*Karma*, Father.'

'But my son —' He took a halting step forward, anguish stitched like a scar across his face. 'Khieu, you don't understand! My son tried to shoot me ... I ... *I killed him*! My God, can't you comprehend that?'

Khieu gazed lovingly at Macomber, his soul drinking greedily in the outpouring of raw emotion. 'As I said, Father. *Karma*. You have extra-ordinary *karma*.'

'I shit on your *karma*!' Macomber cried. Blood returned to his face as anger took him. 'I shit on all your goddamned Buddhist ways! What the hell are they in the face of what's happening to all of us now?'

'Peace,' Khieu said calmly.

And Macomber looked up at him, his teary eyes focusing at last. He felt the beginnings of the emanations coming from his adopted son and, as he felt the rising force of them, a cold fist clutched painfully at his heart, constricting it. His face was a sudden mask and his mind whirled with a thousand questions. 'What ...' For a moment he could not go on, fear and anxiety and, above all, the power of the unknown congealing the words in his throat, choking him. 'What's going on?'

'The end of all things,' Khieu said as he began to move. The light from the hallway was a brilliant vast halo, as if a visible representation of his enormous inner strength. 'You look surprised, Father. I cannot think why. I am what you have made me. Only what you have made me.' His eyes were burning with a dark liquid fire. 'You have fashioned all that you see about you —' His outspread arms like black predator's wings. 'The death of your son ... He thought you were me, you see. I told him I wanted to die.'

'*What're you saying?*'

719

'Oh, the pain I see on your face, Father.' Moving still, constantly moving. 'It is real now. As real as the pain I carry inside me every day. You should die for what you've done to me ... and to Samnang. You betrayed him, Father, then flew in on steel wings to save me ... to pull me out, give me a new life. You killed Sam's murderers but first you killed him. Eliott told me all of it. He –'

'Lies!' Macomber screamed. 'I don't know where he got those ideas. But they're all lies. Eliott hates me. He –'

'He got those *lies* from these,' Khieu said, brandishing the papers and Macomber staggered back, silenced.

'Where?' he whispered. 'How?'

'But really Father, I don't wish death on you. Not you who gave me life when there was only destruction all around me. You who took me out of the hell of war and brought me ... *here*.' Khieu was slipping away, slipping ... 'No, it is infinitely better that you live with what you've done, so that every day, every night when you try to sleep and cannot you will remember the moment of your son's death, reliving it over and over. And when you do sleep there will be only the dreams of that moment, repeating over and over until you cannot bear it any longer and sanity begins to slip away. There is the end of your life, Father.'

Macomber was standing, wide-eyed, wondering how it was that Khieu was no longer under his control. When ... ? Then he remembered. He opened his mouth. 'It began when you went back. I know it did. You must tell me what happened to you in Cambodia. *I must know*!'

'Your time of demanding is gone, Father. Along with your power. It ebbs away from you with every breath you take, with every beat of your heart.' He disappeared into the light, his black silhouette melting away as if it had never existed.

'Wait!' Macomber cried, stricken. 'Don't go!' For he knew, just as he had the first time he had seen Khieu as a teenager – had seen what the boy was capable of – that nothing was possible without him, not the *angka*, not his dream of ultimate control, not the life he had chosen for himself.

And he had chosen this. *Karma*.

The cooling corpse of his son he cradled so gently in his powerful arms was proof enough that this was so. God curse *karma* for all time, he thought, rocking slowly. He longed to get up and go after Khieu but he could not. He could not yet bring himself to let go of his son, as if his presence now would be of some comfort to Eliott.

His mind was reeling. How in Christ's name, he asked himself, had Eliott discovered that diary? It seemed inconceivable to Macomber that this chain of events could have begun, let alone got this far out of hand.

He closed his eyes. He felt the pulse pounding like a triphammer in his chest as if it were riding wildly out of control. He gasped and struggled to maintain air in his lungs.

I must go after him he thought, trying to calm himself. Soon.

Tracy was almost at the top of the stairs when he had the odd sensation of sinking down even though he was still ascending.

He braced himself but even so the shoulder that crashed into him rocked him back against the interior wall. He had an impression of a handsome face filled to the brim with black eyes that raked his face. There were fires alive in those eyes, bright sparks of flame, chips of luminescent colour which for some reason unearthed in Tracy the image of a line of frothy green palms blackened and defoliated by napalm's liquid fire.

The scene was so vivid, so intense in its recreation that Tracy snorted unconsciously in an attempt to rid his nostrils of the remembered reek.

His hands came up, slid off a leading shoulder. The shadow twisted, tried to slide by him along the openwork wooden banister. Tracy shifted his position on the stairs subtly, blocking the other's progress.

The illumination was very bad. There was movement directly in front of him but because of the bad light he could not tell what it was until it was almost too late. The bright spark of reflective metal warned him and he bent his knees, sinking down, grounding himself, forcing the steps beneath his feet to add to the strength in his thighs.

He saw now that the other was gripping a stubby black cylinder in his right hand and, as he flicked it with his wrist, gleaming steel telescoped outward to a length of two feet. Tracy had heard about this weapon but had never actually seen it. It was Japanese, a favourite of the Yakuza, the clannish underworld of modern Japan.

He raised his left arm, the edge of his hand towards the telescoped cylinder. His right hand was cocked, the first two fisted knuckles of that hand ready.

The cylinder came whistling down and Tracy knew that this was the weapon that had been used on Moira.

He took the blow just below his left wrist, his body prepared for it but wincing with the pain all the same. As quickly as the blow came, the cylinder was raised again and he knew he could not survive such an attack for long. No one could.

His right fist flashed out, slamming into the other's chest just above the heart. The almond eyes opened wide as the lips split, pulling back from the white teeth in a grimace of pain. But again the steel stick began its whistling journey downward.

This time, Tracy had more time. He twisted to his right, meeting the attack sideways, the blow slipping by him with just enough margin so that he could reach out with his left arm, wrap his fingers around the shaft of the metal cylinder. He tensed his muscles and the other reacted, knowing he was about to try to wrench the weapon away.

Instead, Tracy attacked with his right fist, his hardened knuckles slamming again into the same spot just above Khieu's heart, the blow delivered from above, the impact all the greater.

Khieu grunted and staggered, off-balance. Tracy twisted his left wrist, bringing the weapon away from the other's grip. It hung from his wrist by a leather thong and Tracy jabbed once again with his right fist, staggering Khieu again, ripping the thong from his wrist.

Now they were both unarmed and Khieu recovered, throwing a rapid series of sword strikes of such speed and intensity that Tracy's attention was fully taken up with the defence.

That was why he did not feel the other's grip on his right elbow until it was too late. The pressure took him by surprise and he was rolled back, off his feet, his right shoulder slamming painfully against the banister.

Khieu followed it up, jamming a lifted knee into Tracy's abdomen, taking his breath away so that all he could do was grip the other by the shoulders and hang on.

They grappled together, two vicious sword-strikes landing across Tracy's chest, vibrating the bone, burning the nerves so that for a moment he felt paralysed, unable to move his arms.

Khieu shrugged Tracy's limp fingers from him, began to move away. Tracy kicked out with his left foot, jamming the arch into the other's ankle, cracking the outside of the protruding bone against the edge of the step above. Khieu's own forward momentum twisted the foot.

It was not enough and Khieu righted himself, crashing the toe of his shoe into the side of Tracy's face, leaning hard into it until Tracy, feeling returning at last to his arms, thrust his balled fist up into the other's crotch.

Khieu doubled over and Tracy regained his feet, moving up the stairs in a semi-crouch, one hand leading. Khieu battered that aside, used both his elbows in the Two Flowers to disengage and regain the initiative. Tracy used a *Hyō*, bringing the elbows together, beginning a series of percussive blows that won him time and space advantage but allowed Khieu to use a *ketaguri*, a leg sweep, to twist Tracy off-balance, then a *yori* Tracy was unfamiliar with.

This style of combat was allied to Sumo and was supremely difficult to master. Tracy had seen some of it when he was in Tokyo, knew a few of the basic manoeuvres. The *yori* was a group of clinches designed originally to displace the combatant's foe from the Sumo circle. but, over the years, others had redesigned it to incapacitate. Its major drawback was that it required enormous strength as well as a draining expenditure of energy. Most instructors at the Mines were of a mind to ignore it for just those reasons.

But this close to Khieu, Tracy again gazed into those strange dark eyes and saw there the edge of madness. That more than anything else broke out the sweat across his hairline. Madness brought its own kind of strength, stamina and way of thinking.

Khieu's *yori* tightened and Tracy felt the pain increasing inside him. The other was slowly squeezing the breath out of him and with every tightening cinch of his grip, less air was allowed into Tracy's lungs.

His muscles strained and heaved in his effort to get free but Khieu's grip was inexorable. Tracy began to pant and black spots danced at the periphery of his vision.

He felt Khieu's enormous power and he wondered at the extent one human being could possess. Dimly he was aware of arhythmic noises from below them. He could not tell what they were but Khieu's attention was diverted for an instant.

Tracy seized that moment, relaxing within the other's grasp to gain the millimetre of room he required. He dropped down, the sudden movement allowing one arm to slip below the cincture of Khieu's *yori*, using the other's reflexive tightening as a response to come away with one arm free, driving it up in a shallow arc, the fingers flat and extended like a sword, using the percussive edge in a throat-strike that sent the other reeling back.

Tracy was aware now of the loudening of the noises from below, the increase in their rapidity making him aware that Thwaite and his team were at the front door, about to break in. And he moved upward to the attack, wanting to end this now because his stamina was waning.

But Khieu had also heard the sounds, had analysed them and as Tracy lunged for him, he flicked out the toe of his shoe at the very last instant, the arc shortened but powerful as it caught Tracy on the point of the chin.

Tracy's teeth snapped shut with a resounding vibration and he was flung backward down a third of the staircase. During that time, he lost a semblance of vision as his eyes closed reflexively.

He staggered, grabbing the top of the banister so that he would not continue his precipitous backward plunge and, righting himself, saw that Khieu was gone. He could not tell whether the Cambodian had gone up or down.

Thwaite and his men would be into the ground floor any moment so he chose to climb upward.

The light was on in the room and Tracy had no difficulty making out the image of Macomber cradling a younger man. Tracy stopped on the threshold as Macomber's head came up, the ice blue eyes attempting to focus, squinting into the light.

'Who's there?' His voice was hoarse and cracked as if he had spent hours screaming into a fierce wind. 'Khieu, is that you? Bastard! You killed my son! *Bastard!*'

'It's Tracy Richter. Khieu's gone. Did he come back up here?'

For a moment, Macomber said nothing. He stared at Tracy and slowly he allowed his son to slide from his arms. He got off his haunches, stood tall.

'Richter?' He took a faltering step forward. 'What the *hell* are you doing here? This is *my* house! How dare you?'

'The police are downstairs,' Tracy said. 'There's a mutilated corpse in your cellar . . . now I see there's another body. That's reason enough.'

'Bastard!' Macomber bit down hard on the word. 'I sent Khieu to kill you. You penetrated the *angka*?'

'The what?'

'The organization. *My* organization.'

Now Tracy understood. 'The one you built from "Sultan".'

'What d'you know about "Sultan", you sonuvabitch? You weren't even around Ban Me Thuot then. You'd disappeared.'

' "Sultan" was my mission, Macomber.'

The tall man staggered as if he had been delivered a lethal blow. 'What are you saying?' His eyes were open wide, his mouth working uncontrollably. 'What are you *saying*?'

'I was your control –'

'Liar!'

'– on "Sultan".'

'You're a goddamned liar, Richter!' Macomber's face was red, a pulse worked wildly on his forehead. 'You were gone by then. God only knows where. But you'd had a belly-ful of the slaughter. I knew that. *Everyone* knew that!'

'Because that's what everyone was meant to believe,' Tracy

said softly. 'I joined the foundation, where you couldn't. "Sultan" was my brainchild. I was the one you crossed.'

The tall man was beside himself. Time seemed to have slipped away, the intervening years as nothing. 'First you kill Tisah and now you tell me ... this.' He was moving again, this time not towards Tracy but off to his left. 'You really *are* a sonuvabitch! I don't know why Khieu didn't kill you but I don't care anymore.' Edging further to his left, into the corner of the room closest to the doorway. 'I'm glad you're still alive, Richter.' Two more steps, three. 'And d'you know why?'

Tracy leapt at Macomber as he snaked down to pick up the thrown knife. He hit the other just as his hand circled the weapon's handle. Macomber was quick. Tracy had forgotten just how quick. The blade turned bright silver as Macomber brought it up through the air, slashing at Tracy's face. He felt a hot swipe but no pain, then wetness crawling across his cheek. Drops of blood flew from the cut as he jerked his head away, bringing his right arm up in a sweep against the inside of Macomber's left wrist, feeling the pressure the other brought to bear.

Tracy chopped inward, felt the block, the balance of momentum changing and he slipped backward, going down on one knee as Macomber hammered him with a kite and then a savage *kansetsu-waza*, meant to dislocate Tracy's shoulder.

Tracy countered with what he knew best, the percussive *ate-waza*, beating a tremendously debilitating tattoo against Macomber's bicep, sapping it of energy.

Macomber dropped that attack immediately, coming at Tracy again with the knife. The shining blade was slightly curved, double-edged, long enough to pierce the heart if properly driven.

Macomber crouched low, circling, feinting once, then twice more before beginning his real attack, thrusting directly inward towards Tracy's exposed abdomen.

There was no time in these close quarter for Tracy to get out of the way or even twist his torso sufficiently to avoid a deep and serious slash so he steeled his mind, ignoring the incoming blade entirely, concentrating on what he had to do. He chose the Third Way to Parry, stepping up *into* the thrust, lifting his left arm in a blur, the fingers straight as a shaft directly on a line with Macomber's eyes.

The tall man reacted immediately, pulling back on his own low thrust, pushing the blade upward instead to counter Tracy's dangerous strike.

Now Tracy used the Chinese Monkey's Body, bringing his arms in so as not to extend them, getting in quickly with his entire body so that he was already *inside* Macomber's next thrust before it could begin.

And now the weapon had been negated, Tracy and Macomber body to body, fighting instinctively, the blows, counters and surges coming with lightning swift speed until the two of them were a blur, a single transitory object within the vault of the room, as if they had ceased to exist within the boundaries of time, fighting within their own tiny enclosed world where only they knew the strictures and where anyone else intruding would be immediately felled.

Tracy's muscles burned with the constant effort and he shook his head to clear his eyes from the stinging of his rolling sweat. Pain blossomed again inside his head, a remnant of Honk Kong and the breath sawed in and out of his lungs like fire.

Explosions burst behind his eyes as he sought to gain a lethal hold. He had entered into this with the idea of bringing Macomber back downstairs for Thwaite. Now he understood what Macomber had known all along. Only one of them could leave this room. It was tomb and birthplace, at once the beginning and the end of the what/had begun fourteen years ago.

He sought an *osae-waza*, one of the immobilization holds, for respite, but Macomber would not allow it, bringing three tremendous kites down on his right shoulder so that the area went completely numb and his arm dropped its hold.

Macomber seized the moment, going immediately for a *shime-waza*, his powerful arm snaking up and around as his right knee spun Tracy completely around, the forearm jammed into Tracy's windpipe. Macomber brought his hands together, the knife's hilt between them, clamped his fingers.

This *shime-waza* was one of the major locks, the ones Jinsoku had taught him the last because they were the most difficult and the most unbreakable.

Macomber's muscles bulged and he grunted like an animal as he jammed his knee again into the small of Tracy's back, arching it even more so that his leverage was increased. It was the final phase of the *shime-waza* and Tracy knew that unless he could break it within the next few fractions of a second he never would be able to summon the strength or the leverage.

It was difficult to think and he was becoming pale through loss of blood to his head. He could no longer feel his feet and that was dangerous.

He used the *Senjō* — as Jinsoku had translated it from the Japanese, the seat of war. *This is not a manoeuvre you use indiscriminately*, the old man had warned. *I am teaching it to you because I want you to survive. You can do that with what I've already given you, I've no doubt. But there may come a time when you have no choice, when death stares you in the face. You'll know it and you'll have the* Senjō.

He needed the floor and the wall. He had both. He twisted, to the left while bringing his left hip down, bending the knee severely so that Macomber was forced to stretch out his spine, lift his heels off the floor if he was to maintain the *shime-waza*.

Tracy pushed upward from the floor, hoping the pressure would be sufficient but not actually knowing until the shift of Macomber's body against his could be felt. Now the wall came into play and he used it as a battering ram of power proportionate with the speed with which Macomber's hip was smashed into it.

The angle had to be just right. Tracy heard the answering crack as the pelvis split under the force of the momentum and the angle the *Senjō* had produced.

Macomber's lower body began to collapse but still he maintained his stranglehold on Tracy's throat, a deathgrip he seemed incapable of relinquishing. He gasped and sobbed with the pain, tears streaming across his face, his hair wet and plastered.

Tracy lifted his right foot, jammed it down on Macomber's left instep with all his might, heaving upward with his torso, twisting to the right simultaneously so that the break in the hip bone widened, the cracked bone grinding together at the lower end of the break as the upper part drew away.

The agony was too much for Macomber. He felt as if all strength was flowing out of his arms, his chest. Pain pooled in his hips, overbalancing him with unnatural weight.

Tracy's knee blurred upward, striking the lower part of Macomber's abdomen just above the cracked bone. It was the last part of the *Senjō* and the most devastating because it sent the internal organs through an area filled with blood and bone splinters. The result of the manoeuvre was that the opponent drowned in his own blood.

Tracy stood gasping, his lungs heaving to regain lost oxygen as Macomber's long form slid like a serpent down Tracy's back, crumpling at his feet. The eyes were open, the head turned upward towards the room's ceiling. There was only an expression of determination there: no fear, no sorrow, not even regret.

Tracy heard the pounding of heavy shoes on the stairs, voices raised in shouts, orders called but he was too exhausted to move or look. He heard his name being called. Thwaite's voice. Well, they would find him soon enough, he thought. For now, he closed his eyes, leaned against the wall. He heard the blood rushing through his ears like the wind.

When Tracy walked out of the building onto Gramercy Park South, the first person he saw was Lauren. She was standing across the street, flanked by a pair of helmeted policemen. Her body was taut with tension and he could see how pale and drawn her face looked in the street lights.

Behind her a crowd had been forming, cordoned off by the cops and, just to her left, the ranks of the news media began to surge towards him. He was too tired to wonder how they had got wind of the story so early.

Lances of light flashed across the pavement as the helmeted police moved to stem the tide of reporters. There were three or four mobile trucks from the networks parked along one of the side streets, long thick cables snaking leading to hand-held cameras.

They saw him coming and started for him but Thwaite, emerging from the open doorway to the house just as the ME's people arrived, waved at his men who closed off the open space between Tracy and the media.

Lauren saw him and broke free of her guard, running across the street towards him. He felt her come against him, grateful for her warmth, her supple arms around him. Pain seemed to melt away, trivialized beneath her touch.

'Thank God,' she whispered. 'Oh thank God.' Her fingertips came up, touched gingerly the cut on his cheek. Her light eyes sought his face, straining for a hint of what had occurred. 'Was it bad in there?'

He nodded. 'Yes.' He gripped her, needing now to feel the press of her body against his, to know for certain that she was physically there, that he was not still back inside the bowels of that house, back inside the war's black heart. 'It was very bad.'

'Come on,' she said softly. He could barely hear her. There were sirens now and the clamour of the press. They passed Thwaite, going the other way as she took him across the street.

They sat on an outcropping just below the black iron fence to the park. Beyond were the black trees, their laden tops swaying slightly in the night breeze. They were thick, blotting out the buildings beyond, the press of people.

He sat with his elbows on his knees, his fingers pushed through his hair. He needed to reassure himself that he was all there, that he had not left a piece of himself back in that nightmare of a house. It was important that he feel whole again.

'Macomber's dead,' he said finally, his voice like the rustle of the treetops above their head. Lauren held him, one arm across his shoulders. Her head was ducked down on its long neck, close to his own. 'I had to kill. There was no other way out.'

Lauren said nothing. She was crying silent tears, feeling the ebb and flow of his emotions billowing like shock waves through her. At last she said, 'What about Khieu?'

'He's gone,' Tracy said hoarsely. 'Disappeared.'

They became aware of Ivory White kneeling in front of them. 'Sorry to break this up,' he said and, swinging her head around, Lauren saw in his eyes that he meant it. 'But the boss wants you.' He threw a glance over their shoulders. 'The situation with the press's starting to get out of hand; he wants the area secured. That means the two of you.'

Lauren nodded. 'Give us a minute, will you?'

White stood up and turned his back on them. They heard him barking orders to a pair of uniforms.

Lauren put her lips against Tracy's ear. 'Are you all right?'

'Yes,' he said softly. He held onto her.

'We've got to get out of here,' she said gently. 'It's time to go.' He said nothing and she looked at him. 'Tracy?'

His head came up and she saw that his eyes were clear. He seemed very calm. 'All right,' he said. And they stood up together. White sensed their movement, herded them off towards Thwaite's unmarked car.

Ahead and further to their left they could see Thwaite. He was the focal point of a bristling knew of microphones thrust out towards him by eager fists. Cameras rolled their video tape, jockeying for a better angle on his face while keeping Macomber's building in the background.

'. . . in an hour,' they heard him say. 'That's the best I can do for you.'

'But what's Mr Richter's involvement?' The question floated on the air, pushed out from the clump of newspeople.

'That'll all be explained at the news conference,' Thwaite said. 'If you'll just be patient –'

'Oh, come on, Sergeant,' another on-air reporter said. 'You've got to give us *something* new. We've already got bulletins interrupting prime time shows.'

'All I can say for the time being is that Mr Richter has been on assignment for the NYPD on a delicate and complex undercover operation. Otherwise, I have no comment.'

'Give us a break. That's a spit in the bucket. You can give us more than that.'

'My heart bleeds for you guys. I know, you're just doing your job. So am I. I've been kind enough to schedule the press conference so you can all meet your eleven o'clock airtime deadlines. I'm a very considerate man. Don't try my patience.'

He backed away from them to a chorus of 'But ...,' 'Now wait a minute –,' 'Can't you tell us –,' 'What about – ?'

'Let's go,' he said to White as he came up to the three of them. He began to hustle them across the macadam to where his car waited. Behind them, the crowd was surging, wanting answers to its eternal questions.

They took off around the piled-up ambulances, police riot trucks and the ME's vehicles. Uniforms were along the intersections of Third Avenue, keeping the traffic moving.

'I thought this was going to be a small operation,' Tracy said.

Thwaite glanced at him in the rear-view mirror, grinned. 'If I let you in on everything, I'd have no image left.' Their siren cleared a path for them downtown. Thwaite's expression changed. 'That was a helluva mess in there. You figured out yet what happened?'

Tracy put his head back against the seat, stared up at the top of the car. Streaks of light played there like shooting stars as they sped past street and traffic lights.

'The ME will have to tell us who the woman was in the basement,' he said. 'But upstairs I can tell you now. The young man was Macomber's son. Somehow Khieu got the son to take a shot at his father. Macomber reacted instinctively – it would have to be that; I know his training – and killed the kid.'

Thwaite expelled a long-held breath in a whoosh of emotion. 'Christ, what the hell did Khieu do *that* for? I mean, how could he?'

'Revenge is the only thing I can think of,' Tracy said.

'I can't understand that.'

'I wouldn't expect you to. There's no analogue in Western thinking but believe me it's what happened. Honour's more important than life to someone like Khieu.' Or Kim, he thought.

'Tell me again about this guy Khieu,' Thwaite said. They were approaching Canal Street and the heart of Chinatown. It seemed apt, somehow. Tracy thought briefly again of the Tanka family and the soft lapping of the water as their junk slid through the bay towards the jewelled shore.

Tracy described the encounter on the staircase, this time

filling in all the details he had omitted when he had first spoken to Thwaite about it inside the house. His head came down and he saw Thwaite's eyes locked on his in the mirror.

'I'm not sure I can believe all this.'

'You've got no choice,' Tracy said.

'It's just,' Thwaite told him, 'that I've got this press conference called for a little over an hour from now. Captain Flaherty – he's my boss – is going to be there, along with the commissioner and the Mayor. I want to have all the facts straight before I put my head in the noose.'

'The important thing now is,' Lauren said, trying to break their deadlock, 'where Khieu is, not what he's done.'

There was a small silence. Ivory White, sitting next to Thwaite on the front seat, fidgeted slightly, shifting from one buttock to the other. Thwaite grunted. 'She's right. But we've got no worries there. We'll find him. This thing's come to an end. I'm not worried about Khieu.'

'Well, you should be,' Tracy said. 'Macomber was just one half of it. Khieu's got all of the *angka*'s knowledge inside his head. He can spring the last stage of Macomber's plan just as if nothing had come apart.'

Thwaite snorted. 'So what? You yourself said he was out after Macomber at the end. That means he hated him; he's not gonna go on with anything.'

'That's where you're wrong.' Tracy sat forward, gripping the top of the front seat. They came to a halt outside One Police Plaza. The city seemed dark around them. 'What he felt about Macomber was personal – very personal. Activating the next stage is business. The two are mutually exclusive.'

Thwaite killed the ignition, swivelled around in his seat to face the back. 'What the hell are you talking about? You hate someone but you follow his orders anyway? Why, for Christ's sake? It's crazy.'

'Only if you look at it a certain way.' Tracy hunched forward. 'Look, Khieu's a Cambodian. That means at some time in his early life, he was a devout Buddhist. I think he still is.'

Thwaite looked at him blankly. 'So?'

Tracy tried not to become impatient. Ever since he had left

Macomber's house he had been thinking about his encounter with Khieu. He had stared into those eyes like pits, had felt the other's strength, probed for his weaknesses. He had been exposed to his spirit: that which made him individual, unique, the person that he was. You could not hide such an intimate thing during combat; your spirit was what guided you, formed all your strategies. Tracy felt he knew Khieu now. It had not taken long; the initial contact had been searing in its intensity.

'So,' Tracy said now, his mind reacing, '*the* prime tenet of Buddhism is an almost fanatic pacifism. A Buddhist priest will not garden himself for the vegetable foods he requires in order to survive for fear he will kill an insect or a worm. He depends upon the gifts of his parishioners in order to eat.'

Thwaite's face was taut. 'Are you saying that this man ... this *monster* who's killed three people we know of ... possibly four ... are you saying he's a *pacifist*?' His tone was unbelieving.

'That's exactly what I'm saying.'

'Then you're out of your mind. One negates the other.'

'No.' Tracy shook his head. 'You're thinking like a Westerner again. In the Eastern mind, so well compartmentalized since birth, the two can co-exist. One does not affect the other. You kill – you learn death from the Khmer Rouge. It becomes political imperative to murder ... to free your country from tyranny. That's what you're told; what you come to believe.

'But you believe in the power of the Amida Buddha because that came first and without it there is no structure to life. You believe in what you *have to do*. You believe in Buddha.'

'That's all well and good for Cambodia,' Thwaite countered. 'But what about here. He's been killing people *here*. That's not the same thing at all.'

'It is,' Tracy said, 'if you're given sufficiently compelling reasons for having to continue the killing.'

Thwaite was silent for a moment. He stared hard at Tracy. 'And Macomber was able to do that.'

'With people – *especially* with people – if you push the right button, you get the desired response. If you find a reason that runs deep enough ...'

Thwaite ran a hand across his face. 'Now just what the hell'm I going to tell them? We've got nowhere to go.'

'Yes we have.'

Lauren's head jerked at the sound of his voice. She knew the tone. In the semi-darkness of the car she could see Tracy's eyes burning like lamps. Her stomach knotted, rolling over and the muscles along the insides of her thighs began to tremble.

'No.' Her voice was a thin reedy whisper. 'No, please.'

Tracy put a hand over hers, squeezed it hard. Lauren opened her mouth but the words would not come. What good would they do anyway? He was set on his course. She shut her eyes tightly to hold back the tears. Destruction. That was what she saw stretching out before her. Death and destruction.

'I can't,' she said, her voice coming to her and breaking. Her head whipped back and forth. 'Please don't ask me to. I can't sit by and ...' Her voice trailed off. Thwaite and White were staring at her. They did not understand; they did not care. What did it matter to them if Tracy died? They did not love him.

She turned blindly away from him, her hand fumbling for the door handle. She jerked on it twice, leaning her shoulder in, before it sprang open.

'Lauren – !' Tracy called.

'No!' she cried. 'It's too much!' And ran for a cruising cab, waving her arms.

There was silence in the car. White turned away, stared at the bleak futurist façade of the police building.

'Want to go after her?' Thwaite said after a time.

'No.' Tracy sat back in the seat, closing his eyes. 'I don't know what I could say to her. She knows me too well.'

'... and the mutilated body of the woman found in the basement of the Macomber house has been identified as Joy Trower Macomber, wife of the late Mr Macomber and younger sister of Senator Vance Trower, Democrat, of Texas. Next of kin have been notified.'

Atherton Gottschalk listened to the authoritative voice of Detective Sergeant Douglas Thwaite with mounting horror. It was all coming out, just like that. Joy dead; Macomber dead, too. How soon before they'd find Kathleen's corpse?

He walked away from the television set, padding across the pile carpet of his New York hotel suite. He had been discharged from the hospital the day before but had decided to stay on in New York. The media attention here was still too intense to walk away from.

Outside the large windows he could see the sparkle and twinkle of Manhattan's West Side lights, across the darkened expanse of Central Park. His wife was in the bathroom, hopefully still soaking in the hot bath.

Gottschalk put one hand up against the glass. He thought about having a drink but he'd already drunk far too much this evening, first at the Republican fund-raising dinner at the Waldorf, then at the reception held for him by the Mayor at the Metropolitan Museum of Art. He would have been there now but he was following his doctor's advice in being prudent about the shock to his body from the bullet's impact. Besides, it was a great publicity ploy, keeping what had happened to him in the media's eye.

He began to shake now, the euphoria he had experienced earlier in the evening totally evaporated. He could not face the thought of his wife knowing what he had done. How would he ever be able to explain it to her?

Gottschalk stared sightlessly at the view he was paying so dearly for. What good was it now? He knew it was only a matter of time before the police were led back to him. He knew quite well how these investigations worked. The police would not have been at Macomber's house at all had they not already known.

The *angka* was dead and him with it. Macomber's death was nothing; that alone could not save him. There were too many links and in an investigation of this magnitude the police would have to be totally incompetent not to discover his own involvement. He knew first hand just how smart cops could be.

He turned from the window, went across the room, pulling the sash of his silk bathrobe tighter around his flat stomach.

He stopped in front of the closed bathroom door, knocked discreetly.

He heard his wife's muffled voice. It sounded sweet. He turned the knob, pushed the door inward. The bathroom was warm and steamy.

Roberta lay with her hair up. Only her head and knees were out of the water.

'Hello, dear,' he said. 'I just came in to say that.' He stood looking at her, wondering. She cocked her head and smiled.

'That's nice, darling.' Her hands appeared through the lens of the soapy water, stirring. 'I'll be out in a couple of minutes.'

'Don't hurry,' Gottschalk said. 'There's plenty of time.'

He went out of the close, stifling room, shutting the door firmly behind him. He went across to the television set. The news conference had broken at last. The announcers were back in the studio, talking about national matters. His name was mentioned twice. He reached out a hand, switched off the set.

Then he went over to the window and opened it. It slid up easily. He thought, fleetingly, floatingly, that it was a good thing he had booked into one of the older, more elegant hotels that still had windows that opened.

It was a long way down but he did not think about that. He felt the breeze on the soft skin of his neck, saw the blaze of lights far out as if at sea, the massed treetops of the park, black and serene.

That was all he thought about as he stepped up on the sill and, with another long stride, crossed over it. And, of course, Kathleen, her body oiled and sleek, shining in the reflected light of the city.

His eyes were open all the way down.

The house on Gramercy Park South was at last dark. The forensic teams had packed up their massive equipment and had gone. So, too, the crew from the ME's office. The police photographer and Thwaite's detective unit had all vacated the premises.

Outside, below the link chain that had been draped across the front staircase, the padlocked front door and the official police investigation notice posted on the shining mahogany doors, a pair of young patrolmen stood and talked to each other in-between shooing the curious on their way.

Above their heads, along the rooftops adjacent to the building, a shadow moved. It was absolutely silent and panther swift. No one noticed as it jumped to the Macomber building rooftop. A moment later it had melted away like a puddle of water soaked into parched earth.

Inside, Khieu slipped down from the attic, his senses questing. When he was certain that he was alone, he came down onto the second storey and softly stole into Eliott's bedroom.

He picked out the precise spot where Eliott had fallen and knelt there, praying as if he were before the image of the Amida Buddha. His mind was whirling even as it sought a quiet peace. He had avenged the death of one brother by betraying another.

He knew it could not be otherwise. The imperative of Sam's spiritual peace had dictated his actions. But the death of Eliott confused and saddened him in a manner he could not fathom. He put his arms around himself, hugging at the warmth.

He felt cold; lost, directionless, a homeless orphan until he remembered that he had not yet carried out Macomber's last order. He had meant to on the stairs for he had no doubts about who he had encountered. But the imminent arrival of those outside had distracted him, turned him away from the completion of his task.

He knew that he could not count himself a true and faithful son to his father unless he strove to carry out his dictates. That was what made him whole, made him what he was, after all. What would he be without Macomber and the *angka*?

He knew he should move, get out of there. But he knew that once he did so he would never return. It was his home; it meant much more to him than the villa of his family in Phnom Penh; it meant more than the rough thatched encampments in the jungles in and around Battambang. *Home*. It hung in his mind for an instant like a perfect jewel, serene in its clarity.

Then the image of Eliott's limp corpse slid upward into the centre of his thoughts and for a long time he could do nothing but weep uncontrollably.

*

Tracy took the Audi 4000 through the Lincoln Tunnel and accelerated into the far left lane. He was remembering Thwaite's face when he had told him.

'The only way you're ever going to get Khieu,' he had said, 'is through me. Macomber told me he'd given Khieu orders to terminate me. He failed on the staircase ... But he'll be drawn back to me. I have no doubts about that.

'Macomber gave him his only structure, save for his religion. And Buddhism alone can't keep him alive. He's got to come after me.'

Thwaite considered this for a moment. 'That's why she left,' he said almost to himself. He was talking about Lauren.

'Yes,' Tracy said. 'That's why.'

Thwaite had turned his head full into the harsh illumination thrusting through the car's rear window as the headlights of an oncoming car washed over them.

'You know,' he said as gently as he could. 'I won't let you do it.'

Tracy ignored him. His eyes were still closed. His mind was racing; his thoughts had gone far beyond this point.

Thwaite leaned over the back seat, tapped Tracy on the knee. 'Listen, pal, for what you did back there I could throw you in a holding cell overnight. I could call it anything I wanted to: protection of material witness; investigation of suspected manslaughter. I'll do it too to get you out of my hair. You've done your part, now let me do mine.'

Tracy had anticipated this and now he told Thwaite what he had held back before. 'You have no choice,' Tracy said, 'because Khieu's a madman.' That was the crimson spark he had seen in the Cambodian's eyes; the element that had shivered him.

'How d'you mean that?' Thwaite snapped. 'Mad in that he's a killer?'

'I mean,' Tracy said, opening his eyes at last, levelling a look at Thwaite, 'he's quite insane. I saw it in his face when we fought on the stairs.'

'You're no shrink, don't give me that.'

Tracy sat abruptly forward, the intense look on his face, startling Thwaite. 'What I know,' he said in a low voice, 'is that

739

I'm the only one who can possibly handle him. For Christ's sake, Thwaite, the man's a walking killing machine! How much more proof do you need? Do you really think you'll be able to find him?' His face was very close to Thwaite's now. 'He's spent his whole life learning how to kill and not be caught. You're not that clever.'

'And I suppose that means you are.'

'Goddamn it, this isn't a contest of egos! We know he's after me –'

'But in the city, we could never put enough men on you. I can't allow it; the danger to you's too great, not to mention any innocent bystanders.'

Tracy nodded. 'Now you're getting the point.' He sat back again in the seat. 'That's why I'm going out to the house in Bucks County. That's my turf; I can control it.' He waited a beat. 'It's also isolated enough so that you and your staff won't have a problem.'

He watched Thwaite in the unnatural light, trying to read the thoughts that lay behind those cold eyes. At length, the detective stirred, turned his head towards White. 'Ivory,' he said, not taking his eyes from Tracy, 'call dispatch. Get the number for the Pennsylvania State Police and the Chief up there in the Bucks County area. Then patch me through. I want to talk to him. I've got a helluva lot of background to fill him in on and not a lotta time to do it in.'

Tracy spun off the Turnpike at Exit 10, paid his toll. It was not Thwaite he was thinking of, however. There were a lot of people now concerned with the far end of Macomber scheme. But Tracy had phoned the Director and, under cover, he had sent a team of computer experts up to New York to attack the Metronics system. These boys knew their way around electronic chips and whatever else went into making up a computer circuit. They'd find it all, eventually.

Tracy recalled what the Director had said about Metronics without Macomber to head it. That it would just disintegrate. He hoped that was not true.

But it was Kim who concerned him now. Tracy had tried repeatedly during the night to get in touch with him, both at his Washington apartment and at the New York City number Kim had given him.

Tracy did not like the fact that Kim had dropped out of sight. Then, just before dawn, the Director had called to tell him that three KGB agents – one of them a VIP – had turned up very dead in a plush hotel in Dallas.

'It's Kim all right,' the Director had said tightly. 'I don't know what's going down but I want you to be very careful. If you need to reach me, I'll be in and out of meetings with State during the next seventy-two hours. Of course we have to try and unruffle Soviet feathers.'

Tracy was in Bucks County. He turned left onto River Road, the brief section of four lanes reduced to two almost immediately. The cicadas were singing their song of summer, shivering the air with molten sound. It made him think of Lauren and their day on the beach, beautiful and stormy.

He saw her eyes and thought of the sea far out where there was no land.

The house came up on his right and he turned off the pitted road. Birds sang and a light breeze brought to him brief whiffs of pine, wild thyme and peppermint. Across the way the cornfield lay barren and empty, stripped of its late summer harvest. The sunlight's warmth was already waning. Winter would soon be here. Bright fires, melting marshmallows on bent blackened sticks. He did not want to spend it without her.

He went up the steps, unlocked the front door. It was six minutes past four.

He went into the kitchen, opened the refrigerator, found only a half-filled jar of mayonnaise, a jar of black apple butter and a tin of sardines whose top had been partially rolled back.

But he found an unopened jar of peanut butter and went at it with gusto. While he ate, he wandered into the living room. He was drawn to the wooden Buddha on the mantelpiece above the tiled fireplace.

His gaze slid downward, past the television set set into the fireplace. There was something odd about the tiles which surrounded the fireplace.

He went down on his haunches to examine more closely what

he saw there. He put his hand out, one finger pressing two points near each other on the surface of the tiles. They were parallel. Dark brown.

With the nail of his forefinger, he carefully scratched away a tiny section of one spot. He brought his finger up, put the tip of his finger into his mouth, tasting it, knowing what the substance was. Dried blood.

He got up, almost as if he were in a trance, and stood in front of the Buddha. Then, carefully, he knelt down so that the points of his knees touched the Mercer tiles.

He knelt as a penitent before his god would kneel, his legs together. The points of his knees covered the two blood spots perfectly.

He rose, thinking, that was what happened. After he beat Moira to death, he saw the figure, came over here and knelt before it, praying. The thought made him shiver involuntarily.

It was almost dark. He turned away from the carved statue, took the jar of peanut butter back into the kitchen. He was no longer hungry.

He went back into the living room and sat down in his favourite chair. He put his head back. Clouds had obscured the lowering sun, the end of the day had turned dull, light like lead. November light. He closed his eyes, listening to the tiny sounds of the house all around him, acclimatizing himself again to the noises of life here so that he could instantly detect any deviation no matter how minute. He wanted to know the moment Khieu slipped in.

He must have dozed off. He had not meant to. He opened his eyes to the dark. Night had come. He sat very still in the chair. His fingers gripped the armrests with unnatural strength.

Something had changed within the house. There had been an alteration – he could not say what yet. A whippoorwill called outside, a branch brushed against the side of the house. These sounds he knew well, they did not disturb him.

A creak of a board overhead, the soft rattle of the casement window in back he had been meaning to repair for a year and a half. These sounds, too, did not disturb him.

It was what he did not hear. The crickets had ceased to sing outside; the house seemed to be holding its breath. He was quite certain he was not alone. He got up, crossed silently to stand in front of the fireplace. The Buddha was at his back.

Shadows filled the room as if poured there from another dimension. Shapes appeared distorted, humped and alien. Stripes of watery light lay obliquely along the bare polished floorboards between the rugs. Beyond them, the back part of the living room was impenetrably black. He heard nothing.

Shadows melted and reformed. Blackness flowed into grey and back again into black. The stripes of light along the floorboards rippled as if seen from under water.

Khieu stood there, dappled, covered like a tiger. Then he shifted and one eye was struck by the light, banded and clear. He cloaked in darkness. He used that element well. As Murano had taught him.

'I knew Macomber well . . . in the old days,' Tracy said softly. 'I knew you would come.'

'I have no desire to kill you,' Khieu said. 'But I am *Chet Khmau*. I have no choice.'

There were echoes in the room Tracy could not explain.

'Why?' He knew the answer but it did not stop him from making the attempt. 'You have been nothing but Macomber's errand boy. Now you have your own life to live.'

'Whatever he gave me,' Khieu said slowly, 'is all I am. Everything else is dead. He killed it all. And yet . . . he was the one who gave me back my life. Can I explain it further? Can anyone explain the unexplainable?'

'No.'

'I . . . no longer think clearly.' The voice contained an odd, floating quality. 'Memory, especially, comes and goes, leaving me without orientation.'

'And the Amida Buddha?'

'The Amida Buddha survives all things.' He shifted slightly. 'He tells us that we must divest ourselves of all worldly encumbrances. For he who lives in purity, free from hope and fear, passion and desire for existence and annihilation, and has attained true knowledge, will make an end of suffering and rebirth and enter into highest Nirvana.'

743

He moved again, just a hairsbreadth. 'I left pain and sorrow back at Macomber's house; love and pity as well.' He looked directly at Tracy. 'I left hate back there too. My mind is filled only with the horror of the present. When that, too, is expunged, I will have fulfilled the Amida's prerequisites.'

Tracy had been right. 'It's this way,' he had said to Thwaite. 'You have two carefully balanced ideas within one mind. They *must* be carefully balanced as well as separated because, as you have said, they are mutually exclusive.

'Something happened quite recently to break down the barriers inside his head. Now the two ideas mix and meld: pacifistic Buddhism and murderous training. But they *cannot* mix, they *cannot* meld. They create, instead, madness.'

And because he came at Tracy from the side, in the darkness which was his staunch ally, he forced Tracy to use the To Move the Shade, a very strong counter to Khieu's *kokyu-nage*.

Khieu, thinking he had seen Tracy's spirit of attack, now closed with a butterfly that put enormous pressure on Tracy's ribcage. The pain was excruciating and Tracy was forced to turn his mind away in order to continue functioning.

To Move the Shade meant feinting a strong attack when you did not see your opponent's strategy – making him believe you had revealed your spirit to him. That belief would cause him to reveal his own strategy.

This, indeed, had occurred and Tracy moved to counter the punishing butterfly. Using his hips and thighs, he undercut Khieu's leverage and, with that, the momentum reversed itself.

Tracy immediately struck with two vicious kites, surprised that they had little effect. But with Khieu's next move, he began to understand and the sweat broke out on him anew.

It was the *chikara-wai chia*, an elaborate outer system of intrinsic energy that Tracy had read about in Jinsoku's well-thumbed copy of the *Ryuko-no-maki*, the 'Book of Dragon and Tiger'. It was, so the old man said, the oldest volume revealing the secrets of the martial arts.

The *chikara-wai chia* was only hinted at, the author declining to describe in detail its awesome power because he felt the system to be far too dangerous as a whole.

The *chikara* energy was something all students of the martial arts strove for — a marshalling of the *inner* forces needed for expertise in all variants from *aikido* to *sumo*. *What should happen, then,* the author of the *Ryuko-no-Maki* posited, *if such a devastating force should be made external?*

How to combat it? Deflect it, even? Tracy had no idea. But he knew what the outcome of his struggle must be now. He had given Lauren the diamond ring because he was certain he was coming back. Now he knew that he was not.

Still he fought on, throwing a series of different *ate-waza*, percussives meant to absorb the opponent's strength, but Khieu's energy level was far too high, far too deep. And, in desperation, he worked the *Yotsu te*, grappling with Khieu, engaging both his arms with his own, trying for a deadlock.

But this, too, the *chikara-wai chia* swept aside and abruptly Tracy found himself flat on his back, his head spinning, his side paining him from the initial attack. He was weak and his breath was coming in short barking pants.

He could feel Khieu's strength all around him, enveloping him, could smell the animal sweat running in rivulets between their working muscles. But most of all he could see Khieu's face hanging like a full and gibbous moon in front of his face. There was no anger there, no hate, none of the elation of imminent triumph. As he himself had said, he had divested himself of all those emotions, leaving them to coat the evil walls of Macomber's house.

What remained was only the essential, a kind of abstract distillation of the martial spirit, carefully honed. Stripped bare. But there was, deep down at the very heart of it, another thing, embedded like a precious pearl.

Tracy could not quite call it a holy light. But there was certainly a transfiguring element to it; the eternal calm of the sky or the sea; an immutability.

It was what he remembered when the pain came, what he clutched to himself as he whirled down an endless chute into the darkness of a river. And in that river, he began to circle lazily around and around, ever slower until all motion ceased.

Lauren parked her '67 Ford Mustang just off the dirt road that ran beside the harvested corn field. She drove it up off the verge, coming to a stop beneath the spreading branches of a large and stately oak so that the car was hidden.

Across the corn field she could see Tracy's house, standing still and dark in the gathering dusk. She had been here with Tracy many times and, in fact, it was the memories of those nights, the quilt pulled high over their heads, talking and making love in continuous succession, that had changed her mind.

When she had run away from him in downtown Manhattan she had been firm in her own mind. The image of his bleak and blasted face as she had stumbled out of Macomber's house on Gramercy Park South had haunted her all through his discussions with Thwaite and White. And when it had become plain to her what he was going to do she had had enough. The thought that she might have to see that blasted face once more or – even worse! – never see his face again, had been too much to bear.

But then, during the long night alone, with her leg aching miserably and sleep a thousand miles away, she had stared up at the light patterns on her bedroom's ceiling. Her ears were open to each and every one of the upper West Side's seemingly endless sounds: sirens wailing, dogs barking, a street fight in sharp guttural exchanges of Spanish, delivered like boxers' blows, a cat screeching, the clangour of spilled garbage cans, the cry of a sick baby. She thought about Tracy. And, at last, knew where he would be tomorrow.

Then, exhausted, she slept as splinters of pink light shouldered their way through the chinked gaps between the filthy brown-stones.

She had chosen to come up on his house from this direction, remembering that there was very little cover here until you came within about a hundred and fifty feet of the house itself. Thwaite's men, who surely would be there as well, could not protect Tracy from that side.

Lauren went across the dirt road into the corn field. Now that she was here, she understood what she had to do. Having come this far, she could not merely be a bystander, watching help-lessly. Inside the house Tracy might be dying.

746

She was going inside and the thought made her legs shake. Her heart pounded wildly. What would she find in there?

She began to walk on stiffened legs across the corn field. She was unconcerned about Thwaite and his team spotting her because she knew they could not show themselves and therefore stop her.

She reached the great shade tree without incident. She was now perhaps a hundred feet from the western face of the house. Now her choice was to go to the front or the back.

She saw no one, heard nothing and this disturbed her. Where were the crickets? She stopped just outside the back door of the house and a moment later, she heard the sharp wheezing sound of the crickets starting up again like a cold engine.

Cautiously she opened the screen door outward, slid herself through sideways, allowing it to fall back gently to rest on her outside shoulder.

She turned the brass doorknob of the inner wooden door with sweating fingers. It was not locked and she pushed the door inward, crossed over the threshold.

She was in the kitchen and she stopped long enough to allow her eyes to adjust to the gloom. Night had fallen outside on her way towards the house but there was a moon and, of course, the stars. Inside, it was darker.

She spent a moment, recalling the layout of the house, then slowly began to inch forward. As soon as she did so, she thought she heard noises. They seemed to be emanating from the living room, off to her right. She moved towards them, as silently as she was able, almost gliding.

She came to the opening to the living room and now she could discern the noises. They sounded like an animal grunting, as if it were feeding off a fresh kill.

There was a partial wall here that she pulled herself around. The windows of the house let in patches of silvery moonlight in distorted angular patterns that reminded her of the eyes of a jack-o-lantern. One of these patches was directly before her and she began to wonder how she could circumvent it.

Then all thought was driven from her mind by the sight of what lay just beyond the spill of moonlight. She saw Tracy on his back, his head to one side so that his face was to her, glowing with the incipient illumination. His eyes were closed and in the absence of sufficient light she could not tell whether or not he was breathing. There was someone standing over him, spread-legged, gasping with breath, sweat or blood, she could not tell which, dripping off the point of his chin.

She gasped involuntarily and his head swivelled. He made a sound deep in the back of his throat and she knew who it was who stood before her. Khieu! She took a step forward into the patch of moonlight and now she heard another cry from him, entirely different in tone.

'*No!*'

It was such a cry of pain that she shivered, even as she moved forward again, crouching, touching Tracy's chest with her spread fingers, sliding them blindly up towards the side of his neck to find the pulse. She could not risk taking her eyes off of him. Khieu. She recognized him as the man who had come to Louis Richter's apartment when she had been there; the man who had had such an extraordinary reaction to her.

'Have you killed him?' she found herself saying. She spat it out, her face distorted with fear and rage. *Where was that artery?*

'I don't know.' His voice was very faint, almost as if he was fading away from her. She checked his position; he had not moved.

She found the artery and the pulse at the same time. Tracy was alive! *Thank God!* a voice whispered inside her head. And she remembered her own words: *I'll come after anyone who hurts you. That's our bargain.* Hot tears traced her cheeks like flame. She had kept that bargain.

She looked up into Khieu's hidden face. 'I'm going to take him out of here.' She did not know what she was saying.

'How have you come back?' She heard his voice, strained, sing-song, almost as if he were speaking a litany. '*Why?*' He moved slightly. 'I left everything behind: envy, greed, hate, fear

748

and ... love. All the human baggage I can no longer afford to carry.' He came forward, bending into the light. *'Why have you come here?'* Again that cry of pain that shivered her spine, contracted her scalp.

At the instant his face appeared in the moonlight, banded by the shadows of the shaking trees outside, Lauren understood that he would not make a move against her. She had a power over him; a power that no one else possessed because he himself had given it to her.

'I'll leave now,' she said softly, because she knew it was what he wanted her to do. He did not want to kill her. He could have done that before. After all, he had killed Louis Richter. She had seen him at the apartment; she had been witness to his ruse. Yet he had allowed her life.

She began to gather Tracy up in her arms. She knew he was far too heavy for her to be able to lift him. She would have to drag him along the floor, back to the kitchen.

'No!'

And she felt his fingers clamp around her wrist. His strength was appalling. Her head whipped up and she glared at him, baring her teeth. 'Yes!' she whispered, pushing force into her voice. 'I'll take him with me.'

'You cannot!' It was the whiplash of command. 'I have been charged with his death. I must see it carried out. I *must.*'

'Then I will stay, too. You'll have to kill me as well.'

'But *I cannot!*'

The agony that flooded his face stunned her. What murderous deeds had he done to deserve the burden of pain he so obviously bore? He was no monster, she saw now. He had killed in order to survive; he found no internal joy in it. Yet, because of him four people were dead and Tracy could be the fifth. What could be more monstrous than that? And yet as she stared into his face, she wondered.

'Then I'll go ... and take him with me.'

'Don't!' he cried. 'Please!' And he began to weep bitter tears, shaking, his arms crossed tightly over his chest, hugging himself.

She began to drag Tracy away, through the moonlight, silver on black.

'Don't . . .'

But there was no force behind it; the command was gone. It was the voice of a child.

And Lauren went on, her mind racing, her body sweating, telling herself that it would be all right, he wouldn't come after them, he wouldn't slit their throats, that she was immune to his power and as long as she kept hold of Tracy it would be all right. *All right, oh God please! Keep us safe!* She prayed, as her mother had always wanted her to, to a God she did not believe in or understand. Still she prayed as she dragged him further and further away from the madman, into the kitchen, through another patch of silvery light. Praying that she would not feel the brief chill wind of his passage as he came for them. As she pulled him past the refrigerator, the table, one arm getting twisted up with the chair leg, dragging it noisily for a foot until she could entangle him.

Gasping and crying and then they were at the back door and she pushed it open, got him at last out of there.

Ivory White had seen the tiny silhouetted figure moving across the corn field and, using his field glasses, had recognized Lauren immediately. He had relayed the information privately to Thwaite who had cursed her with every foul word he could think of.

'What in Christ's name does she think she's doing?' he had asked himself under his breath.

But then he saw her emerge with Tracy. He was in touch by walkie-talkie with the officers of the Pennsylvania State Police who had surrounded the house. He used it now to tell them to move in.

Khieu slipped to his knees, watching the darkness dissolve Lauren into its heart. With her departure, the ache inside of him ceased to be. Seeing her once again, touching her had somehow healed him. His love for her was there, a reality. He had touched it at the precise moment he had touched her. He had felt it,

750

acknowledged it. It had passed through him like the wind. It had reached a place deep inside him, changed that place, and then was gone. At last he had put love aside with all the other emotions. He knew what he had to do.

He got up, turning his back on the entranceway to the kitchen. In the dining area he went to the highboy hutch and opened its glass doors. There were three or four boxes of candles inside. He took them out now, one by one, and began to light them.

Tracy awoke to moonlight on his face. He turned, his head and shoulders aching, and saw Lauren, sitting on the stoop at the back of the house. Her head in her hands. He could not understand what had happened.

He reached for her and she started, her eyes flying open wide and staring. Then she saw that he was awake and broke down, clinging to him, whispering his name softly over and over again.

Tracy picked her up so that they stood together. He was facing the back door. He could see into the kitchen because only the screen door was closed.

He saw a shadow moving in there now and, in a patch of falling moonlight, recognized Kim. Tracy was certain he had not been inside a moment ago; no one had seen him enter, not even Khieu. 'Stay here a moment,' he whispered into her ear. He felt her stiffen.

'Where are you going?' Her fingers gripped him, pulling. She saw his face and her head shook back and forth. 'Not back in there. Oh, God. No.'

He broke away from her. 'Just for a moment.'

'He'll kill you!'

And he saw in her face that she was right. What had she done in there? How had she got him out? He had no answers to those questions. He only knew he had some unfinished business with Kim.

He recognized they were both right and he had to do something about it. 'I'll stay in the kitchen,' he whispered. 'You'll be able to see me all the time.'

She said nothing, knowing that he would go and how he had

751

compromised by what he had just said. She nodded and Tracy left her.

'He's in there, all right,' Thwaite said into the walkie-talkie. 'I don't want to take any chances, Chief. I want tear gas in there first. We'll wait five minutes and then go in.'

'Why wait that long?' the chief of the Pennsylvania State Police said. His voice sounded thin and far away through the mechanism.

'I've got two civilians in the immediate area of the house. I can't signal them for fear of alerting the suspect. We've got to give them time to get clear.'

'Okay,' the chief said, 'but I'll have my hands full containing these television people. I've never had anything like this happen in my command.'

'I'll send one of my men over to help,' Thwaite said, thinking he'd like to get his hands on the bastard in the commissioner's office who leaked the location to the network news people.

'Right. I'd be glad for all the help you can give me in that department.' There was a crackle of interference. 'Don't go away. My men're just about in position.'

'Just tell me when,' Thwaite said.

'Two seconds, one. Now.'

The barrage began.

Tracy and Kim faced each other in the darkness of the kitchen. Ghostly light flickered, filtering in from the living room, waxing and waning along Kim's cheeks and forehead.

'Get away from there,' Kim hissed. 'I'll kill you if you don't let me pass.'

'You're already a dead man,' Tracy said. 'And I'm meant to be the executioner.'

No waver of emotion crossed Kim's features; they were flat planes, going in and out of shadow with the inconstant light.

'If that's what you want,' Kim said, 'come on. I'm going through one way or another.'

Because Kim had used him; because he did not want to kill

752

him, Tracy had to know it all. It was inside Kim's head, he knew. It was up to him to find the right key.

'Kim,' he said, his voice softening, 'd'you remember that time in the jungle when I found you in the Khmer Rouge encampment.' Tracy had worded it carefully.

Now something slid across Kim's face, furtive and momentary.

Tracy knew that was all the sign he was going to get, so he went on. 'We stopped in a clearing,' he said. 'You needed to rest. So did I.'

Kim stared at Tracy, his eyes desperately trying to see beyond the words. 'Yes,' he whispered at last. 'What happened then?' Each syllable seemed wrenched out of him.

Tracy shrugged. 'I don't know. Perhaps I slept for a time; perhaps it was the other way around. Then we got up and went home.'

Kim knew quite well why Tracy had brought up that story of long ago. His hand came up and the calloused pad on his thumb rubbed along the white scar along his neck. Tracy had seen what had happened there in the jungle but he would never tell. He had quite neatly trapped Kim.

'I'm not sorry I brought you into this,' Kim said after a time. 'None of it would've been possible without you. Not with the Director breathing down my neck.'

His eyes glittered. 'But I wanted something more than death for Khieu. I wanted his world to slowly come apart. And you were the honed tool I needed. Only you could've followed my clues. Only you had the expertise to do it.'

Kim's throat contracted until it seemed composed entirely of ligaments, stretched taut. 'His brother . . . his brother deliberately set fire to my family's house. They were Khmer. They hated us Vietnamese. We were *Yuons* to them. Barbarian invaders. But Sam, Khieu Sokha's older brother had an . . . affair with my sister, Diep. He couldn't have her, couldn't perhaps live with the shame of what he was doing.

'So he wiped them out.'

'All of them?' Tracy's mind went cold.

'All save my brother Thu.'

Yes, Tracy thought. It was personal. Very personal. He did not want to allow Kim to go in there. Tracy had been up against Khieu. He knew what the Cambodian would do to Kim. On the other hand, he did not think he had a choice. It was either let him through or kill Kim himself.

He turned and walked quickly out of the house.

Khieu had divested himself of all his clothes and now he sat cross-legged on the rug in front of the gilt-coated wooden Buddha. He saw the great serene face staring down at him and he thought of his childhood *Lok Kru*. Phnom Penh. Summer. The heat in waves, making the tall trees flicker and fade. Heat like a forge. And the insects screaming.

There was flickering light here, too, from the candles he had lit all around him, throughout the living and dining rooms. They, too, gave him comfort, as the image of the Amida Buddha gave him comfort.

He did not start when he heard the *pops* from outside, the chatter of splintering glass. Wind from outside and the candle-light shimmering, wavering, growing dimmer briefly as a number of candles were knocked off their ends. They began to roll.

Flames licked out, dancing across the carpet, the drapes, until finally Khieu became aware of an increase in light, then a diffusion as choking fumes wafted through. He began to cough, his eyes to tear until he began his chants, concentrating on the Amida Buddha and his duty.

'He who is free from all desires, who has a pure heart and has conquered selfishness, he alone is a true disciple of the Enlightened One. Let him therefore strive only for inward perfection; let him cultivate within himself wisdom, serenity and benevolence.'

Kim set foot into the living room and confronted the blazing inferno. Time and space ceased to have any meaning for him. He was lost within the labyrinth of time, hearing the last pitiful cries of Diep as she burned to death, stumbling again over the charred and blackened corpses of his mother and father, his brothers, flames still flickering here and there, running along their sides like tiny demons.

Then a great cracking from above his head, as if the sky itself was crying out in anguish, and the hissing, sparking, heated bar of the crossbeam whooshing down, just missing his head. He watched, dumbfounded, as it struck Thu across the thighs, smashing its great bulk and Diep's half-crushed corpse down on him.

Now Kim was back there again in Chamcar Mon. Now he heard the spirits of his entire family wailing in his ears, crying out for revenge. And now he set off through the crackling flames to get to the figure beyond their licking grinning faces. Hate filled his heart, a black, depthless hatred spinning out of control, consuming his mind as the fire was consuming the house and everything in it. Howling in rage, Kim threw himself forward, hurtling through the first ring of flames.

His clothes began to spark and steam but he ignored that; it had all happened before and he had not died then. His mind, his body, all his energies were focused on the object of his rage. His outstretched arm was aimed at the Khmer's head, seen through the flickering, crackling flames. Kim depressed the hidden stud and the blue blade shot out from its hiding place along the inside of his wrist. It disappeared into the inferno.

Still Khieu Sokha sat, chanting, oblivious to the attack. Kim howled invective, venting his hate as he came on. The entire room was ringed with fire; flames were devouring everything. But Kim felt no pain as his clothes caught fire, felt no heat as the flames licked at his flesh. He was held sacrosant because of his hate, he ran now solely on that.

He had more weapons to use against the Cambodian and he withdrew them, not even noticing his steaming fingers. His back was bare and burning but the intrinsic energy surging within him pushed him on, into that last barrier of intense flame surrounding his foe.

For just an instant he saw that face, the black blind eyes turned his way; he heard the Buddhist chanting almost as a physical vibration shimmering the air. Within that last ring of fire, so close to the fruition of his vengeance, he paused, stunned. He

755

was aflame now but his nerves had already sealed themselves off from trauma.

Kim saw the glow, unearthly and impossible. His eyes goggled and his heart missed a beat. Breath hissed from him like an engine and for that one last moment of his life even his black hatred was gone from him, purged by the sight confronting him.

Then a great roaring filled his ears, an upward whoosh of sparks and a heat so intense he finally felt it engulf him as the charred floorboards gave way, sending him careening downward into oblivion.

How swiftly the flames spread; how easily they ate at the inside of the house, consuming as if famished.

'Let him deceive no one, threaten no one, despise no one, injure no one,' Khieu intoned. 'As a mother her only child, so let him look full of pity and kindness on all beings; let him cultivate this sentiment every day and every hour. As a deep mountain lake, pure and calm, so shall be the mind of him who walks on the Noble Eightfold Path.'

The Amida Buddha called and he felt the pull at his spirit. *'Buddhám saranám gacchāmi, Dammám saranám gacchāmi, Sanghám saranám gacchāmi.'* It was as if his flesh had abruptly loosened, his joints dissolving, his skin flaccid, melting away. At the same time he felt filled with a supranormal clarity of vision and feeling. Not emotion but true *feeling*. The cosmos opened wide its petals to him. He had become loose inside himself. Floating.

His gaze slid down from the Buddha's serene face and he reached forward, turned on the blank face of the television. The dark grey screen, reflecting the dancing flames behind him, blossomed into life like a multi-coloured·flower.

He saw an idiot's face, working soundlessly, hair blowing in the wind, a microphone held before his face. He nodded behind him and the picture changed. He saw a night sky, a country sky. It was lit up by flames. He saw the house within which he sat; he saw it burning.

It was a transcendent moment to see the image transmitted

756

via cathode ray and to be experiencing it at the same time. For an instant he knew that he was watching his own death.

Then he felt the last loosening inside his unfeeling body and his spirit was released. He rose up towards the face of his beloved Buddha. For just a moment, he chased the clouds; he rode the wind, saw the light curve of the world. Then the sky cracked open. It was filled with fire and at last he saw the eternal face of his Amida Buddha change, a glow emanating from it, reaching out to encompass him. He thought of the energy he had once discerned in Preah Moha Panditto. He no longer wondered at it; he no longer stood in awe of it.

He was part of it.

Tracy opened his eyes, heard the sound of the surf, a faraway crash and hiss that nevertheless penetrated the opened windows.

Ocean scents were bright on the air. It was warm, though not uncomfortably so. The semi-detached villa had all the modern conveniences – including air conditioning – since it was part of an exclusive hotel. But they had chosen to keep the old-fashioned ceiling fan going.

He turned over on his side, wincing slightly as he put pressure on a bruise, stared at Lauren's sleeping face. One arm was curled beneath her head, the other between her legs. She breathed slowly and deeply, her eyelids flickering from time to time as she dreamed.

She came awake without his knowing; her hands reached across the narrow expanse between them, searching for the warm areas sleep had placed throughout his body.

Her eyes seemed huge, her coral lips opened slightly. He felt her legs move, twining with his. Already he felt drunk with the contact of their bodies.

'I'm hungry.' Her voice was furry with sleep; she moved closer to him, put her palm over the flesh above his heart. She closed her eyes, listening to the beat increase – vibrations directly from him to her – as she stroked him. She began to purr.

'Lauren,' he whispered, 'I didn't want you to run away. I never meant to make you cry.'

'I know,' she murmured, kissing his palm.

And the curious thing was, Tracy thought now, she *did* know. She seemed to understand what he had to do almost as well as he had himself. But that was impossible, he told himself. How could she have known what Khieu was like?

She murmured something but he could not hear the words. He buried his face in her hair and then he heard her.

'I kept my part of the bargain.'

He held her tight. 'I love you,' he whispered.

Thwaite had misgivings when Melody called him at the office and asked him over to her apartment. He went anyway.

Melody met him on Eleventh Street in front of her building. She was wearing a dove grey pinstripe suit with a pleated white tuxedo shirt underneath, a string silk tie. She wore wide boots of glove leather. Her black hair was pulled back in a long pony tail. She looked like a lawyer fresh out of graduate school.

She smiled when she saw him, leaning slightly forward to kiss him on the cheek, then she hooked her arm through his and they began to walk west. It was not at all as he had imagined.

'I wanted to congratulate you on your promotion,' she said.

'Thanks. But I think it was more of a publicity ploy on the part of the commissioner.' But inside he was pleased. Becoming a lieutenant had always been a dream of his.

They passed the small old church on Fifth Avenue.

'And Tracy?' she asked. 'How is he?'

'Tracy's with Lauren,' he said. 'Away on a long vacation.'

Melody stopped and turned to face him. Sunlight lit her face obliquely and he was struck anew by her features, the contours that had been moulded and fused by her personality.

'That's really why I wanted to see you.' She dropped her arm from his. 'I'm going away, too. To Sunset Key, off the tip of Florida. I've rented a small house for a month but' – her shoulders shrugged – 'I may stay longer. Depending.'

'On what?'

She shrugged again.

'What about the apartment here?'

'I'm getting rid of it,' she said simply. 'I've got plenty of money: I don't need it now. If I ever come back here, I'll find another place easily enough.' She laughed shortly. 'Anyway, I was getting tired of the neighbourhood.' She looked down at her feet, dug into a pocket of her jacket. She thrust a folded slip of paper into his hand, wrapped his fingers around it with her own.

'Here,' she said. 'Take the address. Who knows? You might want it one of these days.'

'Melody, I —'

She smiled tightly up at him. 'Then again you may not. Just do the decent thing, Thwaite, will you? Don't tear it up until after I've gone.' She lifted her face to his, kissed him on the lips.

He felt the contact all the way down his spine; it made him feel warm inside.

'Good-bye, Douglas.' She turned, about to walk away.

'Wait.' Thwaite grabbed her arm, turned her back to him. His face was pained. 'Melody, I don't know. I just don't.'

She stared straight at him, saying nothing. At last she bent her head. 'I have to live my life and you have to live yours.'

'Maybe —' A siren began to wail somewhere north of them and he waited until the crest of sound had passed them by. 'Maybe I could live in your apartment while you were away.'

She thought about this for a moment.

'I have nowhere else to go.'

She knew he was wrong about that but at least now she felt that he might see it for himself. She squinted into the sun and nodded. 'All right,' she said, 'Lieutenant.'

Tracy raced Lauren across the sand, from their doorstep to the crest of the dune. Her body dazzled him, so full of grace and power. She appeared to him to be a fantasy child come to life.

She turned back, wondering why he was lagging behind, and saw how intently he was looking at her. He stumbled over a crop of dune grass and fell face first into the warm sand.

Lauren shrieked like a kid, came rushing back to him, flinging herself down beside him, laughing. He rolled over, kicked at the tuft of grass waving in the gentle breeze.

'Tracy,' she whispered, cupping his face in her hands. 'Oh, Tracy.' He had been laughing, too, thinking how blinded he was to everything else now when he looked at her. He could have gone on laughing, but he kissed her instead, felt her lips opening beneath his, their tongues making electric contact.

His body still ached, the muscles sore, but every day he felt the tension of the past months slipping further and further away. It was partly being here on the hot beach, so far away from New

York. But he recognized that more than anything it was Lauren. He did not think he wanted this time to end.

Their lips broke apart, and Lauren rolled her body over so that she was lying parallel to him. They looked out over the expanse of beach to the cool, creaming waves. When they pulled back to gather again for another rush towards the granulated shore, the wet beach shone and shimmered like gold in the sunlight.

He turned towards her, saw the sea reflected in her eyes. She would not tell him what had happened inside his house after he had been knocked unconscious, saying it wasn't important even though he wanted to know how she had got him out.

At first it had been important for him to know and he had been annoyed. But now he saw that she was right. It didn't matter. He had lived through a nightmare and had awoken from it. That was enough. To know it was over. And to hold her.

'Tracy.' She put her head against him, her unbound hair fluttering like a wing along his skin. 'What about the place where you and Louis once worked. You went back to them.'

'I had no choice.' His eyes traced the line of the horizon, cobalt against turquoise, sharp and unhazed, its back broken by the rough cliffs of Molokai. High up only, clouds raced, chasing each other's tails. 'But the call-up's come and gone for me.'

'Until the next time?' She looked at him, her eyes unusually bright.

'What next time?' He put his arm across her browned shoulders. Now was not the time to speak of such things ... or even to think of them.

There was no one on this vast expanse of white beach except them. The palm tree line was far behind them; it was growing hotter. 'Sometime today,' he said, 'we've got to go swimming.'

'Oh, yes,' Lauren said, moving closer. 'But not now.'

Half a world away, a young Chinese in uniform delivered a packet of documents to the large walled mansion just outside Shanghai. His orders were to deliver it into the hands of a certain official and this he did.

The Monk took the packet, signing for it, using his hand-carved ivory chop. When he was alone, he used a long thumb nail to slip open the packet, revealing its contents. He found inside what he had expected to find: A diplomatic passport, visas and the bogus papers he was ostensibly on his way to America to deliver.

He nodded to himself, placed the packet in the outside pouch of his luggage which was sitting behind the door, waiting. He called for the car. He had deliberately chosen a time when Tisah would be out walking the perimeter of the grounds with the guards she was required to be with.

This was a difficult enough task; he did not think he could continue to lie to her. And certainly to tell her the truth would mean the end of their close and loving relationship. Not because of what he was going to do — he was her father, after all, and she accepted all that he did as was right and proper for an offspring. But she would not be able to understand *why* he did it. She had not his loyalty to China; the motherland's policies were not hers. No, he decided, it was far better to say nothing, to slip away and get the deed over with.

He recalled his summons to the office of Liang Yongquan in Peking several weeks ago. It was one in a veritable warren of such identical rooms within the massive structure of the Bureau of Industry.

However, on that bright hot morning, Liang Yongquan was not in evidence. He was, in fact, rotting in the lightless depths of a prison cell; soon he would be tried and summarily executed for crimes against the state. So said Liang Yongquan's successor.

He was a whip-lean man of middle years named Wu Xilian. The Monk had never heard of him before but that was not so unusual in a government filled with more kinds of political quicksand than could be counted.

Wu Xilian turned out to be a man of dour contenance, lacking even the semblance of humour. The Monk spotted him as a hard-liner immediately. At first that did not worry him overmuch. As a veteran of numerous shakeups within his own department, he knew precisely when to advance and when to withdraw. This was no man to fool with, he knew. But he was unprepared for what his superior had on his mind.

'This Macomber exchange bothers me overmuch.' He possessed the annoying habit of holding his long-necked head as erect as a snapping turtle. This, combined with his rather old-fashioned phraseology caused every statement he made to sound like a lecture.

'I don't see why,' the Monk said evenly. 'I negotiated a price that was more than double what it should have been.' That was the first and last mistake he made with this man.

'I am not,' Wu Xilian said, 'speaking now about *money*.' His inflection gave that last word an unhealthy cast. 'I am referring to the purely *political* nature of what was set up.

'I don't like it or any of the implications I can derive from it. And do you know why?' The Monk wisely kept his mouth shut; he was already getting the hang of this one and though he did not like it he had his duty to perform. 'It has the stink of *personal* aggrandizement about it.' Had Wu Xilian been talking about the devious manoeuvrings of the Soviets, he could not have been more contemptuous.

'Well,' he said after a time. 'I'm waiting.'

The Monk knew he had a fifty-fifty chance of survival now. Desperately he thought of ways to cut down the odds. 'I admit,' he said, starting slowly, 'that there was a strictly personal aspect to the deal that was struck. *However*, I am constrained to point out that the major factor that attracted me to the situation' – he was also wise enough not to mention the name of Wu Xilian's predecessor – 'was the possibility of using an *American* operation to help break down the Soviet-built terrorist network. As it is currently beyond our powers to openly discredit this carefully constructed organism, it occurred to me to acquire a foreign dupe to do the work we obviously could not.'

Wu Xilian contemplated the Monk as if he were a piece in a chess game the man was determined to bring to mate. 'There is something I detest fully as much as personal aggrandizement,' he said slowly so that there would be no mistake, 'and that is a lie.' He put his palms flat on the spotless desk in front of him.

'I demand absolute honesty as well as absolute obedience in my section.'

'Do you wish me to swear an oath of fealty?' the Monk said, somewhat ironically, thinking of his country's feudal past and how little some things had changed though many years and many regimes had already passed this way.

'That is precisely,' Wu Xilian said, 'what I had in mind.'

The Monk sat very still. He could hear the thump–thump pattern of his heartbeat and knew that it was slightly accelerated. He nodded his head in a quick sharp gesture that struck his superior as being military. 'Then it shall be done.'

Wu Xilian's eyes never left the Monk's. They appeared lidless for they never seemed to blink. 'It is not much, really. Not so very much to reach out and touch the life of a Westerner – and an American at that – extinguishing it.'

Wu Xilian's voice seemed to grow in power and strength with every heartbeat. 'I know that Tracy Richter means something to you ... and of course he means something to ... your daughter.' He was almost smiling now. 'I want him out of all our lives. See to it.'

The Monk's Mercedes took him to the governmental airport at Hongquiao where his plane was awaiting him. For New York; that was Richter's home, after all. And if he was not there?

The Monk paused a moment on his way up the movable stairs to the belly of the plane. If Richter was not in New York it would not matter. The Monk would find him wherever he was. The Monk's life and that of his daughter depended on it.

Ducking his head, he disappeared into the tube of aluminium and steel, hydraulics and electronic webs. In a moment he was airborne.

Black Heart

Born and raised in New York City, Eric Lustbader graduated from Columbia University in 1969. Lustbader has had a number of fascinating careers. In addition to having written numerous bestselling novels, including *The Ninja* and *Angel Eyes*, he introduced Elton John to the American music scene. He spent fifteen years in the music industry in various capacities, including working for both Elektra and CBS Records. He is a former writer for *Cash Box* magazine where he wrote lead stories on new rock acts. In that capacity, he was the first person in the United States to predict the success of Jimi Hendrix, David Bowie and Santana, among many others.

Lustbader has taught in the All-Day Neighborhood School Division of the NYC Public School System and has also taught pre-schoolers in special Early Childhood programmes.

Eric Lustbader, who travels worldwide in researching his novels, lives in Southampton, New York, with his wife Victoria Lustbader, who works for the Nature Conservancy.

BY THE SAME AUTHOR

Nicholas Linnear novels

The Ninja
The Miko
White Ninja
The Kaisho
Floating City
Second Skin

China Maroc novels

Jian
Shan

Black Blade
Angel Eyes
French Kiss
Sirens
Zero

The *Sunset Warrior* cycle

The Sunset Warrior
Shallows of Night
Dai-San
Beneath an Opal Moon